WAR OF SHADOWS

The mirror's surface glowed, illuminating Xaffert's face caught in an expression of absolute horror. Blood streamed from his nose, mouth, and ears and his laughter changed to a shriek of pain. Before anyone had a chance to intervene, Xaffert fell to the ground, the mirror still clutched in his hand.

Dagur and Zaryae rushed toward Xaffert, while Piran used a stick to knock the mirror from Xaffert's fingers. "Is he dead?" Blaine asked. He felt disoriented and light-headed as his head pounded. He swayed on his feet before steadying himself against the wall, while trying to keep a worried eye on the mirror, which now lay dim and inert beside the mage.

Dagur knelt beside Xaffert, and his expression grew queasy. "Most definitely. It looks as if his eyes and everything behind them have been burned out."

"Let me make something very clear," Blaine said, fixing Dagur with a look. "I'm willing to give you and your mages sanctuary in exchange for your expertise. But I need to be able to trust you—and that means that you'd better be right when you give me your word on whether or not something is safe to use."

Dagur stood and squared his shoulders. "Unlike Xaffert, when I give you my word, you can stake your life on it."

"I am," Blaine replied. "We all are. And that's why you'd damn well better be right."

By Gail Z. Martin

WAR OF SHADOWS

BOOK THREE OF THE ASCENDANT KINGDOMS SAGA

GAIL Z. MARTIN

orbit

www.orbitbooks.net

ORBIT

First published in Great Britain in 2015 by Orbit

1 3 5 7 9 10 8 6 4 2

Copyright © 2015 by Gail Z. Martin

Excerpt from The Falcon Throne by Karen Miller
Copyright © 2014 by Karen Miller

A CIP catalogue record for this book
is available from the British Library.

ISBN 978-0-356-50493-3

Printed and bound by CPI Group (UK) Ltd, Croydon, CR0 4YY

Papers used by Orbit are from well-managed forests
and other responsible sources.

Orbit
An imprint of
Little, Brown Book Group
100 Victoria Embankment
London EC4Y 0DY

An Hachette UK Company
www.hachette.co.uk

www.orbitbooks.net

To my husband, Larry, and to Kyrie, Chandler, and Cody.
Thank you for making these books possible.

CHAPTER ONE

"TELL ME AGAIN WHY WE LEFT A PERFECTLY GOOD army back at the camp?" Piran Rowse grumbled as the small group followed their guide on a rocky trail to the foothills behind Quillarth Castle.

"For the same reason we left most of the mages behind," Blaine McFadden replied. "The fewer people who know, the better." He paused. "Besides, the soldiers needed time to secure the perimeter and spring any nasty traps Reese and Pollard left for us."

Blaine knew that Piran's real complaint was being out in the open without cover from the soldiers. It had taken half a candlemark's argument to point out that stealth with a contingent of twenty soldiers was impossible. Their goal was to find where the Knights of Esthrane had left magical items for safekeeping, items that might help the mages begin to reverse the damage of the Great Fire. And bringing a large force was sure to tip their hand and complicate matters.

"It's here somewhere," Dillon, their guide, muttered as he moved inch by inch down what appeared to be the solid rock face of the cliff. The wind ruffled Dillon's short-cropped, dark hair. To Blaine's eye, Dillon looked like he belonged in a counting house, and before the Cataclysm, that was exactly where he had been. It made him an unlikely adventurer. Dillon's hands played over the rough stone, lightly skimming the surface.

"It's a big cliff, mate. I hope you remember where the door is," Piran said.

"We're close," Dillon said, paying scant attention to Piran. "Just a little farther—here!"

He pressed his fingers against the rock with his hands held in an unnatural position, and what had appeared a moment earlier to be solid stone shifted enough to allow careful passage inside.

"When was the last time you went in there?" Blaine asked. At a few inches over six feet tall, Blaine stood taller than both Dillon and Piran. Blaine's dark chestnut hair was tied back, revealing intelligent, sea-blue eyes. He was tall and rangy, but years of hard labor had built both muscle and resolve, and months of nearly constant skirmishing had further honed his swordsmanship. Piran was shorter and stockier, and he kept his bald head shaved clean, even in the icy cold. What he lacked in height he made up for in muscle, and in the fighting skills that came with years of soldiering.

Dillon chuckled. "Me? Months ago. Sir Alrik showed me the entrance, and told me that if I went in against his orders, I'd never come out."

"That's comforting," Piran grumbled.

Dillon looked at Piran with exasperation. "I took his meaning straightaway. He meant that the items weren't for me. In fact, he gave strict instructions that I was to tell no one except Blaine McFadden or Lanyon Penhallow what I knew, and then he sent me away and told me to stay away until the war was decided, one way or the other."

"Alrik must have suspected that Reese and Pollard would come calling," Blaine said grimly. "You were his inside man."

"Let's see what Alrik thought was so important," Piran said. He stepped in front of Blaine. "Sorry, mate. I go first. Thick skull, tough skin," he said with a grin that made it clear he relished courting trouble.

"And I've got your back," Kestel Falke said with a jaunty grin. She had a dagger in each hand, better than swords for fighting in the close quarters of the crypt and its tunnels.

"You'll need me somewhere near the front, since I'm the one with the directions," Dillon remarked.

"We need to go in and get out as quickly as possible. The dreams were clear about the danger, and it grows the longer we stay." Zaryae's voice was quiet, meant to avoid attracting the attention of the two university mages in the back of the group. Blaine nodded to acknowledge her warning.

"Just make sure your light shines enough to show the way. I've got no desire to bang into the rocks." Xaffert's curt tone managed to convey both displeasure and impatience.

"Stop fussing. I've got a lantern. And keep your voice down." Dagur brought up the rear, holding his partially shuttered lantern aloft.

"Now, wait just a minute, lad! Where do you—"

"Shut up, or by the gods, I'll put one of these blades in your throat." Kestel turned so that Xaffert could see the glint of her knives and the intensity of her glare. Xaffert looked as if he wanted to say more, then thought better of it. Dagur was barely hiding a snicker.

The group that was heading into the crypt was small but hardly defenseless. Piran was a soldier, and a damn good one before his court-martial. Prison and exile had honed his skills far beyond what the king's army had taught him. Blaine

McFadden, the disgraced lord of Glenreith, had learned a thing or two about combat fighting to survive in the brutal Velant prison colony where he, Piran, and Kestel had been exiled for their crimes. Kestel Falke had earned her exile as a spy and assassin, though her looks and wit made her best remembered as one of the most popular courtesans at court. She, Blaine, and Piran had forged their friendship watching each other's backs long before they returned to their ruined homeland, and it was an old habit that still served them well.

Zaryae, a seer, had been part of a traveling troupe that had joined in Blaine's quest. Dillon was the assistant to the king's exchequer, back when such things as kings, kingdoms, and exchequers still existed. In the ruins of what remained, those days seemed a distant memory, or perhaps a half-forgotten dream. Xaffert and Dagur had been mages at the University before the Great Fire and before the kingdom fell, when the magic worked as it should. As a group, they were a most unusual delegation to be heading into the tombs of the ancient kings to steal back the keys to the future.

Now, in darkness, they moved toward what Blaine hoped might help them rebuild the kingdom. They had restored the magic that was broken in the war, or at least made it possible for the power to be harnessed once more. The Cataclysm that had leveled the castle and killed the rulers had left the kingdom in chaos and anarchy. Blaine believed it would be much easier to rebuild if they could bend the power of artifacts made before the Cataclysm to their will.

"By my reckoning, we're moving back toward the castle. Given the steep angle, we could end up underneath it before too long," Blaine murmured. They had each brought lanterns, making it possible for them to move through the dark and winding passageway.

Kestel had secured one of her knives and now held a lantern in her left hand and a knife in the right. Her red hair was bound up for battle, and her cuirass and plain-spun tunic and trews were the practical attire of a trained assassin. "Obviously, this wasn't supposed to be the main entrance," she said. "Too bad so much of the castle collapsed, or it would have been much easier to get there from inside, but there's too much rubble in the way."

They walked in silence, weapons ready, expecting ambush at every turn. Suddenly, Piran stopped and held up a hand in warning. "Do you hear that?"

Blaine listened carefully. "Voices. Up ahead."

"We're the only living things down here," Zaryae said, breaking her silence.

"But the voices—" Piran protested.

Zaryae shook her head. "Not alive. But very strong." Zaryae's black hair was plaited into a long braid, framing angular features and large, dark eyes. Her dusky skin and faint accent hinted that her homeland had been the Lesser Kingdoms.

Blaine fingered the two amulets that hung on a leather strap around his neck. One was the inscribed obsidian disk that had helped him return magic to the control of men. The other was a passage token given to him by a long-dead soldier, one of the *talishte* Knights of Esthrane. For those with power, they were validation of Blaine's identity, and safe passage among powerful friends.

The passageway ended in a solid wall of rock. Piran swore under his breath, and began to feel his way along the stone surface as Dillon had done outside. Suddenly, a section of the rock swung away, opening into darkness.

"I didn't do that," Piran said, taking a step back. "I swear, I didn't do that."

Blaine could feel the tingle of magic all around them. Before the Cataclysm, his own slight magic enhanced his dexterity in a fight, giving him better-than-mortal speed, but nothing nearly as quick as the *talishte*. His magic had come back, though the restored magic was unpredictable. Now he wished for all the advantages he could get. Old magic flowed around them here, and another power he could not name.

Zaryae placed a warning hand on Blaine's arm. "The spirits are strong—can you sense it? Old and powerful. We must be very careful."

"I think you'd better let me go first," Blaine said, edging past Piran. "Let's hope, between the disk and the Knights' token, that I pass muster."

He stepped out into an ornate tomb. The lantern's flickering light revealed walls covered in an elaborate mural that told the story of the rise and fall of the mage-warrior Knights of Esthrane. One wall was blank, leaving the end of the story incomplete.

In the center of the tomb was a catafalque. Blaine held his lantern aloft and stepped closer for a better look. It was the bier of a warrior, clad in battle armor. The pediment and bier were austere, bearing only the carved figure, and a name: Torsten Almstedt.

Piran gave Xaffert a shove to move him forward out of the passageway. Dagur followed cautiously, gesturing to Kestel and Zaryae that it was safe to step out. Kestel began to walk slowly around the room, taking in the story of the murals. On the other side of the room was a door, and beyond that, Blaine guessed, lay passageways that led farther down beneath the castle.

"Knight Alrik had us hide the items down here right after Penhallow and his servant, Connor, left," Dillon said, glancing around himself as if afraid someone else might overhear. "The

Knight said Penhallow had already been through some of the items down here and figured out which ones were most important. Alrik had us bring down any magic items that were left above."

"Where did you put them?" Piran asked, looking around the room, which was bare except for the catafalque.

"There's a library, down the hall that's outside that door," Dillon said nervously, and pointed to the closed door on the other side of the tomb.

"So the Knights had already hidden the big stuff before Reese captured Lynge," Blaine mused. "Do you think Lynge betrayed them before Reese killed him?"

Dillon drew a long breath. "I doubt it. No, Lynge didn't know what the Knights had done. Reese and Pollard destroyed a lot of the castle, but that closed off the inside passageways to the crypts underneath. When I fled the castle, I kept a watch on the cliffside passageway we just came through. I never saw Reese or Pollard or any of their men near it."

"From what's here, I'd say that Almstedt must have founded the Knights of Esthrane," Kestel mused. "But from the murals, it looks as if he died before they were betrayed."

"Don't touch anything," Zaryae warned. "Our host is watching us, deciding what to make of us."

"Our host?" Piran questioned.

Zaryae nodded, and inclined her head toward the catafalque. "Torsten Almstedt."

The room grew suddenly cold. Outside the door, Blaine heard the low rumble of voices and the clatter of boot steps. He reached for his sword, sure they were about to be attacked.

"Your sword is no use here," Dagur said. He lifted his face to the magic like a hound scenting his quarry. "Not against the dead."

A fine mist appeared from nothing, coalescing between the catafalque and the door to the hallway into the translucent image of a man dressed like the figure atop the bier. The ghost was a man in his middle years with the bearing and stance of a warrior. Almstedt's form may have appeared insubstantial, but here in the crypts, in his place of power, Blaine was certain the ghost could be dangerous. He was just as sure that the sword in Almstedt's hand would be as deadly as any blade in the world of the living.

"We've come to reclaim the items Sir Alrik left here for safe-keeping," Blaine said, stepping forward.

Almstedt's sword swung through the air, narrowly missing Blaine. The blade barred Blaine from moving closer to the door. Almstedt's gaze swept over Blaine. His gaze lingered on the two amulets at Blaine's throat, the disk and the passage token.

"My name is Blaine McFadden, Lord of Glenreith," Blaine replied, willing himself to meet the ghost's gaze. "Nidhud, one of the Knights of Esthrane, is our ally. He gave me this token when I traveled to Valshoa to bring back the magic. Some of the Knights took sanctuary there."

Almstedt listened without showing emotion. *He died long before King Merrill's ancestor betrayed the Knights. In his time, the Knights were the left hand of the king. They had no need of sanctuary,* Blaine thought. *If he exists as a ghost, does he know what's happened in the world he left behind?*

"Tell him why you've come," Zaryae urged.

"We brought the magic back—almost," Blaine told the ghost. "It's not like it was before the war. The magic that returned can be harnessed, but it's brittle...not quite right."

"I fail to see what's causing the delay," Xaffert fussed. He was a sallow-looking man with thinning brown hair and a mon-ocle, and right now he was indignant. "Alrik was the rightful owner of the pieces, and we're acting in his stead." He moved as if to go around Almstedt's sword, but the ghost shifted once more to block his path.

"I think it would be best to wait until our host wants us to proceed," Dagur cautioned. "And from the sound of it, the corridor's not a healthy place to be right now." Shouts and footsteps echoed from the rock, as well as the clang of swords.

"I thought you said no one else can get in down here," Piran whispered. "It sounds like there's a battle going on just outside the door."

"There is," Dillon replied. "The ghosts of the people buried down here are restless. They relive the battles and the betrayals that killed them. Alrik told me that's how Geddy, Lynge's assistant, was killed."

"Now you tell us this?" Piran said, eyes wide.

Dillon's expression was somber. "The ghosts don't reenact their battles all the time," Dillon replied, keeping one eye on the ghost who blocked their path. "When we brought the pieces down here, Alrik was constantly fussing about the time. He must have known when the ghosts were likely to be active. Maybe he figured the spirits could protect the items better than we could."

By the sound of it, the spectral battle beyond the door was drawing to a close, and in a few moments, the tomb was silent. Almstedt lifted his ghostly sword and gestured toward the entranceway, gliding effortlessly through the door.

"I guess he's going with us," Blaine commented.

They moved into the cool, dark passageway. Despite the sounds of pitched battle they had heard just moments ago, nothing in the corridor suggested that anyone had passed this way for quite a while. Almstedt's ghost stood in a passageway to their left.

"He knows the way," Dillon directed. "And keep your wits about you. There are ghosts aplenty. I'm glad I never knew that when I lived in the castle up above. I might not have slept well, knowing what goes on down here."

Wide passageways carved into rock led in several directions, and it seemed to Blaine he had entered an underground city. As they passed the entrances to other chambers, Blaine glimpsed rooms filled with catafalques, and other, larger areas where it looked as if rooms from the castle above, and even whole sections of the city of Castle Reach, had been re-created.

"Alrik told me that the kings and nobles weren't sure they would pass on to the Sea of Souls, given their deeds," Dillon whispered to Blaine. "So they made sure their accommodations here were comfortable and familiar—just in case."

"Can you imagine the secrets buried here?" Kestel murmured, her green eyes shining. She pushed a strand of red hair back into the braid that kept it out of her way. "I wish we could explore."

"The library's just ahead," Dillon interrupted.

"Let's be quick about this," Piran said. "I don't like this place. The sooner we're done and out of here, the better."

"In here," Dillon indicated, using a key from his satchel and opening the door to a room not far from Almstedt's crypt. A warren of corridors led off into darkness. Blaine looked at the flickering light in his lantern and shuddered at the thought of being lost in those dark passageways among warring and treacherous ghosts.

"Let us handle this," Xaffert said as they walked into the room. Xaffert was dressed in clothing that had seen better days. The richly woven brocade of his tunic was badly worn and snagged, stained in places, and his trews were mended awkwardly. Whether the clothing was what remained of his scholarly belongings or, more likely, something he had looted from a deserted villa, Blaine did not know. Xaffert wore his motley outfit with strained dignity, as if the loss of his status and the University itself was almost too much to bear.

Their lanterns illuminated a relatively large room with shelves lining the walls and a worktable with a few chairs. From the way the books and the odd collection of items were stacked on the tables and around the room, it was clear someone had already mined the library for information and then used every surface for the magical items gathered above. On one table lay four cloth sacks filled to the brim.

"Lynge and Geddy brought Connor and Penhallow down here to help you find those disks that you needed to bring back the magic," Dillon said with a look toward Blaine. "I'm not sure what else they took with them, or whether it was helpful, but I'll bet those sacks are full of the items they wanted to come back for."

Blaine could guess. Lanyon Penhallow was a *talishte*, an immortal vampire who had existed for centuries. Bevin Connor, once the assistant to Lord Garnoc before the Cataclysm, had become Penhallow's mortal servant. Both Connor and Penhallow had tracked down several of the obsidian disks that played an important role in helping Blaine restore the magic at Valshoa and bind it once more to the will of men. If Penhallow had gone to the trouble of gathering and safeguarding other artifacts, Blaine was willing to believe they were valuable enough to be worth the risk to retrieve them.

"Let's see what we have," Xaffert said, pushing past Blaine toward a cloth bundle on the nearest table.

"These crypts are full of old power," Dagur said. "Maybe, since the magic remains rather brittle, we might be safest handling the items as little as possible." Balding and thin, perhaps in his fourth decade, Dagur looked more like a tavern master than a scholar, clad as he was in a serviceable woolen jacket, homespun trews, and sturdy boots.

Xaffert fixed his colleague with a glare. "I'm not going to let a few ghosts send me screaming," he said with a sniff. "We're better served knowing what Lord Penhallow and Alrik thought valuable enough to hide down here. That way, if we run into difficulties on the way back, we know what tools are at our disposal."

"I agree with Dagur," Zaryae said. "Even if the artifacts still work as they were intended, using them down here might attract unwanted attention."

Xaffert's contempt was clear in his face. "That's probably prudent for you. What magic you have is untrained. Dagur and I are scholars and adepts, formally educated in the magic arts by the most powerful mages of our era. We're quite well prepared to handle whatever arises."

Blaine was not so sure that Dagur agreed with the older mage. Dagur remained a pace back from the table, and seemed happy to allow Xaffert to take the items out of the sacks as he surveyed the other items in the room.

"Take a look if you have to, but don't spend all day doing it," Piran grumbled. "I want to get aboveground."

Xaffert examined the items from one of the sacks. Blaine stayed back a bit, as did the others, but from what he could see, the magical artifacts did not appear unusual. Half a dozen pieces now lay on the table: a silver chalice, a flat piece of burnished wood carved with sigils, a white-handled boline knife with a curved blade, a dark scrying mirror, a lavishly engraved bell, and a stone censer with carvings. By the lantern light, they looked quite ordinary.

"I find nothing wrong with these pieces, nothing at all,"

Xaffert announced after a few moments. "In fact, I suspect that such basic tools cannot be subverted even by broken magic. It will be a pleasure to have these fine items in our study."

"Just put the bloody things back in the sack and let's get going," Piran said. "We've been down here long enough already."

Zaryae hung back. "The items may have been altered," she said. "We must be careful."

Dagur carefully gathered up the few small items that had spilled from the sacks. Even with the small amount of magic Blaine possessed, he could feel the jangle of power from the items in the room. Yet to him, the magic felt…out of kilter, like a painting hung askew. Piran, with no magic at all, kept his knife and sword at the ready, watching the door to the hallway.

It seemed to Blaine that the shadows crowded more closely around them as they retreated to the corridor. Several times, out of the corner of his eye, he caught a glimpse of motion, only to find nothing when he looked again. Blaine was on edge, and he wondered if the rest of his companions felt the same worrisome tingle in the air, which had grown icy cold.

"What in Raka is that?" Piran growled. Blue-green orbs of light bounced and bobbed, hurtling down the corridor toward the central rotunda, where several corridors led into a larger, open area. The sound of running footsteps echoed from the rock walls. Almstedt moved to stand in the doorway, and beckoned them to come.

"Something that isn't 'in' Raka or the Sea of Souls anymore," Kestel murmured, daggers raised. "And there are a lot of them, blocking the way back to Almstedt's crypt."

The orbs stretched into thin tendrils of light that swirled and shifted, taking on the forms of men, until two spectral armies faced off against each other in the wide chamber. Battle cries rang out as the ghostly soldiers hurtled toward each other, swords and axes raised, colliding with the muffled clang of armor. The combatants might be long dead, but the battle that played out in front of them was as fierce as any waged by living men.

Almstedt's ghost stopped, barring them from approaching the fight. His raised sword made it clear that Almstedt intended to stand his ground. Going back the way they came was not an option.

"I was afraid of this," Piran muttered. "Now what?"

"Dillon—any chance the entrance you and Alrik used to bring the items here is still open?" Blaine asked.

"The upper level where we entered has completely collapsed."

"There's got to be another way out," Blaine said. He looked to Kestel. "How about you? You're the spy. Any great ideas?"

"I heard rumors about secret passageways to the crypts, but I never personally found any," she replied. "I didn't know about the one we used to enter. As for others, even if we found them, are they passable, given how badly the castle was damaged?"

"Let's see what we can find, and worry about the rest later," Blaine said. "Gather up the sacks and whatever items Zaryae and Dagur thought worthy—let's get moving." Xaffert, Dagur, Dillon, and Zaryae gingerly loaded the artifacts into the satchels they had brought, leaving the others free to wield their swords if necessary.

Eager to move away from the spectral battle, Blaine and Piran headed in the opposite direction, back toward the vaults closer to the castle. Their lanterns barely lit their way in the gloom. Doorways opened on either side of the corridor, only to lead into crypts like Almstedt's.

Finally, the corridor widened into another large rotunda filled with catafalques, some ancient and some much newer. The lanterns illuminated the figure that lay carved in marble atop the nearest tomb, and Kestel gasped. "Look," she whispered, pointing. "It's King Merrill."

Merrill had been the king since before Blaine was born, and it was he who exiled them. But Merrill had probably never imagined that he would be the last king of Donderath, or that in his reign, the kingdom would burn, its magic would fail, and the people of an entire Continent would be reduced to desperate subsistence.

"We've got company," Piran said in a low voice.

Blaine looked up to see a young man standing just beyond the torchlight. The man beckoned urgently even as the sounds of battle seemed to close in. Xaffert and Dagur started forward, but Blaine threw out a warning arm to halt them. "Wait. We don't know whose side he's on."

Dillon maneuvered forward. "Yes we do," he said triumphantly. "That's Geddy. Thank the gods, it's Geddy." He turned to the others. "Seneschal Lynge's assistant. He died down here. Now he's come to help us."

Blaine met Piran's gaze and shrugged. Caught between threatening specters and a ghostly guide, they had little choice. "Let's hope he knows where we're going, because those ghost soldiers are getting closer," Blaine said. "Follow Geddy."

Geddy's ghost moved so quickly they were forced to run to keep him in sight. The ghost was tall and angular, with lank dark hair, all slender arms and legs, and although Blaine searched his memories, he could not recall having seen the young man at the castle. He hoped that they had read the ghost's intentions correctly, and that he meant to get them to safety.

Geddy led them through the maze of corridors with confidence, while Blaine struggled to remember their course. The ground was rising under their feet, and they were moving in the right direction to be inside the castle, or at least the bailey walls.

The clang of metal against rock clattered through the empty corridors. Xaffert stood swearing over a jumble of artifacts that had spilled from his satchel. "Pick those things up and be quiet about it!" Blaine snapped.

"You're loud enough to wake the dead, and down here, that's a bad thing," Piran muttered.

"Well, don't just stand there—lend a hand!" Xaffert waved a hand at Dagur, whose expression made it clear he had no desire to handle the artifacts before their power was known. Reluctantly, Dagur withdrew a pair of gloves from his belt and gingerly helped place the objects once more into Xaffert's satchel. Geddy's ghost stood a little farther down the corridor, gesturing for them to hurry.

"Move faster, gents. Our guide's a mite frantic for us to get going," Piran urged. After a few more moments and another crash as Xaffert turned too quickly and his satchel hit the wall, Zaryae strode up to Xaffert. She pulled his bag away from him roughly enough to send his hat flying.

"By Torven's horns! Just give it to me," she demanded. "You're a disaster." Xaffert's protests were muted enough for Blaine to decide that the mage was quite happy having someone else carry the burden.

They had barely gone a dozen steps before Geddy's ghost stopped beside a catafalque. He pointed toward the raised marble tomb, pantomiming moving its heavy carved lid aside.

"What's he want us to do, climb in?" Piran's skepticism was clear in his voice.

"I think that's exactly what he means," Kestel said. "Come on, get to it."

Blaine, Piran, and Dillon set their shoulders to the heavy marble, and Blaine was surprised when it moved easily. He lifted his lantern and peered inside, expecting to see dry bones and rotted finery. Instead, he found stairs descending into darkness.

"In we go," he said, stepping aside to allow Kestel and Zaryae to enter first.

"You expect me to climb into a crypt?" Xaffert huffed.

"You can do what you want," Dillon said. "I'm saving my skin."

Dagur pushed past Xaffert toward the escape route. "I don't have a problem with it, actually," he said. "Honestly, Xaffert, come along."

"We're not waiting on you," Blaine warned. "Are you coming?"

Muttering, Xaffert followed the others. Piran waved Blaine on ahead of him.

Blaine paused in front of Geddy's spirit. Up close, he could see the dark stains on the young man's clothing where a sword had dealt a deathblow. "Thank you," he said. Geddy inclined his head, then gestured toward the catafalque. Blaine climbed inside with Piran right behind him.

Behind them, Blaine heard the thud of boots on the stone floor and the clash of swords. A blue-white light flared, blindingly bright in the gloom of the crypt.

"Help me close this before the ghosts catch up." Blaine nodded toward the handles carved in the bottom of the heavy lid. Together, he and Piran wrested the lid shut, sealing their spectral pursuers behind them.

"Let's hope those ghosts can't walk through walls," Piran said, casting a wary glance overhead. He looked around. "Did anyone notice that Geddy didn't come down with us?"

The catafalque steps led down to a narrow passage. A little maneuvering allowed Piran and Blaine to go first, with the mages taking up the rear.

Dillon, just behind Blaine, held his lantern aloft. "I think I know where this leads," he said. "And besides, there's only one way to go."

They ran along the passageway, stumbling on the uneven floor. The bulky satchels of artifacts were an encumbrance, but too many lives had been lost protecting the items for Blaine to be willing to leave them behind. He ran, expecting any moment to feel a ghostly sword in his back. But the noise of battle receded as they got farther from the crypts, replaced by the sound of their labored breathing.

After a few hundred steps, the passage came to an abrupt end, facing a stone wall with jutting stones offering a ladder upward. "Do you know where we'll come out?" Blaine asked.

Dillon looked uncertain. "Maybe. Late one night, I saw Sir Alrik in the hallway by the exchequer's office. I had to go in the same direction, and when I turned the corner, he was gone. All the doors were locked and the hallway ended in a storage room, so he shouldn't have been able to disappear like that." He paused. "I think there's a panel, somewhere in that corridor, that opens into a hidden passage."

"Yeah, but there's no telling whether it's *this* hidden passage," Piran said.

"Or whether we're coming up under a portion of the castle that's collapsed," Blaine added.

"We'll know soon enough," Kestel said from behind him. "Just climb."

A dark landing at the top of the ladder ended in a blank wooden wall. Dillon edged to the front, and he began to run his hands over the wood. A quiet *snick* of a latch opening brought a smile of triumph. "Got it," he said, and pushed on the door.

It stuck, barely a hand's width open. "It's blocked," Dillon said. Blaine and Piran squeezed forward and put their shoulders against the door. The first shove won an additional inch as the sound of wood grating on rock made it clear what was barring their progress. On the next push, Dagur and Dillon added their weight, shoving the door open far enough that Kestel could slip through.

"It looks like a butler's closet," she said, sheathing her knife and holding aloft the lantern Blaine passed to her. "There's no one here—and it looks like no one's been here for quite a while." She pushed against the wooden crate that blocked the door, and managed to dislodge it, letting the door open to nearly its full span.

"Come on in," she said with a grin as the others stepped out.

Blaine glanced around the room at the shelves that had once held neat stacks of linens for the castle housekeepers. The closet was now a ransacked mess.

"A lot of manors have hiding places—even whole hidden rooms—in case of attack," Kestel said. "Looks like we've stumbled upon one of Glenreith's secrets."

Dillon nodded. "This is where I lost sight of Sir Alrik that night," he said. "It doesn't look as if anyone's been in here, so I doubt Reese and Pollard found it." He smiled. "What do you know? Geddy got us out."

Piran had crossed to the pantry's door and into the corridor, only to find their way blocked by rubble where part of the ceiling had collapsed. "We've got another problem," he said with a sigh. "Since no one knows we're here, no one's going to come dig us out."

"If we straighten up the things that fell, we should have room to move a lot of rock out of the way," Kestel said. She placed the lantern on one of the shelves and then bent to pick up a stack of linens, which she thrust against Xaffert's chest.

"Here," she said. "Be useful. Put those on the shelves, and come back for another load."

Xaffert stammered indignantly. "Now, see here—"

Before he could complete his outburst, Kestel dropped the linens and pressed one of her knives against the mage's throat. "No, you see here," she said in a dangerously pleasant voice. "Either you pull your weight and help move the rocks or we seal you back in that passage and leave you to the ghost soldiers." Her smile was jarringly at odds with her words. "And since no one else knows about the passageway, no one will find you."

Xaffert paled. "All right," he said, "but I must protest your methods."

Kestel sheathed her knife and shoved the linens into his arms. "Protest away. Just keep moving."

Dillon and Zaryae moved to help get the closet's contents back onto the shelves and out of the way. Blaine, Piran, and Dagur created a human chain, handing one stone after another into the room to be stacked against the far wall. After several candlemarks, they had cleared an opening large enough for each of them to hand out the satchels of artifacts and then wiggle through to the other side. It was nearly morning by the time they made their way back to camp.

Kestel seemed to take it all in stride and dusted herself off matter-of-factly, while Zaryae murmured a prayer to the gods. Dagur looked pale and flustered by the ordeal. Xaffert was still sulking. Piran was regaling Dillon with jokes, each one bawdier than the last. Blaine breathed a sigh of relief and turned to Xaffert and Dagur.

"Call the rest of your mages together and let's get an idea of why Penhallow and Alrik thought these artifacts were important," Blaine said. "I just want to know whether or not they still work and whether they're safe to take back to Glenreith."

"Must we work with them immediately?" Dagur asked. "My

books and scrolls are at Glenreith. I'd feel safer working on them there."

"How many times do I have to tell you that, for a mage of power, these items simply pose no danger, even with the new magic?" Xaffert said, exasperation edging his voice. He snatched one of the bags from Dillon and thrust his hand inside, coming up with the dark scrying mirror.

"I really don't think—" Dagur began.

"Take this, for example." Xaffert brandished the mirror like a trophy. "Perhaps you'd like to know whether our road will be clear? Let me have a look."

Zaryae tried to intervene. "Don't! I can feel the power—it's all wrong."

"Nonsense," Xaffert said with a dismissive gesture. "That's like saying that a hammer doesn't work the way it used to. These are mere tools. What matters is the skill of the user."

"The items may be damaged," Zaryae cautioned. "We should be careful."

Xaffert regarded Zaryae before speaking. "My colleagues and I mastered all manner of magical items at the University. I'm quite certain that we can handle the pieces safely, even if the Cataclysm altered them."

"Perhaps we should take this slowly," Dagur cautioned. "We should set a warded circle for protection."

"That won't be necessary," Xaffert replied. He held the dark mirror in front of him in both hands, and his lips moved silently. Blaine felt the tingle of power grow to a roar and it coalesced around the mage, but the magic felt brittle and wild. The air crackled and sparked around Xaffert, who laughed. As the mirror's images changed, his laughter grew fraught with tension until it became heaving breaths.

The mirror's surface glowed, illuminating Xaffert's face

caught in an expression of absolute horror. Blood streamed from his nose, mouth, and ears and his laughter changed to a shriek of pain. Before anyone had a chance to intervene, Xaffert fell to the ground, the mirror still clutched in his hand.

Dagur and Zaryae rushed toward Xaffert, while Piran used a stick to knock the mirror from Xaffert's fingers. "Is he dead?" Blaine asked. He felt disoriented and light-headed as his head pounded. He swayed on his feet before steadying himself against the wall, while trying to keep a worried eye on the mirror, which now lay dim and inert beside the mage.

Dagur knelt beside Xaffert, and his expression grew queasy. "Most definitely. It looks as if his eyes and everything behind them have been burned out."

"Let me make something very clear," Blaine said, fixing Dagur with a look. "I'm willing to give you and your mages sanctuary in exchange for your expertise. But I need to be able to trust you—and that means that you'd better be right when you give me your word on whether or not something is safe to use."

Dagur stood and squared his shoulders. "Unlike Xaffert, when I give you my word, you can stake your life on it."

"I am," Blaine replied. "We all are. And that's why you'd damn well better be right."

CHAPTER TWO

H ERE'S YOUR TRIBUTE...M'LORD." CARR McFAD-
den tossed a leather messenger's pouch at Blaine's feet
and stood back, hands on hips, waiting for a response to his
challenge.

"Open it. You'll find Karstan Lysander's orders to his commanding officers, laying out a battle strategy for his next
offensive—against us, and against your 'buddy' Vigus Quintrel."
Carr did not attempt to hide a victorious smirk. Eight years
younger than Blaine, Carr took more after their father's looks,
with muddy-brown hair and angular features. Soldiering had
hardened his body and dispelled any illusions that remained after
having grown up under Ian McFadden's thumb.

"How did you come by this?" Blaine asked, trying unsuc-
cessfully to keep the bite from his voice. Niklas Theilsson, the
commander of Blaine's army, bent to retrieve the pouch and
opened it, frowning as he reviewed the contents.

"I stole it," Carr said levelly, his voice insolent. "One of
Lysander's messengers got careless. I jumped him and took the
bag." Carr had made no secret of his anger at Blaine for the
scandal that had destroyed the family fortune, even if killing

Ian McFadden had saved Carr and their sister, Mari, from Ian's abuse. A bout of the Madness just before the Battle of Valshoa had added to Carr's edgy unpredictability.

Niklas looked at Carr sharply. "You were supposed to be spying, not waging a one-man war," he snapped.

"Spies bring back information. I don't think he'd have given it to me if I'd just asked. Sir." Carr's tone was still impertinent, but he reserved his contempt for his older brother. It was obvious the packet had required a fight: His knuckles on both hands were skinned and swollen. Carr's lip was split and he had a large bruise on one side of his face, injuries he wore like a mark of honor.

"Of all the wrong-headed, damn-fool stunts—" Blaine began, then stopped to rein in his temper when it was clear Carr was enjoying Blaine's outrage.

"Just doing my part for the war effort," Carr said with a grin that baited Blaine to take a swing at him.

"Before Piran and I have to pull you two off each other—again—can I point out that this appears to be authentic?" Niklas interrupted, with a warning glance to both Blaine and Carr. Blaine and Niklas had been friends since boyhood, and when Blaine's crime sent him into exile, Niklas joined the army in the Meroven War. A few years later, Carr mustered in, seeking out a place under Niklas's command even though Carr was still underage.

Blaine took a deep breath, accepting the wisdom of the warning glance. *Carr wants a reaction, and if I give it to him, he'll do something even riskier next time. But damn, he makes it hard!*

Piran leaned against the wall near the fireplace. They were in what had been one of the exchequer's offices in Quillarth Castle and that was now being used by Niklas as a war room for the portion of Blaine's army stationed at the castle and in the city of Castle Reach. "How do you know the messenger you waylaid wasn't a decoy?" Piran asked, with a deceptively casual tone that Blaine and Kestel knew meant Piran was annoyed.

"I've been shadowing that battalion commander for a while now," Carr replied. "That's his usual messenger, so if he's a decoy, then Lysander hasn't sent any real orders to that division for over a month." His tone dared Piran to challenge him.

Piran shrugged in acknowledgment. "Fair enough." He glanced toward Niklas. "Was the information worth the risk?"

From the look on Carr's face, Blaine was certain his brother had already looked over the documents and knew their value. Niklas took the pouch to the large table in the center of the room and Kestel helped him spread them out.

"I'm not in favor of how you came by these," Niklas said with a stern glance toward Carr. "But I would be happy to stay a step ahead of Lysander. From what I can tell, he's out to make a name for himself."

"Did you know of him—in the war?" Blaine asked, coming around to have a look at the documents. Kestel was already studying them with a practiced eye from her own days as a court spy.

Niklas frowned. "I knew him by reputation. Never met him in person. He won his battles, but he also had the highest casualty rates of any commander in the king's army. His strategies were daring and unpredictable, and he was willing to send large numbers of soldiers to their deaths to make them work." His tone made it clear that he did not share Lysander's perspective.

"He's got to either adjust his tactics or come up with a lot of replacement soldiers," Blaine observed drily.

"Rumor has it, he's agitating the Tingur," Carr said, and grinned as Blaine and Niklas looked up.

"Aren't they the crazy folks wandering around saying that Torven sent the Cataclysm because someone annoyed him?" Piran asked. He had left his spot by the fire to come around and eye the battle map. Before his court-martial, Piran had been rising fast in King Merrill's army. Exile had ended his official career, but Piran's grasp of tactics and strategy was as sharp as ever.

"We know that the Great Fire happened because the battle mages on both sides got out of hand," Kestel replied. "But think about how the Cataclysm looked to your average barmaid or farmer. A green ribbon of fire falls from the sky and destroys most of the countryside, killing the king and the nobles. They wouldn't think about some faraway war. They'd pick the easy explanation—someone made the gods angry." Torven, the god of the sea and underworld, was believed by his followers to be generous to the faithful and merciless to those he disliked.

"The word is that there are plenty of farmers, sailors, and tradesmen whose livelihoods went up in smoke in the Great Fire, and they're milling about looking for something to do," Carr replied. "Some of them join up with the warlord armies, but they'll only take people who can do real soldiering."

"So the Tingur attract all the other people who've got no place left to go and convince them praying to Torven will make it all right again?" Piran mocked.

Kestel shook her head. "I think you're missing the point, Piran. These folks saw their world burn. They want it to make sense, and appeasing an angry god makes the kind of sense they can understand. It gives them a purpose. And if Lysander is clever enough to win their loyalty, he'll have an almost limitless supply of disposable foot soldiers willing to die to make Torven happy."

Blaine felt a chill as he thought through the import of

Kestel's statement. "Sweet Esthrane," he murmured. "They wouldn't stand a chance in a real battle."

Kestel met his gaze. "They wouldn't have to. Lysander could use them to wear down the enemy, and save the real troops for the second wave."

"It takes a sick bastard to use soldiers like that," Niklas muttered. "But from what I've heard of Lysander, it would be like him to try it."

Blaine riffled through the sheaf of parchment from the pouch. "If these orders are real, Lysander's going to send an assault our way in the next few weeks, and it looks like he's interested in seeing if he can break our line to get to Castle Reach."

Niklas nodded. "I saw. Fortunately, he's not the only one who's been recruiting. Word spread after Valshoa. We've taken on enough new recruits to make up for the men we lost in the battle." He met Blaine's gaze. "We can hold the line on the city, and protect Glenreith, too."

"Glad I could be of service, m'lord," Carr drawled, emphasizing 'm'lord' sarcastically. "I'll be heading back to the camp now, with your permission, Commander."

Blaine could see the irritation in Niklas's face at the way Carr intentionally maneuvered to show his disdain for Blaine's authority. And he had no doubt that Niklas would have something to say about it to Carr later, in private. For now, Niklas just gave Carr a glare. "Go. But don't leave camp until you've talked to me. We need to discuss tactics."

"Yes, sir," Carr replied with a salute that was a little too snappy to be serious. As he left, Blaine saw the slight hitch in Carr's gait that was an aftereffect of the Madness, a disease born of the broken magic that nearly killed him.

No one spoke until Carr had left the room. "Bloody hell,

Mick!" Piran exploded. "If he weren't your brother, I'd have loved to wipe that smirk off his face."

Blaine sighed. "It wouldn't do any good. Father beat both of us enough that we're good at taking a whipping." He shook his head. "I understand why he's angry with me. Fine. But I don't understand why he's trying to get himself killed."

Niklas grimaced. "Come on, Blaine. Carr always liked taking risks. He was never afraid to try anything you and I did, even though we were a lot older. And if he could, he figured out how to do us one better. Remember?"

More than one long-ago example came to mind. "Yeah, I remember. But that was different," Blaine objected.

"I agree," Niklas replied. "And I do wonder if the Madness had something to do with it. I've asked Ordel, but he's had so few soldiers live through the Madness that there aren't many cases for comparison." He shook his head. "I don't know whether he's trying to prove something to you, or outdo you, or get himself killed. But he's worse when I try to keep him with the rest of the troops. Letting him go off on patrol—and now, spying—seemed to be the only way to handle him, short of tying him up and putting him in Glenreith's dungeon."

"Maybe you should reconsider," Piran muttered.

Sudden light-headedness made Blaine stagger. From outside the castle came a resounding explosion that made the glass in the windows rattle. "What in Raka is going on?" Niklas muttered, rushing with Piran to look out the window in the direction of the blast.

Kestel hung back, giving Blaine a worried look. "Are you all right?" she asked quietly.

"I'm fine," he said, waving off her concern, although he was far from certain. As soon as he knew he could move without falling over, he joined the others at the window. Smoke was rising from the large tent the mages had claimed as their workspace.

"Looks like it was a good idea to keep the mages out of the castle while they try out the artifacts we brought back," Piran remarked.

"Let's hope no one died," Niklas said.

Kestel still eyed Blaine skeptically. He was reluctant to admit it, but the vertigo worried him. So far, he had not blacked out, but he felt as if his knees might buckle. *What if it happens in battle?* he wondered.

"We'd better go see what happened," Niklas said with a sigh of resignation. "Come on, Piran. Let's find out what they've blown up this time." He looked toward Blaine. "We'll give you a report once we know what's going on."

Kestel waited until the others had gone before she folded her arms across her chest and gave Blaine a level stare. "What's wrong? You looked like you were going to fall over."

Blaine grimaced and turned back toward the window. "It *felt* like I was going to fall over. And I don't know why."

Kestel stepped up behind him and laid a hand on his arm. "How long has it been like this?"

He sighed. "Since Valshoa. Since we brought the magic back."

"Maybe Niklas's battle healer could help," she suggested.

Blaine reached over to take her hand and drew her closer to him. "I've already had Ordel check me over, after we got back from Valshoa." He shook his head. "Nothing. Except that he thought I seemed especially tired and 'run-down' was his term. Made it sound like I hadn't been eating vegetables or something."

Kestel chuckled. "Maybe you need to eat more herring."

Blaine glared at her. "Not if I can help it." After his time in Edgeland, manning the miserable herring boats that supplied the motherland with salted, pickled, and dried fish, he had little desire to eat herring ever again.

"There has to be a reason why it's happening," Kestel pressed. She thought for a moment. "Just now, you looked unsteady an instant before the explosion."

Blaine nodded. "And the same thing happened when Xaffert used the mirror."

He had a suspicion of what was causing the problem, but he desperately wished to be proven wrong.

"Both times there was strong magic," Kestel said.

"That occurred to me, too," Blaine admitted.

"You brought magic back under human control at Valshoa," Kestel said, speaking slowly as she put the thoughts together. "But the last time, thirteen Lords of the Blood anchored the magic. This time, just one."

Blaine nodded again, keeping his gaze focused on the hectic activity as soldiers and healers bustled around the mages' tent. "But if that's the case, how can I fix it?" he asked. "The magic that bound the old Lords of the Blood came down through the eldest son. Except for me, all the others either died in the Cataclysm or the bloodlines died out long ago." He grimaced. "Well, there's the Wraith Lord, but he's a wraith so he can't really help."

"Has the light-headedness changed at all?"

Blaine thought for a moment. "I don't remember noticing it immediately after Valshoa. But it's been several months, and I'd say it's happening more often, growing stronger."

"We need to figure this out," Kestel said, giving his hand a squeeze before she released it and began to pace. "Maybe Zaryae and Dagur can help."

"If they didn't blow themselves up in the tent," Blaine replied.

"Come on," she said. "Let's go find out what happened, and see if we can get Zaryae and Dagur to come up to the castle tonight, once things calm down." She smiled. "Besides, I wanted to make an offering at the shrine. For luck."

"I still can't believe it's come to this."

Kestel stared up at the charred ruins of Quillarth Castle and wiped her eyes with the back of her hand. The wind tangled her red hair around her face, and she brushed it back from green eyes that shimmered with tears.

Blaine slipped an arm around her shoulders. "Even though we heard about what happened, it's different actually seeing the damage up close," he replied.

The once-grand castle was a blackened shell, with most of the structure reduced to rubble. Only one tower and part of a wing remained standing; the rest was a jumble of massive stones. Quillarth Castle had survived a direct strike in the magical onslaught that brought the kingdom of Donderath to ruin, then a devastating fire when the mages of neighboring Meroven had sent their worst against the castle and the manor houses of the nobility. Magic storms had added to the damage since the kingdom's fall. But the last, worst assault had been just two months ago, when renegade lord Vedran Pollard and *talishte* warlord Pentreath Reese had captured what remained of the castle, then took it apart nearly stone by stone to find the treasures Reese believed to be hidden inside.

In an alcove near the castle's once-grand entrance was a shrine with salvaged statues to Donderath's three most powerful gods, Charrot, Torven, and Esthrane. Charrot, the high god, was both male and female, with one head and two faces. Charrot was creation and destruction embodied, the True

Source, and ruled both gods and men. One side of him was the perfect warrior with rippling muscles and broad shoulders. Charrot was handsome, with dusky yellow skin, dark hair, and chiseled features. The other side of Charrot was a beautiful woman with blue skin whose breasts and thighs promised fertility.

Traditionally, Charrot was depicted stretching out his hands to his two consorts. Torven, the god of illusion, was a man whose beauty rivaled that of Charrot himself. Torven ruled the air and sea, darkness and twilight, water and ice, and the Sea of Souls. Esthrane was the second consort, and equaled Charrot's feminine beauty. Artists depicted Esthrane with saffron-colored skin and sorrowful eyes. She summoned fertility from crops and herds and commanded birth and fire. Esthrane was also the master of the Unseen Realm, where wandering and incomplete souls went after death.

A collection of guttered candles, withered flowers, and food offerings lay at the feet of the statues, along with pebbles brought by passersby. Whether the gifts came from supplicants who sought protection or merely wished to give tribute, Blaine did not know. If he had ever believed the gods cared about the affairs of mortals, what he had seen of his ravaged kingdom made such interest unlikely.

Kestel slipped up to the statues and withdrew a small bundle from beneath her cloak. She untied the bit of cloth and took out a hard roll and a bit of sausage. Bowing her head, she knelt before the statue of Esthrane and held out her offerings, murmuring a prayer to the goddess. From a pocket in her trews, she added a few smooth pebbles to her gift, and made a gesture of blessing, then rose to rejoin Blaine.

"I'm with Piran on wondering whether anyone is listening when you do that," Blaine said, taking her arm.

Kestel chuckled. "Then it's good the two of you have me to make offerings for you. I figure it can't hurt."

A deep rumble inside the castle walls quickly became a roar, shaking the ground beneath Blaine's feet. Blaine drew his sword, and Kestel had knives in each hand, ready for the worst. Blaine spotted Piran running toward the disturbance, shouting for Niklas. A cloud of dust rose where part of the castle's inner wall had stood just moments before.

"Let me through," Blaine ordered, shouldering past the guards, with Kestel just a step behind him. "Someone give me a report!" Blaine shouted as they halted just paces away from the damage.

Piran picked his way across the rubble and scowled at Blaine. "The guards were supposed to keep you where it's safe," he said, running a hand over his bald head in frustration. He was covered in rock dust, and there was a smear of blood from a cut on one cheek.

"'Safe' is a relative term," Blaine replied. "What happened?"

Piran muttered a potent oath. "The area's been getting pounded by storms, each worse than the one before. It weakened the wall. That blast from the mages was the last straw."

"Casualties?"

Piran grimaced. "One man broke a leg, maybe some ribs. The battle healer is with him. No one dead, thank the gods."

Blaine looked up to find Dillon heading toward them with a young man behind him. "I've found someone you need to meet," Dillon hailed him. "This is Jodd," he added, with a nod toward his companion. "He was one of the master butler's helpers." He met Blaine's gaze. "He knows his way around the castle, and he's agreed to give us a hand."

"My mates and I sprung all the traps we could find in the tower," Jodd volunteered. He was a half-grown lad, perhaps about fourteen summers old, with a shock of dark hair that poked up at all angles. He looked intelligent and wily, and the grin he shot Blaine was confident and full of mischief.

"Are you certain?" Blaine asked.

Jodd shrugged. "We didn't find no more than what we sprung. Had a right good time of it, too. The blokes who were here before left some real puzzlers, I'll say that for them."

"What kind of puzzlers?" Blaine asked.

Jodd did his best to look nonchalant, though it was clear he was quite pleased with himself. "Trip wires. Parts of the floor rigged to give out when you step on them. Walls set to collapse if you opened the door wrong. We got banged up good, but no one died." From his triumphant grin, it was clear that Jodd and his friends had considered it a fine lark.

"Why would Reese and Pollard bother with traps?" Piran asked. "If they had what they wanted, why not just bring down the walls and be done with it?"

"Because they didn't find what they were looking for," Jodd said with a conspiratorial glance toward Dillon. "They just found enough to make them go away."

Blaine looked from Jodd to Dillon. "I don't understand."

Dillon glanced toward the ruined portion of the castle, and his expression grew somber. "After the Great Fire, when the king and the nobles died, the mages vanished. Seneschal Lynge rallied the servants to salvage what was left," he said. "Then Lord Penhallow came, and Bevin Connor."

"They're friends of ours," Blaine said. Connor had traveled with Blaine's group and earned their trust. Lord Penhallow, an immortal *talishte* lord, was an ally, if not exactly a friend.

"They were looking for the disks that helped forge the magic," Dillon went on. Blaine, Kestel, and Piran exchanged a knowing look. The disks had been critical to raising the magic, and had nearly cost Blaine his life. They were safely locked away at Blaine's manor, Glenreith.

"We know Connor found disks here at the castle," Blaine said.

Dillon nodded. "Aye. When Connor and Lord Penhallow left with the disks, Lynge took me aside and had me work with Sir Alrik. Lynge told me that with Geddy gone, someone else needed to know the secret, in case anything happened to him. Sir Alrik gathered the remaining magic items that had been found, leaving just enough of the less valuable stuff for Pollard to find." He gave a wan smile. "The items we left for Pollard might not have been as powerful as what he wanted, but they were good enough to make him wonder if there might be more if he had time to search harder. That's why he set traps to keep other people out, and didn't just destroy the castle."

"And it's a good thing Lynge and Alrik took you into their confidence, considering what happened," Jodd added.

A chill went down Blaine's back. Dillon met his gaze evenly. "Lynge sent us away when Lord Reese laid siege to the castle. We didn't come back until we heard Lord Reese had been defeated." He looked down. "We found Lynge's body—laid him to rest."

"Thank you for seeing that he got a proper burial," Blaine said. "He deserved a better end." He paused. "Have you told Commander Theilsson about the traps?" Blaine asked.

Jodd looked pleased. "Absolutely! Told him as soon as he arrived, and took him and his men around to show them what we'd found."

"Good work," Blaine replied. He turned to Dillon. "Tomorrow I need to go into Castle Reach, but after that, I'd like to get back to Glenreith. We'll need provisions for the road, and fresh horses."

Dillon nodded. "I'll get started on it," he said, and turned back toward the castle, taking Jodd with him.

Blaine staggered as the vertigo struck again. "Sorry, lost my footing."

Kestel looked at him with concern. "Is the magic still affecting you? We need to figure out how to stop that from happening before we're in battle."

"I suspect that when I anchored the magic, I got tied up in the bond." Blaine replied. "So it's not just breaking me out of the bond—it's making sure that getting me untangled doesn't affect the magic."

Kestel gave him a no-nonsense look. "You mean, making sure that if you get killed, it doesn't destroy the magic again."

"Yeah," he said. "That, too. And I'm sure Pollard and Reese would like to make both those things happen." He could see the worry in her eyes. "But we're jumping to conclusions. Let's see what Dagur or the other mages come up with."

Kestel nodded, and glanced past Blaine. "Just as well. Niklas is headed our way."

"What happened?" Blaine asked as Niklas approached.

Niklas muttered curses. "The mages tried to use another artifact. Good thing they were warded this time, or they might have done more than set off an explosion—although it made that wall fall. As it is, there are two people down with minor burns, and a man with some broken bones from the wall collapse, but Rikard and Dagur seem to think the exercise went well, all things considered."

"How long do you think it'll take to finish securing the grounds?"

Niklas turned to look back at the ruins. "A few more days at most."

"Can you hurry it up?"

Piran laughed. "You put him in charge of your army for a reason. He's good at what he does. Maybe we should let him do it."

Blaine glowered at Piran, then nodded to Niklas. "Just make sure you don't drag it out longer than necessary."

Piran headed back to the wall, and Blaine turned to look at the remaining tower and wing, silhouetted against the sky. "The last time I was at Quillarth Castle, I was in chains," he said quietly as Kestel came to stand next to him. "I never thought I'd outlive either the king or the castle."

It had been nearly seven years since Lord Blaine McFadden had come before King Merrill to be tried for the murder of his father, Ian McFadden. To the court, it did not matter that he had killed Ian for dishonoring his own daughter, Blaine's sister. Merrill exiled Blaine to the Velant prison colony. After three years as a convict and three more as a colonist in the brutal arctic weather of Edgeland, Blaine had returned to Donderath when the war that killed the king and leveled the cities also destroyed the magic.

"Even though we're without a king," Kestel said, "it makes sense to rebuild. Quillarth Castle is located on one of the meridians, so it's a place of power. And it's a stronghold to secure the city and the port. Someday, we'll start trading again with the Cross-Sea powers and the other kingdoms. We'll need a fortress to protect our interests."

"I imagine just getting the city back under control will keep our garrison busy for quite a while," Niklas added.

Blaine shrugged. "That's what you're here for. Glenreith is in pretty good shape now, and well defended," he replied.

"You'll still need all the help you can get for harvest," Kestel replied. "At least our soldiers got enough planted so the manor, the garrison, and what's left of the town won't go hungry."

"It's a start," Blaine acknowledged. "But we've got so much left to do."

Blaine turned his gaze back to Niklas. "What's the situation in Castle Reach?" he asked with a nod of his head in the direction toward where Donderath's capital city sprawled down to the sea.

Niklas let out a long breath. "Even with twice as many men I couldn't get the whole city completely in hand, but we've made a start," he said. "We've secured a corridor from the castle down to the waterfront that includes most of the area that used to be shops, markets, and pubs, as well as the docks."

"Any pushback?"

Niklas swore. "Lots of it. Without the king's guards to keep the peace, and what with so many of the people fleeing the city, the folks who were left fended for themselves as best they could. The city was divided up between bandit gangs, and they each charged a toll for anyone foolhardy enough to cross their territory."

Now that Blaine had a good look in daylight, he could see the fresh marks of recent battle in Niklas's newly healed scars. "First, I took a garrison against the top two bandit gangs, and when we broke them, the others swore fealty, especially the dominant one, run by a man named Folville. He'll keep the others in line."

Blaine's eyes widened. "You accepted oaths of fealty from bandit gangs?"

Niklas grinned. "No, you did. We dealt out death in the name of the warlord Blaine McFadden, and the survivors swore their loyalty to you."

Well, damn. "And does this fealty mean anything at all?" Blaine asked.

"Yes and no," Niklas replied. "Unless you want me to tie up half your army patrolling the city, we can't keep a large enough presence to crack down on all the bandit gangs. But if they swear loyalty to you, those gangs patrol the city to keep out rival gangs—or any of Reese and Pollard's men—and they pay a percentage of their profits to you as tribute."

Before his exile, such an arrangement might have seemed sordid. But after three years in King Merrill's prison colony, Blaine understood the idea of using rivals to gain a balance of power. "Very well," he said. "What else?"

Niklas grimaced. "Reese and Pollard have left a mess behind. We've found an item we think was left as a trap. Dagur thinks it was meant to be triggered by magic. We dug a hole and buried it, and we're going to have the mages see if they can set it off and contain it at the same time."

Blaine raised an eyebrow. "That's rather risky, isn't it?"

Niklas shrugged. "Dagur seems to think it won't be a problem." He grimaced. "Then again, he didn't think trying out this last artifact was going to be a problem, either."

Shouting near the front gate sent guards running. From where Blaine stood, it looked as if someone had arrived unannounced.

"Expecting guests?" Kestel asked with a raised eyebrow.

"Hardly."

Whoever had arrived was heatedly arguing with Niklas's guards. After a while, Piran brought the newcomer over to Blaine at sword's point, with a guard trailing warily behind them. A slender man in patched brown robes strode toward him, his angular features pinched with annoyance, and a pair of wire-rimmed spectacles perched on his sharp nose.

"Well, well, well," Blaine said. "Treven Lowrey. I thought you were staying in Valshoa with Vigus Quintrel." His sidelong glance to Kestel confirmed that she was as wary of the mage's reappearance as Blaine.

"Lord McFadden! Tell this lout to unhand me," Lowrey demanded, glowering at Piran.

Blaine caught Piran's eye. With a sigh, Piran lowered his weapon but did not sheathe it.

"What brings you back to civilization, Treven?" Blaine worked to keep his features unreadable and his tone light, but he felt the same mistrust of the mage that was clear in his friends' expressions.

"I came to beg for sanctuary," Lowrey said, managing to look both defiant and desperate at the same time. "Quintrel sent a delegation of mages to rebuild the University in Lord Rostivan's lands, and I asked to join them, figuring that I could make a break for it once I reached the city."

Kestel fingered one of her knives. "The last time we saw you, you'd decided to throw in your lot with Vigus Quintrel—right before he tried to keep us prisoner in Valshoa."

Lowrey's eyes widened. "One of the biggest mistakes of my life," he said, clutching at his chest dramatically. "Quintrel is a madman. That's why I had to leave—and why I wanted to warn you."

"Why did you think you'd find us here?" Piran asked suspiciously. He still had his sword in hand, and Blaine suspected Piran would be just as happy to give Lowrey a poke.

"I didn't," Lowrey said. "But I was desperate to get out of Valshoa. Once I got to the University—what's left of it—I managed to sneak out for a pint at what passes for a pub these days," he said with a sniff of derision. "That's where I ran into one of the mages I knew from my days as a scholar. He told me he'd gone to ground after the Cataclysm, and wanted no part of organized magic anymore." He gave a conspiratorial smile.

"Seems my friend now sells good-luck tokens and love charms," he said, "and makes enough to keep himself in ale."

"And your point is?" Piran prodded with an unfriendly look.

Lowrey gave a long-suffering sigh. "My old friend told me that some of the other mages had come out of hiding. And I heard they joined up with you."

Out of the corner of his eye, Blaine could see that Dagur and the other mage were watching with a look of concern. Their expressions gave Blaine to believe they were about as thrilled as Piran was to see Lowrey.

"With Reese in hiding and Pollard on the run, I'm not surprised mages have started trickling back," Blaine replied, dodging Lowrey's implied question. "But these days, nothing's safe," he added. He paused. "You said you wanted to warn us."

Lowrey nodded vigorously. "Two things you must know. First of all, Vigus is dangerous. He's allied with warlord Rostivan, and he's trying to gather any magical items he can find and to have the mages figure out how to use them in battle." Lowrey leaned forward, and there was fear in his face that for once seemed utterly genuine. "He's convinced the mages should emerge to rule the Continent," Lowrey said. "And he's mad enough to believe he should be the power behind the throne."

Kestel gave Lowrey a no-nonsense look. "We already knew Quintrel wasn't to be trusted when he tried to keep us prisoner in Valshoa. Anyone who knew Quintrel before the Cataclysm knew he was always—only—out for himself. As for the other part, there are a number of delusional warlords who all think they should be king—why is this news?"

Lowrey lifted his chin and pulled himself up to his full height. "All right, then. How's this? Restoring the magic by himself put Blaine in grave danger, according to Quintrel. If Blaine can't figure out a way to create a broader anchor, it's going to kill him—and he'll take the magic with him. Quintrel wants to own the anchor and control the magic. And he won't rest until he takes Blaine prisoner and has the power for himself."

Several candlemarks had passed since the mages' disastrous experiment and the wall's collapse, long enough for Niklas and Piran to get free of their duties and join Blaine and the others in one of Quillarth Castle's parlors. Blaine paced near the fireplace. Kestel leaned against the wall where she had a good view of the doors. Dagur and Zaryae had joined them, along with Ordel, Niklas's battle healer.

"What makes Quintrel think he found a way to anchor the magic without it going through Blaine?" Niklas asked, with an expression that made it clear his trust of anything Lowrey had to say was highly conditional.

"If Quintrel figured it out, why hasn't he already done it?" Piran added.

Lowrey dropped into a chair, looking miserable. "Because Vigus isn't himself these days," he said, running a hand back through his wild, graying hair. "He was angry when Blaine left—and livid when he found out you'd stolen the thirteen disks," he said, leveling an accusing gaze at Kestel.

"Oops?" she said with false coquettishness. "How did those get in my bags?"

Lowrey gave her a narrowed glance. "I'm not saying you weren't wise to steal them, but it put Quintrel into a fury. I think he knew before Blaine even arrived that using just one Lord of the Blood to anchor the power would create a deadly bond. He probably figured that he could keep Blaine and the rest of you from leaving, or at least control you long enough to find a way to transfer the binding. But you left."

"Damn right," Piran said. "What exactly were we going to do, locked up in Valshoa? Take up stargazing?"

"Quintrel didn't expect the Wraith Lord to force Dolan to help you leave," Lowrey replied. "He thought he could count on the Knights to keep you prisoner. When you left, it meant that the key to magic slipped out of Vigus's control. And he is a very competitive man."

"All well and good," Ordel said impatiently. "But what about the impact on Blaine?"

Lowrey paused, and Blaine reined in the impulse to shake the truth out of the eccentric mage. Lowrey was clearly relishing his moment on center stage. "He wants to get Blaine to ally with him, and in exchange, he'll share what he's discovered."

"You mean, hold Blaine hostage under threat that he support Quintrel or die?" Piran rose from his seat with outrage. Niklas waved him down.

"And you're saying the rumors are true that Quintrel has an alliance with Rostivan?" Niklas asked.

"Yes," Lowrey said. "Quintrel needed an army, and Rostivan needed mages."

Kestel exchanged a glance with Blaine that let him know she questioned Lowrey's truthfulness. *I wouldn't put it past him to have made up the whole story just to get us to take him in,* Blaine thought. *Except that the part about the magic draining me strikes a little too true to be a complete invention.*

"I'm concerned about the effect that anchoring the magic is having on Blaine," Ordel said. "I've healed him on more than one occasion, and his energy has . . . shifted. It feels 'older' than it should for someone of his age and health."

Zaryae nodded. "Three times I've dreamt of Blaine as an old man on his deathbed. At first, I took it as a good sign, that he was destined to live through these troubling times, with many decades ahead of him. The second time, I wondered if his future self had a message for us. The third time, I took it as a warning."

"It is consistent with some of the aftereffects we've seen of the 'new' magic," Dagur added. He gave an apologetic shrug. "We're still figuring out how magic works since the restoration. It's not reliable, fades in and out, and as you've seen, it can be volatile."

"What's that have to do with Blaine?" Niklas asked.

"The mages who are working with the artifacts have to limit their time, because the magic drains them so badly," Dagur replied. "We nearly lost a young mage who worked too long at a time with the artifacts. When we found him, he looked as if he'd been starving in a dungeon for weeks, but it had only been a few candlemarks."

"One mage, working for a few candlemarks with an artifact, and it does *that* to him?" Niklas said. He stared pointedly at Blaine. "And you've anchored all the magic on the Continent."

"What's our option?" Kestel asked. She turned on Lowrey. "You said Quintrel had figured out the secret. How do we get it?"

Lowrey spread his hands. "I don't know. That's the problem. Quintrel wouldn't tell anyone else."

"We'll keep working with the artifacts," Dagur said with a sigh. "Maybe something will turn up."

"That's not good enough," Piran snapped. "If the drain is getting worse, then how long until it puts Mick flat on his back—or worse?"

"It will take the time it takes," Blaine said. "And in the

meantime, we'll figure out how to respond to Quintrel. At least now we have confirmation that I'm having a reaction to anchoring the magic."

"And until we've figured out how to protect you from it, we need to keep you away from powerful magic," Kestel said.

Dagur shook his head. "No, you don't understand," he said. They turned toward him. "It's magic itself that's the danger. How close it is won't matter soon." He looked at them in turn, worry clear in his face. "The bond is growing more powerful. Pretty soon, magic anywhere will take its toll on him. And if it kills him before he can find a new anchor, we'll live through the loss of magic all over again."

CHAPTER
THREE

——

THESE STONES ARE THE KEY TO THE FUTURE OF magic in Donderath." Vigus Quintrel whisked away the cloth covering the top of a worktable to reveal thirteen glowing amber-colored crystals, each about the length and width of a man's hand.

"What are they?" Carensa asked, puzzled. She leaned forward for a better view. "They look like...rocks."

Quintrel chuckled. He was a short man in his middle years, with a balding pate. "Sometimes, important things hide in plain sight," he said. He looked out across the four mages, his most trusted inner circle of advisers. These were the best of the scholars and magic-users who had followed him into self-imposed exile in Valshoa before the Great Fire. The gray-robed mage-scholars peered at the crystals, each roughly the size of a thick candle, trying to figure out what made them glow from within.

"Presence-crystals," Quintrel replied dramatically.

"Those are just old legends," Guran said, giving the glowing crystals a wary look. "No one has been known to use a presence-crystal in centuries." Guran was one of the senior mages, and before the Cataclysm, he had been one of Quintrel's fellows at the University in Castle Reach. Carensa and Jarle nodded their agreement, but Esban, the fourth mage and Quintrel's second-in-command, said nothing.

Quintrel's smile broadened, with an expression that cherished knowing a secret. "You're right. But the Valshoans knew about them—and we found their notes in the archives to make them our own."

"I don't understand," Jarle said. He was in his middle years, similar in age to Quintrel, with graying dark hair and perceptive blue eyes. "How do the presence-crystals affect magic?"

Quintrel's eyes were alight. "Because they are the way to take back control of the magic from Blaine McFadden and anchor it so that it cannot be taken from us again."

Carensa resisted the urge to look to either Guran or Jarle for confirmation that she had heard correctly. To her relief, Guran asked the question that sprang to mind.

"I'm afraid you've skipped ahead of us a few steps, Vigus," Guran said. "I'm not following you."

Quintrel began to pace. His face held a manic intensity. "Blaine McFadden was the last living Lord of the Blood. He came here, to a place of power, a place where the meridians and nodes intersect, and he was able to work the ritual and bind the wild *visithara* magic to become controllable, *hasithara* magic."

"I was there, Vigus. We held the wardings that helped him do it. But these crystals weren't part of the working," Guran said.

"Yes, yes. Be patient," Quintrel admonished. "When McFadden bound the magic, it required an anchor. *He* became that anchor. One man. The last time, and the time before that— and perhaps always—there were thirteen Lords of the Blood.

That's why the magic is brittle. Its mooring is shaky, held only by one man rather than solidly anchored in the bloodlines of more than a dozen lineages."

"That part I understand," Guran said. "But what do the stones have to do with it?" Carensa hid her smile. Guran was enticing Quintrel to explain himself in the way he was least able to resist: being the expert with a clever discovery.

"The obsidian disks that McFadden brought with him had belonged to the original thirteen Lords of the Blood," Quintrel said. He paced faster, and his gestures were quick, almost manic. "They stole those disks when they left us."

They took the disks with them when they escaped, Carensa thought. *Fair enough, considering that they brought them in the first place, except for the one Vigus found.*

"And?" Guran prompted.

Quintrel turned abruptly, his eyes wide. "Don't you see? The disks explained the working to bind the magic. They were a cipher for the maps, and a key to the power." He dropped his voice conspiratorially. "But I had a chance to study the disks before they were taken. And I suspected that they might hold the secret to the biggest challenge to anchoring the magic—how to deal with the fact that twelve of the original lords' bloodlines have died out."

Carensa chafed at Quintrel's roundabout revelation. It was one of her mentor's less admirable traits. In the months she had spent with the mage-scholars in Valshoa, Carensa had come to realize that Vigus Quintrel was a cipher himself.

"And the crystals?" Guran asked, eyebrows raised.

"The Valshoans understood about binding magical energy. And they knew that anchoring it came at a price. The thirteen hosts were needed, or the magic would be too much for them to bear. Anyone who anchors the magic is more closely bound to it. In a way it flows through them like the nodes and meridians. Some gain new powers; others grow stronger in what they already had. But too few people anchoring and all that magic burns them up," Quintrel explained.

Carensa caught her breath. That was something she had never heard before, and it meant that Blaine McFadden had paid a price for bringing the magic back under control far beyond the immediate drain of the working. "Can the anchor be transferred?" she asked.

Quintrel nodded. "That's the point—the manuscripts I found tell us how to do that, and the crystals are the key. I've had a team of mages working out the details. There have been some...setbacks...but we've figured it out, and you see the outcome in front of you."

"Setbacks?" Jarle asked.

Quintrel made a dismissive gesture. "The magic is unstable. There were injuries. But think of what we've discovered," he said, his expression aglow with excitement. "We can transfer the anchor, make it stable, and assure that our mages are the lynchpin for magic for generations!"

"And how, exactly, will we do that?" Jarle's voice was patient, attempting to get Quintrel to focus. Of late, Quintrel had been distracted, prone to wild mood swings, and more volatile than Carensa had ever seen. No wonder the mages of his inner circle had taken to handling him gingerly.

"The crystals have been prepared to accept the imprint of twelve new masters. Twelve new Lords of the Blood," he replied, with a triumphant look. "We'll get Blaine McFadden to return to Valshoa," Quintrel said, agitated with enthusiasm. "Then we'll use the crystals to place twelve of our own as the new Lords of the Blood. Our lineage will bind the magic. It will be as it ought—mages controlling magic."

"I don't think you'll easily convince McFadden to return to Valshoa," Guran said. "What if he refuses?"

Quintrel's expression grew hard. "Then we force him to come." He looked to all of them with the fervor of a prophet. "Don't you see? We stand at a crossroads of history. This is our chance to choose the new Lords of the Blood, the families that will anchor the magic—and have a stake in its binding—for centuries to come."

"You're going to kidnap Blaine McFadden?" Jarle repeated incredulously. "What about his army? His allies? And his assassins?"

Quintrel made a motion as if swatting away flies. "Those concerns are of no regard. I have an agent of my own in place. We'll incapacitate McFadden, spirit him away, and impress upon him the need to cooperate with our plans."

"And once you've used the crystals and created a new quorum, then what?" Guran asked. "Do you just expect McFadden to go about his business as if nothing happened?"

Quintrel frowned. "That's where it gets complicated," he said. He sighed. "We know it's possible to keep the binding if one—or several—of the original Lords dies without an heir. What happens next is really up to McFadden," he said with a shrug. "We may be forced to keep him here until he agrees to an alliance," he said matter-of-factly. "And if that's not an option, I'm afraid we'll be forced to end his line."

Silence fell as Quintrel gave them a moment to consider his last statement. "So much for McFadden," he said finally, as if his last comment was of no particular import. "We've got Rostivan to handle."

Torinth Rostivan was a warlord, and he was Quintrel's newest ally. Carensa was skeptical of the alliance, but she knew Quintrel well enough to keep her reservations to herself.

"You still haven't explained the terms of our new alliance," Guran said warily.

Quintrel's smile broadened once more. "In short, Rostivan does our fighting for us. As he gains power, so do we."

"Why would he fight for us?" Jarle questioned, frowning. "And what makes you so sure he'll include us once he has the power he wants?"

"Because I have a hold over him," Quintrel said simply. He reached into a leather satchel that sat on the table behind him, and withdrew a glass orb. It looked like a scrying ball, with one hideous difference. Preserved in the middle was a mummified human hand clenched in a fist.

Guran's eyes widened and he stared at the orb. "What in the name of the gods is that? Vigus, what have you done?"

Quintrel's smile grew brittle. "I did what I had to do to ensure us a future in the new order," he snapped. "This artifact puts Rostivan under my control. He is unable to defy me—and with mages to be my eyes and ears, he won't be able to make a move without my knowing it."

"Where did you find that…thing?" Jarle asked, his voice a horrified gasp. Carensa peered at the orb with a mixture of fear and fascination. The glass appeared thick and quite solid. The hand was withered and gray, though not as fragile as the old bodies Carensa had seen in the tombs. Instead, the hand looked like it had belonged to a very old, wizened man, preserved as it might have been when it was severed.

"It was buried deep in the Valshoan catacombs," Quintrel replied. His mood had soured, and Carensa guessed that he was not happy at the reaction from his senior mages.

"Perhaps it should have remained there," Jarle replied. "Such things are not to be meddled with, even for mages."

"We are above such superstition!" Quintrel shot back, his

face coloring with anger. "It's a tool, nothing more." He held the orb in his left hand, and his right hand smoothed over it, as if he were petting a cat. Quintrel did not seem aware of the motion.

"How did you bind it to Rostivan?" Carensa asked, doing her best to look like the attentive student she had been when she had first won his favor. Quintrel quieted, and managed a thin smile.

"A very good question. We had to experiment, and with the magic as it is, the price was dear," Quintrel replied. No one was willing to face his wrath by asking, but Carensa was certain they were all thinking the same question: *How dear?*

"Although the glass seems solid, it can melt when the hand wills it," Quintrel said. "With the proper incantation, offering, and ritual, it will accept a token of the intended target. In this case, I had managed to gather a lock of Rostivan's hair. That hair is now clasped in the hand, and until it is released, Rostivan will be under my influence." Quintrel was quite pleased with himself, but there was a cruel glint in his eyes that Carensa found disturbing, and new.

"When the *hand* wills it?" Guran echoed. "Vigus, that's not a bound *divi*, is it?"

Carensa's eyes widened. She had heard of *divis*, old spirits that were neither god nor mortal, stronger than wraiths, far more powerful than ghosts. Spirits that had existed since before the world was formed. Long ago, mages had hoped to bind *divis* to their call, hoping to amplify their own magic through the power of the captive spirit. Legends abounded of the horrible fates that such mages met. *Divis*, as Carensa recalled from her studies, tended to extract a price for their services, higher than anyone wanted to pay, and the *divis* thrived on chaos and destruction.

"There's nothing to fear," Quintrel said. There was a mocking undertone in his voice. Carensa looked closely at him, and saw that he wore a small orb on a strap around his neck. The orb glowed with a faint yellow light, and Carensa was willing to bet it was also part of the *divi*.

"The *divi*—or whatever animates the magic of the artifact—is quite assuredly subordinate to my will," Quintrel assured them. "As is Rostivan."

Something Quintrel said earlier finally made an impression on Carensa. She smoothed a hand over her short red hair, pushing a strand behind one ear. "Vigus," she said, intentionally keeping her tone nonthreatening, "what did you mean about mages being your eyes and ears around Rostivan?"

"Didn't I tell you? I've arranged for six of you to accompany Rostivan back to his stronghold in Torsford, and to be his mage-advisers as he wages war," Quintrel replied in a tone that suggested his announcement was no more controversial than speculation about the weather.

Guran and Jarle both spoke out at once. "We are not battle mages!" Guran argued.

"Vigus, such things ought to have been discussed before committing us," Jarle chided.

Quintrel's eyes darkened with anger. "My first concern—my only concern—is the welfare of this community of mages. We were tools of warfare under King Merrill, and the Cataclysm was the result of placing mages under the control of non-mages. That is why in Rostivan's new order, we are equal to the generals. And that is why I—not Rostivan—am in control."

"You want to use Rostivan and his army to gain political power," Carensa said quietly. Once, she had been one of Quintrel's most promising pupils. *Perhaps*, she thought, *she had learned her lessons too well*. "Instead of a warrior king having puppet mages, you intend to have a puppet warrior."

Quintrel's smile was more of a snarl. "Very good, Carensa. You were always quick with your lessons."

"How are we to be your eyes and ears if we're in Torsford?" Jarle asked. It was clear to Carensa that the older mage was treading carefully, although with Quintrel's temper of late, it was difficult to know what might send him into a rage.

"You'll be going to Torsford, to set up the new University there," Quintrel replied blithely. "When Rostivan has need of you to accompany his troops, you will go with him—and report back to me. Rostivan will be here tomorrow to gather you and your things. Take everything; you probably won't be returning to Valshoa."

"Why not?" Carensa asked, trying to hide her confusion and alarm.

"Because I intend for our mages to return to the outside world and claim our rightful place," Quintrel said. "Oh, I'll leave a few here to maintain Valshoa in case we should need access to the meridians and nodes here, but I don't believe we'll need to hide here once Rostivan secures power—and we have a new anchor for the magic. With a stronger anchor, the magic should lose its brittleness, and our power will be secure," he said with a triumphant smile.

Before any of the stunned mages could think of another argument, a man cleared his throat behind them. Carensa and the others turned to see General Dolan of the Knights of Esthrane standing in the doorway.

"A word with you, Vigus."

Quintrel looked annoyed. "It's not a good time, Dolan. I'm instructing my senior mages."

"I'm of the opinion you've been avoiding my messages,"

Dolan replied. "I'm afraid this cannot wait. I've come to tell you that the Knights of Esthrane are leaving."

Quintrel looked as if he might explode. "This is entirely unacceptable!" Vigus Quintrel adjusted the spectacles on his thin nose. "Completely unacceptable!"

"We made no guarantee that the Knights of Esthrane would remain in Valshoa forever," Dolan replied. Though he was a centuries-old *talishte* warrior-mage, Dolan looked no older than his late thirties, with dark hair cropped short in a soldier's cut and a body toughened by war. Everything about his manner made it clear that he was a man who was used to being in command.

"We had an arrangement," Quintrel shot back. He stood a head shorter than Dolan, with a bald head and a slight build. The quarreling pair reminded Carensa of two dogs warring for dominance. Quintrel was one of the most powerful mages in Donderath. Dolan was a mage in his own right, and *talishte*, giving him the additional abilities of the undead. A duel between them would be catastrophic.

"All things end," Dolan replied. "My soldiers have deliberated the matter since McFadden raised the magic. We have been in exile for two generations. The reason for that exile is gone. Donderath would benefit from our return as peacekeepers."

"And kingmakers?" Quintrel challenged. "That's your plan, isn't it?"

Dolan looked askance at Quintrel. "What interest do we have in mortal kings?"

"Plenty, when they hunt down and murder your Knights," Quintrel snapped. "Is McFadden to be your puppet king?"

"You waste my time," Dolan replied. "Remain in Valshoa, if that's what you want. It has been our prison long enough. My Knights are readying for departure. I came to give you the courtesy of supplying notice. It was not my intent to ask your permission."

"Then go," Quintrel's expression was ugly. He turned his back on Dolan. "You'll quickly find that the world outside is no kinder than when you went into exile."

"I did not expect to find kindness," Dolan replied. "I expect to be useful. We will depart shortly." With that, Dolan strode from the room.

Carensa traded a nervous glance with Jarle. Quintrel's mood, mercurial at best, was certain to turn vicious after such a public loss.

For several minutes, while Carensa and Quintrel's senior mages waited nervously, the master mage said nothing. He paced the small room, head down, hands clasped behind his back. From his facial expressions, it was clear he was having a heated dialogue with himself. Carensa found herself holding her breath.

Finally, Quintrel rounded on them, his face still flushed with anger. "Dolan and his group have chosen to abandon us," Quintrel announced. "He thinks the Knights of Esthrane will be welcomed as the salvation of Donderath," he added, contempt clear in his words. "I believe he will be sorely disappointed."

Carensa and the others said nothing, unwilling to send Quintrel further into rage. "We don't need the Knights," Quintrel muttered. "Dolan and his Knights didn't build Valshoa. They inherited it—stole it, really—from the original Valshoans." Quintrel's agitation showed in his short, shallow breaths, the ruddiness of his face, and the way his hands reflexively opened and closed.

"What would you have us do to prepare?" Jarle asked. If anyone could talk Quintrel down from one of his rages, it would be Jarle.

"Prepare?" Quintrel nearly shrieked the word. "Are you implying that we will be damaged by the Knights' defection?"

"Of course not, Vigus." Jarle had been one of Quintrel's inner circle for many years, a supporter long before the war, when they were both scholars at Castle Reach's university. He was also one of the first to be chosen by Quintrel for the journey to Valshoa. "But it will cause some disruption until we adjust."

"We will get along just fine without Dolan and his men," Quintrel replied through gritted teeth. "We don't need the help of untrustworthy *talishte*."

"Perhaps, in light of this development, you may want to rethink our relationship with Rostivan," Jarle said. "After all, losing the Knights removes some of our military support."

"Our plans do not depend in any way on Dolan and his Knights!" Quintrel exploded, wheeling to face Jarle. Quintrel's right hand rose suddenly, and the closed fingers of his fist snapped open and spread wide.

Jarle dropped as if struck, his eyes wide, mouth taut with pain. A hard glint came into Quintrel's eyes. "Don't doubt me, Jarle. You, especially, should know what I can do."

Quintrel let his hand fall, and Jarle slumped to the floor. Quintrel's gaze swept the other mages, and his mouth twisted into a thin-lipped half smile.

"Don't allow your fears to make you weak," he said. "Our time is near, and we will rise ascendant." With that, Quintrel swept from the room, leaving Jarle and the others behind. Esban, Quintrel's second-in-command, followed a moment later.

Carensa rushed to where Jarle lay. To her relief, he was still breathing, and his pulse was steady. "Jarle? Can you hear me?"

Jarle moaned, but did not move. Carensa looked to Guran.

"Help me," she said. "I can't get him back to his quarters by myself."

Guran and Carensa got under Jarle's shoulders and managed to half carry, half drag the injured mage to his quarters. *When did everything go so wrong?* Carensa fretted as they moved through the narrow corridors of the ancient building. *Vigus was supposed to be our protector. What happened?*

They made their way through the narrow corridors. Valshoa was an ancient city, hidden in a mountain valley. More than a thousand years ago, the city had been built by mages who wanted isolation in which to study their craft. Murals and frescoes, mosaic floors, statues, and bas-relief panels chronicled the history of those long-ago Valshoans. Deep beneath the ground, currents of raw magic power, 'meridians,' flowed across the world. Where two or more meridians crossed, a 'node' formed a potent well of energy. Mages could draw from the energy of the nodes and meridians to extend their power. Beneath Valshoa, a confluence of meridians formed a very powerful node.

Jarle's quarters were sparsely furnished. The few personal possessions were a testament to how quickly the mages had fled to follow Quintrel to refuge during the last, chaotic days before Donderath's collapse.

"Let's get him into bed," Carensa ordered, and Guran helped her maneuver Jarle to lie down. "I'll make sure he gets supper, and some whiskey to bring back his color," she added worriedly.

Guran made a gesture of warding, sealing the door behind them and shrouding the room so that they could not be heard outside. "It's going to take more than whiskey to deal with Vigus when he's like this," Guran said quietly.

Carensa struggled with Jarle's blankets to get the older mage comfortably settled. Jarle managed a weak smile. "Thank you," he murmured.

"That was brave of you—and foolish, given the mood Vigus was in," Carensa chided.

"I thought perhaps he would still listen to me," Jarle replied, and sighed.

"Increasingly, he listens to no one," Guran said. "Even Carensa can't sway him as she used to."

Carensa gave a sad smile. "I think you overestimate my skill with that," she replied. "I was just one of his pupils."

Guran raised an eyebrow. "One of his favored pupils," he corrected.

Carensa sat down on the edge of Jarle's bed. Guran leaned against the wall. "It's getting worse, isn't it? These last few months, since Blaine and his friends left and the magic returned, Vigus hasn't been himself."

"And now we have a good idea of why," Guran replied. "Drawing on the power of a bound *divi* is always risky. But to do it now, when the magic is so unstable—"

"You think the *divi* is what's changed him?" Carensa asked.

"Either the *divi* or one of the other artifacts he's dabbling with," Guran answered. "It's the most logical explanation." He sighed. "He's become obsessed, and his obsession borders on madness."

"Vigus always thought highly of himself," Jarle said, his voice still not at its usual strength. "That's one reason he clashed with the king's mages and the University senior scholars. The thing that annoyed them was that Vigus really was as good as he thought he was."

"I've never known him to take opposing opinions well," Guran said.

"But Vigus wasn't so cold—so willing to sacrifice people's lives for the magic—until after Blaine came," Carensa said quietly.

"You knew McFadden, before the war, didn't you?" Jarle said.

Carensa nodded. "We were betrothed, until he was exiled. Our families lived near each other. I've known him since we were children."

"You're right about the timing," Guran replied. "Vigus was his usual egotistical self until the magic was restored."

"But if it were just the magic itself that pushed him over the edge, wouldn't we all be fighting like mad dogs?" Jarle mused. "Or dead—like the ones who were too quick to try out the artifacts after the magic came back."

Carensa remembered. She had helped bury those mages, and the others who, during the first weeks and months after the magic was restored, discovered the limitations of the new power the hard way. "The magic's become more stable since then," she protested.

Guran shook his head. "It's still brittle. The power waxes and wanes. If that happens when you're channeling a lot of power, it's a good way to end up dead—or damaged."

"I don't think it's the magic that's changed Vigus," Jarle said. "I think it's the artifacts. Think about it. Before the magic was restored, Vigus was interested in saving the artifacts and scrolls to preserve old knowledge. It's only been since the magic returned that he's been interested—obsessed, really—with using the artifacts to gain political power. And he no longer cares who gets hurt."

"But the artifacts weren't evil to begin with. What changed?" Carensa asked.

"The magic changed," Jarle replied. "The artifacts aren't evil now, they've just been corrupted. Like spoiled meat. It's not evil, but it still might kill you."

Guran nodded. "I believe that's it exactly. I think this *divi* globe is the most likely culprit." He paused. "And Vigus has changed in another way. He never showed any interest before in ruling the kingdom. He just wanted the mages to be free to practice their magic. But now..."

Guran didn't have to finish his sentence. They knew what he meant. *Now Vigus wants to be the kingmaker, and the power behind the throne.*

Once Carensa was assured that Jarle was recovering, she returned to her quarters, deep in thought. Her small room looked much like Jarle's. A few personal mementos were all she had of her life before Valshoa. There was a small oil painting of her son and husband, both of whom lay buried in the rubble of her family's manor house. Beside the oil painting was a small silver box, and in it, the betrothal ring Blaine McFadden had given her before he had been exiled.

Several books and scrolls lay neatly stacked on the shelf above the desk, along with a parchment and quill. Her cloak, hat, and scarf hung on a peg near the door, and underneath was a pair of leather boots. In the trunk at the foot of her bed were a few changes of clothing and a new set of bed linen and towels, all she needed in the simple life of a scholar. It would be easy to pack to go to Torsford, although Carensa felt heartsick at the reason for leaving.

A knock at the door startled her, and she was worried to see Guran standing in the corridor. "Is Jarle worse?"

Guran shook his head, and Carensa motioned for him to enter, closing the door behind him. Once again, Guran made a warding to keep them from being overheard. "I just wanted to come by and make sure you were all right. We were all pretty upset by what happened."

Carensa offered Guran the chair at her desk, and she sat on the edge of her cot. "I don't understand why Vigus has decided that Blaine is suddenly the enemy," she said with a sigh. "Just a few months ago, he was happy to help Blaine restore the magic. Why Rostivan? We don't know anything about him."

"Before the war, Torinth Rostivan was a smuggler, and during the war he appears to have made a lot of money supplying both sides," Guran said with distaste. "Now he fancies himself a warlord."

"Why him and not Blaine? Blaine already has an army in place."

Guran shrugged. "I think Vigus sees McFadden as a rival."

"You think Vigus has set this all up to go to war against Blaine?"

"I think that's exactly what he has in mind."

Carensa was quiet for a moment, thinking through what Guran said. "Why choose me for the group to go to Torsford?" Carensa asked. "I've got very little power. My magic helps me translate languages. That's hardly battle worthy."

Guran's gaze fell to the small paintings on Carensa's desk. "Does Vigus know you were involved with McFadden?"

"Yes." She sighed, and drew her knees up, hugging them to herself. "Blaine's exile dishonored his family, and me. My... notoriety...limited the potential suitors." She shrugged. "I withdrew from everyone. My father got me tutors, trying to find something to interest me. That's how I met Vigus. Then Father finally found an older man who needed my dowry money. I had no choice about the marriage. I never really loved my husband, but I did love our son."

"They died in the Cataclysm?"

Carensa nodded. "I nearly did, too. The manor collapsed and I woke up trapped in the rubble. Vigus got me out and brought me here."

"So you had no idea McFadden had returned."

Carensa shook her head. "None at all, until he arrived here. I thought Blaine died in Velant."

"You helped McFadden and his friends defy Vigus to leave," Guran said.

Carensa lifted her head. "Yes, I did. I made my choice to be a scholar, and I have no desire to change that. Blaine's made his choices, too. But I'll always wish him well. He sacrificed everything to save his family from that brute of a father. I would do anything to protect him."

Guran met her gaze. "Be careful, Carensa. McFadden is only valuable until Vigus can figure out how to keep the magic bound without him." He paused. "At least Vigus has a reason to keep McFadden alive. Others might find it to their advantage if he—and the magic—went away permanently."

Late that night, Carensa's dreams were dark. *Once again, she was pinned beneath the rubble of Rhystorp, surrounded by the smell of fire and death. Grief seized her, but she had no tears left to cry. She was resigned to dying alone in the darkness, numb to fear. And then, after she had accepted her fate, the stones that sealed her into her prison shifted, sending light and air and, most importantly, hope. Vigus Quintrel had spoken to her, calmed her, kept up a quiet, confident one-sided conversation until he could remove her from the wreckage.*

But in this dream, Quintrel was livid, and in his grasp was the orb, with its withered hand and bound divi. *He held the orb aloft, and it blazed like lightning, filling the sky with green ribbons of fire. Quintrel and the* divi *became the Cataclysm.*

Screams woke her. Carensa sat upright in her bed, clutching the covers to her chest, heart thudding. Before she could question whether the screams were real or imagined, she heard the shrieking once again. Worried, Carensa hurriedly wrapped herself in her robe and gathered her slippers, rushing out into the corridor. More mages began to appear in their doorways. Many quickly retreated, shutting their doors again. A few ventured into the corridor, but hung back, wary.

She found Vigus Quintrel in his sitting room, tearing at his hair, ripping his clothing, and screaming curses like a madman. He hurled a vase across the room, barely missing Guran and Esban, who had edged into the room.

Carensa maneuvered close. Once, they had been friends as well as tutor and student. It was dangerous to trade on that old bond, but Carensa hoped that it might help her calm Quintrel long enough to discover what had gone so terribly wrong.

"Vigus." Carensa moved closer to where Quintrel sat. A tankard sailed over her head, slamming against the far wall. "Vigus, please. Tell me what's wrong."

Quintrel threw an inkwell against the stone fireplace, sending a spray of ink across the room. "They're gone," he said, breathing heavily.

"Who's gone?" Carensa asked. "The Knights? But you knew they were going."

Quintrel shook his head disconsolately. "No, no," he moaned. "They're all gone."

"Vigus, who's gone?" Carensa pressed, close enough now that she laid her hand on Quintrel's arm. He looked utterly distraught.

Quintrel turned to her, a look of complete misery and loss clear in his expression. "The presence-crystals. And the manuscripts that go with them. Gone, stolen."

CHAPTER
FOUR

I'VE ARRANGED FOR A MEETING WITH FOLVILLE IN public; hopefully, he'll swear his fealty to you," Niklas said. It was after eighth bells, and they were gathered in the parlor once more. Dagur and the mages had gone back to their work, reluctantly taking Treven Lowrey with them.

Blaine stood near the fire, a glass of whiskey in his hand. Piran was sprawled on a divan, while Kestel watched from the window, looking beyond the castle walls into the darkened streets of the city.

Blaine looked to Niklas. "Right now, I feel like I 'need' to be in at least three places at once," he said. "Can you spare the soldiers for Kestel and me to ride into Castle Reach?"

Niklas nodded. "If you're going to be lord of your land, not to mention a warlord, your people need to see you in the forefront. Makes them less likely to follow an upstart who wants to make trouble."

"I'll work with Niklas, Mick, if it takes a load off your mind," Piran said.

"It might lessen Mick's worry, but what about Niklas?" Kestel jibed.

Piran ignored her. "Don't forget—we've got Geir and the other *talishte* soldiers, who can make a big difference in getting the castle secured—hopefully before the next big storm."

Kestel turned away from the window. "Dagur said there's another storm coming. The question is—can the mages predict when?" She shook her head. "I'm sure the mages King Merrill used to control the weather never realized that they'd cause an even bigger problem. Lucky us; we get to live with it."

"All the more reason for Blaine to meet with Folville and deliver the warning. Our soldiers can help batten down the city and get people to safety," Niklas said.

Blaine grimaced. "I'm still getting used to this whole 'lord' thing. I really and truly thought I had given that up."

"*You're* still getting used to it," Piran replied. "Some of us didn't even know you *were* a lord for how many years, Mick?"

Kestel rolled her eyes. "You're never going to let him live that down, are you?"

Piran grinned. "Nope."

Blaine took a sip of his whiskey. "I'm worried about the storms. They could destroy what's left of the wharves and wipe out a lot of what's been rebuilt."

"What about *talishte*? Can they lend a hand?" Kestel asked.

Niklas nodded. "I don't have a lot of *talishte* soldiers, but I've reassigned some of Geir's men to split their time between rebuilding here at the castle and in the city." Geir was a *talishte* on loan to Blaine's service from Lanyon Penhallow, who had decided he had an interest in seeing Blaine secure his position.

"We can't possibly evacuate Castle Reach," Blaine said. "There are too many people. "

Kestel met his gaze. "No, but we can warn them."

"I'm going to send Captain Hemmington with you," Niklas said. "He's the one who brokered the arrangement with Folville, so he's known to them. He's from Castle Reach, spent some time in the city gangs himself, then joined the army before the war. They respect him."

"That helps," Blaine said.

Niklas grinned. "It won't hurt that you're bringing one of Donderath's most notorious assassins with you," he said with a nod toward Kestel.

Kestel grinned. "Reputation is everything in the assassin business," she said, feigning boredom.

Somewhere nearby, mages were drawing on the meridians. Blaine could feel it, and it added to his fatigue. If he shut his eyes, he could sense bright spots in the darkness, places he knew magic was being worked.

It must have shown in his face, because Kestel gave him a worried look. "It's the magic again, isn't it?" she asked.

Blaine tossed back the rest of his whiskey and nodded.

"I don't get it, Mick," Piran said. "You only ever had a bit of battle magic. If you're this connected to the magic, why didn't it make you a mage?" Piran and the others from Velant still called Blaine 'Mick,' the name he had taken in prison, when Glenreith and his former life seemed lost forever.

Kestel moved away from the window to stand closer to Blaine. "We don't know for certain what toll harnessing the magic took from the last group who did the working," she said. "But the scrolls said the original Lords of the Blood came away from Mirdalur with new abilities. And yet they weren't all mages, either. King Merrill certainly wasn't a mage, or Blaine's father, or any of the former Lords of the Blood, come to think of it, except for the Wraith Lord," Kestel said. "Maybe whatever the new abilities are, it's something that will show up over time," Kestel mused.

"Perhaps," Blaine said, unwilling to discuss the subject more, at least for now. "But right now, Folville is our focus. We'll leave for the city tomorrow, as soon as you get the horses ready to travel," Blaine said.

"If the mages are right and we still have a day or more before the storm hits, it's long enough to make a difference." He fell quiet for a moment.

Kestel looked at him and frowned. "You've got something else on your mind."

Blaine sighed and nodded. "I know I need to be here, but I feel like I should be at Glenreith. They're likely to be hit by the storm, too."

"Dawe's taking care of it," Kestel assured him. "Trust your friends, Mick. We have your back."

The guards at the gate waved their party through as Blaine and the others headed for Castle Reach. Captain Hemmington was a sober-looking man in his late twenties with short-cropped dark hair and a wary expression. Blaine thought that Hemmington looked like someone who had seen real action and would never sleep well again.

The main road into Castle Reach had once been bordered by the villas of the minor nobility in the section just outside Quillarth Castle. A little closer toward the city were the homes of prosperous merchants and sea captains, with more modest homes at the base of the hill. On most days before the Great Fire, the road had been busy with peddlers and travelers, carts full of provisions headed to market to sell or coming from market loaded with purchases, and people on foot or horseback going about their business.

Now the road was empty. Many of the once-grand homes had been burned in the Great Fire, and those that remained standing bore soot-scars and broken windows. Looters sacked any of the villas and homes that had not burned.

"A copper for your thoughts," Kestel said.

He sighed. "It's hard to take this route and not remember being herded down here in chains for the ship to Velant," he said. He looked to the side to meet her gaze. "Do you think about Edgeland much, since we're back?"

Kestel gave a wan smile and nodded. "All the time. I wonder how Engraham and his mother are doing, and whether Ifrem is still running the pub. And I hope that with magic restored, they have what they need to get by." She sighed. "I miss the people—but not the weather!"

Blaine chuckled. "No, not the weather. I hope that leaving was the right thing to do."

Kestel looked at him askance. "You really question that? You brought back the magic."

Blaine had returned his gaze to the road ahead of them. "And what has that done? Donderath is as much at war as it ever was, only now it's between warlords carving up what's left for themselves."

"It's only been a few months since the magic was restored," Kestel reminded him. "Even the weather is still adjusting. And don't forget," she pointed out, "when the magic came back, so did healing and all the other little magics that made life a lot more bearable. Especially in Edgeland."

Blaine sighed. "I know. And I try to convince myself of that. But it's more difficult some days than others."

Near the edge of what had been the merchant district in Castle Reach they were met by a small contingent of soldiers. Captain Hemmington moved ahead to greet them, and spoke quietly with the head of the city guard.

"Lord McFadden, welcome to Castle Reach," a man said,

stepping up to welcome them. "I'm Captain Larson." Larson was a plain-looking man in his early thirties, with a head of thinning, yellow-blond hair and light-blue eyes.

"I'm afraid we bear bad news," Blaine replied. "Big storms are headed this way. We've come to warn you, and prepare the city."

Larson met his gaze. "Do we know when they'll hit or how damaging they'll be?"

Blaine shook his head. "The seers said it would be soon, likely a day or so. The storms will be strong. Flooding and damage could be bad."

Larson sighed. "Then let's get started warning people and see how many will go to high ground." He spoke to two soldiers and sent them ahead to gather the rest of the garrison. The two men ran off, leaving the others to follow at a more dignified pace.

They made their way through the twisting cobblestone streets. At a high point in the road, it was possible to look across most of the city of Castle Reach. Blaine stopped for a moment, taking in the sweeping vista. Two soldiers rode toward them and stopped, making a crisp salute.

"Is it arranged?" Larson asked.

The lead soldier nodded. "The garrison will meet you in the city square. And Captain Hemmington's man has gotten word to William Folville that his lord desires a meeting."

A few moments later, they were in the plaza that was at the heart of Castle Reach. Hougen Square had once been the center of daily life for residents of Castle Reach. On three sides of the square sat the temples to Charrot, Esthrane, and Torven. The square itself was made of paving stones set in a mosaic pattern with a large fountain in the center from which city dwellers drew their water.

Before the Cataclysm, the temples had been imposing

structures. Seekers traveled across Donderath to make their gifts and plead for favors from the High God and his consorts. On the fourth side of the square was the Tariff House, the king's authority over all the ships in port. It had been a majestic building with soaring pillars and larger-than-life statues.

Now the once-white temples showed black streaks of soot where the green ribbon of fire from the sky had touched them. The roof of Charrot's temple was missing, and several of the columns had crumbled. Esthrane's temple had lost a wall, leaving the inner court exposed. Only the front façade remained of the temple to Torven. In the center of the square, the fountain still functioned, but the stone tile around it was cracked and scorched. Across the way, the Tariff House had received a direct hit from the Great Fire, destroying half of the building and badly damaging the remaining part of the large structure.

"There's a lot of activity around Torven's temple," Kestel noted, nudging Blaine, who turned to look. A crowd of several dozen robed men and women were bringing a steady stream of offerings to place in front of Torven's statue, and across the open square, Blaine could hear their chants and songs. "Are they Tingur?"

"How do we tell the Tingur from regular worshippers?" Kestel asked quietly.

Blaine watched the crowd, wondering the same thing. "I don't know. We'll have to be careful."

The garrison of soldiers Niklas had assigned to help keep peace waited in the plaza. Blaine swung down from his horse to regroup with Captain Larson. Kestel joined him a moment later.

"Where would you like us to begin?" Larson asked.

Blaine grimaced. "I'm going to need help from you and your men to warn the residents and get as many people as possible to higher ground, someplace they can shelter themselves from wind and water." He paused. "We've brought soldiers with us who can lend a hand."

Larson let out a long breath. "And you said the storms are coming soon? Even with help that's not an easy order, m'lord. A lot of the buildings that survived the Cataclysm are in poor shape. Most buildings in the lower third of the city nearest where the wharves were have been damaged so badly that the upper floors aren't habitable. The tunnels still exist below the city, but they're likely to fill up with water."

"That's why we're relying on you and your men, Captain," Blaine said. "General Theilsson will send what men he can spare, but he's going to be stretched thin. Is there anyplace people can take refuge?"

Larson thought for a moment, turning to look over the city's roofs. Finally, he nodded.

"The northeast side of the city didn't get hit as hard as the section near the wharves or just below the castle," he replied. "There are buildings out that way that might be safe on the upper levels, and some large barns and warehouses where we might get people to shelter."

He shook his head. "There's no way, m'lord, that we can get all the people in this city to shelter there."

"Then save the ones you can," Kestel urged. The wind gusted through the square, swirling leaves around the fountain and raising dust clouds in the corners.

Larson nodded. "Aye, m'lady." He chewed his lip as he thought, then turned to his men.

"Gorett, Taben—start moving food and blankets to the barns on the northeast side. There's a storm coming."

Larson turned to the other soldiers, who stood in ranks, awaiting orders. "Strong storms heading our way. Gonna be floods, heavy rain, maybe worse." He paused. "I want teams of two spread out through the city. Shout a warning at every marketplace, every intersection, every square. Send the people up the hill to the granary barns on the far side of the city. No wagons, no carts—just what they can carry."

Larson's men hurried to carry out his orders. Larson cast a glance toward the sky. "How long did your mages say we had to prepare?"

Blaine followed his gaze. Clouds were rolling in, and the air had grown colder. The wind had picked up, and there was an undeniable bite in the air. "A day, if we're lucky."

Larson gave him a skeptical glance. "You sure about that, m'lord? The sky's grown much darker just since this morning."

Blaine felt a prickle of foreboding as he stared at the gray clouds. He had spent three years in Edgeland aboard the herring boats, and in the dangerous northern seas, being able to read the weather was the difference between making it back to shore alive and being lost at sea. And right now, if he had been aboard one of the herring boats, Blaine would have been ready to head for home.

He drew Larson over to the side, where they could speak without their voices carrying. "Tell me; how long have the Torven worshippers been gathering like that?"

Larson glanced over toward where the group began another chant and knelt in supplication. "They've been filing in now for a little over a week. We're not sure what it means, or whether it's just how some folks are dealing with everything that's been going on."

Blaine briefed Larson on what they knew about the Tingur. "Don't assume they're friendly."

"Thank you for the warning." Larson said, then rallied his men and headed out to begin evacuating the city.

"Lord McFadden." One of the soldiers who had accompanied Blaine and Kestel approached. "We've made contact with William Folville of the . . . guild. You asked us to let you know," the soldier said. Kestel barely hid a snicker at the polite term.

"And?"

"A meeting has been arranged a candlemark from now at the old Rooster and Pig. Folville said he was certain you would know where that was."

"Do you think it's a trap?" Kestel asked.

Blaine shrugged. "Right now, he's got more to gain by working with us than against us. It's an arrangement of necessity. He and his gang are the best of a bad lot. But we don't have enough soldiers to enforce the law. Folville's got enough of a following to be able to keep worse elements at bay."

Kestel nodded. "Where will he stand, I wonder, if Lysander or one of the other warlords attacks?"

Blaine chuckled. "With his own interests. And I intend to make sure he sees that his interests are closely aligned with ours."

It should have taken only half a candlemark to cross Castle Reach and get to the Rooster and Pig. But with the dock road under water and the other roadways still littered with fallen rocks and debris, nearly a full candlemark had passed before Blaine and his party reached the old shipyard where the remains of the tavern stood.

Kestel gave a sad smile. "The Rooster and Pig had the best bitterbeer in all of Donderath," she sighed. "And the best illicit gambling parlor in Castle Reach."

Blaine raised an eyebrow. "Oh?"

Kestel chuckled. "You knew Engraham, the tavern's owner, before he and Connor washed ashore in Edgeland?'

Blaine nodded. "Like everyone else, if I had business in

Castle Reach, I did my best to stop for bitterbeer at the Rooster and Pig. I never joined in the wagering, although I'd heard rumors that it went on."

The group rounded a corner, and what remained of the Rooster and Pig came into view. "It looks a little better than the last time we were here," Kestel observed.

Before the Great Fire, the Rooster and Pig had been a prosperous tavern. The front of the house drew city dwellers of all types, from the sailors who were in port with the merchant ships, to the dockhands on the wharves, to farmers in town to sell wares at market. In the back, the wastrel sons of the nobility gambled away their fortunes, cheered on by their courtesans and hangers-on.

The Rooster and Pig's red roof had always been visible from halfway across the city, and its bright-blue shutters always made Blaine think of it as a garishly made-up strumpet. It was too loud, too crowded, too smoke-filled—and just right. Before the Cataclysm, Engraham held court at the bar, serving up drinks and platters of fresh fish with a never-ending supply of good conversation and wit.

"Sorry, but I never had the opportunity to be one of those debauched young noblemen," Blaine replied. "I didn't get into Castle Reach that often, and I truly came for the bitterbeer."

Kestel chuckled. "Believe me when I tell you, the company in the back room was overrated." She paused. "I wonder how Engraham is doing up in Edgeland?"

"If he's selling bitterbeer, he's probably a wealthy man by now," Blaine replied, only partly in jest.

When Blaine and his friends arrived on the ship from Edgeland, they had come directly to the ruins of the Rooster and Pig. Engraham had given Connor directions to a small stash of weapons and valuables stored in one of the tunnels beneath the pub, and they had needed the supplies after their journey.

Then, the Rooster and Pig was a tumbledown heap of burned beams and scorched brick, its windows shattered, its roof a pile of wreckage. As Blaine and the others rode closer, it was obvious that someone had attempted to rebuild.

The roof had been replaced. Glass was hard to find, so wooden shutters covered the windows. The brick was marred by scorch marks and soot, stained by years of use, but the tavern's walls stood straight and strong. And by the look of it, the Rooster and Pig was open for business once more.

"Keep a sharp eye out. Make sure we don't get any surprises." Blaine instructed the two soldiers who had accompanied them.

"I've got your back," Kestel murmured. "Just be your charming self."

Inside the Rooster and Pig, it was clear that the revived pub was only a shadow of its former glory. From the sharp smell of raw liquor, Blaine guessed that the distilling skills of the new owner were still being developed.

Kestel wrinkled her nose. "Smells like the rotgut we used to brew in Edgeland."

The fireplace blazed, adding the scent of burning wood to the smell of unwashed bodies and candle smoke. The pub was busy, and serving wenches brought out trenchers of stew and plates of baked fish that looked passingly edible.

"There's our man," Blaine said with a nod.

William Folville sat at a table in the far corner of the pub. He was a lean man with a sharp, rodent-like face, and long, skinny arms. Folville was likely the same age as Blaine, just a few years shy of thirty. If so, he had already lived unusually long for someone who was the leader of one of the city's most notorious—and successful—gangs of thieves.

"Lord McFadden," Folville said with a lopsided smile that showed a row of crooked, blackened teeth. "Welcome to my parlor." He eyed Kestel as if trying to figure out why a woman was wearing not just a man's tunic and trews but a soldier's cuirass and a bandolier of knives.

"M'lady," Folville said. "Please, have a seat. I understand we have business to discuss."

"I'll stand," Kestel said, taking up a position behind Blaine that mirrored the stance of the two strongmen who stood behind Folville. For a moment, Folville looked as if he meant to make a jest, but something in Kestel's gaze made him reconsider.

"You asked for a meeting," Folville said, turning his attention to Blaine. "Why?"

"We've been gathering the mages who've finally come out of hiding," Blaine replied. "Our far-seers predict a series of powerful storms heading across the ocean for Castle Reach. The garrison is telling everyone in the city to either move to higher ground or head inland as soon as they can."

"We're not going anywhere," Folville replied, meeting Blaine's gaze levelly. "If the people from my ward want to go, we won't get in their way. But I'm not going to run."

"If the seers are right, and Castle Reach gets hit with a surge tide that reaches up to Quillarth Castle, the whole lower half of the city will be under water," Blaine said. "There's nowhere to hide."

"*If* the seers are right," Folville repeated. "But what if they're wrong? Look, Lord McFadden, we've kept our part of the bargain. We've pushed back against the Badger Group and the Red Blades to keep the city from having one battle after another over territory. And right now, my followers control three-quarters of Castle Reach, including the waterfront."

He shook his head. "We pull back, storm or no, and it won't

just be the sea rushing in. The Badgers and the Blades will snap up that territory, kill anyone loyal to me—and to you—and we'll have to retake it square by bloody square."

"What's your plan, then?" Blaine asked. "If the storms were coming down from the mountains instead of in from the sea, we could get people into the tunnels. But that high a tide together with winds and heavy rain will flood the tunnels."

Folville's dark eyes glinted with the challenge. "My men have been reinforcing the upper levels of the tallest buildings that survived the war. They don't look like much on the outside, but inside, we've shored up the supports, strengthened the floors, replaced beams in the roofs."

"You expected storms?" Blaine asked.

Folville laughed, and the two bodyguards chuckled. "Hardly. We figured them for towers that could give us command of key streets and plazas, plus a view so we could see who might be coming our way."

"You're preparing for war," Kestel said.

Folville looked at her as if trying to figure out her place. He nodded. "Yeah. The Badgers have gotten pushy. They've been brewing whiskey and trying to sell it in our areas, and I've had a couple of my men turn up dead near Badger territory. Personally, I think someone's helping them."

"Who?" Blaine asked.

Folville shrugged. "If I knew that, I'd have already killed them."

"No suspicions?" Kestel probed.

Once again, Folville studied her features. "I know who you are. You're Falke, the assassin."

"Right you are," Kestel replied. Blaine saw Folville's two bodyguards startle, as if it had not occurred to them before this that Kestel's presence was not for show.

"You did time in Velant," Folville added. "For murder."

"Only the one they knew about," Kestel said brightly. She met Folville's gaze. "There were lots they didn't."

The implied threat did not seem to rattle Folville, but his bodyguards looked wary, if a little surprised. *They each out-weigh Kestel a couple of times over, but I'd bet on her in a fight any day,* Blaine thought, suppressing a chuckle.

"How many buildings do your people control?" Blaine asked. "Could you shelter people on the upper floors?"

Folville hesitated for a moment, and then nodded. "Not the whole city, but a lot of people. It wouldn't be comfortable, but if it gets as bad as your mages say, they won't drown."

"The far-seers think it's going to be a series of storms," Kestel said. "It's payback for what the king's mages used to do to keep bad storms away from the kingdom. Now nature's straightening itself out, and we're in for it until things get sorted."

"We've got supplies laid in," Folville replied. "That's one way I make sure the people in my ward stay loyal when the other gangs come around trying to push into my streets. My people don't go hungry. They work for me and stay loyal, and I'll make sure they have clothes on their backs, shoes on their feet, and food in their bellies."

"Will your supplies get flooded?" Blaine pressed. "If the storms hit like we're expecting, it's going to be a while before you'll be able to get new provisions."

Folville shrugged. "Some might. If we've got a day or two, my men can move most of what might be in danger. Most of what we've got should be safe."

Outside the Rooster and Pig, Blaine could hear the wind howl. A loose shutter banged against the wooden walls. Above the wind, Blaine heard the sound of chanting, and what sounded like a large crowd singing. Some of the patrons in the

Rooster and Pig shifted to see out the pub's windows. Folville gestured to one of his bodyguards, and the man took a few steps to look out the window. He returned a moment later, scowling.

"It's those damn Torven troublemakers," the burly man growled. "Got a big crowd down by the water."

Folville looked up at the bodyguard. "Go get some of the other men. Run those bastards out of my territory."

The bodyguard nodded. "We'll get it done," he promised, and shouldered his way out of the crowded pub.

"What do you know about them?" Blaine asked Folville.

Folville cursed. "Very little, and even that's too much. They showed up a couple of weeks ago, around Torven's main shrine. Pretty soon, there were more of them, and then even more. Next thing I know, they're causing problems."

"What kind of problems?" Kestel asked.

Folville spat on the floor. "We caught a couple of them trying to break into one of our storehouses. They've been causing disturbances, making prophecies. We don't need that. My men roughed them up plenty good. Maybe the others will get the message."

"Anything else?" Blaine asked.

Folville muttered a few more curses under his breath. "Nothing I can prove, but every time there's trouble, those damn Tingur have just left. Had a warehouse catch on fire. One of my men saw two of those robed men nearby just before the flames caught. We've been having more problems than usual with the Badgers and the Blades, and I can't shake the feeling that the Tingur have something to do with it."

"Rumor has it Karstan Lysander might be using the Tingur, giving them aid," Blaine said.

"What in Raka does Lysander have to do with a bunch of loonies?" Folville asked.

"We think Lysander's using them to find the weak points," Blaine replied.

Folville let loose a string of curses. "I knew it! I figured those blighters for trouble. My men run them out of my ward whenever they show up, but they keep coming back. I always thought they were planning something."

Just then, a tremendous crash shook the Rooster and Pig. The floor shook hard enough to send tankards tumbling and beer sloshing. Women screamed and men got to their feet in startled alarm. Kestel drew her sword, as did Folville's bodyguard. Blaine and Folville were on their feet, expecting an attack.

They followed the crowd to the door. "Damned if the old shipworks didn't collapse," one man said as the tavern's patrons shoved to get a better look.

Blaine was tall enough to see over most of the people in front of him. He remembered the old Donderath shipworks, a large building that before the Cataclysm had been the pride of the kingdom, turning out the majestic sailing vessels that made up Donderath's cargo fleet and navy. Since the Great Fire, the building stood empty and abandoned, hunched on the edge of the waterline.

Now the old shipworks was a pile of rubble, with dust still rising from its sagging walls and splintered beams.

Just in the time they had been inside the Rooster and Pig, the sky had turned an ugly shade of gray. The wind had been brisk on their trip into Castle Reach. Now it lashed the waves into whitecaps and swept down the cobblestone streets, driving leaves and debris in front of it. The waves pounded against the new seawall, splashing nearly to its rim. Rain fell, and from the look of the sky just a little farther out to sea, the isolated drops were likely to become a torrent very soon.

"I think the mages were right about the storm—and wrong about the timing," Kestel murmured. "I don't like the look of those waves."

Blaine shook his head. "I spent too long out on the boats in Edgeland. That's a storm sea." He looked to Folville. "We need to start getting people to shelter."

Folville stared out at the angry sea. "I think you're right." He climbed on one of the benches and clapped his hands loudly.

"There's a storm coming," he shouted. "A bad one. Get inland, or up high. Don't wait."

The Rooster and Pig's patrons gave Folville an incredulous look. "I'm not afraid of a little rain," a man said, lifting his tankard. "And besides, where better to sit out a gale than with plenty of ale?"

Most of the others chuckled at his joke, but Blaine heard the nervousness beneath the laughter. A few of the pub's customers headed out the door, fighting against gusts of wind to make their way up the street.

Folville turned to Blaine. "Whether you planned to or not, you won't be going back to Quillarth Castle tonight. You wanted to warn us. Well, m'lord, we're warned. And I'd be much obliged if you and your men can help me save my people."

"Get inside! Go now!" Blaine shouted to be heard above the howling wind. His voice was raw and he was soaked to the skin. Kestel stood near the door to the tall brick building, encouraging dazed city dwellers to move more quickly.

"How many more can you fit in there?" Blaine shouted.

"A few dozen more, not a lot," Folville replied. "This is our last building. Anyone who doesn't make it in here is going to need to head farther north, to the warehouses."

Folville was drenched, hair clinging to his thin face, his cloak a sodden mass of wool. Captain Hemmington and his men were farther down the plaza, helping a stream of miserable men, women, and children make their way through the high winds and sleeting rain toward shelter. A thin scrim of ice coated everything, making footing treacherous.

Blaine eyed the warehouse. It was an old building, sturdy enough to have escaped the Great Fire largely intact. A soldier jogged up through the rain to where Blaine stood. "Captain Hemmington sent me to tell you that the water is getting higher, m'lord. We've evacuated people from the lowest streets."

Blaine nodded. "We're going to have to get to shelter ourselves soon."

"Aye, m'lord. I'll let him know." The soldier headed back toward Hemmington's position, nearly losing his footing several times on the slick pavers of the plaza.

Blaine eyed the stragglers. Over the course of several candlemarks, Folville's people, along with Hemmington's troops and Larson's garrison, had urged thousands of residents to get to safety. Blaine was unsure that the high winds might not drive the storm surge high enough to pose a danger even to those on the second floor of buildings within sight of the sea.

"The third floor is full," Kestel reported. Her hooded cloak had kept her relatively dry, but Blaine could see that her lips were tinged blue with cold. "Fourth floor still has some room."

Kestel eyed the people still trying to make their way across the plaza.

"I think they'll be the last," Blaine said, following her gaze. "I suspect everyone else has found somewhere to batten down."

Blaine glanced at the sky. "Not any too soon, I wager. We haven't seen the worst of this yet."

An intrepid bell ringer had stayed at his post. As the last of the bells tolled the candlemark, Captain Hemmington and his exhausted soldiers herded the final stragglers into the building. Larson had sent word that he and his soldiers would hole up in one of Folville's other shelters.

"It's getting hard to stand against the wind," Hemmington said as he sent his men on ahead of him into the warehouse. He shook the sleet from his cloak like a wet dog. "Too bad we can't use the first floor, too, but it's sure to flood."

Once, the structure had been a warehouse, before the Great Fire. Then it sat damaged and abandoned before Folville's men took it for their own, replacing or boarding up broken windows, shoring up its supporting beams and patching its ruined roof. They would be high enough to escape the storm surge, Blaine thought, but he wondered whether the building would hold against the winds, which seemed to grow stronger minute by minute.

Men and women, entire families, old and young, crowded into the shelter. They had felt the storm warning in their bones and brought only what they could carry. Some clutched wailing infants and terrified small children. A few hung tenaciously on to dogs they refused to leave behind. Most came only with the clothes on their backs or a small bag of hastily gathered belongings.

Blaine struggled to close the door against the wind. The downstairs shutters had been secured, but they banged against the sill. Rain struck like small pebbles being tossed against the siding.

"Let's find a place upstairs where we can see what's going on in the city," Blaine said.

They climbed the steep, narrow steps, stopping at each landing to look in on the people sheltered on that floor. Some milled about, or spoke quietly in small groups. Others huddled over crying children or tried to calm disoriented elders. Though it was cold outside and growing colder, the press of bodies warmed even the large, open room.

"You have provisions?" Blaine asked.

Folville nodded. "I've got men on each floor to make sure the provisions are rationed evenly. With luck, we won't be here long enough to need them."

Blaine eyed the refugees. Most had a bleak, hopeless look, as if this last round of hardship, on the heels of the Great Fire and the Cataclysm, was nearly too much to bear. A few sobbed quietly. The third floor was as crowded as the second. Despite the large number of people, it was strangely silent, quiet enough to hear the wind battering the building. From time to time, something crashed against the brick or shattered against the wooden shutters, hurled by the wild winds outside. Those nearest the windows flinched, but others, lost in their misery, did not react at all.

Blaine and Kestel worked their way over to the fourth-floor windows facing the sea, but darkness and driving rain made it impossible to see out. "How long do you think it'll be until the storm gives out?" Kestel asked, slipping up beside Blaine.

He shrugged. "Hard to say. If we're lucky, maybe it will be over by daybreak."

The question, of course, was what would be left after the storm passed. People had just begun to rebuild. Devastating storms could undo all that. If the storms continued, residents would abandon Castle Reach, leaving the former seaport deserted.

Blaine and Kestel returned to the first floor, where they found Hemmington and his soldiers, as well as Folville. One of the soldiers peered through a broken shutter. "I pity anyone who's out there. The wind is driving a lot of garbage around. Looks like it's ripping the tile off some of the roofs."

"Hopefully, not ours," Folville said. The old building creaked and wind whistled through gaps, as if the entire structure was moaning. Lanterns cast a dim glow over the large rooms. The air smelled of smoke and lamp oil.

Hemmington posted two soldiers on watch by the door. "I'm less worried about people breaking in than water seeping under the door," he said. "You see a leak, I want to know about it."

Time passed, and no more bells tolled. Without the bells, it was impossible to gauge how long the storm raged. "We've got water coming in," the watchman shouted in the middle of the night. Blaine climbed to his feet and saw water pouring in under the door from the flooded street.

"Get upstairs," Blaine ordered.

"Water's still rising," the guard said. "I'm betting the seawall didn't hold."

Blaine and Kestel made their way back up to the fourth floor. The building had been used for storage, and with the sudden storm, casks and boxes were pushed up against the walls to make room for all the people. Old lumber leaned against the wall, along with boards and a battered door that had seen better days. Cartons of provisions lay stacked against one wall, covered by tarpaulins.

The wind rattled through the tiles on the roof and battered the warehouse with its full strength. Harried mothers tried to soothe squalling, frightened children. Men passed the time playing cards or dice. The crowded room smelled of wet wool and unwashed bodies. Fear was tangible, even on the faces of the soldiers.

One of the soldiers climbed up the stairs to make a report.

"No one is going anywhere. The entire first floor is flooded almost to the ceiling. The street's just as bad, maybe worse with the current. There's nowhere to go."

Kestel slipped through the crowd, talking to a mother with small children in one corner or speaking quietly with a group of men huddled along the wall. Folville and Blaine did the same, trying to keep the frightened people as calm as possible. All around them, the old building creaked louder as it strained against the storm.

Huddled in the large room, mothers held their children near. Blaine could hear voices chanting prayers, while others sang softly to themselves, rocking back and forth to blot out the sound of the storm.

A crash overhead brought the room to a standstill. One loud crack after another sounded, followed by something that sounded like a hail of heavy stones rattling down the building's roof.

"We're losing the tiles," Blaine said to Folville. "Just how well did your engineers reinforce this building?"

Folville paled. "We fortified it for a ground assault. We weren't expecting the danger to come from the sky."

Another crash sounded overhead, and another.

"So they just replaced the roof. They didn't do anything to make it strong enough to withstand an attack," Blaine said pointedly.

"No. They didn't."

Water dripped from the ceiling. As the crowd tried to move away from the water, it quickly became apparent that new leaks were everywhere.

"We've got to start moving people down below," Blaine said to Folville, eyeing the water stains on the ceiling. "We're going to lose the whole roof if these winds keep up."

"I think you might be right," Folville said nervously.

"We're going to get you down below, where you can stay dry," Blaine shouted above the murmur of voices. "It will be crowded, but you won't be wet."

The murmur grew to a loud buzz as everyone spoke at once. Folville put two fingers to his mouth and let out an ear-piercing whistle. "Quiet down!" he shouted.

"The stairs are narrow, so line up," Blaine yelled. "Bring your things. Let's move." Kestel and the guards roused the fearful and hesitant. At the doorway, Blaine and Folville barked at the group to keep moving in single file. The line moved slowly. Blaine eyed the roof and listened to the wind outside.

A strong gust of wind slammed against the warehouse, making the building shudder. Overhead, Blaine heard a deafening crack and saw the far corner of the ceiling begin to ripple.

"Get down the stairs now! The roof is going!" Blaine shouted.

Kestel and the guards shouted at the laggards, dragging those too terrified to move. More of the tiles peeled away, opening holes to the storm. The temperature plunged as the cold wind swept in, driving the rain with it.

"Go, go, go!" Blaine shouted.

The terrified stragglers surged forward, and Blaine heard the guards below yelling for people to move faster or be trampled. A huge gust howled across the broken tiles, stripping them away.

"Move!" Blaine shouted.

Kestel grabbed an old woman by the arm and dragged her toward the stairs. The guard scooped a pregnant woman into his arms and headed for the door. Blaine went after a woman with two small children. The little girl tried to pull out of her grasp, shrieking in fear, and the boy had lost a shoe and was hobbling, crying to go back for it.

Pieces of heavy tile fell from the ceiling, crashing against the floor and sending shards into the air. The guard dropped to his knees as one of the tiles caught him across the back. Folville went after the downed man, dragging him toward the exit.

"You've got to move!" Blaine shouted above the wind. He slung one child under each arm, expecting the mother to be just a step behind him. With every passing moment, more of the roof tore away, and he feared that if the wind stripped off their remaining shelter, he and the others might be swept away.

A section of tile smashed to the floor between Blaine and the young mother. She crumpled, bleeding where the tile had struck her in the head. Kestel and Folville ran toward him from the stairwell. "Take them! I'll get her!" Blaine yelled, thrusting the screaming, panicked children into their arms.

More of the roof fell with every moment. Blaine grabbed a discarded door that lay propped against the wall, holding it overhead like a shield. Tiles slammed down on him as he dodged toward where the woman lay. Shards of tile pelted him, slicing through his pants below his cloak.

Blaine slung the woman over one shoulder, shielding both of them with the door. The wind whipped through the room, pelting them with sleet. Blaine struggled to keep his footing against the gusts. Just as they neared the stairs, the rest of the roof gave way with a groan and a thunderous crack. Broken tile and timbers showered down, and the full gale force of the winds ripped through the exposed room.

Folville was waiting in the doorway. "Come on!" he screamed above the wind. Kestel appeared next to him, and the two of them reached to take the woman from Blaine. Blaine felt the wind drag him backward, ripping at his clothing. He grasped the door frame with both hands, pulling himself toward the opening, but his strength was no match for the power of the wind.

Folville grabbed one arm and Kestel grabbed the other, yanking Blaine toward them with their full might. The three of them collapsed against the far wall of the stairwell, near where the injured woman lay on the landing. Folville picked her up and headed down the steps. Kestel followed, then Blaine, who was limping where a large chunk of tile had struck him in the leg.

"Let's hope that your engineers did better with the lower floors," Blaine muttered as they edged their way into the crowd on the third floor.

The buzz of conversation stopped as they entered. The injured woman's two children cried out in greeting and rushed toward her, breaking loose from the arms of an old woman who had been holding them. Folville spoke quietly to one of his guards who stepped up to take the woman from Folville's arms.

"Find a healer—we've got to have at least a hedge witch in this crowd," Folville instructed.

He turned toward where Blaine and Kestel stood. Then without a word, Folville went down on one knee in front of Blaine. The room fell silent.

"I never got the chance to swear fealty to you like I said I would," Folville said. "And to tell you the truth, until tonight, I wasn't sure I wanted to. You could have gotten killed saving that woman," he said. "That convinced me." He bowed his head and awaited Blaine's response.

Blaine hoped he did not look as uncomfortable as he felt. "As Lord of Glenreith and Lord of Castle Reach, I accept your fealty, William Folville. Swear to me your loyalty and your sword."

"I swear, m'lord," Folville replied.

"And I swear to you, William Folville, that you will have my protection and aid. May the gods hear our pledges and hold us to our words," Blaine finished.

Someone in the room began to cheer. Another person joined in, and then another until the whole room was cheering. Folville looked up at Blaine, who nodded his permission to stand. Together, they looked out over the room of people, who stared at them expectantly.

"Lord Blaine McFadden has sent his troops to protect us and his provisions to feed us," Folville said, shouting above the wind that still roared with the fury of the storm outside. "Castle Reach has not been forgotten. Storm or no storm, Castle Reach will survive," Folville said. "I have sworn my allegiance," he continued. "Now swear yours. This is your lord."

To Blaine's amazement, one by one, the room's occupants knelt, leaving Blaine, Kestel, and Folville standing. Even Folville's strongmen and Hemmington's guards knelt. Blaine sincerely hoped that his discomfort was not clear in his face.

I never rehearsed this part, he thought. He drew a deep breath and found his voice.

"I accept your allegiance," he said, looking out at the crowd. "But what I need is your help. The city's barely begun to rebuild and now the storms will set it back. This storm is bad—it's likely there will be others. Folville will need your help to rebuild, and to resist those who will try to keep the city— and Donderath—on its knees." He paused. "Please rise—and help Castle Reach rise again."

The sound of cheers followed them to the second floor. Folville announced his new-sworn fealty and asked for the same show of loyalty that the group on the floor above had made.

"You handled that nicely," Kestel murmured, giving his hand a squeeze.

"It's not something I trained for in Velant," Blaine replied.

She met his gaze. "I'd argue that the man Velant made you is better suited to rule than you might have been before."

Hemmington strode toward them. "We've distributed rations for supper, and some of the men used buckets to gather rainwater for drinking." He nodded toward the opposite corner. "We've set up more buckets for latrines on each floor." He grimaced. "It's not going to be pleasant, but there's no helping it. We'll just send the slop out the window and let it wash away with the floodwater."

"I'll see what General Theilsson can spare for troops to lend a hand with the cleanup and rebuilding," Blaine replied. "But we're getting hit with the storms everywhere, and there aren't enough troops to assign to the building crews and still have a fighting force for defense."

Hemmington's expression told Blaine that he understood. "We'll have to manage," he said. "That's the army way. Never enough men or resources to do what has to be done, and some-how, it gets done anyway."

The storm outside continued its fury, but as the first light of dawn filtered through the shutters, Blaine realized that the winds were not as wild as they had been the night before. Floodwaters filled the first floor, but did not rise to the top of the steps. Hemmington cautiously opened one of the shutters on the city side of the building just after sunrise. Blaine, Kestel, and Folville crowded around him.

The street below ran with filthy water higher than the windows of the first floor. The current swept bits of wood, animal carcasses, tree limbs, and flotsam, along with more than a few corpses.

Blaine looked out across the city toward the sea. Many of the buildings had lost their roofs. Some of the buildings collapsed under the pounding of the wind. Before the Great Fire, the Plaza of the Kings had boasted a large statue of King Merrill and several of his ancestors. Those statues still stood when Blaine and the others had taken refuge the night before.

Now floodwaters swept as high as the huge carvings' heads. One statue, a monument to King Hougen, used to have an arm upraised, holding a torch. The torch had snapped off, leaving only the broken stub of a marble arm. In the center of the plaza, all but the finial on top of the fountain was covered by swirling floodwaters.

"It's going to take a while for those waters to recede," Kestel murmured.

Blaine nodded. "And you realize, Niklas and Piran have absolutely no idea what's become of us. By now they're probably worried and angry."

Kestel chuckled. "Niklas, yes. Piran probably holed up in the castle with a bottle of spirits and a deck of cards. By now, he's probably won the crown jewels."

Kestel was quiet for a moment. "It's not the city we left," she murmured, staring out over the broken buildings. Floodwaters ran down to join the angry gray ocean, which seemed to be trying to swallow Castle Reach whole.

"No, it isn't," Blaine agreed. "But now we have the chance to remake it to our liking. If we survive."

CHAPTER
FIVE

VEDRAN POLLARD STOOD NEAR THE FIREPLACE, holding a goblet casually in one hand. He was dressed as if he had just come in from the hunt, with high leather boots and a well-fitted waistcoat. Pollard was in his late fourth decade, but his hair had gone white when he was still a young man. Hawk-faced, with sharp gray eyes and angular, uncompromising features, Pollard's silver, close-trimmed beard added to his aristocratic bearing.

"Welcome," Pollard said, moving away from where he stood near the fire. The guard closed the door and faded back into the shadows along the wall. Other bodyguards, dressed in black, waited in silence.

Pollard chuckled. "Do come in." He moved to pour amber liquid from a decanter into a goblet and held it out. "Brandy?"

Larska Hennoch regarded the drink suspiciously, then seemed to decide that Pollard had better things to do than poison him, and accepted the glass. "If you wanted to talk to me, you could have just set up a meeting," Hennoch said. "Kidnapping my son wasn't necessary."

Pollard looked at his guest for a moment without speaking.

Hennoch had the physique of a boxer and carried himself like an alley brawler. He wore a patch over one eye, lost no doubt to the wound that caused a long, jagged scar from his hairline down to his chin on the right side of his face. When he arrived, Hennoch wore an impressive array of weapons, all of which Pollard's men had impounded. Even without his weapons, Hennoch looked the part of a notorious highwayman.

"I wanted to make sure I had your full attention," Pollard replied. "What happens to your son is entirely up to you. Cooperate, and he's merely come for fostering in the household of Lord Reese. Prove difficult, and you'll find his ransom very dear indeed."

Hennoch glared at Pollard. "I'm listening."

"You've set yourself up as a warlord," Pollard said, moving around the room as he spoke. "I would like to propose a deal."

Hennoch's lip curled. "Why me?"

Pollard shrugged. "You control the smuggling network and the thieves' guild in a twenty-league area. No goods or people move through your territory without you knowing about it and charging for the privilege. You've killed your rivals or forced them into fealty. And you've collected a sizable fighting force who owe allegiance to you. You're the kind of man Lord Reese likes to deal with."

"So why isn't he here?"

Pollard sipped his brandy. "Lord Reese has other matters to which he must attend. He has left this matter to me." *If Hennoch was gauging how difficult it might be for him to get the jump on Pollard, he might be surprised at the outcome,* Pollard thought. More than one dead man had mistaken youth for skill. The presence of *talishte* bodyguards, standing motionless in the shadows of the room, might also temper Hennoch's actions, even if the life of his son did not.

"This venture will amass a good bit of money—something that's more difficult to come by now," Pollard continued.

"True enough," Hennoch replied. "What is it you want from me?"

"Ally with Lord Reese and me, and we'll cut you in for a generous percentage of the spoils," Pollard said.

"I already get all the spoils," Hennoch shot back. "You want me to hand over my money and kiss your ring? For what?"

Pollard pressed on a panel in the wall that swung open at his touch. It was about a foot square, and inside was a large brass horn, like an ear trumpet. "Beneath this manor house are a maze of cells," he said offhandedly. "They're used to store—and interrogate—prisoners. This speaking tube connects directly to one of those rooms. It permits us to hear exactly what is going on far beneath us."

A scream sounded from the bell of the trumpet, followed by the sound of a young man's voice begging for mercy. Hennoch blanched, and launched himself at Pollard, only to be easily restrained by two of the *talishte* bodyguards.

"That's my son!" Hennoch snarled.

Pollard nodded, his expression unchanged. "Yes, it is. And the comfort of his stay here is entirely up to you."

The two bodyguards still gripped Hennoch by the shoulders, immobilizing him. Hatred glinted in Hennoch's eyes. "So if I don't agree, you'll kill my son?"

Pollard met his gaze. "Eventually. He's a strong young man. I'm sure the guards here would enjoy a meal or two from his blood. He might find a way to serve as a blood source for a while, or for the amusement of the jailers," he said with ennui, purposely turning his back on Hennoch. "Or perhaps he could be brought across to serve Lord Reese in immortality."

Hennoch let out a string of obscenities, then sagged in his captor's hold. "All right," he agreed sullenly. "I'll do it. Just don't hurt my son."

"Fulfill your part of the bargain, and he'll earn rewards—better food, better treatment, perhaps even a room above-ground," Pollard replied. "Cheat us, or fail to fulfill your obligations, and he suffers for it."

"I understand."

Pollard turned to look at his visitor, and regarded the hatred in Hennoch's eyes with satisfaction. "Very good. We have an understanding." He paused, and swirled the brandy in his glass. "There is one more condition."

"Which is?"

"You and your troops will be at my disposal and that of Lord Reese. You will muster when we call for you, and fight with full effort when we need your assistance." Pollard's eyes narrowed. "Your men will not act in any way to undermine our interests, and you will provide no support or protection of any kind to Blaine McFadden."

Hennoch let out a long breath, and Pollard could not tell whether the man was relieved by a less burdensome require-ment than he had expected, or surprised at the scope of the demand. "All right," Hennoch replied. "We're your men." He met Pollard's gaze. "Aside from your cut of the profits, and fighting when you call for us, the rest of our business goes on as it was?"

Pollard spread his hands as if the answer was obvious. "Of course. We have no plans to interfere in your territory—unless we have reason to believe you are not keeping to your side of the bargain." He glanced toward the silent speaking tube, and Hennoch flinched.

"I'll keep my side of it. Make sure you keep yours. I want my son safe," Hennoch agreed in a rough voice. He gave Pollard a baleful look.

A thin smile touched Pollard's lips. "You have my word."

A candlemark later, long after Hennoch had been escorted from the manor house, Pollard was seated at the desk in the parlor he had claimed as his office. He had taken the ruins of Lord Arvo's manor at Solsiden for his headquarters. The Battle of Valshoa had forced Pollard to flee Reese's manor at Westbain. But Lord Arvo, unlike Reese, had been a Lord of the Blood, and the mage strike by enemy mages that killed most of Donderath's nobility had severely damaged much of the once-great home.

Half of the old mansion survived, as well as an underground maze of cells and storage areas, enough to set up a functional camp. Any luxuries that could be stolen or scavenged had gone into making the parlor and meeting room as impressive as possible, suitable to the aspirations Lord Reese held for the future.

Pollard sat at his desk with his cloak around him, since the fire struggled to heat the damaged room. Broken windows were difficult to replace, but boarding up every cracked pane blocked out light, so the rooms were drafty, even at night when the heavy draperies were closed. *It was as bad as being on campaign,* Pollard thought, *only without any hope of it getting better once the army came home.*

A light knock at the door made Pollard raise his head. Kerr, his assistant, stuck his head into the room. "Shall I bring your dinner and a pot of tea now, sir?" Unflappable, organized even amid the chaos of postwar Donderath, Kerr kept Pollard's world functioning smoothly. The last several months had sprinkled gray in Kerr's dark hair, and lean times had given Kerr, who had always been slender, a more gaunt appearance, but his brown eyes held the same shrewdness as always.

"If there's food and tea to be had, I'm ready for it," Pollard replied, and leaned back in his chair.

Kerr chuckled. "It's not as good as the best we've had in times past, and not as bad as the worst we've eaten to make do. Cabbage and leek stew with a few stray bits of venison if you're lucky, some cheese, and a hard roll from the flour the men found at the mill."

"I'm so damn cold I don't care what's in the bowl so long as it's warm," Pollard replied.

"I'll bring it right away," Kerr said. "And Captain Nilo asked me to let you know he'll come by as you requested after sixth bells."

"Show him in when he gets here," Pollard said. "We've got a lot to talk about."

Kerr inclined his head in acknowledgment. "As you wish, sir."

Pollard let out a long breath after Kerr left the room and sat staring at the closed door for a few moments, lost in thought. Bending Hennoch to Reese's will was a small but necessary victory. It would take more than that, much more, to achieve their goals, especially after the rout at the Valshoan foothills.

Kerr brought the stew along with a pot of steaming tea, and hungry as he was, Pollard ate slowly to savor the warmth as it thawed his numbed fingers and brought heat to his extremities. *Is that what taking blood does for Reese?* Pollard wondered. *Does it warm him like soup warms a mortal, or is there more to it than just sustenance?* He was as unlikely to get an answer to his musing as he was to ask the question.

When the bowl was empty and the pot of tea finished, Kerr returned to clean away the dishes. "Captain Nilo is waiting outside," he said as he gathered the napkin and dishes onto a tray and replaced them with a bottle of brandy and two glasses.

"Show him in," Pollard replied. He removed the stopper from the bottle and poured a generous amount into each glass. Before the war, Pollard had prided himself on having brandy that rivaled the king's for quality. Now he was grateful to get the awful rotgut that his men distilled whenever they could scrape together something to ferment. *Calling it 'brandy' was an undeserved compliment,* Pollard thought, but it reminded him of better days.

Captain Nilo entered after a brisk knock, and strode across the room. He was ten years Pollard's junior, with dark hair and wary blue eyes. Nilo was also Pollard's best strategist, and his only confidant.

"I take it Hennoch agreed to terms?" Nilo said in greeting.

Pollard nodded and gestured for Nilo to sit in one of the two chairs near the fire. Pollard took the glasses of brandy and came around the desk, offering one to Nilo and taking the other for himself as he settled into the remaining chair. It was only a bit warmer this close to the fire, not enough for Pollard to immediately set aside his cloak.

"He's with us, for now at least," Pollard replied. "Though we'll need to make sure we have spies among his men. He wasn't quite as upset about his son as I expected. There may come a point where he decides to sacrifice the boy to achieve other goals. I want him to know we're watching."

"Done." Nilo took a sip of the brandy and tried not to make a face at the taste. "What have you heard from Reese?"

Pollard stared at the fire without answering for a moment. "Very little. I don't know where he's gone to ground. He was badly damaged, even for a *talishte.* There's no way to tell how long it will take him to recover." He paused. "So here we are, licking our wounds, trying to recover enough strength to own a piece of the new Donderath." His frustration was clear in his voice.

In the Battle of Valshoa, Blaine McFadden's forces had their own *talishte* fighters, both the Knights of Esthrane and volunteers from Lanyon Penhallow's brood. Reese had held his own, only to be badly burned when one of the catapults lobbed a flaming pitcher of oil that exploded close to him. A younger *talishte* would have been immolated, but Reese's age enabled him to survive, though he was severely injured. Since then Reese had gone into hiding to heal.

"What can you sense through the *kruvgaldur*?" Nilo asked, with a glance toward where Pollard's long sleeves covered the many scars on his forearms made by Reese's fangs. Few outside Pollard's inner circle knew for sure that part of Pollard's fealty to Reese demanded that he offer up his blood to be read by the *talishte* lord, though many had heard rumors that *talishte* could read memories from the blood of a living person. That was enough to spark rumors and speculation among the troops. Reese could see Pollard's memories in his blood, providing an efficient way to make a detailed report and an effective means to reinforce the chain of command. The blood taking also created a bond between *talishte* and mortal, the *kruvgaldur*, which could allow for a level of telepathic connection.

"Not much," Pollard replied. "It's been months since he's taken blood, and the bond weakens over time."

"Does it weaken for him, too?" Nilo asked. "If so, that means you may have a bit more freedom than usual."

Pollard shrugged. "No way to know. I suspect we would each sense if the other died. I've felt a light touch in my dreams, but nothing coherent."

"And if he doesn't recover?" Nilo asked with an expression inviting Pollard to speculate.

"We lose an ally—and a liability," Pollard replied, and took a sip of his drink. "There are rumors that Reese may have angered the Elders. If so, his survival may be more precarious than we thought." The fact that, even now, Pollard was unwilling to speak freely was evidence of just how wary he was of his *talishte* master.

"Elders?"

Pollard let out a long breath. "It's not something *talishte* speak of directly around mortals. It's a ruling body as well as a tribunal formed long ago to protect the *talishte* by punishing flagrant crimes against mortals. The idea was that if the *talishte* policed themselves, dealing with anyone who drew attention by, say, wiping out a village, it would avoid persecution by the king, like what happened in King Merrill's grandfather's time. They're the oldest and strongest of their kind, and their word is law. I gather that attracting their attention is never a good thing."

"Why would they be angered at Reese?"

Pollard grimaced. "Before the battle, Reese challenged Penhallow in the presence of the Wraith Lord. He entered the Wraith Lord's lands without invitation and attacked his brood."

"Are they angry that he lost at Valshoa?" Nilo asked.

Pollard shook his head. "Some of them, perhaps. Reese had supporters among the Elders, although so did Penhallow. But remember, the Wraith Lord helped McFadden, and Reese brought an army against McFadden's forces. I'd lay money on the odds that Reese didn't win any favor for his involvement."

"Reese and his *talishte* are assets," Nilo said, speaking slowly as he thought through his words. "But if we lose him, does it change the objectives?"

Pollard sighed. "No. But it's going to take time to rebuild. Right now we're at a disadvantage. We're hemmed in to the south by Penhallow's allies, our troop strength is still depleted after Valshoa, and with Reese still recovering…" His voice trailed off.

"We've got Hennoch's allegiance. I've sent a courier with an invitation to Karstan Lysander to meet about an alliance. With Hennoch and Lysander, our armies will easily replace what we lost at Valshoa, perhaps more." Pollard was certain Nilo could read the anger in his voice. "If we consolidate our power, we'll be ready to strike when the moment is right."

"We'll want to move as soon as we can," Nilo said, setting his drink aside and leaning forward, his elbows on his knees. "I've heard from our spies. McFadden didn't lose nearly as many soldiers as we did, and he's gathered enough new men to make up for what he lost. And one more thing—McFadden is recruiting mages."

Pollard turned to look at Nilo. "Oh, really?"

Nilo shrugged. "They seem to be finding him one or two at a time. They've probably been in hiding."

Pollard drummed his fingers as he thought. "Reese wanted to keep McFadden from restoring the magic," he said after a long pause. "He failed."

"McFadden had help," Nilo replied drily. "Penhallow, Voss, the Knights of Esthrane. He wouldn't have survived alone."

Pollard shook his head. "Even Quintrel helped him, though no doubt I'm sure he had his own agenda. So what is Quintrel up to now that the magic is restored?"

"I imagine he wants what everyone wants these days—control over what Donderath becomes," Nilo replied.

Pollard licked his lips as he thought. "That creates an opportunity."

"How so?"

Pollard finished his brandy and rose, pacing the room as he spoke. "The new magic may eventually favor a different kind of mage than before," he said. "Surely mages can also adapt."

"I doubt very much they'll adapt to catching on fire."

Pollard grimaced. "No, but there may be a particular type of mage or a level of skill that can work with the new magic as it now exists. That's what we want to find, and recruit mages of that type before anyone else has found the key."

"That would give us control of the magic," Nilo said, a slow smile spreading across his features. "Which could gain us Lord Reese's objective by a different means. What we control, we don't have to reckon with as a force against us."

"At least, not for a while," Pollard replied. "Military secrets are the most fleeting of all."

A hesitant tap at the door silenced their conversation. Pollard turned as Kerr leaned into the doorway. "Sir," he said, "something has been left on the doorstep. We saw no one arrive or leave. Perhaps you'll know what to make of it."

Pollard frowned and exchanged a glance with Nilo. "What is it?" he asked.

Kerr stepped into the room, carrying a tray with a single, white mask, the kind lords and ladies donned for masquerades at the palace. Yet this mask had none of the festivity of those party favors. The mask on Kerr's tray would cover the full face, leaving no features to tease onlookers into guessing its wearer's identity. The expression was grim, even intimidating.

Pollard went cold at the sight, and caught his breath sharply.

"Sir, do you recognize it?" Kerr asked with concern. Nilo stood and walked over, staring at the mask in confusion.

"The party season ended in Donderath a long time ago," Nilo joked nervously.

Pollard shook his head, struggling to regain his composure. "It's no joke," he said in a hushed voice. "Reese mentioned that the Elders are always masked, each one a different color. This is a warning, and a message. Reese has been taken by the Elders for trial."

"And what does that mean for us?" Nilo asked.

Pollard imagined that he could feel the bite scars tingling on his forearms. "It means," he said, "that either we are free of our mercurial master or the Elders decide that our fate hangs in the balance with his."

CHAPTER SIX

"S O MANY PEOPLE DEAD, FOR A FEW BOXES OF TRIN-
kets." Bevin Connor looked at a trunk full of magical items
and shook his head. Connor brushed his dark-blond hair from
his eyes. He was of average height and build, although the last
year had added muscle as he learned to hold his own with a
sword. He was passing fair in looks, though hardly the first to
be noticed in a room. Curiosity and a quick wit were easy to see
in his blue-green eyes.

"Worthless trinkets, for the most part," Lanyon Penhallow agreed. "Not too different from the way many wars go,
unfortunately."

Just a few days before, Connor and Penhallow had been
among the armed force that besieged and won Westbain from
Reese's loyalists. With Traher Voss's mercenary army in support of Penhallow's troops, Reese's men could not hope to hold
the manor without risking that it might burn around them.
The cost in lives had been significant, especially for Reese's soldiers. Connor had almost felt sorry for the troops inside the
walls, outnumbered, under siege, and trapped by fire, men who

had almost certainly been abandoned by their lord and whose lives were considered forfeit for Reese's strategic advantage.

One look at the miserable captives in the dungeon ended Connor's sympathy for their captors.

"Any idea where Reese is hiding?" Connor asked.

Penhallow shook his head. "We know he was badly injured at the Battle of Valshoa. That kind of injury takes a long time to heal—even for a *talishte*."

They stood in the manor house at Westbain that used to belong to Reese's family. Before the Great War, back when King Merrill presided over a thriving kingdom, Westbain had been one of the old homes, its stern façade and thick walls making a statement about its owner's wealth and power.

The mage fire that fell from the heavens on the night Donderath was destroyed took its toll. One wing had burned, leaving a central structure with four fairly habitable floors, plus cellars and a dungeon below. It was obvious, as soon as Penhallow's forces had taken possession of the building, that Reese's priorities had been the crypt and dungeons.

Connor pushed a strand of hair back from his face. "Do you think that the items can be cleansed, now that magic works again?" Connor asked, eyeing the trunk warily. He had been present at Valshoa when Blaine McFadden harnessed the wild magic and made it possible for men to bend that power to their will. And he had seen firsthand, in the months since then, that the magic had returned broken and dangerous.

"Perhaps," Penhallow replied. The *talishte* lord appeared no more than a decade older than Connor, in his late thirties at most, yet he had existed for centuries, long enough to see magic rise and fall and rise again. Dark hair and dark eyes were accentuated by his pale skin, and his angular features and confident bearing gave him an aristocratic appearance even when dressed, as they both were this day, in functional tunic and trews.

"I guess I should take comfort in the fact that you've seen this kind of thing happen before," Connor said.

A trace of a sad smile touched the corners of Penhallow's lips. "If it pleases you," he replied, "although 'comfort' isn't the word I might have chosen."

Just in the last year, Connor had seen enough that he had a hint of what Penhallow meant. Connor had witnessed the death of his mortal master and the king, and fled for his life as the kingdom burned. His life as an assistant to Lord Garnoc seemed like a half-forgotten dream.

When the mage strike on Donderath brought the kingdom to its knees, Garnoc had charged Connor with the task of protecting two items—an obsidian disk and a map. That task had taken Connor to the frozen top of the world, to Edgeland, where he had met Blaine McFadden and returned with McFadden and his friends to put things right. Becoming Penhallow's mortal servant had been unexpected, as had discovering his own ability as a medium. That talent for allowing the spirits of the dead to speak through him made Connor the perfect sometime host for the Wraith Lord.

"What of the mages down below?" Connor asked, forcing himself back to the unpleasant reality at hand.

"There's little we can do for them," Penhallow replied, an undercurrent of anger in his voice. "Several are near death. Voss's healers can't do anything except give them drugs for the pain and speed them on their way to the gods." He shook his head. "Those who went mad are beyond our help."

"Can any of them be saved?" Connor asked, horrified.

"Doubtful," Penhallow replied, though he appeared to take no satisfaction in the statement. "I imagine the mages were either lured here with promises of wealth and power, or captured. Probably the latter." He paused.

"Which brings up an interesting question: I wonder what Quintrel and his mages are making of the fact that the 'new' magic can be deadly?"

Connor quelled a shudder. "I don't know, and I don't care. I didn't trust Quintrel, and neither did Blaine." He grimaced.

Penhallow frowned. "Unfortunately, the magic is taking a toll on Blaine. I can feel it through the *kruvgaldur*."

"What do you mean, 'taking a toll'?" Connor asked, worried.

"The magic was never meant to be anchored by just one man," Penhallow replied. "Out of necessity, when Blaine brought back the magic at Valshoa, he unintentionally channeled the full strain of anchoring the power through himself." Penhallow shook his head. "I worry that it's too great a strain. I can tell from our bond that it's depleting him, burning him out."

"What choice does he have?" Connor replied.

Penhallow shrugged. "None, at the moment. But it's not an idle concern. Blaine won't be able to sustain the magic alone for long. As we gather mages, finding a new anchor needs to be a primary concern. We dare not wait too long."

Connor looked out the cracked windowpane across the courtyard of the fortified manor. By the torchlight, he could see Voss's soldiers bustling about their work, taking inventory of the items being seized from Reese's storage buildings and triaging the wounded.

Reese had not only prepared for a siege, he was laying in provisions for a war. Storage areas above- and belowground were filled with weapons, supplies, and foodstuffs that Reese, a *talishte*, did not require but that would be necessary for a human army. Other areas, like this workroom, were full of stolen manuscripts and scrolls, pilfered magical items, and looted treasures.

"You know, I thought Lowrey was awful when he admitted to having stolen a few dozen books from the University and the noble houses that hosted him before the Great Fire," Connor said. "He had nothing on Reese." Connor shook his head in amazement as he looked around the room.

"I doubt Treven killed for any of his treasures," Penhallow replied. "And we already know that Reese felt no such limitations."

"Lanyon, a word with you?" Traher Voss stood in the doorway, a burly man in his middle years whose broad shoulders nearly spanned the door frame. Connor had heard his heavy tread coming down the hallway. To sensitive *talishte* hearing, it probably sounded like stampeding elk.

"What do you need, Traher?" Penhallow asked as he turned and gestured for Voss to join them.

Before the Cataclysm, Traher Voss was someone Connor had heard of, but never in his life expected to meet. Renowned in some circles for his military prowess, infamous in others for his well-known preference for fighting in support of the highest bidder, Voss was legendary, if not notorious. He was also a longtime associate of Penhallow's, and someone to whom Connor owed his life, indirectly, twice over.

"What do you want us to do with Reese's soldiers?" Voss asked. He was a commanding figure, even though his uniform was stained with blood and dirt from the battle and there was a streak of soot across one cheek. A fringe of close-cropped graying hair ringed a balding pate, and piercing dark eyes seemed to catch and analyze every movement.

"The Wraith Lord will handle the *talishte* soldiers," Penhallow replied. As if anticipating Connor's concern, Penhallow turned and met Connor's gaze. "Don't worry. He won't require your assistance for that."

Connor felt a surge of relief. Allowing the disembodied Wraith Lord to possess his body was one of the unpleasant tasks of being a medium. He did not relish the idea of being the mortal host of an immortal and angry Elder passing judgment on renegade *talishte* fighters.

"And the others?" Voss asked. Connor knew Voss meant the mortal soldiers Reese had gathered for his army.

"How many are there?" Penhallow asked.

"Too many to glamour," Voss replied matter-of-factly. "The good news is, most of them aren't bonded by the *kruvgaldur*. We checked for that."

Penhallow ran a hand back through his dark hair, a mortal gesture that death did not erase. "Dozens or hundreds?"

"There were thirty-six survivors when we accepted their surrender," Voss replied. "They were all that remained of the garrison Reese abandoned when he went into hiding. Some of them realize they were set up to take the fall for their lord, and they say they're willing to change their allegiance."

"What about the rest?"

Voss shrugged. "Some men can't admit when they're wrong, or when they've been played for a fool. There are a handful who are snarling insults from their cells, telling us what Reese is going to do to us when he comes back for them." He shook his head. "Poor, dumb bastards."

Connor had witnessed Penhallow's compassion, and his cunning. He had glimpsed ruthlessness and remorse. Now a shadow seemed to fall across Penhallow's features, and his eyes took on a hard light.

"Accept surrender from those who will swear fealty. Have a *talishte* read their blood to make sure they're telling the truth.

Those who won't swear fealty need to understand that we don't have the manpower to guard prisoners or the supplies to feed them." He paused. "Give them time to reconsider, and then hang the holdouts."

Voss's face showed no emotion. "Those were my thoughts, but I wanted to check with you first."

"Unfortunate, but necessary," Penhallow said. "Anything else?"

"We've confiscated a nice cache of weapons and supplies, which always come in handy, especially the food. There were horses in the stables, good ones, so we'll take them and the wagons. I wish I could say we also found a large number of full casks of brandy, but unfortunately, that's not the case," Voss replied.

Penhallow nodded. "Very well. Carry on."

It was silent for a few moments after Voss left the room. Connor's thoughts churned. Voss and Penhallow were men who had seen more than their share of war. Their decision to deal with Reese's soldiers was well within military tradition, he knew. They didn't have to offer the chance to switch sides, and had they not been able to assure a change in loyalty by reading the blood of the captives, such grace might not have been extended at all. When he served Lord Garnoc, he had been present at enough of King Merrill's council meetings to have heard the lives of thousands of soldiers decided after heated debate.

Intellectually, he knew the decision was sound. Yet he hated hangings, and had gone out of his way to avoid the public executions that were held before the Cataclysm in Castle Reach's main square, events many others regarded as entertainment.

"Death is a necessary part of war, Bevin," Penhallow said quietly.

Whether the *talishte* read his thoughts through the *kruvgaldur*, or guessed them from Connor's expression, did not matter. The comment still made Connor wince. "I know," he said. "I don't fault the logic. It just all seemed much more distant and…academic…when I served Lord Garnoc."

"And yet, the men who died as a result of those council meetings are just as dead," Penhallow replied.

Connor nodded. "I know. But I don't have to like it."

Penhallow regarded him for a moment, and there was a sadness in his eyes Connor had rarely glimpsed before. "No. That speaks well of you. And know this—the decision never gets easier to make."

Penhallow's words only partly allayed the concern Connor felt. He knew that his real fear centered on the meeting to which he and Penhallow had been summoned later that night.

"Has the Wraith Lord told you more about what we're to do tonight?" Connor asked, knowing that Penhallow could easily read his worries.

Penhallow shook his head. "No. My role is as a witness. You will play a much more pivotal role if he needs you as his host."

Kierken Vandholt had been a *talishte* mage for six hundred years when he used his magic to save the life of King Hougen, Donderath's king four centuries past. His loyalty cost him his soul. By exchanging his own soul for that of the king's at the instant of Reaping, he cheated Etelscurion, the Taker of Souls, master of the Sea of Souls. The goddess refused Vandholt eternal rest, but Esthrane, a more powerful goddess, took pity, giving Vandholt sanctuary in the Unseen Realm, dooming him to a half-life existence as a wraith, neither living, dead, nor truly undead. King Hougen's heirs grew to fear Vandholt's power, murdering his living descendants and sending Vandholt into exile. Now nearly one thousand years old, Kierken Vandholt was better known as the Wraith Lord.

"That's what makes me nervous," Connor replied. "I get to be the Wraith Lord's borrowed body while he plays prosecutor for Pentreath Reese in front of the oldest and most powerful *talishte* on the Continent. I can't help worrying that the Elders will be wondering how I'd taste as a snack."

"There are valid reasons to be concerned over tonight's event," Penhallow replied. "Fearing that you will become a 'snack,' as you put it, is not one of them."

"I'm the one with warm blood," Connor said, not feeling reassured.

"Possessed by one of the most powerful *talishte* the Continent has ever seen," Penhallow reminded him. "I know that hosting Kierken takes a toll on you. But you know better than anyone that he has always protected you in exchange."

Even when it was his own presence inside me that nearly burned me up and dried me to a husk, Connor thought, indulging what he considered a moment of well-deserved pique. "That's true," he conceded. "But you have no idea how frightening it is on this end of the bargain."

Penhallow's expression softened. "Actually, Bevin, I do. Or did you forget that the *kruvgaldur* is a two-way bond?"

Connor felt his cheeks color at the reminder. "I understand that what is being asked of you is difficult, even unreasonable," Penhallow continued. "You have shown uncommon courage, above and beyond what ought to be asked of you. And I regret that we must ask too much of you yet again."

"It's not really like there's a choice, is there?" Connor replied quietly. "There isn't anyone else who can do the job. I can, so it falls to me. That's how it works."

"I know it's scant consolation," Penhallow said, "but you will be privy to something no living mortal has ever seen: the convocation of the Elders and their judgment on a powerful *talishte*."

"What if they decide they don't like the idea of having a mortal witness?" Connor asked, finally getting up the nerve to voice the question that had bothered him all day. "You and the Wraith Lord are very powerful, but if they came after me, could you really promise me I'd make it out alive?"

Penhallow's gaze met his, and Connor saw just how seriously the *talishte* took his question. "I will protect you with all my power, Connor. Even if I cease to exist. The Wraith Lord, I believe, has made you a similar oath. It's the most we can promise."

Connor let out a long breath. "I know, and I'm not ungrateful. I'm just—"

"Frightened," Penhallow finished for him, placing a firm hand on Connor's shoulder. "You would hardly be sane or reasonable were you not."

"The Elders are going to determine Reese's fate, aren't they?" Connor asked. The ride to the Wraith Lord's manor at Lundmyhre would have taken two candlemarks in good weather. In the sleeting rain, it took considerably more. Connor was chilled to the bone.

Penhallow frowned. "The Elders have authority to punish Reese for crimes against immortals. That includes waging war against the Wraith Lord at Valshoa, and attacking my brood on several occasions."

"I was there," Connor replied, doing his best to keep his teeth from chattering.

The fact that Reese might be punished for putting the *talishte* in danger rather than for the loss of mortal life was not lost on Connor. "They've called him to be sentenced, but they haven't declared a verdict yet. So there's the chance that Reese might not be punished at all, isn't there? Where would that leave us?"

The tightness around Penhallow's mouth told Connor the *talishte* was far from certain of the outcome. "If the Elders refuse to pass judgment, they might also refuse to place special protection over Reese. Other *talishte* would still be able to destroy him—without fearing the Elders' wrath."

They rode with an escort of Penhallow's *talishte* soldiers and Traher Voss's mortal fighters until they reached the borders of the Wraith Lord's lands. Connor followed Penhallow through the tangled undergrowth to Lundmyhre, once a grand manor and now an overgrown ruin.

Cold mist coalesced into the shape of a man. Connor recognized the sense of presence even before the features became distinct. This was Kierken Vandholt, *talishte*, warrior, and Wraith Lord.

To Connor's surprise, General Dolan and Nidhud of the Knights of Esthrane moved out of the shadows to stand with the Wraith Lord. If Penhallow was surprised, he did not show it.

"Welcome," the Wraith Lord said. He was of medium height, broad-shouldered, with the stance of a warrior, clad in clothing out of fashion centuries ago. The mist made his features indistinct, but Connor had no problem calling Kierken Vandholt's face to mind. After all, Vandholt had inhabited his thoughts and possessed his body on more than one occasion.

"Gentlemen," Penhallow said with a nod to Dolan and Nidhud. He looked back to the Wraith Lord. "To what do we owe the reinforcements?"

The Wraith Lord's chuckle held little mirth. "Not exactly 'reinforcements,'" he said.

"I've withdrawn my soldiers from Valshoa," Dolan replied, meeting Penhallow's gaze. "The situation has grown undesirable."

"I don't imagine Quintrel was happy about that," Penhallow said.

Dolan's mouth tightened. "No. He wasn't. And I suspect he was even less happy after we left," he added, withdrawing a black bag from beneath his cloak. "Quintrel used old Valshoan manuscripts to figure out a way to anchor the magic outside of Blaine McFadden. These," he said with a nod toward the bag, "are what he called 'presence-crystals,' artifacts he needed to work the magic necessary to shift the anchor."

Connor let out a low whistle, then realized he had been audible and fell abruptly silent. Penhallow chuckled. "Eloquently put, Connor." He looked to Dolan. "Quintrel hadn't had a chance to do the working yet?"

Dolan shook his head. "He would have needed to kidnap McFadden to make that happen." He paused. "Anchoring the magic is a strain no one man was meant to bear. If the anchor doesn't shift, it will eventually kill McFadden."

Penhallow eyed the bag. "Do you think it's possible to work the ritual somewhere besides Valshoa? Could you and mages loyal to McFadden create that new anchor?"

"I believe it's possible," Dolan replied. "But we would need the right place to make the working, a place of power. Perhaps the crypts beneath Quillarth Castle, or even better, Mirdalur."

"Blaine tried to bring the magic back at Mirdalur and it nearly killed him," Connor objected before he could stop himself.

Dolan nodded. "True. But the magic was wild then, and McFadden was unprepared for the working. The crystals, together with the obsidian disks and the restored magic, might yield a very different outcome."

Dolan returned his attention to Penhallow. "I believe that Quintrel has fallen under the sway of a corrupted artifact," he said. "A globe with a bound *divi*."

The Wraith Lord looked up sharply. "A *divi*? What in Raka is Quintrel doing with a *divi*?"

"Nothing good, that's for certain," Penhallow replied. "You say it's affected him?"

Dolan's expression was grave. "It's making him unstable and volatile. If he persists—and I think he will—it will drive him mad."

Penhallow frowned. "What brings you here?"

Dolan looked from Penhallow to the Wraith Lord. "Nidhud told me about what McFadden has done since Valshoa. He would seem to be an honorable contender for power." He paused. "I would like to propose a deal to McFadden. I will ally my Knights with those Nidhud leads and support him—on one condition."

"Say on," the Wraith Lord said warily.

"I will not allow the Knights to be exiled again," Dolan said. "So in exchange for our support, I would ask that one of the new Lords of the Blood be chosen from among the Knights of Esthrane, and that the Knights hold seats on McFadden's senior council."

Penhallow and the Wraith Lord exchanged a glance. "We aren't the ones who can make that decision, but if Blaine agrees, we'll support you," the Wraith Lord replied.

Dolan nodded. "In that case, I will send Nidhud to Glenreith to make our offer. And I will go to Mirdalur."

"Why Mirdalur?" Connor could not contain his curiosity. Dolan looked at him and raised an eyebrow.

"Is your servant always so forthright?" he asked Penhallow drolly.

"Always," Penhallow replied. Connor blushed, but held his ground.

Dolan regarded Connor with amusement. "Mirdalur is an exceptionally powerful place. I am not convinced that its usefulness is over."

"I'll send Geir to let Niklas Theilsson know there may be new allies," Penhallow said. "Once we finish securing Westbain, Connor and I are due to travel to Glenreith."

"Nidhud will bring word," Dolan replied. "Travel safely. Donderath is a dangerous place." With that, he and Nidhud were gone. Connor could not suppress a shiver. *If a talishte mage-warrior considers travel dangerous, what does that say for the mortals?*

Penhallow turned his attention back to the Wraith Lord. "What should we expect tonight among the Elders?"

"The Elders are assembling at the Circle. *Talishte* loyal to me will bring Reese to us there." The insubstantial figure turned toward Connor. "I may need to ask to use your form once again," he said. "I will need you only if we are attacked, and I will do my best to return the form to you unharmed."

Not far beyond the ruins of the Wraith Lord's fortress stood an ancient circle of large stones in the center of a forest clearing. Connor had not quite decided whether the stones themselves were magic, but he feared venturing close to them, and hesitated to step within their circle.

The Wraith Lord led them directly into the center of the stones. It was clear they were no accident of nature. The spaces between the huge stone rectangles were even, and their width was uniform. The moon hung directly above one of the tallest stone rectangles, illuminating cryptic carvings.

They waited in the darkness. Connor blinked, and twelve black-robed figures appeared, each wearing a different color satin mask. The masks hid the entire face, and the color of the masks was duplicated in the gemstone pendants each wore at the throat of their robes.

"Who called us?" The speaker was a tall figure with a deep-red satin mask and a large ruby pendant.

"I did," the Wraith Lord said. "Pentreath Reese has waged war against me and against Lanyon Penhallow. For that, I demand he be punished. I have brought Penhallow as witness."

"Lord Vandholt—you have brought a mortal among us." The speaker was a smaller figure with a saffron-colored mask and pendant. Connor wondered if the speaker were female.

"Penhallow's servant serves as my host when needed," the Wraith Lord answered. "It is my right."

The Wraith Lord had not bothered to ask either Connor or Penhallow to leave behind their weapons, but Connor found that he took little comfort in the sword at his hip. Given the speed with which these oldest *talishte* moved, Connor knew that he could not hope to even draw his blade before they would be on him unless the Wraith Lord possessed him.

"You are not unknown to us, Lanyon Penhallow." Sapphire-mask said. "Some might say you have a troubling history of inserting yourself into the affairs of mortals."

If the comment ruffled Penhallow, he did not show it. "I have found it advantageous, not only for my own part but also for the defense of the *talishte* as a whole, to maintain ties to influential mortals," Penhallow replied. "A word or two in the right ear at court, a small payment here or there, and many problems are solved before they ever begin."

"Yet you don't make the same investment into the dealings of your own kind. How interesting." The onyx-masked figure's voice was neutral, but there was an edge of implied threat that made the hair on the back of Connor's neck prickle.

Penhallow shrugged. "I'm not interested in politics. I've found, over the centuries, that the things that pose a threat to me also threaten the survival of our kind."

"What is this threat that is so great, you risk yourself to summon us?" Emerald turned to face Penhallow.

"It is against the law of the Elders for a *talishte* to make an unprovoked attack on another *talishte*," Penhallow said. "Yet Reese attacked me and my brood in my crypt, burned the safe haven, and destroyed many of my get."

"He sent armed men into my territory to attack me and my guests," the Wraith Lord added, "and allied with Vedran Pollard to wage war against Penhallow and myself at Valshoa."

"Reese would have preferred magic to remain out of reach," Onyx replied. "He hoped that by attacking you, he could stop Blaine McFadden from restoring the magic. He failed."

"What has this to do with us? We are *talishte*, not mages." Saffron's impatience was clear.

"It has everything to do with us, my lords," Penhallow said. "When magic functions, we benefit as much as any of the mortals for conveniences small and large. We use magical protections to guard our day places, and ward intruders away. When harvests are good and famine is rare, feeding is better."

Connor tried not to flinch at that last comment.

"Magic is restored. Why trouble us?" Sapphire challenged. "We want nothing to do with your squabble."

"I came to ask your judgment on Reese," the Wraith Lord replied. "Reese's attacks against me and against Penhallow are a violation of our law. He has defied the Elders."

"We have only your word for these attacks," Emerald answered. "It sounds like a personal squabble, hardly a matter for the Elders."

"Reese sent a team of assassins into my sanctuary," Penhallow said. "Reese and Pollard sent an army to besiege the fortress of my associate, Traher Voss, with the express intent to capture me and my servant. Surely an army escalates this far beyond a 'personal squabble.'"

"What would you have us do? Give him the final death?" Ruby challenged. "Place you in protective custody?"

The latter suggestion sounded far more like imprisonment than protection to Connor, who struggled to say nothing. *I'm in way over my head*, he thought. *We'll be lucky to make it out of here alive.*

"I petition the Elders for Reese's final death," the Wraith Lord said, looking from one Elder to the next as if to challenge a reply. "Punish him as he deserves."

"Is that all?" Saffron mocked. "You presume that your cause to bring back the magic puts you in the right, and that Reese is clearly wrong. I disagree. We are immortals. We do not require the convenience of magic. Magic enables the survival of the weak. Let hardship cull the herds, so that only the strongest blood survives."

"You romanticize misery," Emerald replied. "Immortality doesn't make privation less unpleasant. Hardship means that there's less blood to go around. Soon our people are fighting among themselves for territory to have sufficient prey for them and their broods to survive." He shook his head. "I do not want to see a return of those days."

"The last time the magic died, it took more than a generation to bring it back," Sapphire said. "It was a struggle to feed ourselves and our broods," he added. "I have no desire for that to happen again."

"This is not about magic. It is forbidden for a *talishte* to strike against an Elder, yet Reese has sent his men against me.

I claim my right as Elder to bring charges against him," the Wraith Lord said. "I call for your judgment."

"Shall we hear the defendant's side?" Emerald interrupted. "Since we took Lord Reese prisoner at the Wraith Lord's behest?"

Three *talishte* guards brought Pentreath Reese from the shadows outside the stone circle. Reese's wrists were bound. Despite the rapid rate at which *talishte* healed, Reese still showed evidence of the damage done in the Battle of Valshoa. Even after several months of healing, Reese's skin was puckered and discolored from the fire that had nearly destroyed him. One side of his face was nearly burned away, along with most of his right ear. His hair had grown back in patches here and there in the scar tissue. Reese walked with a new limp, and held one arm as if it were painful to move.

He's had several months to heal, and he's talishte, Connor thought. *If he looks this bad now, I'm glad I didn't see what he looked like right after the battle.*

"Elders. I appeal to you," Reese said. He shot a glare in the direction of Penhallow and the Wraith Lord. "I've done nothing that warrants this imposition on your time." His body might have tested the limits of endurance, but it was obvious that hardship had not dimmed his will.

"Speak your case," Emerald said.

Reese squared his shoulders. "Without magic, *talishte* would not be subservient to mortals. Magic enables mortals to amplify their strength. It upsets the natural order. I had no hand in the destruction of magic. But when that destruction came, I saw the opportunity for our kind to regain their rightful place in the order of things."

Reese looked from one masked face to another. "We are the top predator. And to the victor goes the spoils." He looked toward Penhallow. "Yet Penhallow and the Wraith Lord would deny us our victory. They act against our kind, allying with mortals to give those mortals magic once more, magic they will use to hunt us and destroy us."

"Had we convened before the Battle of Valshoa, your plea would have had merit," Sapphire-mask replied. "But magic has been restored. Your aggression toward mortals could bring retribution on all of us. You brought assassins against Lord Penhallow, and armed men against the Wraith Lord. How do you plead?"

"My lords," Reese said, spreading his hands in supplication. "What I did was out of desperation, in an attempt to protect all *talishte*. I identified a threat to the *talishte*, and I acted on it, with the intent to protect our kind," Reese said, raising his head. "I will not apologize for that."

"And in the matter of allowing troops under your control to attack the Wraith Lord, one of the Elders?"

Reese struck a conciliatory note. "My lords," he said, "I had no way to verify that the Wraith Lord was in possession of his mortal servant. We suspected such claims were a ruse by Penhallow to force our troops to retreat."

"Then let us vote," Saffron said. "End the conjecture."

The Wraith Lord turned to the assembly of Elders. "We have been convened here to determine whether or not the Elders shall levy punishment upon Pentreath Reese for attacks against Lanyon Penhallow and the Wraith Lord. How say you?"

"I must remind the Elders that a vote of condemnation demands the final death," Saffron said. "There is precedent, in times of extreme unrest, to show forbearance." He paused. "I vote for punishment, but not death."

"I believe Pentreath Reese deserves the final death for his actions," the Wraith Lord said, facing Reese. "Guilty. Death."

"This is nonsense." Saffron replied. "Release Reese and end this farce."

"Punishment." Ruby and Brown spoke at the same time.

"I see a larger issue," said Amber. "Our numbers are few. If we *talishte* are going to survive, we cannot pass final judgment on one another for matters that, in a century or two, will seem trivial. I vote for censure, with imprisonment, even torture, but not death."

"I see nothing wrong with Lord Reese's actions." Aubergine's voice was sharp. "I vote to absolve Lord Reese of all charges."

"Death," said Silver.

"Death," added Gold.

"Death," Gray voted.

"Censure without death." Jade sounded bored with the proceedings.

"Death," Onyx replied.

"It appears we have a tie." The Wraith Lord looked to Emerald. "How do you vote?"

Emerald looked at Penhallow in silence for a moment. "I agree that Reese's actions were…unwise. But these are unstable and dangerous times, and the old ways may need to be reexamined." He paused. "In normal circumstances, the attacks would warrant death," Emerald said, leveling a stern gaze at Reese, who had the good grace to look abashed.

"Yet we do not live in normal circumstances," the Elder continued. "Our numbers are few, and many of our kind were destroyed in the Great Fire. We cannot replenish those numbers quickly. For that reason alone I am loath to destroy one of our older *talishte*. It is with hesitation that I vote…censure with punishment but not death." Emerald paused. "But should Reese repeat any of these crimes against the Elders, he shall receive final death without trial."

In less than the blink of an eye, Onyx withdrew a stake from the folds of his cloak and drove it into Reese's heart. Reese's eyes widened and his mouth opened, but he made no sound as he crumpled to the ground.

"Lord Reese—you are under censure by the Elders for attacks on Penhallow and Kierken Vandholt," Onyx said. "Such actions, if repeated, will result in the final death. The Elders have spoken."

"Let him have the punishment given to Hemming Lorens," Onyx ordered. "Let him be bound with rope made from rowan-wood fibers. Let masterwort be burned and the ashes sprinkled on his skin and all around him. Make a tincture of moonflower and allow it to seep into his clothing and bonds. And when he is immobilized, place him in the oubliette beneath my manor. For his crimes, he shall starve there for fifty years. This is the word of the Elders."

As quickly as they had assembled, the Elders vanished and took Reese with them, leaving the Wraith Lord, Penhallow, and Connor standing inside the stone circle.

"Will the black-masked Elder carry out the sentence?" Connor asked, still shaking.

Vandholt nodded. "Onyx is trustworthy," he replied. "Imprisoning Reese at his own manor makes me more certain the punishment will be carried out."

"You're immortal, ancient, and powerful. Why bother with the masks?" Connor's fear made him impudent.

"Because we are not indestructible," Vandholt replied. "Even I can be destroyed." He paused. "We Elders rule on the affairs of the *talishte*, beings who, after many centuries of existence, often believe themselves beholden to no one. Those whom we rule against have supporters who may take vengeance in the name of their master."

"So the Elders are afraid?" Connor asked incredulously. He realized what he said aloud and blanched, aware of the company he kept. "I'm sorry—it's just that it's difficult to think of beings like the Elders feeling fear, with all their power."

Penhallow met his gaze. "The night of the Great Fire, do you believe King Merrill was afraid? And the other lords of the realm, did they feel fear?"

Connor felt his face redden. "Of course. They were men. Powerful, but still men."

"And so are we," the Wraith Lord said. "Men...and a few women...who have great power, yet we have no real desire to go to the Sea of Souls while existence is still within our grasp."

"I'm sorry," Connor said. "I spoke rashly."

"You spoke honestly," the Wraith Lord replied. "Yet it is good for you to remember the discretion you learned at court. Not many among our kind will answer you as candidly—or without offense taken—as Lanyon and I."

"Setting Connor's question aside," Penhallow said, "what repercussions do you foresee?"

Kierken Vandholt turned to face Penhallow. "Perhaps nothing. Perhaps war. We'll see what kind of loyalty Pentreath Reese commands from his followers—and his master."

CHAPTER SEVEN

THANKS FOR MEETING US." VERRAN DANNING stood in the shadow of a large oak. Borya and Desya were just a pace behind him, bodyguards as well as companions in espionage.

"I don't know why I've got to freeze my nuts off in the woods," Niklas muttered.

"Because it won't do for people to see you with us if you want us to be your spies, now will it?" Verran asked.

"What have you got for me?" Niklas asked.

"Lysander is definitely moving his forces for an attack," Borya said, his Flatlands accent clear in his voice. "From every-thing we've seen, I'd place my money on a strike against Glen-reith or maybe one of the northern warlords, such as Verner or the Solveigs."

"He's recruiting—maybe a better word is 'conscripting'—soldiers from the pubs and taverns," Verran added. "More than once we've seen Lysander's men come into a pub, strike up a conversation with a young, able-bodied fellow, and then they leave together—and the young man isn't seen again."

Desya leaned closer. "And that's not all. Not long after Lysander's army comes through, several robed 'priests' of Torven show up, and get the townsfolk and farmers all stirred up. Next thing you know, most of the layabouts who didn't have aught to do follow them off to petition the gods, or some such nonsense." He pushed an errant lock of black hair out of his eyes and grinned. "Don't think it leaves much doubt that Lysander is also recruiting the Tingur."

Nearly two months had passed since Verran, Desya, and Borya had proposed their daring scheme and won grudging approval from Blaine and Niklas. Verran Danning, master thief and sometime musician, was one of Blaine's comrades from Velant. He was the first to admit that combat wasn't his strong point, but stealing—either provisions or information— was. Borya and Desya were brothers, cousins to Zaryae and onetime acrobats in a traveling group of performers that had helped Blaine on his quest to restore the magic. They had proposed creating a new caravan of erstwhile minstrels and performers to travel among the farms and towns, eyes and ears for Blaine and Niklas.

"Admit it, Niklas," Verran said with a grin. "Our little ruse is paying off." Verran was slightly built, with dirty-blond hair that stuck out at angles like a scarecrow, and pale-blue eyes that were alight with relish for the game.

"You're enjoying this far too much," Niklas grumbled. "If you get caught, you'll see that it's not a lark."

"Oh, we're quite well aware of that," Borya replied, his expression growing serious. The twins' eyes had the unnerving yellow irises of a cat, an unfortunate effect of being caught in the wild-magic storms. "We've dealt with our share of brigands on the road."

He smirked, and let his hand fall to the grip of the long knife in a sheath on his belt. "We consider ridding Donderath of those blackguards to be a bonus. We take care of ourselves."

Even if Verran was not much of a fighter, Borya and Desya were experienced with swords. Geir had assigned several *talishte* fighters who were also musicians to accompany the spies, and Niklas had likewise found soldiers who could pass for performers for additional backup. The arrangement had paid off handsomely with valuable information.

"What else?" Niklas asked, rubbing his gloved hands up and down his arms over his cloak to warm himself.

Verran and the others exchanged a wary glance. Niklas caught the look, and frowned. "What?"

"It's Carr," Verran said. "That bloke's going to get himself killed. He steers clear of us, but we've caught sight of him one place and another, always where he's got no business being."

"Like where?"

"In one town, he showed up to one of the gatherings where Lysander's 'priests' were calling for the faithful to take up arms," Borya said. "Kept to the back, faded away before they left, but I thought I saw him shadowing them afterward."

Niklas swore under his breath. "Anything else?"

Desya nodded. "Aye. Turned up in a wayside tavern a few weeks ago, playing the sot." At Niklas's raised eyebrow, he shook his head. "Oh, he wasn't really drunk. Guess he wanted people to think so to get them to talk in front of him." He grimaced. "Worked a little too well. A couple of men tried to relieve him of his coins."

"Almost relieved him of his life with the thrashing he took," Verran added, "but he fought his way out without needing our help." He shook his head worriedly. "Damn fool. Is he trying to impress Mick, or spite him?"

Niklas sighed. "I don't know. He wasn't this reckless as a soldier. Maybe it's from his bout with the Madness, or maybe it's in his blood—Ian was known for his temper." *Or maybe he still has a touch of the Madness*, Niklas thought to himself, recalling how it had affected Carr. Few who had been struck had survived, and most who lived through it did not escape undamaged. Fortunately, now that the magic had been anchored again, the outbreaks had all but ceased.

"I don't want to be the one to tell Mick his brother's dead," Verran said with a pointed look. "Carr's going to push his luck too far."

"Agreed, but there's nothing any of us can do about it, short of locking him up at Glenreith, which isn't going to happen," Niklas said. He pulled a small bag of coins from inside his cloak. "Good work," he added. "This should cover your provisions for a while."

Verran tucked the bag into his shirt and grinned. "I'll take your coin, mate, but we earn our way. The twins put on a good show with all their damn-fool twists and flips, and the other musicians and I usually earn drinks and dinner for our table at the pub. The magic may not be perfect, but I've got some of the gift back."

"Mind you don't get too well-known," Niklas cautioned. "You wouldn't want anyone to take too much interest in you."

Verran chuckled. "No danger of that," he said. "And we take pains to look appropriately shabby. Just your average down-on-our-luck vagabonds," he said with a smile.

"Keep an eye out for Lysander's supply lines," Niklas said. "Especially if he's going to come after us, I want to know how we can cut the bastard off and starve him out."

"Will do," Borya said. "From what we've seen, once his priests recruit the Tingur, they go back to what's left of their farms and villages and turn over anything they can get their hands on to Lysander."

"Clever son of a bitch," Niklas said. "Watch yourselves— mages say there are more storms coming, and bad ones, too."

Desya nodded. "No surprise there. We've ridden out the last few in barns and cellars. Do you think that once the magic has time to settle, it'll get better?"

Niklas shrugged. "No way to tell. Zaryae and the mages are convinced it's payback for the king's meddling with the weather before the Great Fire." His breath fogged with the cold, and the air was bone-chillingly damp, on the cusp between rain and sleet.

"We'll keep our eyes open," Verran assured him. "Good luck with Lysander." With that, he and the twins headed back to the caravan, and Niklas saddled up for the ride back to the camp.

Ayers was waiting for him in his tent. "News?" his second-in-command asked.

Niklas peeled off his damp cloak, standing near the small brazier that took the worst of the chill off inside his tent. He rubbed his hands to warm them as he related what he had learned.

Ayers nodded. "One of our *talishte* brought an update from Castle Reach. Folville says the Tingur seem intent on storming the gates at Quillarth Castle, even though they're hardly armed to breach the walls," he said. "His bet was it was a ruse to draw you off while Lysander is busy elsewhere."

Niklas nodded. "As we figured. We left enough soldiers at the castle that I'm not worried. With the walls rebuilt, they can hold out against quite a bit, and I doubt the Tingur have siege engines handy."

Ayers grimaced. "Let's hope not." He paused. "Oh, there was

one more bit of news, passed through several hands from our man at Solsiden."

"Oh?"

"According to him, Pollard approached Lysander for an alliance."

Niklas raised an eyebrow. "That's interesting. Any idea why?"

Ayers shook his head. "I suspect it's because Pollard needs muscle. No word on Lysander's response, but he seems the type to play both ends against the middle."

Niklas sighed. "And we'll find out soon enough just how good a gamesman he is."

By tenth bells, the army camp was quiet. Fires were banked for the night, lanterns were out except for the kitchen tent, where cooks and bakers prepared for the next morning. Three soldiers walked the perimeter on patrol as usual. Which was exactly what Niklas was counting on.

Inside the tents, the night was far from 'usual.' Soldiers sat fully clothed, armored and armed, ready for action, silent in the darkness. Niklas's small contingent of mages had constructed a passive warding, a protection that would only flare into power if the camp's boundaries were trespassed by hostile magic.

"It's been a candlemark," Ayers murmured. "What if the Tingur decide to strike another night?"

Niklas shook his head. "They'll come. The scouts agreed with Verran. The Tingur are close. And a division of Lysander's army isn't far behind."

"Let's hope it's only a division."

"Intruders!" A man's shout and the clang of swords were all the signal the waiting soldiers needed.

"Go!" Niklas's voice carried on the night air, echoed by commanders down the line. All of the patrols were locked in battle, and while their attackers outnumbered them at first, those odds were rapidly shifting. Soldiers streamed from the tents, jumped from tarpaulin-covered wagons, and ran to battle from their hiding places throughout the camp.

"It's about time we had a good honest fight," Niklas muttered. The night was crisp and clear, though moonless. Then again, given the number of torches their Tingur opponents were wielding, the soldiers hardly needed moonlight to find their enemy.

"Go home!" Niklas shouted at the three shabbily dressed men who began to close on him when he joined the fray at the edge of camp. "Leave now, and we won't follow you. Save yourselves."

The only reply was a guttural war cry as the men began to run, holding their scythes and axes aloft.

The Tingur with the scythe swung wildly, like a drunkard reaping wheat. Niklas sidestepped the man's first assault, then thrust with his sword, easily getting under the man's arm, sinking his blade between the ribs before the scythe blade could come close to him. He kicked the man's weapon hand, knocking the scythe out of reach, then brought his boot down hard, assuring that even if the sword strike was not fatal, that Tingur would not be taking up arms until his bone had healed.

"Behind you, Captain!"

Niklas pivoted, just in time to block a swing from a bearded man with a brush-cutting blade who barreled toward him, rage and terror in his eyes. The blade struck Niklas's sword, sending a shudder down his arm, and he saw surprise in his attacker's eyes.

"You should have stayed home," Niklas muttered, drawing a

short sword with his left hand and dealing a series of blows that sent the Tingur back several steps, as the man began to realize that the attack might not be the rout he had expected.

Blow after blow hammered the bearded man's blade, quickly enough that he could barely parry. Niklas knew that hand-to-hand, his burly attacker had the advantage. With blades, all Niklas had to do was await the opportunity.

"Run while you can," Niklas advised, continuing his onslaught. Down the line, out of the corner of his eye, he could see his men advancing step by bloody step.

"Not while you breathe," the Tingur responded. Niklas had scored a deep slice on the man's forearm, and another to his shoulder, cutting through his thin cloak. *He's got strength, but not speed,* Niklas thought. *Just wait for the opening.*

The bearded man was tiring. His swings grew more erratic, wider. Niklas saw his chance as the attacker overextended, giving Niklas the opportunity he needed. His first strike took off the attacker's arm at the shoulder; the second swing took his head.

Blood-spattered and angry, Niklas stepped over the corpse, ready for the next attacker. One glance told him that the Tingur's numbers had dramatically decreased. No doubt some had fled for their lives. Judging from the corpses that littered the ground, too many of them had tried to stand their ground, and died for their foolhardiness.

Intuition prickled at the back of Niklas's mind. "Close ranks!" he shouted to his men, and the soldiers rallied, filling the gaps in their line.

Only several dozen of the Tingur still remained. Blood-ied and outnumbered, their sharpened farm tools no match for swords, their fates were sealed. From the looks on their faces, they knew it. In better times, Niklas would have called for their surrender and sent them back to their villages roped together like convicts, counting on shame to keep them out of the next battle. But their villages were gone, and supplies were scarce, too precious to waste feeding prisoners. He wondered if the Tingur's attack would bring them accolades from Torven, because their sacrifice brought their mortal master no gain.

Niklas caught a glimpse of motion in the shadows behind the handful of Tingur still on their feet. "Reinforcements coming in!" Niklas shouted as a wave of newcomers ran for their line.

These men were not Tingur. Though they lacked the uniform of a proper army, the fact that they were real soldiers was clear in their every movement. *The rumors were right,* Niklas thought, with a mixture of anger and revulsion. *Lysander sends in his greenest troops, the Tingur, to wear out the enemy before his real soldiers attack. Bastard.*

Then the attack came, and there wasn't time to think at all.

"You're in our way." The soldier stood a head taller than Niklas, with a scarred, shaved head and a smashed nose.

"We'll fix that for you," Niklas said between gritted teeth. He launched himself at the man, landing a slash to his forearm. *He's used to people turning tail at his size. He's come to the wrong place.*

All of Niklas's fury over the slaughtered Tingur and his annoyance at having a good night's sleep ruined found expression in his sword. His first strike drew blood. His second tested the speed of his attacker's reflexes, and the third told Niklas all he needed to know about the man's reach.

Niklas dropped back, then feinted left. His attacker was a breath too slow to deflect the slice Niklas's sword tip put in his shoulder, but he returned a pounding series of parries that scored cuts on Niklas's arm and nearly got inside his defense. Niklas felt the warm blood seeping through his torn shirt, running down his forearm.

"I'm going to have your head," the burly man gloated. "Put it on my pike as a trophy. And I always take a finger from kills, to remember them." He grinned. "Got fifty so far. Room for more."

"Fifty was just another day in the Meroven War," Niklas muttered. He moved right, but the bald man was faster than Niklas expected, and he scored a deep jab to Niklas's side.

"I take the fingers off before the head, so they're alive when I do it," the man added. His reach was just a bit longer than Niklas's, and Niklas barely evaded the swing that went for his neck.

The cold night air smelled of blood and offal. The torches of the Tingur guttered in the dirt, or lay smoking and extinguished beside their corpses. New torches, borne by both sides, cast the trampled field in shades of flame. They stank of oil and soot, sending a haze of smoke across the battlefield.

The bald man was broad-shouldered and muscular, with powerful arms. Niklas watched his attacker strike, and as he evaded the blow, he dodged left and behind. He had just a second's grace, but he gambled that his attacker's powerful swing came at a price.

Niklas dove forward, sword angled just under the enemy soldier's shoulder blade, betting that the man was too muscle-bound to be able to parry in that direction. The tip of his blade sank deep, driven farther by the attacker's own momentum as he tried and failed to swing at Niklas in a spot he could not reach.

Niklas's second blade slid into the soldier's side, below the ribs, and Niklas gave it a twist for good measure. Warm blood poured from the wound over Niklas's hand, but his own blood had soaked his shirt and trews, growing sticky in the cold.

The bald man stumbled, then sank to his knees, and Niklas barely got his blades clear before the soldier pulled him along with him. Wary, Niklas swung again, taking off the soldier's sword hand at the wrist.

"No trophies this time," Niklas said, staggering back a pace. He caught his balance, then lunged, watching as his sword sent the bald head tumbling into the dirt. The body swayed for a moment, headless, then collapsed in a widening pool of blood.

Despite the cold, sweat ran down Niklas's back. In the darkness, it was impossible to guess how many men Lysander had sent against them, but he hoped that the spies were right that it was just a portion of Lysander's troops, and not his entire army.

Where is Lysander? Niklas wondered, pressing a hand against his side to staunch the bleeding. *Or couldn't he be bothered to come to his own battle?*

Then he saw him. Karstan Lysander looked just as Niklas's spies had described him: a big man with a thick neck and coarse, fleshy features. He was astride a warhorse, back from the line of battle, watching from an outcropping that was safely removed from the bloodshed.

Getting his men to do the bloody work for him, Niklas thought. Anger boiled over, and he took a running step in Lysander's direction, but the pain in his side made him stagger. His hand was still pressed over the wound in his side, slick with blood, and Niklas knew he would not be the one to give Lysander chase. *Not today.*

The battle had turned as Niklas fought the bald man. No Tingur remained to be seen on the field, and as Niklas managed to stand, he realized that his men had turned back the assault. A horn blared near Lysander, a call for retreat, not a trumpet call of victory.

All around him, Niklas's men surged like a wave behind the retreating soldiers, hard on their heels, giving chase until Niklas heard Ayers shout for the trumpeters to signal a halt. Bloodied, injured, but triumphant, Niklas's soldiers jeered obscenities at the remnant that withdrew.

Yet as Niklas looked around, the cost of winning had been dear. Dozens of his own men lay dead among the bodies of the Tingur and Lysander's soldiers. Blaine's army had held their own against the invaders, but with the Tingur to strike the first blows, Lysander had exacted a heavy price.

He doesn't need to win, Niklas realized. *Damn him. All he needs to do is strike, damage, and retreat enough times, and wait for us to weaken. While he sits at a distance, watching it play out.*

"Captain!"

Niklas managed a tight-lipped grimace in acknowledgment. No matter that Blaine had given Niklas the title of general. For the men who had served with him in the war and followed him across a continent to come home, Niklas would always be 'captain.'

"Good work," Niklas said as Ayers and two other soldiers caught up with him. "We ran them off."

"You're hurt," Ayers said.

"Nothing Ordel can't patch up," Niklas replied. He took a step toward Ayers, and stumbled. One of the soldiers got under his uninjured arm to steady him.

"Go find Ordel, tell him to come to the Captain's tent," Ayers ordered the second soldier. He turned his attention back to Niklas. "Can you walk?"

"If we don't take the long way home," Niklas said, although he was beginning to feel light-headed, and the edges of his vision were blurring black. He was about to say more, but everything went dark.

"You're lucky."

Niklas heard Ordel's voice before he opened his eyes. The pain in his side was nearly gone, though Niklas felt weak, and every muscle ached. "I don't feel lucky."

"If you weren't lucky, you wouldn't be feeling anything. You'd be dead," Ordel reproved him archly. "If you'd lost a little more blood, I guess we could have had you turned *talishte*, but I'm not sure there would have been enough left for a decent meal."

Niklas repressed a shiver. "Don't even think about it." He paused. "How many men are down?" He looked at the healer, who was sitting in a chair in Niklas's tent next to his cot.

"Enough that I'd prefer not to fight another battle in the next couple of days if there's a choice," Ordel replied. "After that, they'll be fine. If it's any consolation, we took more of theirs than they got of ours."

"That's something."

Ordel nodded toward a small side table beside the cot. "Brought you some food. Eat a little at a time, and promise me you won't try to get out of bed until I come back to check the dressing on that wound." He glared at Niklas. "If his sword had gone a bit to one side or the other, I might not have been able to fix you up. Remember that."

"I'll try," Niklas muttered.

"This came for you, but I thought you should be conscious before I gave it to you," Ordel said, passing a sealed parchment envelope to Niklas.

Niklas frowned, looking at the handwriting. "It's from Blaine."

Ordel sighed. "I know that. The *talishte* who delivered it said as much. What's inside?"

Niklas broke the seal and quickly scanned down over the crowded, angular script. He looked up, sure Ordel could read the concern in his face. "We're to bring the soldiers and meet up with Blaine at the Citadel of the Knights of Esthrane," he said, glancing at the paper one more time to reassure himself of what he had read.

"What do the Knights need McFadden for?" Ordel asked.

Niklas shook his head. "Not the Knights. Blaine picked the Citadel because it's neutral territory. He's called Verner and the Solveig twins for a summit. And he wants us there to back him up."

CHAPTER
EIGHT

—————

"IT'S BEEN A LONG TIME SINCE THE CITADEL OF THE Knights of Esthrane was considered 'neutral territory,'" Piran said as he reined in his horse. Beside him, Blaine eyed the old structure. Deserted a century ago when King Merrill's grandfather declared the Knights to be traitors, the Citadel was in good condition compared to many structures of similar age after the Great Fire.

The Citadel's large tower had been spared in the Great Fire because the building was not home to one of the nobility. Since then, it had endured the magic storms. Here and there, Blaine could see scorch marks, and cracks in the massive stone where a direct strike had hit the tower. Yet the tower's base looked undamaged beyond the neglect of years.

A week had passed since the flood in Castle Reach. Blaine's time had been taken up with negotiations to bring the warlords together, while Niklas and his men had battled Lysander to a standstill. Now, Blaine eyed the skies warily, afraid to trust in the mages' prediction that they had a few clear days before more storms came their way.

Since Nidhud and the Knights of Esthrane had returned

from exile, none of the other warlords could claim the Citadel as their own. The Knights had gone to ground for the daylight hours, but come nightfall, they would return. Blaine suspected that knowledge that the Knights supported him encouraged the other warlords to consider cooperation.

"At least they came," Niklas replied. He had left Ayers in charge of mopping up after the Lysander skirmish, and brought several dozen soldiers to the Citadel for the summit. "And we've got a balance of power. Equal forces."

"How sure are we no one is bending the rules?" Kestel asked, surveying the area warily.

Niklas gave a grim smile. "Dagur and the mages are watching the area. Or, more precisely, they're scanning the area behind us to make sure we don't get blindsided. If any large force moves anywhere near this place, he'll signal us. More importantly, he'll signal the mages, who stand ready with the rest of the troops." And come nightfall, Blaine knew that Nidhud would be waiting with a contingent of the Knights of Esthrane, as would Geir and several of the *talishte* from Penhallow's brood, just in case.

"Do we know whether the other warlords have mages, too?" Piran asked. "This could go very wrong very quickly."

"No one of power other than Tormod Solveig," Niklas replied. "At least, according to Dagur." He paused. "Rumor has it Solveig's a mage, but beyond that, we don't know much about him."

"And I can tell you that no one's calling on the magic nearby. If they were, I'd feel it. Enough talking. Let's go in." Blaine swung down from his horse. He removed his sword belt and scabbard, and handed them over to Niklas. "Keep it handy, just in case."

Grumbling to himself, Piran did the same, as did Kestel, although Blaine was certain Kestel had not given up all her weapons. Then again, he thought, Piran probably had some extras handy as well. That thought cheered him as they walked toward the Citadel.

Niklas's men had set up the meeting place: a bare table and three sturdy chairs for the warlords, with room for the bodyguards. By design, the meeting area was austere. Fewer decorations meant no place to hide assassins.

The flat area next to the tower might once have been a gathering place or a garden. Now it was open on three sides, dotted here and there with fallen stones and rubble. Niklas's men had chopped back the overgrown vegetation.

Blaine ascended the dozen stone steps that led to the meeting place. He was glad to reach the high ground before the other warlords, using the few moments of lead time to assess his 'guests.'

To his right, Sindre Verner moved up the stairs. He was not a tall man, but he looked as if he had done hard labor, with powerful arms and sturdy shoulders, and he walked like a man who had spent a lifetime in the army. Like Blaine, he had a cloak against the spring chill and wore a leather cuirass and vambraces. It was what Blaine would have expected from a soldier. The two bodyguards behind Verner were large men, but they held themselves like soldiers, shoulders squared, back straight, eyes forward.

That fit what Blaine knew of Verner. According to Niklas, Verner had been a major in the king's army during the Meroven War, a man of reasonable honor, though reputed to favor whiskey too much on occasion. Verner's broad features and florid coloring seemed to back up the story. Still, Niklas said Verner had a reputation of demanding nothing from his men that he did not require of himself. That boded well, Blaine thought.

To his left, Rinka and Tormod Solveig walked up the steps with stately grace. The two shared a resemblance that made it clear they were brother and sister. Crow-black hair and eyes and pale skin might have given Blaine to wonder if they were *talishte*, had it not been full sunlight. Both Rinka and Tormod were dressed in leather armor that had definitely seen use.

Unlike the serviceable pieces Blaine and Verner wore, the Solveigs' armor looked to have been custom-made to provide excellent defense while making an indelible impression. Rinka's leather had been dyed red, so that at first glance, it appeared she was already awash in blood. Tormod's leather armor was black, tooled with runes.

Their two bodyguards were dressed in worn leather armor, mismatched pieces that had likely been assembled from multiple owners. The bodyguards moved with a lightness that suggested they might be as equally skilled at thieving as fighting.

While Verner was an unknown in Blaine's experience, Blaine knew the Solveigs by reputation from Velant. The brother and sister had been exiled for running brothels and gaming houses in the three largest cities west of Castle Reach. As Blaine recalled, King Merrill's soldiers were happy to look the other way in return for generous bribes.

The Solveigs' success ended when the king sent a regiment to demand long-overdue taxes. In Edgeland, it was rumored they ran a profitable prostitution and gambling racket and bribed guards well enough to get away with it. They had returned to Donderath on the same ship as Blaine. Clearly, the Solveigs saw a profit to be made.

Verner gave Blaine and his friends a long, scrutinizing look. "I knew your father when he served in King Merrill's army. I always said he deserved to be murdered; I just didn't expect his son would be the one to do it."

Blaine shrugged. "I had my reasons."

Verner nodded. "I'm sure you did."

Rinka's gaze was on Kestel. "I don't remember anything about bringing our own assassins with us," she said. Her voice had a raw quality to it, as if she favored whiskey, or had once nearly been garroted.

"Congratulations on running such a successful business in Edgeland," Kestel replied.

Rinka shrugged. "Actually, it was easier in Edgeland. The guards always had money for women and liquor. Here, no one has money for much."

Blaine broke the impasse and pulled out his chair to take a seat, prompting the others to do the same. It was clear that just showing up to the meeting had expended this group's reservoir of trust.

"I want to propose an alliance," Blaine said. "My army controls from Glenreith south to Castle Reach, including Quillarth Castle and the seaport. The Solveigs control the area to the north and west of Glenreith, to the Pelaran River." He looked to Verner. "Verner controls an arc of land from just beyond Glenreith and Mirdalur, west to the Solveigs'. Allied, we would control a crescent through the heart of Donderath, including the two most valuable trade routes and the key roads between the coast and the river."

"We already control those areas," Rinka replied. "What do we gain from an alliance?"

"Safe passage, for one thing," Blaine replied. "Together, we can encourage merchants and caravans to move freely through our territories, without fear of being stopped at the borders from one holding to the next.

"Our mages have also confirmed that the severe storms happening now are because King Merrill's mages used magic to control the weather before the Great Fire," Blaine continued. "They're likely to continue until the natural currents stabilize, which means we're in for a rough ride. Our chances for surviving are much better working together."

"Strength in numbers," Verner added. He leaned forward, looking to Blaine and then to the Solveigs. "We're not the only warlords to consider alliance. I have heard that Torinth Rostivan has made alliances in the far north, between his lands and the Riven Mountains."

Blaine and Kestel exchanged glances. *Valshoa is in the Riven Mountains*, Blaine thought. *That confirms what Lowrey said and it means Quintrel really is preparing for a return to civilization. Interesting.*

"Larska Hennoch's been in talks with Lord Pollard. Together, their army controls from east of the Arkala twins and Lysander to the foothills of the Riven Mountains," Rinka said, leaning back in her chair and affecting boredom. Blaine was quite certain that despite her appearance, she was actively engaged in sizing up the opportunities.

"Pollard and Reese were weakened at the Battle of Valshoa," Blaine said. "We beat them back, and shattered their army. Lord Penhallow controls Westbain now, and the territory from there to Rodestead House and north to Lundmyhre. Counting Traher Voss's land, that extends their hold down to the coast."

Verner made a sign of warding at the last name. "I want nothing to do with Lundmyhre," he said. "The place is cursed."

"I already have an understanding with both Lord Penhallow and the Wraith Lord. Those lands are in friendly hands," Blaine replied.

That bit of news got a wary look from Verner and a raised eyebrow from Rinka.

"Your proposed alliance sounds wonderful," Rinka said in a tone that conveyed deep skepticism. "What does it cost us?"

"We agree to allow free passage for trade between our

sovereign areas," Blaine said, rolling out a map he had brought showing the proposed boundaries of the alliance, "so we gain from increased trade, and agree to forfeit some passage fees."

Tormod leaned over to whisper to Rinka, who nodded. "Worth considering," she replied. "What else?"

"There is an agreement for mutual protection," Blaine said, meeting first Verner's gaze and then Rinka's, followed by Tormod's. "If Torinth Rostivan has allied with Vigus Quintrel and his mages, we all face a significant threat from the north. And if Hennoch is allied with Lord Pollard and Pentreath Reese, then once Reese recoups his losses, be assured they will look to expand their territory." He paused. "And I think we have all seen Lysander's tactics. He's aggressive, and he doesn't care how many people he has to kill to get what he wants."

"What do you propose?" Verner asked. Now that the topic turned to military matters, he seemed in his element.

"First, that none of us will ally with Rostivan, Lysander, Hennoch, Pollard, or Reese," Blaine said. "We are allied *against* them."

"And?" Rinka prodded.

"I'm confident that Penhallow and the Wraith Lord can hold their area without our help. But if Hennoch and Rostivan want trade routes, we've cut them off from the river and from the coast. Eventually, they'll want to change that," Blaine replied. "And Lysander seems to be out to grab as much territory as he can get. In the short run, I would expect them to make a push to test our strengths while things are still in flux. This alliance will help us hold our borders."

"We've got a lot of rebuilding to do, crops to plant and harvest if we want to eat," Verner said. "We can't afford to have our men fighting continually."

"Verner's land and my land buffer McFadden's territory

from Rostivan and the west," Rinka said. "Why will McFadden care if we get attacked on our borders?"

"I'll care because if you fall, I have one less ally when the attacks come my way," Blaine said with a pointed glance toward Rinka. "If Hennoch, Rostivan, and Reese ally—even without Lysander—they could crush any of us individually. But we are allied, and have the support of Penhallow, Voss, and the Wraith Lord, we can hold back the attack."

"What of their lands? Rostivan, Lysander, Reese, the Arkalas, and Hennoch. Do we hope to capture them?" Rinka was watching both Blaine and Verner closely, as if weighing an internal judgment.

"I have no desire to expand my territory," Verner replied.

Blaine met Rinka's gaze. "If you want more land, take as much as you can west of the river. I want to see Castle Reach prosper and make sure my people can go about their business."

"There is one more thing," Blaine said. "It concerns magic."

Rinka's eyes narrowed to slits, and Tormod straightened. Verner shifted in his chair. "What about magic?" Rinka demanded.

"You're the one who brought the magic back, aren't you?" Verner asked, drumming his fingers on the table. "It's fixed."

"No." Everyone turned to look at Tormod. "Not like it was."

Tormod glared at Blaine. "The magic isn't right. It's...broken, unpredictable. We've lost two of our mages when they tried to use the power. One of them went mad. The other"—he paused and took a deep breath—"the other burned to death. The fire came from inside him. From magic."

"We know," Blaine said. "I was going to warn you—and offer an alternative."

"I've never held much with magic," Verner said. "Didn't care for battle mages before the Meroven War, and a great deal less since then. But I understand that an army needs every weapon it can get."

Blaine nodded. "We're up against a group of mages who were quite powerful before the Great Fire, and who have plans, I believe, to become powerful again. Their leader, Vigus Quintrel, wants power."

"Magical power?" Rinka asked. The tilt of her head revealed her distrust.

Blaine shook his head. "Quintrel sees a world where mages are in control."

Rinka sniffed. "Wouldn't it help if his magic actually worked?"

Blaine shrugged. "We don't know whether the new magic is really still broken, or just changed into something different from what it was before. Sooner or later someone will figure out how to fix it, or how to use what it's become. Quintrel will use those mages against us."

"What do you want from us?" Tormod challenged.

"Information," Blaine replied. "If your mages find and use magical objects, share what happens. If you get the magic to work, tell us. We're going to need to ally our magical forces the same way we ally our troops."

Rinka and Tormod conferred quietly. Verner was silent for a moment. Finally, Verner looked up.

"I think we should go farther," Verner said. He looked from Blaine to Rinka. "Right now, our mages are experimenting. Some of those experiments won't turn out well. If our mages are working separately, and an idea doesn't work, three mages could die, one in each group. They have no way to share information."

He leaned forward. "But if they work together—at least until they figure this all out—then the bad experiments take a lesser toll. The good experiments get shared. Once they understand what they're dealing with, our mages come back to their own territories, to protect our holdings."

Blaine nodded. "I like that. The mages would also know each other's power, which would make it easier if they had to work together against a common threat."

"Exactly." Verner leaned back, pleased with his contribution, as if daring Tormod to object.

"The mages in this central location become hostages of a sort," Tormod said. "Each group, under the eye of the others, within the reach of each warlord, just in case." He gave a cold smile. "In the last war, the mages created a weapon they couldn't control. This time, we make sure they have more...supervision."

"Then, are we agreed to this alliance?" Blaine asked, looking to the others in turn.

Rinka and Tormod conferred quietly for a moment, while Verner appeared deep in thought.

Verner was the first to break the silence. "I'm in."

Rinka and Tormod ended their whispered discussion and exchanged a final glance. Rinka met Blaine's gaze. "We will ally with you."

Just then they heard hurried footsteps on the stone stairs. The Solveigs' bodyguards moved closer protectively, as did Verner's soldiers, but Piran and Kestel moved toward the stairs as Niklas hurried toward them.

"My lords," Niklas said with a hurried bow. "A large force is moving toward us from the north. We think it's Rostivan. I hope you've worked out your differences, because within a candlemark, we'll be under attack."

CHAPTER NINE

"HOW DO WE KNOW YOUR PEOPLE DIDN'T STAGE this attack?" Rinka demanded.

Niklas fixed Rinka with a glare. "We don't control the lands north of this point. Rostivan's the one I'd guess is behind it."

"Perhaps our time is best spent preparing for defense," Verner suggested acerbically.

"It's also the best way to prove our intent is firm," Blaine said. "Do we stand together against the threat?"

"Time's wasting," Piran broke in. "Let's kill them first and figure out why they came later."

Tormod gave an appreciative grin. "I like how you think."

Blaine looked to Verner and Rinka. "Let's make sure our generals are working together on this. It's likely our enemies are going to use this as a test. Will you introduce Niklas to your generals and authorize them to work with him on defense?"

Rinka and Tormod exchanged a few whispered words. Rinka looked up. "Under whose command?"

Blaine forced down his frustration. "If the commanders agree on a strategy, they can each command their own troops."

Verner stared at Niklas for a moment as if taking his

measure. "I agree. And I'll take you to my general right now," he said, giving Rinka a look as if to force her agreement.

"Come to our camp when you finish," Rinka said, meeting Verner's stare like a challenge. "We will make sure our general cooperates."

It did not take long for the ruins of the Citadel to become a battleground.

"The next time you set up a warlord council, pick a place we can actually defend." Piran kicked the dead soldier's body clear of his sword. Blaine rolled the headless corpse of another enemy fighter out of his way, and looked around the battlefield to see where they could jump back into the fray.

"Defensible sites tend to make treachery easier as well," Blaine retorted. "More cover, more places for someone to hide." With a nod, he indicated a knot of fighting where three of his soldiers were barely holding their own against four of the enemy, suggesting that was where they were needed next.

Piran gave a loud, off-key war cry that startled the rival warlord's fighters, and charged at a dead run, with Blaine only a step behind. Out of the corner of his eye, Blaine could see Kestel slipping through the lines, intent on her prey. Although she was an accomplished sword fighter, Kestel preferred to send a throwing knife into an enemy soldier's back, or finish off the enemy's dying and wounded fighters with a slash to the throat.

The broad, flat plain north of the Citadel was now a killing field. Torinth Rostivan's identity was confirmed as soon as his battle flag came into view. The flag showed a *gryp*, wings unfurled and fanged maw opened wide, with talons extended for the hunt.

"Tell Kestel to leave some of the wounded alive," Piran said through clenched teeth as he deflected a strike from his opponent. "We can't interrogate the dead."

"You tell her," Blaine countered, parrying a blow from the soldier he fought. The numbers were now equally matched between the four of Blaine's soldiers and the four enemy fighters, and Hennoch's troops were getting the worst of it.

"She'll take it better from you," Piran retorted.

"When have you ever known Kestel to take orders from anyone?" Blaine replied.

Rostivan's forces outnumbered the allied warlords' combined troops they'd brought with them to the Citadel, but to Blaine's eye, their soldiers were better trained. Above the din, Blaine could hear Niklas shouting to rally their soldiers for an advance. The generals had made the most of their slight warning. Verner's soldiers hooked around to the left, pushing a wedge of Rostivan's men into the waiting swords of both Blaine's troops and those belonging to the Solveigs.

"Poor, dumb bastards," Piran muttered as he pulled his sword free of the soldier he had just cleaved from shoulder to hip. "Does Rostivan give them a sword and a jug of grog and tell them it makes them warriors?" His tone was flippant, but Blaine could see anger in Piran's eyes.

Verner's troops were farthest away, but the skill with which his front line was driving Rostivan's soldiers into the waiting blades of the allies suggested a tightly coordinated fighting unit that was skilled in battle. Blaine caught a glimpse of Verner sprinting between battle zones, climbing onto a ruined wall to direct the battle, and bet that the warlord's cavalier attitude toward his own safety made him popular with his men. Niklas, by comparison, was a cagey strategist and a survivor. Small teams of his soldiers attacked clusters of enemy fighters.

"Something about those two makes my skin crawl," Piran

said, and Blaine followed his gaze to where the Solveig siblings were fighting alongside a dozen of their soldiers against a line of Rostivan's men. Rinka was as accomplished with the sword as Kestel, and Tormod's fighting style showed that he had gained his skill in battle.

Even by Velant standards, Rinka and Tormod fought dirty, skills likely won in tavern brawls and prison fights. The Solveigs moved with feral grace and strength, cutting down their attackers mercilessly. But when three more of Rostivan's soldiers joined the fray, the odds tilted against them.

"Piran—over here!" Blaine shouted. They had crossed half of the distance between them and the Solveigs when Blaine stopped cold, staring at what he saw.

Rinka was moving in a swift, deadly circle around Tormod, who had gone still, face impassive. Though Rinka executed her moves with the grace of a dancer, her sword strikes were lethal.

Tormod's features grew tight with concentration. Blaine felt a surge of magic and a sudden, blinding headache that caused him to stumble. One of the corpses on the ground began to rise, then a second, and finally a third struggled to its feet and jerked toward the attackers. Rostivan's soldiers cried out in alarm and fell back. The corpses began to tremble, limbs quaking and bodies shaking as if taken by a seizure. In the next instant, the dead soldiers exploded, spraying Rostivan's men in gobbets of blood and drenching Rinka and Tormod in gore.

Rostivan's soldiers ran screaming.

"He's a necromancer," Piran muttered.

Before Blaine could reply, a raw-throated scream cut through the air. A wild-eyed young man careened toward Blaine, broadsword raised. He was within striking distance, and the blade fell with enough power to cleave bone.

Blaine parried, blocking the swing. The force of the strike

shuddered painfully down his arm. The enemy soldier's eyes were wide with fear, and the panicked ferocity of his strikes made up for what he lacked in training.

Blaine parried again, watching for the opening he somehow knew was coming. The fighter swung high, and Blaine's sword went low, slicing across the man's belly and spilling his entrails in a steaming mass down his legs and onto the ground. Fear shifted to pain and disbelief as the man's eyes widened, and he grasped at his gashed abdomen, vainly attempting to stuff the slick mass back through the bloody slit. He groaned and fell to his knees. Blaine swung once more, taking the soldier's head from his shoulders in one clean move.

Piran was fighting off an attacker, but it was clear that the field of fighters had thinned. Bodies littered the ground, but the majority of those still standing were on their side. Rostivan's flag was down, and his troops departed as quickly as they came, a retreat instead of a rout, giving Blaine to wonder about the intent behind the attack.

"Nothing like sealing a treaty in blood," Kestel said, joining them. Bloody long-bladed knives dangled in her crimson hands. Her face, arms, and armor were spattered with blood.

"The Solveigs are necromancers," Blaine said, scanning the horizon to find the twins. "Or at least, Tormod is."

Kestel frowned. "And his power worked?"

"He animated three corpses, but before they could do more than stand, they exploded," Blaine replied. "No way to tell whether that's what he intended or not."

"As long as it was effective," Kestel said with a shrug.

"Did you leave us any prisoners to interrogate?" Piran asked, eyeing Kestel's bloody blades.

Kestel made a show of wiping her blades clean and sheathed them with a flourish. "A few. Enough to be valuable for information, but not a chore to feed." She gave a jerk of her head in the direction in which Rostivan's soldiers had retreated. "Somehow, I doubt their warlord will negotiate for them."

Piran looked to Kestel. "Who's got the prisoners?"

"Niklas sent a team of men to collect them," Kestel replied. "I thought you'd want to be there when he questions them. He said he'd bring them back to the Citadel and wait for us there."

Not a bad move, Blaine thought. *If the prisoners won't talk on their own, come nightfall, the* talishte *can read their blood.*

Rinka and Tormod were rallying their soldiers to determine their losses, and farther down the field, Verner's second-in-command was doing the same. Behind them, Blaine heard Niklas shouting for his troops to gather.

"Rostivan had more men. The odds were with him," Kestel said, looking out over the field of bodies.

"He had green recruits," Blaine said, anger coloring his voice. "None of the men I fought were old enough to have mustered into the army during the Meroven War. I think it was a test to see if the alliance would hold."

"I think there's more to it than that, Mick," Piran said. "I think Rostivan came looking for you. After all, he's allied with Quintrel, isn't he? And you mucked up Quintrel's plans when we left Valshoa." He looked out over the battlefield. "I think Rostivan retreated because he didn't expect us to have reinforcements." He shrugged. "Maybe his spies got it wrong. I don't think he came here looking for a big battle. I think he came after you."

They fell silent as they walked the rest of the way, alert for trouble. Blaine mulled Piran's observation, validating it with every savaged body they stepped over. *It doesn't make sense for Quintrel to want to kill me*, Blaine thought. *If I die, the magic could be broken forever. So what's he after? And how do I factor into it?*

Niklas was waiting for them when they returned to the Citadel, along with Rinka and Tormod. Half a dozen men knelt on the stone landing, wrists bound, hands atop their heads. Behind them, double the number of guards held the prisoners at sword's point.

"Verner and some of his men went after Rostivan's troops, at least to make sure they were really leaving," Niklas said. "I expect he'll join us when he can." He nodded toward the captives. "I figured you'd want to hear the answers," Niklas said. His uniform was streaked with dirt and blood, and one sleeve was torn, exposing a bloody gash.

Niklas turned toward the prisoners. "Your lives have been spared—for the moment—to tell us what you know," Niklas said. "If your information is valuable, your life will be longer. Refuse to talk, and we have no reason at all to keep you alive." He paused. "Help us, and swear allegiance to one of the allied lords, and we'll get you a healer and let you live. Otherwise…" He let his voice drift off, but his meaning was clear.

Niklas stopped in front of one young soldier whose eye was nearly swollen shut. "What can you tell me, soldier? Your master sent you to die. You owe him nothing."

The soldier hesitated.

"Your commander abandoned you, ran off to save his skin. Talk to us, tell us what we want to know, and you can live."

"Rostivan knew you were going to be at the Citadel." The voice came from another soldier, a dark-haired young man whose face was drenched in blood from a scalp wound.

Niklas turned his attention to the captive. "How?"

"He's got spies everywhere," another soldier said.

"It's McFadden he really wants." The first soldier spoke up. "We were told what he looked like, and offered a gold piece each if we captured him."

Blaine and Piran exchanged a glance. "Why McFadden?" Niklas asked the prisoner.

"Rostivan's orders were to capture McFadden or wound him so he could be taken," the soldier replied.

"His orders?" Kestel repeated. "Orders from whom?"

The soldier shrugged. "That hocus up in the mountains, I guess."

"Vigus Quintrel. That explains it," Piran muttered.

"How big of an army does Rostivan have?" Niklas probed. "Speak up, lads; tell me what I want to know and save your own lives."

"Big," the first soldier replied. "Most of the fellows are like us, got nowhere else to go. Rostivan promised we could take new land once he beat the warlords."

Rinka and Tormod moved into view, and abruptly, the first soldier paled and shied back. "Don't hocus me! I saw him. He made the dead rise!" the man said, staring in terror at Tormod. Tormod gave the man a chilling smile that showed his teeth.

"Where else is Rostivan planning to strike?" Niklas prodded.

"He doesn't tell us nothin' but where we're to march that day," one of the other soldiers put in.

"Where do you march?" Niklas pressed.

"Back and forth, and back again, it seems," the soldier replied. "Sometimes, we go to a tumble of rock and he tells us to dig and see if we find anything. Says he wants anything 'hocus-like,' whatever that means."

"What kind of 'hocus things' does Rostivan want?" Niklas asked.

The dark-haired soldier with the scalp wound seemed happy to elaborate. "Bone or stone carved with odd marks, round pieces of black stone. Things that look odd, like normal folk wouldn't use them."

"And did you find any of those kinds of things?"

"Here and there, not all at once," the first soldier replied. "Whatever we found, we gave it to our captain."

"What else can you tell me?" Niklas glanced up and down the line of desperate captives.

Eager to save their skins, the soldiers passed along bits of gossip and wild rumors, but nothing particularly useful. When they had exhausted their tales, they slumped, awaiting their fate. Niklas met Blaine's gaze and nodded. Blaine returned the nod.

"You've been helpful," Niklas said. "Lord McFadden keeps his promises. I'll have our healers take care of you. But you must swear fealty, renouncing your previous lords, and we must be able to assure that your oath is true."

A skinny blond man with a crooked nose looked up. "How ya gonna do that? Hocus us?"

Niklas shook his head. His expression grew sober. "Tonight, our *talishte* allies will join us. A *talishte* can read truth or lies from a man's blood."

The captives looked terrified at the thought, yet none seemed to think death preferable enough to volunteer to be executed instead. Niklas gave quiet instructions to the guards, who pulled the captives to their feet and led them away toward the camp where the healers were located.

Blaine turned to face Rinka and Tormod. "You never mentioned you were a necromancer," he said tersely, meeting Tormod's gaze.

Rinka shrugged. "You never mentioned that it was you who restored the magic," she said. "Yet here you are, the last living Lord of the Blood."

"Were you able to raise the dead before the Cataclysm?"

Tormod gave a knowing smile. "Before the Great Fire, like

most mages, my abilities were different. What matters is what I can do now."

In other words, our allies are keeping their secrets to themselves, Blaine thought.

Several candlemarks passed before Niklas joined Blaine, Piran, and Kestel in the command center Niklas's men had hastily set up in one of the Citadel's less-damaged rooms. Niklas looked worn and tired, and he still had not changed from his bloodied uniform.

"Have a drink, mate," Piran said, passing his flask to Niklas.

Niklas dropped into a chair and took a swig. "Thanks," he said, handing back the flask. "But I'd need about a cask more to make an impact."

"Any sign of Rostivan?" Blaine asked. He sat on a wooden crate near the fireplace. Kestel stood close to the hearth, warming her hands.

"Verner's men chased him for a candlemark, but there wasn't much point beyond that," Niklas said tiredly. "I still want to know why he's going after Blaine in particular."

"Like the soldier said, it's got to have something to do with Quintrel," Kestel said. "But that doesn't explain why Quintrel turned on us after Blaine brought the magic back at Valshoa. Until then, Quintrel seemed like an ally, leaving us clues, helping Blaine work the ritual. Then he tried to force us to stay."

"Odds are, he knew about the anchoring," Blaine said. His hand brushed one temple, but that did nothing to ease the headache that still pounded. "Maybe he figured he'd just keep me in Valshoa indefinitely, and then he would control the anchor and maybe the magic itself."

"Do you think he's guessed what the anchoring is doing to you?" Kestel asked, watching him with concern.

"He knows." Niklas slouched in his chair, head back, eyes shut. "And I don't think there's any doubt that Quintrel sent Rostivan to capture you."

Blaine and Kestel exchanged a glance. "Why do you say that?"

Niklas sighed. "Geir caught up with me not long after sundown, when I was reviewing the troops. Seems General Dolan's had a falling out with Quintrel and left." He opened his eyes and looked at Blaine. "According to Geir, Dolan believes Quintrel's gone mad, pushed 'round the bend by some kind of corrupted artifact. And since Quintrel couldn't keep you in Valshoa, he's bound a *divi* spirit and he's got something called 'presence-crystals' he thought could bind the magic to new Lords of the Blood."

"Do you think that's possible?" Kestel asked, turning toward Niklas. She looked from Niklas to Blaine. "If the magic can be re-anchored, that could stop the drain on Mick."

Niklas shifted in his chair, leaning forward with his elbows on his knees. "Dolan seemed to think it can. He didn't just leave Valshoa—he stole the crystals and the manuscripts that went with them."

Piran let out a low whistle. "I bet old Vigus is stewed about that."

"Murderous, I'd say," Blaine replied.

Niklas nodded. "Geir says Dolan's sent Nidhud our way with a 'proposal.' Dolan's already worked out some type of an alliance with Nidhud and Penhallow, and as Geir understands it, eventually we need to return to a place of power to do the ritual—maybe Mirdalur."

Piran made his opinion clear with an impressively creative string of curses. "Not that place again! We nearly died the last time."

Niklas shrugged. "That was last time. Cheer up. Geir said Dolan's also looking at the tunnels under Quillarth Castle."

"Lovely," Piran exploded. "We nearly died there, too. Can we find a place to try this where we haven't all almost been killed?"

"Probably not," Kestel replied. "Because it's got to be a place of power, where the nodes and meridians are just right, and there aren't too many of them. Valshoa's out, for obvious reasons. At least Mirdalur and Quillarth Castle are solidly inside Blaine's territory."

"What's the proposal? Do you know what Dolan wants in exchange for helping us?" Blaine asked. He expected to be tired after a battle, but not as bone weary as he was feeling now. His head ached, and his body felt feverish. Blaine was certain the magic had something to do with it.

"Geir didn't have details, but I gathered Dolan wants assurances that when a ruling body is formed, the Knights—and the *talishte*—will have seats at the table."

"Not an unreasonable request, given the help Penhallow and the Wraith Lord have already provided," Blaine said. "And if the Knights are reliable allies, all the better. I'm sure Dolan wants to make sure there's no repeat betrayal."

Niklas nodded. "I don't doubt it. And while I'm fine with the arrangement, I suspect there will be some who balk at bringing the *talishte* into the formal power structure."

"Let them," Blaine replied. "I've got enough people trying to kill me, they'll have to stand in line."

CHAPTER
TEN

———

CARENSA, I'M SO HAPPY YOU'VE COME DOWN TO the Workshop." Vigus Quintrel's smile was broad and, as far as Carensa could tell, genuine. "Come in, come in. Let me show you around."

It had been quite a while since Carensa had been down to the building Quintrel claimed as his own private Workshop. Just a handful of mages were permitted inside, and invitations to guests were few.

Quintrel had chosen a building left behind by the builders of the city long ago, the Valshoans, who had died out in centuries past. The secretive Valshoan mages had sealed their doom with their insularity, refusing to leave their mountain refuge and forbidding outsiders from visiting. By the time the Knights of Esthrane had sought sanctuary, there were only a few Valshoans left, and they had permitted the Knights to stay, just as many years later, the Knights had permitted Quintrel and his band of rogue mages to hide within Valshoa's boundaries from the Cataclysm Quintrel had predicted.

The Cataclysm had not entirely skipped over Valshoa, but the valley's protections were strong enough to keep the city from being completely destroyed. Many of the ancient buildings were still standing, though time and the battering of magic storms had taken a toll. Some of the grand structures were only ruins. Without the Knights in residence, Quintrel's small group of mages were just a few dozen in a city built to hold thousands. The empty streets and lingering silence made Carensa feel as if Valshoa existed outside of time and space, cut off from everything else. The emptiness was eerie, as if they were the last survivors in the world, a possibility Quintrel had thought possible.

"I'm flattered to be invited," Carensa said. That was true, in part. She had always wondered just what mysteries Quintrel and his senior mages explored in his Workshop. Lately, as Quintrel had become more withdrawn and snappish, and as rumors of dark endeavors had begun to circulate, Carensa had been glad her magic had not been deemed useful for Quintrel's experiments. Now she was both curious and wary, even though Quintrel at the moment was his eccentrically charming self.

"I'll give you the tour, and show you some of the things we're working on. Then I'm hoping your talent with translation can help me solve a puzzle," Quintrel said.

It would be so easy to take Quintrel at face value, Carensa knew. For a time, she had looked at him with awe and a touch of hero-worship. He had taken an interest in her as a pupil, given her hope and purpose to lift her out of the bleakness after Blaine's exile, rescued her from the rubble after the Great Fire. She had believed him to be a great man and a mage of extraordinary power, as well as a visionary leader. Disillusionment came hard.

"I'll certainly give it a try," Carensa said, wary of making any promises. Quintrel of late was not the scholar she once knew. Time, ambition, and the bound *divi* had changed him. She hoped her venture into his private Workshop would give her some idea of just how drastic that change had been.

Half a dozen mages worked at long tables or hunched over manuscripts at carrels. Some of the mages she knew well, others she barely recognized. But she frowned as she searched the room. Initially, Quintrel's 'special projects' team had numbered close to a dozen.

"Where are the others?" Carensa asked, hoping she sounded innocently curious. "Do you have other Workshops?"

Quintrel did not turn. "No other Workshops. You know how the magic's been since it came back. Not entirely reliable. A few of our projects didn't go as planned."

Carensa had suspected that would be the answer. She already knew several mages had died helping Quintrel discover the secrets of the presence-crystals Dolan had taken. But Quintrel's casual acceptance of death made her shiver. *Would the old Vigus have been so nonchalant?* she wondered. *I didn't think so back then. Now, I wonder.*

"Take a look at this," Quintrel said with fatherly pride. He pointed to a map in a damaged, gold-leaf frame. "What do you see?"

Carensa peered at the map. It was a little bigger than a foot square, and as she squinted to see detail, she recognized it as a map of the Valshoan mountain pass. "It's a map of where we are," she said, straightening.

Quintrel chuckled. "Exactly. And no matter where you are, it will be a map of that area. Not only that," he said triumphantly, "but it will show you anyone within three leagues of your position. Possess this map, and you'll never be lost, never be ambushed."

Carensa nodded, genuinely impressed. "Nice. Was this something your team found, or made?"

Quintrel glowed with pride. "It's a found object, one of the things we've retrieved going into the abandoned Valshoa buildings." He shook his head. "The Knights left most of the city alone, other than to make sure it was secured from outsiders." He swept an arm to indicate the valley, with its hundreds of structures. "Who knows what marvels are out there?"

He turned and gave Carensa a conspiratorial wink. "That's why some of the mages will stay behind when the rest of us return to the outside. I don't think Valshoa has given up all its wonders yet."

In spite of herself, Carensa began to relax. Quintrel seemed much like his old self. They came to a large, open area, where several of the mages had gathered. A warding circle was drawn on the floor, and Osten, a thin, angular man dressed in mage robes, stood inside the circle holding a metallic egg-shaped artifact.

"This should be good," Quintrel said, grinning. "Osten's about to test the artifact. If this works, it could be quite useful—especially for a mage-assassin."

Carensa frowned. "What does it do?"

Quintrel's grin broadened. "It allows the holder to move from one place to another without crossing the area in between. Osten's going to test it on a very limited scale, getting it to move him from one side of the circle to the other."

"Is that safe?" Carensa asked. "The magic's still brittle."

Quintrel gave a dismissive gesture. "We have to adapt to how magic is now, at least until we're able to re-anchor the power. It means a new kind of approach for a new type of power."

Carensa decided against arguing. Quintrel's exceptional mood was giving her access, and she planned to report what she discovered to Jarle and Guran. And to be honest, the potential for a magical object such as the one Quintrel described intrigued her.

"Could it take you anywhere?" she asked.

Quintrel shrugged. "We're not entirely sure yet. The old scrolls we found seem to indicate that you have to be either within your line of sight or at least plan to end up someplace you've been before. This is our first test."

Carensa gave Osten credit for bravery, given how unpredictably magic and artifacts had performed lately. The experiment could go wrong in an untold number of ways. From inside the warded circle, Osten shot the onlookers a wide grin, and Quintrel nodded for the attempt to begin.

Osten held up the metallic egg and began to chant, invoking words of power. The silvery metal began to glow, and he held it to his chest, clasped between his hands. The light grew brighter, escaping from between his fingers, and in a blinding flare, Osten disappeared.

The onlookers gasped, then cheered as Osten reappeared an instant later on the far side of the warded circle. The cheers turned to chuckles, and Carensa repressed a giggle. Osten had reappeared, but his robes had not.

Osten blushed scarlet, dropped one hand to cover his groin, and rolled his eyes good-naturedly as Quintrel released the warding. Amid the ribbing and jokes, one of the mages tossed Osten a cloak. He covered himself and then handed off the artifact, making a quick exit.

Carensa wiped tears of laughter from her eyes. *By Torven's horns! I haven't laughed in such a very long time,* she thought.

A mage handed the metallic egg back to Quintrel, who held it up, marveling at the object. "Not a bad first test," he said proudly. "We don't know its range yet, and obviously, the clothing piece is a problem."

"It would pose a few difficulties to appear naked behind enemy lines," Carensa agreed, still chuckling.

"Well, there might be something to be said for the element of surprise," Quintrel agreed.

Carensa found herself laughing easily, falling into old patterns. The blink of yellow light at the collar of Quintrel's shirt brought her back. The small orb Quintrel wore beneath his tunic kept him linked to the bound *divi*, reminding her that despite appearances, Quintrel was not himself.

She looked around, hoping and dreading to catch a glimpse of the *divi* orb. Carensa did not spot it in the Workshop, but that did not surprise her. Quintrel was unlikely to entrust an artifact with a hold over his soul to a place of common access, even among the privileged few who could enter the Workshop.

"This is the piece I'd like you to take a look at, Carensa," Quintrel said, calling her attention back to the present.

Quintrel took down a scroll from one of the shelves near the back of the room and held it out to her. Carensa took it gingerly. The parchment was yellowed and very old, and she feared it might disintegrate at her touch.

"I've had the others take a look at it," Quintrel said, "but they can't read it. We think it's an old form of Valshoan."

Carensa carefully spread out the scroll on one of the empty worktables. "Can't your *divi* read it?" she asked.

Quintrel's hand went to the glass orb on the strap around his neck. "*Divis* are powerful, but not all-knowing."

Carensa fell silent, staring at the unfamiliar words in an alphabet and script she had never seen before. She placed her hands on the manuscript, and brought the magic of her gift to the forefront. Her fingertips tingled on the old parchment, as if she could feel the ink itself, and gradually, to her sight, the script began to rearrange itself as she stared at the document, translating itself into the language she had willed her magic to use.

An essay on the techniques of transmogrification, the document began. Carensa blinked, reading slowly so as to fully understand what she saw.

Sweet Esthrane, Carensa thought. *It's a working to turn men into unnatural creatures, like the magicked monsters that came through the wild-magic storms.*

She swallowed hard. There was no doubt in her mind who the target of such monsters would be, not after the last rant Vigus had gone on about Blaine McFadden.

"Any luck?" Quintrel asked, looking over her shoulder.

Carensa glanced down at the manuscript, afraid that somehow her gift might have translated it for Quintrel to see, but without her magic applied to the text, the words were as alien as before. "It's very old," she said. "And I'm so new with my magic. Are you sure there's no one else who can translate it?"

Is it a test? Carensa wondered. *Vigus doesn't trust anyone these days. Maybe he's testing my loyalty. Maybe he already knows what it says—or at least suspects—but he wants to see what I'll do.*

Quintrel shook his head. "You know you're the only one with translation magic," he replied. "We have some mages who have learned to read old languages by rote, or who speak other tongues, but no one who can translate a dead language without a cipher."

Then there is no way in Raka I'll give you the translation, Carensa decided. "I'm sorry, Vigus. I've tried. It just isn't working. I guess my magic isn't as strong as we hoped."

For a split second, Quintrel looked like he might burst into a rage. The *divi* orb flared, and the light in Quintrel's eyes was not altogether sane. He stiffened, and grew red in the face, and she feared he might lash out at her, either with magic or with his hands, which had balled into fists at his side. After a moment, he took a deep breath and allowed himself to relax.

"That's all right, Carensa," he said. "It is an exceptionally old piece. All magic has its limits." He sighed, and seemed to shutter away his rage. He turned to her with a smile, only now she could see how forced and false it was.

"Would you like to see our real breakthrough?" he asked. Something about his voice made Carensa wary.

"What is it?" she asked, trying to keep her tone light. Any illusion that Vigus Quintrel was still the same man she had known before the Cataclysm was gone. She did not know this stranger, but what she had seen of him frightened her to her soul.

Quintrel led her down a hallway and into a windowless room lit by torchlight. A man Carensa had never seen before sat tied to a chair in the center of the room. On the other side of the room sat the large *divi* orb with its withered hand, as if it were the prisoner's jailer. The orb glowed a sickly yellow, and Carensa wondered if it were indeed watching over the bound man.

"Who is he?" she asked, alarmed. She looked closer, but nothing about the man was familiar. He was dressed in a tunic and trews that might have been military issue but had seen a lot of wear. Nothing about him, from the cut of his clothing to the style of his shoes to the way he wore his hair, suggested that he was a mage, let alone one of Quintrel's rogues.

"We found him exploring the cliffside near the mountain pass," Quintrel said with a dismissive gesture. "I've had him truth-read. He admits he was looking for a way in. He's not allied with any of the warlords—that had been my first concern."

Quintrel regarded the prisoner with disdain. "He's just a common thief. But we can't let him leave."

Carensa turned to look at Quintrel. "We have mages who can alter memories," she said quietly. "Surely he could be made to forget, and left outside far from where you found him."

Quintrel looked at her as if her remark disappointed him. "There are few of us, and many thieves. It needs to be known that people who come sniffing around for secrets don't come back." He looked toward the prisoner. "But he is the perfect way to test the power of the *divi* orb before we meet with Rostivan."

The thief tried to rock the chair and loosen his bonds, but Carensa knew the knots were tied expertly and spelled tight. She bet he was in his early twenties, and from the look of him, he had not had a decent meal in days. His clothing was dirty and torn, and he looked terrified and defiant.

"Vigus, you're powerful enough to be merciful," Carensa urged.

"Mercy won't achieve our purpose," Quintrel replied. He walked over to the prisoner and slowly circled him. From the look on Quintrel's face, he was enjoying the young man's terror. Suddenly, Quintrel reached out and snatched several hairs from the man's head, then walked toward the large *divi* orb.

As Carensa watched, the solid sphere around the withered hand shrank back like melting ice, and the fingers reached up to accept a few strands of the prisoner's hair. Quintrel murmured a word under his breath, and the sphere became solid once more. Next to the large orb lay a smaller sphere on a strap, similar to the one Quintrel wore.

"The *divi's* power links from the hair I've given to the orb, putting the wearer under my control," Quintrel said. Unlike his own small orb, which glowed yellow, the orb in his hand pulsed a faint red. Quintrel crossed to the prisoner and tied the strap around the man's neck, then loosed the captive's hands with a slash of a knife through his bonds. The thief's ankles were still tied securely to the chair. He had no hope of escape, but Carensa suspected his lot was about to go from bad to worse.

Quintrel stepped back to stand next to her. A few of the other mages had gathered behind them.

"What is that thing?" the thief shouted, pointing at the large *divi* orb, which was glowing a more vivid yellow. "And what have you put on me?" He grabbed the small orb with one hand and tried to yank it off, but no matter how hard he pulled, he could not break the strap, nor would the sphere allow him to lift it off over his head.

"Get this thing off me!" he yelled, tearing at it until the leather strap cut into his neck and left bloody marks. Blood pleased the *divi*, and the yellow glow grew brighter.

"He can't remove it," Quintrel remarked. "Not without my permission." Quintrel smiled. "And now I control his every move. As I will control Rostivan. Observe."

Quintrel murmured something under his breath. With one hand, he clasped the small orb that hung at his throat, and with his other hand, he formed a fist and brought it up sharply again and again.

With a nauseating crack of bone and a wet smack of fresh blood, the prisoner's fist slammed into his own nose. The man howled in pain, but the fist rose again and again, flattening his nose, blackening both eyes, slamming hard enough into his own mouth to leave deep cuts from his teeth on his knuckles and loosening several teeth in the process.

"Vigus, please," Carensa said, plucking at Quintrel's sleeve.

"He is completely under my control," Quintrel said, and the light that animated his eyes was cold and cruel. The prisoner continued to pummel himself, first with one fist and then the other, until his screams grew hoarse and died to a whimper. Blood flowed down his face in streams from his ruined nose, his swollen eyes, his split and torn lips.

"Under the call of the *divi* orb, he believes himself to be in control," Quintrel said, narrating as if it were just another demonstration of routine magic. "So he can't understand why his body has suddenly turned on him. He has no idea he's being controlled."

A shiver went down Carensa's spine. *Is your* divi *orb so different?* she wondered. Quintrel seemed blind to the possibility that, like the prisoner, he too might be controlled by an outside force. Carensa stole a glance at the large orb. It glowed brightly, a deep, vivid yellow, as if the blood brought it alive.

"There's nothing he won't do," Quintrel said. "He is powerless to resist." Quintrel walked over to one of the worktables and picked up a slender boline knife. He took one of the prisoner's hands, and closed the man's torn fingers around the bone handle so that the man held the blade toward his own chest.

"Vigus, you don't have to do this," Carensa said, willing herself not to throw up.

"I want you all to believe in me, believe in what we can do with an army at our command," Quintrel said, sweeping the small crowd with his gaze. He paused to wipe the blood from his hands on the prisoner's discarded cloak.

Quintrel walked back to where the others stood. "Watch," he said.

With that, Quintrel clenched the small orb with his right hand while his left hand made a fist and brought it sharply toward his chest.

Carensa watched in horror as the prisoner drove the thin, sharp blade deep into his own chest, staring at the knife as if some corner of his brain still fought for autonomy. Blood washed down the man's chest, and a cold smile came to Quintrel's lips.

"He's mine, until the last breath," Quintrel said, forcing the hapless thief to stab the blade again and again, hilt-deep, into his own flesh time after time.

"Sweet Charrot and Esthrane, enough!" Tenneril blurted. He was one of the mages Carensa had recognized in the outer workroom, a bookish man whose specialty was charms and talismans. Tenneril looked as if he might faint. He had gone deathly pale, and his eyes were wide and shocky. "Please, Vigus. Enough," he begged.

Quintrel turned a cold glare on Tenneril, and the man shrank back. "You disapprove?"

Carensa had no desire to see a repeat of Quintrel's attack on Jarle. She did not think Tenneril's heart would take it. Recklessly, Carensa took hold of Quintrel's bloody sleeve.

"Vigus! I think my magic broke the code," she said, doing her best to look as excited as she could manage, when all she wanted to do was crawl into a corner and retch. "The manuscript! I think I can translate it for you."

Quintrel hesitated, torn between his greed to know what the manuscript revealed and his desire to punish Tenneril for his outspokenness. In the end, greed won out.

"Show me," he said in a hoarse voice, and Carensa could see the strain in Quintrel's face as he tried to rein in his rage.

"Vigus—what do you want us to do with the body?" one of the mages asked hesitantly.

Quintrel did not turn back. "Dump it where the crows will feast on it," he replied.

Carensa led the way out of the room, eager to leave behind the slumped form of the bloodied young thief. She heard Tenneril's murmured thanks, and glimpsed others crowding closer against the frail, older mage, no doubt fearing that the confrontation would not be good for his heart.

She had seconds to come up with a convincing lie. *I can't give him the real translation,* she thought wildly. *He'll use it to go after Blaine, and anyone else he wants to eliminate. No man deserves that kind of power, especially not the 'thing' that Vigus has become.*

Carensa knew she would have to be careful. *Vigus is clever. He'll smell an outright lie. I'm sure he knows what the manuscript ought to contain, so I can't tell him it's something else. I'll have to alter it, just enough, so that it doesn't work.*

She set her jaw, knowing there was a price to pay. *I could get someone else killed, if the magic goes wrong, or if Vigus goes into a rage because it doesn't work. By the gods! I never asked to be in this position!*

Quintrel reached down the scroll once more, and again Carensa laid it out on the table. Slowly, making it seem as if the translation was coming with difficulty, Carensa worked out each word as Quintrel hung over her shoulder, giving her his full attention.

"Master Quintrel—" one of the Workshop mages called.

"Not now!" Quintrel snapped.

"But Master Quintrel—"

Quintrel rounded on the man with a snarl. "I said 'not now'!"

Breathing hard from the exertion of restraining his temper, Quintrel turned back to Carensa. "Go on," he urged, and the hunger in his eyes looked less than human. He had beckoned for one of the other mages to come over and write down everything Carensa said. The rest of the mages left their work and came to stand around them, except for Tenneril, who had not rejoined them.

Silently offering up a prayer to Esthrane to guide her, Carensa continued her halting 'interpretation.' At each instruction, she paused as if working out the wording, then read aloud the opposite of what the manuscript set forth. Worried that strictly giving the opposite of the instructions might somehow still make it work, Carensa did her best to hopelessly muddle the directions while still maintaining a ring of authenticity.

When she finished, she glanced at Quintrel, as if seeking his approval. In reality, she wanted to know whether or not he had seen through her deception. His eager expression gave her to know that he believed he had the tool he wanted.

"Excellent," Quintrel said. "Well done, Carensa. We'll work with this; see what we can make of it." He beamed at her. "You've handed us a powerful weapon. Be proud of your gift."

Carensa managed a smile. "I hope the Old Ones got it right," she said. "I wish we knew more about the manuscript's author. It would be nice to know whether it really worked as planned."

"We'll figure it out, I have no doubt of it," Quintrel said, nearly ecstatic with triumph. "And if this works, we have more manuscripts for you to work with." He went to a shelf in the corner of the room full of scrolls and an odd assortment of objects and pulled out a silver bracelet in the shape of a serpent and a bone carved with runes, along with several parchment scrolls.

"You can start with these," Quintrel said, handing the items to Carensa. "We've vetted the objects—they're safe. But we're not sure about the full range of their uses because no one can read the manuscripts where they've been mentioned." He bestowed his most charming smile. "So we're depending on you, my dear."

"Master Quintrel!"

They looked up to see Havilend, a rotund, older man, standing just inside the doorway to the next room. He had been the mage calling for Quintrel's attention before, and he looked terribly upset.

"What is it, Havilend?" Quintrel snapped.

"It's Osten. You need to come quick."

Grudgingly, Quintrel went where Havilend beckoned, and the other mages followed. Carensa looked down at the silver bracelet in the shape of a serpent and a bone carved with runes. *The day is coming when I'll need to make a stand,* Carensa thought. *I can't fight Vigus with my translation magic! But if I had a weapon or two, I might be able to stop him with the right opportunity. It's time to start gathering what Guran and I will need when it comes time to make our stand.*

She wrapped the items Quintrel had given her in her shawl, then hurried to catch up with the others. Carensa tried to peer over the mages who had crowded around the room where they had taken Osten. Worry gnawed at her. Osten had been the mage who demonstrated the translocation spell. From Havilend's expression, something had gone wrong.

"By the gods!"

"Charrot protect us!"

"Torven keep us!"

The mages murmured protections and prayers as they crowded into the small storage room off the main workroom. Osten—or what remained of him—heaved in a gelatinous blob on the stone floor. His features were flattened and distorted, as if his skin remained whole, but there were no longer bones supporting his body.

Osten was alive, trapped in his trembling flesh, unable to do more than moan, without bones to work his jaw. His eyes darted back and forth in panic, pleading.

"I don't think the translocation artifact worked as well as we thought it did," one of the mages behind Carensa observed.

"We can't just let him suffer like that!" Carensa argued.

But before she could protest, Osten's shapeless body began

to shudder violently, then started to come apart. Not in an explosion, but as if the invisible bonds that held his form together decided little by little to let go, scattering him in small, quivering bits, until he gave a final moan of agony and disassembled completely into a thick slurry on the stone floor.

Vigus never vetted the object before he gave it to Osten, Carensa thought with a sick feeling in the pit of her stomach. *The artifact Osten used was corrupted. It wouldn't have worked for anyone. So I'd best be careful with the pieces he thought were safe to give me. But by Esthrane, I'll find artifacts to help me bring Vigus down when the time is right. For Osten's sake—and all the others.*

Quintrel gave a frustrated snort, and turned on his heel. "Somebody get a mop and clean up the mess," he said, striding past the astonished onlookers and out of the workroom.

CHAPTER ELEVEN

"IT'S NOT HEALING." KERR SAID IN A WORRIED voice.

Vedran Pollard eyed his longtime valet with frustration. "Then try something else. There's got to be a poultice to set it right."

"Perhaps a healer—"

"No one else must know about this," Pollard said, meeting Kerr's gaze. "No one. Do you understand?"

Reluctantly, Kerr bowed his head in acknowledgment. "Of course, sir."

Pollard looked down at the open wound on his chest, right over his heart. The wound had appeared a week before, in a moment of blinding pain. Pollard had taken many an injury on the battlefield, some that had taxed the abilities of healers to mend, but nothing had been so agonizing. He collapsed, and when he regained consciousness, he found the raw, red wound.

"Does it look any better—or worse?" Pollard asked. By now, Kerr was used to his tempers and moods. If he heard the hint of anxiety that colored Pollard's voice, Kerr knew better than to show it.

"There doesn't appear to be any change, sir," Kerr reported. "I'm stymied as to why it refuses to heal, yet hasn't soured."

"Could it be magic?" Pollard wondered aloud. "The way it appeared out of nowhere, along with this damn itching." Beneath his sleeves, his forearms were scratched raw from a persistent itch that no balm soothed. The rest of his body, except for his face, fared no better. Pollard was no stranger to poisonous plants and biting insects. Nothing he had ever encountered was as maddening as the red pinpricks that now covered his body.

"I've heard of nothing like it among the troops—either the wound or the rash," Kerr replied. "Surely if it were mage-sent, they would have wanted to incapacitate the army and not just the commander."

"Perhaps," Pollard said. "And if it were something here in the manor, then it should have affected someone else as well."

Kerr shook his head. "I haven't heard of anything, sir. And if it were something catching, I would have caught it from tending you."

Pollard let out a long sigh. "It's worst at night. Woolen shirts are no help at all."

"Perhaps once the weather warms, some heat and sunshine will help," Kerr offered. He gathered the supplies he had brought, tucking them back in a canvas bag. "Shall I bring you another pot of tea? That variety is supposed to be quite good for the skin."

Pollard nodded, and buttoned up his shirt. "It helped, a bit."

"Very well, then," Kerr replied. There was something desperate about his stiff formality, but it was a ritual to which they both clung, through wordless agreement. Proper etiquette was one of the last vestiges of a civilized time that was gone and might never come again.

When Kerr left him alone in the parlor at Solsiden, Pollard permitted himself the luxury of collapsing into one of the wing chairs. He had a private theory about where the wound and the rash had come from, and that it was the same source as the nightmares that had troubled his sleep every night since he had collapsed.

Word had come, in a tersely written note delivered by messenger, that Pentreath Reese had received the judgment of the Elders, to be staked through the heart and confined in an oubliette for fifty years. That was the night the wound appeared. Pollard's right hand went to cover the raw, round ulcer. Just the circumference one might make a wooden stake, above where one might slip such a stake. Pollard was certain that the strong *kruvgaldur* bond he shared with Reese was responsible for both the physical marks and the terrifying dreams.

Since the wound appeared, Pollard's dreams had verged on madness. Images came to him of people he did not know, places he had never visited, and times long before his birth. So much blood. The darkness was suffocating, and the hunger and thirst overwhelmed him. *If this is what I can look forward to for the next fifty years, I may as well fall on my sword*, he thought bleakly.

"There has to be some way to free him," Pollard muttered, thinking aloud. Self-preservation, more than loyalty, added urgency. He had come to an additional realization that he would not speak aloud: *If the bond is this strong, then if Reese dies, so do I.*

Agitated, Pollard shifted in his chair. No position was comfortable, but some were more tolerable than others. He went to scratch his shoulder, then barely restrained himself. Even with his nails clipped short there were bloody trails across his skin where he had given in to the unrelenting itch and later came to regret it.

It's the price to be paid for the other parts of the bond, he thought, forcing down his fears. *Even Kerr and Nilo have commented that I'm aging more slowly. I've got the vigor of a man ten years younger. Reese told me the* kruvgaldur *would extend my life and strength. But with as often as he's fed from me and as deeply, I don't doubt that my soul is bound to him.*

Kerr coughed to announce that he had returned, and set a tray with the tea on a table between the two wing chairs. He poured a cup for Pollard and set it aside. "Captain Nilo is here to see you, sir. Shall I show him in?"

Pollard straightened and reached for the tea. *Tea for the skin, and whiskey for the dreams*, he thought. "Send him to me."

Kerr went to fetch Nilo, and Pollard finished his tea, then stood and poured himself a slug of whiskey.

Outside the damaged manor house's stone walls, the wild winds blasted down from the northern plains, rattling the broken glass in the upstairs windows and slamming the splintered shutters against the masonry. Solsiden had not fared well in the Cataclysm, and the storm that battered it now was likely to increase the damage.

"Nasty storm," Captain Nilo observed as he entered. Nilo's cloak and his pants were sodden and his face was reddened with cold.

Another gust of wind battered the manor. Pollard sipped the glass of whiskey and stared out the window in the study. Tonight's storm sounded as if it might rip the slate from the roof. "At least we're not in a tent on some godsforsaken field," he muttered.

Nilo smiled and took a sip of his own drink. "Hennoch's

sparing us some of that. Although we'll need to go back out soon enough."

Pollard nodded. "I know. I'm just not looking forward to it."

Overhead, through the ruined windows on the second floor, the wind howled and sent something crashing to the floor. In the few months since Pollard had taken Solsiden for his own, the scarce resources had gone toward fortification, not toward restoring the damage the old manor had sustained since the Great Fire. Parts of the upper floors were badly damaged, but the main floor and cellars were usable, as well as the sturdiest barns and dependencies. Now the old manor served as a headquarters for Pollard's army and a depot for crucial supplies.

"How long do you expect Hennoch to keep his word?" Nilo asked. He walked away from the fireplace and settled into one of the worn wing chairs still within the warm glow of the fire.

Pollard shrugged moodily. "For as long as we keep his son alive—or until he decides he can make do without him."

"The storms are getting worse," Nilo observed. "Magic caused them; now the question is, can they be stopped?"

"If so, my mages don't know how," Pollard said with a sigh. "Nothing they've done has worked, and two died in the trying."

He paused. "I have some of Reese's brood searching out the mages who haven't aligned with other warlords. They'll bring the mages across, which binds their fealty to us. If we couldn't keep the magic from coming back, now that it's returned, we need to be able to hold our own."

"If the magic doesn't function the way it did before, perhaps the weather won't, either. This could be 'normal' for the foreseeable future," Nilo replied.

Pollard shuddered. "Let's hope not. Makes it miserable to field an army when it's like this."

"I have a report from the units," Nilo said, drawing out

several pieces of folded parchment from inside his jacket. "About Hennoch and Lysander."

Pollard crossed to a small table and topped off his whiskey, then paced near the fire. "Give me the gist of it. I don't have the patience to wade through the rest."

Nilo unfolded the parchment and scanned down through the lines of cramped writing. "One of the reports comes from Hillard, our man inside Hennoch's troops. He's with the healers, so he moves freely around the camp and on occasion gets pretty close to the commander." Nilo gave Pollard a pointed glance. "Which will come in handy if Hennoch stops cooperating."

Pollard nodded. "Good. Go on."

"They've had some problems with the Arkala twins, the brother warlords to the northwest," Nilo replied. "The area north and east of Mirdalur is still disputed. The Arkalas want it, and so does Karstan Lysander, as well as Hennoch."

Pollard raised an eyebrow. "My money's on Lysander."

Nilo shrugged. "Too soon to tell. The Arkalas have a small army, but they're well trained and they have a knack for making lightning raids where they score their objective and then disappear."

"*Talishte?*"

Again, Nilo shrugged. "Apparently not, since the raids occur in the daytime as well. From what Hillard says, Hennoch is getting annoyed at the Arkalas, because they've been disrupting supply lines. Hillard believes Hennoch will want to make a strike sometime soon against the Arkalas."

"Interesting. What about those damn Tingur?"

Nilo scanned down through the missive. "Jonn believes Lysander is behind them. He says that there are a lot of small groups wandering the roads since the magic storms and the Great Fire."

Pollard frowned. "How are the wanderers turning into Torven fanatics?"

Nilo sat back and took another sip of whiskey. "Jonn thinks Lysander is sending spies who pretend to be holy men among the wanderers and telling them that Torven will save them if they demonstrate their devotion."

Pollard gave a humorless chuckle. "Amusing. And apparently effective."

Nilo shrugged. "Apparently, Lysander's men put on a good show."

Pollard grimaced and began to pace. "Lysander's smarter than I gave him credit for. The Tingur give him a large number of disposable soldiers to wear down his enemies."

"Where's Lysander himself in all this?" Pollard asked. The whiskey and the fire warmed him, but the old manor was drafty enough that the harsh winds outside leeched any heat from the building.

Nilo gave a wolfish smile. "According to Jonn, the man in Lysander's army, Lysander has his eye on the entire north. He's been using the Tingur to probe for weaknesses, and for good measure, he's sent them into all the other warlords' territories to make trouble."

"Lovely. Be sure to tell the troops that any Tingur spotted are to be killed on sight," Pollard replied. The cold damp of the storm had turned his voice gravelly, and the rough whiskey didn't help. Word had already spread in the camp that the quickest way to the lord's favor was to find and deliver a bottle of spirits or wine from before the Great Fire.

Nilo chuckled. "That's already a standing order." Nilo watched him for a moment. "What of Reese?" he asked.

Pollard let out a long breath. "Reese is at the bottom of an oubliette with a stake in his heart."

Nilo's eyes widened. "Destroyed?"

Pollard shook his head. "No. But incapacitated for fifty years."

"Damn." Nilo pondered for a moment. "What does that mean for us?" The look he gave Pollard made it clear that he was also wondering, *What does it mean for you?*

Pollard shrugged. "A little more freedom—and somewhat more danger."

"The troops won't need to know," Nilo said slowly, formulating a plan as he spoke. "Reese rarely showed himself to them except in battle. We can cover that."

Pollard nodded. "His *talishte* fighters will know, but they will keep that secret since it's not to their advantage for the mortals to know their weakness."

"Do you expect him to escape?"

Pollard began to pace once more. "I expect him to seize whatever opportunities come his way," he replied. He eyed the whiskey, then turned away. There wasn't enough whiskey in the entire kingdom to make things right.

"Is this an opportunity?"

Pollard shook his head. "Maybe. I don't know. As much as the Great Fire was. Which is to say, it's up to us to find the opportunity in the middle of the flames."

Nilo toyed with his drink for a few moments. "Reese believed he had supporters on the Elder Council."

Pollard grimaced. "Apparently, not enough of them."

Nilo's fingers drummed against his glass. "Lysander appears to be planning a strike against the Solveigs and Verner. That might draw McFadden into the open."

"Maybe. More likely he'll send Theilsson. I'll be interested to see how Verner and the Solveigs fare." Pollard sat down in the other wing chair and set his glass aside. "What's your take on their strengths?"

Nilo frowned. "I don't know much about Verner. Whether or not he can hold on to his territory remains to be seen. The Solveigs know how to play rough. They won't be easy to break, especially if it's true that one of them is a necromancer."

"Do we have a spy in their camp?" Pollard asked.

Nilo shook his head. "No. Or at least, not currently. We've had three spies, and they've all ended up dead."

"Interesting."

Nilo made a face. "Not the word I would have chosen. The men I sent were too good to be easily caught out. I don't know whether they're using mages or whether the twins have some kind of ability to truth-sense, but something's afoot. Makes them damn difficult to infiltrate."

Rain beat against the windows, loud enough that when the wind shifted, the noise was sharp and startling. Gusts made the embers fly and the flames dance. Pollard watched the fire for a moment.

"There are too damn many players in this game," he muttered. "We need to reduce the number. Get a message to Lysander. Try again to get him to meet with me."

Nilo raised an eyebrow. "Easier said than done. Certainly he's been approached by others?"

Pollard shrugged. "Perhaps. Or not. Hennoch's troops buy us time while we rebuild our own, but he's a small player compared to Rostivan and Lysander—or McFadden, when you add in Voss's soldiers."

"We have a surety on Hennoch," Nilo said. "His son. What do you propose we use to 'encourage' Lysander?"

Pollard smiled. "*Talishte* fighters. I've been in contact with Reese's brood. Many of them want a chance to avenge our loss at Valshoa. They have no desire to see Penhallow and the Knights of Esthrane in control."

"Maybe we'd be better off if Reese's brood figured out how to free their master," Nilo said with a nod toward the wounds Pollard hid beneath his shirt.

Pollard gave him a sour look. "Since they, also, suffer for his sins, I'm sure the thought has occurred to them. I've been told as much, though opportunity is lacking. For the moment, escape appears unlikely. But think of it—we offer Lysander what he doesn't have, *talishte* fighters. Even a small number can turn the tide of a battle." He sniffed. "Much better than the rabble Lysander attracts."

"I'll send the messenger," Nilo said with a shrug. "And we'll see what happens."

Three days later, Pollard sat in the back room of a roadside tavern that had likely seen better days even before the Great Fire. It looked as if the building had collapsed and been cobbled back together again with odds and ends. The only thing rougher than the building itself were the men who gathered inside. One look assured Pollard that they were brigands, highwaymen, or worse. And all of them had fallen over themselves to show deference to the large man who sat across the table from Pollard.

"Your offer has some merit," Karstan Lysander said, setting his tankard aside. Pollard knew Lysander's reputation, and he wondered whether Lysander had heard about him, too.

"I'm assuming that eventually, Blaine McFadden's claims will pose an inconvenience," Pollard said. "The *talishte* I can bring to our arrangement would pose a sizable advantage."

Lysander took a draw from his pipe. Pipe weed, like brandy, had become increasingly difficult to acquire since the Cataclysm. Substitutes for both were usually quite inferior. From the acrid smell, Pollard assumed that Lysander was loath to give up his pipe, regardless of the quality of the pipe weed. "An advantage, to be sure, against mortal soldiers," Lysander said, and exhaled a cloud of smoke. "But against McFadden...it would take quite a force to make a difference if the Knights of Esthrane are truly on his side."

Pollard made a dismissive gesture. "The Knights are formidable, yes, but few in number. Penhallow, it's said, has shied away from creating as large a brood as many other *talishte*."

Lysander took another drag on his pipe. His eyes were half-closed, enjoying the smoke, but Pollard knew it would be a mistake to think Lysander's reflexes were dulled or his attention truly diverted. From the weapons that hung from his belt to the scars that covered his hands and marred his face, Lysander's entire appearance spoke of danger.

"You're not *talishte*. Rumor has it, your *talishte* master has been banished—imprisoned—by his own kind. Why should his brood follow you into battle?"

"Lord Reese's brood have no love of McFadden or Penhallow—or the Knights of Esthrane," Pollard said. "Alone, they are too few in number to affect the course of events. But allied with a powerful army, they can help alter circumstances to their liking," he replied.

Lysander shook a strand of greasy black hair away from his pipe. The odor of a stable clung to him as if he had not bathed in quite some time. Everything about him offended Pollard, everything, except the opportunity he presented for revenge.

"McFadden routed your army at Valshoa," Lysander said offhandedly, as if discussing the weather. "It's said you—and Reese—barely made it out alive." He gave a raspy chuckle at the inappropriate word choice. "Larska Hennoch does your bidding because you have his son as a prisoner." He paused.

"What hold do you think you have over me?" There was no mistaking the danger in his voice.

"None," Pollard replied, though he had already thought through how that might change. Insinuate Reese's *talishte* into Lysander's ranks, have them prove their merit and gain enough trust to get close to him, then bind him with the *kruvgaldur* to Reese—and by default, to Pollard.

"I don't accept gifts," Lysander said, watching the smoke from his pipe waft toward the ceiling beams. "They're just hobbles, disguised. But your proposal has merit, and I see where you stand to benefit. Much better to trust in a man's self-interest than in his generosity, I've found."

"Do we have an understanding?" Pollard asked.

Lysander's gaze shifted to regard him, a look of cold calculation. "Yes, we have an understanding," Lysander replied. Something in his tone made Pollard wonder if he completely understood just what that 'understanding' would cost him.

CHAPTER
TWELVE

WHEN CONNOR WOKE, IT WAS NEARLY NOON. He had grown accustomed to having his days and nights shifted; it was a necessary accommodation to serving a *talishte* lord. Still, he could not shake a bit of guilt over not rising at dawn as was his custom when he had served Lord Garnoc. He sighed and threw off his covers. *Those days are long gone.*

Although much of Westbain had been damaged, in the Cataclysm and then in Penhallow's siege, most of the main wing was intact. Connor's room was in relatively good shape, and after weeks of sleeping in crypts and on hard ground, having a bed and a mattress was a true luxury.

It's reached a sad place when waking up and realizing I'm not being shot at means it's going to be a good day, Connor thought.

A figure flitted behind him in the mirror, there and gone, and Connor felt a sudden chill. "I can see you," he said to the empty room. "I mean you no harm."

Since he had become the Wraith Lord's human host, Connor's skills as a medium had grown stronger. Where he had merely sensed disquieting presences before the Great Fire, now Connor could sense the trapped souls that roamed the kingdom.

Connor stretched out his senses and the spirit shied away, but the contact had been enough to tell him what he wanted to know. This ghost was not strong enough to try to possess him. *If it's going to haunt my bedroom, then I'm glad I don't have to worry about it possessing me in my sleep.*

Connor made his way downstairs, taking in the smell of cooked bacon and freshly baked bread. Once the fighting had ended, Reese's mortal house servants had crept out of hiding. Penhallow and Nidhud had made sure that no one with a *kruv-galdur* tie to Reese remained, something that affected only a few of the servants. The others swiftly swore their allegiance to Penhallow and got back to work. Penhallow had introduced Connor as Westbain's new seneschal.

"Good morning, m'lord," the cook said as Connor came down the back stairs into the kitchen. "Have a seat and I'll put your breakfast out for you."

The cook was a plump, gray-haired woman who seemed to enjoy her own cooking a little more than she should. She set a plate of hard-boiled eggs fried in a coating of sausage in front of him, along with a dollop of mustard and a hunk of still-warm bread. Then she poured him a cup of *fet* from a pot simmering on the hearth. "Lots to do today," the cook said.

"That there is," Connor replied. *Gods above!* he thought. *I've gone hungry and eaten scraps too often to ever take a meal for granted again. And I'd best enjoy it when the opportunity presents itself, because there will be hungry times again.*

"How long did you serve Lord Reese?" Connor asked.

The cook looked away. "It's not a test," Connor said quickly. "Lord Penhallow has given me the task of getting the manor functioning again, and I'm trying to learn about the people who remain."

Connor saw caution in her eyes. She was wise to be wary. A

careless word, repeated to the wrong person, had brought many a servant to grief. "I started here when I was a young girl, as a scullery maid," she answered. "And I've been here ever since."

"Were you free to go?"

This time, she took longer to reply. "In a manner of speaking," she said. "Lord Reese chose one person from every family in his holdings to serve at the manor. We were a surety for him, and our families for us."

Hostages, Connor thought. *Once again, Reese lives down to my expectations of him.*

"What happened to the rest of the servants?" Connor asked.

The cook sighed, and looked careworn. "Some died in the Great Fire. The strong young men, Lord Reese conscripted for his soldiers."

She hesitated, and her features seemed shadowed. "Lord Reese was badly injured in the Cataclysm. He was trapped beneath the rubble, and when he emerged, he didn't allow anyone to see him until he healed." The cook paused, longer this time. "He sent for any of the servants who had been injured or those who were old. We never saw them again."

He fed from them, Connor thought. *He used them like cattle, against their will, and drained them to heal himself.*

"Lord Penhallow is a very different man," Connor said.

"So I've heard." She met Connor's gaze. "Tell me. Was Lord Reese destroyed?"

Connor shook his head. "No. But he is in a dungeon, bound by spells and chains."

"He'll be back, you know," she said, turning away. "You'd best prepare."

Connor suspected that few of the servants would be willing to give more help than absolutely necessary lest they be charged with betrayal should Reese regain control. And Connor had no doubt, despite the ruling of the Elders, that somehow, Reese would slip the noose.

He stepped out of the kitchen into the servants' hallway. The mortal servants regarded Connor warily, no doubt sharing the cook's fears. They returned his greeting in monosyllables, and answered his questions with as few words as possible. The servants might not be active enemies, but they were at best unreliable allies.

The spirits of the dead were all around him as he moved through Westbain's corridors. Connor shuddered to think about the spirits haunting the dungeons. *I'd feel much safer if we had a necromancer with us, since the Wraith Lord isn't here to keep the peace.* He remembered the spirits on the path to Valshoa that had tried to possess him. Only the Wraith Lord's power had prevented them from overpowering Connor and seizing his body. *What do you know? I actually miss the Wraith Lord. If he's inside my head, at least no one else can be.*

Westbain's topmost floor held the servants' quarters. Connor began his daily walk-through at the top and worked his way toward the dungeon. He could feel the ghosts swirl around him in the corridor. He was certain they knew he could see them, though the mortal servants either ignored the ghosts or did not sense their presence.

Outside, Voss's soldiers were working hard to repair the damage to the outer wall. Connor wished they were faster. If Reese were to get free, Connor wanted thick walls and a lot of flaming torches between him and a vengeful vampire.

When Westbain was built, its second floor would have held suites of rooms for favored guests and parlors for their leisure. Now the area was claimed by mages Blaine had been happy to supply at Penhallow's request.

"Hello, Caz. Find anything interesting?" Connor asked as he entered the room. This was one of the rooms the mages had made into a work area with a long table littered with bits of gem and bone, glass orbs and metal talismans, carved wooden figures and leather-bound books, and a few mummified remains that Connor did not want to view too closely.

Caz looked up and grinned. "Hello, Bevin. I mean, Seneschal Connor," he added. Caz was about Connor's age, early twenties, with hazel eyes and dark-red hair. Before the Cataclysm, Caz and Connor had frequented the Rooster and Pig together, enjoying some of the best bitterbeer in all of Donderath.

"Good morning, Bevin." Alsibeth, a clairvoyant, looked up and gave a distracted wave. Back when Connor would make a trip into Castle Reach to bring back a bucket of bitterbeer for Lord Garnoc, Alsibeth could usually be found in the back corner of the pub, reading the futures of her customers from candles, still water, and bells. Before the war, she cut a flamboyant figure in brightly colored silks, with violet eyes and waist-long dark hair.

Now, Alsibeth's hair was cut to shoulder-length, and small gold hoops replaced the long chandelier earrings. The silks were gone, save for a scrap she used to tie back her hair, and she wore a long tunic over loose trews. Alsibeth walked with a new limp, and Connor had glimpsed scars from a bad burn on one forearm.

"Come to check up on us?" Alsibeth teased.

"Just making my rounds," Connor said. Alsibeth's talent was foresight. Caz's magic was reading signs and sigils, along with practical magic, like keeping milk from souring and banishing pests from crop fields. Rolf was one of the senior mages, and his specialty was scrying. Horst was a mage-scholar, one of the teachers at the University before the Great Fire with a magical ability for solving puzzles, ideally suited to study the manuscripts Reese's men had stolen from the mages' libraries.

Rolf and Horst were deep in conversation over an old manuscript, and barely looked up as Connor entered.

On the other side of the room, Volker and Kai waved their greeting. "Good morning, Seneschal Connor," Kai called.

She was a motherly woman with gray-flecked brown hair and a grin that might have been impish on a younger woman. Kai's power lay with weather magic. Volker was a thin, angular man whose specialty was unlocking hidden codes. Volker seemed as gloomy as Kai was pleasant. They made an odd pair.

"Can the seneschal spare a few moments?" Caz asked. "There's a pot of *fet* on the hearth and a few clean tankards by the fireplace."

Connor poured himself a cup and returned to where the others were working. "Any amazing discoveries?"

"Only that Reese had terrible judgment about magical objects," Caz said with a grimace. "Look at this trash! No respecting peddler would have taken this stuff." He gestured toward the motley assortment of objects that covered the table. "Half of it's broken. Some of the things don't make any sense at all." He pointed to a cracked wooden tankard. "Was he expecting a magic tankard that brewed its own beer?"

Connor chuckled. "If you find one, save it for me, will you?"

It felt good to be at ease with people who would have been his peers in the old days. Since the Great Fire, Connor had been in the company of lords and *talishte*, immortal spirits and powerful mages, but few real friends.

Caz grinned. "Only if there are two of them."

Connor looked at the pieces that littered the table. "Reese killed a lot of people to get these pieces," he said. "Is it all worthless?"

"Not necessarily." The voice came from behind Connor. Rolf looked better suited to loading cargo on wagons or pitching hay. He was a little taller than Connor, but broad through the chest, with strong arms and a thick neck.

"Meaning?" Connor replied. He took a long drink from his cup of *fet* and grimaced at the bitter taste.

"We're still trying to figure it all out," Rolf replied. "The magic didn't come back exactly the way it was before, so all these objects are dangerous unknowns."

Caz nodded vigorously. "Very dangerous. The problem is, even Alsibeth can't always tell what's going to happen, with the way the magic is now. Mages have died just trying to use the simplest objects for the most basic workings."

Connor frowned. "Why bother with the objects at all?"

"Good focusing objects help a mage concentrate his or her power," Alsibeth replied. "A well-crafted magical item can make a mediocre mage strong and a strong mage exceptional."

Connor caught Caz's gaze. "Try not to burn anything down, please?"

"We'll do our best," Alsibeth promised. Caz nodded, but Rolf did not look certain of success.

After his conversation with the mages, Connor headed for the first floor, to check on the kitchen staff and then see what he could make of the records that remained from Reese's exchequer.

A woman's scream echoed from the stone walls. It came from the hallway toward the deserted east wing. Connor started toward the sound at a run. The scream sounded again. He had only gone a short way down the hall before he realized that the corridor had grown icy cold. Connor slowed, growing wary.

He threw open the double doors to a suite of rooms. The suite's fine wall coverings hung in tatters. The room had been stripped of its furnishings, and its draperies hung faded and torn against the windows. An oil painting over the mantel showed a pretty young girl with a world-weary expression.

Connor caught a glimpse of motion out of the corner of his eye. Two spirits, one male and one female, faced off against each other in the middle of the room. It was obvious that they were arguing. The woman's ghost raised her chin defiantly, and the man's jaw was set. Connor could not hear their words, though it was obvious that they were screaming at each other.

The man's hand lashed out, striking the woman on the jaw. She fell against a writing table, sending quills and other instruments scattering. One hand scrabbled behind her, and her fist closed on a small knife. With a howl of rage she launched herself at the man and plunged the knife deep into his chest. He threw her out of his way, and she lost her footing. Her head hit hard against a table, and she dropped to the floor.

The scene vanished, leaving Connor alone in the room.

I don't want to know how often this show repeats, Connor thought, escaping to the corridor. He was shaking. The scene had seemed so real, the spirits so lifelike, that Connor could not help feeling guilty for not taking action. *There's nothing I could do to change what happened,* he thought. *It took place a long time ago.*

Connor looked around himself. He was in a shabby section of corridor. At the end of the hallway, chunks of rock littered the floor where parts of the ceiling had fallen, and rough wooden beams barricaded the walkway where Westbain's other wing had collapsed.

The winter wind whistled through cracks in the barricade. Something wordless cautioned him not to turn his back. Connor stared into the shadowed end of the corridor, and the hair on the back of his neck began to rise. The air grew heavy, and the temperature plummeted as the shadows began to roil.

An ink-black wave of darkness swept toward him, fast as breakers in a storm. The darkness was opaque, blotting out everything behind it. Connor ran toward the lights and safety of the main house.

Connor felt a low rumble, and heard something growling.

He sensed that the blackness was hard on his heels. Suddenly, the darkness rushed over him, sweeping him into it like the tug of a powerful undertow. The shadows had weight and strength, and Connor thought that he might be crushed in its press.

Let me in! A man's voice sounded in Connor's mind.

Get out of my head, Connor snapped.

I can make this painful, or easy, the voice replied. *But I have waited too long without a body to let you go.*

I'm using this body. You can't have it.

The voice gave a harsh laugh. *I wasn't asking permission,* the voice replied. *I just wanted to know how much I was going to need to hurt you.*

The spirit thrust itself into Connor's mind with a force that made him gasp. Pinpoints of light flashed in his vision. A specter formed in front of him, a large man with heavy-lidded eyes and a face with jowls like a bulldog's. His lips formed a perpetual pout, and the set of his mouth was harsh. The man's eyes had held a flat, dead glare, and glinted with casual cruelty.

I see we'll have to do this the hard way. The spirit forced itself against Connor's shape as if it were squeezing into a too-tight suit of armor. The man's ghost shoved and twisted, taking pleasure in the pain he caused in his rough entry. Connor bit back a scream.

I warned you.

Connor felt a tide of anger well up inside him, fed by his anger at Reese, and the long-unspent fury at the mages who had sent the Cataclysm and destroyed Connor's world.

Get…out…of…my…head! The words summoned up every bit of energy in Connor's being, calling to every strand of untested power, rage made all the more potent for its long suppression.

Connor felt that rage well up inside him as his magic flared in his mind. Rage and magic melded with sheer willpower in one massive push, throwing the intruder out of his mind, casting the spirit free of his body.

The effort left Connor gasping on his hands and knees, but he lifted his head defiantly, expecting the spirit to try once more, doubting that he had the strength to fight him off again.

The large man's spirit took visible shape once more, its fleshy features twisted in an expression of fury. *I will destroy you,* the spirit vowed. *I will crush every memory. Nothing of you will remain.*

The ghost began to rush toward Connor. But just as it gathered speed, a blast of wind roared through the corridor, sudden and violent enough to make Connor throw up his arms to protect himself. A glowing specter stood between Connor and the ghost, a broad-shouldered man in full armor, holding a glowing sword in each hand. Power rippled from the apparition, and fury.

This was Kierken Vandholt, the Wraith Lord, and he was very, very angry.

You tried to take something that does not belong to you, the Wraith Lord thundered.

The fat man's ghost dared not rise. *M'lord, I beg you—*

Silence! the Wraith Lord roared. *I have no interest in your defense. I felt what harm you worked against my servant. His pain was mine. And now, my vengeance shall be his.*

The ghost's image waxed and waned, and Connor wondered if the spirit was trying to flee. If so, the Wraith Lord possessed the power to keep him from doing so. By now, the fat man's ghost was on his knees, sobbing and pleading, promising to make amends and bargaining with offers of hidden treasures.

The Wraith Lord did not slow his advance, and Connor was grateful that he could not see Vandholt's face.

Mercy, my lord, I beg of you, the corpulent man pleaded.

I will show you the mercy you showed my servant, the Wraith Lord said in a cold voice. He lunged forward, and one of his glowing blades skewered the ghost through the belly. With his other hand, he plunged the second blade down through the apparition's head and into his chest.

It would serve you well if I left you like this for eternity, the Wraith Lord said in a low rumble. *I have read your spirit, and this is not the first time you have forced yourself into a mortal's consciousness. But it will be the last.*

The fat man's mouth worked silently, his eyes wide with pain and utter terror. If Connor had ever questioned the stories that Kierken Vandholt walked the Unseen Realm with the permission of Esthrane herself, this ability to punish the incorporeal dead removed all doubt.

You threatened to snuff out every glimmer that remained of my servant's self, the Wraith Lord said. *You intended to steal his body and destroy his soul. You do not have that power. But I do.*

The fat man's ghost made a strangled bleat, and winked out of sight, drawing the darkness with him like a shroud.

The Wraith Lord stared at the empty space where the ghost had vanished for a moment, then turned toward Connor. Dimly, Connor was aware of a rustle behind him and hushed voices that fell silent with one look from the Wraith Lord. Kierken Vandholt strode over to where Connor knelt. Vandholt's expression changed, softening to one of concern.

Are you damaged?

Connor shook his head, still at a loss for words. He managed to climb to his feet. "Thank you. If he had come at me a second time, I don't think I could have fought him back."

I felt the intrusion and your pain, the Wraith Lord said. *The bond between us goes both ways, a* kruvgaldur *of spirit if not blood.* He paused. *That you were able to throw him off at all is quite unusual. I have met very few mediums who could muster that kind of power, even with their lives at stake.* He chuckled. *You continue to surprise me, Bevin.*

"Thank you," Connor repeated. "I didn't think you could help. I'm far away from your lands."

Kierken Vandholt inclined his head in acknowledgment. *You are most welcome. I am not bound to my lands, but I choose to stay close since it gives me comfort. I could not allow you to be destroyed. I have cost you a great deal. But I also watch over those under my protection.* He frowned. *Be wary, Bevin. Westbain is a dangerous place.*

With that, the Wraith Lord's image disappeared.

Connor heard a gasp behind him and turned to find Alsibeth and Caz staring at him with a mixture of fear and incredulity.

"We heard you cry out," Alsibeth said, recovering her voice. "Something kept us from reaching you. We could hear you, but everything was dark. Then…" She struggled for words. "Was that the Wraith Lord?"

Connor nodded. The adrenaline that had sustained him in his life-or-death battle was draining fast, leaving him completely spent. "We have an…understanding," he said.

Alsibeth chuckled. "You are a man of surprises, Bevin Connor. The night of the Great Fire, the omens told me that you would play an important role in what was to unfold. I had no idea what that meant."

"Believe me, neither did I," Connor muttered.

CHAPTER THIRTEEN

S ENESCHAL CONNOR!"
Lieutenant Aurick, commander of the contingent of guards Traher Voss had left to guard the captured manor, ran a few steps to catch up with Connor. "Good to see you up and about again, sir," Aurick said.

"Glad to be back," Connor replied. It had taken him a full day to recover from his run-in with the ghost.

"Thought you'd want an update on the construction when it's light enough to see what's been done, since Lord Penhallow won't be available until after dark," Aurick added. Aurick was a sandy-haired man in his late twenties, just a few years older than Connor, but with the look of a man who has been soldiering since he could carry a sword. He had the plain, pleasant face of a farmhand, although old battles had flattened his nose and given him a nasty scar across one cheek.

"Let's take a look," Connor said, grabbing a cloak. Overhead, gray clouds threatened snow. Connor shivered.

"We're nearly done repairing the break in the south wall," Aurick said, pointing. The Great Fire had caused some of the damage, and the rest was the result of the assault Voss and Pen-hallow had led against Reese's defenders.

"That's good," Connor said, eyeing the expanse of wall. One breach was repaired, but several more remained. "How soon do you think your men can get to the rest of the breaks?"

Aurick drew a deep breath. "We're working day and night, sir. The problem is, the original wall was reinforced by magic, and when the Cataclysm knocked out the magic, parts of the wall collapsed." He shook his head. "If they'd built the wall right, we wouldn't have so much to fix." He sighed. "A few more weeks, at least, sir—if the weather stays good."

"How will you defend the manor in the meantime?"

Aurick pointed down beyond the walls. "My men are raising earthworks and digging a dry moat. We'll get abatis and bar-ricades in place as well."

Connor nodded. "That's more than we've got now. I have a bad feeling about having those gaps open."

Aurick gave a grim chuckle. "Me too, sir. I like a sturdy wall between me and the enemy."

"Do I need to ask Voss for more men?"

Aurick shook his head. "Commander Voss and the rest of the troops are busy at Rodestead House, sir. I'd like to think that by the time anyone could ride there and return with rein-forcements, we'll be done."

"I hope so, Lieutenant," Connor responded. "I don't think any of us will sleep well until the walls are up."

Shouting drew their attention toward the main gate. A group of robed men and women were arguing stridently with the guards, who were blocking their attempt to enter. Connor and Aurick hurried closer to the action.

"No one gets inside without permission of Lord Penhallow."

A burly guard stood toe to toe with a tall, thin man in a roughly woven robe. Connor looked at the newcomers. At least a dozen people, all dressed similarly to their spokesperson, looked as if they had been living out of doors and in rough conditions. Their hair was matted, their robes were frayed and smudged with dirt, and several wore rags wrapped around their feet instead of shoes.

"We are the Tingur," the man said, "followers of Torven. And we have come to make offerings at the manor shrine."

Two more guards had joined the first man, and together they presented a solid wall of brawn. Other guards were drawing close, in case reinforcements were needed.

"I don't care if you're Charrot, Esthrane, and Torven and all the household gods," the guard replied. "No one gets in without permission from Lord Penhallow."

The thin spokesperson glowered at the guard. "Don't jest about the gods," he warned. "We don't need permission of a lord to make our offering—and we refuse to recognize a lord who is not among the living."

The guard was clearly reaching the end of his patience. "*You* might not be among the living if you don't leave here *now*. You're not getting in, not unless Lord Penhallow says so."

For a moment, Connor feared that the robed visitors might rush the guards. That was bound to end badly, since the guards were already worn to short tempers. The guards drew their swords, and at that, the waiting soldiers closed ranks.

The thin man raised his hands toward the sky. "Torven, consort of Charrot, lord of the Sea of Souls, bring down your curse on those who prevent offerings from being made to your name. Scourge them with fire, and flay the flesh from their bones that all may know that you are ascendant among the consorts, and your power is unmeasured."

"Are you done yet?" the guard demanded. "You'd best be moving on. We've already seen fire, and all the flaying's been on our part, so if you know what's good for you, you'll leave. Now."

The soldiers had formed shoulder-to-shoulder ranks, swords drawn, and at the guard's challenge, they moved a step forward.

The tall man lifted his head defiantly. "We will return, and we will enter. Torven will have his sacrifice."

"Yeah, maybe the cook will burn dinner. That'd be a burnt offering for you," the guard said. "Now, be on your way."

Grumbling their displeasure, the Tingur moved away from the gate. The soldiers did not disband until the wanderers were out of sight, and when the extra men went back to their duties, the lead guard ordered the heavy gates to be shut, although it was still early in the day.

"Can they get through the breaks in the wall?" Connor asked.

Aurick shook his head. "Not unless they've got an army with them. We've got barricades and soldiers at each breach point."

"So there are more of these... Tingur?" Connor asked.

"We've seen small groups on the roads in the last few months," Aurick replied. "We've been so busy fighting brigands and trying to repair what the Great Fire destroyed, we didn't pay a lot of attention."

"Ask your men to keep an eye out for more of these Tingur. I want to know what you hear," Connor said.

Aurick grinned. "That we can easily do, sir."

Aurick headed toward the repair crew while Connor walked back to the manor house, deep in thought. He hurried up the cracked steps to the manor house, happy to get in out of the cold. As he hung up his cloak, he sighed. *I've put it off as long as I can. There's no avoiding going into the dungeons today.*

Connor knew where the entrance was to the levels beneath Westbain. He had made it a point to studiously avoid them, entering as rarely as he could. He took a deep breath and squared his shoulders. *I'm a visitor, not a prisoner.* His stomach tightened as he descended the stone steps. Every step deepened a feeling of despair.

A shrill cry startled him, and he drew his knife, advancing cautiously. Yet when he reached the bottom of the stairs, he saw that nothing had changed since his first visit. Healers, not jailers, moved among the cells.

For a moment, Connor watched the men and women who bustled through the tight corridor between cells that had been converted to sickrooms. His previous visits had not lasted longer than a few minutes, enough to assure himself that the dungeons were no longer filled with Reese's prisoners and that everything was being handled in an orderly fashion. The resonance of the ghosts whose spirits filled the dungeons had caused him to turn around and leave, but today Connor had resolved to make a complete walk-through, regardless of discomfort.

"Seneschal Connor." A man in his middle years with graying reddish hair moved to greet him. "We were wondering when your duties would permit you to come our way." The man spared him a tired smile. "I'm Berus," he said, and swept an arm to indicate the rows of cells. "And this is as close as you'll ever want to come to the Unseen Realm."

"Come with me," Berus said, leading the way through the narrow corridor. The stone around them was dark with moisture and mold, and a smell lingered, the odor of wounds gone bad.

"The night that Westbain fell to our forces, Lord Penhallow ordered the healers to see to the prisoners in the dungeons."

Berus shook his head. "As you can imagine—or if you're lucky, maybe you can't—things were very bad down here."

"I'm actually surprised that Reese's men left anyone alive—or sane," Connor said.

Berus nodded soberly. "Had *talishte* soldiers not intervened as quickly as they did, I'm certain Reese's men had orders to kill all the prisoners. Even so, for some, it was too late."

Connor looked at the scarred and bandaged men who lay on pallets in the cells. Most were missing an ear or several fingers, marks of the torturer's craft. A few sat head in hands, rocking and moaning to themselves. "What about them?" Connor asked.

Berus sighed. "Our healers and mages will try everything within their power to heal them. If that is impossible, they will make sure that their passage to the Sea of Souls is painless."

"Were you able to learn anything?" Connor asked.

Berus gave him a skeptical glance. "Are you serious? Any information these men might have had is buried beneath so much pain that it will be amazing if they remember their names. Reese broke them physically. *Talishte* read their blood and glamoured them into collaborating against their will. Then when magic was restored, Reese used it to strip out any remaining information and leave the husks behind."

Connor knew what it was like to have a *talishte* read his blood. He did not want to imagine how it would be to have that process done by force. He stared at the prisoners with a mixture of pity and horror.

"Let me know if there's anything you need," Connor said, looking at the dying prisoners and the healers laboring to ease their pain. "If I can get it for you, I will."

Connor trudged up the stone steps from the dungeon deep

in thought. He was halfway up the steps when he heard a crash overhead and the manor felt as if it rocked on its foundation. Above and below him, he heard people cry out in shock and fear. A flurry of dust rained down on him. Connor began to take the steps two at a time, bursting from the entrance to the lower floors into a crowd of servants who were huddled toward the back of the manor's first floor.

"What's going on?" Connor demanded. Some of the younger maids were crying. Several of the men were bleeding from gashes on their faces and chests. Everyone was covered in dust. He saw a heap of rubble partially blocking the main entrance to the manor.

"Don't know, m'lord," Orwin, one of the kitchen boys replied. "We heard a loud noise, and the rock in the front of the manor came tumbling down. Nearly killed Ned over there," he said, and nodded toward where another of the kitchen boys sat against the wall while the cook tried to bandage a cut on his scalp.

Penhallow would not be awake for several candlemarks, Connor thought. *Aurick's the only one who might know more— and he's out there.*

Another crash shook the manor, shattering glass and bringing down a chunk of ceiling plaster. Connor growled a stream of curses. He turned to Orwin. "Get everyone down below-ground. Go!"

He spotted two of the men who hauled supplies for the kitchen staff. "You there. Help me move the wounded."

Connor and the other two men began sifting through the heavy plaster, throwing the rubble off two women who had been caught beneath the collapse. One of them, a scullery maid, cradled a broken arm. The other woman was heaving for breath.

"Gentle!" he admonished his helpers as the maid cried out

when one of the men tried to lift her. "There are healers in the dungeon. You'll all be safer belowground."

"The dungeon! I'm not going down there!" The maid's eyes widened in terror. No doubt rumors of what became of Reese's prisoners had been whispered among the servants.

"If you stay up here, I can't promise more of the manor won't fall on you," Connor replied. "Everyone else has gone below."

"You won't make us stay down there, will you?" The maid began to wail and fight against the man trying to help her to the steps.

Connor grabbed her by her good shoulder. "Once the fighting's over, you can all come up again. Now, get down there!"

Connor turned back toward the manor's entrance. Another crash made him lose his footing, but he struggled to remain standing.

We're getting pounded by a catapult, Connor thought. *But whose forces want Westbain?*

He chafed at not being able to find Aurick and learn what was going on, but Connor knew his first responsibility was to get the servants to safety and secure the manor from fire. The front hall was full of rubble from where part of the ceiling had fallen, and the large windows in the great room left a hail of shattered glass on the floor.

"Get to shelter!" Connor shouted as he ran down the hallway. "Go belowground. You're not safe up here!" Dull thuds outside gave Connor to suspect that Aurick's men were returning fire. Connor glimpsed servants emerging from their hiding places under tables and in wardrobes, clinging to each other in twos and threes, making their way toward the steps to the lower levels. He paused in the kitchen long enough to make sure that the fires were banked. *The last thing we need is a house fire,* he thought.

Connor paused at the bottom of the stairs to the second floor. He had intentionally headed for the servants' stairs since they were in the back of the manor and had only a few small windows, making them less exposed than the sweeping staircase in the front entrance. Another loud crash made the floor shake beneath his feet. He heard glass break, and winced at the sound of something fragile smashing to the floor.

Connor's heart was thudding as he sprinted up the steps. He reached the second floor and kept low, staying to the center of the corridor, hoping that if the manor took another hit, any debris would fall before they could break through the manor walls. A gust of cold wind blasted across the hall, and he knew that at least some of the rooms had lost the glass in their windows.

Connor dove into his room and grabbed his cuirass and helmet from a trunk at the bottom of his bed. He had not expected to need his armor once they reached Westbain, and had felt uncomfortable wearing his sword at all times. Now he was glad his armor was handy and that his sword already hung from a scabbard at his belt. Connor stayed low as he strapped on his cuirass. He pulled on his helmet, and crawled over to the window, daring to look out onto the front of the manor.

From this vantage point, Connor could see that a force of approximately a hundred soldiers had brought two catapults into position on the other side of Westbain's wall, just beyond the partially constructed earthworks and dry moat. While the barriers worked to keep the invaders at a distance, they also made it more difficult for Aurick's soldiers to get close to the opposing side.

The soldiers Traher Voss had left behind to guard and rebuild Westbain were seasoned veterans, both from the Meroven War and from skirmishes with brigands and rival warlords.

Aurick's men numbered about the same as the invaders, and Connor could see that they had taken up positions within what remained of the manor's walls. It was obvious that Aurick had rebuilt with an eye toward defense. Catapults that Connor did not know existed had been rolled out to respond to the attack. Soldiers manned the barricades that filled in the broken places in the defensive walls.

"I need to get out there. I'm not doing any bloody good up here," Connor muttered, keeping low as he ran for the corridor and down the steps.

He dodged down the second-floor corridor, wondering whether the mages had gotten to safety or whether they were out with the troops. Inside the workroom, he found Alsibeth hunched over a scrying bowl while Caz helped Rolf prepare for a working with a length of rope to set a warded area and candles to mark the quarters.

"Bevin! What are you doing here?" Caz looked alarmed.

"I could ask the same. I'm trying to make sure everyone in the house gets to safety. And you're not safe here," Connor replied. He looked around. "Where are the rest of the mages?"

"The others volunteered to go out with Aurick's men. We needed more tools than we could haul with us, so we stayed behind," Rolf said.

"What can I do to help?" Connor asked.

Rolf shook his head. "You're not a mage."

"Maybe not, but I can still lend a hand." He glanced out the window. "Can you tell who's attacking us?" Connor asked. He had not been able to identify either uniforms or flags from the soldiers he had seen from the window, and he wondered if the force arrayed against them was organized enough to even have insignia.

"It appears to be Karstan Lysander," Alsibeth replied without looking up from the shallow bowl filled with water that held her attention. "I'm trying to see whether there are reinforcements coming, but I can't see clearly."

"Lysander?" Connor echoed. "I thought he was staying unaligned."

"Apparently not," Rolf replied. "If you're going to stay, come over here. We need a third person to triangulate the power."

Connor went to the place Rolf pointed. He had watched enough of Blaine's preparation at Valshoa to recognize that Rolf had set a warded area with rope and salt around their work space. "What are we doing?" Connor asked.

Rolf spared a look from his preparations. "There's a mob out there—but we don't think it's a true army. All of Alsibeth's scryings point to Lysander, and he may be recruiting and provisioning these people, but either he's not much of a warlord, or they're not his real forces. Take a look."

Connor moved to the window and tried to get a better view without putting himself at risk. Before, he had only focused on the size of the force. Now, bearing Rolf's comments in mind, Connor could see that the enemy 'soldiers' looked more like a riot than any kind of disciplined military force. The crowd shouted curses and jabbed their swords and torches into the air with fervor, but the longer Connor watched, the less organized the mob appeared.

"Someone's provided them with weapons, and those catapults aren't something angry villagers put together," Connor said. "They're military equipment."

"As I said, Lysander could well be provisioning them and whipping them into a frenzy," Rolf replied.

"Soldiers or not, those catapults are doing some real damage to the manor," Connor noted. "We've got several servants with injuries."

"But that's all they're doing—loading the catapult," Rolf pointed out. "There's no move to scale the earthworks, no split force to attack the flank—nothing I'd expect from a real military commander."

"Then why the attack?"

"Lysander could be using mobs to find his rivals' weaknesses," Alsibeth said, raising her gaze from the pool of water. "It's a cynical—and rather brilliant—move, assuming you don't mind sacrificing large numbers of peasants in the process."

Connor stared back at her. "You think he's deliberately whipping up the people to riot, knowing that many of them will die, to soften up his enemies, and then his troops can sweep in behind and take the fortress with fewer casualties?"

"Exactly," Alsibeth replied.

"The Tingur," Connor said, remembering the rabble who had confronted Aurick. He looked to Alsibeth and Rolf. "What if Lysander has convinced the Tingur to fight for him as some kind of holy war, in Torven's name? Penhallow and Blaine have the support of the Knights of Esthrane. That would make them the Tingur's enemies, if they serve Torven." In all of Donderath's stories of their gods, Torven and Esthrane were rivals for Charrot's attention. And while Esthrane was willing to curtail her power, Torven was prone to chaos and self-interest.

Rolf nodded soberly. "That would be a clever way to get someone else to do his dirty work. Lysander wouldn't be the first to use a mob for his own purposes."

Outside, Connor heard the answering thuds of Aurick's catapults. The Great Fire and Penhallow's previous bombardment had left the troops with no small amount of rubble to be used as ammunition. Each time the catapults would send a deadly hail of rock, wood, and debris flying toward the mob, a few people would fall, the crowd would scatter and then regroup, angrier than before.

"I hope we're right," Rolf said, "because if they're not trained soldiers, that opens up some opportunities."

"Like what?" Connor asked.

Rolf grinned. "Real soldiers will hold their positions. Let's see how disciplined the mob really is."

Another crash shook the manor. "If you think there's something we can do to help, we'd better start while the manor is still standing," Connor said.

Rolf nodded. "Very well. Step over the cord and salt—mind not to disturb them. We're going to try some battle-mage tricks, and see if our new artifacts will help."

Connor and Caz got into position, and Rolf closed the circle. He held up a glass pyramid. "We've been working with this piece for a while, and it's been fairly stable."

"Fairly?" Connor challenged.

Rolf ignored him. "I'm going to start with something irritating but harmless—fleas." He grinned. "Let's see how well the Tingur hold their places." He looked to Connor and Caz. "The sending part of this is a little tricky—that's why I need the two of you for me to draw energy from."

"What do we need to do?" Connor asked.

"Relax—if you can. Be willing to open your minds to me," Rolf instructed. "Chant with me—it will bring your energy into alignment with mine. I'll use the pyramid to concentrate the magic and redirect it, and if everything goes as it should, every flea in the area should feel compelled to descend on our visitors."

Connor took a deep breath as Rolf began to chant. Caz joined in a moment later, and Connor did his best to follow their lead. Outside, the pounding of the catapults continued, although the attackers seemed to need longer to regroup from the last round of bombardment from Aurick's men.

Everyone seems to want to drain something from me, Connor thought. *The mages want energy. Penhallow wants blood, and the Wraith Lord wants my body.* He forced the sour thoughts away, focusing instead on taking deep, regular breaths until he felt his body relax a bit and his attention was diverted from the sounds of fighting outside.

"Keep chanting," Rolf instructed. "I'm going to make the working now." Connor focused on repeating the same words and cadence as Caz, trying to block out what Rolf was saying so as not to get distracted. Rolf's chant was a counterpoint, and within the wardings, Connor could feel power building.

Connor wasn't a mage, but he had been in the presence of strong magic many times. He knew its signature. The hair on his arms and on the back of his neck seemed to be standing on end. His skin prickled as it did when lightning was about to strike nearby. Connor felt the blood rush in his ears. As Rolf spoke the words of power, it seemed as if the air suddenly rushed out of the warded space, leaving it still and drained.

A sudden tiredness washed over Connor. Caz staggered, and Connor reached out to steady him. "I'm fine," Caz assured him, but Connor thought the young mage looked pale.

"Your magic worked," Alsibeth said, a hint of pride in her voice. "Let's see how many folks stick around for the fight when they're scratching themselves raw."

Rolf released the warding. Caz found a chair while Connor edged up to the window. Even at a distance, he could hear cries going up from the rival force, and although he could not see exactly what was going on, the people on the other side seemed to be milling around more than before. He chuckled. "If we can run them off, it's a damn sight better than killing them, especially if they're not real soldiers," he said.

"That's my thought, but if they come back, we'll have to step things up a notch," Rolf replied.

They waited. As Connor watched, some of the crowd trickled away down the side streets and alleys, perhaps hoping to get away from the fleas. "It's working," Connor reported. "There are fewer people out there than there were a couple of minutes ago."

"And it's taking them longer to fire back," Caz pointed out. "That's a good thing."

Aurick had taken advantage of the lull. He stepped up his bombardment, lobbing whatever he could find toward the mob, hoping, Connor was certain, to break their resolve.

"Uh-oh," Connor said. "They're reloading."

From what Connor could see, about a third of the mob had disbanded, but the ones who stayed had returned to their post, regardless of the discomfort. "What in Raka are they loading up?" Connor wondered as he watched the catapult crews struggle to lift two squirming sacks of burlap into the mechanisms.

"We've got to stop those launches," Alsibeth said suddenly. She looked down, intently focused on her scrying bowl. "I don't know what's in them, but it's deadly. Rolf—what can you do?"

Rolf deliberated for only a moment before he snatched down what looked to Connor to be a metal-and-glass lantern from a shelf filled with a hodgepodge of artifacts and magical objects. "Get back into the circle," Rolf commanded, his tone grim. "I'm going to see if I can channel fire and burn those bags out of the sky."

"We haven't vetted that piece yet," Caz pointed out worriedly.

"No time like the present," Rolf replied. With Connor and Caz in place, Rolf hurriedly raised the warding.

"You don't know it will work the way it should," Caz protested.

Rolf fixed him with a pointed glare. "Then it'll be on my head if it doesn't. All you two need to do is chant."

Connor wasn't sure what scared him more, the sight of those writhing, twisting sacks being loaded into the catapults, or Rolf's determination to proceed into the unknown.

"There is death," Alsibeth said, her gaze fixed on the water. "No matter what choice is made."

Rolf began the chant. Caz and Connor took it up a moment later. Unlike the last time, the chant seemed rough and fast. Connor could feel the power welling up like a storm surge. Rolf was speaking quickly, and his low voice was like a pounding war drum. Connor could hear fear in Caz's voice, and wondered if the others could hear the same in his. Alsibeth had left off scrying and raised her voice in the chant. Connor wondered if she feared that the power Rolf was raising might need the extra help to control.

Two catapults thudded, launching their squirming loads toward Westbain. Rolf raised the lantern, and spoke a word of command.

Fire blasted from the lantern, shattering the glass in the window, torching across the sky toward the enemy lines. The fire lanced through one of the burlap-bound sacks launched by the catapult. A nightmarish shriek echoed from the walls of the manor as the burning bundle tumbled to the ground.

"Rolf, let it go!" Connor urged.

Rolf had not moved. He held the lantern aloft, his hands like claws. His expression was resolute, and he stared unblinking toward his objective.

Alsibeth screamed. Connor chanced a look again toward the window. The stream of fire continued its blast, arcing to touch down where the catapults had sent their deadly missiles into the air. Flames burst across the flatlands, incinerating the mob that had not already dispersed. Rolf remained motionless, his gaze fixed on the lantern.

Then Connor realized that Rolf was no longer breathing.

"He's dead." Connor reached out to grab Caz's arm. "Whatever that damned lantern did, it pulled the life out of him—and it'll come for us next unless we do something!"

"Break the warding, Alsibeth," Caz said, his eyes taking on a determined glint. "I'll handle the lantern."

Alsibeth shouted the words of power, and Connor felt the energy shift. He stepped backward, purposely kicking away the rope that had defined the workspace and smudging the protective line of salt.

"Stand clear!" Caz tackled Rolf, shoulder-slamming into the older, heavier man. The fiery blast went wild, and Caz screamed as it caught him on one side. Alsibeth dove for the floor. Caz brought one fist down hard against Rolf's still-outstretched hands to dash the lantern to the floor. The lantern smashed and went dark. Caz and Rolf tumbled to the ground and lay still.

Connor ran to Caz, pulling him off of Rolf's body. He dropped to his knees, checking Rolf for a pulse he did not expect to find. But when he rolled Caz over, Connor let out a low moan of despair. The lantern's fire had seared one side of Caz's body, burning away his hair, charring the skin on his face, chest, and arm. Caz groaned, a guttural sound that reminded Connor of a death rattle.

"Caz!" Alsibeth cried, crawling over to the injured mage. Alsibeth appeared unharmed, though her hair was wild and her skin was ashen.

"We've got to get him down to the healers," Connor urged. "It's too late to help Rolf."

A feral growl rumbled down the hallway, and claws scratched against the stone floor.

Connor climbed to his feet, drawing his sword. Whatever was scratching its way down the corridor was getting closer.

"Go!" Alsibeth shouted. "I'll stay with Caz."

"I don't even know what's out there," Connor retorted.

"Monsters," Alsibeth said, gentling Caz's unburned hand into her lap. "That's what was in the last catapult assault. They restrained some of the magic beasts long enough to fire them toward us. It was the last thing I saw before the scrying went blank."

Monsters. Connor had heard the tales that Blaine and the others told of having faced down the monsters that wild magic had unleashed across Donderath.

"Stay here. See what you can do for Caz." Connor tightened his grip on his sword. If the beast had reached the manor house, then it had somehow gotten past the soldiers. Going to look for the monster was better than having it find them where they were.

Connor flattened himself against the wall next to the door, and chanced a look down the corridor. He could see something moving in the shadows, something the size of a large dog. He frowned. *The sack that the catapult launched was much bigger than a dog. Could they have sent multiple monsters?*

From outside, Connor heard men shouting and the clang of swords. A howl unlike anything Connor had ever heard before rose above the shouts, to be answered again and again.

The thing in the hallway scented the air, then raised its head and gave an answering cry that sent a shiver down Connor's spine.

The sounds of fighting outside the manor told Connor that help was unlikely to come in time. Connor doubted Alsibeth had the strength left for a magical assault. It was still daytime, so there would be no assistance coming from Nidhud or his Knights, or from Penhallow. The Wraith Lord came and went on his own whims, not to be counted on.

I can buy us time, Connor thought. *That's worth something.*

Connor pivoted out into the hallway at the same moment when the thing seemed to scent him. It rose crab-like on six spiny, jointed legs. The scratching Connor had heard was the beast's hard carapace and its clawed feet. Its white shell gave it the look of bleached bones. The body of the thing was oval-shaped and thick. Altogether, the beast was the size of a full-grown mastiff, and when it scented Connor, he learned one more thing about it.

It was fast.

Connor saw the beast scuttling toward him, moving with a sideways, swaying motion all the more terrifying for its speed. Connor braced himself, sword held in both hands, positioning his body to keep the thing from getting to Caz and Alsibeth.

Now would have been a good time for some of Rolf's fire, Connor thought. The thing was on him with the speed of a bounding wolf. Connor hacked at it with his sword, aiming for the joints.

His sword grated against the hard surface, and although Connor had brought down his blade with his full strength, it did not slice through the leg. Two large, faceted eyes watched him, unblinking like a spider, and the thing's legs clicked as they lashed at him, slicing through his shirt with their sharp tips.

Connor set about himself with his sword, slashing with all his might. His blade bounced off the body of the thing, but found purchase in one of its forelegs, where the blade sliced into the joint that attached the leg to the body. One of the white, bone-like legs snapped off and fell to the floor in a jet of bluish ichor.

The beast screeched an earsplitting sound that echoed in the confines of the corridor. Connor was bleeding freely from a dozen gashes where the thing had cut him; the scent of his blood sent the creature into a frenzy. It came at him with its five clawed legs flailing, fast as whips and surprisingly strong. Like fighting a swordsman with extra arms, Connor could only parry part of each strike, and with every attack, the creature scored more deep cuts on his arms, chest, and thighs.

If its claws are poisoned, I'm a dead man, Connor thought. He grabbed a board that lay near the entrance to the mage's room, using it as a makeshift shield. It spared him a few strikes, but it was impossible to block all of its legs at once.

Connor's sword sliced off another of the creature's legs. The beast shrieked and skittered backward, then launched itself at Connor once more. He angled his sword so that the tip struck the thing in its underbelly, hoping to find a weak spot. But the tip of his sword scratched down along its rigid exoskeleton without causing damage.

The beast was chattering wildly, a high-pitched, staccato noise. It reared back and its maw opened wide, a circular hole filled with rows of sharp teeth. *It would take forever for that thing to eat me,* Connor thought.

Despite his fear, Connor was tiring quickly. No one from downstairs had run to his aid, leaving him to assume that the soldiers were busy with their own problems, and the servants had gone to the dungeons. *Perhaps the creatures got to them first.*

Alsibeth slipped out of the mage's workroom and stood behind Connor. She held a lit oil lamp in one hand. "Caz needs more help than I can give him—but I might be able to help you," she said. "I've got an idea."

"I could use a good one." Connor's shirt and pants were soaked with blood. One of the creature's sharp legs had sliced across one temple, barely missing his eye and sending a rivulet of blood down the side of his face. Blood trickled down both his arms, and his hands looked as if they had been sliced by knives.

"These things, the *ranin*, they don't like fire," Alsibeth whispered.

Connor dared not take his eyes off the creature long enough to spare her an incredulous glance. "Burning down the manor isn't an option."

"We won't have to," Alsibeth replied. "Just follow my lead."

"Watch out—it moves fast," Connor warned.

Alsibeth gave him a canny look. "I'm counting on it."

The next time the *ranin* came at him, Connor dodged so that he had his back to the door of the room Alsibeth had indicated. It was another workroom, but rarely used, so that all that was in it was a small worktable and a few chairs. On one end was a large stone fireplace as tall as Connor's shoulders and as wide across as his outstretched arms. The fireplace was dark, although someone had left wood stacked inside should a fire be needed.

The beast sprang at Connor, and he barely kept it from getting past him to Alsibeth. "Whatever you're doing to do, do it quickly!" he shouted.

Alsibeth grabbed the table and flipped it on its side so that it was between them and the creature.

"That won't hold it," Connor cautioned.

"Doesn't have to," Alsibeth replied. "Here's the plan. I draw that thing toward the fireplace. You be ready behind the table, and when the *ranin* is in place, shove that table as hard and as fast as you can to trap it inside the fireplace. I'll throw the lamp in with it, and with luck, that thing will go up in flame without taking the rest of us with it."

"It's worth a try. I've got nothing better."

"Get ready," Alsibeth said, eyeing the way the creature bobbed back and forth like a duelist sizing up an opponent. "Go!"

Alsibeth dodged toward the fireplace, and the creature swiveled to follow her motion. Connor hurled himself against the table, putting his shoulder against the edge and pushing the flat surface of the upended tabletop toward the *ranin* and the fireplace as fast as he could move. At the last moment, Alsibeth dodged aside, and Connor slammed the table against the creature, knocking it into the stone firebox.

Alsibeth lobbed the oil lamp over the top of the table. It hit the back of the firebox and shattered, dousing the *ranin* with oil and flames. Connor kept the table shoved up against the opening.

"We did it!" Alsibeth shouted as the creature squealed, hissing and popping in the flames and trying to hurl itself against the table to get free.

Connor turned toward her to reply, but no words came. Three of the creature's razor-sharp claws protruded through the wooden tabletop, lancing deep into his chest and belly. Connor stared down at the wounds in shock, and then tumbled backward into darkness.

CHAPTER
FOURTEEN

"ARE YOU CERTAIN WE'RE IN THE RIGHT PLACE?"
Ayers asked skeptically.

"This is Mirdalur," Niklas replied. "And yes, I'm certain."

Ayers cleared his throat. "It doesn't exactly look the way I'd expected, that's all."

Niklas chuckled. "Maybe you just need to use your imagination." It would require quite a stretch of anyone's imagination to envision the ruined old manor and its tumbledown grounds as a hub of magical power. Despite Blaine's stories of his first failed attempt there to restore the magic, and Dolan's conviction that Mirdalur was the best site to anchor the magic, Niklas was having the same challenge as Ayers when it came to seeing the wreckage in a different light. But Blaine's orders had been clear, that Niklas and his men were needed to help Dolan ready the site, and Niklas made those orders plain to his men as the commission of their commander and their lord.

Once, Mirdalur had been a grand and imposing manor. Four hundred years ago, the Lords of the Blood had convened here to bind magic to the will of men. Time had not been kind to the manor in the centuries since then. The high stone walls were shattered, and the keep was an overgrown pile of rubble. Weeds and brambles had taken over what remained of the ruined manor and its dependencies. Scorch marks blackened the cracked stone from the Great Fire. In the center of the bailey, a broken fountain and shattered statues lay half-submerged in murky water.

"Not much left, is there?" Ayers said.

Niklas shook his head. "No, there isn't. Then again, the Great Fire only did part of the damage. From what the Knights of Esthrane say, the worst of this happened a hundred years before the Lords of the Blood anchored the magic, when they had their own version of the Cataclysm and magic went rogue."

"And they went without harnessed magic for a century?" Ayers replied. "Damn. It's been less than a year since the Cataclysm, and it feels like forever." He stared at the blackened stone. "I can't even imagine what that would have been like."

Torches lit the perimeter of the main manor grounds, and dotted the inner courtyard. An orange ribbon along the horizon tinged with gold signaled sunset.

"A century of wild magic, wreaking havoc. Magicked beasts, dropped out of nowhere from the storms, hunting in the shadows." Niklas's voice held horror and awe. "It's amazing anyone survived long enough to try to restore the magic."

"I'd have felt better if Sir Dolan had chosen Quillarth Castle for the ritual," Ayers said, turning his back to the wind as it gusted. "I felt relatively safe there. Here"—he gestured to the overgrown ruins—"it feels too exposed."

Niklas clapped him on the shoulder. "And that, my good man, is why we're here. We're the day workers, making sure nothing interrupts the Knights of Esthrane, or attacks them while they sleep."

Ayers gave him a sour look. "Can't say I'm completely happy with the assignment, but we've had worse."

"That we have." Niklas shared Ayer's apprehension about the *talishte* mages. Like most soldiers, neither Niklas nor Ayers had magic of their own, and that bred an innate suspicion of anyone with more than hedge-witch powers.

Niklas walked to a crumbling cistern and looked over the side. He could barely make out a ledge around the inside wall.

"That's how Lord McFadden and them got in, down the well?" Ayers asked, leaning over for a good look.

"Yeah. They didn't know about the other passageway, and it had collapsed, so they couldn't have gotten in that way anyhow," Niklas replied. "At least Dolan doesn't have to go down the hard way."

Ayers snorted. "Wouldn't be bad for them. *Talishte* can fly."

"Not all of us." Geir's voice behind them startled both men. He was tall and thin, with dark, shoulder-length hair that was caught back in a queue. Though he appeared to be in his early twenties, like his maker, Lanyon Penhallow, Geir was centuries old. "Some can only levitate."

Niklas glared at him. "If you're off the ground, it counts as flying."

Geir chuckled. "Maybe so." He looked to Ayers. "But the point is, we've cleared the passageway, and posted guards inside. We'll just need your assistance during daylight hours."

Niklas nodded. "We've got your back. How long do you think it will take your mages to figure out whether or not the presence-crystals will work here?"

Geir grimaced. "No idea. With luck, it will go easier than at Quillarth Castle."

Ayers shuddered. An attempt by one of the *talishte* mages to work a binding spell with a crystal similar to the ones Dolan had stolen had gone horrifically wrong, flaying skin and tissue from the doomed mage as he writhed in a circle of incinerating magical power.

"Anything would be easier than that, if you don't mind my saying so," Ayers muttered.

"Quite true," Geir replied. "But we remain hopeful."

Considering the circumstances, Niklas was quite happy not to have any magical abilities. He was about to reply when he heard a shout from the perimeter.

"Hey, Captain!" Carr's voice echoed across the ruined courtyard.

Niklas looked up to see Carr hauling a large burlap sack behind him, the right size and shape to hold a body. Geir raised an eyebrow, but said nothing. Ayers muttered a curse under his breath.

Carr looked worse for the wear. One eye was nearly swollen shut, and a nasty gash ran from the edge of his eyebrow to his chin on the right side of his face. The sleeves of his shirt were shredded, and stained with blood. Yet he wore a triumphant expression as he dragged the sack to Niklas. "I've got a report for you, sir."

Niklas bit back several replies that came to mind. "What's in the bag, and how many rules did you break to get it?"

Carr brandished a knife and slit the bag open. A monstrosity tumbled out. Its skin was the color of a corpse trapped underwater. Gelatinous, lidless eyes stared from a misshapen face that seemed to be largely snaggle-toothed maw. Wicked claws protruded from nightmarishly long, slender arms. Muscled legs, with taloned feet, suggested the monster had been fast. "Brought you a present, Cap'n."

"Where did you get that thing?" Ayers asked, his voice caught between terror and wonder. He dared to peer closer, then drew back at the stench.

"About a day's ride from here," Carr reported. "Didn't go down easily. Fortunately, they hunt alone."

"You got lucky," Geir observed coldly. Any retort Carr might have made died in his throat at the look on Geir's face. "Normally, *chrolutes* like that hunt in packs. Lord Penhallow has *talishte* patrolling the forest to destroy these abominations. We knew one had escaped. Had it been with the six others our men killed, you would not have survived."

"One was plenty," Carr replied, anger bright in his eyes. He kicked the corpse a few inches closer to Niklas. "It savaged a village before I brought it down."

Whether that was true, or whether it was an exaggeration Carr invented to save face, Niklas had no way of knowing. "You're supposed to be spying, not waging a one-man war," he growled.

Carr's head snapped up. "I didn't go looking for trouble. I was on my way back from shadowing some of Hennoch's men when that thing attacked me. Running away wasn't an option, so I stood my ground."

Niklas sighed. "Go see Ordel. Don't waste time—if it's been a day already, those slashes could go sour."

Carr gave an exaggerated salute and turned on his heel, leaving the rotting carcass behind him. Niklas wrinkled his nose at the pungent odor. "Damn him," Niklas muttered.

"It might have happened the way he reported," Geir said, although skepticism tinged his voice. "Fewer beasts are appearing, since there aren't as many magic storms now that Blaine has mostly restored the magic, but some are still stalking the forests and the wild places."

Ayers swore under his breath. "I've fought my share of these, between those winged beasts and the bug-things. Never want to see one again, that's for certain."

Niklas nodded. *Gryps*, the flying beasts, and *mestids*, the insect-like monsters, had taken a toll on his troops. He had lost several dozen men to their claws, and his soldiers had kill-on-sight orders. "I'll be glad when they're gone," he said, though he was certain he would see them in his nightmares for the rest of his life.

"Until the magic is better anchored and stabilizes, the storms will continue—and more beasts will slip through," Geir said.

"We've got plenty of torches and pitch," Niklas replied. "And my men set up some of our smaller catapults, so we can lob those torch-balls that worked well the last time the beasts attacked."

Geir nodded. "I'll warn the *talishte*, so they know that surprising your men could be deadly." He paused. "I came up to request that you assign at least one healer and half a dozen soldiers to the underground areas."

Niklas frowned. "Expecting problems? We plan to make sure we stop unexpected visitors up here."

"I'm more worried about the safety of the mortal mages who came with us," Geir replied. "Dolan was unhappy about having them accompany us, but the Wraith Lord insisted. He was worried that a *talishte* might be able to use artifacts without harm that would damage a mortal. And since McFadden is mortal—"

"You brought some mortal mages along to test your theories," Niklas said drily.

"If it helps, they volunteered." Geir's expression made it plain that he shared Niklas's skepticism.

"That accounts for the healers," Ayers said. "Why do you need guards?"

Geir shrugged. "Our mages will be concentrating on the

magic. If any intruders were to slip past your men above and interrupt the workings, it could go badly for all of us."

Niklas preferred not to think about that too hard. "All right. I'll assign them. But I'd like to go down there with them and see the lay of the land."

Geir nodded. "I would have been surprised if you hadn't asked." He gestured for him to follow. "Get your team together and I'll take you down."

Niklas and his guards followed Geir around to a hidden cleft and down a narrow stone passageway, angling deep beneath the manor's walls. Geir might be able to see in the dark, but Niklas and the soldiers were glad to have a lantern to light their way over the rough footing, along the narrow and winding route through long-abandoned cellars and piles of rubble. They eventually emerged in a large ceremonial hall, lit by more than a dozen torches in sconces along the walls, a stark contrast to the rooms and passages they had used to enter. The floor and the walls had been chiseled smooth. Carved into the walls at intervals were the symbols for the thirteen constellations, and the floor was set with pavers in an elaborate labyrinth.

Niklas spotted Dolan and Nidhud on the other site of the ceremonial chamber, deep in discussion. He also recognized Dagur, one of the mages who had been with them at Quillarth Castle, and two other mages whom he remembered from the castle but whose names escaped him. Against one wall of the chamber, a makeshift table had been erected of boards and barrels, and it was covered with manuscripts and artifacts.

"Hello, General Theilsson," Dagur greeted Niklas. "Welcome to the workspace."

Niklas looked around at the carved rock walls. The ritual chamber felt ancient, and even though he had no magic of his own, the hair on the back of his neck prickled in the presence of strong power.

"How's the research going?" Niklas asked, with a nod of his head toward the table and its manuscripts.

Dagur gave a nervous smile. "We'll know pretty soon. Another candlemark or so, and we'll be ready to try a working with Lord McFadden's focus crystal."

Niklas frowned. "Blaine has a focus crystal?"

Dagur shook his head. "Not young Lord McFadden. His father. Or maybe, his grandfather. Geir brought it to us from Glenreith, and said it had been found in the same trunk as the obsidian disks."

"You have the disks, too?" Niklas asked. "Kestel Falke brought them back from Valshoa."

Dagur chuckled. "So I heard. And yes, we have them with us. General Dolan and I have been conferring on the manuscripts, and we believe we see a way for the pieces to work together."

"Are you the one who gets to test the theory?" Niklas asked, raising an eyebrow skeptically.

"No. Brandur will try the working, because his magic with artifacts is stronger than mine," Dagur replied. "We're not going to try the entire anchoring magic—that would be too risky. Brandur is going to try to use the focus crystal and Ian McFadden's obsidian disk and see if he can get the magic to shift at all. Our hope is that with the disk and the old crystal together, he might be able to pin down just a bit of the magic, even for only a few minutes. That would confirm that Quintrel was on the right path with the new presence-crystals." He sighed. "The rest of us will strengthen the wardings, do our best to contain the power, and keep Brandur safe."

Niklas had heard Blaine's account of how disastrously the

attempt to restore the magic at Mirdalur had gone. "I'll be wishing you luck," he replied.

Dagur paused. "We've worked defensive magic around the manor compound as well, just in case," he added. "I won't claim that the magic will keep out a full army, but it should deflect interest from anyone who happens to wander by."

"I'll take all the help we can get," Niklas said, though he privately doubted that the boundary would do much to keep out the troops of any warlord determined enough to march soldiers all the way to Mirdalur.

Later that evening, Niklas was among the guards who stood watch over the ceremonial chamber. He had sent Ayers above with the rest of the soldiers to secure Mirdalur's perimeter, and come below once he was assured that preparations to defend the compound were completed. *If we're going to guard them, I want to know what's going on,* Niklas thought, wondering if he looked as uncomfortable as he felt.

"Think it's safe, Cap'n?" one of the soldiers asked in a hushed voice. "I mean, us being here and not mages or *talishte,* you know."

Niklas chuckled. "We're soldiers. We don't go places that are safe."

"Guess you're right, sir," the man admitted. Niklas recognized him as one of the men who had trekked across most of Donderath with his soldiers after the end of the Meroven War. The young man had seen his share of combat, but magic, Niklas knew, was an altogether different threat.

"Just stay out of the way of the mages, and you'll probably be fine," Niklas said, though he doubted his own advice.

Dagur and Brandur were talking near the entrance to the labyrinth. Dolan and the rest of the Knights of Esthrane had taken positions around the outside of the labyrinth, and as he looked, Niklas realized that thirteen mages were actively taking part in the ritual, one for each Lord of the Blood.

He had expected to see the other mages holding Quintrel's presence-crystals, or wearing the obsidian disks, but those artifacts were nowhere to be seen, except for the single disk on a leather strap around Brandur's neck.

Niklas eyed the mage who was about to do the working. Brandur was in his fourth decade, with graying dark hair and a plump, avuncular face. He looked more like a village healer than a mage from the Castle Reach University, and Niklas could picture the man raising a tankard of ale in a wayside tavern. From Brandur's expression, it was clear the mage understood the danger of what they were about to attempt. Dolan came over to speak to Dagur and Brandur, before turning to give a nod of approval to the waiting mages and returning to his place outside the labyrinth.

The focus crystal was an orb about the length and width of a man's hand, made of a clear mineral with a yellow cast. Brandur held the crystal in front of him like a candle, and Niklas thought he saw it pulse with a faint glow. The mage began to walk the labyrinth, pausing to touch the crystal to the obsidian disk at intervals along the path.

The glow inside the focus crystal grew brighter with each turn of the labyrinth. Brandur and the other mages began to chant softly, growing louder each time Brandur followed the convoluted path in another spiral. Near the center, Brandur stopped at one of the thirteen places where the path widened, and Niklas wondered whether it was the spot where Blaine's long-ago ancestor had taken part as a Lord of the Blood.

The chanting grew louder, and one of the mages began to pound a rhythm on a hand drum that echoed from the chamber's rock walls, making it feel as if the ritual space throbbed with a heartbeat of its own. The torch flames wavered, and the air grew colder. The cold air stirred through the underground room and carried the smoke from the torches in a spiral that picked up speed until it was swirling hard enough to stir their hair and flutter the mage's clothing.

Brandur did not seem to notice, although the unlikely wind sent strands of hair across his face and tugged at the sleeves of his robe. His chanting grew faster and louder, and he had a look of fierce concentration, gaze riveted on the focus crystal, which by now was glowing so brightly that Niklas could not look at it directly.

Dolan looked alarmed, and Niklas saw the *talishte*-mage exchange a worried glance with Nidhud, but neither moved to break the circle or halt the ritual. Niklas gestured to his soldiers to step back, until they and the healers had flattened themselves against the wall as far from the magic as they could get. *We're spectators, and the ones who'll clean up the mess when it's over*, he thought, *but there's not a thing we can do to help before that.*

Brandur's entire form had taken on the yellow glow of the focus crystal, as if a golden light shone through skin that had become translucent. The glow became brighter, and Niklas had to squint against the light to look at Brandur. His whole body began to tremble, and then the light exploded from his chest, spraying the chamber with gore as Brandur's flesh sizzled and hissed with the heat of the power being channeled through it.

A moment later, the charred remains collapsed to the stone floor, a pile of ash, hair, and bloody, burned cloth. The air smelled of blood and burned meat, and the soldier next to Niklas retched. Niklas swallowed hard to keep from doing the same. Next to the heap lay the focus crystal, soot-streaked and ashy, but apparently undamaged. The obsidian disk lay nearby. The leather strap was charred, but the disk itself looked unchanged.

Dolan and the other mages stayed where they were until the drumming and chanting stopped. Nidhud spoke in a language Niklas did not understand, and walked widdershins around the labyrinth, gesturing and murmuring as he went to release the wardings. Only when he finished did Dolan and Dagur rush toward where Brandur had stood.

Niklas joined them, staring in horror at the remains. "I thought you said you had this figured out," he snapped.

Dolan regarded him as if he were a distraction. "Obviously not. This is quite unfortunate."

"Unfortunate!" Niklas repeated, almost choking on the word. "I'd say it's a lot more than unfortunate."

Dagur said a prayer of blessing over Brandur's ashes, consigning his spirit to rest in the Sea of Souls. He sighed, and then looked up at Niklas. "Of course it is," he said tiredly, climbing to his feet. "We will mourn him."

"I'm sorry about your dead mage, but my concern is keeping Blaine McFadden very much alive," Niklas retorted. "If the way the magic is anchored is killing Blaine now, burning him to a crisp isn't the answer we were looking for."

Dagur winced. "We know that." He turned to Niklas with a weary expression. "When you hear us say the magic is 'fragile,' this is what we mean. It hasn't come back quite right, even though it's been restored. Sometimes, the magic isn't as strong as it was, and other times, it comes back with more power than we ever could have imagined."

"The artifacts were not damaged," Dolan said, still kneeling next to the ashes. "And there was a shift in the magic, in the last moments, before the power surged."

Dagur nodded. "I felt it. Just as poor Brandur lit up like a torch, the magic suddenly felt more stable, 'cleaner' somehow, though it flooded through him as if a dam had burst."

"Perhaps that's something to consider." Nidhud had slipped up behind them so silently that Niklas did not hear his approach. "Before we decide this working failed utterly, I suggest we consider whether it was a matter of intensity rather than improper technique."

"Brandur won't be around to hear the answer," Niklas replied. "And I'll be damned if I'll let Blaine step into that labyrinth before you have it figured out."

He might have said more, although he knew speaking his mind to a room full of mages and *talishte* was likely unwise. But before he could go on, a soldier appeared at the mouth of the entrance tunnel, and a sound like thunder boomed overhead, sending down a fine shower of dust.

"We're under attack!" the soldier said. "General Theilsson— we need you."

Niklas drew a deep breath and nodded. "I'll be there," he said. He looked to the soldiers he had brought with him. They all looked shaken by what had transpired. "Stay here," he said. "Make sure no one gets down that tunnel."

He turned back to Dolan and Dagur. "Blaine doesn't have a *talishte* life span for you to figure this out," he warned. "And if he dies before the magic gets a new anchor, your power goes with him, so you'd best get this right soon."

Before they could answer, Niklas followed his soldiers up the tunnel, less concerned about the battle in front of him than the struggle waged by the men behind him.

"Report!" Niklas shouted as he broke out of the gloom of the tunnel and into the cold night air. At the first sign of attack, his soldiers lit the torches that ringed Mirdalur's courtyard. Keeping the area dark was the strategy when they hoped to go undiscovered, but now that the fight was on, mortal soldiers needed light.

"Soldiers incoming from the northwest," the guard who had fetched him replied.

"Whose?"

"Not sure, sir. The scouts said possibly Larska Hennoch's soldiers, by the look of them."

Niklas swore under his breath. "If it's Hennoch's men, then Pollard's behind it, even if he doesn't have the balls to be here himself. How many men—and do they have *talishte*?"

"That's where we're lucky, sir. Only about twenty-five."

That meant Niklas's troops outnumbered the intruders, especially with the *talishte* fighters Geir had supplied. "There'll be twice as many next time if any of these sons of bitches survive," Niklas said. "Tell the men, 'No quarter.' Find them and make sure none of them make it back to report."

"Aye, sir." The soldier sprinted off to pass the message. Niklas drew his sword and ran toward the action. From the look of it, a patrol had happened upon the activity at Mirdalur and decided to have a closer look. He set his jaw, determined to make it their last look.

Niklas took on one of the two attackers battling Ayers. "Not exactly what I had in mind tonight," Ayers muttered, blocking the advance of his opponent.

Niklas parried, setting the enemy soldier he battled back several paces with the force of his strikes. He was in a foul mood from the debacle in the ritual chamber, and the attack gave him someone to take it out on. His opponent's sword skills were adequate, but lacked the edge Niklas had gained in the bloody combat on the Meroven front. Now those skills combined with Niklas's rage, and he slashed his way through the enemy onslaught, giving no quarter. He spotted Geir and some of the *talishte* soldiers joining the fight, and hoped that would help make quick work of the attackers.

Off to one side, he glimpsed Carr battling a soldier twice his size. *He's supposed to be recuperating in the healers' tent, not getting himself killed out here on the field,* Niklas thought.

His opponent took advantage of Niklas's momentary distraction to land a gash on Niklas's shoulder. Niklas responded with a pounding series of blows, getting inside the man's guard more than once to open deep cuts on his chest, arm, and thigh. He swung once more, bringing his blade down with bone-splitting power across the soldier's wrist, severing his hand. The man froze with shock and Niklas thrust forward, sinking his blade deep into the soldier's chest.

He shook the dying man's body loose from his blade just in time to see Carr feint in one direction, only to land a lethal strike with the short sword in his left hand as the attacker misjudged his intentions. Carr's sword slashed across the soldier's belly, spilling shit and guts down the front of his stained trews. One more slash, and Carr drew his blade across the man's throat, adding a torrent of blood to the offal. The attacker slumped to the ground, and Carr stepped over his body to engage the next attacker.

Carr was holding his own, but it was clear to Niklas that Carr was not fully recovered. He was tiring, his strikes broader and off the mark, his gait almost drunken. Carr's opponent sensed the opportunity, and came at him fast. A series of quick, tight strikes meant to distract and disarm got inside Carr's guard more than once, opening bloody slashes down his arms.

Breathing hard, his face twisted into an angry grimace, Carr bellowed a war cry, coming after the enemy soldier in a rage of two-handed swings. The first swing cut the soldier's sword arm to the bone, while the second cleaved through his shoulder. Another swing caught him across the ribs, deep enough that Niklas could hear the steel skitter against bone. The soldier dropped his sword and fell to his knees. Carr struck again, taking the entire sword arm this time, and rammed his blade through the fallen man's throat.

"Carr! That's enough. Carr!" Niklas shouted as he closed the distance between them. Carr kept on slashing, landing blow after blow although the soldier lay dead and nearly dismembered. Carr stood over the body, bloodied to the elbows and spattered head to toe in gore, heaving for breath as the killing rage drained from him.

"Stand down, soldier. That's an order," Niklas snapped, pushing back his horror and focusing on the wild-eyed young man he had known all his life who now seemed a complete stranger.

Exhausted, his rage spent, Carr's swords dangled from his hands as he stared at the blood-soaked remains.

The battle was limping to an end. The area around Mirdalur's walls was littered with the bodies of enemy soldiers. Geir emerged from the tree line dragging two corpses by the arms. Ayers directed two of their men to work their way across the downed fighters, administering a deathblow. The night air stank of blood and sweat.

"Drop your swords, Carr," Niklas said. Carr remained motionless, eyes wide, puffing gusts of steam as he tried to catch his breath. After a delay, the crimson-stained blades dropped from Carr's hands, but Carr did not move.

"Do you know where you are?" Niklas asked, more concerned than ever.

"Mirdalur," Carr replied, his voice slightly slurred.

"You don't have to fight anymore tonight," Niklas said,

doing his best to reassure him. "The attackers are dead. You won. We won. It's over now."

"I got him," Carr said, staring at the butchered remains at his feet. "I got him."

Ordel came up behind Niklas. "Let me handle this," he murmured. Ordel whispered a word Niklas did not catch and made a subtle gesture, and Carr dropped to the ground, unconscious. Only then did Ordel stop to look at the carnage around them.

"Sweet Esthrane, did Carr—"

Niklas nodded. "Yes. I saw him do it, but there was no stopping him. If that wasn't a blood frenzy, I don't ever want to see one."

Ordel knelt beside Carr, feeling for a pulse. "He's alive. I see he got himself cut up again," he added with a sigh. "And we'd only just patched him back together."

"I'm afraid you'll have to mend him again," Niklas replied. "I don't know whether he just worked out his frustrations with a little more vigor than most, or whether I need to worry more about him than I already do," he said. "He wouldn't stop hacking," he added quietly. "He wasn't finished."

Behind them, Ayers had the matter well in hand, shouting orders and sending the soldiers to clean up the area. Geir returned with two other *talishte* to help, meaning the bodies would be disposed of promptly. Ordel sat back on his heels and looked at Carr's still form.

"I can heal the gashes," Ordel replied. "But what's driving him, making him reckless—I don't even know where to begin."

"He's not the first soldier to take things to extremes," Niklas replied.

"Have you seen anyone take things quite as far? Ever?" Ordel challenged.

Niklas looked away. "Once or twice. We all thought they

were madmen; maybe they were. If they wanted to die, they got their wish."

"I'm sorry, Niklas. I know you grew up with both Carr and Blaine, and I know you feel responsible for him, but it's out of your hands," Ordel said. "I can fix him up, and he'll hare off again. Unless you're ready to clap him in irons, that's what will happen as soon as he's well enough to walk. He'll go out on another mission, with or without permission, and one of these times, he won't come back."

Niklas let out a long, ragged breath. "I know that," he replied quietly. "But in a few days, I'm supposed to go up to Glenreith for Blaine and Kestel's wedding. I don't want to have to spoil the day by giving Blaine bad news."

Ordel grimaced. "Look at the bright side. Maybe Carr won't want to go with you. I suspect he won't be the most welcome guest, after the last time."

Niklas turned so that the wind swept past him, carrying the stench of death with it. "Blaine won't give up on him," he said. "Oh, the two of them will fight like wildcats, and Blaine's plenty sore at the way Carr's acted the fool, but he won't cut him off."

"Maybe he should."

Niklas nodded. "Maybe. But he won't." He wished the bitter cold wind could cleanse him, and knew that was too much to ask even of the gods. "Come on," he said finally. "Let's get him back to camp."

CHAPTER FIFTEEN

NEAR AS I CAN TELL, THE MAGIC IS BURNING YOU out, using up your reserves. Your body can't survive this for too long. It's not possible to get enough rest or food to make up for what it's taking," Zaryae said, standing back to have a look at Blaine. "So figure every day is a step closer to your grave until we can change the way the magic is anchored. Your bond with Penhallow will help, but the energy he can feed you through the *kruvgaldur* isn't enough to counter the drain."

"You're certain the magic is causing it?" Kestel asked sharply.

Zaryae grimaced. "From the signs I find, yes." She met Blaine's gaze. "So it's not something you can put off solving. You'll do no one a favor dying before your time."

"Can it be stopped?" Blaine asked. "Or slowed?" He wondered if he looked as tired and worn as he felt. It had been so much easier to blame the discomfort, fatigue, and headaches on the constant skirmishing and the storms than to think about them being a price to be paid for anchoring the magic. A steep price.

"That's what we're here to find out," Rikard replied. Since Dagur had left Glenreith to work with Niklas and the Knights,

Rikard was now the senior mage in charge. Thin, fussy, and short-tempered, he had been a mage in a noble house before the Great Fire. Rumor had it he survived by hiding in a barn, something Rikard hotly denied.

They were gathered at Glenreith, Blaine's lands, in the rooms he had outfitted for the mages' workshop. Glenreith had two manor houses: the original home, now largely in ruins from time and the effects of the Great Fire, and the new house, still several centuries old and damaged from the Cataclysm's toll. Little of the old, original home was still standing, but part of the first-floor wing remained, used for storage until Blaine reclaimed it for the mages.

The walls of the main room were stained from age and the elements. Glass had been replaced in the windows, and the floors had been scrubbed, but the rooms still smelled of disuse. The fireplace barely seemed to take the chill off the room. Several scarred worktables and a collection of mismatched stools and chairs gathered from around the manor furnished the rooms, together with a variety of lamps and lanterns. The mages' sleeping quarters were in the new manor, though Blaine saw they had set up cots in the second room for long workdays.

"You think a null-magic charm will help?" Blaine asked warily. "What if it knocks the magic loose again? Having it anchored is bad, but having it out of control is worse. We don't need that again."

"It will be out of control if we don't get the anchoring right and the strain of it kills you," Kestel reproved. "Or if someone decides to kill you to get rid of magic once and for all."

"How can magic 'null' magic?" Blaine asked.

"The same way a forest fire may be contained by starting another, controlled fire along its edge," Rikard replied. "The original fire can't 'jump' the second fire and the fire brigade has to be careful to make certain the new fire can't spread. Eventually, both fires run out of fuel and die out."

"A null charm counters magic with other magic," Treven Lowrey said, and his tone warned them he was about to launch into professorial discourse. He had not yet forgiven Rikard for being named senior mage, an honor Lowrey coveted. "But since the 'tamed' magic you've anchored is the source of the problem, perhaps a bit of 'wild' magic—properly contained— might be enough to blunt the effect of the anchoring."

Zaryae sighed at the two master mages' posturing and looked away. The other three mages, Artan, Nemus, and Leiv, busied themselves with their projects to avoid being dragged into the fight. By now, Blaine assumed, they should be used to it. Rikard and Lowrey seemed incapable of breathing the same air for more than ten minutes without sniping at each other.

"If the null charm works, it could blunt the effects of the magic until you can find a way to change how the power is anchored," Kestel said.

"How reliable are the manuscripts you used to create the null?" Zaryae asked suspiciously.

"It would take very careful adjustment   if it could be done at all," Artan mused. He was short and squat as a cistern, with a broad face and small, piggy eyes.

"A stasis charm, perhaps?" Nemus asked, joining the group. Long-limbed and jug-eared, Nemus loped across the room. "Maybe something that would shield Lord McFadden from magic used around him, while not disturbing the anchor itself."

Lowrey peered at Blaine over the top of his wire-rimmed spectacles. "Can you tell whether the workings we're doing here in the manor are affecting him?" he asked, glancing at Zaryae.

"Of course it's affecting him," Zaryae replied, tossing her dark braid over one shoulder as she spoke. "Just keeping the magic harnessed is part of the drain. Any magic that's done near him—large or small—makes it worse, and the closer it is, the harder it goes on him."

"I am sitting here, and I can hear you," Blaine interrupted drily. "And since I'm the poor bloke who has to live with the bond, I get a say in what we do about it," he added.

"Then, tell us what you want, Lord McFadden," Rikard said. "And we will endeavor to do it."

Blaine sighed. "Finding a different way to anchor the magic is the important part. I know that Dolan thinks he's onto something at Mirdalur, and maybe he is. But there are two parts. 'Where?' Dolan may have answered. 'How?' is the piece we don't seem to know yet—and time is running out."

"Quintrel was certain that the presence-crystals and the obsidian disks would be enough, together," Lowrey said.

"Quintrel was being controlled by a *divi*," Kestel retorted. "That means we can trust him even less than usual. Who knows what the *divi* really wants?"

"We had the disks at Valshoa, and it wasn't enough," Blaine replied. "The Wraith Lord is the only one who actually remembers the last time the magic was restored. They'd used the disks, but since he didn't help prepare the chamber, he told Dagur that he couldn't be certain other artifacts weren't involved."

Rikard held up a small lead box. "This is the null charm, or more correctly a dampening charm. It doesn't remove or block magic altogether. I tried it personally, to no ill effect, either while I wore it or when I removed it."

"We all tried it," Artan said. "Well, all of us except for him," he added with a glare toward Lowrey.

"It was essential to preserve someone in their unaltered condition," Lowrey said with a sniff. "I volunteered to forgo any beneficial effects for the sake of the experiment."

Blaine doubted that 'beneficial effects' had been uppermost in Lowrey's mind, but said nothing.

Lowrey rolled his eyes. "Here," he said. "Give it to me." He snatched the charm from Rikard and slipped his head through the leather loop that held it. Everyone stood in silence for a moment while Lowrey did a turn in place.

"See?" He said. "No harm done." He removed the charm and held it between his hands for a moment. "No negative energy at all," he said. He put the charm into the box and slipped it into his pocket.

"The point being, four—five—of us have tried the charm and suffered no harm," Rikard replied testily.

Zaryae nodded. "I can attest to that," she said. "I checked the mages who used it before and after they wore the charm. The charm lessened their magical ability, but didn't remove it completely. When they took the charm off, their power returned to its previous strength, and no one suffered ill effects."

"All right," Blaine said, reaching out his hand. "Let's get this over with. Give it to me."

Rikard clucked his tongue and shook his head. "Not quite like that, m'lord. Precautions must be taken."

He led them into a small room off the main work space. A circle had been marked with salt and rope in the center of the room. Blaine noted a variety of protective stones, crystals, and dried herbs hanging from the room's rafters, and the air smelled of burned sage.

"If you'll stand in the center of the circle—step over the warding, don't smudge it," Rikard warned, "then open the box and remove the charm. If you feel any untoward effects, replace the charm in the box and close it."

Zaryae stood just outside the circle. "I don't know what effect the null charm will have on my ability to sense your safety, but

I will watch over you the best I can," she said. "If something worries me, I'll signal. If I do, put the charm away."

Blaine nodded. Kestel touched his arm and gave a wan smile. "I'll keep an eye on the door. No one will bother us." He gave her hand a squeeze.

Rikard looked around. "Where's the charm?"

Lowrey withdrew the box from his pocket. "Not to worry," he said. "Step across the warding, and I'll hand it to Blaine."

Blaine squared his shoulders and took a deep breath, then stepped into the circle. Lowrey came close enough that his toes touched the line, and handed the box to Blaine, then backed away.

Blaine flipped the box open and withdrew the charm. His heart was pounding, and he had to think to slow his breathing. Nervous energy tingled through his skin, making him jumpy and sending his thoughts racing. It took conscious effort to be aware of how the magic felt, the tingling energy that coursed through his blood, a feeling that had become oddly familiar, and then he focused on what was going on outside the circle.

Zaryae was closest, watching him with concern, but so far she was making no gestures to indicate danger. Kestel stood to the side of the door, a blade in each hand, her back against the wall, eyes on Blaine within the circle. Lowrey had retreated until he was in the farthest corner of the room, watching Blaine as if he might burst into flame at any moment. Artan, Nemus, and Leiv stood a pace or two behind Zaryae at the three other quarters of the circle, intently watching to see what would happen.

"It's wrong," Zaryae said, eyes widening. "Blaine! Something's wrong. Close the box!" Her words were drowned out as Lowrey backed into a worktable full of metal bowls, sending them all scattering across the wooden floor in a cacophony. Nemus gestured for Rikard to look at one of the artifacts, which was pulsing with blue light. Artan stepped up to take Rikard's place.

For an instant, Blaine felt a release as the pressure of anchoring the magic lifted. The strain melted away, the tingling fire faded, and a sense of well-being filled him, clean and rejuvenating.

Without warning, the pressure returned, smothering and heavy. Blaine's heart raced, and he struggled to draw shallow breaths. His blood felt like it was on fire, energy coursing through his body. He stumbled, almost dropping the heavy leaded box. Outside the warded circle, Zaryae was calling to him and gesturing. Kestel started toward the circle, but Lowrey blundered into her way. Dimly, he heard them arguing.

The artifacts on the table suddenly activated. Some pieces flashed colored light, while others began to tremble or hum. Nemus, Leiv, and Rikard circled the table, doing their best to contain the errant objects.

Streaks of light crackled from the box and charm in Blaine's hand, sizzling across the room. Wood burst and glass shattered as the light flared, arcing in every direction. One of the bolts hit Artan and he fell, screaming, clutching for the seared skin of his back where his robes had been burned away.

The guards pounded at the door, but it was locked, a precaution to keep the ritual from being interrupted. Kestel and the others had thrown themselves to the floor to stay out of the way of the streaks of light, but Kestel was crawling toward the circle, trying to get to Blaine.

"The warding's broken!" she shouted.

Smoke and the tang of lightning filled the air in the room. Wind gusted in through the broken window. Another arc struck perilously close to Rikard, who shrieked and dove beneath the heavy worktable. Lowrey cowered in the farthest corner, watching through the space between his arms, which he had put up in front of himself to cover his face and head.

Zaryae crawled toward Rikard and grabbed him by the collar, hauling him out of his refuge. "Counter the magic!" she ordered, and hurled him toward the circle.

Blood thundered in Blaine's ears. His vision dimmed, limned in darkness. Chest heaving, he dropped to his knees, struggling to close the box. The heavy lead lid clanged shut, and Blaine collapsed, falling facedown on the wooden floor as the shouts around him faded into silence.

Blaine woke slowly, fighting off coldness as frigid as the winter sea. His body felt as leaden as the null charm's box, inert and too heavy to move. After the way his heartbeat had hammered in his head, it now felt sluggish, as if his blood were too thick to move easily. Breathing came easier, but every movement hurt. The headache was back, pounding and relentless. He yearned for the peaceful darkness, but it had receded beyond his grasp. Blaine lay still, not yet ready to try to open his eyes.

"He's coming around." Rikard sounded tired.

"Can you tell if the working did any damage?" Kestel barely controlled her anger. *She's angriest when she's frightened*, he thought.

"We'll know soon enough, when he wakes up," Rikard replied.

Blaine opened his mouth to say something in response, but all he managed was a groan. Opening his eyes was a struggle, but he managed to get them half-lidded, enough to see. He was back in his room at Glenreith, in the new mansion. Kestel paced the floor at the foot of his bed. Rikard stood on the other side, arms crossed, looking much less sure of himself than the last time Blaine had seen him. Lowrey watched from the other side of the room. Artan, Nemus, and Leiv were not present.

Kestel stopped pacing and turned to look at him. Her expression made it clear that if he did not recover, Rikard probably would not remain in good health. She took Blaine's hand. "He's warming up," she said, although Blaine himself still felt thoroughly chilled. "Heartbeat is steady," she added, pressing her fingers into the groove in Blaine's wrist. "Breathing isn't as shallow."

"I don't understand," Rikard muttered, and from the way he said it, Blaine bet that this was not the first time. "Five of us tried that null charm personally, in the same warded circle, under the same room protections."

"None of you were a Lord of the Blood, or were anchoring all the magic of the Continent," Kestel snapped. "That might account for the difference."

Rikard shook his head. "I don't know. Maybe. But we have no better way to test the artifacts, and at least we ruled out several much more dangerous approaches before Lord McFadden could get hurt."

"'More dangerous'?" Kestel's voice was strained. "His heart stopped. How does it get more dangerous?"

"The bickering can wait," Rikard chastised. "What matters is that he's stable, and getting stronger." He sighed. "The magic that holds the anchoring is back. For an instant, in the circle, it was gone. Now I can feel the magic flowing through him.

"And that's what I think caused the problem," Rikard went on. "For that instant, all that power, the wild *visithara* magic, was anchorless again, and then it surged to root itself, and the shock of it caused the reaction."

"Whatever caused it, we still don't have an answer, and Blaine can't go on like this forever," Kestel replied through gritted teeth. "So we need a different answer, and we need it fast."

"I know, I know." Rikard actually sounded contrite. "I was just so sure..." He shook his head. "I'll go back and have another look at the null charm, and then the manuscripts. We might have had the right idea, just not gotten the right charm or the best conditions." He gathered his cloak and opened the door to the hallway. "I'll let you know what I find."

It's so much easier to listen than to speak, Blaine thought. But once Rikard left, Kestel turned her full attention to him.

"That didn't go well." His voice was scratchy, and his mouth was dry, but he managed to get the words out.

Kestel laid a hand on his shoulder. "You didn't die. It could have gone worse."

"Where's Zaryae?" Blaine asked.

"In her room, resting," Kestel replied. "She said she didn't feel well. And she said to tell you she thinks the charm became corrupted." She sighed. "Zaryae's blaming herself. At the last minute, she had a vision of danger, but it was too late to stop what was happening." She shook her head. "I didn't want to say anything in front of Rikard, but tomorrow, I want her to take a look at that charm. I'd like to see what she can read from it."

Kestel let her fingers drift across his cheek. "Judith and Mari were in to see you," she said.

"I don't remember," Blaine murmured.

"Mari said that Dawe needs to talk to you, once you're up to it," Kestel added. "There's another big storm coming." She stood and stretched. "Zaryae is going to help the mages cast preservation spells on the provisions."

Blaine groaned as he shifted position, and Kestel looked concerned. "How do you feel?"

"Awful."

Kestel chuckled. "You keep giving us a scare."

"Me, too."

The door to the hallway opened and Niklas peered in. "Kestel, can I see you for a moment?"

She squeezed Blaine's hand. "I won't be long." She gave him a worried look. "Dolan had better be right about Mirdalur, and Rikard needs to figure out the magic, because things can't go on like this," Kestel fretted, and left with Niklas.

"It won't," Blaine replied, slipping back toward sleep. *It can't. Because we'll either fix it or I'll die.*

Blaine was half-asleep when he heard the click of the bolt thrown in the lock. He was groggy, and in the lee of the botched magic, it was hard to think clearly. Dimly, he remembered that Kestel was gone, but he strained in the gloom to make out the figure that stood near the door.

"Don't fight the magic," Lowrey said quietly. "You'll sleep soon enough."

"Not...going...to sleep," Blaine managed.

Lowrey gave him an unsettling smile. "Yes, you are," he said. "Don't blame Rikard for what happened. I changed the charm he gave you. It was supposed to kill you." He shrugged. "But since it didn't, here we are."

"Why?" Blaine asked hoarsely. He felt as if he were struggling through a haze.

"Vigus has no need for you since Dolan stole the artifacts and the attempts to kidnap you failed," Lowrey said, moving toward him. "He'd rather see you dead, and the magic gone wild again, than lose control of the anchor."

Lowrey pulled a long, thin knife from his robe. "Since magic alone didn't work the last time, we'll do this the old-fashioned way."

Blaine struggled to rise, but invisible hands pushed him back. His confusion was not lost on Lowrey. "You didn't think I had it in me, did you?" Lowrey mocked. "None of you. Not even Penhallow, I wager."

His expression turned ugly. "Lowrey, the lackey. Lowrey, the joke. You don't know how many times I wanted to show all of you what I could really do."

"You...Quintrel...all along," Blaine whispered.

"Very good," Lowrey sneered. "You're smarter than you look. Took you long enough. Vigus said it would."

Blaine threw himself to one side, managing to fall off the bed on the side opposite Lowrey. Lowrey swore at the inconvenience. "You don't have to suffer. I just want to finish what I started. When your heart stops, you'll barely feel it."

Blaine struggled against the magic that held him. Lowrey had increased the strength of the invisible bonds, so that even rolling was beyond what Blaine could manage now. Lowrey reached the bed, and circled it. A few more steps, and it would be over.

The door to Blaine's room blew apart, sending a hail of splinters flying. Zaryae and Rikard stood outside, with Kestel a step behind and Niklas running to catch up.

"What in the name of the gods?" Lowrey blustered.

Kestel's hand flicked, and two daggers embedded themselves into Lowrey's chest.

Lowrey snarled and sent a blast of power toward the spot where Kestel had been standing. Zaryae and Rikard blocked the strike. Kestel was gone, moving in a blur as she dove and rolled, coming up behind Lowrey and sinking a shiv deep into his back. Her right hand moved too fast to follow, drawing a blade across Lowrey's throat. She jerked her shiv free and pushed Lowrey forward. His head lolled to one side, and his body collapsed to the floor in a pool of blood.

Rikard raised his hand, and an arc of power struck Lowrey's body, causing it to shrivel and blacken as if burning on a pyre. "That's for Artan," he muttered.

Kestel crossed to the empty bed and circled it. "Blaine's alive! He's over here, on the floor."

Free of Lowrey's geas, Blaine was struggling to his feet as Kestel bent to help him up. Niklas and Rikard reached him seconds later. "You all right?" Niklas asked, looking him up and down for signs of blood.

"Almost wasn't," Blaine rasped. Lowrey's magic no longer constrained him, but he felt the rough power of the botched working in every muscle and sinew.

He dropped heavily into the bed as the world around him spun. "How did you know?" he asked.

Bloodied to her elbows, Kestel sauntered over to Lowrey's cloak near the door and wiped her blades clean. Then she walked over to the washstand and calmly rinsed the blood from her arms.

"Thank Zaryae," she said. "Niklas came to get me because he thought Judith was calling for me. But when we got to the kitchen, Judith said she wasn't. That's when Zaryae came looking for us because she had a premonition, and we found the door to your room was locked from inside."

"Quintrel sent him," Blaine said, closing his eyes. "If Quintrel couldn't own the anchor, he wanted to destroy it."

"Figures," Niklas muttered. He glanced toward Kestel. "So all those stories I heard, about Falke the Assassin, they were true."

Kestel's lips quirked in a smile. "You bet. And the best stories never got told."

"I'm really, really glad you're watching his back," Niklas said. "But to spare you some of the trouble, I'll post two guards at all times outside the room."

"I'm not leaving here without Mick," Kestel said, flopping down on the other side of the bed.

"We'll make sure the room is warded—properly, this time," Rikard added. "And now that we know Lowrey tampered with the null charm, we'll start again. I do think it will work—when we don't have someone working against us."

"Thank you," Blaine whispered, too tired to keep his eyes open. "I didn't think I was going to make it out of that one." Kestel might have responded, but by then, Blaine was asleep.

Blaine insisted on sitting up the next day, and forced himself to eat the food Judith sent for him. Dawe Killick came in on the heels of the servant who took away the breakfast dishes.

"Good to see you awake and breathing," Dawe said with a grin. Tall and lanky with dark hair and a lopsided grin, Dawe had been one of Blaine's inner circle in Velant and as a colonist in Edgeland.

"Good to *be* awake and breathing," Blaine replied. His voice had lost its scratchiness, and the all-over achiness had faded, but Zaryae had cautioned him to rest, and for once, he did not feel like arguing.

"I'll make it easy on you," Dawe offered. "You sit there while I talk. Nod if you like it, shake your head if you don't. That way Kestel can't have my head for bothering you on your sickbed."

Blaine chuckled. "Go ahead."

"Whenever I haven't been in the forge, I've been working with Edward and one of Niklas's lieutenants on getting provisions," Dawe said. "We've sent teams of soldiers to gather whatever seed, tools, livestock, and food was left behind. And when I'm not forging weapons, I've been working on hoes, plows, and the other tools we'll need to get crops in the ground and tend them till harvest."

"Thank Charrot," Blaine said. *I'm the lord of the manor, but I've been so busy with war, I haven't been here long enough to see to the things that need to be done so we can eat,* Blaine thought.

"I'm much more useful here at Glenreith in the forge making swords than out on the field swinging one around," Dawe said. "I have no illusions about my skill as a warrior." Dawe grinned. "But I'm getting better at brewing whiskey, which Mari and I have been working on." Dawe sat back in his chair. "It's going to be a while before we see good wine again, considering what the Great Fire and all the fighting did to the vineyards. But Mari's been helping Edward and some of the servants with plans to make wine out of whatever fruit and berries we can grow or gather, come harvest.

"We haven't had a lot of grain to spare for ale, but with luck, a good harvest will fix that," Dawe continued. "But we did scavenge beets and potatoes and we've managed to brew up some drinkable liquor.

"If we can keep it up, we'll not only have wine, ale, and liquor for our own use, but it's something we can trade for anything we can't make." He sighed. "Until the crops are in and producing, we don't have much to barter with."

"What about the forge?" Blaine asked.

Dawe grinned. "Niklas's lieutenant found some soldiers with blacksmithing experience. He sends them up to me here a few days a week to help forge weapons and tools, and I go down to the camp the other days to help the farrier shoe the horses."

Blaine nodded to keep up his side of the conversation, moving gingerly to keep his headache from getting worse.

"We're not the only ones trying to get crops in the field and rebuild," Dawe went on. "We've been sending soldiers out to the villages and farms on your lands, to warn them and help them prepare for the storms. If their crops and livestock get destroyed, we won't be able to grow enough on the manor's fields to supply the household, the army, and the surrounding villages, too.

"Been shoring up our own barns, too. Have to, with how bad the storms are, and how often they come. I sure hope you can fix that somehow, Mick," Dawe added, "because it's bad, and it's getting worse." He brightened. "And then there are the plans for the wedding, but Kestel and Judith swore me to secrecy."

"Everything set?" Blaine asked.

Dawe nodded. "Everything's ready. Now we just need to get the groom back on his feet." Dawe sobered. "One thing you should know, Mick. Carr's back. Just got in last night, looking like he'd been dragged by a wagon, but he's here. He's acting cagey, but I don't think Niklas knows where he is."

He looked worried. "Be careful. Even Judith's nervous, although she won't send him away. Kestel's not letting him out of her sight. Even so, watch your back around him, Mick."

"Thanks for the warning. I'll watch out."

"I know he's your brother, but I wouldn't count on that if I were you," Dawe cautioned.

I don't, for anything but trouble, Blaine thought.

CHAPTER
SIXTEEN

"IF I DON'T COME BACK, KILL THEM." VEDRAN POL-lard glanced at the hostages, and then at the two soldiers he had brought with him to the meeting. Two bound men knelt on the exposed stone of what had once been a granary threshing floor. Roden Holcumb was Torinth Rostivan's second-in-command, and Nias Dovar was Karstan Lysander's right-hand man. Both had been given as sureties for the negotiation that was about to begin. And both men stood a good chance of dying if the meeting did not go as planned. It was a simple and ruthless way to assure that none of the participants tried to eliminate the others while they were all gathered together.

"Don't take too long. I get bored easily," Piet replied. Pollard glared at him.

Pollard had given up Nilo Jansen and Larska Hennoch as his hostages for this meeting, and while he was ambivalent about Hennoch, he would hate to lose Nilo. Rostivan had also given one hostage to Pollard and one to Lysander, so that all three of the warlords had a pressing reason to act in good faith.

"Right now, their safety is our ticket out of here, so I expect them to be completely undamaged unless things go badly wrong," Pollard said, the warning clear in his voice.

Rieulf and Piet, two of Pollard's best soldiers, were part of the small personal security contingent permitted by the terms of the meeting rules. They bound the hostages and removed their weapons, then gestured for them to sit, and took up places on either side of the men.

"It could be a trap," Rieulf said.

The thought had occurred to Pollard numerous times on the journey. "It could," he allowed. "Which is why I suspect all three of us have mages watching with far-sight, and sharp-shooters on the perimeter. I'd wager that trust isn't big for any of us," Pollard replied.

He pulled his cloak around him and looked across the open plain. It was flat and featureless for as far as the eye could see. In the distance, Pollard could make out a gray line around the outskirts of the meeting area, out of archer range. Those were the backup troops, in case something went wrong. He assumed that the other warlords had armed their men to the teeth as he had done, and he further assumed that the other two would cheat, as he had also done. He hoped the reinforcements were not necessary. Things could get messy.

Long ago, a large granary had stood on this ground. Large stone slabs were now all that remained of the storage barns and threshing floors. Everything else was long gone. The land was situated close to the boundaries of all three of the represented warlords, a wasteland of little economic or strategic importance, and hence sparsely populated and unfortified. It was as close to neutral ground as could be found in Donderath.

Karstan Lysander stood in the center of the cordoned-off area, large and imposing. He was not a handsome man by any stretch of the imagination, nor could even vast sums of money make him so. To Pollard's eye, he guessed that he and Lysander were close to the same age, old enough to be very dangerous. Lysander stood half a head taller than Pollard and twice as broad, a bull of a man, who looked like he was accustomed to getting his way through size and sheer will.

Torinth Rostivan was just a bit shorter than Lysander, though likely a decade younger. He was built solidly, with intelligent dark eyes and short, graying brown hair. He was pox-scarred, and missing part of his left ear, and he wore the disfigurement like a mark of valor. Rostivan was reputed to have be a successful smuggler before the Meroven War, and looked the part.

"We're here," Pollard said, lifting his chin. He met Lysander's gaze and then looked to Rostivan. "And we're freezing our asses off in this wind. Let's make this quick."

"I want the Arkala twins dead," Lysander said.

"So, kill them." Rostivan shrugged. Kaleb and Johan Arkala had carved out a piece of northern Donderath south of the Riven Mountains and north of what had been the kingdom's major east-west trade route. Before the Cataclysm, that land would have been valuable for the traders and caravans that traveled its boundaries and for the mines in the foothills of the tall mountains. Now its chief value lay in the fact that it had been secured out of the area otherwise controlled by the three warlords.

"At the moment, the bulk of my forces are keeping the Solveigs and Verner busy," Lysander snapped.

"Send your rabble against them," Pollard replied, referring to the Tingur. "Just like you've sent them against Westbain and Castle Reach. Your forces are the largest."

"And stretched the thinnest," Lysander replied. "It's time the two of you start holding up your part of this alliance."

"And what do we get out of it?" Rostivan demanded. "Will

we share in the Arkalas' land? I doubt they have much else of value."

Lysander rounded on Rostivan. "You get to live, without my soldiers hounding you night and day," he growled. "Our truce means you don't have to watch your back every moment. And it means that when the time is right to bring down McFadden and Penhallow, as well as the Solveigs and Verner, we all benefit from the spoils."

Rostivan glowered. It was clear he was used to giving orders, not taking them. His fists balled at his sides, and his face flushed with anger. Lysander regarded him coolly, as if daring Rostivan to make a move.

"Gentlemen, please," Pollard intervened. "The Arkalas are hardly a prize worth fighting over. They're a mere annoyance, a thorn in the foot." Diplomacy came hard to Pollard, but years at court meant he could manage a truce, especially when his eye was on a prize. Right now, Rostivan and Lysander both had larger forces than his men and Hennoch's combined, and if anyone could break Blaine McFadden, it would be these two warlords. Until Reese managed an escape, keeping Lysander and Rostivan focused on McFadden's threat was Pollard's best chance of success, and he had no intention of seeing it slip away in a pissing contest.

"So why don't your men attack?" Rostivan demanded.

Pollard shrugged. "We will. But I suggest that an even better solution would be to team up against them," he said, allowing his lips to curve in a devious smile. "You've made an alliance with mages," Pollard said with a glance toward Rostivan. "Try them out against a quarry where the stakes are low. It might be wise. Vigus Quintrel was never known to be dependable. Best to know early on if you've been sold a pig in a poke."

He saw anger glimmer in Rostivan's eyes at the suggestion

that he might have been unwise. Just as quickly, the anger subsided—suspiciously quickly, Pollard thought, for a man with as high an opinion of himself as Rostivan was said to have.

"I don't see what Quintrel has to do with this," Rostivan countered.

Pollard sighed. "Word has it you've made a bargain with Quintrel and his rogue mages. Sure, he has a reputation, but have you actually seen what they can do in battle?"

Rostivan sneered. "Enough to kick your ass and fry your biter master at Valshoa."

Pollard had expected the insult. "Actually, Quintrel was locked away with McFadden trying to bring back the magic. He had almost nothing to do with the battle itself. Lord Reese was injured by the Knights of Esthrane, and fire bombs sent by McFadden's allies." He raised an eyebrow. "So really, no one actually knows whether Quintrel can deliver on his promises or not."

Again, Rostivan's temper looked about to get the best of him, when he took a deep breath and regained control. Moderation was not something for which Torinth Rostivan was known, and two such incidents with sufficient and deliberate provocation made Pollard suspicious.

Pollard nearly missed the glimmer of light. He caught a glimpse at the edge of his vision, something beneath Rostivan's tunic that sparked with light for just a second, then fell dark again. Lysander did not seem to notice. Pollard might have dismissed it had he not thought Rostivan's behavior to be suspicious.

There's something off about him, Pollard thought. *And I know something about being controlled by my master. I wonder if dear old Rostivan has a geas on him. It would be like Quintrel, from what I've heard. And the dumb bastard doesn't even suspect.*

The thought of Rostivan being played for a fool lightened Pollard's mood despite the biting wind and dropping temperatures.

"So how about it?" Pollard challenged. "Why not put your mages to the test, and my soldiers will sweep up the scraps?" He had annoyed Rostivan enough, so giving him a sop did not bother Pollard. Not if he got what he wanted. And right now, from the look on Lysander's face, Pollard could see that he was gaining points for getting Rostivan to deliver results Lysander desired.

"Suits me," Rostivan replied, and Pollard guessed that meant it suited Quintrel as well. Rostivan looked at Lysander as if attacking the Arkalas was his own idea. "I wouldn't be surprised if my army alone is enough to destroy the Arkalas, but if there's anything left, Pollard and Hennoch are welcome to handle the cleanup. I think you'll see just what a valuable ally I've made in Quintrel and his mages."

For an instant, Pollard's pride burned, but rationality quickly won out. *Lysander is the tool, not the craftsman,* Pollard reminded himself. *Rostivan even more so. They'll keep McFadden hemmed in while we wait out Reese's fortunes and rebuild my army. If we're lucky, by the time my troops are back up to full force, Lysander and Rostivan will have done all the hard jobs. Then all that remains is getting rid of them.*

Lysander looked at Rostivan. "You brought your soldiers against McFadden, the Solveigs, and Verner at the Citadel of the Knights of Esthrane. What did you learn?"

Rostivan shrugged. "Together, they're formidable. That's one of the reasons I was open to this alliance. Tormod Solveig is a necromancer, although how great his power is, I'm not sure."

Lysander raised an eyebrow. "We knew he was a mage. But he's been tight-lipped about the type of magic." He looked to

Pollard. "Can a necromancer harm your *talishte*? If so, their use to me is limited."

Pollard shook his head. "*Talishte* are not dead, they're undead. The magic of the Dark Gift animates them. The Solveigs have far more to fear from *talishte* soldiers than the other way around."

Lysander regarded Pollard skeptically. "We shall see," he said. "What of McFadden?"

Pollard shrugged. "His army is growing, and Niklas Theilsson is an able general. With the backing of Voss and Penhallow, they pose a serious threat. With the additional support of the Solveigs and Verner—and the Wraith Lord's meddling—he's your most dangerous adversary."

To focus Lysander and Rostivan on eliminating McFadden, Pollard could set aside his pride, at least for a while. Long enough to get what he wanted. *With luck, they'll not only destroy McFadden and his allies, they'll destroy each other at the same time, leaving the field open for us.*

"We're agreed, then," Lysander said. "The bulk of my forces will move north, toward the Solveigs. The Tingur will continue to harry McFadden's allies where they can. Their destructiveness is unpredictable, but damaging enough that the enemy has no choice except to divert resources to protect themselves."

Rostivan nodded. "I'll lead the attack against the Arkalas, then join forces with you against Verner and McFadden."

"We'll finish up with whatever you leave behind of the Arkalas, and watch your flank," Pollard said. "And my offer of *talishte* fighters remains open. You can be certain McFadden will have *talishte* among his troops."

Lysander thought for a moment, then gave a nod. "Very well. Send me no more than a dozen, and make sure they understand not to feed from my troops."

Pollard regarded him coolly. "They're not dogs. Your troops have nothing to fear."

Lysander shrugged. "Perhaps not, if your master can so easily be taken prisoner and held against his will."

Pollard bristled, then brought his temper under control. *I need Lysander. For now. Later, the 'dogs' can feed at will, once we have what we want.*

"I'd like my men back, unharmed," Pollard said, since the meeting was clearly at an end.

"All the hostages will be returned before anyone leaves the area," Lysander said. "Have your soldiers send the hostages into the center area, so that everyone may see all six men alive and well." He gave a curt nod. "We each have our orders. Let's get to it."

Despite his vow to keep his pride and his temper in check, Pollard was fuming as he walked back to his men. *Lysander is just as much rabble as his Tingur,* Pollard thought, striding across the dry grass. *When the reckoning comes, it will be very sweet.*

His return was the signal for the two hostages to be released. Pollard watched them walk toward the center of the field, and kept an eye on Nilo and Hennoch, assuring himself that they were both unharmed.

"Any signal from the mages?" Pollard asked. Not all of his mages were *talishte*, and he had brought two of his far-seers along with the personal guard, dressed as soldiers, to keep watch and alert him to the threat of ambush.

Rieulf shook his head. "We've been watching, but there's been no signal."

Pollard let out a long breath. "Very well." He looked to Piet, a mage with the ability to scan minds at a distance. "What did you learn?"

Piet's gaze scanned the waiting soldiers around the meeting circle as each group waited for their hostages to rejoin them. "We're beyond the range for my most accurate impressions," he said quietly. "So I can't tell you exactly whose thoughts I scanned, although I can separate the impressions by which group they belonged to."

"Yes, yes—just tell me what you heard."

Piet chuckled. "What I 'heard' from Rostivan's troops was impatience, anger, annoyance at Lysander for an alliance they consider of less than equal partners."

Pollard nodded. "What else?"

Piet considered for a moment. "Lysander's men, on the other hand, are quite certain they are the victors of this arrangement, and some of them are already counting their spoils." He shook his head. "Rostivan's men are loyal because they believe him to be a competent leader with a good chance of success. With Lysander's troops, it's different. Perhaps he has a bit of charm magic himself. They look on him as a god, swoon at his orders, and consider themselves lucky to serve him."

"No wonder he's been effective drawing the Tingur to his cause," Pollard muttered. "Let's see how much they 'swoon' when the time comes to clip his wings."

Nilo and Hennoch were nearly back by now, and Pollard wished they would hurry. His wounds from Reese made it difficult to move without wincing, and only his steel will kept him from betraying his pain. Beneath his armor, his skin burned from the tormenting rash, which grew worse with sweat and the chafing of armor. Pollard wanted nothing more than to go back to his rooms at Solsiden, drink a whiskey, and see if Kerr could do anything to ease his suffering.

"Let's not do that again, shall we?" Nilo said, still rubbing his wrists. Pollard could see the rope burn. Hennoch looked ready to fight, and Pollard was certain the indignity of being a hostage galled him, especially given his son's precarious situation.

"My apologies for the inconvenience," Pollard said with a trace of sarcasm. "We got what we wanted. Lysander believes McFadden and his allies to be the main threat. Rostivan will lead the assault on the Arkalas, and we come in behind them to take care of the stragglers, minimizing the danger to our troops."

"They think we're weak," Hennoch growled. "That's why they left the easy job to us."

Pollard chuckled. "When it's to our advantage, they can think what they like. Our forces are reduced from what they were, what they will be again. In the meantime, we need to conserve our strength. Let Rostivan and Lysander take the losses and clear the path. I'll take dented pride and live soldiers if the alternative is bragging rights and a pile of corpses."

Hennoch glowered, but did not contradict him, perhaps making a similar bargain to assure his son's safety.

As quickly as the group convened, they scattered, though it seemed to Pollard that the ride back to Solsiden was interminable. Every movement pained Pollard as the armor rubbed against his wounds. He could hear Reese screaming in the back of his mind, and he doubted the impression was imagined. Nilo said nothing, but Pollard was sure his second suspected. Pollard was adamant that Hennoch should know nothing of his weakness, and so he forced himself to sit tall on his horse, and move as if nothing was wrong.

It won't do for Hennoch to get any ideas, Pollard thought. *We need him, and the only hold I have is fear.*

Several candlemarks later, when Pollard and his men had returned to Solsiden, Vedran Pollard stared into the fireplace as he sipped his whiskey. It dulled the pain, a little. Of late, that was the best he could hope for. Kerr had treated his wounds and bandaged him, and a warm dinner was some recompense for the cold day afield.

He and Nilo had been over the events of the day during supper, and despite the fact that they both agreed it had been a coup for their side, Pollard found he could not muster a celebratory mood.

Far too much left undone, too many places where the road could fork before we reach the destination, he thought. Age and experience had taught him to wait until a victory was firmly in hand before declaring the winner. All too often, the outlook could shift in a matter of moments. *I prefer reasonable doubt to false certainty,* he thought, taking another drink and letting the liquor burn down his throat. *Safer in the long run.*

A knock at the door startled him. "What now?" he snapped, setting aside his drink and rising. Kerr opened the door, his expression apologetic.

"M'lord Pollard, two of Lord Reese's men to see you."

Pollard cursed silently, aware that *talishte* hearing would pick up even a muttered expletive. He looked up as two *talishte* strode into the room.

"Vika and Demian," Pollard said. He intentionally made eye contact, knowing that they disliked the fact that his *kruvgaldur* bond to their maker meant he could not be glamoured by them. "I'd wondered if you had gone into hiding."

Vika looked the older of the two, though Pollard knew they were each centuries old. Vika had been the wastrel son of a minor noble three hundred years ago, before Reese selected him to be among his courtiers. Demian had been a soldier, the younger son of a prominent noble house. His turning had come on the battlefield, when Reese had brought him across as reward for how fiercely he fought despite his wounds. Pollard knew that both men were among Reese's inner circle within his brood, and he was equally certain their appearance here was not to inquire about his health.

"You've heard about the ruling?" Vika asked.

Pollard nodded. "The question is, can it be overturned?"

Uninvited, Vika and Demian moved farther into the room, and Pollard moved to stand by the fireplace, partly for warmth and in part because it encouraged the two *talishte* to keep their distance. Some of Reese's get had made it clear that while they accepted the need for human collaborators, they considered them mere servants. Reese himself swung between treating Pollard as a valued partner and not hiding the fact that Pollard continued to exist at Reese's sufferance. Pollard was unsure to which group his visitors belonged, and was not in the mood to take chances.

"Overturned?" Vika said. "Unlikely. The Elders aren't in the habit of reconsidering their opinions."

"But the Elders are not of one mind," Demian added. "We hear that there is dissention among the lords. It's said that the vote was very close, and several members of the council were not pleased with the outcome."

Pollard gestured toward the two chairs that faced the fireplace, and the men sat down.

"Tell me." Pollard leaned against the wall and crossed his arms.

"The dealings of the Elders are not usually shared with mortals," Vika replied.

Pollard scowled at him. "After serving your maker for as long as I have, I'm no longer completely mortal. And since you came to me, I assume there was a purpose. If I'm to serve my lord, I need information."

Vika nodded. "Lord Reese has supporters among the Elders. We have heard that there is a schism among the Elders. Some would see the council disband entirely, believing it serves no purpose as the kingdom now stands."

"Would that help or harm our cause?" Pollard asked. Court politics had been difficult enough to follow. *Talishte* politics was even more convoluted, especially when the grudges could stretch over centuries.

"Word has come to us from some of the old *talishte* that the fortress where Reese is imprisoned can be breached," Demian said. "The Elder who serves as his jailer will not change his mind, but he cannot hope to stand against several of the other Elders if they make their move."

"And will they?" Pollard challenged. He was tired and cold and his body ached from wounds that were not his own. He was having a bad day, and the two uninvited guests were first in line to bear the brunt of it. "From what I've seen of *talishte* politics, it's every man for himself. Why would they bother?"

Vika chuckled. It was not a pleasant laugh. "Who's to say that freeing Lord Reese would not be in the best interests of these Elders?" he asked. "Penhallow and the Wraith Lord have made enemies among some of the old ones with their support for McFadden. Their king making has stirred old anger." He clucked his tongue. "The kind of king they would place on a throne would not align with our interests."

Pollard swore. "Of course not. Penhallow likes giving mortals real power. He wants them to limit us. I don't doubt that doesn't sit well with the Elders."

"Those with the power to attempt to free Lord Reese are biding their time," Demian said. "The more that internal fighting weakens the mortal factions, the greater the likelihood our side will prevail." He leveled a gaze at Pollard. "Your role in this is to ensure that the other warlords are too weak to pose a danger to Lord Reese when he returns."

"If you'd been paying attention, you would know that is exactly what I've been doing," Pollard snapped. "I've set forces in motion that should set the other warlords at each other's throats. It won't be long."

Vika nodded. "Very good."

"Are Reese's get in any shape to fight?" Pollard challenged. "I understood that damage to the maker harmed those he brought across."

Demian looked uncomfortable, as if Pollard had ventured into something he did not wish to discuss. Vika merely nodded. "Our lord suffers greatly," he said. "And those of us marked by him suffer with him, until he can be freed." His pointed look made it clear that Vika knew exactly what kind of damage Reese's imprisonment had caused for Pollard, and likely shared it.

He's also got the talishte *stamina to bear it,* Pollard thought darkly. *And while my bond with Reese has made me harder to kill, it's not the same as full* talishte *strength.*

"What would you ask of me, to help you free Reese?" Pollard asked.

"Be ready," Vika warned. "It would be good to weaken the mortal armies as much as possible, because if Lord Reese should succeed with his escape, it may plunge the *talishte* into civil war."

CHAPTER
SEVENTEEN

"WE NEVER SAID WE WERE BATTLE MAGES," Carensa muttered. She pulled her cloak close around her. Guran and Jarle rode with her, along with three more mages, all of them handpicked to accompany the army. The rest of the mages remained at Rostivan's Torsford headquarters to finish setting up the University.

Guran's ability of far-sight was a classic battlefield skill and had recently been put to the test when he accompanied Rostivan to a parlay with the other warlords. Jarle could manipulate objects at a distance. Carensa's ability to translate might be useful. Holgir, a big man with the soulful look of a poet, was a weather mage, though his skill lay more with predicting storms than causing or stopping them. Tall, skinny Dag was good with illusion. Gunvar was an enhancer, able to strengthen the magic of those around him. Carensa could not fault Rostivan's choices, though she heartily wished she had not been among those selected.

"A copper for your thoughts," Guran asked.

Carensa mustered up a halfhearted smile. "Trying not to

think about what it is we're supposed to do when we get to where we're going."

Each of the mages wore a cuirass. Carensa had two wicked-looking knives. Dag carried a sword, and looked as if he knew how to use it. Jarle and Guran both had long, curved knives. Gunvar carried a bow and a slingshot. Holgir's ax was strapped to his saddle. Even so, Carensa hoped they were as far as possible from the actual fighting.

"Rostivan assured us that we won't be riding into battle," Guran said.

Jarle fixed Guran with a look. "You mean, Quintrel directed Rostivan not to take us into the fight." Rostivan wore the amulet Quintrel had given him, one Quintrel had promised the warlord assured success in battle and personal protection. And for as long as the *divi* in Quintrel's corrupted artifact found Rostivan useful, those promises were probably true, Carensa thought. In the meantime, she and the other mages were Quintrel's spies, sent to make sure Rostivan did not try to remove the amulet or change the agreement.

"What would happen, if someone removed a charm like that?" Carensa asked, being intentionally vague in her phrasing. She glanced around to make sure none of the others were listening.

"It can't be removed—without consequences—unless the *divi* lets go," Guran replied quietly.

"What kind of consequences?"

"Dire ones."

Carensa shivered, and returned to the original topic. "Rostivan may not intend to take us to the battle, but the fighting may bring itself to us," Carensa replied. She paused. "Do you know anything about the Arkala twins?"

"I've heard a little," Gunvar replied. "No idea whether it's true. I heard they were traders, maybe smugglers, before the war. Supplying weapons to both sides, and making a handsome profit."

"Stands to reason that they might become warlords," Jarle replied. "But are they looking to expand their territory, or just hold on to their land? Because Rostivan definitely wants to own as much of northern Donderath as he can get."

It seemed to Carensa that they had barely set up their tent when Rostivan strode through the entrance, followed by a lieutenant.

"The troops move out at daybreak. I'll expect you to be awake before then, and ready," Rostivan snapped. "I didn't bring you out here for you to sit on your asses. Quintrel promised me you could help me win battles."

"What exactly are you expecting of us?" Jarle asked.

Rostivan glowered at him. "Scrying, for one thing. I want to know where the Arkalas are before we strike. They're like rats, always scurrying out of reach."

Up close, Rostivan was even more imposing than what Carensa had viewed from afar. He was taller than any of the mages except for Holgir, broad-shouldered and strong. His face bore the scars of old pox, and one ear was missing a chunk, like an alley cat who had been in too many fights to count. Rostivan had a cunning look, and a hard set to his chin.

"Where do you want me to look?" Guran asked.

Rostivan glared at him. "Tell me where the Arkalas' troops are, how far away. I want to know how many tents in his camp, how large a force, anything at all that might give us an advantage."

Guran completed the warding and walked over to the scrying bowl. He closed his eyes, whispering his words of focus.

Then he opened his eyes and leaned forward, staring intently into the still water of the bowl. No one spoke. Even Rostivan watched with cautious interest. Carensa could glimpse fleeting images in the water, but scrying was not her gift.

After a time, Guran stood and turned toward Rostivan. "There is a large encampment. I saw a field of tents, and many men on horseback."

"Can you tell the size of their troop strength?" Rostivan interrupted impatiently.

Guran shook his head. "No, but from what I saw, our forces appear well matched."

Rostivan frowned, obviously unhappy with the vagueness of Guran's answer. "What else?"

"I saw what might be catapults, but I can't be certain," Guran replied. "It doesn't work like a telescope."

Rostivan's features darkened. "Then try again. I need to know what we're going up against."

Guran met Rostivan's gaze. "I can try again, but there is no guarantee that I'll see anything more than I saw before. Magic isn't precise."

"You've given me no more than I could get from a scout," Rostivan growled. "Quintrel promised me that you could provide me with superior information."

Guran bent over the scrying bowl once again. This time, Gunvar stood behind him with a hand on his shoulder, enhancing the magic. The water grew darker, like spilled ink. Carensa saw fear on Gunvar's face, and he lifted his hand from Guran's shoulder, breaking their connection. Still, Guran stared into the bowl, entranced.

Guran suddenly straightened and began to speak in a clipped, guttural language that was not the common tongue of Donderath.

"What's he saying?" Rostivan demanded.

Carensa let her magic flow toward Guran. "It's a warning," she said. "From the Arkalas. They warn us to leave now, before we die."

Gunvar reached over and tipped the edge of the scrying bowl, breaking the connection. Guran slumped to the floor.

Rostivan's expression hardened into determination. "I'm not going to let those upstarts get the better of us. Be ready to ride at dawn." He swept from the tent, with the lieutenant a step behind.

Gunvar laid Guran out on the floor. "How is he?" Carensa asked.

Guran gave a low moan. "I feel like someone has been poking at my brain with a pike," he muttered.

"We've got to be careful," Jarle said. "The Arkalas have strong mages, too. And like it or not, we're now enemy targets."

"Are the Arkalas waiting for us?" Jarle asked as the mages climbed to their hilltop outpost overlooking the battlefield.

"They know we're coming," Guran said. "Their mages have been watching."

Their equipment was simple: a lightweight folding table for a workspace, and the implements and artifacts they had been willing to carry in their packs. Five soldiers made the journey with them. At the top of the hill, the soldiers gathered large stones for archers' blinds.

Dag warded the top of the hill with sage and salt. He spoke to the winds at the four quarters, and set an illusion that made it easier to look away from the hilltop than to see it clearly.

"I'm not sure what good I can do," Carensa fretted. "Not much chance for needing a translation up here."

Jarle shrugged. "Count yourself lucky."

Carensa found a place to stand near the crest of the hilltop beside a large oak tree. In the valley, the two forces arrayed against each other. The land between their hilltop and the Arkalas' camp was fairly flat, with the Arkala camp to the north and by a wide creek to the west. Tall grass and scrub bushes covered the ground, dry and brown from the winter. The snow was gone, but the ground was frozen solid.

Dag walked over. "Learn anything?"

Carensa nodded. "Look at the camp. I don't think the Arkalas intended to dig in and make it a permanent holding. There aren't many buildings, no stables or large corrals." In the distance, Carensa heard the sound of trumpets. "It's starting."

Jarle had moved to the edge of the warding. He looked out over the battlefield, selecting his targets. "Let's see what I can do," he murmured.

Jarle concentrated on a stand of trees that lined the road between the enemy camp and the battlefront. He held out one hand, palm open, his face tight with focus. He made a sudden fist, then wrested his hand to the side, and four large trees fell across the roadway just as a contingent of soldiers passed beneath them.

"Got them."

Holgir was watching the sky. "There's a storm coming, and it's not changing course. We'd best be done by the time it hits."

Guran had his scrying bowl in front of him. "No additional troops headed this way," he reported. "That may mean Lysander isn't going to meddle." He paused. "Rostivan's wearing the amulet. I can sense the *divi*'s power, even at this distance." He swore under his breath. "Plenty of men will die today, but it won't be Rostivan."

Jarle closed his fist again and splintered a small bridge

between the Arkalas' camp and the battlefield. That would force the men and horses to ford the wide creek, leaving them vulnerable to Rostivan's archers. Jarle's look of triumph made Carensa think he was enjoying his role far too much.

A sudden violent stomach cramp sent Carensa to her knees. Guran and the others dropped to the ground, too, holding their arms across their bellies, rolling in pain.

Gunvar reached out to lay a hand on Dag. "Can you repel it?" he asked, his voice tight. "I can give you strength."

Dag looked dangerously pale, his features taut with pain, but he nodded, and drew a shuddering breath. A few seconds later, the pain subsided. "I strengthened the wardings," he said. "That should hold them out."

Carensa gasped for breath, rolling over onto her side and trying to muster the strength to stand. "Jarle," Carensa said, "can you tell where the Arkalas' mages are?"

Jarle scanned the horizon. "There," he said, pointing. "That stone building." He smiled. "Let's see what mischief can be made." He stretched out his magic, concentrated, and clenched his fist. A cloud of dust rose where the building had been. "They may need to find another location," Jarle commented.

A moment later, a burst of power sent a tremor through the hilltop. Carensa staggered to keep her footing.

"Can you hold the warding?" Carensa asked Dag.

Dag shrugged, deep in concentration. Below on the battlefield, it was difficult to figure out who might be winning.

"Time to strike back," Jarle muttered.

"Wait!" Carensa said. She pointed to the battle below. "I think their mages are trying to distract us from the real issue. Look—the Arkalas have Rostivan's troops at a standstill."

Jarle set his jaw. "Let's see if we can kick up a little dust."

"First, the catapult," Jarle said. The catapult's shaft splintered, sending its load of rocks and debris down onto the soldiers at its base.

"One down," Jarle muttered. A few moments later, the second war machine lay in ruins. Jarle staggered. Gunvar and Carensa helped him sit down.

"The farther the object, the more energy it takes," Jarle replied. "I don't think I'd still be able to do this if Gunvar weren't helping."

Carensa looked out across the battlefield. The lines of fighting surged and fell back. Bodies littered the field, which had had grown dark with blood, yet neither side had scored a decisive blow. The afternoon was far spent, and the shadows were lengthening.

"If Rostivan is to win, he must win before the night is through," Guran said, breaking the silence. He was bent over his scrying bowl, deep in concentration. "I see the tide turning if the battle continues until morning. If that occurs, Rostivan will lose."

Carensa stared out across the battlefield. The wind had picked up out of the south, blowing toward the enemy camp. It swept across the land, bending the grass that had not been trampled in the fighting. She turned to Jarle.

"Fire," she said. "Can you catch the grass on fire just behind the Arkala troops?"

Jarle stared at her. "If the wind shifts, our men will burn!"

Holgir shook his head. "It won't—not anytime soon. The storm is coming up from the south."

"I think the storm is the key," Carensa explained. "If it hits before Rostivan strikes a decisive blow, the Arkalas will somehow turn that to their advantage. But if we could start a fire behind their lines, the winds would carry it toward their camp. That would pull their mages off whatever they're doing with the battle, and trap the soldiers between Rostivan's line and the flames. The bridge is out on the creek, so they can't go in that direction to escape. Rostivan could bottle them up."

Jarle nodded. "It could work."

She looked to Guran. "You can get a message to Quintrel through the crystal, can't you?" she asked. Guran nodded. "Can you ask him to nudge Rostivan to begin moving his troops to squeeze the Arkala soldiers between the camp and the stream?"

Guran looked down at one of the artifacts on their work-table, a piece Quintrel had entrusted to him in Valshoa before coming to Torsford. It appeared to be a crystal scrying orb, nothing anyone would find unusual among mages. Unless someone looked closer, and sensed the yellow flickering light that sparked inside the orb, or felt the aura of controlled power that radiated from the small globe. In reality, it provided a way for Guran and Quintrel to communicate, even when separated by distance.

"Yes," Guran answered, and hesitated just an instant before taking the orb in his hand. He closed his eyes and grimaced. "It's done."

"Let's get to it," Gunvar replied. "I'm cold and I'd like to go home."

"Gunvar, can you draw from me to help Jarle?" Carensa asked.

Gunvar frowned. "Maybe."

"Then do it," Carensa said. "I haven't expended as much power as the rest of you."

Jarle stood facing the Arkala camp. Gunvar stood with a hand on Jarle's shoulder, while Carensa clasped Gunvar's other hand with hers. Jarle took a deep breath and stared into the twilight, focusing on a strip of land between the rear of the Arkala forces and the camp.

After a moment, Jarle cursed. "I'm tired, and I'm not strong enough right now to cast past the warding," he said. "We'll have to drop it for me to send the fire."

Guran nodded his assent. "Do it. Just get the damn thing back up as quickly as you can."

Carensa felt an odd tingle, like crossing a woolen carpet in winter. The sensation grew stronger, radiating through her body, growing more and more uncomfortable until she longed to break the contact.

Dots of flame flared to the rear of the Arkala forces. Soon a solid line of fire stretched behind the enemy. Men shouted in panic as the fire spread, and the rear line of soldiers tried to put out the fire before it reached the camp.

Newly energized by the enemy's turn of luck, Rostivan's commanders pressed forward, driving the Arkala army back against the flames. The winds remained steady, blasting the fire toward the Arkala camp.

Rostivan's troops blocked their escape. Those who had remained in the camp made a panicked attempt to douse the flames, then fled on foot. Within minutes, the entire camp was ablaze.

On the battleground, the Arkala soldiers fought for their lives. Rostivan pressed his advantage, forcing the enemy to choose between fire and sword. Some tried and failed to leap across the flames. Others launched themselves at the Rostivan forces, nothing to lose.

No matter how the wind whipped or the flames danced, Rostivan's troops moved in lethal discipline. Line after line of Arkala soldiers fell to their swords. Some tried to swim the creek, only to be cut down by Rostivan's bowmen. Jarle sent waves of flame, keeping the retreating troops on the run, hemming in any escape routes. Without the warding, the wind was sharper than before, and very cold. Clouds had rolled in, blotting out the moon.

Night had fallen. Guran lit a lantern, keeping it heavily shaded. Dag and Holgir laid out several torches, but did not light them. The wall of flames sent a red glow into the night sky.

Suddenly, three dark shapes loomed on the other side of the circle—Arkala mages, come to exact their revenge. Pain staggered Carensa and she cried out as she fell to her knees. Guran collapsed, knocking his scrying bowl to the ground. Dag and the others writhed on the ground. Carensa felt as if the fire was inside her veins, burning her from the inside out. She gasped for air. It hurt too much to scream.

Jarle's face contorted. He dragged himself onto his knees, and made a wild sweep with one arm. Guran's bowl flew through the air, slamming against one of the Arkala mages, who staggered back a pace.

The magic wavered, just long enough for Dag to draw his sword and lurch toward the enemy mages, swinging with all his remaining might. Holgir sent his ax cartwheeling through the air. It landed, blade-deep, in the chest of one of the attackers. Gunvar grabbed the slingshot on his belt and rose to his knees. He scooped up several stones and sent them flying through the air in quick succession, dropping the second mage.

Jarle launched himself at the mage who had cast the attack, grasping him around the shoulders, muttering a chant. The enemy mage began to buck and kick, his hands scrabbling in the dirt, as blood gushed from his mouth and nose. Jarle kept chanting. The attacker stiffened and arched, then he fell still. Jarle collapsed beside him.

Carensa had both knives in her hands. As she watched Jarle and the mage in horror, a strong hand grabbed for her from the shadows. All the anger she felt at Jarle's death and at the bloodshed of battle welled up in her. Carensa wheeled, slashing with her knives. One of the blades struck a glancing blow to her attacker's arm, but the other went deep into his belly.

Carensa's attacker lurched after her, one hand pressed against the gash in his belly, a sword raised in the other. Carensa stumbled out of his way, knowing that her knives could not hold off a swordsman.

Guran struggled to his feet, lunging toward the swordsman with his long knife. He brought the blade down and across the attacker's neck, slitting his throat. The man staggered one step farther, then collapsed.

"Where in Raka were our guards?" Dag demanded.

Carensa was covered with blood, though little of it was her own. She was certain, even before Gunvar checked, that Jarle and his opponent were dead. On the battlefield below them, Rostivan's troops pursued the Arkala stragglers as the fires burned.

Dag and Holgir lit the torches and walked to where the other two Arkala mages lay. Holgir's ax had neatly severed their heads. They continued down the hillside until Carensa could see four bodies sprawled on the ground.

"Offhand, I'd say our guards are dead," Dag replied. He nudged one of the bodies with his boot.

"What killed them?" Carensa asked.

Holgir bent closer to the bodies. "Magic. Poor bastards."

"Obviously, they decided that trying to take us out would be a greater strategic victory than anything else they were doing," Gunvar said, stepping over one of the guards' corpses. "Perhaps we should be flattered."

Except that Jarle is dead, Carensa thought. *He won't be here for the victory celebration.*

"For all we know, we've spent so much blood against a small force while the real attack occurs elsewhere," Dag said.

Guran shook his head. "Hardly likely. I've been scrying, remember? It would have been very difficult for a force of any size to slip by completely unnoticed." He looked down toward the dead soldiers with chagrin. "A small group of assassins, cloaked by magic, is another matter entirely." They were silent as they returned to the crest of the hill, staying alert for other enemies in the darkness.

Dag and Holgir dragged Jarle and the dead soldiers into a nearby trench, then stacked stones over them as a cairn. The Arkala mages they left for the crows. Guran and Carensa collected what was left of their gear. The battle was over.

"We need to get down the hill," Holgir said, raising his head to scent the air like a hound after a fox. "Storm's coming fast."

To their surprise, Rostivan was at the bottom of the hill. It was impossible to guess his mood from his expression. Carensa glimpsed the leather strap that held the amulet, though the charm was hidden beneath his cuirass. Even in the torchlight, Carensa could see that Rostivan's armor was covered with blood, and from the stiff way he held himself, she bet some of it was his own.

"You took losses today?"

Guran nodded. "We lost Jarle, the one who could move objects at a distance. Most of us were injured. Our guards were killed by enemy mages."

Rostivan nodded. "Unfortunate." He paused. "Your man Jarle, he sent the fire?" He did not wait for an answer. "A good tactical move. It made a difference."

It bloody well saved your ass, Carensa wanted to say.

"Figure out what could have gone better today, and find a way to make it work next time. I'll send to Quintrel for a replacement," Rostivan continued. "He'll be heading to the city soon." With that, he strode away.

He'll send for a replacement, Carensa thought as she swung up on her horse. *Like a wagon, or a sword.*

CHAPTER EIGHTEEN

CONNOR WOKE SLOWLY. THE SHADOWS TRIED to drag him back into darkness. He would have been content to float in the moonless place where he did not dream, but something was pulling him away. Caught between two powerful forces, Connor let them battle it out, too exhausted to care whether he sank or rose.

"Bevin." A voice called to him from far away, and Connor knew that he should obey it, but it seemed too distant to lay claim on him.

Connor. A second voice, sterner than the first, sounded inside his head. He knew this voice, too, but he could not find the energy to move toward the sound of his name.

"Bevin." The first voice again, a command this time, instead of an invitation. "Follow my voice. You must wake."

"You should have turned him." The second voice, spoken aloud this time. Not to him, Connor thought, but to the first speaker.

"I swore I would not."

"What good is your word if he dies?"

"He isn't going to die. He's bound to me."

"He doesn't have the strength to rise from the shadowland on his own, Lanyon. We must wake him."

"It's too soon, Kierken."

"Better too soon than too late."

Connor suspected that he needed to keep eavesdropping, but it took so much effort to pay attention, and he was so very tired. Bits of memories surfaced. A hallway. A fireplace. Something that looked like a white, shell-covered creature from a nightmare. And then pain, fire, and blood. So much blood.

"Wake him, Lanyon. His wounds are healed. The longer he stays in the shadows, the more they lay claim to him."

"Perhaps you're right." There was a pause. "Bevin. It's time to get back to work. Wake now. You've rested long enough."

At the voice's command, the shadows parted. Connor longed to keep the darkness enfolded around him, but it slipped away like tendrils of smoke. Smoke. Fire. The smell of something burning came back to him, along with the hiss and spit of roasting meat. "Bevin. Come back. Now." The familiar voice had steel in it, and the order was one Connor could not disobey. Every fiber in his body felt compelled to follow that voice and do its bidding.

The last of the shadows slipped away. Connor drew a deep breath, and was surprised to find that it did not hurt to move. *It should hurt. It hurt before.*

Connor could feel his chest moving with every intake of air. His heart pounded in his ears, louder than usual. He felt smooth sheets beneath the palms of his hands, and he realized that he lay on a mattress, not the hard stone floor.

With a groan, he opened his eyes. His body felt stiff, as if it had not moved in a very long time.

"How do you feel, Bevin?" Lanyon Penhallow sat next to Connor's bed, looking worried. The room was dimly lit by a single lantern, and just behind Penhallow, Connor could make out the faint gray outline of Kierken Vandholt, the Wraith Lord.

"Foggy," Connor rasped. His throat was dry and his lips were parched. "Did I die?"

Penhallow hesitated. "It was very close," he said finally. "You lost a lot of blood. Kierken reached you too late to do more than hold tight to your spirit. By the time I awakened, you were beyond what the healers could do."

"Did you turn me?" Memory returned with consciousness, and while Connor was unclear on what had happened right before he had nearly died, he was quite certain that he had not wanted to become *talishte*.

"Not exactly."

"What do you mean, 'not exactly'?"

"You are still mortal," Penhallow replied, choosing his words carefully. "But you are a little less mortal than you were."

"What in Raka does that mean?" Connor met Penhallow's gaze. Most mortals avoided looking a *talishte* in the eyes for fear of being glamoured. Connor's susceptibility to glamouring had waned as the *kruvguldur* strengthened. Now he was angry enough to care little for the consequences.

"It means that he's bound your life force to his Dark Gift," the Wraith Lord said. His voice was a low whisper, and Connor knew that Vandholt was expending extra energy to be seen.

"You're speaking in riddles," Connor said, falling back against the mattress. "What you've said makes no sense to me."

Other than feeling tired and weakened, Connor felt the same as before the fight with the creature. *Then again, I have no idea how it feels to be* talishte, he thought.

"I took the healing a step further than before," Penhallow

said quietly. Connor thought he heard hesitation, something unusual for his vampire lord.

"You were within a few breaths of dying," Penhallow continued. "I knew that you didn't want to be turned. I would not turn you without your permission. But I didn't believe you wanted to die, either. There was a middle ground, but it required a few compromises."

"Like what?" Connor asked suspiciously. He reminded himself that Penhallow had always been a fair and kind master, and had—on more than one occasion—risked his own safety and nearly his existence to protect Connor. Vandholt had also saved his life and the lives of Connor's friends. Gratitude didn't make it easier to hear what Penhallow had to say.

"Allowing me to read your memories from your blood created the first *kruvgaldur* between us," Penhallow replied. "Saving your life last year, when I gave you my blood, made that bond stronger. Just healing the wound itself this time wouldn't have been enough. You needed blood."

"And you gave me yours," Connor said.

"Kierken possessed your body to hold on to your soul. I gave you just enough blood to strengthen you without turning you." He looked away. "It is a fine line."

"So I'm not quite mortal, and not quite *talishte*," Connor summed up.

"Had you died before we finished, I'm afraid that the turning would have been complete despite my intentions," Penhallow replied. "You did not."

Connor was silent for a few moments, reining in his anger and trying to think through what Penhallow had said. "What does it mean, to be like this? How am I different?"

"You'll be harder to kill, for one thing," the Wraith Lord replied.

"Why?"

Penhallow met his gaze. "Because part of what I am sustains you. The Dark Gift sustains me, and through me, it sustains you."

"So without you, I'll die."

"Yes." Penhallow paused. "And if you are destroyed, I will be severely harmed. The bond goes both ways."

Connor swore under his breath. "Look, I'm grateful for all both of you have done. And I'm glad I'm not dead. But I don't know exactly how to feel about this."

"If we hadn't saved you, you wouldn't be around to worry about it." The Wraith Lord's voice was terse.

Connor sighed. "I don't know if you can understand. It's been so long since either of you were mortal. I've been changed."

"It means that you will age more slowly," Penhallow replied. "You will be immune to much of what sickens most mortals. Your reflexes will not be *talishte* fast, but quicker than before. Sight, smell, hearing will be enhanced. You'll be stronger than you used to be. The sun will not destroy you, though your skin may mind its light more than before. Yet you're still alive. You do not need to feed on blood."

"And my life depends on your existence."

Penhallow nodded. "Yes. We are bound together, and that bond cannot be severed except by death." Penhallow was being quite patient, Connor knew. And he heard in Penhallow's voice a note of sadness and regret.

Connor let out a long breath and turned away. "I can't say that I would have chosen differently. But it bothers me not to have had a choice."

"I know that," Penhallow replied. "But I can't tell you that I'm sorry for saving your life. I value you, your service, and... I believe you have an important role yet to play in what becomes of this kingdom. We both understand what it is to serve something bigger than ourselves, whether it's a lord, or a commander, or a king. In service to that cause, sometimes sacrifices need to be made."

Connor could not fault Penhallow's logic. Even so, it stuck in his craw. A new question occurred to him.

"You said that what you did will extend my life. By how much?"

Penhallow shrugged. "*Talishte* don't age. That's why we appear as we were when we were turned. It's part of the Dark Gift. You are not *talishte*, and yet the Dark Gift sustains you through me. Aging will slow dramatically for you because of our bond. It may easily add eighty to one hundred years—perhaps more—to your life span, and your body won't be ravaged by old age. You won't remain forever young, but your body will not reflect your true age."

Connor drew a deep breath and let it out again. It would take a while, perhaps a long while, to sort out how he felt about what had happened, but there was no changing it. And as angry as it made him not to have had a say in the matter, Connor also knew that Penhallow, as his lord, was not required to ask him for his opinion. *I've been given a gift,* he told himself. *It may not be a gift I wanted, or one I would have chosen for myself, but it is still priceless. And there's no changing it, so I might as well get used to it.*

"All right," Connor said. "The decision's been made. And despite everything, I'd rather not be dead. So…thank you both for saving my life. And the rest, I'll figure it out as we go."

"Rest now," Penhallow said, placing his hand on Connor's shoulder. "As soon as you're well enough to travel, we'll be going to Glenreith."

"For the wedding?" Connor asked.

"Yes, and because I need to see Blaine. He's been injured. Seems our 'friend' Lowrey betrayed him. Tried to assassinate him. Fortunately, it didn't work. Lowrey's dead."

"Lowrey? But he stayed at Valshoa..."

"I don't know the details, just what I felt through the *kruv-galdur* and what I was able to get through Geir," Penhallow replied. "The magic is still taking its toll, draining Blaine. Our time is running out."

Penhallow and the Wraith Lord left Connor to rest, and when he woke again, Alsibeth was watching him with concern. Connor managed a smile. "I'm glad you made it," he said. "I was worried there for a while."

Alsibeth chuckled. "I had a little more cause to worry about you than the other way around. And I'm glad you made it, too."

Memories returned in a jumble. "Rolf?" he asked.

Alsibeth shook her head. "Dead."

"And Caz?"

Alsibeth swallowed hard. "He was burned too badly. There was nothing the healers could do except end his pain. His wounds were more than Penhallow could heal without turning him. He chose to move on."

"What about the Tingur—and those creatures?" Connor asked.

Alsibeth gave a sad smile. "Rolf didn't die in vain, although I don't think he intended to die at all. The artifact he used to focus fire was corrupted. We hadn't had time to validate it before he tried to use it. It worked—better than he ever expected."

She looked down at her hands. "Rolf meant to burn the sacks full of monsters that the Tingur catapulted toward the manor.

He hit one of them—thank the gods—or we would have more of those things running loose. Rolf didn't expect the artifact to drain his life. He was dying—and I think he knew it. He missed the second sack, but he hit the Tingur with a wave of fire, incinerating them."

The assault on Westbain had cost their side too many lives for Connor to feel regret. "Were there other creatures than the one we fought?"

"Three," Alsibeth replied. "Two of them never made it into the manor. Aurick's men fought them. Several soldiers died."

Belatedly, Connor remembered that he was the seneschal. "What about the servants? Did they survive?"

Alsibeth nodded. "Nearly all. Most of the injuries were minor."

"And the soldiers?" Connor's memories were coming back a little at a time, and as Alsibeth was talking, he recalled his conversation with Aurick right before the attack.

"There were casualties," Alsibeth replied. "But his men held the wall. Aurick asked after you, when everything was over. He sends his wishes for a quick recovery."

Thanks to Penhallow's 'gift,' Connor had no doubt that he was likely to recuperate at record speed. He made an effort to sit up, but Alsibeth laid a hand on his shoulder and gently pushed him down.

"Lord Penhallow was quite explicit in his instructions. You are to rest—in bed—for the remainder of the day," Alsibeth said archly. "He assured me that he would know if you didn't. He said to tell you that you'll need your strength for the trip to Glenreith." She laid a hand on his arm. "Be careful, Connor. My dreams have been dark. I fear you have powerful enemies who haven't yet shown themselves, beings that aren't for mortals to meddle with."

Then again, I'm no longer entirely mortal, Connor thought. "I'll take care," he reassured the seer. "Alsibeth," he said after a pause. "What else do your visions say? Can you see what lies ahead?"

The night of the Great Fire, Lord Garnoc had sent Connor to the Rooster and Pig to seek Alsibeth's counsel. Castle Reach had abounded with self-proclaimed mystics and clairvoyants, but few had the power they claimed to possess. Garnoc had been certain that Alsibeth's gift was genuine, and the warning she had given Connor to bear back to his master had been chillingly correct.

"While you were... sleeping... I read the portents," Alsibeth replied. She gestured behind her, and Connor squinted to see in the room's dim light. He could make out a shallow bowl and several partially burned candles, and he remembered that one of Alsibeth's ways to divine the future was to drip hot wax into cold water and read the omens in the shapes that the wax made as it hardened.

Alsibeth gave him a tired smile. "I can't give you the answers you want, Connor. But I do sense that McFadden is still at the center of what is to come. The outcome is unclear, but I'm certain your fate remains tangled with his—and with Penhallow."

"At least I'm on the right side," Connor said. Despite Penhallow's healing, Connor felt a tiredness that he was sure had more to do with mental exhaustion than physical stamina, and let sleep take him.

CHAPTER
NINETEEN

Y OU WEREN'T THIS NERVOUS WHEN WE WERE
fighting monsters," Piran said, shaking his head.

"That was war. This is marriage," Blaine replied.

Piran raised an eyebrow. "You mean there's a difference?"

Blaine rolled his eyes and chuckled. Blaine stood in Glenreith's great room, dressed in the most presentable outfit he could scavenge.

The long table in the center of the great room held a feast of roasted venison, freshly baked breads, pastries, cheeses, and dried fruits. Blaine argued against straining the manor's scant resources, but his aunt Judith and Edward, Glenreith's seneschal, turned a deaf ear. Garlands of woven straw and cuttings of pine and fir decorated the walls and table. Candles gave the room a festive glow, and a fire roared in the room's huge fireplace.

Outside, another storm raged. Blaine counted it as a blessing; the storm made it highly unlikely that anyone would attack, perhaps not for several days to come.

Blaine's closest friends stood behind him: Niklas, Piran, Dawe, and Verran. Edward opened a door into the corridor to admit the bride and her party. Judith was the first to enter, followed by Kestel. Blaine's sister, Mari, and Zaryae followed behind Kestel. Mari carried a sword that lay flat on her upturned palms.

"Blaine McFadden, is it your intent to make a handfasting with Kestel Falke?" Judith McFadden Ainsworth asked when the bridal party reached the place where Blaine stood. Judith was a handsome woman in her middle years, and tonight, between the soft light of the candles and the extra effort she had taken with her appearance for the wedding, it was possible to glimpse the beauty she had been in her younger years, before hardship and sorrow had taken their toll.

"It is," Blaine said. He was nervous enough that he feared his voice might crack like that of a half-grown boy.

"Kestel Falke, is it your intent to make a handfasting with this man?" Judith asked.

"Yes," Kestel replied, meeting Blaine's gaze. "It is."

Kestel wore a borrowed gown of sapphire blue. Blaine guessed that Judith and Mari had remade the gown from one of Judith's dresses. The dress flattered Kestel's red hair and light skin, and its cut showed off her toned body. Kestel's hair was twisted into complicated braids that circled her head, and a line of kohl outlined her green eyes. In better days, gold and gemstones would have completed the bridal clothing, but anything of value that Judith and Mari owned had long ago been sold.

"Present the groom's gift," Judith instructed.

A blush crept into Kestel's cheeks as she turned to take the sword-gift from Mari. Holding the sword flat on her open hands, Kestel offered it to Blaine. On the end of the pommel lay one of the rings Dawe had forged for them.

"I accept your intention, and swear my intention on this blade that nothing separate us but death itself," Kestel said.

Blaine accepted the sword, and Kestel took the ring from the pommel, sliding it onto Blaine's finger. "This I have sworn," she said.

Niklas stepped forward, holding a similar sword, but this one was wrapped with a silken cord. Blaine took the sword and held it out to Kestel.

"I honor your acceptance, and swear on this blade that all I own, I will share with you until death parts us," Blaine replied. Kestel took the sword, and Blaine lifted her hand and slipped the ring into place. "This I have sworn," he echoed.

Judith unwrapped the silken cord from around the blade. Blaine and Kestel clasped their left hands and held them up while Judith twined the cord over and around them.

"By your intent, and in the sight of all the gods and the spirits that be, you are wed," Judith proclaimed. "And may the gods above and below bless your union." It was an old tradition in Donderath that a village's matrons, the 'wise women,' readied brides for their weddings and spoke the words of binding. Judith's eyes glittered with joy.

Judith unwound the silk cord, and bent forward to kiss their clasped hands in blessing, then grinned broadly and turned the newlyweds to face their guests. "Tonight, we have something fine to celebrate."

Verran, who had just returned to Glenreith the night before, pulled a pennywhistle from inside his vest, striking up a pleasant tune. The small crowd of friends clapped and cheered.

"Best of everything to you," Borya said as he and Desya stepped up to greet them. Zaryae wrapped an arm around each twin's waist.

"We're honored to be part of your celebration," Zaryae said.

Kestel leaned forward to give her a kiss on the cheek. "Glenreith is your home now. That makes you family."

Dawe wasted no time moving to stand with Mari, and Blaine wondered how long it would be before the two of them made their own handfasting. Robbe, Mari's four-year-old son with her late husband, had already gathered a handful of sweets and gone to enjoy his ill-gotten bounty underneath the table.

"My congratulations to both of you," Geir said, making a low bow to Kestel. "I haven't been a guest at a handfasting since my mortal days." Geir's smile hid the tips of his long eyeteeth. A slight ruddiness to his complexion suggested to Blaine that Geir had already fed, though Edward had made sure to have a flagon of fresh deer blood so that Geir and Penhallow could join in the feast. Geir's dark hair hung loose to his shoulders, and he looked attired for court in a black waistcoat and pants.

"Best wishes to both of you," Lanyon Penhallow added, giving Blaine's hand a hearty shake and leaning forward to kiss Kestel on the cheek.

"I'm really happy for you two," Connor said, grinning. Penhallow, Geir, and Connor had arrived the night before, and their presence was one of the reasons Blaine and Kestel had planned an evening ceremony.

"I see Niklas is taking no chances," Geir added, with a nod toward the soldiers who stood guard at each entrance to the great room.

"People are most vulnerable when they're happy," Kestel replied. "One of the first lessons an assassin learns," she said.

Connor chuckled. "She's the perfect match for you, Blaine," he said. "What better partner for a warlord than an assassin?"

"My thinking exactly," Blaine said, and leaned over to kiss Kestel.

By now, Dawe had slipped over to sit near Verran, and pulled a hand drum out from a bag on the floor. Borya and Desya joined them, and retrieved a lute and a larger drum from the same bag. Blaine had met Zaryae and the twins on his quest to restore the magic, and after their support for him cost the life of two of their troupe, he had invited Zaryae and the twins to make Glenreith their home.

Kestel walked over to the musicians and whispered to Verran. Verran changed the tune he was playing to one of the up-tempo circle dances that Kestel loved, and she strode across the room to take Blaine's arm.

"A dance for the bride?" she asked, grinning broadly. Blaine let her lead him away. Judith and Edward danced with abandon, while Mari laughed affectionately as Dawe stumbled through the steps. Connor gallantly squired Zaryae, and Blaine was surprised that he knew the complicated steps.

"Come dance with us!" Kestel called to Piran, who watched the dance from the safety of the far wall.

"I'm not drunk enough to dance," Piran replied, raising a glass of ale to let her know he was working on it.

Verran and the others played one dance after another until the dancers were winded and even Kestel begged off. Blaine escorted her to the table heaped with food—a true luxury in postwar Donderath.

"Judith and Edward have outdone themselves," Kestel said.

"I believe my aunt is quite smitten with your charms," Blaine replied, helping himself to the roasted venison and a piece of bread. "As is the lord of the manor."

Kestel looked down the table of food. "I notice there's no herring. An oversight?" She gave an evil chuckle.

Blaine groaned. "You know, when we left Edgeland, I swore I'd never eat another herring again," he said.

"Did you forget that most of those herring were shipped home to Donderath?" Kestel asked in her sweetest voice.

"I managed to push that from my thoughts," he replied.

"Zaryae told me that she had a dream about Carr," she said quietly. "She mentioned it while we were getting ready. She said it was a warning." She looked up into his eyes. "She believes he's a danger to you."

"I appreciate the warning," Blaine said, "but right now, Carr poses the biggest danger to himself." He sighed. "Niklas is watching him. He's off somewhere on patrol. And I'm sleeping with the most dangerous assassin in all of Donderath."

Kestel flashed a lascivious smile. "Let's get back to our celebration, so we can get to the sleeping part," she added with a wicked look in her eye.

When they returned to the center of the room from the banquet table, Zaryae and Connor were deep in conversation. Judith stood watching the festivities with Edward close by her side. The hard years since Blaine's exile had changed the nature of their relationship, and they no longer made a pretense of not being a couple. Verran had struck up another tune, with Borya and Desya joining in enthusiastically. Dawe had abandoned his drum for Mari's company, and they stood off to one side, talking quietly.

"A copper for your thoughts," Kestel said, gently elbowing Blaine in the ribs.

He hugged her close and kissed the top of her head. "Just feeling amazed and lucky to have made it this far," he replied. "Even threadbare and down-at-the-heels, Glenreith still feels like home."

When the dancers were finally exhausted, Piran pulled out dice and cards. Since none of his friends would play him for money, Piran settled for using dried beans, and the wagering commenced. Even Judith and Edward got into the game. Kestel and Piran traded good-natured barbs, Verran cheated every chance he got, and somehow Dawe managed to win more hands than anyone else.

Blaine was content to watch Kestel do the betting. It was good to have the Edgeland crew back together again. Though it made sense for them to play their separate roles in the war effort, he missed having his friends around him on a daily basis. Seeing his Edgeland 'family' and his Glenreith family meld so seamlessly made him happier than he had been in a long while, despite the dangers of the world beyond the manor's walls.

A commotion in the front entrance hall brought the festivities to a standstill. A gust of cold wind swept into the great room, and they heard the large doors shut.

"Let me through," a man's voice demanded. "I'm the groom's brother."

Blaine and Kestel exchanged wary glances. "Go on with the party," Blaine said. "Niklas and I will take care of Carr." Niklas was already moving across the room. Blaine joined him and together they headed for the door. Geir and Penhallow followed at a distance, just in case.

Carr strode into the room. He was dressed for the storm, with a bulky fur-lined leather coat. Snow clung to his boots and fell from his hat and shoulders. But what caught everyone's attention was the bound and gagged prisoner slung over Carr's shoulder. Carr shrugged, barely bothering to break the man's fall as he tumbled to the ground and rolled to Blaine's feet.

"I brought you a wedding present," Carr said. The challenge in his eyes was unmistakable.

Zaryae knelt next to the prisoner and pulled back enough of the blanket around him to feel for a pulse. "He's alive," she reported. "But not quite right."

"He's one of Hennoch's favorite lieutenants," Carr replied. "I met him in a tavern and drugged him with a potion I got from a hedge witch." He nudged the body with his boot, but the prisoner did not respond. "There's an amulet around his neck that will make him answer any questions you ask of him, once the potion wears off." He paused.

"Am I too late to say 'congratulations' to my brother and his new wife?" Carr asked with an insolent smile.

"Of all the stupid stunts to pull..." Niklas began.

Kestel laid a hand on his arm, and shot a warning glance at Blaine. "How did you get him away from the other soldiers?"

"I seduced him—or at least, that's what he thought I was doing," Carr replied with a hard glint in his eyes. "I already knew all about him, and it wasn't hard to arrange to accidentally befriend him in the tavern. He figured I was just another trollop, and after a couple of drinks, he was ready to go." He smiled unpleasantly. "I gave him a different ride than he expected."

Blaine saw how much the last few months had changed Carr. Since the Madness, he had grown too thin, making his angular features sharper. If Carr were to bother to clean up, his looks would be better than passable, with a hint of danger that could make him attractive to someone who liked to take chances.

"So no one saw you leave with him?" Kestel pressed. Espionage was a business she knew well.

Carr laughed. "Oh, everyone saw us leave together. And they were pretty sure where we were going, from the catcalls. So no one would have missed him for several candlemarks, and by that time, we were long gone."

"Why him?" Though Carr had made his disdain for Kestel clear, her attention seemed to gratify him, averting an outburst of temper.

Carr gave her a crafty look. "He's one of Hennoch's top men.

He'll know about Hennoch's troop sizes, his strategies, maybe even what Pollard's up to." He leveled his gaze at Geir and Penhallow. "I figured you can ask him all he remembers while he's magicked, and then have one of them," he said with nod of his head, "read his blood and get the rest."

Blaine knew the others were waiting for his reaction. As much as he felt like throttling Carr, the prisoner's information could be valuable. And Carr had already made his point, disrupting the wedding and putting a damper on the festivities. Blaine resolved to curtail the damage.

"Let's get him downstairs and locked up—keep two guards on him until we can get back to him," Blaine said to Niklas, who signaled for soldiers to do what Blaine ordered.

"I wouldn't wait too long," Carr called after them. "The potion's effective, but toxic. I've had to dose him a couple of times on the way here. It'll wear off in another candlemark or so, and he'll be dead by morning."

Blaine and Niklas looked at each other with a glance that said they knew Carr had maneuvered them into a corner. "All right," Blaine said. "Let's get him downstairs and get this over with."

"I'm coming with you," Kestel said. "Verran and the twins can keep the music going. We'll come back when we're finished."

"I'll be glad to lend assistance," Geir volunteered. He looked to Carr. "What did you drug him with?" Carr named several plants. Geir shrugged before picking up the prisoner. "None of those should harm a *talishte*. I can read his blood once you're through with the interrogation."

"I would also join you, if you allow?" Penhallow asked.

Blaine gave a nod, knowing without a word through the *kruvgaldur* that Penhallow wanted to protect him. *This bond takes some getting used to,* he thought to himself.

Blaine doubted that after the interrogation and the prisoner's execution, he or Kestel would feel much like rejoining the party.

Judith slipped up beside Blaine and laid a hand on his arm. "Go on. I'll make sure your guests have a good evening." Blaine took Kestel's hand and followed the others to the cellar.

The new manor house had no need of a dungeon. But it did have windowless storage rooms with solid wooden doors, and it was to one of those rooms that Niklas directed Geir to take the prisoner. They found a nearly empty room and a chair and unloaded the groggy prisoner, tying his arms to the chair before cutting the bonds at his wrists. Perhaps the prisoner thought they had shown mercy, but Blaine knew it was to make it easier for Geir to find an artery when the interrogation came to an end.

"Ask him your questions," Carr prompted. "Between the drugs and the amulet, he'll tell you anything."

Blaine glared at Carr. Niklas moved between them and faced the prisoner.

"What's your name, soldier?"

"Lieutenant Runi Melkir."

"What lord do you serve?"

"Lord Hennoch, and his liege, Lord Reese and Lord Pollard," Melkir replied.

Niklas nodded. "What are your orders?"

"We're to harry Blaine McFadden and block him from accomplishing his objectives," the man replied in a slurred voice.

"What are those objectives?" Niklas pressed.

Melkir was silent for a moment. "Doesn't matter," he answered finally. "We're to get in the way. Find out what his men are doing at Mirdalur, block supplies from going into Castle Reach, burn out villages loyal to him. Whatever it takes."

Niklas looked at Blaine. "Pretty much what we expected," he murmured. He turned his attention back to Melkir. "How did you know about Mirdalur?"

The drugged man gave a sluggish chuckle. "Lord Pollard hears things," he said. "He has spies."

"Who are your spies? Who gives you information?" Kestel asked.

The prisoner gave Kestel a puzzled look. "You're a pretty lady," he slurred.

Kestel gave him a warm smile that did not reach her eyes. "Tell me who gives you information," she repeated, using a flicker of her own magic to encourage him to answer.

"Steen the tinker," he said finally, in a drunken mutter. "Teodor—he's a thief. And Vinsi, the peddler."

"That's very good," Kestel praised, with a glance to make sure that Niklas had committed the names to memory.

"How many men are in Hennoch's army?" Niklas asked, nodding as Melkir replied with a number. If Melkir was correct, Hennoch's forces were smaller than those Niklas commanded.

"And then there are the mages," Melkir muttered.

"What about the mages?" Blaine pressed.

Melkir was fading fast. His voice had dropped to a whisper, and his skin was ashen. "*Talishte*...turn the mages they find... makes them loyal to Reese and Pollard. Find where they're hiding." His last words were almost too quiet to hear.

"Get your questions in fast, he doesn't have much longer," Carr prodded. Kestel gave him a murderous look.

"Perhaps this is where I come in?" Geir said, looking to Penhallow, then Blaine, for confirmation. "I don't think the man can tell us more than he has, but I may read things from his blood that he has forgotten he knew—or that he overlooked."

"You'll see that he sleeps?" Kestel said, knowing that Geir took her meaning.

"Aye," Geir replied with a nod. "And he won't wake."

The prisoner hung limply against the ropes that held him, and would have fallen had he not been bound. Geir knelt beside him and raised the man's left forearm in his hands.

"It's time for you to rest," he said in a low, smooth voice that Blaine knew would be heavy with compulsion, glamouring Melkir to Geir's will. Melkir took a deep breath and slumped, eyes closed.

Geir looked to Carr with an expression that made his opinion of the situation clear. "If you ever put us in this position again, I will read *your* blood once I'm finished with the prisoner's." Carr had the good sense not to speak, but anger was clear in his gaze.

Blaine swallowed hard as he watched Geir drink from the prisoner. Geir paused after a few moments, and Blaine guessed it was to process the images the blood had revealed. After a moment, Geir bent his head once more and did not stop until Melkir was dead.

"I can sketch out what I saw later," Geir said, rising without a fleck of blood on his mouth. "There was more about troop strength, outposts, supply lines that could be helpful." He shook his head. "I saw his memories. Pollard has Reese's *talishte* looking for any mages who haven't already sworn fealty to a warlord. Once they're turned, they owe Reese allegiance for several lifetimes, and their magic is guaranteed to be in support of whatever he wants."

"Lovely," Kestel said drily.

Geir looked to Blaine and Niklas. "There was one more

thing, something that Melkir didn't understand, so he didn't realize what it meant. He overheard Pollard assure Hennoch that Reese would be rejoining him very soon."

"I thought Reese had been sentenced by some *talishte* tribunal," Blaine countered, frowning.

Penhallow nodded. "He was. The Elders passed judgment on him, and he's to be imprisoned in an oubliette for fifty years. No small punishment, even for an immortal." He paused. "The imprisonment should be secure, even against other *talishte*."

"Maybe Pollard was lying," Kestel said. "Trying to make Hennoch think Pollard still had Reese's backing."

Geir shook his head. "Remember—I saw what Melkir saw. It didn't look like Pollard was spinning a tale." He met Blaine's gaze. "I think we have to face the very real possibility that Pollard—and some of Reese's *talishte* supporters—believe they can free him." He gave Penhallow a grim look. "I know this doesn't make you happy—and it certainly won't please the Wraith Lord."

"What about him?" Niklas said, gesturing toward Melkir.

"He's dead, but most assuredly not turned," Geir replied. "You can deal with the body as you wish."

"I should make you bury him," Niklas said, glowering at Carr.

"He had valuable information," Carr countered. "And this is war. People die."

Niklas bit back a retort and turned to the soldiers. "Take the body to the refuse trench, and cover it with rocks. It will do." He looked back at the others. "I can't justify putting soldiers at risk to bury him outside the fence."

Blaine eyed Carr. Anger at the disruption of the wedding mingled with repulsion at the prisoner's treatment, and concern over Carr's sanity.

"You didn't have to come." Blaine knew that the sharp tone

in his own voice masked his disappointment. Long ago, he and Carr had been close.

"I make it a point never to miss food," Carr said. He took a swig of whiskey from a flask he withdrew from a pouch on his belt.

Carr had made it clear that he would have preferred Blaine stayed in Edgeland. Judith and Mari had welcomed Blaine and his friends back to Glenreith. *Carr doesn't seem to realize that without the army, Glenreith would be easy prey for Pollard's troops.*

Carr tipped his flask in salute. "If you'll excuse me, I'm going to get some of that venison, if there's any left." While Niklas was talking quietly with the soldiers, Carr slipped up the steps.

Niklas shot him a glance that gave Blaine to know that his old friend had guessed his thoughts. "Quit blaming yourself for Carr's bad decisions," Niklas said. "He's not a child."

Blaine sighed. "I know. I just wish he weren't so out of control. And short of chaining him up in the cellar, I'm not sure how to stop him. We don't have the extra guards to assign him a jailer."

"Even Judith can see that Carr hasn't fully recovered. I'm not sure he ever will." Niklas shook his head. "Fortunately, he's only putting himself at risk—at least so far. I've tried confining him to quarters, setting him to hard labor, cutting his rations, and he pulls the same kind of fool stunt as soon as he's free. I have no desire to flog him, and I doubt it would work anyhow," Niklas added. "The only time he isn't disruptive is when he goes out on a scouting mission, but it's always a toss-up as to whether or not he'll come back again. He seems to up the stakes every time he leaves." When Blaine said nothing, Niklas paused, then went on. "And you'll be happy to know," he added, "Folville's men are holding their own in Castle Reach.

They've had some problems with the Tingur, but nothing they can't handle. I guess Lysander's had his sights set on other targets." Before Blaine could answer, Niklas gave him a pointed glance. "This is your wedding day. Let me worry about Carr. Your bride is waiting."

Blaine nodded. "Thanks," he said, though Kestel looked as concerned over the situation as he felt. Niklas headed up the steps, but Penhallow laid a hand on Blaine's shoulder.

"Stay a moment," he said. Kestel hung back, making it clear by her stance that whatever was to be discussed would include her as well.

"I feel your strain," Penhallow said quietly, meeting Blaine's gaze. "The anchoring is taking a toll."

Blaine nodded. "Not sure yet what to do about it, so I just keep fighting. But we'll have to figure it out before too long."

Penhallow nodded. "Dolan and Nidhud are working out the ritual to anchor the magic, but the way magic is right now makes it difficult." Penhallow looked as if he had been under a great deal of stress, something unusual for a *talishte*.

"Connor is different," Blaine said, and he thought that for a second, he saw a flash of guilt in Penhallow's eyes.

"It was necessary to save his life," Penhallow replied. "Connor came very close to death." He grimaced. "I fear Bevin is still coming to terms with the situation." They fell silent for a moment, and then Penhallow spoke again. "Nidhud spoke with you of the Knights' proposal?"

"Yes. It was actually what I had hoped would happen anyway," Blaine responded.

"Nidhud and Dolan are certain Mirdalur is the place where the ritual will be most effective," Penhallow said.

"I'll be heading back there with Niklas after the wedding, at least until I'm needed elsewhere," Geir added.

"Once Dolan is ready, and the mages here feel like they've got it worked out, I'm willing to give it a try," Blaine said. "I'll be very happy to have the anchoring resolved."

Penhallow nodded. "I think we all will." He grinned. "But for now, go back to your wedding and forget all this. You're on home territory, and for the moment, no one's attacking. The storm should keep it that way for a day or two, at least. Geir and I will stay on watch."

"And if the information the prisoner provided is valid, it might give us an edge the next time we face off against Hennoch. That's more than we've been able to say for the last several months," Geir said as he clapped Blaine on the shoulder. "Enjoy it while it lasts. The winds will shift soon enough."

Geir and Penhallow headed back upstairs, leaving Blaine and Kestel alone on the steps. "Someday, when all this is over, I'll take you on a proper wedding trip," Blaine promised.

Kestel chuckled. "Where is there to go? We've already been to the edge of the world."

"There is that," he admitted. "Maybe we'll find out that there's somewhere that didn't fall to pieces in the Cataclysm."

At the top of the steps, Blaine took Kestel in his arms and kissed her. "Maybe someday, we can create a place where you'll be able to really relax without worrying," he murmured.

Kestel squeezed him tight and leaned into him for a moment. "I can't say that I've ever known what that feels like. But it's a nice thing to imagine."

Blaine took Kestel's hand as they walked toward the great room, where Verran and the others were still playing music. "I wish I could have seen Glenreith before the Great Fire," Kestel said, looking at her surroundings. "It would have been nice to see it in its heyday."

Blaine made a face. "Assuming you could have come on a

day when my father wasn't at home," he replied with a sigh. "And to be honest, though Carr doesn't remember it this way, Glenreith had seen its best days before Father's time. Merrill tolerated father because of his military service, but no one liked him."

"At least your aunt was able to keep the servants on," Kestel added. "It would have been impossible for Judith and Edward to hold things together with just Carr and Mari."

Blaine nodded. "Really, where was there to go? A few of the servants went to look for family after the Great Fire, but most of those came back. Judith did her best to make sure everyone was fed and sheltered. And since the Cataclysm, there are precious few supplies to be had even for a pile of gold."

Despite the candlelight, Blaine could see that the hall looked shabby. Paintings and tapestries that Blaine remembered were missing, sold to raise the cash Judith had needed to keep the manor functioning.

"You seem far away," Kestel observed.

Blaine managed a self-conscious smile. "Just remembering. I've often wondered what would have happened if Father had died on a hunt, or fallen over with a bad heart. I would have taken over the lands and title, and the manor might have had a few prosperous years before the world went up in flames."

"Maybe," Kestel said. "I've wondered something similar about the night I was caught by the guards. Then again, odds are we'd have both been killed by the Great Fire."

"Probably so," Blaine conceded. "I just don't like knowing that I left them in a lurch."

Kestel stopped him with a hand on his arm and met his gaze with determination. "Gods above, Mick, you saved their lives."

"Carr certainly doesn't see it like that," Blaine replied.

"Carr may be more like your father than you want to admit,"

Kestel said. "If you can't bring yourself to believe that Carr has changed so much, then blame the Madness."

Blaine led Kestel to the large window. Moonlight was bright on the snow. From the front gate of the protective walls down to the army camp in the valley ranged a no-man's land, a wooden stockade patrolled by the army that Niklas commanded. Farther down, Blaine could see Arengarte's roof and what remained of the old grist mill.

"Carr's eight years younger than I am," he said. "When we were children, we spent as much time as we could as far from here as possible to get away from Father." Blaine smiled sadly. "Mari tagged along."

He pointed down toward the valley. "We would go fishing, or hunt rabbits, or imagine the most amazing adventures out in the woods." He sighed. "Carr used to beg me to make a lean-to and let us live there, away from Father. But I knew that sooner or later, we had to come back."

"You were close then?" Kestel asked quietly.

Blaine nodded. "Carr was only six when Mother died. Mari was just ten. I ended up becoming the parent to both of them." He was quiet for a moment, remembering.

"I learned how to draw off Father's attention so that he'd come after me in his temper. When I couldn't keep them safe, I learned to bind up the wounds, and I found a healer who would treat us in exchange for food we stole from the kitchen." Blaine shook his head. "When we were without a tutor, I read to them, made sure they learned their lessons." He fell silent again for a bit. "I would have died for them."

"You nearly did," Kestel said. "If Merrill hadn't known what your father was really like, you would have hanged. You did everything that you could. Mari adores you," she added. "You can see it whenever she looks at you. You're her hero."

"It never really occurred to me that things could get any worse," Blaine replied. "And the day I killed Father, I didn't really think at all. I just wanted to make sure he never hurt Mari again. If Carr even crossed my mind, I would have thought about him not having to worry about getting beaten again." He shook his head. "I never meant to ruin his life."

Kestel took Blaine by the shoulders. "If it hadn't been for you, Carr wouldn't have a life to ruin," she said. "If anything ruined Carr's life, it was your father."

A fierce look burned in Kestel's eyes. "Those nobles who ostracized your family, who do you think hired me as an assassin to do their dirty work for them? My specialty was killing abusive, philandering husbands and making it look like an accident."

"Now I'm doubly sorry I didn't know you back then," Blaine replied, but the humor of his quip never reached his eyes.

"Your noble peers weren't horrified that you murdered someone," Kestel said, temper flaring in her eyes. "They were offended that you did the deed yourself, in broad daylight, and refused to deny it."

Kestel stretched up to kiss his cheek. "You're a good man, Mick. But you worry too much, even for a warlord. Carr will find his way, either here with you, or on his own."

Everyone in the room clapped when Blaine and Kestel rejoined the wedding party. Dawe pressed a glass of whiskey into Blaine's hand, while Mari offered the same to Kestel. Blaine wandered over to where Verran, Borya, and Desya sat, taking a break from the music. "I never thought you would actually make it back to Glenreith in time for the wedding," he said. "How's the traveling-minstrel business?"

"Never a dull moment," Verran said, in a tone that made it clear that not all of the excitement had been welcome. "Borya and Desya can hold their own quite well in a bar fight, and I've been glad more than once for the soldiers and *talishte* you sent along with us." He grinned. "By the way, the *talishte* musicians Geir sent us are rather amazingly good."

"I'd expect that even you'd improve with a couple of life-times' practice," Piran said with a grin, joining them. Kestel kicked his shin with a look of feigned innocence, and Piran mock-glowered at her. Blaine sighed, unable to resist smiling at the long-running friendly feud.

"Lysander and Rostivan seem to be the ones we have to worry about," Borya added. "Penhallow's forces took over Reese's old manor at Westbain, and the alliance between Penhallow, some of the Knights of Esthrane, and Voss seems to have that corner of Donderath under control, at least for now."

"Did you get any feel for the size of the armies, or how well provisioned they were?" Blaine asked, sipping his whiskey.

Borya shook his head. "No. We went around them because we were afraid we'd be conscripted if we were seen."

"Probably a good idea," Kestel agreed.

"Of course, no one would want to conscript musicians and actors," Desya added. "What use could we be in a fight?" His feral grin made the irony of his statement clear. Blaine had seen both the brothers in battle, and knew just how lethal they could be. Even Verran, whose fighting usually was limited to throwing rocks, could hold his own. The guards and *talishte* who accompanied them were even better equipped.

"It's harder to put spies in place now," Kestel said, and took a sip of her drink. "Before the Cataclysm, it was easy to have someone sign on as a servant or get an invitation to a ball." She shook her head. "These warlord groups are going to be tight-knit."

"And if we can think of having *talishte* or mages screen new recruits, I imagine it's occurred to the other warlords, too," Piran added.

"I think we've had as good cover as anyone would get," Verran said. Blaine glanced at his old friend. Verran looked a bit thinner and scruffier since he had been on the road, but it was clear in every word that he was relishing the action. "No one gives us a second glance." He shrugged. "It's like we're invisible."

"And we made good money performing, too," Desya said with a grin. Borya jabbed him with an elbow. "Hey!" Desya protested. "Any money we earn is money Blaine doesn't have to shell out to keep us in the field. We might even turn a profit."

"Don't let him fool you," Borya said. "He means we had money for ale."

"My minstrel friends and thieving partners are enjoying the adventure," Verran said. "And they add an air of authenticity."

"You mean, they're running from the law," Piran said drily.

Verran shrugged. "What law? But running, yeah, that, too."

"We're not always paid with coin for our effort," Desya said. "Everyone barters now. But we do usually take in enough in vegetables to have a nice stew for dinner," he added.

"Is the countryside functioning at all?" Kestel asked, eager for news.

Verran shrugged. "If you mean, does it look like it did before we were shipped off to Velant? No. It looks like it was blown up and burned down and then drowned."

"But it's amazing how creative people can be when it comes to necessities," Borya chimed in. "The pubs loot what they can find to make their vats, and they brew beer, but you might have to be desperate to drink the stuff."

"Which, it appears, people are," Desya added. "And with people paying for their ale with turnips or chickens or whatever, the pub master throws it all together in a pot and makes stew."

"How many chickens does the whorehouse charge?" Piran asked. Kestel kicked him again. "Ow!" he exclaimed. "What did I say? Just wanted to know the going rate."

"We didn't inquire," Verran replied. "But the two oldest professions—pubs and trollops—are getting back to business. Not much else, because there's naught to sell and nothing to pay for it with—a person can only use so many turnips."

"We're going back out tomorrow," Verran said.

"What about the storms?" Kestel asked.

Verran shrugged. "We'll get by. We always do." He managed a daring grin. "It's not like we're going to see anything to match what we've lived through in Edgeland, after all."

"For the gods' sake, come back in one piece," Blaine replied. "Stay away from the other warlords, and don't poke your noses where they're likely to get chopped off."

Verran grinned and gave a mock salute. "As you wish, M'lord Mick. And—thanks. We really do want to do something useful." He raised his pennywhistle. "But first, a little more music."

CHAPTER TWENTY

B Y THE TIME NIKLAS AND CARR RETURNED TO the camp at Mirdalur, the wind had become a force to fight against. Freezing rain began to fall, and the temperature had grown colder. The gray sky was dark, though it was still early in the day, far too early for Dolan and the Knights to be awake.

"Let's get the horses inside," Niklas said. "It's time to hunker down."

Niklas and Carr shook off the worst of the rain and headed into an old stone barn that had been patched up to serve as a barracks. Niklas's men had shored it up with enough repairs to make it habitable for the time it took to make Mirdalur ready to anchor the magic.

"There are a couple of card games going if you want to join in," Ordel, the senior healer, said in greeting.

Niklas managed a tired smile. "Depending on how long we're stuck in here, I might just be tempted." He looked up as the timbers overhead creaked and groaned as the winds battered the structure. "How long do you think the repairs will hold if the storm gets worse?"

Ordel shrugged. He was a decade older than Niklas, and the

hardships of the last few years had taken their toll. To Niklas's eye, Ordel looked tired.

"We'll see," Ordel replied. "The walls weren't in good shape, and we didn't have time to really repair them." He sighed. "You know what they say, 'Only a fool fights the wind.'" He paused. "How is it, up above?"

Niklas shrugged. "Winds are almost too strong to stand against. Freezing rain."

"Let's hope the ice doesn't put too much weight on the roofs."

Niklas grimaced. "I can only worry about so many things at once." He walked over to where the mages clustered together in one corner of the room. "Any news?" he asked.

Dagur looked up. "All the signs point to a long run of storms, some from the north and others coming up from the coast."

Niklas nodded. It was what he had expected, but it didn't hurt to ask. "If you can't shift the storm, can you protect our men and supplies?"

Dagur brightened. "That we've done. We've placed a preservation spell on the supplies, and protection spells on the barns." He grimaced. "Problem is, the magic is flickering like a candle—probably because of the storms. So we've placed the wardings, but there's no guarantee they'll hold."

Ayers walked up from behind Niklas. "Glad the two of you made it back," he said with a nod toward Carr. "Everything go well at the wedding?" One look at their expressions, and Ayers gave a low whistle. "Well then, maybe we should discuss something else."

"I didn't get the chance to tell you everything I found out on my last scouting trip," Carr said, lifting his chin defiantly. "There are Tingur, plenty of them, on the move."

Niklas turned his full attention to Carr. "How close? How many? Headed where?"

"When I spotted them, they were headed northwest, toward the Solveigs' lands," Carr reported. "I shadowed them for as long as I dared. They're a tight bunch, and I didn't think that I could infiltrate them, even if I knocked some bloke over the head and stole his robes."

Thank the gods for small favors, Niklas thought. He had noticed that Carr had fresh bruises on his face and raw scratches on his hands when he showed up at Glenreith, but at the time, Carr's prisoner had been the focus of attention. *I'm betting that Carr had a closer call than he's letting on.*

"Here's another thing," Carr added, and his expression gave Niklas to suspect that Carr had withheld this bit of information to get himself back into his commander's good graces. "There were messengers going back and forth between Lysander's camp and the Tingur. That's how I found the Tingur in the first place."

"Do you think they were headed here?" Niklas asked.

Carr grimaced. "It's possible. But if they stayed on their course toward the Solveigs, I'd bet Glenreith is a more likely target."

Niklas swore under his breath. "So one way or the other, we'll be fighting them soon."

"There's food and ale near the fire," Ordel said, with a nod in the direction of where Niklas's soldiers had added a fireplace and chimney to take the chill from the damp old barn. The small hearth was no match for the large space or the frigid wind outside.

As Carr walked away, Niklas noted that his limp was more pronounced.

"That boy has a real strong death wish," Niklas muttered.

Ordel sighed. "I suspect that's true." He paused. "We have very little knowledge of how the Madness affects survivors. He might not be fully in control of himself."

"I feel like I'm watching him attempt suicide over and over again until he gets it to work," Niklas said, running a hand back through his hair. "If it were anyone but Carr, I'd say that he was bucking for a promotion. Or that he was showing off for the rest of the troops."

"Carr's young," Ordel replied. "I suspect you had a few reckless moments yourself."

Niklas shook his head. "This is different. It's like each time Carr does something foolhardy and it doesn't kill him, the next time he ups the stakes. And sooner or later, he'll get his wish."

Ordel jerked his head toward the large, open barracks. "Go on. Do a walkabout. You'll feel better."

The barn had been nothing but old stone walls when Niklas and his men arrived at Mirdalur. It lacked a roof, and the floor of the loft had long ago rotted completely away, as had many of the supporting timbers. There were actually two parts to the old barn: the main section, which once had a high loft, and a single-story side building that was probably used for tack or storage. The soldiers slept in the large barn, while Niklas and the mages had claimed the smaller building as a command center. Niklas was glad he had put his soldiers to work shoring up both the barn and a nearby stable, since their tents would have been no match for the brutal storm, and their horses needed shelter.

Still, as the winds howled across the roof, Niklas watched the old stone walls with a wary eye. *Those walls have stood for a long time,* he argued to himself. *If they outlasted the Great Fire, surely they'll make it through a few more storms.* The timbers creaked again, and the wind outside howled, a worrisome sound.

Niklas was just about to head from the small building into the larger barn when there was a loud crack followed by the roar of falling rock. Men screamed, and rock dust billowed through the large open area.

"What in Raka was that?" one of the guards asked.

"I don't know, but I'm going to find out," Niklas said. He set off at a run as men crowded toward him, choking and waving at the clouds of dust. Ordel appeared out of the mayhem at his side.

"I figure you're going to need a healer," Ordel replied.

Niklas and Ordel fought against the tide of frightened soldiers. Niklas nearly gagged on the thick dust. "Clear the way!"

"Roof's falling in on us, Captain!" one of the soldiers said as Niklas pushed past him. "Rocks coming down—one of the walls just let go."

Niklas made it halfway across the barn before the cause became clear. "Sweet Esthrane and Charrot," he groaned, looking at the heap of rubble. Part of a wall had collapsed with a tumble of building stones and timber. More was in danger of falling with every icy blast of wind, and their shelter against the elements was now open to the rain and cold.

"It's the ice," Ordel said. "Those walls weren't in good shape, and after all they've been through, the ice was probably the last straw. All it would have taken was for the magic to flicker when the walls were under stress."

"We've got men under there," Niklas said. "We've got to get to them." He looked around. "And we need to get the others to shelter." He sighed. "Whether Dolan likes it or not, I say we send them into the tunnels down below."

By now, Ayers had caught up to them and was swearing under his breath as the extent of the damage became clear. "If we're not careful, we risk bringing more of it down on top of us."

"We've got to get in there," Niklas said. "There could be

survivors." He looked to Ayers. "Get half the men to shelter in the tunnels—try to keep them away from where the Knights are sleeping for the day. We'll take shifts, one group digging while the other group gets warm and rests. And send me the mages. Maybe they can help."

Ayers nodded and headed off, shouting orders as he went. Three soldiers shouldered their way through the crowd, and Niklas recognized them as being his best engineers.

"What can we do to get through to the men on the other side?" Niklas asked. "We've got to get in there, but I don't want to bring more of the roof down on us."

One of the engineers turned toward Niklas. "It's the wind and the weight of the ice that brought the wall down," he said. "The problem is, we could begin digging, and have more rubble fall."

Niklas nodded. "If we wait until the storm passes, we're not likely to pull anyone out alive."

Signar, the senior engineer, was a broad-shouldered man with graying temples who looked more than a decade older than Niklas. He stroked his close-cropped beard as he thought. "It would help if we could get a team outside," he said. "What we really need to know is whether there's another wall waiting to fall in."

A gust of wind blasted through the opening in the wall. "No one's going to be able to stay out long, between the wind and the cold," Niklas said.

"You had the right idea," Signar said. "We'll work in teams, take shifts."

"You've got a team," Carr said from behind them. "I'll go."

"Me, too," another voice answered.

"And me." Voice after voice echoed the phrase.

"I'll go with them," Signar said. "If there's another wall waiting to collapse, we either need to shore it up or bring it down in the opposite direction. Then we can start removing the rubble."

"I don't want to lose men to exposure on top of what we've lost to the cave-in." Niklas replied.

"Neither do I," Signar said. "I'll do my best not to let that happen." He looked to his fellow engineers. "Kornus and Poul—stay here with the captain and see what you can do."

"I need some of you to circle around and see if anyone got out on the other side," Niklas ordered. "Those are your friends under there. The sooner we get to them, the more men live through this. Go."

Niklas paced and then he stopped and looked at Ordel. "Does your healing magic tell you if we've got wounded in there?" he asked.

Ordel closed his eyes for a moment. "Yes. Several."

"And dead?"

Ordel paused for a few moments. "Harder to sense. But... there aren't as many alive as there should be."

"Damn."

Ordel opened his eyes. "It may not mean the rest are dead," he cautioned. "Perhaps they managed to escape."

Signar returned after half a candlemark. "Well?" Niklas demanded.

"One of the walls of the barn partially collapsed, bringing a section of the roof with it," Signar replied. "The others aren't in good shape. We think we've got them supported enough to hold while we dig for survivors." He eyed the beams overhead. "I think it's wise to move the men underground. The less time we spend here, the safer we'll be."

Niklas drew a deep breath. "All right. Go. Make sure you give the same news to the men on the other side. And let them know I'll send up fresh troops in a candlemark or so."

Signar nodded, then took off, shouldering his way through the crowd.

Niklas turned to the others, who had gathered close, trying to hear. "Listen up! We're going to form two lines, and we'll pass the rocks hand to hand to clear the area." He moved to the front of one of the lines. Ordel moved to the back of the area with the other healers to prepare to care for the wounded.

"Put your backs into it!" Niklas said, handing a heavy chunk of rock to the man behind him, who turned and passed the rock down the long line of men. From the grim looks on their faces, Niklas could see that the men understood the urgency.

"Got my shoes and got my pack," one of the men behind Niklas sang out above the howl of the wind.

"Headed out, ain't comin' back," the others responded.

"Got my sword and got my shield," the soldiers on the left side of the corridor sang.

"Left my home and left my fields," those on the right responded.

The call-and-response was an old one, well-known to soldiers in the Donderath army. Hearing it lifted Niklas's heart. No one knew how many verses there were. That chant had carried them from the Meroven border, mile upon weary mile. The verses ranged from silly to obscene, but the cadence was a comforting heartbeat. And today, as they passed rubble down the line, it was the defiant chorus that refused to give in to death itself.

Niklas lost track of time. One of his lieutenants came forward to relieve him. Exhausted, Niklas nodded in agreement, but instead of resting he stood to one side, watching the line, determined to remain part of the rescue effort until he was certain of the fate of the men trapped by the cave-in. Dagur and the other mages walked up and down along the walls that remained, reinforcing their wardings.

After a while, Ordel led fresh troops to relieve the men in the lines. "Go get warm and eat something," Ordel ordered. "You'll be coming back before long." He looked at Niklas. "I sent a relief team outside as well. You should go for a while, too. You can't stay here all night," Ordel said when he reached Niklas.

"Watch me." Niklas's hands were white with rock dust and streaked dark with blood from dozens of places where the sharp stone had cut his skin.

"You've been at this for three candlemarks. Let someone else take a turn, and come back when you've rested. You're no good to your men half-dead," Ordel argued in a low voice.

Niklas gave him a sidelong glance that let Ordel know just what he thought of the advice. Niklas's shoulders and back ached, as did his lower body from bending and lifting. His hands were a cut-up mess. "Just a little while longer," Niklas said. "The men underneath—they don't have much time left."

"It may already be too late," Ordel replied. "In which case, killing yourself won't help."

Niklas nodded, and shook a sodden lock of hair out of his eyes. "I know that. But we're going to keep digging as long as there's a chance we've got men alive in there."

Ordel nodded. "We'll patch up the other group and send them back in a candlemark or so," he replied, heading back toward the tunnels.

"Watch out!" the man behind Niklas shouted. The pile of rubble shifted, and men scrambled back.

"We're getting closer, Captain," the soldier shouted. "Not much longer now!"

The men behind Niklas gave a weary roar of triumph. Niklas was bone tired and every muscle ached, but the thought that they might be close to success gave him a surge of energy. Behind him, the soldiers swung into a new chorus of the cadence.

"Get back!" Dagur's voice barely carried above the rowdy chant. "Get back now, all of you!"

A loud boom sounded, and more of the damaged wall began to tumble toward them. Niklas gave the men behind him a shove with all his might. Chunks of stone rained down on them. Hoarse screams and shouting carried above the wind. The cold air was choked with dust.

"Move back!" Niklas shouted, ending in a fit of coughing as the rock dust filled his lungs. The dust was thick enough that it was almost impossible to see. Somewhere in the blinding grit and lashing winds, Niklas could hear men scrambling for safety, cursing and shouting. He stumbled blindly, and his feet caught on debris that might have been stones from overhead or the bodies of fallen comrades.

Something hard and heavy slammed into Niklas, catching him low in the back and sending him sprawling. He probed over his head with his fingertips, only to find two large timbers that both sheltered him from the worst of the collapse, and trapped him beneath it.

Niklas smelled blood and urine, and the pungent odor of entrails. He put a hand to his aching head, and his palm came away sticky with blood. Niklas carefully shifted, seeing how much room he had to move his legs. The effort sent pain arcing down his back intense enough to make him cry out. He gasped, then choked on the dust. Somewhere in the darkness, he heard men calling out for help.

"Can you hear me?" Niklas shouted. "Sound off if you hear me!"

"Jacobs."

"Renden."

"Jonsen."

"Pattersen."

One by one, men called out their names in the darkness until Niklas had counted eight other men trapped in the new collapse.

"Can't move my legs, Cap'n," a man called back. "Can't feel them, neither."

"I can move, I think," another soldier answered. "But I'm wedged in and I'm scared I'll bring the rest down on me."

"Sit tight," Niklas responded. "Ayers and the others know we're here. They'll come after us."

Rubble blocked out wind and light, and Niklas lost track of time. Overhead, he could hear rocks grinding and falling. The air beneath grew warm and stale, and Niklas's body cramped. Even if he could shift, he was afraid it would worsen the collapse. Fatigue eventually won out and allowed him restless sleep.

He woke with a start, and fought down panic. It was too quiet. Niklas wondered whether the others were sleeping, dead, or unconscious. Lying amid the rubble, Niklas let dreams take him. Memories of his boyhood at Arengarte seemed as fresh as if they had happened yesterday.

"Got a shovel, got a pick," distant voices sang out.

"Dig in deep and make it stick," other voices answered.

"Gonna get the captain free," the first voices responded.

"Pour some grog and one for me," came the reply.

The impromptu verses shook Niklas out of slumber. "Wake

up!" he called, his voice a dry croak. "Did you hear that? They're digging for us!"

"I think we've lost Jonsen, Cap," Renden said. "When I gave him a shake, he's cold and he didn't say nothin'."

"Let them know we're down here," Niklas said. "Give a shout!" They called out as loudly as they could, coughing and gagging in the dust.

"They're alive down there!" Ayers's voice carried, muffled through the rock and debris. "Pick up the speed, boys. Let's get them out."

Metal scraped on rock as the rescuers pried the rubble loose. Niklas ducked at a shower of small stones and dust that tumbled down from overhead. *Please don't let them get us crushed*, he thought. *Not when they're this close.*

Fresh, cold air rushed into the space where Niklas and his men were trapped, and they greeted it with weary cheers. Every stone the rescuers removed sent a shudder through the precarious support that held up the timbers over Niklas's head. He tried to wriggle forward, but the pain made him gasp. Night had fallen.

"Be careful. If those timbers shift, we die," Niklas rasped.

"Don't worry, Captain. We're working on it." Niklas recognized the voice. It was Liam, one of the *talishte* soldiers.

"Hold still," Liam said, carefully wriggling through the hole the others had cleared. He maneuvered so that he had his back against the timbers that angled over Niklas's head. "All right," Liam called to the rescuers. "Go ahead. I can hold this."

Stone by stone, the opening grew larger until Niklas could make out the shadowy shapes of men in the torchlight.

"There were eight of us when the roof came down," Niklas told Liam. "Take the worst-off first."

Liam shook his head. "We've got to take you out in the order we come to you, Captain. The mages are helping hold this pile up, but it's been shifting, and the storm hasn't helped. They're going to have to start nearest the entrance and work their way back."

Even as Liam spoke, Niklas saw two figures carefully lift a man's body and carry it out through the hole the rescuers had made in the debris.

"Watch the arm! I think it's pinned," Renden cautioned as the figures returned for him. Niklas heard the sound of rocks grinding against each other, and the timbers groaned ominously as the rescuers tried to free Renden.

"It's crushed. I can get you out, but I can't move the rock without bringing everything down on our heads," one of the rescuers cautioned.

"Do it," Renden replied. His voice trembled. "Just do it."

A moment later, Niklas heard the dull thud of steel on bone and a man's raw scream. Soldiers carried Renden out, the bleeding stump of his arm soaking his dust-caked shirt. Patterson crawled out, followed by Jacobs.

"Time to go," Liam said.

"There were eight of us," Niklas said.

"Only five alive," Liam replied. "Sorry."

Two *talishte* soldiers crawled through the cramped space to get to Niklas. "When we take you out and Liam lets go of those timbers, this whole place is likely to come down," one of the soldiers said. "We've got to be fast, so we might not be gentle."

"Understood," Niklas said, bracing himself.

Pain shot through his body as strong hands pulled him free. Niklas cried out. The hands tightened their grip, and then he was moving fast, supported by powerful arms, as the rubble roared down behind them.

In the next heartbeat, Niklas lay in the corridor on the hard stone floor, staring up at the ceiling. He was shaking from pain and cold, but he was alive. Ordel knelt next to him. Down the corridor, Niklas could hear the voices of the other battle healers. Ordel put a hand on his shoulder.

"Don't move. I'm trying to figure out what you've done to your back. If you stay still, you might get to walk again."

"How are the others?" Niklas could taste rock dust and blood in his mouth.

Ordel's expression was grim. "We lost Jonsen. The rock opened up a gash in his leg and he bled dry. Renden lost part of his arm, but I think he'll be all right." He grimaced. "Except for the arm."

"And the others?"

"Don't you think you should be worrying about yourself right now?" Ordel said.

"Not until I know. What about the others?" Niklas argued.

Ordel sighed. "We got five of you out alive. The other three might have been alive after the cave-in, but they didn't make it long enough for us to get to them. I'm sorry."

"Damn." Niklas paused. "How did the *talishte* soldiers get here?"

"Dolan woke when our men went into the tunnels. We're lucky he looks before he strikes," Ordel added with a grimace. "Ayers explained what happened, and as soon as the sun set, Dolan sent the *talishte* to help."

"I owe him. Ayers was right. We were running out of time."

Ordel nodded. "The mages told Ayers none of you would make it out alive if we kept digging without the *talishte*."

Niklas shivered. "Even so, it was too close."

Niklas fell silent as Ordel worked on him, struggling with himself to ask the question he most feared. "What about my back?" he asked finally.

Ordel nodded. "You took a hard wallop. You're purple from your waist to your ass. Everything's bruised to a pulp, but you didn't break your back and your spine's not damaged." He shook his head in amazement. "You're one lucky son of a bitch."

"Is the storm over?"

"Pretty much," Ordel replied, bandaging a deep gash on Niklas's leg. "The worst of the storm ended about a candle-mark after the wall fell."

Niklas listened, trying to make sense of what he heard. Wind no longer howled past the chimneys and the vents. But instead of silence, the air was filled with the shouts of men and the clang of swords. He tried again to sit up, and once more, Ordel pressed him back.

"What's going on?" Niklas demanded.

Ordel swore under his breath. "Damn Tingur. Carr must not have spotted them all. They were waiting for us when the storm ended. Don't ask me where they sat out the wind. That's all I know."

Niklas cursed. "I should be out there."

Ordel fixed him with a glare. "You should be thanking the gods that you're alive and still able to walk. The Tingur are a dangerous nuisance. Trust your men to do what you've taught them to do."

"I should still be out there with them," Niklas growled.

"You're bruised enough," Ordel observed, sitting back on his haunches. He took a flask from his belt and helped Niklas sit up long enough to take a drink. It burned down Niklas's throat.

"Let me give you something for the pain—something stronger than this," Ordel said, gesturing with the flask. "It'll let you sleep, and you'll heal faster."

"I want to see what's going on," Niklas insisted. He gritted his teeth and forced himself to a seated position, then gasped at the pain. Still, he waved away Ordel's restraining hand. "I may not be able to fight, but I want to be where my men can see me."

Ordel let out a long, frustrated breath. "The only way you're going to get up those stairs today is if someone carries you. You're in no condition for crutches. I've been working on you for two candlemarks, and you could undo everything. For what?"

"My men are up there. I should be with them," Niklas said. He tried to stand, and fell back with a curse.

Ordel glared at him. "You've made your point. Sit down. I'll get someone to help you, if you don't mind bruising your dignity along with your ass." He strode down the corridor and returned a few minutes later with a soldier and Walker, one of the healers.

"Take the Captain up where he can see what's going on outside," Ordel ordered. "Make sure he stays under cover. He shouldn't be on his feet, let alone fighting." He looked at Walker. "If he tries to join the battle, knock him out. I'll take full responsibility."

"Yes, sir."

"Don't make it too comfortable for him. He needs to be down here resting." He fixed Niklas with a glare. "The longer you stay up there, the longer it'll be before you're actually healed enough to be any good to anyone. Your choice." With that, Ordel turned and walked away, snapping orders at the other healers.

"I'm going to need some help," Niklas admitted. The pain nearly made him pass out as the men lifted him to his feet.

"Sir? Do you want to sit back down? You've gone pale," Walker asked worriedly.

"Just get me up there," Niklas muttered between gritted teeth. It took all his concentration not to black out. Every step hurt, and his ribs ached from the strain of being supported by the two men. They made their way to the outside and stood in the cover provided by the ruins of the barn. Whether the winds had flattened part of the stockade wall that surrounded the camp, or whether the Tingur had brought it down while the camp was undefended, Niklas had no way to know, but through that break in their defenses streamed dozens of ragged, wild-eyed men.

Above the fray, Niklas could hear Ayers shouting orders. "I need a better view," Niklas growled, frustrated by the ruined wall that both protected them and blocked their line of sight.

"Ordel was very clear—"

"I heard what Ordel said," Niklas snapped. "But I'm your captain, and I want to see what in Raka is going on!"

"Yes, sir." Walker helped Niklas shift position. The soldier who had accompanied them was standing guard.

"How many of them do you figure there are?" Niklas muttered.

Walker's eyes narrowed as he counted. "Hard to tell, but at least a few dozen that we can see, probably more."

Niklas cursed under his breath. "Can't you bring them down with dysentery or make them break out in boils or something?"

Walker looked horrified. "Maybe some healers can, sir. I'm not that powerful. And we're not supposed—"

"I know you're not supposed to use your magic to make people sick," Niklas snapped. "But making the enemy sick stops them from making our boys dead. Is there something you can do?"

"I've never tried to do anything like that before, sir," Walker replied.

"Just try," Niklas replied. "And you can tell Ordel that I ordered you to do it."

"Yes, sir."

Walker stared at the breach in the wall where the fighting was most vicious. His face grew taut with concentration, and his eyes took on a glassy look. "The magic's not good," he murmured. "It's flickering. I'm having trouble holding on to it."

"Try."

Ayers was near the forefront of the fighting, shouting insults at the attackers and orders to his own men. The Tingur were armed with farm tools and clubs, but what they lacked in proper weapons they made up for in rage. They fought like wild men, shouting their devotion to Torven, caught up in ecstatic fury.

Walker raised one hand, his eyes still fixed on the break in the wall, and began to chant. The cords in his neck grew visible with the strain, and his chant grew faster. One of the Tingur screamed and collapsed. Another, and then another dropped to the ground, writhing and vomiting blood. Niklas's soldiers gave a shout and pressed forward. Niklas glimpsed Carr at the forefront of the fight, stepping over the bloody bodies of the fallen Tingur to give chase.

If he comes back alive, I'm going to kill him, Niklas thought, watching as Carr ran bellowing after the retreating Tingur.

Ayers and the soldiers surged forward as the Tingur forces fell to their knees in surrender or ran in disarray. Even as they turned and ran, some of the Tingur collapsed as Walker's magic found them. They dropped to the ground, flopping like gigged fish, blood fountaining from their mouths, streaming from ears, eyes, and noses.

"They're gone," Niklas said, too exhausted and in too much pain to feel exultant about the victory.

He turned to Walker, who stood stock-still, arm upraised, unmoving. Tears streamed down Walker's face, and he had gone pale. His voice was rough as he continued his chant.

"You can stop now—they're gone," Niklas said, worry beginning to prickle at the back of his neck. "You did it. You turned the battle for us. We won."

Walker's chant rumbled on, reaching a crescendo as if he had not heard a word Niklas had said. He wrested his outstretched hand closed in a fist in a sudden, violent movement, and gasped. His head fell forward, chin to chest, and his arm lowered, but otherwise, Walker was motionless except for heavy, labored breathing.

Niklas watched Walker carefully. "Walker?"

Walker lifted his head slowly, and his expression was baleful. "I did what you ordered, Captain. Only because the magic isn't right, the working went wrong. I meant to make them ill. But that's not what happened."

Niklas felt a growing cold that had nothing to do with the weather. He glimpsed horrors in Walker's eyes. "What did you do?" Niklas asked quietly.

"The magic ruptured their bellies and ripped their entrails apart," Walker replied, his voice tight with his struggle to hold on to his sanity. "*I* ripped them apart," he added, loathing clear in his voice. He was breathing shallowly, trembling.

"So at the end—" Niklas started. Walker cut him off.

"At the end I finished what I started," Walker said in a voice that sounded nothing like his own. "They were suffering. They could have lain there for candlemarks, dying in agony. So I snuffed out their light."

Walker's eyes had the wide-pupil, glazed look of someone in shock. He had not heard Ordel come up behind Niklas. He glanced at Walker, who appeared more unhinged with every passing moment, then to Niklas, then beyond them to the dozens of bloody corpses that littered the camp near the break in the wall. He shot an icy glare at Niklas, and approached Walker carefully.

"You've been through a lot," Ordel said gently. "Let's get you down below." He reached for Walker's arm, but Walker wrenched it away and backed up a few steps.

"Don't you understand? I didn't mean to kill them," Walker said pleadingly. "I only wanted to bring them down. It wasn't supposed to work like that." He swallowed hard, his voice ragged. "I didn't even know that could happen until I felt them tearing apart."

Ordel nodded. "It's not your fault," he soothed. "The magic is unpredictable. There's no way you could have known. Please, come below. I can help you forget."

Walker was shuddering uncontrollably, his breath coming in sobs. "I don't deserve to forget," he snapped. "I should be out there burying those bodies myself. *I* did that to them. I'm supposed to be a healer, and I ripped those men to shreds."

"I take responsibility," Niklas said. "I gave the order. I forced you to do it. And you saved lives—you saved our soldiers."

"I felt them die," Walker whispered. "I felt the first one die, and I didn't stop. Torven take my soul, I didn't stop and I knew what was happening." He wavered on his feet as if he might collapse. Ordel had moved several steps closer. He grabbed Walker's arm.

"Sleep," Ordel commanded. Walker's eyes rolled up toward the back of his head and his body fell to the ground.

"What in the name of Torven did you make him do?" Ordel snapped.

Niklas was leaning against the ruined wall, trying to remain on his feet. He stared at the fallen healer, and let out a deep breath. "I ordered him to slow down the Tingur," he replied. "I didn't expect him to kill them. I just wanted him to make them sick." His legs were shaking so badly from the strain of standing despite his injuries that he let himself slide down the wall to sit, and even that brought a gasp of pain.

Ordel knelt next to Walker. "He's a healer," he said reprovingly. "He wasn't even an army healer. He's never seen action before."

"I was trying to save our men," Niklas said, and the pain, weariness, and self-reproach came out as anger. "I didn't know. And he did save lives on our side. First blood is always the hardest." *Sweet Esthrane, I sound hard and bitter*, Niklas thought.

Ordel picked Walker up in his arms like a wounded child. "I'll see what I can do for him, blur the memories, try to make sure he wakes up in better shape." His feelings about the subject were clear in his face. "I'll send someone back up for you."

Ayers came around the side of the wall just as Ordel disappeared in the cellars. "Glad you're alive, Captain," he said. "But you don't look so good."

Niklas let out a deep breath, and tried to ignore the lancing pain. "How did it go?"

Ayers grimaced. "I don't have a count yet. Fewer dead than wounded—on our side, at least. The Tingur come at us like wildcats just let out of the bag, but they're lousy hand-to-hand. I think they get most of their hits in because they're so damn unpredictable."

He paused. "What happened, at the end? All of a sudden, the Tingur went down and started purging blood. It scared me shitless."

Niklas told him. Ayers was silent for a moment. "War goes like that," he said finally. "If you live through the battle, the dead get their vengeance in your dreams."

"What about the rest of the Tingur?" Niklas asked.

"The ones who didn't die ran off. They're not much more

than a mob," Ayers said. "I don't know what Lysander's promised them, or how they think that getting themselves killed in battle helps out Torven, but it's a bit like slaughtering mad dogs. Easy and horrible at the same time."

"There's one more thing," Ayers added. "Carr and a handful of men went after the Tingur. I called for them to stop, but they kept going. There weren't enough of our men to run the Tingur to ground, but they might have wanted to shadow them back to their camp."

"Damn." Niklas paused, trying to catch his breath when a spasm in his back nearly made him black out. "When Carr gets back, I want to see him."

"If he comes back," Ayers replied. "He didn't bring all his gear back to camp with him, so my bet is he'll go out scouting again. How do we know the difference between when he's out spying and when he's gone rogue?"

"Good question." Niklas shifted, and bit back a curse at the pain. "I think Ordel is going to leave me up here as long as possible to make me suffer for what happened to Walker," Niklas said. "I'd be much obliged for some help."

Ayers got under his arm and Niklas choked back a cry of pain as he rose to his feet. "I have a flask down with my things," Ayers offered. "Let's get below, and I'll fetch it for you."

"Much obliged," Niklas grated through clenched teeth. "Whiskey will help," he said. *But it won't, not really,* he thought. *Because when you sober up, the dead are still just as dead.*

CHAPTER
TWENTY-ONE

―――

J ARLE WAS YOUR FRIEND, AND HE'S DEAD," CARENSA
said, daring to stare down Vigus Quintrel.

She had been back at Torsford for a day, not yet physically recovered from the last battle, though she doubted she would ever forget the bloodshed she had seen. Now, alone in the mage's workshop with Quintrel long after the others had gone to bed, Carensa could not hold back.

"And I have already told you how sorry I am that such a thing happened," Quintrel replied. Carensa could almost believe him. Quintrel's voice was appropriately sincere, his manner just the right degree of concerned. *Almost.* Calculation glinted in Quintrel's eyes, something that had not been there before. *Or,* she thought with a sigh, *she had been too naïve to see it.*

"You're influencing Rostivan, so it wasn't really his decision to take us to the battlefield. It was yours." Carensa knew she was on dangerous ground. Yet if anything of the old Vigus remained, Carensa felt duty-bound to be his conscience.

Quintrel turned away. "We must make it clear that an alliance with us—as equals, not as servants—has its benefits." He softened his tone. "These are desperate times, Carensa,"

Quintrel continued. Carensa could still hear the charisma in his voice, though it no longer swayed her.

"There's a moment when the wind is changing, when a ship has to fill its sails or miss its chance," Quintrel went on. "This is Donderath's moment. The old ways are gone. The slate has been wiped clean. We stand in a moment of remaking, when the future of the entire Continent is as malleable as putty." His eyes were alight with passion—or madness.

"Can't you feel it? We are alive at this moment for a reason, Carensa. We are mages at this moment because destiny has willed it. We have an opportunity that only comes once every millennium—to change the course of history and make of it what we want."

Funny, she thought, *I never realized how he calculates every word, every gesture to get a response. It's like he's rehearsed it all for effect. Nothing is spontaneous.*

"I know that the kingdom is a tinderbox," Carensa said, choosing her words carefully. "Rostivan set the Arkalas back on their heels—for now. But what about Lysander? Or the Solveigs? All I see is squabbling for territory as everything falls to Raka around us."

Quintrel looked at her with pity. "That's because you don't have the gift of foresight. Chaos is a process when great things are born. It's a forge, a crucible. It makes us stronger so we can seize the best the future offers." The orb with its *divi* spirit hung in a pouch on a leather strand around Quintrel's neck. Even with the string drawn shut, Carensa could see a glow from the top of the pouch. The *divi* was listening.

He's speaking in platitudes, Carensa thought, *the kind he might use to whip a crowd up into a fervor. When did I become immune?*

"It didn't make Jarle stronger," Carensa said quietly. "It made him dead."

"Jarle wasn't strong enough for the future that's coming," Quintrel snapped. "The more you and the other mages help Rostivan, the more we prove our worth. We need soldiers to keep the peace and defend our interests," Quintrel explained, his eyes alight with the promise of his vision. "And they need to understand that without us, they cannot get and keep the power they desire." The *divi's* glow surged and then dimmed. Carensa was certain the spirit was paying attention.

"Rostivan considers us disposable—and replaceable," Carensa said, lifting her chin. "Is that how you see us?"

Quintrel's expression softened into a smile, and for an instant, it was easy to believe he was the same mentor who had rescued her from the Great Fire. "Carensa. How can you doubt me? You could never be replaced. Each of you have such special gifts. You are all precious."

His voice is saying all the right things, but his eyes are cold as ice, Carensa thought. *And he brought two new mages with him, one to replace Jarle and a spare. Vigus is the only mage who isn't disposable. The rest of us are just tools to accomplish his vision.*

"I'm glad to hear you say that, Vigus," Carensa said, ducking her head so that Quintrel did not meet her gaze. She did her best to suffuse her voice with the admiration she once felt. But she knew her eyes would give her away. "It was such a shock, being in the battle. I don't think I'm quite recovered yet." Once, Quintrel had doted on her as a promising pupil. Now Carensa bet on the fact that his pride would not allow him to see that the student no longer trusted the master.

"First blood is difficult," Quintrel replied in a fatherly tone. "But when you look at the temporary difficulty from the perspective of the grand vision...well, it changes how you see everything."

Oh, it has, Carensa thought. *But not in the way you intended.* "We should have the University up and functioning in a week or two," Carensa said, changing subjects. She turned away, gesturing toward the library, but it was really to avoid making eye contact with Quintrel. "What then?"

"We must solve the problem of anchoring the magic," Quintrel replied. "We've made two attempts to bring McFadden to us, and both failed. Dolan has the crystals, but oddly enough he hasn't used them yet. We need to act before Dolan can make a move."

"How?" Carensa asked warily.

"If we can't control McFadden, we must destroy him," Quintrel replied. "That's why we must make our own people the dominant power in Donderath—and then the Continent." Enthusiasm warmed his voice. "We'll adapt to deal with the magic as it is now. Imagine a king of our choosing, with our mages at his side, creating a new kingdom as it should always have been, with mages coequal to the king."

Is that what the divi *has promised you?* Carensa thought. *And you believed it? Because I don't see the* divi *sharing power, and how can a return to magic chaos and the storms help us?* She drew a deep breath. *This is against everything we worked for; the Vigus I thought I knew was too smart to fall for that,* she thought. *Vigus and the rest of us are being used as pawns.*

"That's a lofty vision," Carensa said, hoping she sounded appropriately impressed. "But if you destroy McFadden, how do you know it won't make the magic wild again?"

Quintrel's hand shifted unconsciously to the *divi* orb in its pouch. "McFadden is a Lord of the Blood," he replied. "Blood magic is the oldest and most powerful. I've been studying. And if we can't capture McFadden, then I believe we can make his death serve us." A strange light glinted in Quintrel's eyes, the same as the glow from the *divi* orb.

"What does the University have to do with it?"

"The mages in the last war didn't properly understand how magic was bound. Now we do. McFadden harnessed magic, but that magic is different. We need mages who can work with this new magic. And we must transfer—or wrest—magic's anchor away from McFadden. He's the weak point. Even if it means his death." Quintrel sighed. "If only Lowrey hadn't failed..."

Carensa held her breath to avoid speaking. *Lowrey? Vigus, what have you done? It was bad enough when you wanted to lock Blaine up, maybe for the rest of his life. But to kill him and risk the loss of magic, the return of the beasts, and the storms, when you worked so hard to anchor the magic to him?*

"How?" Carensa asked. *If he trusts me, he'll tell me the truth. Or else he sees right through me, and he's setting me up.*

"Ally with his enemies, break his allies." His smile was predatory, the glint in his eyes not altogether sane.

Carensa warmed her hands at the fireplace. She had taken a sudden chill. "Is Rostivan strong enough to do that?"

"By himself, no. But allied with all those who see McFadden as a threat...definitely." He paused. "We've already made overtures to Lord Pollard and Lysander."

I knew Vedran Pollard, Carensa thought. *He was a nasty, backstabbing son of a bitch before the Great Fire, and I doubt his temperament has improved.*

Quintrel gave a mysterious smile and leaned back in his chair. "Our mages help them win their battles, then feed information back to me, and exert control."

And if Pollard and Lysander realized we were betraying them, they'd kill us in a heartbeat, Carensa thought.

Quintrel smiled reassuringly. "Don't worry, Carensa. Once you make up your mind to do whatever it takes, victory is certain. Rostivan wants to win. He's open to any proposal that gets him power." He paused. "That desire makes him easy to control. You might even argue that being manipulated by the *divi* to get what he wants falls under 'whatever it takes.' It's not difficult to tempt someone who goes willingly."

Whatever it takes, she thought. *How many people's deaths are factored into that equation? By Esthrane! He's just declared that no price is too high to get what he wants. And I'm going to be right in the middle of it.*

Quintrel got to his feet. "Rostivan and I are due to meet. He spoke well of your involvement at the battle, Carensa. You impressed him. That's important. The *divi's* control is subtle; Rostivan isn't a mindless puppet on strings. The coercion works best when he believes he is making up his own mind." He paused. "I trust you're recovered from the exertion of the outing?"

Carensa managed a smile. "I'm just a little tired."

It was impossible for her to read Quintrel's expression. Quintrel would be a formidable adversary. Whether or not he knew it, that's exactly what he had become.

"But after all the effort you put into helping McFadden bring back the magic, if you kill him, won't it all be for naught?" She did her best to make the question sound completely academic.

"Magic wasn't always harnessed for human use," Quintrel replied, falling into the tone he used to lecture students. "Go back far enough, and the Lords of the Blood didn't inherit their power, they seized it on their own. Since McFadden won't cooperate with us to let us join with him to re-anchor the magic, then we must do the same." He met her gaze, and his eyes were alight with ambition and madness.

"Kill McFadden, and the slate is wiped clean. No mortal

Lords of the Blood remain. The *divi* has helped us find old records. With its help, we can name our own Lords of the Blood, cement our own dynasty of mages, shape magic as we deem it should be," he said with the fervor of a convert.

"Can you do that? Truly?" Carensa replied, aghast. "Name your own Lords of the Blood?"

Quintrel nodded. "It's what McFadden will have to do, if he lives long enough to try to re-anchor the power. And if he gets that chance, it will lock us out of true power for generations, unless we kill his chosen. And that will become much more difficult once they have been anointed Lords of the Blood."

Carensa tried to hide her shock. She replayed the conversation with Quintrel in her mind. *Vigus isn't just a danger to Blaine. He's a danger to the mages, to the soldiers, and to Donderath. And I have absolutely no idea what to do about it,* she concluded with a sigh.

That evening, Carensa sat by the window in her room, watching the rain. *I remember watching the raindrops run down the windowpane when I was a child,* Carensa thought, keeping the same raindrop in view as it made its way down the glass. *How much less complicated things were then!*

She rehashed her alternatives, and found none of them to be promising. Going against Quintrel head-on was impossible. Even with the brittle new magic, his power was much stronger than hers. An outright coup would just mean death, her own and the deaths of any who came to her aid. There would only be one opportunity, and it would likely be fatal for both Quintrel and his attackers. *My magic is translation. I can barely light a candle with magic. What can I possibly do?*

The knock at her door startled her. Carensa reluctantly left her chair and went to greet her visitor. Guran stood in the doorway with a pot of tea.

"I didn't think you looked well at dinner," he said. "I brought you some tea. May I come in?"

Carensa moved to the side to allow him to enter. "That's very kind of you," she said. "I don't think I've quite recovered from the battle."

Guran placed the tray on her desk, and poured a cup for each of them. "Should I be worried?"

Carensa shrugged. "No more than before," she replied. With Quintrel in the building, it was unwise to speak plainly. And even though she knew Guran could temporarily block them from being overheard, Carensa did not know whether or not Quintrel could sense it. She did not want Quintrel to question her loyalty. Too much was at stake. *I don't dare have Vigus doubt me. If he isn't completely sure of me, I won't have the access when I need it. We have to be very, very careful until then.*

Carensa shook her head. "I just never expected to be anywhere close to a battle. And then, to see Jarle die…" It required no acting on her part to look distressed.

"Dag said that Vigus paid you a visit," Guran said neutrally.

He suspects, Carensa thought. *Now we begin the cat-and-mouse game of saying things without saying them.*

Carensa weighed her words. She would need to give Guran information he would interpret correctly, while having the conversation be utterly innocent should they be overheard.

"He wanted to see how I was doing, and to tell me a little more about his plans," she replied.

"Oh?"

"He helped me put the pieces together about where we fit with Rostivan," Carensa replied. "We'll be training battle mages for the allies Vigus hopes to make—Pollard and Lysander."

"I suspect it's going to take a lot of conversations to make this happen," he said, with a meaningful glance that told Carensa his agenda differed from Quintrel's.

She nodded. "We'll all have to take a look at how our magic comes into play and what we can do to have an impact."

"These kinds of things take shape best with a core team. Too many people and it gets unwieldy," Guran agreed.

"The smaller the better," Carensa agreed. *Then again, if Vigus goes around expounding on his 'vision' too often and too loudly, I suspect those allies' spies will carry the word back before we have a chance to do anything.*

Guran took a deep breath, steadying himself. "Well, I've kept you long enough. But I'm glad for the news."

"Thank you for the tea," Carensa said, laying a hand on Guran's arm. He put an arm around her shoulder.

Carensa closed the door behind him and bit back tears of disappointment and frustration. *How did things go so wrong so quickly?*

She stared at the fire, watching the flames flicker. *There's going to be a bloodbath, and I've got to find a way to stop it. One way or another, I've got to stop Quintrel before he can work his plan.*

Carensa watched nervously as Rostivan pulled Quintrel into discussions behind closed doors. They had expected to meet with Quintrel to discuss plans, but Carensa and Guran were left chafing, wondering what their masters had in mind.

"Be ready to go in a candlemark," Quintrel told Carensa and Guran when he emerged from his private conversation with Rostivan.

"Go where?" Carensa asked, alarmed. She and the others

had just returned from the battlefield, and Carensa had hoped they would have a few weeks to recover before being sent on another task.

"Diplomatic mission," Quintrel replied with a wave of his hand. "Essential business. Utmost urgency."

"Why us?" Guran asked suspiciously.

Quintrel looked at him as if the answer were obvious. "I need a translator and a far-seer. Don't worry—we'll have a contingent of guards to assure our safety on the road."

Neither Quintrel's assurances nor Rostivan's guards were likely to assuage Carensa's worries, but she said nothing. Her bags were still packed, so readying herself for the journey took only minutes. Carensa stared out the window of her room at the snow, sorting through the possibilities, uncomfortable with any of the reasons for the journey that she could devise.

"Where exactly are you taking us, Vigus?" Guran pressed as they rode away from Torsford.

"The Kells Mill Lyceum," Quintrel replied offhandedly. At the throat of his tunic, the *divi* orb pulsed a bright yellow, something Carensa had come to understand meant that the spirit that resided inside it was pleased. Anything that pleased the *divi* worried Carensa.

Guran and Carensa exchanged a look. "That's on the border of Karstan Lysander's lands," Guran warned. "What could possibly be worth the risk?"

"You'll see," Quintrel answered, spurring his horse onward. Carensa sought counsel in Guran's expression, but he merely shrugged, looking as uncomfortable and perplexed as she felt. With a heavy heart, she snapped the reins, her worries as dark as the snow clouds on the horizon.

The village of Kells Mill was a three-candlemark ride from Torsford. Carensa was glad for her heavy cloak, hat, and scarf.

She huddled down into her cloak against the wind, but kept a wary eye on the roadway and the hedgerow. Brigands now ruled Donderath's highways, once safeguarded by King Merrill's soldiers. Rostivan's team of ten soldiers seemed paltry to Carensa, who had heard tell of bandit gangs of two or three times that many men, preying on anyone foolish enough to journey the shattered kingdom's ruined roadways.

Once, Kells Mill was a prosperous town with a large grist mill that drew farmers and merchants from miles around. Carensa looked at the deserted fields and abandoned farms along their route, feeling a familiar pang of sadness. Some of the barns and homes had burned in the Great Fire; others might have been destroyed in the Cataclysm. But for many, Carensa guessed that their desperate owners just walked away to seek their fortune somewhere, anywhere, else.

"Why Kells Mill?" Guran probed. Quintrel had been maddeningly silent for the entire ride. Carensa and Guran had chatted quietly with each other, but neither felt free to speculate on the question that was uppermost in their minds.

"Because it's neutral ground," Quintrel replied. He refused to say anything more until the village's bell tower came into view. The longer they rode, the more worried Guran looked. Given his abilities, that gave Carensa deep cause for concern.

Before the Cataclysm, the Kells Mill bells would have rung out the candlemarks for farmers and villagers alike. Now the tower was a ruined, blackened hulk, scorched and broken where the Great Fire had touched it. The bell tower sat in the center of the village, which was surrounded by a high stockade fence patrolled by guards.

"I'm not sure about how neutral this ground is," Guran murmured as they rode through the village gates.

Carensa had to agree as she looked from side to side. Few

people walked along the village streets, and those she saw were soldiers. The suspicion she had tried to dismiss since they left Torsford loomed large, and she could no longer ignore it.

"Does your gift tell you anything?" Carensa asked Guran quietly.

"You won't like it."

"We're going to meet with Lysander, aren't we?" she said.

Guran nodded. "Almost certainly."

Quintrel rode down the main street of the village with Carensa and Guran behind him, flanked by guards who also took up the rear of the procession. They approached the largest building still standing in the village, a home that Carensa guessed must once have belonged to the richest man in town. The home looked hard used, damaged by the Great Fire and repaired by workers less skilled than those who built it. Now it appeared to have been pressed into service as a headquarters for the most dangerous warlord in Donderath.

Four uniformed soldiers blocked their path. "State your purpose," the ranking soldier demanded.

Quintrel waved his hand in dismissal. "We are here by arrangement with Lord Lysander. Step aside and let us pass."

The soldier leveled an appraising glance at the team of guards that accompanied Quintrel. "They stay out here," he said. "You three, dismount and approach."

Not exactly a warm welcome, Carensa thought.

"Lord Lysander has placed a condition upon his agreement to meet with you," the soldier said, and as they walked closer, Carensa could see insignia indicating that the man was a captain.

"I agreed to no conditions," Quintrel bristled.

The captain shrugged. "Perhaps not, but the condition remains."

"What is it?" Quintrel demanded.

The captain held out three agate disks with hollow centers, strung on three separate leather lanyards. Even at a distance, the disks gave off a strange magical aura that Carensa found uncomfortable.

"These are null amulets. They dampen magic," the captain said. "You will wear them if you wish to meet with Lord Lysander."

Carensa expected a challenge from Quintrel, but instead, the mage-scholar gave a tolerant smile. "Of course," he said as if the request was customary. He allowed the captain to place the amulet's strap over his head, and gestured for Carensa and Guran to do the same. Carensa noticed that the *divi* orb no longer glowed, nor was it visible at the neck of Quintrel's tunic.

Carensa felt a physical jolt as the amulet touched her skin. She was one of the least powerful of Quintrel's mages, and her magic—translating languages—seemed insignificant compared to the grander power of the others. Carensa had the uncomfortable feeling of being partially blind, constrained as if someone had rolled her up in a heavy blanket that blocked motion, sight, and sound. Just like when the magic had died. She could not guess what it felt like for Quintrel or Guran, but from Guran's expression, she suspected he was also decidedly uncomfortable. Quintrel did not seem to be affected, and his mood was buoyant.

The captain escorted them through the old home's scarred front hallway and into a room that might once have been the office of the well-to-do merchant or gentleman farmer who owned the house. The ravages of storms, fire, and errant magic had taken a toll on the house and its furnishings, dimming its former grandeur.

"So you're the mage I've heard about." Karstan Lysander

sat behind a large, solid wooden desk. He did not rise to greet them, and there were no chairs to welcome visitors. A fire burned in the fireplace, barely taking the chill from the room. Lysander spoke with a heavy accent, one Carensa searched her memory to place.

Carensa studied Lysander, trying to match the reality to the legend. Karstan Lysander was a large man, broad-shouldered and thick-necked. His dark eyes were cold and it almost seemed possible to see the calculations going on behind them. No one would consider him handsome. His face was fleshy, like the wild hogs that roamed the countryside. In the close confines of the warm room, an unpleasant odor hung about Lysander that made Carensa want to wrinkle her nose. Yet from his heavy boots to his sturdy weapons to the scars that marked his hands and face, no one could doubt Lysander was a warrior.

Standing behind him was another man, in mage robes, who looked vaguely familiar to Carensa. Nothing in the mage's face betrayed any recognition, and Carensa struggled to keep her own features impassive as she put the face with a name. *Dro Hastins,* her memory supplied. *At least, that's what he called himself back in Castle Reach, before the Great Fire. He was one of Quintrel's hangers-on.*

"My lord," Quintrel said with a bow. "We are honored."

Lysander looked at him with curiosity. "You requested a meeting. I'm here. What do you want?"

Carensa glanced at Quintrel in alarm. Vigus Quintrel's opinion of himself was as grand as his magic, and she had never known him to permit anyone to speak so dismissively to him. Yet to her amazement, Quintrel did not look perturbed in the least.

"To be blunt, we wish to further our alliance."

Carensa stifled a gasp. Guran looked alarmed. But Quintrel continued as if the request was nothing out of the ordinary. Lysander regarded Quintrel with heavy-lidded eyes, unreadable.

"You're already aligned with Rostivan, and he's helping rid me of some unwanted pests. What need do I have for mages?" Lysander challenged. Carensa finally recognized Lysander's thick accent: It was common in the region nearest the Meroven border. Before the war, many of the mountain villages had kept to themselves for so long that they spoke an unusual dialect not found anywhere else in Donderath. It was rumored Lysander had drawn on Meroven mercenaries to swell the ranks of his army, in addition to the Tingur. Carensa chafed at the effect of the magic-dampening amulets, since it hindered her ability to easily understand the whispered conversation between Lysander's captain and a guard at the door.

"I suggest a grander alliance, and I am empowered by General Rostivan to extend an offer of truce and to negotiate further, on his behalf," Quintrel continued smoothly.

"I would be more likely to accept your surrender than your truce," Lysander growled. "What do I need from you that I can't do on my own or that Rostivan hasn't already promised?"

"Real magic," Quintrel replied. "The kind of magic that turns the tide of battles." Quintrel was at his charming best, and Carensa thought she caught a hint of a glow from the *divi* orb. The light lasted for a fraction of a second, but it left Carensa wondering whether the *divi* was constrained at all by Lysander's amulets.

"I had my fill of magic in the Meroven War," Lysander replied.

"Perhaps," Quintrel said agreeably. "But what will you do when you go up against Tormod Solveig? Animating the battlefield dead is child's play to a necromancer of his power. What happens when he decides to wrest the living soul from your soldiers?" Quintrel asked.

"McFadden's assembled his own mages, and he's allied with the Knights of Esthrane," Quintrel continued. My mages know those Knights, studied their magic. How will you stand against such powerful *talishte* mages without mages of your own?"

Lysander glowered at him, but did not end the conversation. "What do you propose?"

"Protection spells for you and your soldiers," Quintrel said. "Magic to turn back the undead. Wardings *talishte* cannot cross. A translator to make it easier for you to communicate with your Meroven mercenaries. A far-seer, who can look beyond the scope of mortal vision. And a priceless gift for you to make you impossible to kill—if you will accept it."

Interest and skepticism flickered in Lysander's black eyes. "Interesting. Tell me about this 'gift.'"

Quintrel smiled and leaned forward, warming to the tale. "Such a gift was given by the first Knights of Esthrane to King Hougen many years ago, and the king did not die until he removed the charm," Quintrel said.

"You've heard the tales, no doubt, about Randuvil the Destroyer?" Quintrel added. Carensa recognized the name as belonging to the most storied warlord in Donderath's history, an invincible fighter who conquered nearly the entire Continent. "This amulet was created from manuscripts we found in Valshoa made by the maker of Randuvil's talisman. Those manuscripts have been hidden away for hundreds of years, which is why no one in all these centuries had such a charm."

He shrugged. "I brought it to give to you, but it can't work in the presence of these amulets," he said, as if that settled the matter. "It must be attuned to you, something that can only be done in your presence." He paused. "It's of no consequence. I can take it back with me."

Carensa could almost hear Lysander's internal struggle. Greed glinted in his eyes, and she knew Quintrel had been cagey enough to determine what Lysander would find irresistible. After a moment, Lysander nodded.

"You may remove your amulets," Lysander said, and Carensa guessed that caution had lost out to avarice. Once again, Carensa thought she saw the barest glimmer of the *divi* orb, but it was gone as soon as she blinked.

Carensa felt as if a heavy weight had been lifted from her chest as she removed the amulet and set it aside. Guran also wasted no time removing the talisman, nor did Quintrel. Lysander's guards felt compelled to move a step closer from their stations along the walls, but the warlord motioned for them to stand down.

"Show me," Lysander rumbled.

Quintrel reached inside his coat and withdrew a velvet pouch with elaborate, arcane embroidery in golden thread. "Quite literally, a gift worthy of a king," Quintrel said, holding it aloft.

"Just think: the power of Randuvil the Destroyer, for you," he said, staring at the pouch in awe.

I'll give him credit: Quintrel's a showman, Carensa thought. Quintrel was reeling in Lysander like an expert fisherman, and from the naked desire in the warlord's eyes, the bait was working.

"Mage! Your assistance is required." Lysander's voice brought Hastins to the forefront. "Test this item with your magic. Tell me what you find."

Carensa held her breath. If Hastins had parted faith with Quintrel, there was no way a mage of any power could help but sense the *divi*'s presence. Hastins's betrayal would mean certain death for her and for Quintrel.

Hastins looked bored, even slightly contemptuous, as he reached out to take the pouch from Quintrel. He weighed the velvet pouch in his hand, passing his other palm above it, then closed his eyes, as if focusing his magic. After a moment of silence, Hastins looked to Lysander.

"He speaks the truth," Hastins said. "The amulet is as he has told you. I sense no ill intent." Hastins handed the pouch back to Quintrel as if it were of little interest.

"Give it to me." Lysander's voice was husky with hunger.

"As you wish," Quintrel said, making a shallow bow. Somehow he managed to keep his glee from showing in his face. Lysander was falling for it, just as Quintrel knew he would. And Hastins was in on it, Carensa realized, Quintrel's man on the inside.

Of course, she thought. *Hastins was Quintrel's infiltrator. He's working with Quintrel to make Lysander trust the orb, and he lied about the amulet being safe because Quintrel told him to lie. That's also how Quintrel could make a* divi *orb tied to Lysander—Hastins supplied him with something of Lysander's in order to bind him.*

Quintrel withdrew a small crystal orb much like his own *divi* sphere. This orb was much smaller, its surface etched with sigils and runes. Carensa could read the magical language. The markings would bend the sphere's wearer to Quintrel's will. Instead of a leather strap, the new orb was on a length of braided silken cord.

"Isn't it beautiful?" Quintrel said with a sigh, as if he were looking on the face of a lover. Lysander's gaze fixed on the orb, which as of yet showed none of the *divi*'s spark.

"My lord Lysander," Quintrel said, presenting the orb and its pouch with a flourish.

"Just imagine, m'lord," Quintrel continued. "You will become Randuvil's heir. Generations will celebrate your victories. Your name will be legend."

Lysander lifted the small orb and peered at it. "I see nothing extraordinary," he said, giving Quintrel a piercing look.

"That's because it must be activated to your personal energies," Quintrel replied with a smile. "It will attune itself once you wear it."

For a moment, Lysander looked conflicted, as if some inner warning fought with his desire for immortality. Greed won, and Lysander slipped the silken cord around his neck. The small orb lay on his breastbone, and after a few breaths, a yellow light flickered from its depths. At the same instant, Carensa saw an answering glimmer from the *divi* orb beneath Quintrel's tunic.

"The orb is your protector," Quintrel advised. "Never remove it. It will not only extend your life and give you luck, it will guide your decisions and visit your dreams with secrets that will allow you to rule over other men."

And it will worm its way into your brain and your soul, putting you entirely under the control of Vigus Quintrel, Carensa thought. From the unabashed avarice in Lysander's eyes, she concluded he was a man who had made more than one Raka's bargain in his life.

"A royal gift indeed," Lysander replied as one hand absently stroked the orb. The *divi* had begun its work. He looked to Quintrel, and the hardened glint came back to his black eyes. "What boon do you ask in exchange?"

Always ask the cost first, Carensa thought, though she did not think Lysander worth her pity. *Never trust a mage's gifts.*

"A place at the table, m'lord," Quintrel said, playing to Lysander's self-importance. Carensa marveled that Quintrel could set aside his own grand opinion of himself long enough to be someone else's lickspittle, but she guessed the mage had decided the outcome was worth the temporary abasement.

"When you come into your power, dominating the other warlords, I ask that you name mages to your council. We would advise and protect you, and in return, be protected by your power," Quintrel asked with such a convincing show of humility that Carensa thought she might retch.

"And what of Rostivan?" Lysander asked, a canny look coming into his black eyes.

"Surely you will need clever proxies to wield your power and subdue dissent," Quintrel replied. "Lord Rostivan and I discussed such matters before my party set out. He acknowledges your primacy, and wishes to serve in the role to which he is best suited: as a military man enforcing order."

"And Rostivan would accept that?" Lysander said shrewdly. "He fights hard for a man who doesn't want to be king himself."

Quintrel did not hesitate. "There are many ways to wield power," he answered. "Rostivan is a man born to do battle. He has no love for administration, for council meetings and court ceremonies. Honor him as your foremost general, and he will have the power and prestige he desires."

Clever, Carensa thought. *Quintrel sets Lysander up as the would-be king without saying so, and positions Rostivan as his right-hand military commander and himself as the king's left hand.* As much as Carensa had grown to dislike Quintrel, she could not deny his brilliance.

"And if I decide to accept your gift, and deny your request?" Lysander asked, growing suspicious too late in the process.

Quintrel gave his most unassuming smile. "You're not the kind of man who makes a misstep like that," he said mildly. "Together, we are invincible. You've gained your power by choosing your allies wisely. This alliance will make you the supreme power in Donderath—a kingdom to shape to your liking," he added. "I assure you, m'lord, you will gain the victory you so richly deserve," Quintrel said confidently.

Funny, Carensa thought, *Lysander believes that's a good thing.* But she had a suspicion that the reality of Lysander's victory would be exactly, and mercilessly, what he deserved.

CHAPTER
TWENTY-TWO

B RING THOSE HORSES AROUND!" VEDRAN POL-
lard shouted above the din of battle. It felt good to swing
a sword again, to be back in the thick of the fight. Battle made
him feel alive, unlike the slow administrative death of oversee-
ing Solsiden.

Soldiers reined in their mounts to comply, and the line
shifted as Pollard pressed the Arkala forces for ground. Rostivan had weakened the Arkalas, and Pollard had mustered his
troops quickly, so that before the weary and bloodied Arkala
forces could return to their fortifications, they found an army
standing in their path.

Pollard brought his sword down hard. His blade bit through
the foot soldier's leather armor and into the sinew and tendon
of his shoulder. He fell to the side, his blood soaking the dry
winter grass.

Pollard's soldiers cut their way through the Arkala front line,
leaving a wake of corpses and severed limbs behind them.

This is where I belong, Pollard thought, though his muscles
ached with every jarring blow. All of his disappointment with
Reese found its way into the honed steel blade. *Insufferable*

talishte *son of a bitch, leaves me to clean up his mess,* he ranted to himself as his sword rose and fell, splattering his cloak with blood.

Reese left me to take the fall, to handle the war he started, to deal with his sorry brood. Anger coursed through Pollard's blood, winning out over fatigue, over pain. *And then his damn bond curses me to feel his wounds,* Pollard's mental tirade continued as he slashed his way through the infantry. *I did not fight this hard to be some biter's lackey!*

Perhaps the best of the Arkala troops had fallen in their battle with Rostivan. That would be a charitable excuse for the poor showing the soldiers made, and the slaughter Pollard's forces dealt out. Pollard soldiers were intent on making an example of the Arkala troops, giving no quarter.

Pollard's body knew the rhythm of battle. His sword rose and fell, like a scythe winnowing the harvest. Being on horseback in the thick of the fight, awash in the battlefield smell of blood and offal, surrounded by the cacophony of steel on steel and men's death cries, this was what Pollard had missed in those gray weeks at Solsiden.

"Don't let them get past you!" he shouted, rallying his men when the line left too much room between riders.

He had brought only a portion of his army, and still they outnumbered the Arkala forces. The doomed men fought with valor. Few tried to run, and Pollard's men rode those cowards down, trampling them with their warhorses' heavy iron shoes. The other soldiers fought with fury. *Hopeless pawns,* he thought, watching as line after line of advancing troops fell to the sword.

"Bring me the Arkala twins!" Pollard thundered.

In the distance, he heard trumpets sound retreat, but for the press of soldiers already committed to battle, the reprieve sounded too late. As the men behind them ran for their lives, the men in the front lines knew they could die fighting or die fleeing. They hurled themselves at Pollard and his men, slashing wildly with their blades, tearing at the horses and their bridles with bloodied hands, their faces twisted in rage.

Pollard's horse shied as one of the enemy soldiers dove toward it, sword upraised. Pollard reined in his mount, veering sharply, and thrust with his sword, using the soldier's own momentum to gut him like a fish. The man's entrails spilled onto his boots, steaming in the cold spring air, and his sword clattered from his hand as the soldier grabbed for his guts, pressing them against his slit belly, his mouth opening and closing as he fell to his knees.

Another soldier came at Pollard from the left, shouting obscenities. Pollard pivoted his horse, angling his sword to take the running man through the slit of his visor, feeling the bite as steel connected with bone. He had barely yanked his blade free as the man tumbled to the ground, jerking spasmodically.

Pollard brought his horse up onto its hind legs, then let it plunge down, heavy hooves crushing the dying man, sending a spray of gore that coated the horse's underbelly and sent gobbets sliding down Pollard's slick black boots.

"A gold piece and a cask of ale for anyone who brings me the Arkala twins!" Pollard shouted, his voice raw. Gold had little worth in the wreckage that was Donderath, but ale held its value. The challenge seemed to inspire the troops, who left off trampling the abandoned front line and sent their horses charging after the retreating troops.

Poor dumb bastards, Pollard thought as he watched the fleeing army. Hennoch's troops waited just beyond the rise, poised to cut them down. Pollard smiled grimly. He had sent Hennoch and his men in a flanking maneuver two days before provoking the battle. According to his spies, three thousand Arkala troops had gone against Rostivan's troops and Quintrel's mages. Fifteen hundred had limped away, burned and bloodied. Pollard was ready to finish the battle.

Arkala commanders shouted orders above the chaos, but their men were too panicked to respond. Some threw down their weapons and fled. Pollard watched them run, knowing what awaited them.

After today, the Arkala brothers will no longer pose a threat.

Pollard left it to his own foot soldiers to work their way among dead and dying enemy soldiers, slitting throats and looting bodies. His horse picked its way among the corpses as if the stench of death offended it.

Some of the Arkala troops fled east. Pollard let them run. A few of Pollard's soldiers made a sport of chasing after the terrified foot soldiers, herding them back and forth between their horses like cattle, letting them gain ground and then closing the gap. They rode up behind the terrified soldiers, jabbing them with the point of their swords before riding the hapless bastards down. The last hopes of the desperate retreat were dashed by the solid line of Hennoch's fresh troops, armed and mounted, ready to mete out judgment.

"Bring me the twins, and it will go that much easier on the rest of you," Pollard shouted.

Some of the Arkala troops, seeing a fresh army before them, sank to their knees in surrender. Others launched a suicide attack, unwilling to go down without a fight. In the center of the fray, still surrounded by their doomed troops, were two dark-haired soldiers fighting with a skill and intensity that set them apart. It was impossible to dismiss them as mere conscripts.

"Take them!" Pollard bellowed. "I want the Arkala twins alive!"

Pollard's troops converged on the two men, who were battling for their lives. The Arkala loyalists rallied around their commanders, fighting in vain to hold off wave upon wave of enemies, only to fall beneath the flash of swords and axes. The Arkalas were fighting back-to-back, massively outnumbered.

Pollard signaled impatiently to one of the mages who had ridden up behind him. "Those two," he said, pointing. "I want them."

It would be like the willful twins to deny him his victory by cutting each other down, Pollard thought. He was not about to be denied. The mage went still, his brow furrowed in concentration, and brought his outstretched hands in a loud clap. Across the battlefield, the Arkala twins fell as if poleaxed.

"Bring them to me!" Pollard's ragged voice carried across the distance.

Soldiers piled onto the downed warlords, binding their hands behind their back. Two guards dragged the Arkala twins roughly to their feet as the others kept the last desperate enemy soldiers at bay as their leaders were dragged away.

Pollard watched the two captives with little sense of triumph. *A turn of fortune, and the roles could be reversed,* he thought. At this point, nearing his fifth decade, Pollard had few illusions left. *We're all captives of one sort or another.*

At sword's point, the twins fell to their knees, defiance clear in their faces. "We do not yield to you," the twin on the left snarled. Birth made them identical; war distinguished them. The twin who spoke had a flattened nose and a scar that cut across his left eyebrow. The other twin had lost part of an ear and had a deep cleft in his cheek that was the reminder of a long-ago sword stroke.

"It matters nothing to me whether you yield or not," Pollard replied. "Your forces are dead or dying. And soon, you will join them in the Unseen Realm."

"Go to Raka," the second twin growled. "Death in battle carries no shame."

Pollard stared at his captives, debating the question he had mulled throughout the battle. *I could drag them back to Solsiden in chains, break their bodies, perhaps even have* talishte *turn them. Could their spirits be broken? In time, all can. But is there an advantage to it greater than slaughtering them here? Either way, they become martyrs. And either way, they're dead.*

"You've failed," Pollard said, his voice as cold as the harsh wind. "Your men are dead. Those who ran like cowards met General Hennoch over the next rise. No army will survive you, no one will be left to sing your praises or venerate your name. It ends here."

He swung his sword for the twin on the right, and the blade bit into the man's neck, jerking as it encountered the bone and tendon. Pollard did not strike again, and the prisoner fell to one side, blood darkening his armor, body quivering, denied a quick and painless death.

The other Arkala twin paled, but his expression remained defiant. "I am not afraid to die."

"Good," Pollard remarked. He swung again, angling the sword so that it hit the spine at the base of the skull but did not cut through the throat. The last Arkala brother toppled slowly. His spine was severed where it would paralyze his body from the throat down, stopping his breath and stilling his heart. But it would take a bit for the realization to reach his mind, which would be the last to go. Pollard saw a range of emotions flicker in the dying man's eyes. Rage, at being cut down. Defiance, even now. Mortal terror of the darkness that lay beyond the light vanishing from his eyes.

"Take the bodies," Pollard ordered, cleaning his sword on the cloak of one of the dead men. "Post them in gibbets outside Solsiden. It's cold enough, they'll keep for quite a while, I think." With that, he turned his back and swung up on his horse.

Back in camp, Pollard walked to his tent, cheered by his men for their victory over the Arkala forces. Pollard acknowledged their cheers with a distracted wave, intent on reaching his tent before he collapsed.

A guard parted the flaps for him, and Pollard nodded his thanks. Once the flaps dropped, hiding him from the view of outsiders, Pollard staggered. Kerr rushed to him, getting under his shoulder and helping him to his campaign chair near the brazier in the center of the tent.

"M'lord, are you injured?" Kerr's concern was clear in his face.

Pollard gasped in pain as Kerr rushed to remove his armor. The wounds he had taken in battle did not warrant more than the requisite attention. Pollard had long grown accustomed to the sting and ache of battle damage. But as Kerr lifted his cuirass and then removed his tunic, it was plain that his chest and arms were a seeping mass of boils, with the raw wound over his chest now festering.

"Oh, m'lord," Kerr moaned, voicing the anguish Pollard's pride would not let him articulate.

"Whiskey," Pollard groaned. Kerr went to the side table and

filled a glass four fingers full, then returned and pressed it into Pollard's hand. Pollard knocked it back in two gulps, gasping as the raw liquor burned down his throat.

"I can get you the healer—" Kerr began.

Pollard shook his head. "There's no cure for this, save Reese's escape," he said, his voice gravelly from the damp and the whiskey. "Even magic won't help." Pollard had broken down and allowed one of the healers to try. But even the magic could not heal or help his sympathetic wounds from Reese.

"Let me see what I can do," Kerr said, and he began to bustle around the tent, removing the items from the trunk at the foot of Pollard's cot that he would need to make the poultice. Before a candlemark was gone, Kerr had applied an unguent and bound up all of the affected skin, then helped Pollard slip into a loose tunic that would neither aggravate his wounds nor reveal them to an onlooker.

"How long can this go on?" Kerr asked, pressing a fresh glass into Pollard's hand.

"Fifty years," Pollard replied matter-of-factly. "Or until we can find a way to free my…master." He hated the word, but there was none other that would suffice. When the bond of thralldom was cinched so tightly that to wound one was to scar the other, it was time to forgo euphemisms.

"Eat," Kerr chided. "To survive this, you must remain strong."

Kerr ducked his head out of the tent for a moment and spoke a word to the soldiers, then returned. "They'll have a hot trencher for you as quickly as a runner can retrieve it," he said, fussing like a mother hen.

Pollard let him fuss. He was too exhausted to object, and his body was wounded more than his pride. Although he had not taken serious damage in the fight, his joints and muscles ached in ways they had not when he was a younger man. Armor had blocked the worst of the strikes, but the bruises from those blows would blossom in shades of blue and purple, aching to the bone for weeks. Even riding, something he had loved ever since he could sit a horse, now meant that he would fight stiffness in his legs for days. *There's a reason warriors die young*, he thought.

He did not realize just how hungry he was until Kerr set the steaming trencher in front of him. It was venison stew, standard rations for an army on the move, but it smelled edible, and it was warm. Tonight, Pollard felt as if he had taken a chill to the bone. Perhaps it was the realization of just how completely he was Reese's man. Perhaps it was the whisper of mortality, that today he had been wielding the sword, and that someday he would be the one kneeling. Intellectually, he accepted that. But viscerally, the primal urge to survive fought that knowledge with every fiber.

"Commander Jansen to see you, sir," Kerr said. His inflection gave Pollard to know that if he did not feel well enough to receive company, Kerr would make the requisite excuses. For anyone else, Pollard might have begged off. Not for Nilo.

"Show him in."

Nilo followed Kerr into the tent and took off his cloak, setting it to one side. He drew up the other campaign chair while Kerr poured him a drink. Nilo did not speak until Kerr left them alone.

"Gods above, Vedran. You look awful!"

From anyone else, Pollard would have taken offense. He knew that Nilo spoke the truth. "It's the bond," he said miserably, sipping at his second glass of whiskey.

"Did you take damage?"

Pollard made a dismissive gesture. "Minimal. You?"

Nilo shook his head. "I let the foot soldiers take the brunt of it this time. We did our best to drive the bulk of the enemy into Hennoch's troops. Let him have the casualties. It weakens him and saves our troops."

"Learn anything new?"

Nilo sipped his drink. "Nothing solid. I'm working on it."

Pollard nodded, thinking as he took another drink. The liquor warmed him, and it numbed the worst of the pain. There was little a healer could do for him, and he did not dare let it get out how badly he was injured, or by what cause. Yet another indignity visited upon him by his master, he thought dourly.

"What of Reese?" Nilo asked after a long pause. "Have you heard anything more?"

Pollard drew a long breath and let it out again. "Not since the Elders sent word about his sentence. But in my dreams, I hear him. He suffers greatly."

"And there is nothing you can do?" Nilo asked.

Pollard shrugged. "Nothing *I* can do, but there are plans in the brood to test the security of Reese's prison."

"Do you know details?"

Pollard shook his head. "*Talishte* are a closemouthed bunch. I was surprised to know of the plans aforetime. But I believe they'll make their move soon."

"You think Reese can sense it through the *kruvgaldur*?"

"I'm certain of it," Pollard replied, draining the rest of his second glass. Only now was the rough whiskey beginning to take hold, blunting his pain and dulling his memory. Under normal circumstances, his tolerance for drink was high. In conditions like these, it would take half a bottle to give him the peace he craved, but he dared not risk the price of the after-effects. Reluctantly, he set his empty glass aside.

"Is that a good thing?" Nilo asked.

Again, Pollard shrugged. "Reese's *talishte* won't remain loyal to us much longer without him present. He's their true lord. Without them, we're at a disadvantage." He swore. "We're still not recovered from the loss at Valshoa. We need more time to regain our strength. And we need Reese to buy us that time."

Pollard shifted and winced. Nilo looked at him with concern. "Can the healers do nothing?" Nilo asked quietly.

Pollard sighed. "No, and it was a waste of a good healer. Kerr is trustworthy, but if word were to get out…" He did not need to finish his sentence. Nilo understood.

"Regardless of where his real feelings lie, Hennoch performed well for you," Nilo reported. "He made a complete rout of the enemy, and his spies played an important role in trapping the Arkalas."

"Good for him," Pollard replied without emotion. "Do you think he'll betray us?"

Nilo shrugged. "You have his son. It depends on how far he's willing to be pushed, and how willing he is to lose his only son."

"Fair enough." Pollard stretched, then grimaced at the pain. "Was there anything else?"

"We've spotted Tingur on the move, but we don't know where they're going," Nilo replied. "I've had men watching them, but they're damn difficult to infiltrate. It's certain that they're supporting Lysander, and willing to fight for him. We still don't know whether they're truly a cult of Torven or just desperate rabble. But they give Lysander an edge in battle."

"Stay on them," Pollard instructed. "Perhaps their devotion is genuine, perhaps not, but such things are easily used by others."

"Hennoch also reported something odd that I think you'll want to know about," Nilo continued. "A team of his men vanished on patrol."

"Vanished?" Pollard said, raising an eyebrow.

Nilo nodded. "Disappeared—soldiers, gear, and horses. No trace of their bodies."

Pollard frowned. "Where?"

Nilo met his gaze. "That's the interesting part. Their route took them near Mirdalur."

"Mirdalur, huh? That is interesting," Pollard replied. "I'll ask him about it. That bears looking into."

Nilo nodded. "My thoughts exactly." He stood. "I'll let you rest," he said. "If there's any news to tell, I'll bring word in the morning."

Pollard nodded. "Much as I have reason to dread returning to Solsiden, I do miss a real bed. Sleep well. I shan't."

"I want to see my son." Larska Hennoch glared at Vedran Pollard. "I've done yer bidding, and I'll do more, but I want to see my boy."

Three days had passed since their triumph over the Arkala twins. Now the rotting corpses of the twins hung in gibbets outside Solsiden's gate, the smell mercifully dampened by the cold spring wind. Loyal though they had been, the Arkala forces could not regroup from their defeat by Rostivan quickly enough to escape the combined armies of Pollard and Hennoch. To Pollard's knowledge, there had been no survivors.

"I've had good report of your troops," Pollard said. "Commander Jansen tells me your men fought well, and held their line. You played a role in our victory. You're to be commended." His tone conveyed grudging approval. It would not do for Hennoch to value himself too highly in this bargain.

"All I ask is to see my boy."

"That can be arranged." Pollard walked to the door of his study and leaned outside, speaking a few words to the guards.

"Have a seat. These things take time." Pollard gestured to one of the chairs by the fire. Hennoch gave him a skeptical look and then cautiously went to sit down.

Pollard poured two glasses with the rough brew that passed for whiskey these days. He carried them to the small table between the chairs by the fire, and took one for himself, motioning for Hennoch to take the other.

"A toast," he proposed. "To victory. The Arkalas have fallen. So will the others who stand in our way."

Hennoch raised his glass dutifully. "To the future," he said, but his expression was unreadable.

"Tell me about the soldiers who disappeared."

Hennoch's eyes betrayed his surprise, although his expression was schooled to reveal nothing. "It happens," he said off-handedly. "Men go out on patrol, or on a mission. Sometimes they don't come back."

Pollard nodded. "It happens. And when it does, you find out who cost you your soldiers and you make the bastard pay for it." He paused. "So...what have you learned?"

Hennoch looked uncomfortable. "We realized they were missing right when we rallied to move on the Arkalas," he replied. "I sent two scouts back to find out whether the men are missing or just runaways." His tone grew harsh. "We'll figure it out, and whoever is responsible will pay."

"My sources tell me the missing soldiers' route took them near Mirdalur."

Hennoch nodded. "Aye. Old ruins."

Pollard's gaze was intense. "Much more than that. Mirdalur has strategic importance. I want to know whether it's being used again, and who's using it."

Hennoch looked confused, but nodded. "Aye. That's easy enough. I'll take care of it as soon as we move camp."

Easy enough—unless the Knights of Esthrane are behind this, Pollard thought.

"I've delivered the Arkalas as we agreed," Hennoch said, returning to their original conversation. "Now I'd like to see my son."

Before long, two guards escorted a young man into the room. Eljas Hennoch was sixteen summers old. He resembled his father in the face, though he had yet to gain muscle. His clothes were clean, as was his hair and skin, and Pollard silently congratulated himself at having the foresight to move the prisoner to better quarters immediately upon his return. The implied threat of the guards was not lost on the elder Hennoch as the group stopped just inside the doors.

"Father!" Eljas cried, then stopped, drawing himself up and holding his head high.

"You look well," Larska Hennoch replied. To Pollard's eye, it seemed as if each was fighting the urge to embrace, unwilling to let their captor see just how much of a surety they were for each other.

"I am fed and warm," Eljas replied. Although Eljas was young, it was clear to Pollard that he had been schooled in what was expected behavior for a noble hostage. He conveyed little emotion, and made no plea for his release.

For his part, Larska Hennoch eyed his son with cold appraisal, taking in the hollow of his cheeks, the color of his skin, searching for evidence of mistreatment or neglect. "As it should be," the elder Hennoch replied. "Have you been moved to suitable quarters?"

"I do not complain," Eljas answered. Pollard knew Eljas had been moved from the dungeons into a locked and guarded room aboveground after Hennoch had agreed to terms. The windows were barred and the confines of the room were likely to be the young man's world for quite some time to come, but so long as Hennoch played the faithful loyalist, Pollard had given word for Eljas to receive food and clothing befitting his station, as well as the books that were the young captive's only request.

"He's been the perfect houseguest," Pollard said smoothly, and saw a twitch at the corner of Hennoch's eye. "I gave you my word. You keep your part of the bargain and I'll keep mine. Under the right conditions, Solsiden is a comfortable home, and I am a gracious host." He knew that both father and son read the implied threat.

"I'll let your mother know I've seen you," Hennoch said in a gruff voice. "She prays to the gods for your safe return."

"The gods have little to do with it these days, I fear," Eljas replied stiffly. "Our fates lie in our own hands."

Pollard gave a nod, and Eljas's guards escorted him back to his confinement. Hennoch stood staring at the doors for a moment after they had closed. "He knows his duty," he said quietly. "And so do I."

"Then all is well," Pollard replied. He paused. "Tell me, what new reports do you have of the Tingur? Where are they causing problems?"

Hennoch returned to his seat. He licked his lips and took a sip of his drink. "The spies tell me that they're crazy men, people who have nothing to lose, who've thrown their lot in with the prophets and left what little they had."

"Anything else?"

Hennoch savored his drink for a moment before answering. "The rumors are growing that Lysander has men among the Tingur, and that he's using them to do his bidding."

"The rumors are true. They're his personal army of fanatics." Pollard replied.

Hennoch met Pollard's gaze, and in his eyes Pollard saw the cunning of an experienced soldier. "Not a bad idea. A mob doesn't have to be skilled to cause damage," he said. "Or to overrun a garrison. All it needs are enough men reckless enough to care little for their own safety." He raised an eyebrow. "Such fervor is a weapon if one knows how to wield it."

CHAPTER
TWENTY-THREE

THERE WERE TWO THINGS I NEVER WANTED TO see again after Edgeland. Herring and snow," Piran said. Piran and Blaine waited with their troops just behind a rise before heading into battle. Snow was falling, and from the look of the clouds, it would get worse before the weather would clear. The wind whipped at Blaine's cloak and stung his eyes.

Beyond the rise, they could hear the sound of battle. Lysander's troops had launched their offensive against the Solveigs three days ago. Verner had brought his soldiers to support his allies, and Lysander had promptly fielded more men. The *talishte* messenger the Solveigs sent had arrived at Glenreith exhausted even for one of the undead, with the urgent summons for help. Blaine and Niklas had mustered as large a force as they dared to take and still leave Glenreith defended, and headed north at a brisk pace to join in the fight.

"Looks like you're out of luck," Blaine replied.

Down the line, Blaine could see Niklas standing in his stirrups, shouting the order to advance. A bugle call cut through the cold winter air, answered by the shouts of men and the pounding of hooves as their forces started up the rise and down the slope, swords aloft.

Blaine and Piran rode with the mounted soldiers, the advance guard sent to inflict as much damage as possible to open a hole in the line for the foot soldiers. Blaine's magic enhanced his fighting skills, and since the anchoring, he had gained foresight, a few seconds' advance warning of where his opponent would move next. The magic, together with the practice he'd had of late, made him a much more formidable opponent.

Blaine rode into the fray, cutting a swath through the enemy soldiers. The battlefield was already littered with bodies, and the stench of corpses rose despite the cold. Blaine's horse picked its way across the frozen dead, past heaps of offal and snow dyed a bloody black. Sprawling out over the battlefield, Blaine guessed that nearly twenty thousand men fought for their lives, though few, he wagered, had any goal loftier than to be alive come nightfall. Lysander's soldiers attempted to make up for their lack of skill with sheer numbers, making their every gain hideously expensive.

"Where in Raka are the mages?" Piran grumbled, his voice barely carrying across the deadly landscape.

"They're active," Blaine replied. "I can feel it." The bond between the restored magic and his singular blood had grown stronger. His headache and the tingle in his blood, in reaction to the magic, had begun before they were in sight of the battlefield, and by now was nearly enough to make him vomit. "Not just our mages. Someone else is using mages, too."

The Solveigs? Tormod was a mage, but surely if he were going to bring his power to bear, he would have already done so, and precluded the need to draw in Verner and Blaine. Perhaps the magic was even more brittle than usual, or perhaps Tormod's power was balky.

Across the battlefield, Niklas rallied the troops for a move deep into Lysander's line. Behind him, the Solveigs held their own, rebounding with the reprieve from their allies. Blaine held up a hand to shade his eyes against the glare of the snow. From what little he could make out, Verner's line looked overrun.

Shouting to Blaine's left made him rein in his horse, alert for an attack. "Tingur," he muttered as a tide of peasant berserkers hurtled toward them wielding scythes and sickles.

Piran turned his horse. Blaine rose in his stirrups. "Protect the rear! We can't let them pass!"

The Tingur launched themselves into the fray fully committed. Three men ran at Blaine despite his armor and his huge warhorse. Blaine reined his horse in, and it reared, kicking with huge, heavy hooves. One hoof caved in the skull of a Tingur soldier before the man came close enough to do damage. Blaine brought his sword down hard on the shoulder of another man. The blade sank deep into tendon and bone, cleaving down to the man's breastbone. The Tingur took a stumbling step, clutched at his bloody chest, and fell face-forward into the muddy snow.

Like the tide, the Tingur were relentless, single-minded, and unstoppable. They surged forward, shouting and cursing and calling out to Torven as they swung their scythes and waded into bloodshed.

"There's no end of them!" Piran shouted, barely hacking down one attacker before another threw himself at his mount.

"They bleed just like the others," Blaine called in response, slashing with his sword, sickened by the waste of life, though the fervor in the Tingurs' eyes gave him no choice.

Four Tingur came at him at once. Skilled or not, there was

danger in numbers. Piran was pinned down by another group. Even with a good warhorse, a solitary man was at a disadvantage with lunges and thrusts coming from so many directions at once. Blaine brought his sword down, severing an attacker's arm, and then slashed, slicing through his throat. That soldier fell aside, but another was ready to take his place, undeterred by the body he stepped over to get at his objective.

Blaine kept his huge horse in motion, signaling with the reins for the stallion to kick with his heavy iron shoes. One kick took off the top of a soldier's skull, while a back-kick sent another man flying through the air with a blow to the gut vicious enough to burst internal organs.

Blaine's sword clanged down on a battered scythe aiming for his horse's ribs. The warhorse sidestepped, forcing the soldiers to back away or be trampled. The Tingur swarmed, surrounding Blaine and Piran, heedless of their own safety. As soon as Blaine cut one man down, another pressed forward to take his place.

Are they bewitched? Blaine wondered. *How can anyone want the favor of the gods this badly?*

Yet despite their recklessness, nothing about the attackers appeared coerced, and Blaine could not sense a geas on them. Blood matted his horse's coat, covered his boots, and turned the ground black. Blaine was bloodied to the elbows, though so far, he had managed to avoid taking any serious damage himself. He thanked his magic for that, and the new precognition that had come with working the anchoring ritual.

Two of the Tingur charged Blaine at once. Blaine slashed with his sword and tried to maneuver his horse into striking range of the man on the right, knowing as soon as he did that the other man was going to go for his horse. Blaine attempted to adjust, but he couldn't move the horse fast enough as the man on his left darted forward, getting under Blaine's guard and landing a deep slash down the side of Blaine's horse. The horse shrieked and reared, and the other attacker threw himself under the massive animal, lurching forward with his blade and sinking it deep into the horse's belly.

Blaine's mount screamed in pain and crashed down, trampling the Tingur that had dealt the blow, but the damage was done. Blaine jumped from the saddle as the horse staggered, whining pitifully, and stumbled forward, then collapsed, blood streaming from its underbelly.

Fury raised Blaine's resolve, coupled with the pain of the pounding in his head. Practice, skill, and battle magic took over, and the glimpse of future-sight meant his body seemed to know where to go even before the thought was fully formed in his mind, or before the attacker's moves betrayed his intent. One soldier after another fell to his blade. Blaine forged past exhaustion, cutting a swath through the enemy ranks, though with each candlemark, he could feel the drain of strong magic being used nearby.

Piran shouted curses as he thrust and parried, keeping the onslaught at bay. He had also lost his horse, and without that advantage, the odds improved in favor of their attackers.

"I swear they spawn from the dead!" Piran shouted as another wave of wild-eyed peasants hurtled toward them. Blaine and Piran were not yet fighting back-to-back, but it wouldn't take many more onslaughts for that to happen. Yet whenever Blaine dared glance across the battlefield, all he could see were soldiers fighting for their lives.

The wind whipped down from the high ground. Snow fell steadily, ankle-deep and rising rapidly. The snow made it difficult to see far across the battlefield, but it also slowed the Tingur's advance on the slippery ground. The storm narrowed

Blaine's focus, so that the assault on the Solveigs' line or on Verner might as well be on the other side of Donderath. All that mattered was what lay in front of him, and what might emerge unexpectedly out of the storm.

Despite his heavy cloak and the exertion of battle, the wind was bitter cold. Blaine could see it taking a toll on the Tingur as well. Torven's fanatical followers looked as if they had abandoned their farms and gone off adventuring without bothering to pack a change of clothing for the season. None of them looked to have proper boots or cloaks heavier than a woolen blanket, and some of the fighters already showed signs of frostbite.

Blaine chuckled. "It's a warm day in Edgeland, don't you think, Piran?" he shouted.

"Balmy," Piran replied. "Almost picnic weather."

Compared to what Blaine and Piran had survived in the far north, Donderath's extreme weather was not daunting. Blaine had faced far more brutal conditions as a convict, dressed in more ragged clothing than the Tingur. That memory fortified him, though he was far from comfortable. Yet despite the blasting, icy winds and the steady snow, the Tingur did not let up on their assault.

Blaine could hear the sounds of battle through the snow-shroud that cut off their visibility. Though the roar of the wind muted the clang of swords and the shouts of soldiers, the din carried on the frigid air, reminding them that if they failed to hold the Tingur here, Lysander's troops might well break through the Solveig line.

"Now would be a good time for the mages to do something clever," Piran muttered.

"They're doing something, and it's powerful," Blaine replied as a wave of pain nearly staggered him. "I'm just not sure what it is, or whose mages are doing it."

Do they need a clear line of sight to work their magic? Blaine wondered. *If so, the snow is going to make them useless. I hope no one gets inspired to send fire or lightning until they can make bloody certain whose soldiers they're frying.*

Niklas's voice carried despite the wind, and others relayed his shouted commands down the line. Their troops pressed the Tingur back toward the main battle lines, forcing them into the path of Lysander's advance on the Solveig fortifications.

The slippery, wet snow and the frozen, snow-covered corpses made footing treacherous. Blaine slipped as his boots hit ice, and stumbled over bodies hidden by the snow. *At least we're moving forward*, he thought grimly. *The Tingur are retreating.*

Adequate armor and warm clothing gave Blaine's side a decided advantage. The Tingur stood a good chance of dying from exposure before they fell in battle. Their stubborn refusal to surrender stoked Blaine's anger, since they stood between him and a warm fire.

An explosion shook the ground. In the distance, a column of flame flared against the gray, snow-laden sky, sending up a plume of smoke that was visible even in the storm. The fiery column was blindingly bright, widening with every second for a moment or two before it vanished as suddenly as it had appeared. Blaine felt the blast of magic like a physical blow. He stumbled, giving an opening to the Tingur he fought who slashed with his wide-bladed knife.

Anticipated victory shone in the Tingur's eyes as Blaine parried a second too late, taking a gash on his forearm. Blaine swore and knocked the blade away, but not before his sleeve stained red with blood, leaving a trail of crimson on the snow.

The blast of magic rallied the Tingur. Blaine was feeling the strain of the rapid march to reach the battle and the fatigue of combat. He feared that the drain of his connection to the magic slowed his reactions and muddied his thoughts. His sword felt heavy, and his body ached. As he had learned to do in the mines of Velant, Blaine focused his anger on keeping his body moving, one step at a time, intent on making an end of it so that he could go home.

Blaine felt a sudden surge of magic like lancing pain, and he lost his footing. His attacker saw the advantage. The Tingur swung again, and Blaine managed to deflect the blade before it bit into his shoulder, sensing where the Tingur planned to strike through his new ability. A predatory smile spread across the Tingur's face.

"Tired, are you?" the Tingur taunted, mistaking the reason for Blaine's sudden slump. "Just stand still, and I'll send you to your rest."

Sheer tenacity made Blaine rally, lashing out with unexpected speed. His blade caught the Tingur across the wrist, slicing across bone and tendon, and the harvesting knife fell from the man's hand, giving Blaine an opening to drive his sword deep into his opponent's chest. The Tingur stared in astonishment at the blood that flowed down his chest as Blaine yanked his sword free.

"I thought I had you," the man gasped, hands pressed to his bloody chest as his knees buckled under him and he fell face-first into the trampled snow.

Blaine staggered back, still off balance from the powerful magic that vibrated through his body. He could feel the burn and hum of the magic deep in his mind, and he wondered if he could have survived the fight had it not been for the few seconds of foresight. *Will the foresight remain, once we properly anchor the magic?* he wondered. *If it stays when we've worked the new ritual, will it get stronger? And just because the last Lords of the Bloods gained new abilities, will it work the same way when we do the ritual this time?*

"What in Raka was that?" Piran said as he and Blaine battled their way forward one bloody inch at a time in the bitter wind.

"More importantly, whose side sent it?" Blaine replied. He was shaking from the resonance of the bond, and struggling to catch his breath.

The bodies of newly dead Tingur fell atop the snow-covered heaps of past days' battles. Steadily falling snow covered the dead. But while the storm limited visibility, the sound of battle was a constant beacon.

"Push harder, lads! We've got them on the run!" Blaine shouted. The command echoed down the line. Those still on horseback drove the Tingur ahead of them, sending them stumbling over treacherous footing, trampling them when they fell.

The Tingur's unpredictability was more dangerous than their swords. Now that their confidence in a quick victory was dashed by the number of their fellows who lay dead, panic replaced triumph. They fled the battle, stumbling into the thick of the chaos as they careened into Lysander's advance.

The wind shifted, giving Blaine his first clear view of the battlefield in quite a while. His side had advanced. Lysander's soldiers fought the Tingur to push them out of their way and clear a path for the assault on the Solveigs' fortification. That trapped the Tingur in a no-man's-land between Blaine's troops and Lysander's forces.

Blaine's soldiers charged with a battle cry, overrunning the Tingur stragglers and attacking the flank of Lysander's army. It took Lysander precious moments to realize that he could not afford to devote his army's full attention to scaling the Solveigs' walls. And in those moments, the battle began to turn.

"Where in the name of the gods is Verner?" Piran grumbled. The snow closed in around them once more, isolating them.

The buzz in the back of Blaine's mind grew louder. He

staggered, and Piran reached out to steady him. "It's the magic, isn't it?"

Blaine nodded. "It's here and it's strong, though I'll be damned if I could tell you what the mages are actually doing."

"Sweet Esthrane!" Piran yelped. "What's going on?"

Blaine followed Piran's gaze. The main group of their soldiers were fighting valiantly. But at the outer ranks, the soldiers stumbled and milled about in confusion as if drunk. As Blaine shouted to them to rouse them, Lysander's troops rode in to cut the men down.

"They looked bewitched!" Piran exclaimed.

The battle shifted, and the wind dropped suddenly, clearing the air. Blaine got his first good look at the battlefield in several candlemarks.

The Solveigs' fortress still stood, damaged from the assault. Any surviving Tingur had either run away or been absorbed into Lysander's army. On the far side of the battlefield, where Verner's troops had been, was a blackened crater.

"Oh my gods," Piran swore. "Do you think…"

Blaine stared at the charred ground before the snow closed in once more. "I don't think we're going to be getting any help from that direction," he said quietly.

The hum in Blaine's mind grew deafening, and pain drove him to his knees, threatening to black him out. Overhead, the sky exploded in flame. The soldiers on the edge of Blaine's group caught fire like tinder, and their agonized screams sounded above the wind. In that moment, when the air felt thick as deep water and it was hard to breathe, Blaine understood.

"It's the mages," he managed, trying not to retch or pass out. "They're spending their magic defending us against the kind of strikes that destroyed Verner."

Piran helped him to his feet, though Blaine's head swam

and his body felt leaden. The magic tethered through Blaine's blood drew from his life force, and Blaine was weakening. Gritting his teeth, Blaine raised his sword, signaling for the troops to charge, and they surged against the Lysander troops, seizing the moment when Lysander's mages would be too spent to launch another attack.

Blaine's head snapped up at a cry from across the battlefield. The portcullis on the Solveigs' fortress was raised, and armed men poured out with a fierce roar.

Renewed by the appearance of fresh troops, Blaine's soldiers took up the shout, pushing past exhaustion to make one last press against the Lysander forces.

Once more, Blaine felt the painful buzz of magic. In the space between where Blaine's troops held the line and where the Lysander army began, the snow trembled. From beneath their icy shrouds, the dead shuddered and woke. Here and there, ragged, bloody hands thrust up from the trampled snow, struggling free.

Cursing and scrambling, the Lysander troops scrambled back. Blaine gave a feral grin. He could feel Tormod's necromancy sending its tendrils of power out to the fresh dead, waking them from their slumber, calling them to arms. Seeing the enemy flee in fear was worth the pain the magic caused.

Curses and cries of alarm rose above the storm as the snow-covered corpses struggled to their feet, lumbering toward the terrified Lysander line. One last service the dead could do for their brothers-in-arms and that was to send their killers into retreat. Mottled with the cold, covered in blood, marred with the gruesome death wounds that had sent them to the Sea of Souls, they'd been called by Tormod Solveig to a final duty.

"Those dead are our men," Blaine shouted, raising his sword like a battle standard. "Let's do them proud. Forward!"

With a roar, Blaine's army surged forward, as the Lysander

troops recoiled from the frozen corpses that staggered toward them. The animated dead moved slowly, but as more and more struggled from their frozen graves, they formed a front line that had nothing to fear from the enemy troops.

Blaine watched the lurching corpses in fascinated horror. He knew that Tormod was controlling them like a master puppeteer, that the dead had not risen on their own, and that he and his men had nothing to fear, and yet he shuddered. Blaine let the dead men take the lead, driving Lysander's soldiers back with a buffer of fighters who were beyond the harm of mortal weapons.

For a moment, the line held. The corpses stopped. They stood, pale as the snow, trembling. With a muted bang, hundreds of corpses exploded at once. Frozen gobbets of gore splattered Lysander's soldiers as the bodies blew apart. Bone and tissue, hair and skin rained down on the enemy troops.

Blaine's soldiers surged forward, followed by the Solveig troops. Lysander's army ran, stumbling and falling over the corpses that littered the snow-covered field, terrified that more of the dead would rise up to take their vengeance. Blaine snagged a riderless horse and swung up into the saddle. He saw Piran do the same. Together, they led the charge. Lysander himself was nowhere to be seen, and his mounted officers spurred their horses to full speed, outpacing the hapless infantry.

The storm abated one more time, clearing just enough to afford the fleeing troops no cover. Blaine and Piran were in the vanguard, with the rest close behind. They took out their anger on the stragglers, cutting them down without quarter, trampling the bodies of the fallen as they pursued the rear guard of Lysander's army. As they fought their way through the chaos, Blaine felt the buzz in his mind grow distant. He was exhausted from the weather, the exertion of battle, and the pull of magic, but he kept up the pressure on the retreating troops, bringing his sword down again and again, sending more of the enemy soldiers to the Sea of Souls. It was taking effort for Blaine to stay in his saddle, but he was resolved to see the battle through to its end.

Harried by the dead and pursued by the living, Lysander's troops retreated, leaving their stragglers behind. Blaine's men chased the enemy to the foothills. Exhausted, cold to the bone, and weary of battle, Blaine and Piran led their portion of the army back to rendezvous with Niklas, who was standing with Rinka Solveig.

Rinka's blood-red armor did not stand out against the stained and sullied snow. Tormod was nowhere to be seen. Rinka eyed the retreating Lysander troops. "That was bloody expensive," she said.

"I'd say we put a crimp in Lysander's plans," Blaine replied. "We definitely took a toll on his troops. Thank Tormod for us."

Rinka grimaced. "My brother enjoys this kind of thing."

"I don't think Lysander will be coming back today," Blaine replied.

Rinka looked at him. "Not today. But we haven't broken him."

"What about Verner?" Blaine asked.

Rinka jerked her head in the direction of the blackened crater. "Mage strike. Killed about a third of his men, injured a lot more. We've got medics getting the survivors to shelter."

"Our mages had their hands full keeping that from happening to us," Blaine replied. He looked out over the battlefield. "Let's get my troops to shelter, and we can plan our next move from there."

CHAPTER
TWENTY-FOUR

POLLARD DID THIS?" CONNOR LOOKED AROUND the ruined grounds. The sturdy gate hung askew from its hinges, its iron bars twisted and bent. A fortified inner door lay battered into splinters. A battle took place here. But there were no corpses, no newly dug graves, and no scorched pyres.

Penhallow nodded. "Not Pollard himself. One of Reese's brood, on Pollard's orders. That's why there are no casualties. They were turned."

On a gut level, Connor suspected that Penhallow was right. "Why?" The Wraith Lord also accompanied them, though he was visible only when he chose to show himself.

Penhallow looked out over the moonlit ruins as the Wraith Lord answered Connor. "Pollard and Reese hoped to keep McFadden from restoring the magic. They failed—and their loss at Valshoa cost them dearly. Pollard needs an army. He has far too few men left to wield the kind of power he desires."

"Pollard's forces must have used magic of their own to overcome the mages," Connor said.

Penhallow nodded. "Which means that they've figured out

how to use the 'new' magic without destroying themselves. Or they got lucky." He paused. "I suspect it's the latter. Pollard couldn't stop magic from returning, so now he's got to have mages of his own, thoroughly loyal, if he hopes to win any future battles."

"And if the mages are turned, they've no choice except to be loyal," Connor finished the thought. A small group of mages who had survived the Cataclysm and escaped both Quintrel and Reese had made a new home for themselves in a converted granary. They had politely turned down an alliance with Penhallow, and with any warlord, they insisted. They merely desired to practice their craft. For that, they had been slaughtered and brought across against their will.

"Do you think Reese will escape?" Connor asked.

Penhallow shrugged. "Nothing is certain. He can afford to be patient. After all, he can outwait the mortal players. Pollard's lifetime is extended as Reese's servant. He, too, has time. He'll need it to rebuild an army, and time for his fledglings to adjust and gain strength."

"Does Reese really have the support of some of the Elders?" Connor walked through the wreckage of the mage's retreat. Scrolls and parchment were strewn everywhere. Tables and shelves were filled with glass vials, abalone shells, tins of herbs, and other mage tools, but anything that might have been a relic or magical artifact appeared to have been taken. Some of the vials and tins had been knocked to the floor and scattered.

"I believe at least two of the Elders support his ideas, maybe more," the Wraith Lord replied. By moonlight, the ruined compound looked even more forlorn. Pollard's men had left nothing of value behind. "Whether or not they will back him in fact as well as in theory remains to be seen."

The granary was the third incident in the last few weeks. "I didn't think it was easy—or wise—to turn a lot of people at once," Connor said.

Penhallow shook his head. "It isn't. Fledglings are vulnerable while they get accustomed to the Dark Gift. Many of them don't survive the transition. If Reese's brood are turning all the mages they've taken, it's a very risky proposition."

"But they would be ultimately under Reese's control," the Wraith Lord replied. "Which may be his intent."

"Can we stop him?" Connor asked.

"From killing mages? Probably not," Penhallow acknowledged. "Even with Voss's army supporting us, we'll be busy enough holding Rodestead House and Westbain, plus Voss's lands, and now sending a contingent to Mirdalur."

He shook his head. "Each of the warlords has gathered mages," Penhallow replied. "We've taken in our share, and so has Traher Voss. Pollard is targeting mages who refused alliances." He shook his head. "This is a very dangerous time to decide to be independent, if you lack an army to back it up."

"Is there any way to warn the mages?" Connor mused.

Penhallow grimaced. "Pollard's strikes don't leave survivors. So there's no one left to spread the word about what happened. I doubt the other mages would listen."

"Which is why we haven't had a mob of mages arguing to be protected." Connor sighed.

"We'd best keep going," Penhallow said. "Nidhud will be expecting us at Mirdalur, and so will Traher Voss and his men. I'm anxious to see how Dolan's research is coming, and whether he thinks Blaine can anchor the power soon."

"Let's hope Dolan's been successful. The magic is too fragile to remain this way much longer," the Wraith Lord replied. "And McFadden's time is running out unless the anchor can be shifted."

* * *

By the time they reached Mirdalur, Niklas Theilsson and his soldiers had left for battle north of Glenreith, and Traher Voss's men had taken their place. Connor and the others found Nidhud and Dagur waiting for them in one of the reclaimed cellar rooms of the old manor.

"For a place that stood abandoned for so long, Dolan and the mages have managed to make it more livable than I would have expected," Connor remarked. Several of the underground rooms had been cleaned of debris and set up for the use of Dolan and his mages, both the *talishte* warriors of the Knights of Esthrane and a dozen mortal mages.

"McFadden, the Solveigs, and Verner pooled some of their mages and had them working at the Citadel," Dagur said. "We felt their work would be more useful here, and they would be easier to defend. They've been a great help," he added, "and with the rumors of mages disappearing, they were happy for the additional protection."

Connor shook his head. "Those aren't rumors," he replied, and told Dagur what they had seen on their way from Westbain.

"Then I'm doubly glad the mages joined us," he replied. "The Knights have been kind hosts."

Nidhud chuckled. "And your mages have enabled us to progress much faster," he said. "An excellent alliance." He turned to Penhallow. "Welcome. Good to see you've arrived safely. You'll be glad to know the repairs and fortifications at Rodestead House are nearly complete," he reported. Rodestead House, Penhallow's manor, had been badly damaged by the Cataclysm.

"Good to hear," Penhallow replied. He accepted a goblet of deer's blood from a tray on one of the worktables. Connor was quite happy with a glass of whiskey. "And what from Voss? I assume news came along with his troops."

Nidhud nodded. "His men are guarding Rodestead House, as well as Voss's own fortifications. These troops arrived a fortnight ago, at the request of Niklas Theilsson. He's gone to support McFadden in the north, along with Rikard and the mages who stayed with Glenreith and the army." He paused. "As for Voss himself, he sent word that he would love a chance to finish what we started at Valshoa."

"I don't doubt that," Penhallow said, smiling. "Let him know that he'll get his chance against Pollard again, though they're the least of our worries for now."

Nidhud reached for a goblet and took a sip. "Dolan is getting closer to a solution here," he said. He gestured for Connor and Penhallow to join him at the worktable. Connor found a plate with sausage, bread, and cheese set out for him, as well as a flask with more whiskey. After the long ride, he was grateful for the refreshments, and he ate quickly.

"It's taken us quite a while to examine the artifacts you hid in the crypts beneath Quillarth Castle," Dagur said. "I'm glad you managed to keep them out of Reese's hands, although some of the pieces are corrupted enough that they're no use to anyone."

"We had very little time," Penhallow replied. "We gathered what we could and secured them."

Nidhud nodded. "That's where it's been valuable to have mortal and *talishte*-mages working together. Having the *talishte* mages reduces the deaths and injuries when pieces are tainted, and the mortal mages give us an idea of whether or not McFadden could safely use an artifact."

"What have you found?" Penhallow asked.

"I'll show you," Nidhud said, rising and gesturing for them

to follow him. He led them into another, more crowded work-room. Dolan and several mages looked up as they entered.

"Glad you're here," Dolan said brusquely. "We've nearly figured this out, I believe."

Penhallow and Connor crowded around the table, where thirteen crystal rods and obsidian disks were scattered, along with yellowed manuscripts, a piece of wood covered with carved sigils, an ornate boline knife, and a stone chalice.

"Those are presence-crystals," Dolan said, indicating the rods. "I took them along with the manuscripts that Quintrel thought were the key to creating a new anchor. McFadden already had the thirteen obsidian disks. But we suspected something was missing, and we were right."

"The disks and crystals will create the anchor," Dagur said. "But what we've learned—from the Valshoan manuscripts and from some that we found in the crypts at the Citadel—make it clear these other artifacts are needed to create the new Lords of the Blood." He looked to Connor. "And we'll need your help—along with that of the Wraith Lord—to make it happen."

"How?" Connor asked.

The Wraith Lord had been listening. He stood near the fireplace, where his ghostly form was half-hidden by the shadows. "I was among the lords at Mirdalur. But I inherited my disk from my father, and his fathers before that. Even I don't know how the Lords of the Blood were created."

Dolan nodded. "We realized that the Lords of the Blood were either special because of their magic, or made special because they took part in the binding ritual." He leaned back and took a sip from his goblet. "But we did have a clue—the thirteen onyx disks.

"The disks were made for the Lords of the Blood, handed

down through generations. They weren't just artifacts to call and bind the magic," Dolan continued. "They were the story of how magic was originally bound, split into thirteen parts, and put into code for safekeeping. And together with some of the artifacts we've recovered, we believe we've discovered how to create new Lords of the Blood."

"Your mages deciphered them?" the Wraith Lord asked, his gaze sharp. "And are they certain of their conclusions?"

Dolan nodded. "As certain as they can be, without putting what they've found into practice."

"If you're wrong about this, Blaine McFadden dies," Penhallow said.

"I'm well aware of that," Dolan replied archly.

"That's where these other pieces come in," Dagur said excitedly. "The key was combining that sigil wood with the disks. It held the words of power and the ritual instructions for binding blood to magic." His eyes gleamed with the discovery. "It's blood magic, very old and strong."

Dagur gestured toward the table. "That knife and the chalice have matching sigils," he explained. "Words of power open the ritual and activate the chamber, drawing on the meridians."

"The knife draws blood from each of the thirteen participants," Dolan continued. "It's mingled in the chalice, where it awakens the chalice's power. Pouring the blood onto the sigils that are carved in the ritual chamber floor connects the power to the meridians."

"And where do the Wraith Lord and I come in?" Connor asked.

"The Wraith Lord is the only one who has seen the ritual completed successfully. We'll need you to be part of the anchoring," Dolan answered.

*   *   *

Connor slept fitfully. Dagur provided a cot for him in the room shared by the mortal mages, where a small fireplace drove away Mirdalur's persistent chill. Connor's dreams were dark, shifting from visions of flame to memories of being buried alive. When he woke, the sun was just struggling above the horizon, barely visible behind the thick gray clouds.

"I hope you and Lord Penhallow weren't planning to go anywhere soon," Dagur said as Connor got dressed. "Looks like we've got another storm heading our way."

Connor shook his head. "We're here until Niklas returns, maybe longer. Penhallow and the Wraith Lord believed we were needed."

Dagur nodded. "As usual, his instincts are good."

"I don't know what I can do to help. I'm a medium, not a mage."

Dagur smiled. "You—and Penhallow—are among those McFadden wants for his thirteen."

Connor stared at Dagur in shock. "Me? I'm just Lord Penhallow's servant."

Dagur seemed to be enjoying his shock. "You're also the Wraith Lord's host. And McFadden says he trusts you, that he's seen you show a lot of courage."

"Who else is to be among the thirteen?" Connor asked, still sorting out the news.

"I don't know that he's chosen them all," Dagur replied. "His mates from Edgeland, and General Dolan, plus Niklas Theilsson."

"Blaine's married to Kestel, so that's one bloodline," Connor said, thinking aloud. "Piran, Dawe, and Verran he trusts with his life."

"It wouldn't be a surprise for him to choose his strongest allies," Dagur added. "It seals the compact, and binds them together."

Connor nodded. "Voss maybe, then. Perhaps one of the Solveigs, and Verner."

Dagur shrugged. "Perhaps. But you were one of the people he was certain he wanted."

"That's going to take some time to get used to," Connor replied.

Dagur moved to respond, then froze. A look of confusion turned to terror, and with a cry of pain, he fell to the floor, holding his head in his hands.

Let me in, Connor, the Wraith Lord's voice sounded in his mind. *I can protect you. We're under attack.*

Connor steeled himself and nodded. "Go," he murmured. He felt the cold mist of the Wraith Lord's presence envelop him, and the jarring dislocation as Kierken Vandholt's consciousness took possession of his body.

You're stronger, better able to withstand me, the Wraith Lord noted, and Connor knew the change was due to Penhallow's last healing. *That's good. We have a battle to fight. I'll tell you what I'm doing as we go. Please don't fight me, we don't have time.*

"What about Dagur?" Connor asked. Dagur rocked back and forth on the floor, insensible, moaning in pain.

"The enemy's using magic against the mages," the Wraith Lord replied. "We can't do anything about that, but we can fight, and we must protect the *talishte* and the ritual chamber."

The Wraith Lord ran down the corridor and up the steps to the bare entrance room, then burst out into the wan daylight.

Voss's mercenaries were fighting soldiers whose garb Connor recognized all too well. *Hennoch,* Connor thought. *Damn.*

The smell of smoke hung in the cold air, not the distant

smell of cooking fires or the scent of the mage's fireplace but an acrid, heavy stench of burning oil. A wall of fire rose behind the ruins of Mirdalur's manor house. Voss's soldiers fought a force that easily outnumbered them by half. No soldiers could be spared to extinguish the flames without dooming the others to die by the sword. Behind the battle lines, Connor made out the shapes of wagons bearing huge casks.

The mages are down. The talishte *are trapped by the daylight, and the soldiers are fighting for their lives. It's up to us to put out the fire.*

Mirdalur survived the Great Fire and the Cataclysm, Connor thought. *If Hennoch's soldiers break through the line, they'll make sure the whole place burns. Smoke will kill the mages. Fire will destroy the* talishte, *the artifacts, and McFadden's last chance to anchor the magic.*

All right, then. What can we do? Connor asked the Wraith Lord.

I've got a plan.

It had better be good, Connor retorted in his mind.

The Wraith Lord chuckled. *First, we need weapons. I'll head down to where Dolan and the others are sleeping. We'll take what we need.*

"Stealing the weapons from a team of *talishte* warriors isn't a recipe for a long life," Connor muttered.

The Knights can't use their weapons, because it's daylight. The other soldiers are occupied, and the mages may die if we don't get things put right. We're the only ones free to stop that fire. Win this, and Dolan will forgive you.

Connor let the Wraith Lord direct him through unfamiliar corridors and stairways to the deep crypts where Penhallow and the Knights slept. Their weapons were nearby, and Connor took what the Wraith Lord wanted: a bow with a quiver of arrows, and a crossbow and quarrels.

We'll need something from the mages' workshop, the Wraith Lord said. *Don't stop, don't fight me, no matter what you see. We don't have much time.*

"I'm terrible with a bow," Connor grumbled to the Wraith Lord.

But I'm quite good with one, the Wraith Lord replied.

They reached the entrance to the mages' rooms and Connor had to keep himself from fighting to stop in his tracks. The mages lay on the floor, some pale and still, others rocking and moaning in pain. *We can't do anything for them here,* the Wraith Lord said. *But if we succeed, their pain ends. We must hurry!*

The Wraith Lord found the substance he wanted, a cake of white powder, and took a small burlap sack as well. Then he grabbed a bucket of pitch near the fire, and a handful of rags.

We'll tie a bit of rag near the head of each arrow, then soak the rag in pitch, the Wraith Lord explained. *We're going to fight fire with fire.* Connor watched his hands as the Wraith Lord made quick work of it.

Now we need to find the highest point we can facing the pond that's just beyond the courtyard, the Wraith Lord advised. *We'll put the mage's powder in the sack and tie it onto one of the quarrels.* Connor watched, eyeing the arrow skeptically.

Mirdalur's main house was a ruin. Its broken walls stood like an empty shell, with its roof and most of its flooring long gone. The Wraith Lord and Connor came up from the cellars and heard the battle unfolding around them. Smoke hung heavy in the air, and the fiery wash of oil from the wagon casks burned closer to the house and its crypts. Connor knew that if the upper portion of the manor burned, the mages and the Knights would die.

The Wraith Lord studied the stone walls until he saw what remained of a staircase. The stone supports and bits of old timbers still stuck out from one of the walls. He slung the bows across Connor's back and started to climb.

The stone was old and covered with dirt and moss, making the footing treacherous. The Wraith Lord slipped, barely catching himself with a handhold on another stone that ripped at Connor's skin and nails. The wall gave him cover from the fighting, but they could hear the clang of steel and the shouts of the fighters. The first empty window in the ruined wall was still far above him.

We'll have to climb faster! the Wraith Lord advised.

"We nearly fell," Connor muttered. "You won't break if you hit the ground, but my body will."

You've got my strength and agility, and the resilience you gained from Penhallow's bond, the Wraith Lord reminded him. *That makes you harder to kill.*

Difficult, but not impossible, Connor grunted in his mind, as he stretched to grab the next handhold. The smoke was growing thicker, and Connor could hear the flames licking closer to the manor. The oil fed the fire, and the dry grass enlarged it. Heat from the flames raised a sweat on Connor's forehead despite the cold day.

An arrow zinged past Connor's head, narrowly missing his scalp. A second arrow sliced through the skin on his upper arm, nearly making him lose his grip. Despite the cuirass he wore to protect his torso, Connor knew that most of his body was vulnerable to a keen-eyed bowman.

They were still low enough to the ground to drop without breaking a limb, and as the smoke drifted his way, the Wraith Lord took advantage of the temporary cover to hide Connor, disappearing from the sniper's sight.

We need to get high enough to have a clear shot into the pond, the Wraith Lord reminded Connor.

"We also need to avoid becoming a pincushion," Connor muttered. He paused to think. Mirdalur had been slowly deteriorating for decades, helped along by the Great Fire's devastation. Yet the buildings were made of solid rock, built to withstand assault. Wooden interiors might have disintegrated, but the walls of the fortress had been built as a stronghold for the ages.

"I have an idea," Connor said.

The Wraith Lord read his thoughts. *Let's try it,* the Wraith Lord responded.

Keeping Connor's head down, the Wraith Lord moved from one protected vantage point to another, until he saw their objective: a narrow old bell tower that stood on the intact side of the ruined keep.

The Wraith Lord dove from cover, getting several yards closer to the bell tower before the sniper spotted him. An arrow bit into the frozen ground at his heels, and another narrowly missed him, skimming his shoulder closely enough to rip his shirt without raising blood. He ducked behind a ruined stone wall and then ran a zigzag path as fast as he could for the dark doorway at the bottom of the bell tower. He heard the twang of an arrow, and warm blood flowed down over his left ear from where the sharp tip had opened a slice in his scalp. Another arrow hit his right thigh, biting into his leg and darkening his trouser leg with blood.

Limping and swearing, the Wraith Lord moved into the darkness of the tower. Too late, they saw the shadowy form waiting there.

"Where do you think you're going?"

Connor's eyes took a moment to adjust to the light, and in

that instant, his attacker swung. The Wraith Lord reacted, executing a deadly series of parries and blows that took his opponent by surprise. The enemy soldier got in one lucky blow, opening a slash across Connor's chest that made him gasp in pain. Connor could feel the Wraith Lord's anger coursing through his borrowed body. Only then did the attacker realize that his opponent's skill far outstripped his expectations. In the next instant, the enemy soldier was dying, with Connor's blade in his heart.

Trust me, Connor, the Wraith Lord said as he eyed three long, rusted chains that hung from high in the bell tower's rafters. The heavy bells were gone, but the chains remained, connected to the iron yoke far above. Connor wiped the blood from his face and grimaced as he put weight on his injured leg. He could feel the pain of his injuries beginning to throb as the Wraith Lord grasped the shaft of the arrow in his leg near the skin with one hand and cut off most of its length with his sword.

"If we can climb one of those chains, we'll have a view of the pond," Connor mused aloud. "And the bell tower is a more protected climb than the wall we tried before."

Unless an archer follows us and shoots from below.

"Very funny," Connor grumbled. The tower was cramped, the size of a small room at the bottom, growing narrower toward the top. He doubted that the area where the bells had been was much wider than his shoulders. The Wraith Lord sheathed his sword, adjusted his bow and quiver into the center of his back, and squared his shoulders.

Here we go, the Wraith Lord said, and took a running leap to catch the largest bell chain. Connor bit back a cry as the pain from his injured arms and chest spiked. They dropped down, and fell as Connor's injured leg gave out under him.

We can do this, Connor, the Wraith Lord encouraged. Connor gritted his teeth and felt himself dragged to his feet. He could hear the battle outside, and he knew that their ability to change its course decreased with every passing moment. Eyeing the chain as if it were an opponent, the Wraith Lord ran and jumped again, Connor stifling a cry as he caught the chain, willing the Wraith Lord and his injured body not to let go.

The Wraith Lord wrapped his legs around the chain and inched up its length, hand over hand, using Connor's good leg to help hold him in place. The Wraith Lord shook blood out of his eyes, and Connor tried not to think of how much blood he had lost. It would not do to get light-headed at the top of the bell tower. His ragged breathing echoed in the confines of the tight space.

We draw on your new strength, the Wraith Lord encouraged him. *Remember: You are no longer fully mortal.*

Connor had already thought about the enhanced abilities Penhallow had promised would come from his tighter bond. Whether it was the strengthened *kruvgaldur* or merely that with experience and mortal fear, Connor had grown more cussedly stubborn, they kept on climbing. Connor's arms shook with the effort, and his legs ached from gripping the chain, even with the Wraith Lord in control. As they ascended, the stone walls brushed his shoulders in the narrow passage. Connor did not think he would ever be able to straighten out his fingers again, since they had cramped into claws from holding on to the chain.

The bell chain swayed. They were nearly to the top, and he had begun counting every handhold as the Wraith Lord climbed, anything to keep his mind off the pain and his height above the ground. If the Wraith Lord's grip gave way, he doubted that anything could save him.

"How come you can't fly like normal *talishte*?" Connor muttered.

The Wraith Lord's chuckle sounded in his mind. *'Normal'* talishte. *You never cease to amaze me, Bevin. But even among immortals, not all talents are equal. Flight was not one of mine.*

Connor's head rose above the sill of the bell tower window. In the distance, they could see the pond. *Just a bit more*, the Wraith Lord murmured.

Metal creaked, then gave way. The chain grew slack in his hands and fell away with a rush. For an instant, Connor fell, too.

He never figured out whether he reacted out of survival instinct or whether the Wraith Lord knew what to do, but his arms and legs thrust out, stopping his fall by bracing himself against the narrow stone walls. His howl of pain echoed up the rock tower, but despite his shaking limbs, his body did not buckle. Biting into his lip so hard he tasted blood, the Wraith Lord began to inch his way back up the tower.

At the top of the tower, they found the remains of a platform used by long-ago bell ringers. Its heavy planks had been treated in pitch to withstand the elements, and Connor heaved himself onto it, praying to all the gods that it would not give way beneath his weight. For a moment, he lay still, gasping for breath, shaking from head to toe. Then he gathered his wits and crawled on all fours to where he could see the horizon.

We're going to fire that arrow with the white powder into the pond, the Wraith Lord instructed.

"Are you mad? I can't hit that from here!" Connor protested.

I can.

Connor fought down his instincts and took a deep breath. He mentally stepped back so the Wraith Lord could take full possession of his movements without distraction. With a skill and grace born of lifetimes of practice, the Wraith Lord armed the crossbow and took aim. Relegating himself to a corner of his mind, Connor watched as the Wraith Lord sighted the target and squeezed the trigger, grabbing for a handhold with faster-than-mortal speed as the crossbow's kick nearly sent them tumbling to the stone floor far below.

Prepare! The Wraith Lord's voice warned. Connor stared after the quarrel, utterly confused.

"Prepare for what?"

The Wraith Lord threw Connor down and covered his head with his arms. The arrow dipped beneath the surface of the pond, carrying the burlap bag filled with the powder cake. A heartbeat later, the pond exploded with a loud boom, sending a wave of water over the banks, dousing the flames in a large area.

Connor was still reeling from the shock, but the Wraith Lord had readied the regular bow and one of the pitch-soaked arrows. The Wraith Lord got to his knees, drew the bow once more, and let the arrow fly. Connor felt the Wraith Lord's deep satisfaction in the sheer physical ability to handle the weapon. He loosed the rest of the arrows in quick succession, aiming for the nearest of the two oil wagons. The arrow's flames stuttered and flickered for a moment on the old, oil-soaked wood, then the cask itself caught fire, and its keepers raised a shout, scrambling to get clear. With a roar, the cask exploded into a shower of oil that engulfed the wagons and splattered nearby soldiers with flaming liquid.

That's enough of that, the Wraith Lord said. *Now to get down.*

"I'm with you on that one," Connor murmured. The Wraith Lord seized the stronger of the remaining two chains, winding his legs around it. Then he slid down the chain, barking the skin on his palms, as Connor's injured shoulder and thigh threatened to black him out. At last, he dropped to the ground and fell once more as his leg buckled on him.

Let me handle this. The Wraith Lord shrugged out of the bows and dropped the quiver, drawing Connor's sword. *The fight isn't over yet.*

Buoyed by the Wraith Lord's power, sustained by the stamina from his strengthened bond with Penhallow, the Wraith Lord ran into the courtyard, sword raised. Billows of black smoke rose from where the oil casks had exploded. Voss had sent thirty men to protect Mirdalur; to Connor's relief, he could see most of them on their feet and fighting. Hennoch's soldiers might have outnumbered the mercenaries, but from the corpses Connor counted on the ground, the mercenaries were doing better than holding their own.

"Let's send these sons of Raka straight to the Sea of Souls!" the Wraith Lord shouted with Connor's voice, wading into the fray.

If the soldier the Wraith Lord attacked estimated the skill of his opponent by judging Connor's appearance, he was in for a rude shock. On the battlefield, Connor gave up all semblance of control, watching the battle unfold while his body moved of its own volition. Centuries of the Wraith Lord's existence as *talishte* had made him a battle-hardened warrior, exulting in the fight, ruthless in his tactics. Now that skill animated Connor's body, moving him with utter confidence, making him oblivious to pain, besting his opponent in just a few merciless strokes.

Two more enemy soldiers came at Connor, and the Wraith Lord laughed. It was a cold, harsh sound without pity. Blood spattered Connor's face and arms as the Wraith Lord swung at the first soldier, slashing him across the chest. They pivoted, blocking a swing from the second soldier as the Wraith Lord drew the knife from Connor's belt, fighting two-handed with a skill Connor knew he could never hope to muster himself.

The Wraith Lord possessed *talishte* speed and strength. His hapless opponents realized too late that Connor was not what he appeared.

"By Torven! What are you? You fight like a biter, in the daylight!" one of the men swore as he found himself parrying frantically.

"I am your executioner," the Wraith Lord muttered through gritted teeth. He delivered a series of bone-jarring swings, coming at the soldier faster than the man could react. One swing bit deeply into the man's shoulder, letting his sword arm hang by a shred of sinew. The next swing severed his head. Then with a dizzyingly quick pivot, the Wraith Lord scythed the blade toward the second soldier and lunged, taking him through the heart.

Connor's arms were blood-soaked to the elbows, and blood spattered his hair and face. The Wraith Lord grinned, reveling in the familiar cadence of battle, rejoicing in the sensuality of having a physical body. And to Connor's concerned amazement, he did not feel as utterly spent as he expected from the possession.

Penhallow told you; you're harder to kill now. Not quite human—something more.

That would bear thinking through on another day, but for the moment, Connor accepted the boon. He stood surrounded by corpses, breathing hard. Soot mingled with sweat and blood running in rivulets down his face. Despite the cold, his shirt clung to his back. As far as he could tell, little of the blood was his own, except for his leg, which hurt like a son of a bitch.

The battle had turned. The casks' explosion had taken several of the enemy soldiers, coating them in oil and setting them ablaze. Voss's mercenaries dealt out a harsher reception than Hennoch's soldiers expected, and Connor's sudden appearance, along with the Wraith Lord's deadly prowess, helped to change the odds. Only a handful of the attackers remained on the field. The Wraith Lord and the mercenaries ran the stragglers down. Hennoch's soldiers, knowing they were going to die, fought with insane fury, desperate to inflict damage.

I would have been mincemeat, Connor thought. Without the Wraith Lord's possession, he had gained enough skill with a sword to hold off an attacker of average ability, but never in a lifetime did Connor expect to acquire the Wraith Lord's deadly grace and speed.

Which is why I'm doing the fighting, the Wraith Lord replied. He swung once more, bringing his blade down with a powerful swing that cleaved his attacker from shoulder to hip.

All around them, the bloodied courtyard had grown quiet. Black smoke still drifted in the wind, but the flames had been washed away or stamped out, so that they posed no threat to those inside the manor's cellars. Voss's men made their way across the battlefield, slitting throats. To one side, the oil wagons' flames guttered like a spent candle.

"Good fighting. I didn't expect that from you." Annik, the commander of Voss's soldiers, strode up to Connor. "By Torven! You're injured."

"I'll probably live," Connor said, though as the Wraith Lord withdrew some of his control, the pain returned in a blinding flash. "How did your men fare?"

Annik shrugged. "Lost a couple. Voss will be sending reinforcements soon. Still, hate to bury any of my men. But they made the enemy pay, and there's no shame in that," he said, looking out over the bodies that littered the ground. The glint in his eyes and the set of his mouth told Connor that Annik was no stranger to battle.

"Do you think they'll be back? Hennoch's men?" Connor asked, looking toward the still-smoking oil wagons.

Annik shrugged. "If not him, someone else. Good thing, too, or my men and me would be out of a job." He walked away, chuckling at his own joke, stepping over bodies and shouting orders to his men.

You did well, Bevin, the Wraith Lord's voice echoed in Connor's mind. *Now I will get you to safety, and leave you once I am assured of your care. I think you'll find the recovery to be a bit easier than in the past.*

Limping so badly that his injured leg dragged, Connor stumbled toward the keep and the tunnels below. One of Voss's soldiers spotted him and ran to support him under one shoulder, helping him to the shelter of the ruined first floor as the full extent of Connor's injuries began to make themselves felt.

"We need a healer!" the soldier shouted, waving for one of Voss's battle healers to attend. As the healer headed toward him, the Wraith Lord slipped free of Connor's body. To Connor's surprise, he was not burning up with fever from hosting the spirit, and his heart was not pounding dangerously, though every muscle and sinew in his body seemed to burn and he was light-headed from the blood loss.

Harder to kill. Not quite mortal, Connor thought. *This will take some getting used to.*

CHAPTER TWENTY-FIVE

M ASTER QUINTREL! WE'VE CAUGHT A SPY."

Vigus Quintrel glanced up as a guard came to the doorway of the study at Torsford. Carensa and Guran, who were conferring with Quintrel, turned to see the newcomer.

"Where did you find this spy?" Quintrel asked.

"Prowling the edge of the camp. Do you want us to interrogate him, or just kill him?"

With a sigh, Quintrel stood. He set his drink aside, and cast a lingering glance toward the fire before turning toward the guard. "Bring him to me. I'll decide."

A few moments later, two guards returned, dragging their unconscious prisoner. A tall young man with muddy-brown hair slumped between the guards, bound at the wrists and ankles. From the blood on his shirt and the dirt on his trousers, Carensa guessed that he did not go down easily. One of the guards reached down to grab the prisoner's hair and pull back his head so Quintrel could see him.

An unexpected resemblance made Quintrel hesitate. Carensa caught her breath, trying to muffle a gasp of recognition.

"Esban," he said, calling to his second-in-command, "does he remind you of anyone?"

Esban studied the prisoner's features. "If I didn't know better, I'd guess he might be related to Blaine McFadden."

Quintrel turned to Carensa. "You knew the McFaddens well. Do you recognize him?"

Carensa fought down panic, hoping she could keep her voice even. "I don't know, Vigus. It's been so long. People change and he's young. I can't say for certain."

Quintrel's look told her that he was sure she was holding back. "Let's play this a little differently, shall we?" Quintrel mused aloud. "Take him up to the guest rooms—one with bars on the windows. I'll have a servant bring up wash water and a fresh change of clothing. Cut him loose, but keep a guard on the door. When he comes around, tell him to clean up and get dressed. He'll be my guest at dinner tonight." He turned and leveled a gaze at both Carensa and Guran. "And so will you."

A puzzled look passed between the guards, but they did as they were told. The prisoner hung limply in their grasp, but Carensa could not tell whether the young man was playacting or was still unconscious. The door closed behind the guards, and Quintrel turned to Carensa and Guran.

"I'll want your help interrogating the prisoner," he said offhandedly. "He may be no one of importance. In which case, executing him won't matter to anyone. But he might be valuable to us, either for what he knows or for who he is. And I am going to find that out."

"We can help," Guran said smoothly. Carensa nodded, avoiding meeting Quintrel's gaze directly. "But perhaps we should go back to the workroom with the information we were discussing before the interruption. Let us get cleaned up before dinner."

Quintrel gave a curt nod. "Go on. I'll send someone for you."

Carensa realized she was holding her breath when they reached the hallway, but she said nothing, trying to force herself to remain calm as she and Guran made their way back to the workroom.

"I'm not feeling well," she said, knowing Guran could see her distress. "I need to lie down before dinner."

"I'll convey Vigus's instructions to the mages, and stop by with some tea," he replied, with a knowing look that let her know he recognized her distress.

Carensa made her way through the hallways with her head down, not wanting to attract attention. She let herself into her room and collapsed against the door. Tears started, and a sob welled up in her throat. "Oh, Carr," she murmured. "What have you gotten yourself into?"

Several candlemarks later, Quintrel waited in the parlor along with Carensa and Guran. A private dinner had been set for four on a small table. Guards waited in the shadows. Quintrel wore one of his scholar's robes, embroidered with runes and inlaid with velvet and silk to show his rank. Carensa and Guran had worn clean but unpretentious work robes.

Two guards escorted the prisoner to the parlor. He looked to be in his late teens, but hard work and battle had put muscles on his long limbs. Carensa wondered if Quintrel could even question his decided resemblance to Ian McFadden.

"Won't you join us for dinner?" Quintrel invited, gesturing to the table. Rostivan's steward had set out a meal of venison, roasted beets and turnips, bread pudding with dried fruit, and a carafe of brandy. It was a rare feast these days, and hunger was clear in the prisoner's eyes.

Warily, Carr made his way to the table. His gaze flickered to the guards who stood silently in the darkened corners of the room, and he did not miss the click of the lock as his escort locked the door behind them. Then he saw Carensa, and he froze, though she kept her face impassive.

Don't say anything, she thought. *It will be worse for both of us if you do.*

"Sit, please." Quintrel seated himself and gestured for the others to do the same. With a flourish, Quintrel placed a napkin on his lap. A steward appeared to fill their plates from the serving platters. The steward poured them each a goblet of brandy before retreating from sight.

"I don't believe you came to pay a social call," Quintrel said. His voice was cordial, but there was threat beneath the civility.

"The manor is quite nice," Carr replied with a half smile that said he knew they were playing a game. "But I don't believe you're the original owner."

"You're correct. This was better suited to our needs," Quintrel replied. He cut a piece of meat and ate it. "Please, eat. If I intended to poison you, I wouldn't have wasted good venison on it."

Perhaps Carr figured that he was unlikely to leave alive, no matter which scenario played out, or maybe he was just hungry. He made short work of the food on his plate and allowed the steward to fill it a second time, though he merely sipped his brandy. *Does he figure this for a last meal?* Carensa wondered. *If so, he's quite cool about it.*

"I want to know who you are," Quintrel said.

Carr sipped his drink. "No one important."

Quintrel's smile was taut. "Let me be the judge of that." Quintrel barely moved his hand, but Carr froze in his seat, eyes panicked. Another moment, and Carr's hands went to his temples.

"Get out of my head!" Carr managed, though his words ended in a gasp of pain.

Carensa's hands gripped her chair, and she bit her lip until it bled. *I can't challenge Vigus, not directly. And if he believes I favor Carr, I'll have no chance to help Carr—or Blaine. Gods above, I hate this!*

"Carr McFadden," Quintrel said, leaning back with a look of satisfaction. The *divi* orb glowed brightly on its strap around Quintrel's neck. Carensa did not doubt that the *divi* had enjoyed the pain Quintrel had caused. Carr shook his head, pale and angry. "Did your brother send you?"

"No. I came on my own." Carr replied. His voice was insolent.

"I could have warned you that showing up unexpected might lead to a less than friendly reception."

Carr must not have gone down without a fight, Carensa thought. One eye was darkening to purple, looking swollen and sore. His lip was split, and his knuckles were scratched and red. From the stiff way he had walked to his chair, she guessed that he had taken a thorough pummeling, perhaps even some bruised or broken ribs. Still, he was handling the situation like a seasoned courtier. Or an utter madman. Knowing his father, either was possible.

"Carensa, can you confirm what I've read from him? Is this really Carr McFadden?"

Carensa met Carr's eyes, wishing that her gift were telepathy, willing him not to speak out of turn. "I told you, Vigus, it's been years. Maybe. I don't know."

Quintrel's expression suggested that he was reserving judgment. "Why did you come here?" he asked Carr. "I'm sure you know your brother and I aren't on friendly terms."

"Just curious, I guess," Carr replied evenly.

"Did it occur to you that our archers might have shot you on sight? Or that the guards might have hanged you as a spy without asking questions?" Quintrel pressed.

For the first time, Carr met his level gaze. "I have stared down the maw of *gryps* and looked into the mouth of Raka when the Great Fire fell. Pardon my saying so, but not much scares me after that."

What would Ian's madness coupled with Blaine's courage produce? Carensa wondered. Meeting Carr's gaze, she thought she might have the answer.

"There's not much left for you at Glenreith, is there?" Quintrel said offhandedly. "I mean, things started to fall apart when Blaine was exiled, and it's never really recovered. At least you had the title—"

"I don't see that titles mean much since the Great Fire," Carr replied. "What matters is whether or not you can hold on to what's yours and protect your own. And so far, Glenreith has done that—even against you."

Quintrel allowed himself the ghost of a smile. "I can offer you something better," he said. "A commission with Lord Rostivan, for one thing. You've seen enough battle to be an officer."

Carr took a sip of his brandy. "Officers are just big targets, with their armor and warhorses. I like it on the ground, where I can run or hide."

Quintrel chuckled. "It takes a man who's seen real combat to understand that." He took another sip of his brandy. "I don't really care why you came here," Quintrel said. "But now that you're here, you've got a decision to make. You know things that could help me defeat Blaine and stop the fighting. Help me, and you'll have a place in the new order that I bring to Donderath."

Carr met Quintrel's gaze. "We make those same kinds of

promises to the spies we catch back at camp. But no one's going to trust a turncoat. So I suspect you've just wasted an excellent venison dinner."

Quintrel raised his glass in salute. "Well said—and true enough. But there remains the matter of your life and freedom. You can offer what you know willingly, and extend your life in some comfort as my 'guest.'"

He met Carr's gaze. "Or we can use magic to take whatever you don't give freely." He paused. "We even have a *talishte* or two around who can read memories from your blood. Everything you know will be mine—one way or another. You decide how painful the process becomes."

"Betray my brother and his allies, and you'll put off my execution for a bit, is that the offer?" Carr's voice stopped short of baiting Quintrel, but it was clear that he harbored no illusions.

"What do you care? By all accounts, there's no love lost there."

A shadow crossed Carr's face, there and gone before Carensa could quite decipher it. "What's between Blaine and me is personal. Betraying him—and my commander—to the enemy is something else entirely," Carr replied.

"Your presence here betrays him," Quintrel said smoothly, finishing his glass of brandy. "He threw away his lands, title, and betrothal to save your sister. Why wouldn't he throw down his sword for you?" The *divi* orb pulsed with a dim glow. Carensa wondered if Carr could see it. The light had grown stronger throughout the conversation, as if the spirit inside the orb was excitedly waiting for something.

Carr looked away. "If you have to ask, you don't know us very well. Trust me on this. Blaine won't die for me. Not now." There was a certainty and sadness in his voice that gave Carensa to know that Carr was not bluffing.

"I have some questions for you," Quintrel said to Carr, and there was a hint of steel in his voice. "Answer them, and you can remain here indefinitely as an honored guest. You've got nothing waiting for you at Glenreith. Ally with us, and everything you lost will be regained."

Carr met Quintrel's gaze. "No."

Quintrel made a motion with his hand, and Carr's chair pivoted away from the table. Carr moved to rise, and found that he could not. He struggled against the invisible bonds that held him, and a satisfied smile touched Quintrel's lips.

"Now, about those questions," he said quietly. "How many soldiers are sworn to Blaine McFadden?"

"I never counted them."

Quintrel's fingers twitched, the *divi* orb flared, and Carr screamed as three ragged gashes ripped down through his shirt and the flesh of his chest, staining the torn cloth red with blood.

Carensa started from her chair, but Guran grabbed her wrist, silencing her with a warning glance.

Quintrel's expression was far away, and Carensa guessed that he was rummaging through Carr's memories for the answer. Carr screamed again, hands struggling as if he were trying to fight off the intrusion. Carr writhed, fighting the power that held him, but Quintrel's hold remained firm.

Quintrel brightened. "At least a division's worth. That's valuable."

Carr slumped in his chair, glaring at Quintrel. Quintrel regarded him with curiosity. "Let's see what you know about your allies."

Quintrel motioned, and Carr went rigid with pain, pale and wide-eyed. Another set of bloody claw marks raked down his right arm. Carensa could tell Carr was trying not to scream, trying to avoid giving Quintrel the satisfaction, but in the end, Quintrel's will won out. This time, Carr screamed until he was hoarse as the *divi* orb flared brightly, throbbing like a heartbeat.

Carensa gripped both arms of her chair, feeling as if she might pass out. The guards in the room assured that neither she nor Guran could physically overpower Quintrel. She knew her magic was no match for Quintrel's. *Guran might be strong enough, perhaps, but what then?* she thought frantically. *We can't cross Quintrel unless we're willing to kill him, and if we do, his loyalists will carry on without him.*

"The more complex the information, the more digging it takes to rip it out of your mind," Quintrel said, with the tone of a bored lecturer. "Thank you for confirming that Tormod Solveig is a necromancer. That's helpful to know, although his tricks won't be as useful against Rostivan's troops. Useful also to know that Verner's forces have been essentially wiped out. Very useful."

Carr's breath was ragged. His hands balled into fists. Blood streamed from the gashes the *divi* had torn.

Quintrel paused, as if he were listening to something the rest of them could not hear. Carensa wondered if the *divi* was feeding him suggestions. "Let's find out more about McFadden himself."

Quintrel stood in front of Carr, hands on hips. "What effect has anchoring the magic had on McFadden?"

Carr gave Quintrel a baleful look. His body tensed, and it looked to Carensa as if Carr was determined to fight Quintrel's intrusion.

Quintrel's hand moved. The *divi* light was blindingly bright, and this time, it played across Carr's features as if it sensed his determination to balk.

Three new bloody gashes slashed across Carr's face. A second swipe opened new slashes on his chest. Carr's whole body trembled with his struggle to block Quintrel, a fight he could not hope to win without magic. His screams echoed in the small room, and even Guran blanched. Carensa wavered in her chair, dizzy from holding her breath, trembling with rage.

Quintrel tilted his head as he received his answer, a surprised and pleased expression on his face. "He's dying," Quintrel said as a triumphant smile touched his lips. "That's what you've been trying to hide. Anchoring the magic is killing him. Strong magic nearby wounds him." He chuckled. "It doesn't matter what his troop strength is. If magic is his bane, we can use that against him."

Carr hung limply against the invisible bonds that held him. His hair covered his face, and Carensa could not tell whether he was conscious. Only his shuddering breaths reassured her that Carr still lived.

"Vigus, please! Give him time to reconsider," Carensa said. "You've made your point. He could still be a valuable ally, but he's worth nothing if you kill him."

Quintrel gave Carensa an evaluating gaze, and for a moment she wondered if his *divi* would rip into her mind, wrest her secrets, and see how much she hated him. She hoped her expression was hopeful and guileless, but she doubted she was that good a liar.

"For your sake, Carensa, I will offer him mercy," Quintrel said finally as the *divi* orb dimmed. He strode over to where Carr slumped in his chair and pushed his head up.

"I'll give you two candlemarks to think over my offer. Cooperate, and your stay here can be comfortable and long. Fight me, and I will rip every secret from your mind, and the *talishte* will feast on your memories."

Quintrel signaled the guards, who walked toward Carr. He

made a gesture, and Carr's bonds vanished. He tumbled to the floor. "Guard his door. No one gets in. No one," he repeated, looking directly at Carensa. The two guards grabbed Carr by the arms and dragged him out of the room.

The door closed behind Carr, and Quintrel began to pace. "What's the real reason Carr McFadden's here?" Quintrel wondered aloud, frowning. "Do you really think McFadden would risk his brother as a spy?"

"From what he said, there's bad blood between them," Guran noted. Carensa was grateful that Guran responded. She did not think she could speak without her voice giving her away. Her throat ached from choking back tears, and her nails raised bloody half-moons in her palms.

"Interesting," Quintrel replied. "Do you know why?"

Guran shook his head. "No. But if I had to hazard a guess, I'd say that McFadden left the rest of the family in the lurch when he killed his father and got sent off to the end of the world. I imagine the young man's prospects dimmed dramatically at that point, along with the family fortune."

Quintrel looked to Carensa. "You knew the whole McFadden family. What do you make of it?"

Carensa had steadied herself enough to appear disinterested. "Carr was a lot younger, always getting in the way," she said with a shrug. "There were too many years between Blaine and Carr for them to be close." She paused. "Things were hard on the family after Blaine's exile. Guran's right; the scandal hurt Carr's prospects, and banished the family from court."

"So why assume Carr McFadden is a spy?" Guran said. "His brother mucks things up, destroys the family reputation, gets exiled as a murderer, and then comes back six years later and expects a hero's welcome and reclaims the title. Perhaps Carr was less than pleased to see him."

Quintrel reached for his glass and took a long sip of brandy. "I had been thinking along the same lines. He could be valuable. Certainly he has information about McFadden's plans and troops, maybe about the magic as well. If we can gain his trust, stoke his anger, perhaps he'll tell us what he knows."

Guran shrugged. "And if he won't, you'll get your answers the hard way." He paused. "Do you think he's much use as a bargaining chip? Would McFadden care that we have his brother, if it's true the two didn't like each other?"

"Obviously blood only counts for so much with McFadden, since he was willing to kill his own father," Quintrel replied. "If you mean, would McFadden trade himself for his brother? I doubt it."

"Which brings us back to wondering about Carr's reasons," Guran replied. "Maybe he's figured out that there's no place for him in the new lord's plans."

Carensa knew what Guran was doing, and she appreciated it. By making Quintrel question Carr's motives, Guran hoped to make Carr more valuable alive than dead, buying time. And by keeping Quintrel engaged in conversation, Guran helped Carensa avoid answering any questions that might increase Carr's danger.

"Younger sons shouldn't be shocked by that. It's possible he began to count on keeping the title once McFadden was exiled," Quintrel remarked. "For all the good it would have done him."

Quintrel knocked back the rest of his liquor. "Wounded pride has cost many a king his crown," he observed. He looked to Carensa. "What else can you tell me about Carr?"

Carensa shrugged. "I really never paid him much attention at all," she lied. "But he was always reckless. Then again, he was Ian's son. That's in the blood."

Quintrel seemed to debate the matter for a moment in his

mind, and then he let out a breath and gestured for them to move on. "Any other news?" he asked.

Guran nodded and set his empty glass aside. "One of our *talishte* spies just got back from the north. Said that Lysander went up against the Solveigs and got pushed back. On the bright side, Verner is no longer a problem. Our mages with Lysander got in a direct hit. McFadden and Theilsson showed up and turned the battle."

Carensa repressed a smile at Guran's skill. He was feeding Quintrel enough information to cover them, but framing it in a way that strengthened Blaine's position.

Quintrel frowned. "For a man who was supposed to be dead, McFadden causes a lot of trouble." He leaned against the mantle and toyed with his empty glass. "Our forces, combined with Lysander's, should outnumber McFadden's army. We will need to ensure future attacks are more coordinated."

"If you want to be rid of McFadden, why not just wear him down with magic?" Guran asked. "He's the sole anchor—strong magic drains him. Send enough of it against him, you could bleed him dry, so to speak, without needing to lay a hand on him."

Quintrel swore under his breath. "Too costly, too uncertain. We would badly drain ourselves in the process, leaving us vulnerable should one of McFadden's allies attack." He shook his head. "Assassination is easier to arrange—and much less expensive."

"When you're counting battle forces, have you figured in Voss's soldiers?" Guran asked, expertly pivoting the conversation now that he had gotten the information he wanted. "At Valshoa, Traher Voss's army made quite a showing."

"Voss," Quintrel spat. "He's a problem. Still, he's not a mage."

"Don't discount the *talishte* helping McFadden. You'll have to factor them into your plan," Guran said. "Penhallow, the Wraith Lord, the Knights of Esthrane."

Quintrel made a dismissive gesture. "A small number to worry about."

"I don't think we dare ignore them, Vigus," Guran replied. "They can do damage out of proportion to their numbers."

Quintrel stroked the *divi* orb, and it seemed to purr under his attention. What he heard from the *divi* Carensa did not know, or want to know, but Quintrel seemed satisfied with the answers only he could hear. "There are ways for the magic to remove that threat," he replied. "I'm not worried about *talishte*."

"What about Pollard? Fostering an alliance there could increase our troops as well," Guran said. "Our *talishte* say Reese has been imprisoned by his own. Reese wanted to stop the magic from coming back. It's back. Pollard is tricky enough to change his plans when the winds shift." Carensa only half listened to their discussion, trying to figure out a pretense to get in to see Carr.

Quintrel nodded. "I've directed Rostivan to ally with both Lysander and Pollard. It suits our purposes. Pollard's always hated the McFaddens," Quintrel added. "Even if magic wasn't at stake, I suspect Pollard would be trying to expand his lands at their expense."

"He has reason to side against McFadden," Guran pointed out. "Pollard's troops took a beating at Valshoa. He went off to lick his wounds. Without Reese, he'll have no control over the *talishte*. He's in need of allies."

"Vedran Pollard and Ian McFadden were cut from the same cloth," Carensa said. "Don't turn your back on him."

Quintrel chuckled. "I won't need to worry about that," he replied, fingering the strap that held the *divi's* orb.

"What new plans do you have for Lysander?" Guran asked.

Quintrel gave the matter some thought while he finished his drink. "I have a few options in mind. Let's see what I can learn from McFadden's brother. There might be something that chooses our course for us."

"We'd best get back to our work," Guran said. "Especially with more fighting sure to be happening soon."

Quintrel nodded. "Yes, of course. But I want both of you with me when I call for the prisoner. I want to know what you make of what he tells us."

"You're certain he'll cooperate?" Guran asked.

"I'll have a *talishte* with me," Quintrel replied. "He'll cooperate—one way or another."

Carensa was grateful that they passed few people in the corridors. She hung on to her composure with sheer willpower, and her control was slipping quickly. Guran opened the door to one of the workrooms and glanced around to assure that it was empty. He muttered words of power and warded the door for silence.

Carensa collapsed into a chair, weeping. Guran knelt beside her. "I can't keep the warding up long. Vigus will sense it—if he doesn't already."

"What he did...the *divi*..."

Guran nodded and let her cry into his shoulder. "I know. I saw. I've known Vigus for decades. He has an ego. He can be thoughtless. But it's new for him to use magic to torture someone." He shook his head. "I don't think that's all Vigus's doing. He's been corrupted by the *divi*."

"Maybe," Carensa allowed, drying her tears on the back of her hand and daubing her face with her sleeve. "But Vigus opened himself to the *divi* to get what he wanted. He didn't worry about who got hurt. I can't forgive him for that." She drew a ragged breath. "I can't forgive him for what he did to Carr. Gods above, Guran! Carr's just a boy."

Guran took both her hands in his. "He's a soldier, Carensa. You heard him. And he chose to come here as a spy. He knew the risks."

"He didn't know Vigus could rip his thoughts from his mind," she argued.

"Maybe. But he has to know that *talishte* can read a person's blood," Guran replied. "Or that he could be hanged—or worse—if he got caught."

"We've got to do something," Carensa said miserably. "Vigus won't leave him sane."

Guran met her gaze. "You've got a choice to make, Carensa. Save Carr, defy Vigus now, and it's over. You won't be able to help Blaine. Vigus will cast you out, or lock you up. And you'll have no way to stop what he's planning, when he's at the forefront of a massive army trampling his way across Donderath."

"How can we stop that?"

"I don't know yet," Guran admitted. "But I do know that you've got to make a choice. Save Carr, or save Blaine. You can't save both of them."

He gave her a warning shake of his head, and dispelled the warding. "I like the progress you've made on the translation," he said, rising. "Keep at it—you're almost done."

Carensa nodded miserably. "I will," she said, her voice choked. "Thank you."

Guran shut the workshop door behind him. Carensa slumped across the table, her head on her arms. The tears were gone, leaving behind cold rage and the closest thing she had ever felt to pure hatred. *Guran's right,* she thought. *Even though I don't want to admit it. I can't take the risk of saving Carr and losing the opportunity to strike at Vigus when the chance appears to turn the tide of battle. I may not be able to save Carr, but by all the gods, large and small, I will avenge him.*

The candlemarks passed too quickly, and Quintrel sent for Guran and Carensa to meet him at the room where Carr was imprisoned. With Quintrel was Stanton, a dark-haired *talishte* Carensa recognized but did not know. She memorized his face, for later. For the reckoning.

Two guards stood in front of the door to Carr's room, and when Quintrel nodded, one of them turned the key in the lock. When they entered, Carr was nowhere to be seen.

"Where is he?" Quintrel demanded of the guards, who stared at the empty room, wide-eyed. Carensa felt a surge of hope.

"No one left the room after we locked him in," the senior guard replied. "And the window hasn't been tampered with."

Stanton made a careful circle of the room. "I believe I've found the problem."

Stanton stood by the garderobe, which was hidden from view by a curtain. He threw back the cloth to reveal Carr slumped next to the stone seat, with both arms thrust into the hole.

The senior guard grabbed Carr by the shoulders and pulled him back. Carr's head lolled, and his body tumbled from its perch. Carr looked unnaturally pale, even before the lantern light revealed a new set of cuts, long, straight gashes that ran from wrist to elbow on each forearm.

The guard felt for a pulse in Carr's neck, then looked up. "He's gone, m'lord."

Quintrel turned to Stanton. "Can you—"

Stanton shook his head. "No. If we had reached him at the moment of death, perhaps. But I can't read the dead, nor could I read still blood, even if it hadn't flowed down the castle wall by now."

"He must have had a blade hidden on him that was missed," Guran said.

"If so, then I suspect it's at the bottom of the chute as well," Stanton remarked. "An unexpected complication. But he may still be valuable."

"We've lost our leverage," Quintrel snapped. "I fail to see the value in that."

Stanton turned to him. "He can still be used to send a message." He looked back down at Carr's body. "I can get him to Glenreith before daybreak, drop him off in front of the manor. I don't think it will take McFadden long to figure it out. He has a temper; perhaps this will goad him into something rash."

"And if it doesn't?" Quintrel challenged.

Stanton shrugged. "You'll still have scored a blow close to home. McFadden won't let that go. And when he strikes back, we will be ready."

CHAPTER TWENTY-SIX

———

"A RE YOU CRAZY?" KESTEL LEVELED AN ANGRY glare at Blaine. "Have you forgotten what happened the last time you were at Mirdalur? Or at Valshoa? Both times, you nearly went up in flames."

Blaine's small war council gathered in the parlor at Glenreith. Niklas leaned against one of the bookshelves, arms crossed over his chest, a dour look on his face. "It's doubly risky since Hennoch and Rostivan expanded their territories. You'll be back in the same situation you were when we first met up—a small group, trying to sneak past the patrols." He glowered at Blaine. "And you know how that ended."

"The alternative is waiting to anchor the magic until we've battled Lysander and Rostivan—and maybe Hennoch—to a standstill," Blaine said.

"I don't think Hennoch is cause for too much concern," Niklas replied. "The word I've gotten from Verran's spies is that Reese is still imprisoned and Pollard's forces have not fully recovered after the Battle of Valshoa. Hennoch isn't strong enough to make much of a difference—at least, not yet."

Piran sat on one of the couches with his feet propped up on

the footstool, toying with his knife. He appeared distracted, but Blaine knew Piran was not only paying attention, he was uncertain about the chances for success.

"If anchoring the magic is killing Mick, I don't see how there's really a choice about what to do first," Piran drawled without looking up.

"Swapping one thing that's trying to kill Mick for something else that's almost certain to succeed isn't much of an improvement," Kestel snapped.

Geir stood near the fire. Its glow gave a hint of color to his pale skin, though he could not draw comfort from its warmth. "The fact remains," he said, "that as long as Blaine is the only anchor for the magic, the magic is as vulnerable as he is."

"Anchoring the magic might make you less of a target for Quintrel," Niklas offered. "After all, once the magic's anchored, killing or kidnapping you doesn't gain him anything."

Blaine made a dismissive gesture. "Knowing Quintrel, he won't give up that easily."

"Are you certain the ritual can be done at Mirdalur?" Piran asked.

Niklas nodded. "Nidhud and Dolan investigated the Citadel, and also went into the crypts beneath Quillarth Castle." He shook his head. "They were lucky to get out in one piece. There are reasons why those levels beneath the castle were off-limits for so long. The dead are dangerous—even to *talishte*."

Kestel swore under her breath. "Am I the only one who thinks this is a bad idea? Mirdalur is on the edge of Hennoch's territory. Even if Mick survives the ritual, we could come up in the middle of a battle. And we don't dare take a full complement of troops with us, because that would call Hennoch down on us for certain." Kestel was pacing at the far end of the room, and Blaine knew from her gestures that she was both angry and frightened.

"How do we keep a working of that level a secret?" Blaine asked. "Kestel's right—moving troops to protect ourselves is essentially a declaration of war. For Quintrel or anyone with magical abilities, what we do will be like lighting a bonfire. Even if we could slip in unannounced, after we finish— assuming it works—every mage in Donderath will feel it." He shook his head. "That's the hard part about trying to anchor the magic before we've won the war."

"How do you even know this will work?" Kestel challenged. "I know you can't anchor the magic yourself much longer. But if you're wrong about how it's done, it could kill everyone involved."

"So what do you get out of this whole 'anchor' thing, Mick?" Piran asked, looking up. "I mean, it makes you a target for every warlord on the Continent. You've nearly gotten fried several times, with one more shot coming up, it seems. Does it make you a mage? Will you be able to fly or walk through walls? Cheat at cards without getting caught? Seriously, Mick—there ought to be something in this for you."

"If we can anchor it properly, I get to go on living," Blaine answered drily. "And the short answer is: it doesn't do much for me, beyond having the magic working again. From everything we've found, when it's done right, the Lords of the Blood all come away with some extra abilities—things like King Merrill's truth-sensing. But it didn't make them mages before, and it probably won't make them mages now if they weren't already before the ritual. Maybe it's because the magic is still brittle, but the only difference I can see so far from anchoring the magic myself is having a few seconds of foreknowledge before someone attacks." He shrugged. "And maybe that's all there will ever be."

"Sounds like a bad bargain, Mick," Piran said, shaking his

head. "I'd never have gone for it." Kestel snickered. "What?" Piran demanded.

"Oh, nothing," Kestel said with a wave of her hand. "By all means, keep talking."

"Let's look over that list again," Niklas said. "Your new Lords of the Blood."

Blaine let out a long breath and nodded. "Start with me, and you, and with the Wraith Lord, who was a Lord of the Blood when he was mortal."

"So that really means Connor," Kestel supplied. "Since we need Lords of the Blood who actually have blood."

"True. Connor's done a lot to make this possible." Blaine said. "He and the Wraith Lord together are valuable allies."

"Penhallow is a good choice," Piran said. "It can't hurt to have your strongest allies included."

"Good of you to think so, since you, Dawe, and Verran are all on the list," Kestel said, playfully swatting at Piran's bald head.

"Why aren't you?" Piran challenged.

"Because the real power of the Lords of the Blood lies in anchoring the magic over generations, and since I'm married to Mick, that would create only one Lord in the next generation, not two," Kestel replied, rolling her eyes. "As it is, House McFadden will ultimately be represented twice, since Dawe's asked Mari for a handfasting this summer."

"We're sure *talishte* can be a Lord of the Blood?" Niklas asked.

"They were before," Kestel responded. "Kierken Vandholt was already *talishte* but had not yet been made a wraith."

"We believe the bond stays with the *talishte* until the ultimate death," Geir added.

"Did Borya and Desya decide which of them wants to be the lucky one?" Piran asked.

"Zaryae decided it for them. Said that Borya was the first twin born, so it's his job," Kestel replied with a chuckle.

"She didn't want to have the honor?" Niklas raised an eyebrow.

Kestel shook her head. "Blaine approached her first, because of the magic. Zaryae declined because she hasn't decided whether or not she wants to wed." She shrugged.

"Dolan is a good choice, to secure the allegiance of the Knights of Esthrane," Geir said. "As is Traher Voss—a valuable man to have on your side."

"Tormod Solveig makes sense," Kestel agreed. "And there, the decision between Tormod and Rinka had to do with Tormod's magic. They talked about it, and thought Tormod was the better choice."

"Too bad Verner didn't survive the last battle," Piran commented.

"His son did," Niklas pointed out. "Birgen was commanding part of their army elsewhere when the mage strike hit his father's troops. He's agreed to be one of the thirteen."

"Which leaves one more," Blaine said. "We've got representatives of the *talishte*, and from the mages, plus old friends and allies. That's why I chose Folville."

"Quite a set of rogues, if I do say so myself," Niklas said. "And I think you've just answered our question with the names on the list. We're going to have to fight the war to a conclusion before we can anchor the magic, because we can't hope to assemble all of those people at Mirdalur until we've dealt with Lysander and Quintrel. We'd be inviting a massacre."

"All your allies in one place, tied up with a magic ritual that will kill them if anything goes wrong—he's right, Mick," Piran agreed. "You might as well paint a target on our backs if we try to fix the magic before the war is decided."

"Not much of a choice," Kestel said, grimacing. "Anchor the

magic, and we probably all die. Keep on fighting, and we don't know how much of a toll the magic will take on Blaine."

"Dolan and Nidhud are confident that they've figured out the transfer and anchoring process, once we can assemble the group," Geir said. "Dolan has the presence-crystals and manuscript he took from Quintrel, plus the disks. And since then, he's found more information beneath Quillarth Castle and in the hidden rooms at the Citadel, details that Quintrel didn't know. Put it all together, with a Lord of the Blood in a place of great power, and they're sure it will work."

"And we can be pretty certain that if Quintrel had found the rest of the pieces, he would have either offered it up when Blaine did the ritual at Valshoa, or used it for himself to try to take control of the magic away from Blaine," Niklas said. "I don't think Quintrel would be resorting to allying with warlords if he could get what he wanted with magic."

Piran looked up. "So just one of the last Lords of the Blood was a mage, right? But all of them came out of it with some kind of extra abilities. So how will it change us? And what about Mick? Does he get to keep his battle magic and foresight, or will that change, too?"

"Dolan's gone over the manuscripts carefully, researching that point," Geir said. "From all accounts, only Kierken Vandholt was a mage before—or after—the ritual at Mirdalur four hundred years ago. And remember, magic had been gone for a hundred years when they restored it. So when the small magics started to manifest, in people who had been without magic for generations, it seemed miraculous. And those who participated in the actual ritual came out with new, small magics that provided a survival advantage."

"Like Blaine's foresight or King Merrill's truth-sensing," Kestel said.

"I'm certainly not a mage, but I've always had a small dollop of magic that made me a little faster, a little stronger in a fight, better reflexes than when I'm not in battle," Blaine said. "Since Valshoa, it's like I can see a few seconds ahead, sense an attack before I'd normally be able to know it was coming." He shrugged. "It's not huge magic, but it's helped keep my head on my shoulders. When everything's said and done, I wouldn't mind keeping those abilities, or even having them expand. If I'm going to stay in the warlord business, I'm fine with an unfair advantage."

"You could also say that your new bond with the magic heightens your awareness of when power is being used nearby," Kestel speculated. "That might be handy, if it didn't drain you so badly. Maybe when the magic's properly anchored, if you keep that ability, it can give you a warning without damaging you." She gave a wicked smile. "Being able to keep tabs on who's using magic and where they are could make you a hard man to kill."

"That'll take some getting used to," Piran mused. "I've made it this far without any magic at all." He grinned. "Maybe my new magic will make me irresistible to the ladies."

"Don't get your hopes up," Kestel said. "There's not enough magic in the world to make that happen." Her grin softened their long-running friendly bickering.

Geir looked up abruptly, as if summoned by a call only he could hear. "Excuse me," he said, already making his way to the door. "I'm needed outside."

"Is there anything—" Niklas began.

Geir shook his head. "Not yet. Stay inside." With that, he was gone.

"Something's gone wrong," Blaine said, crossing to the window. "Remember—my bond to Penhallow includes Geir." The door flew open and Mari came running into the room, trailed by Dawe.

"He's dead! By the gods, Blaine. Carr's dead!"

Blaine looked from Mari's tearstained face to Dawe's grief-stricken expression.

"It's true, Mick," Dawe said quietly. "You'd better come down. He's in the entrance hallway."

Kestel touched Blaine's arm in a gesture of support. Blaine took the stairs two at a time, leaving the others behind him as they hurried to follow. He slowed as he reached Glenreith's entrance hall. Judith knelt, sobbing, beside a figure wrapped in burlap. Edward knelt next to her, one arm protectively around her shoulders. The older man was weeping. A guard stood just inside the doors.

"What happened?" Blaine asked, stunned.

"A *talishte* dropped the body in front of the gates, sir," the guard replied. "Two of ours gave chase."

Blaine nodded absently, although he barely heard the answer. He knelt next to Carr's body. Carr's eyes were open and staring, his skin unusually ashen, even for a corpse. Deep gouges across his face and chest were mute testimony to torture. Blaine looked up, feeling grief war with rage. "They drained him?"

Edward folded Judith against his chest as she sobbed, and shook his head. "Look at his arms, Blaine," Edward said.

Blaine lifted one of Carr's arms and turned it palm up. His hand was dark with dried blood, but not from the bite marks Blaine feared. Two raw, deep parallel gashes sliced from Carr's wrist to his elbow, slashed into the veins.

"I don't understand," he muttered, barely able to frame his thoughts aloud. "Why would he kill himself?"

Kestel knelt next to him, staring at Carr's body in silent grief. Piran stood behind Blaine, on guard. Mari leaned against

Dawe, looking as if she might collapse. Niklas was the last to join them.

"By Torven's horns," Niklas murmured. "What in Raka happened?"

Edward gestured toward the body. "Inside the burlap, he's wrapped in one of Rostivan's battle pennants."

Blaine felt grief and anger roll through him like a crushing tide, robbing him of breath. "How in the name of the gods did they catch him?"

"Carr was spying," Niklas replied, his voice rough and choked. "He took off on his own. He's been missing since the last storm." He shook his head. "Blaine, you have to believe me. I would never have sent him anywhere near Quintrel or Rostivan. Short of clapping him in irons or locking him in the dungeon, there was no stopping him. I ordered him to stay away from the warlords. We haven't seen him in a fortnight."

The front doors slammed open. Blaine and the other fighters were on their feet, weapons at the ready, before they recognized the newcomers. Geir and two of his *talishte* soldiers dropped a bound man on the entranceway floor.

"Here's the one who dropped off the body," Geir said, leaning down to jerk the prisoner to his knees. "Tell Lord McFadden what you know," he commanded.

"Or what?" the prisoner countered. "You're a hundred years too late to kill me."

Geir leaned down to whisper in the man's ear. The smirk on the captive's face dimmed and vanished.

"And that is how Hemming Lorens existed, in agony, for more than sixty years," Geir finished, standing. "We can do the same for you."

"That won't be necessary," the prisoner said, his voice strained.

Blaine walked over to stand in front of the captive *talishte*.

The prisoner had the look of a hungry stray dog, with dirty-brown hair that fell lank across his face, a gaunt face, and a body too thin for its height. "What happened to my brother?" Blaine demanded.

The prisoner licked his lips. "They caught him spying outside Torsford and took him to Vigus Quintrel. Quintrel figured out he was your brother, and offered him a deal. He refused."

"How did he die?" Blaine asked in a dangerously quiet voice.

The *talishte* licked his lips, a gesture from his mortal days. "Quintrel wanted information. The spy wouldn't give it to him, so Quintrel used magic to take what he wanted. Quintrel gave him time to reconsider and tell him everything, or a *talishte* would read the rest from his blood."

"Carr knew what would happen if a *talishte* read his blood," Niklas said. "He'd seen it happen to the spies we caught. And if he was able to withhold anything of value from Quintrel's magic, all his secrets would be in the blood. So he made that impossible."

"What do you want us to do with the prisoner?" Geir asked.

Blaine drew a ragged breath. He could think of a long list of things that he wanted to do to avenge Carr, but none of them would change anything. The room was silent, awaiting his decision.

"Can you read another *talishte*? If so, read him, then execute him. If not, go ahead and kill him," Blaine said tonelessly. "Just get him out of my sight."

Geir nodded, then pulled the prisoner to his feet, and the soldiers escorted them out. Blaine swallowed hard, trying to pull himself together.

Kestel moved beside him. "It means that, in the end, he didn't betray you," she said. "He chose his fate so he couldn't be turned by one of Quintrel's *talishte*, or used as a bargaining chip."

Judith dried her tears on her sleeve and stood, once more calm and controlled. "We'll take care of him," she said with a catch in her voice. Mari left Dawe's side and slipped up to take Judith's hand.

"There's room out by the oak to bury him with the rest of the family," Judith added. "Near where your mother is buried."

"The ground is still frozen," Mari protested.

"Geir and I can take care of it," Niklas replied. "That's not a problem."

Blaine nodded, not trusting himself to speak. So many emotions warred inside him. Grief, for what was lost. Anger, at Carr's headstrong recklessness. Rage, over Quintrel's cruelty. He settled on rage, since it was the most productive.

"Quintrel brought him here to goad us into war," Blaine said finally. "I won't let Quintrel push us into fighting before we're ready. But when the time comes..." He did not have to finish his sentence. He saw the same hunger for vengeance in their eyes that he knew they saw in his. "When the time comes," he repeated quietly, "Quintrel belongs to me."

After sunset the next day, Blaine led a solemn procession to the burying ground by the large oak. Ian McFadden's grave was on the far right, set apart. Judith had seen to Ian's burial after Blaine's imprisonment, and the distance between the elder McFadden's grave and those of the rest of the family was a measure of her scorn.

The new grave was on the left, near the lonely stone that marked Blaine's mother's grave. Blaine's grandparents were buried here, and his ancestors long past, back to the first McFaddens who built Glenreith. Behind the McFadden graves were the modest resting places of the servants, some of whose families had served at Glenreith for generations.

Geir and Niklas had made good on their word. Despite the

frozen soil, they had dug a proper grave. Judith and Mari had bathed Carr's body, dressed him, and wrapped him in a shroud. Edward and Dawe saw to a coffin, a rough pine box.

Blaine, Niklas, Piran, Dawe, Geir, and Edward shouldered the coffin. Kestel, Judith, and Mari followed them, then Rikard and Leiv, and most of Glenreith's servants, along with a contingent of guards for protection. Judith took the role of Wise Woman, the elder who spoke the final blessing over the dead and consigned the body to rest in the Sea of Souls.

Blaine watched the simple ceremony, numb with shock and loss. Even rage seemed insufficient. As much as he desired Quintrel's death, Blaine knew from experience that it would not make anything right. He took his turn with the other pall-bearers shoveling dirt into the grave, listening to the sound of the clods striking the wooden box, the most final sound in the world. When the grave was filled, Blaine and the men hefted stones to make a cairn. Judith, Kestel, and Mari set out candles, food, and wine as an offering to Esthrane and Torven, the gods who controlled the Sea of Souls and the Unseen Realm.

Blaine paused for a moment as the others headed back to the manor, watching the candles flicker in the wind. Kestel slipped her arm through his. "Come back to the house," she urged. "There's nothing more you can do here."

Blaine nodded. "I know."

Kestel looked up at him earnestly. "Mick, this is not your fault."

Blaine sighed. "Sometimes I think that when I killed Father, it was like I pushed a big boulder off the top of a mountain, and it tumbles faster and faster, destroying everything in its path."

Kestel gave him a level look. "You didn't start the war with Meroven. You didn't cause the Great Fire, or the Cataclysm. And if you hadn't been exiled, you'd have died with the others, and there's no telling when—or if—the magic could have been restored."

Blaine shook his head. "No, I'll grant you that. But it's caused no end of misery for my family, when all I wanted was to stop their pain." He gestured toward Carr's grave. "I thought I was saving Carr and Mari. I didn't."

Kestel pulled him around to face her. "For the gods' sake, Mick! Mari's done well for herself. She has a fine son, and she's made a good match with Dawe. Carr chose his path, and for all we know, perhaps he took more after your father's temperament than you—or Judith—want to admit. I don't know whether he was taking crazy chances to prove himself, or whether he was looking to get killed, but in the end, he didn't betray you. He made his choice. He did exactly what you did when you killed Ian, except you got lucky and he didn't. Let him rest, Mick. There's work to do."

Blaine stared at the cairn a moment longer, then nodded and turned, taking Kestel's hand for the walk back to the manor. He noticed that two of Niklas's guards waited a discreet distance away, and trailed them as they headed down the path.

They found Verran, Borya, and Desya waiting in the great room, along with the other members of their minstrel-spy team.

"We just got in, Mick," Verran said, his face still ruddy from the cold. "Dawe told us what happened. I'm so sorry."

Blaine nodded curtly. "Thank you." He frowned, and glanced at the group. "You're back sooner than you expected. Problems?" By his count, no one was missing.

Kestel hugged Verran in greeting. "Have you eaten? Everyone's been rather distracted. Let me go see what I can find." She bustled off to rouse the servants.

Verran returned his attention to Blaine. "Forces are moving.

Everything we've seen says both Lysander and Rostivan have their armies headed north."

Blaine nodded. "Zaryae predicted the same. Niklas is rallying the troops, and Voss has men on the way. Geir sent *talishte* messengers to the Solveigs and Verner's son."

"Good," Verran nodded. "Because all the conversation we've heard says this is the deciding battle."

"Folville sent a runner last night," Niklas said, walking up behind them. "With all that was going on, I didn't say anything. There've been Tingur attacks in the city, but Folville's men and our guards have handled it. Then all of a sudden, about three days ago, the Tingur disappeared. Folville thinks Lysander plans to use them in a battle elsewhere."

Blaine swore. "Lovely. But at least we know in advance."

"It gets worse," Borya added. "We've heard tell that the Tingur have found a way to use magic to bind the magicked monsters to their bidding. They capture the beasts and keep them contained, then loose them on their enemies." Borya had lost a cousin to the powerful talons of a *gryp*, a leather-winged predator spawned by one of the wild-magic storms.

"Just what we need," Niklas muttered.

"There've been more Tingur problems in the countryside," Verran said. "It's gotten pretty bloody. Some of the villages have run them out of town, and there's been talk that the Tingur hanged some villagers in revenge. We made sure to spread the word that the Tingur support Lysander."

"That might explain why we've had a large number of new recruits in the last few weeks," Niklas said. "I blamed it on hungry bellies." It was the point in the spring when the food put by for the winter was growing scarce, and new crops were long in the future. "But maybe the Tingur annoyed enough folks they decided to join up with us."

"Right about now, I'll take good news wherever I can find it," Blaine said. He looked to Verran as Kestel beckoned from the hallway for the newcomers to come and eat. "Go get some food. We'll find places for everyone to stay. Enjoy it while it lasts; we'll be heading out to battle in a couple of days."

Later that evening, Rikard approached Blaine, Kestel, and Niklas in the parlor.

"We believe we've worked out a solution to your magic problem," Rikard said. "Well, not a full solution—that won't happen until you can alter the anchoring. But a way to help you make it through the next battle without the magic taking as much of a toll. And this time, there's no one working against us."

Kestel gave him a narrowed glance. "How sure are you?"

Rikard chuckled, expecting her reaction. "Leiv, Zaryae, Nemus, and I have all attempted use of the item, with no ill effects. And after what happened the last time, I have the pendant in my pocket. I'm not going to let it out of my sight."

Blaine and Niklas exchanged a look, and then Blaine rose. "All right. Show me."

"Those artifacts Penhallow secured in the crypts under the castle have proven their worth," Rikard said as Blaine and the others followed him to the mage's workroom. "It just took a little digging."

Zaryae and Leiv were waiting for them. Nemus stayed behind in the workroom. Artan had died of his injuries, and with Lowrey's treachery, only the four were left. Zaryae looked at Blaine with concern as he entered.

"The magic makes your dreams restless," she said, scanning him with her gift.

Blaine hesitated, then nodded. "It's getting worse."

"One more way it drains you," Zaryae agreed. "Your tether to the magic never sleeps. At first, your mind could hide that from you. But as time goes on, it wears you down." She gave a sad smile. "Like a cistern with a leak. Only a little water leaves at a time, but soon enough, the whole well empties."

"Show us what you've found," Kestel said. "The sooner we can decide the battle, the sooner Mick can go to Mirdalur and stop the 'leak.'"

"We can't use a traditional null charm for Lord McFadden because of the effect it might have on anchoring the magic, and on his battle magic," Rikard said. "Unfortunately, Lowrey destroyed the only dampening charm we'd found when he corrupted it," he added with a grimace.

"We went through the bags of artifacts that were brought up from the crypt. Dagur left most of them here, since he only wanted the ones that might affect making a new anchor." He gave a crafty smile. "And we got lucky."

Rikard held up a round agate circle on a braided leather-and-twine cord. "I know it doesn't look like much. Magically, it doesn't feel like much either, until you realize that the magic sort of 'slides off' the charm like rain on slate."

"We thought it deflected magic," Leiv said, with more enthusiasm than Blaine had seen the quiet mage show over anything. "But that's not the only thing it does. Watch."

Rikard slipped the amulet's cord over his own head, and gave Leiv a nod. Leiv stood back, then raised his hands and sent a streak of light toward Rikard's chest. It flashed against the amulet and returned to Leiv, stinging him in the shoulder. Leiv shook his arm and rubbed his skin where the light hit, but he was grinning widely.

"Of course, I didn't use anything like the energy that got bounced around the last time," Leiv said. "Didn't want to hurt anyone. But you see what happens—magic slides off and then bounces back to the sender. Handy, don't you think?"

"If Blaine insists on going to the battlefield—" Zaryae began.

"I do," Blaine interrupted.

Zaryae nodded in acknowledgment. "Then we've got to keep the magic from wearing you down, and I think this is our best bet." She gave a dangerous smile. "Of course, Rikard and the rest of us will be going with you, and we'll be focused on taking out the other mages."

"General Theilsson was good enough to spare a messenger for us to summon our fellow mages from the Citadel," Rikard said. "They'll join us for the battle as well. We expect them here tomorrow, and we'll work out our strategy then. But our goal will be to strike hard and fast at the mages with Rostivan and Lysander to put them out of the battle first."

Which might include Carensa, Blaine thought with a pang. *Sweet Esthrane, I hope Quintrel's not mad enough to send her into battle.*

"Let's try out what you've got," Blaine said.

Rikard took the amulet from around his own neck and draped it over Blaine's head. Blaine settled it onto his chest so that it hung nearly at heart level. Kestel, Niklas, and the other mages remained on the other side of the wardings.

"First, we'll see if the charm works the same for you as it did for the rest of us," Rikard said. He gave a nervous glance at Kestel and Niklas. "I assure you, the strike I send will sting but do no worse damage." He gave a dry chuckle. "Remember, if it bounces back, it hits me."

"Send it," Blaine said, taking a deep breath to steel himself. Rikard raised his hand, and a brilliant flare of light arced from his palm. It crackled toward Blaine, sliding aside at the last minute and sizzling back toward Rikard, striking him in the arm.

"It works!" Kestel said, grinning.

Zaryae frowned and closed her eyes. She spread her hands, palm down, and looked as if she were listening for something she alone could hear. "I sense no change in Blaine's energy levels from the strike," she said. She opened her eyes. "Of course, Rikard expended very little power. Still, it bodes well."

Rikard rubbed his palms together and licked his lips. "Which brings me to the other thing we wanted to try," he said nervously. "We thought it prudent to gauge how well Lord McFadden reacts to powerful magic nearby, and whether the amulet blunts that impact."

Kestel looked dubious, but Blaine nodded. "Better we find out here than to get knocked off my horse in battle," he said. "What did you have in mind?"

"A simple trial," Rikard replied. "We'll raise a warding around Blaine, so that our magic can't harm him directly. We just want to see how he reacts to being in the presence of strong power. Of course, the amulet won't raise a warding—that would be too constraining. But the amulet should be able to protect his body, and most importantly his mind and his life energy."

Kestel's glare told Blaine what she thought of the idea, and Zaryae looked worried. Niklas looked to Blaine and shrugged. "Up to you."

Blaine let out a long breath. "I'd rather land on my ass here where I can recuperate than expect protection and get flattened in the thick of the fight." He nodded. "Let's give it a try."

Kestel gave Rikard a look that made the mage pale, no doubt thinking about the fate that had befallen Lowrey. "I promise you, Lord McFadden, we will minimize the impact."

Blaine shook his head. "Don't. We need to know what this amulet will—and won't—do. Better here than elsewhere."

Rikard nodded nervously. "As you wish, m'lord," he said, though his gaze slid sideways to Kestel's glower.

Rikard, Zaryae, and Leiv took up places at an equal distance from each other along the outside of the circle. "We aren't going to make a direct strike at Lord McFadden," Rikard explained. "We're just going to raise a lot of power quickly, and see how it affects him while he's wearing the amulet." He met Blaine's gaze. "Then we'll have him remove the amulet, and see what happens when we do it again."

Blaine nodded, and Rikard signaled the others. Each called down power in his or her own way. Rikard chanted quietly under his breath as he raised his hands, and his entire form began to glow. Zaryae closed her eyes, singing to herself, and Leiv swayed back and forth, fingers working in complex motions as he gathered his magic.

A milky curtain of pure power shot up to the ceiling, shimmering white, glowing like the Spirit Lights of the far-north sky. Tendrils of mist-like energy wafted back and forth through the center of the circle, winding and curling around Blaine but leaving him untouched. Blaine caught his breath and staggered back a step, but when Rikard shot him a worried glance, Blaine shook his head, signaling them to continue.

The coruscating wall of power glowed brighter, crackling with energy, glistening like the trapped power of a winter storm. Blaine paled and wavered on his feet, but did not fall. He nodded to Rikard.

This time, the power rippled like a waterfall, with a rush and crash of a thundering cataract. Blaine could barely make out the worried faces on the other side. He could sense the amulet straining against the power, like listening to a rainstorm pouring down on the roof overhead. Yet every time the power closed in, Blaine felt it slide away, as the amulet deflected the worst of the strike. Blaine could feel the magic shift back and forth, what the mages called 'fragile.' The energy poured out full strength, then dropped out for an instant, back again almost too quickly to notice the gap. Gradually, the protection of the amulet wavered, and Blaine gasped, falling to his knees.

Abruptly, the power vanished. The sudden disappearance of the energy gave Blaine to realize just how much he had been straining against it. When the power winked out, he fell forward, as if he had set himself against a headwind that suddenly quelled.

Rikard ran toward him, waving the others back. Blaine was already on his hands and knees, shaking his head to clear it.

"How do you feel?" Rikard asked. Blaine related what he had noticed as the power escalated, and Rikard nodded.

"The power we raised was substantial, more than we could sustain for long under battle conditions," Rikard said. "There will be more mages on the battlefield, but our side will work to blunt the enemies' strikes, so unlike this test, all that power will not come to bear on you."

"If we're lucky," Blaine said.

"Do you still want to try it without the amulet?" Rikard asked.

Blaine fingered the agate circle, and shook his head. "No. You've made your point. I could sense the power that the amulet was holding back. I know that feeling; I've felt it before in the thick of things. And I know I would have collapsed a lot sooner—and felt much worse—without the amulet." He managed to get to his feet without help.

"What if I wore a null amulet?" Kestel asked. "It wouldn't block Blaine from using his own magic unless we were very close together, but if he has a deflecting charm, and I have a null charm, it might give us one more advantage in battle."

Rikard nodded. "I can arrange that."

"Thank you," Blaine said.

Rikard gave a wan smile. "The greatest thanks would be your safe return, and an end to the fragile magic."

"I'll do my best to make that happen," Blaine said, tucking the amulet under his shirt. He was happy to accept the hot cup of *fet* Kestel pressed into his hands from a pot on the hearth. Blaine sank gratefully into a chair, feeling as if his legs had become jelly, trembling all over from the exertion of the test.

"That decides it," Kestel said. "I'm riding with you."

Blaine moved to protest, but to his surprise, Niklas nodded. "Sorry, Blaine. I've got to agree. Kestel's got a big stake in making sure you live through this, and from what we've seen, even with the amulet, you've got a weak point the enemy can exploit." He paid no attention to Blaine's annoyance. "And I'm also going to make sure you've got at least three bodyguards whose sole job is to make sure you come back alive."

Blaine wanted to argue, but he sighed and nodded. *There's more at stake here than my pride. Niklas is right. It's not enough to win the battle. If I die, the magic could still be lost for good.*

CHAPTER
TWENTY-SEVEN

"THESE ARE THE ARTIFACTS POLLARD'S TROOPS found with the Arkalas," Torinth Rostivan said, and a soldier dumped out a bag of objects onto a table in the mages' workroom. "I want to know what they do, and how we can use them as weapons."

Carensa looked at the motley collection of items and wondered what had given Rostivan the idea that any of them were magical. From where she stood, near the back of the room, it looked like a pile of junk.

Vigus Quintrel stood near the table, and he eyed the objects, then nodded. "I'll need a place we can work that won't damage the building if something goes wrong," he said. "One of the outbuildings."

Someplace that won't matter if we blow it up, Carensa thought.

"I can have the men clear out one of the storage buildings," Rostivan said. "What else?"

"Where are the mages Pollard's people captured?" Quintrel asked.

"Sedated, chained, and under watch with *talishte* guards," Rostivan replied.

Quintrel nodded. "Bring them to me, once night falls. The guards as well. They'll help us figure out the use of these items."

Rostivan raised an eyebrow. "You expect them to cooperate?"

The smile on Quintrel's face was unpleasant. "They won't have a choice."

By dusk, the work space was ready. It was a small stone-walled building with heavy wooden rafters and a slate roof, as fireproof as anything could be built. The building was windowless, and no more than thirty paces by thirty paces, meaning that any magic worked here would be close and personal. Torches hung in sconces around the walls of the room, enough to give light but not heat. Smoke collected up at the peak of the building's ceiling, and hung heavy in the air below.

Carensa was dressed warmly beneath her cloak, but the damp cold of the outbuilding still seemed to get into her bones. Her fingerless gloves helped, but she still shivered, both from cold and from anger.

Four hapless mages sat bound, blindfolded, and gagged against the wall of the stone room. They were all male, and they looked as if they had fought their capture. Several of the captured mages bore bruises on their faces, split lips, or blackened eyes. Their robes were stained and dirty, bloodied in places. One of the men slumped, defeated. Two of the men seemed resigned to their fate, leaning back against the wall, waiting for whatever befell them. The other mage strained against his bonds and chewed at his gag, still fighting.

Carensa could not look too long at their prisoners without feeling her anger rise at Quintrel, so she studied the *talishte* guards instead. Before the Cataclysm, she had only rarely glimpsed individual *talishte* at a distance, usually among the guests at a noble's party, since they had been unwelcome in King Merrill's court.

"Remove his blindfold," Quintrel said, pointing to the angry mage. It was like Vigus to choose the hardest one first, Carensa thought. Quintrel—or the *divi* who now controlled him—would want to break the rebel, as a lesson to the others. She cast a wary glance toward the specially made brass-bound chest Quintrel had personally carried into the workroom. Its top was open and the front of the chest folded down, revealing the large *divi* orb on a velvet cushion, like a god seated on a throne.

One of the *talishte* guards walked over and unwrapped the rag that blindfolded the mage. Now that she could see his face, Carensa saw that he was perhaps a few years older than she was, a tall, lanky man with angular features and dark eyes. He stared at Quintrel balefully, and Carensa guessed that only the magic worked in with his bonds and gag kept him from making a suicide attack on them all. She couldn't blame him.

"Did you make the warding full strength?" Quintrel asked with a sharp glance to Guran.

"It'll hold," Guran said. "I've got no desire to go up in flames," he added. In the center of the workroom, Guran and Gunvar had drawn a warded circle with chalk and charcoal, then reinforced it with a braided mage cord. Candles were set at intervals around the outside of the circle, and between the candles lay bloody pieces of a freshly slaughtered rabbit, torn apart to feed the working. The *divi* liked blood.

"Put him under compulsion," Quintrel ordered. "Take away his will."

The *talishte* guards regarded Quintrel with a look that told Carensa they were following orders from Pollard, not responding to please Quintrel. She dared not meet their gazes, but it was clear in their expression that they did little to hide their disdain.

One of the *talishte* guards reached out, his hand moving

faster than sight could follow, and grabbed the rebel mage by the chin, forcing the man to meet his gaze. Reflexively, the captive shut his eyes.

"Open your eyes or I'll cut away your eyelids," the *talishte* said quietly.

The captive mage opened his eyes, and the position in which the *talishte* held his head gave no choice except to meet his gaze. "You will comply with what Mage Quintrel orders you to do," the *talishte* said. "You will follow his orders exactly. You will make no move to disobey, either by action or inaction. Do you understand?"

The rebel mage nodded. His body, tight with anger only moments before, had relaxed, and his face, which had been twisted with rage, was slack and vacant.

"He'll do as you order," the *talishte* said, stepping back. Carensa could see a bruise starting where the guard had gripped the man's chin.

"Cut his bonds and have him walk into the center of the warding, stepping over the circle," Quintrel said to the same *talishte* guard.

The *talishte* regarded Quintrel for a moment, as if to remind the mage that he obeyed by choice, and walked over to the angry prisoner. He grabbed the man by his bound hands and jerked him to his feet, where he swayed for a moment before getting his balance. The *divi* orb glowed at the neckline of Quintrel's tunic, and Carensa thought sickly that the spirit was enjoying itself at the captives' expense.

The prisoner did not move as the *talishte* unlocked the chains around his hands and feet. His stare was blank, and Carensa wondered if deep inside himself, he knew he was being compelled, or whether all sense of self had been sublimated to the *talishte*'s will. She doubted the latter. It would have been too merciful.

The *talishte* gave the mage his orders, and the man walked into the center of the warding, careful not to smudge the protective markings. Quintrel walked over to a table that had been placed near the large *divi* orb, where the captured artifacts lay. He selected a steel torque. It was a flat semicircle of dull-gray metal, large enough to fit around a man's neck and lie over the collarbones, half a hand's-width wide. Quintrel lifted the item with wooden tongs, and in the firelight, Carensa could see etchings of runes and sigils covering its surface. Even at a distance, the collar felt wrong, tainted—and powerful.

"Order him to invoke it," Quintrel said. The *talishte* complied. Something flickered behind the captive mage's eyes, fear that was stronger than compulsion, but against his will, his body moved. The mage's lips formed words of power, and the runes on the collar glowed with an inner fire.

The collar flared, and the captive mage screamed. His body began to shake, trembling from head to toe. His skin writhed as if it had a life of its own, bubbling and heaving as it wrenched itself free.

"Call a shape to his mind," Quintrel ordered.

The *talishte* closed his eyes, and his features grew taut with concentration. Once again, the tortured mage's skin heaved and quivered, and as Carensa watched in horror, flesh took new form as the bones and muscles remade themselves.

Through it all, the skull had remained intact, enabling the mage to shriek in agony. His cries echoed off the stone walls, deafeningly loud. Guran blanched, and Carensa thought she might pass out. Gunvar, whose magic enhanced the power of others, slumped to the floor, unconscious. Carensa knelt beside him, long enough to assure herself that he was still breathing.

When she stood and looked into the circle once more, a nightmare creature hunched where the doomed mage had stood. It was the same bulk as the man had been, but the body had been remade. The creature sat on thick, powerful haunches with long-fingered forefeet and hind feet that ended in black, curling claws. The overall form was shortened and thickened, as if what had been height had been forcibly remade into muscle. The skull no longer resembled that of a man. Its jaws protruded, overfilled with the sharp teeth of a predator. Yet the eyes remained the same, eyes that met Carensa's gaze and begged for death.

"It still possesses magic," Quintrel said. "Force it to embed the collar."

The *talishte*'s expression was neutral. Perhaps, Carensa thought, his master had willed him to do worse. Once again, the *talishte* concentrated, and the mage in the circle screamed. Beneath the collar, the skin tore apart, until the steel rested on blood and muscle. Just as quickly, the skin re-formed, sealing the collar beneath it so that it bulged like a deformity around the creature's neck.

"Keep him under compulsion, and have him leave the warded space—carefully, don't smudge the marks," Quintrel ordered.

Given no choice by the *talishte* that held him in thrall, the creature limped out of the warding, as if uncertain how to make its newly formed legs work. The muscles looked capable of great power, but at the moment, the beast shuffled awkwardly, trying to adapt to walking on all fours, as if the brain had not changed as fast or as radically as the rest of the body.

One glimpse at the eyes had been enough to assure Carensa

that despite the changes worked on the body, the unlucky rebel mage had been left sentient, aware of what he had been and of what was done to him. She shivered, holding herself tightly, willing herself to partition off a cold place in her mind for the hatred that coursed through her, the anger and disgust she felt at the sight of what Quintrel had become. She and Guran avoided looking at each other, or at their fellow mages.

It could just have easily been us he decided to try out his new 'toys' on, she thought. *It might have been us if the captives hadn't been convenient. I don't think there's any sentiment left in him.*

Quintrel stood next to the large *divi* orb with its withered hand encased in the sphere of glass. In the center of the orb, Carensa caught flashes of light like flying embers, but even unwillingly, at a distance, she could feel the orb's greed for blood.

At Quintrel's direction, the *talishte* forced the creature to squat in front of the *divi* orb. The orb flared, snaring the transformed mage in a burst of green light that lit up the ruined face, snaring the mage-thing's gaze. Fresh screams tore from the creature's throat, hoarse howls of pain unbearable to hear. From where Carensa stood, it looked as if the last resistance drained from the creature's body, and when the green light faded, nothing of the human it once had been remained in its gaze.

"The mage's consciousness, and his ability to do magic, have been extinguished," Quintrel said. "Present your master with a beast of war, my gift to him to use as he sees fit." He bent down to pick up the chains that had bound the tall mage's wrists and looped them around the beast's neck like a leash.

"I'd cage it soon, if I were you," Quintrel cautioned, holding out the leash to the *talishte*. "Once the shock wears off, you'll find it to be as fierce as the *gryps*, and smarter than the wolves."

The *talishte* guard took the chain and gave it a tug, and the beast shambled forward, more agile now that no vestige of humanity struggled with how to move its transformed body. Carensa and the rest of Quintrel's mages stared at their master in horror, and only now did Carensa realize that her face was stained with tears.

The captive mages had been spared the sight of their comrade's transmogrification by their blindfolds, but their blindness made the horror even worse with imaginings, and they shrank back against the wall. The smell of urine and shit told Carensa that at least one of the men had soiled himself in fear.

"Well," Quintrel said calmly, dusting off his hands, "we know what that artifact does."

Carensa stole a look at Guran. His expression was schooled to be neutral, but she glimpsed fury in his eyes as his color returned. She knelt next to Gunvar, and wondered if Quintrel had used the mage's power to magnify the magic of the artifact without seeking permission. Gunvar's breathing was shallow and his skin was pale, as if he had lost blood.

"If you use him again like that, you'll kill him," Carensa snapped. "And if he dies here, we won't have his magic to draw on in battle." She had no desire to ever go out with the army again, but she bet that Quintrel would be more likely to preserve a valuable fighting asset than to save Gunvar out of sheer compassion.

"As you wish," Quintrel said with a shrug. "I don't think I'll require his help with the next piece."

"You're not going to continue, are you?" Guran said, staring at Quintrel in horror.

But Quintrel was already using the wooden tongs to select a new artifact from among the pile. "Of course I am," he replied as if the question was irrelevant. "Who knows what we might discover?"

That was entirely the point, but Carensa knew it was useless to argue, and she had no desire to draw Quintrel's ire. Sickened as she was to be a spectator, she forced herself to feel nothing, allowing cold rage to settle into her bones, closing off her heart, deadening her feelings. *I must remember,* she thought. *I must record what happens here, as a witness to these deaths, so that someone knows what took place.*

This time, Quintrel removed a steel-and-silver gauntlet and vambrace from the pile. It was a fearsome piece of armor in itself, with a vambrace to encircle the forearm and hinged plates in the gauntlet that covered the individual fingers, ending in short, sharp knives.

"That one," Quintrel said to another of the *talishte*, pointing to one of the captives who was huddled, weeping. "Take him."

Once again, a *talishte* guard removed the blindfold of his victim, compelled him to rise against his will, and loosed his bonds. "Fit this on his right arm," Quintrel directed, and the *talishte* complied, as the mage captive looked on in terror but unable to resist.

When the captive was again within the warded space, Quintrel nodded to the *talishte*, who ordered the prisoner to speak the artifact into action. For a moment, the mage's terrified gaze locked onto Carensa's, and she saw that he knew he was going to die.

The vambrace and gauntlet took on a silver glow, and the mage stiffened, then moaned in pain. As Carensa watched in fascinated horror, the vambrace melded with the man's arm, encasing the skin in steel, molding itself to the hand, wrist, and fingers. The mage relaxed, and flexed his hand, twisting his wrist and moving his forearm to see just how maneuverable the artifact was. The steel fit like skin itself, and the knife-edged fingertips had grown longer into talons. For a moment, all was well.

Carensa felt the magic around them fluctuate. That was not unusual since the magic had been restored, but imperfectly. It was part of the brittleness that made the 'new' magic so unstable and dangerous, something mages like Carensa and her fellow scholars feared. Magic interrupted was often deadly to the mage who cast it.

The vambrace's silvery glow reddened, and the mage in the warded circle shouted in alarm, trying to tear the vambrace and gauntlet free. It clung to his skin, warming to a dull red, and the mage tore at it, leaving bloody tracks down his upper arm as he tried and failed to get his fingers under the armor to rip it away.

Quintrel made no move to end the test. The smell of roasting flesh was unmistakable as the vambrace burned into the mage's arm and the man began to scream. Inside the warded circle, the desperate mage cast one spell after another, chanting words of power, all in vain.

A few moments later, the vambrace slid off, leaving behind charred bone, and the mage collapsed, sobbing and trembling. His hand and forearm were blackened like that of a corpse on a pyre, and the wound was cauterized below the elbow. Yet the gauntlet and vambrace still glowed, brighter now than before. Carensa could hear the man's sobbing pleas for death, even from inside the circle's wardings.

"If he wishes for death so badly, let him activate the piece once more," Quintrel said diffidently. "Do it."

The *talishte* made a gesture, and the prisoner stared at the cursed artifact as if looking into the maw of Raka itself. Then against his will, the mage began to call the armor to him, and in the middle of the call, Carensa sensed that the mage gave up resisting, realizing that he was about to gain the death he coveted.

Carensa saw understanding dawn on the mage as he stared at the gauntlet and vambrace, realizing that it had gained power by consuming his flesh and that he could command it, but only at the cost of his skin and sinew.

"Come," he ordered the cursed armor, and the vambrace skittered over to him, using its metallic fingers to move it across the floor. The mage held out his blackened arm. "Fit," he said, and the armor backed itself onto his arm, adjusting itself to the lack of flesh and muscle, becoming a metal hand and arm.

"How long can the piece remain like that?" Guran asked, curious despite his revulsion. "That level of magic has to take a toll."

"That would be good to know," Quintrel mused, as if the question had not already occurred to him. "A warrior might be willing to forfeit an arm for a better replacement. But I wonder how hard a bargain the piece drives?"

Within fifteen minutes, the captive had begun to go gray in the face. Another ten minutes, and his breathing became ragged. Gradually, his face grew gaunt, and as Carensa stared in sickened fascination, she realized that little by little, the mage was growing thinner.

"It's consuming him," she murmured.

Guran nodded. "It's meant for onetime use, I wager. A desperation weapon, when the warrior knows he'll die one way or the other and just wants to take the enemy down with him."

"Can he release it? Would that change anything?" Carensa asked, her voice barely above a whisper. The dying mage heard her, locked his gaze with hers, and she saw that he had no desire to release his spell when death and freedom were quite literally within his grasp.

"Probably not," Guran replied. "Even if he wanted to."

Carensa had seen bodies charred by flames after the Great Fire. In the tombs and caves where she and Quintrel had hidden as he took her to refuge in Valshoa, she had looked on the mummified corpses of the long dead. The mage in the warded circle reminded her of those corpses as his cheeks hollowed and his skin wrinkled over shrunken limbs. His eyes were sunken, and the flesh of his face pulled tight and thin over bone.

With a final moan, the mage fell back, and the skin withered like leaves in a fire until all that remained was blackened bone, and the gauntlet and vambrace clattered to the stone, empty and sated.

Quintrel released the warding, and used the wooden tongs to remove the deadly armor. "A pity," he said. "The curse limits its usefulness." He set the piece to the side. "I'll inform Rostivan not to waste his best men on it."

At Quintrel's nod, the same *talishte* guard removed the mage's skeleton, and stepped back with the other undead soldiers. Quintrel returned to the table of artifacts, and returned with an amulet of brass on a braided leather strap. He gestured toward the next mage to become a victim of the artifacts, and once again a *talishte* guard removed the blindfold, glamoured the mage, and released his bonds.

"I suspect that I know what this artifact does," Quintrel said. "Just not its limits." He shook his head as the *talishte* began to herd the captive toward the warded circle.

"No need for that, not this time. But I would like two of you to hold him, one on each arm," Quintrel said. He dangled the amulet in front of the lead *talishte*. "Take this and fasten it around his neck," he instructed.

He clucked his tongue when the *talishte* hung back. "You're undead. This particular amulet has no power over you." The *talishte* gave him a skeptical look, then took the piece by its leather straps and fastened it around the prisoner's neck. Despite the compulsion, the captive mage looked terrified, having heard if not seen what happened to his former companions.

"Hold his arms out," Quintrel ordered. "And hold him tightly." The two *talishte* soldiers each took a wrist and stretched the mage's arms out, holding him open and vulnerable.

Quintrel looked to the lead guard again. "Run him through."

The *talishte* raised an eyebrow, then drew his sword. Carensa gasped as the soldier plunged his blade deep into the mage's belly, tearing through skin and organs, ripping through to the other side.

"Vigus, no!" Carensa cried out despite herself as the mage sagged in the hold of his captors, blood streaming from the wound.

"Watch," Quintrel said.

Carensa felt bile rise in her throat as she stared at the mortally wounded mage. The brass amulet glowed amber, and as Carensa watched, the flow of blood stopped and the skin began to knit itself back together.

"Again, in two places this time," Quintrel ordered, and the soldier sprang forward, driving his sword through the man's naval and out through his spine, then withdrawing his bloody blade and sliding it cleanly through the ribs and heart.

The mage's body jerked in spasms. He screamed in pain, his legs useless beneath him, his ragged clothing sodden with blood. Once more, a heartbeat later, the amulet glowed again, stronger now, bathing the man's body in its amber light. Strength returned to his legs, and as Carensa listened with her magic, beneath the rapidly healing skin, the ravaged heart returned to its steady beat.

"You've proven your point, Vigus," Guran growled.

Quintrel regarded him with disappointment. "It's not enough to know a weapon's strengths and capabilities," he said archly. "One must also know its point of failure."

"Cleave him shoulder to hip," Quintrel ordered. Carensa turned to hide her face against Guran's chest, and Guran wrapped his arms around her, shielding her from having to watch as the *talishte* brought his sword down with undead strength and the terrified mage screamed in panic. Carensa winced as the cry was cut short, struggling not to launch herself at Quintrel in a futile gesture of fury.

This time, it took the amulet longer. "He's healing," Guran murmured. "It's like it never happened."

Carensa drew a ragged breath and let it out again, calling on all her limited magic to sustain her and strengthen her. She gently shook off Guran's protective embrace with a nod of thanks, and turned to see the captive mage begin to breathe again, regaining his footing, still held in the iron grip of the two impassive *talishte* guards.

"Interesting," Quintrel mused. "Take off his head."

The *talishte* hesitated. "Even we cannot withstand such a blow," he warned Quintrel.

Quintrel shrugged. "The Dark Gift is just one type of magic. Let's see what the talisman can do."

"As you wish." The *talishte* strode forward, and the mage attempted to stand to his full height, awaiting and accepting his executioner. With one clean stroke, the *talishte* swung his sword in a silver blur, and the captive's head fell backward as his body sagged forward, blood spurting from the severed artery, spraying his blood-soaked captors with gore.

"Quickly," Quintrel ordered. "Lay him down and put the head back into place."

The *talishte* did as they were ordered, arranging the headless body on the floor and laying the severed skull atop the ruined neck. The amulet hung in place, blood-soaked and dull, its amber glow gone. They waited for several minutes, but the amulet appeared to be as dead as the mage himself.

"Well," Quintrel said with a shrug. "At least we know its limits."

Carensa glanced toward the table and then to the one remaining mage. As if he guessed her thoughts, Quintrel chuckled. "There's no need to test the other artifacts," he said. "Several of them have no magic at all now, whether or not they had power previously. The others hold a trifling amount, not worth the risk of using for what little benefit they might present."

"What do you mean to do with him?" Guran asked, with a nod toward the last captive mage. The man had curled into a fetal position, sobbing quietly, trembling so hard Carensa could see the shaking from where she stood.

"Don't worry," Quintrel assured Guran. "He has a purpose." At his nod, the *talishte* soldiers hauled the last mage to his feet.

"Bring him here," Quintrel instructed them when they had removed the blindfold and glamoured the captive. Under the *talishtes'* compulsion, the prisoner walked on his own to where Quintrel stood next to the large *divi* orb.

"Kneel," Quintrel ordered, and the man fell to his knees, so that his head was on level with the sphere with its monstrous, withered hand.

"Open your eyes wide," Quintrel instructed the prisoner. "And behold."

"What are you doing, Vigus?" Carensa asked, afraid of the answer.

"Giving him his freedom," Quintrel replied as if the answer were obvious.

The large orb flared, and so did the smaller sphere on its

strap at Quintrel's throat. Carensa saw their light reflected in her master's eyes, or perhaps, shining through them from inside, where the *divi*'s rot had taken hold. The kneeling prisoner's body went rigid, bathed in a foxfire glow, and hoarse screams tore from the man's throat.

Quintrel stepped back, and Carensa saw that the light shone on the prisoner's whole form, which had begun to shimmer and waver. The screaming stopped. The captive's body grew less solid, flattening as if it were a drawing on parchment, stretching and narrowing so that soon it was a pulsating column of light.

The *divi* orb surrounding the withered hand receded, and the light streamed in, absorbed by the severed bone and withered skin, feeding the *divi* with the mage's death. Satisfied, the crystal swelled to encase the hand once more in its solid orb, and the light winked out and the captive mage was gone.

Guran took Carensa's hand, lending her his strength and support. She could feel the stiffness in his muscles, and knew he reined in the same deadly anger she strained to control.

Not yet, but soon. Carensa was not sure whether the thought was her own or whether Guran was able to send his thoughts to her through their clasped hands, but she nodded her understanding.

Once and for all, Carensa vowed. *For these deaths and all the others, no matter the cost, I will find a way to stop Vigus and make him pay.*

CHAPTER
TWENTY-EIGHT

D AMN THE MAGIC!" NIKLAS MUTTERED.
Midday, and the battle was taking its toll. Bodies covered the valley so that it was hard to step without putting a foot onto a corpse. Blood made the ground sticky in some places and slippery in others, and the whole thing smelled like an abattoir.

Bodies hung on angled pikes, a macabre forest of bitter fruit. Not a candlemark before, Niklas had seen dozens of his men charge ahead at full speed, believing they were ambushing a feckless group of stragglers. They ran at full speed, swords raised, a victory cry on their lips. Magic hid the truth. Only when the sharp stakes ripped into their chests and savaged their bellies did the illusion waver and fail. By then, dead eyes no longer saw, dying soldiers were past caring.

"Be glad magic comes with limitations," Ayers said, sounding just as weary.

"It didn't seem very 'limited' when they were gigging themselves like frogs," Niklas muttered.

The battlefront was shifting. Several candlemarks' hard

fighting drove Rostivan's soldiers back, and Niklas's mages were making a counterstrike of their own. Rikard was able to make blazing fireballs appear out of nowhere, and he harried the enemy troops for as long as he could, scattering their formations and lighting unlucky soldiers on fire.

"I hate battle magic," Niklas growled. "Saw too damn much of it on the Meroven front."

"We all did," Ayers said as they moved with the rest of the unit, re-forming for the next strike. "It's sloppy. The mages can't send a plague of boils or some such unless the two sides are separated, which means they can't do much in a pitched fight. Using magic drains mages so badly they're not good for long, and with the way the magic is now, even a strong mage can't do what he used to."

Niklas grimaced. "Be thankful for that last bit. We've seen what mages can do." He was thinking of the green ribbon of flame that descended the night of the Great Fire, magic that worked too well for the battle mages on both sides, and left a shattered, cindered Continent in its wake.

Niklas heard the thud of distant catapults. "Incoming!" a voice shouted.

Dozens of white, stone-like lumpy balls rained down on them from the enemy catapults. "What in Raka—" Niklas muttered.

The 'stones' unfurled crab-like legs tipped in lethal claws, moving with infernal speed. Niklas and Ayers slashed with their swords, finding the beasts' carapaces as hard as any cuirass.

"Where in the Sea of Souls did the *ranin* come from?" Ayers yelped.

"Nowhere good," Niklas said grimly, swinging two-handed at the creatures. "They're fast sons of bitches."

The *ranin* scuttled toward him, waving its dangerously sharp claws. Niklas jumped out of the way, but a claw tore at his pant leg, and he did not want to think what it would have done to soft flesh.

"I can't even find the eyes on those damn things!" Ayers said, slashing with his full might as two of the beasts came at him at once. Niklas was holding three at bay. Down the line, dozens of the miserable creatures had popped through, sent by Rostivan's mages.

"What in Raka are our mages doing?" Niklas demanded.

"That, I think." Ayers nodded in to his left, since he dared not stop fighting.

Dead men jerked down from the pikes that killed them. Staggering like drunkards, a line of corpses shambled their way toward their last mortal task. Eyes unseeing, stumbling on their own entrails, the fallen soldiers slashed their swords at anything that moved in front of them.

"We don't have a necromancer," Niklas said, wide-eyed.

Ayers shook his head. "Don't need one. Didn't bring the dead back to life, just moved their bodies." He gave a jaded chuckle. "Puts on a good show, doesn't it?"

"Enough of a godsdamned show right here," Niklas muttered, bringing his sword down hard to snap the leg from one of the crab creatures. The *ranin* reared up on its other legs, slashing with a long foreleg, and gave an earsplitting shriek.

All around Niklas, soldiers battled the shelled monsters with any weapon available. Niklas and Ayers kept hacking away with their broadswords, crippling the beasts to slow them down, then smashing their hard bodies with rocks.

The crab-things burst apart, spraying a sticky ichor that burned like lye and stank like shit. Niklas swore as the foul liquid sprayed him, giving the dead *ranin* a kick for good measure.

"We're in for some weather," Ayers said with a warning glance at the sky.

"Figures," Niklas said darkly, and just then, snow began to fall.

Behind them, rank upon rank of soldiers fought down the last of the crab-things, or dispatched the dying enemy soldiers with a mercy strike.

"Re-form!" Niklas bellowed, trying to shout above the wind. "Ready!" Voices carried his commands down the line, and footsteps pounded as soldiers got into position. "Charge!"

Niklas and Ayers led the way, flanked by a sea of soldiers. Rostivan's troops, gathering their nerve after the assault by the dead, closed ranks, angry and ready for vengeance.

More catapult thuds echoed, and rocks pelted Niklas's soldiers like rain. Tiny pebbles and stones the size of a man's fist fell out of the sky. Men fell in their tracks, struck in the head, and did not rise. Niklas winced as a rock clipped him on the shoulder; hard enough he was certain he would bruise. Dodging the falling stones slowed their advance, buying Rostivan's forces a few precious minutes.

Niklas looked up to see one of Rostivan's commanders blocking his way. Ayers skidded to a halt, facing a challenger of his own.

"Cut off the head, and the beast dies," Niklas's opponent said with a nasty smile. "What becomes of your army if I cut off your head?"

"Too bad you won't find out," Niklas muttered, lunging at the man before the other could strike. The exchange of a few sword blows made it clear the two were evenly matched in strength and skill.

Niklas blocked a series of savage strikes meant to maim. Shouting his anger and cursing the wind, Niklas gave as good as he got, taking cold satisfaction in the blood his sword raised on his attacker's arm.

The enemy commander returned the favor, coming at him fast, with hard strikes that nearly knocked Niklas's sword out of his hand. A few paces away, Ayers was holding his own with difficulty, struggling against an opponent who seemed to be enjoying every bone-jarring swing.

Murderous focus glinted in his enemy's eyes as Niklas dodged and parried, trying to get inside the man's guard. An instant too late, he moved to block a swing and took a deep gash on his upper arm, sending a rush of blood down to soak his hand.

Niklas drew back a step, ready to make a run at the officer, when his opponent froze, eyes glazed. As Niklas and Ayers watched in consternation, their attackers suddenly turned on each other with lethal frenzy, oblivious to the two men they had just been about to kill. They swung at each other like mad men as blood sprayed into the air, carried on the merciless wind, tingeing the snow crimson. The man Niklas had been fighting gave a roar and brought the blade down so hard he cut through the other soldier's shoulder, sending the severed arm flying into the fouled snow. The maimed man scythed low, his blade connecting so hard with the officer's thigh he hit bone.

The same thing happened all around Niklas and Ayers: Enemy soldiers on the edge of victory suddenly attacked soldiers on their own side with mad-dog ferocity. Niklas had no magic of his own, but he had soldiered long enough to know it when he saw it. He and Ayers backed away from the fight.

Somewhere in the distance, Niklas heard Rostivan's commanders shouting for order, screaming at their soldiers to stop killing each other. Heedless, the soldiers fought with deranged fury, their bloodlust not satisfied until their opponents had been chopped to bits.

As suddenly as it began, the fog lifted from the crazed

soldiers' eyes and they looked about themselves in utter confusion and horror, finding themselves maimed, bleeding, and soaked with the blood of their slaughtered comrades.

"Now!" Niklas shouted, descending on the enemy in their moment of disorientation, finishing the job their madness had begun. Niklas waded into the fray with the grim determination of a butcher culling the herd. His sword swung like a reaper, splashing him with gore. He paused only long enough to wipe the blood from his eyes.

The bewitched soldiers gave little resistance as the realization of their treason sank in. Cursing and wailing like damned men, most of the soldiers either rushed unarmed at Niklas's soldiers or fell on their own swords.

"Poor, sorry bastards," Ayers muttered.

"Pity them as much as you want, as long as they're dead," Niklas replied. A space had cleared in the fighting as Rostivan's troops fell back, desperate to avoid whatever had entranced their fighters. Snow fell thick and fast, whipped by wind that had grown bitingly sharp.

Niklas yelped in alarm. He had been shivering with cold a moment before; suddenly his skin was as hot as if he had been in the summer sun, blistering with fever. Ayers felt it, too, and a sheen of sweat broke out on his forehead.

Niklas was panting, eyeing the falling snow longingly, wishing he could breathe it all into him to slake the raging fever. He stumbled, vision blurring, his tongue swelling in his dry mouth.

"Torven take my soul!" he murmured, sure that he would burst into flames. *This is how we die,* he thought, *broiled in our own juices when our blood boils. Damn the mages!*

From what Niklas could make out, the entire front line

staggered with fever. Niklas fell to his knees, expecting at any moment to hear the swish of a sword's blade angled at his neck.

A frigid wind swept across the bloody field, swift enough to nearly take men off their feet. Shapes rode the wind, and in his fevered haze, Niklas thought perhaps the spirits of his family had come to gather him to the Sea of Souls.

The figures grew closer, and Niklas gasped. These revenants had not come to collect the dead. They came to reap the living. Their forms grew more distinct, and Niklas realized that they wore the battle armor of the recent and long-gone past. Some of the ghosts bore their death wounds. Others were ragged skeletons with sundered armor. Rage animated all of them.

Primal instinct made Niklas duck as the spirits swept past, but they did not come for him. The ghost horde rushed toward Rostivan's men like a flood, clawed hands grasping, teeth chattering, hungry for vengeance.

"They can't hurt us! They're just ghosts!" one of Rostivan's men shouted. He turned to face the spirits, squaring his shoulders and planting his feet, sword held in front of him.

"Come and get me," he challenged.

They came. The gray ghosts swept over the soldier, shrouding him in their mist. The fighter began to scream, terrified shrieks that continued as his skin lost its color, fading to the gray of the dead. His screams filled the air until the breath was gone from his lungs, and the spirits dropped him behind them as they passed.

Another soldier fell, and another. The gray tide grew dark like the storm clouds overhead, and as it darkened, the ghosts became more solid, as did the weapons they carried. Beyond harm, beyond pain, the spirits advanced. The pounding of marching feet filled the air.

Niklas struggled to his feet and shouted for his men to fall back, giving the ghosts room to attack. A few of his soldiers, pale with fear, ran for their lives. Most retreated warily, watching the ghosts with suspicion.

The spirits of the dead marched forward, ignoring Niklas's soldiers altogether. Niklas saw the centuries represented in the different styles of their armor. Some looked to be the recent dead, others wore the armor of a generation or two past. Many were outfitted in clothing from centuries before, and a few might have been barbarian fighters from a time before Donderath was civilized enough for such things as uniforms.

On and on and on the dead came. No battle cries rose from the revenant soldiers, just an uncanny silence remorseless in its purpose. The living screamed and cursed, powerless against the onslaught. *Odd that when the ghosts passed me, I felt no tingle of magic in the air,* Niklas thought, *yet now the air feels charged with power.*

Maybe the ghosts don't need magic, he mused. *Maybe that's Rostivan's side, trying to muster up enough magic to lay the ghosts to rest.*

The wind had grown vicious, whipping the snow that was falling and the snow already on the ground. Against that background, the gray ghosts seemed even more fantastical. Niklas was tempted to dismiss them as yet another illusion, but the screams of dying men—men whose very solid, bleeding bodies fell at his feet—persuaded him of the spirits' reality. Rostivan was in full retreat, yet the ghosts pursued him, moving as fast as a swift courser, easily overrunning men on foot.

Snow masked the distance, but screams carried on the cold air. Hearing the massacre when he could not see it made the slaughter more terrifying. Niklas was surprised that anything could terrorize him anymore. The carnage mortal soldiers had worked upon each other no longer distressed him, although it haunted his dreams. The charge of the dead soldiers almost made him feel sorry for the enemy. Almost.

"Fall back!" Niklas ordered. Until the storm cleared, fighting would be folly, at least for mortals. The ghost soldiers had Rostivan's troops in retreat, and evening would soon fall. Though it was technically spring, the days were still short and the weather wintry.

"Do you think the storm is mage-sent?" Ayers said, struggling out of the winds to appear near Niklas.

Niklas shrugged. "If we believe the mages, they say no one can do much to affect the weather now, between how the magic doesn't work right yet and the reaction from what was done before." The storm clouds made it difficult to gauge time, since the sky seemed dark enough for sunset. Niklas guessed that it was late afternoon, still too early to count on *talishte* help.

Ayers nodded. "Just wondering, that's all. Can't imagine we'll see more fighting tonight, between the ghosts driving Rostivan's men off and it soon being time for the *talishte* to rise."

"That's my thought," Niklas agreed. "We'll fall back to camp and prepare for tomorrow, with double guards on duty in case the snow stops and Rostivan plans a midnight raid."

"Already working on it," Ayers said with a grin. "And tonight, a hot cup of *fet* will taste mighty good. Damn, even cook's stew will taste good, as long as it's hot."

"I rather fancied whiskey myself," Niklas said. His arm ached where he had taken the injury, and the rest of his body let him know it had been hard used. Real luxury would be a steaming-hot bath, but there would be nothing like that unless he survived and returned to Glenreith. The thought of it made him smile.

"Mages have already asked to meet with us once camp is set," Ayers reported.

Niklas nodded. "Very good. Saves me having to round them up. What else?"

"Trying to figure out how many we lost today," Ayers replied. "A lot, but not as bad as it could be."

"We'll regroup with the mages, and the *talishte* when they rise, and figure out tomorrow's strategy. I'll send *talishte* messengers to Blaine with an update and see if that changes his orders for us." Niklas gave a feral grin. "Maybe the *talishte* can even pay a nighttime visit to Rostivan's folks, following up on the ghosts."

Ayers chuckled. "I like the way you think."

Camp was hurriedly pitched, just enough to hold the line and protect soldiers from the elements. The real camp was several miles away, back where they had begun. Niklas was not about to give up the land they had fought to take inch by bloody inch. And he was certain that despite the storm and the ghosts, Rostivan had withdrawn only as far as he had to, with the intent to regain ground lost as soon as possible.

Niklas's tent when they were in the field was the same size as those of his soldiers. His only luxury was that unlike his men, Niklas had the tent to himself. A bedroll, a small brazier, and a trunk were all the goods he allowed himself for the forward camp, less to strike when circumstances required hasty action. Unlike his campaign tent, there was no table, no folding chairs, so his guests had to sit on the ground.

There was, however, a bottle of whiskey. Niklas passed it around for his guests to pour a finger or two into their tankards to warm the blood on such a cold night.

"What in Raka happened today?" Niklas asked. "What was magic, and what was dumb luck?"

His three senior mages—Rikard, Leiv, and Zaryae—sat facing him. Nemus remained outside, watching the magic for any sign of an attack. Ayers was to his right, and Geir had arrived after nightfall with updates from Mirdalur and from the other front, where Blaine and his allies battled Lysander and the Tingur.

"Rikard and one of our younger mages can move objects from a distance," Leiv said. "So they threw some fireballs and rocks, anything to cause a problem and spook the horses."

"We had some large rocks thrown at us," Niklas said, frowning.

Rikard raised his hands, palms out, to forestall blame. "Not us, although Quintrel's mages may have copied, or had the same idea themselves. We made sure to work our mayhem a distance from our troops."

"You can thank Zaryae for that," Leiv said. "She's got an amazing gift for far-sight." He was a bookish fellow, more suited to copying manuscripts than serving on the front lines of a war, yet he had volunteered to accompany the troops without hesitation. He looked simultaneously frightened and amazed to be there. Straight, dark hair stuck out at angles beneath the hood of his robe, and his slightly crooked nose gave him a winsome appearance.

"Did one of you call the ghosts?" Niklas asked.

The three mages shook their heads. "No. But we knew they were coming."

"Explain," Niklas asked. He was tired and sore and cold, and his patience was at an end.

Zaryae frowned, pausing as she searched for words. "The dead are aware of the living," she replied. "Not all spirits pass over to the Sea of Souls, or wander the Unseen Realm. Many remain here, for a variety of reasons. Some places are more haunted than others. This land," she said, gesturing palm up to indicate the valley, "has seen warfare since men first came to the Continent."

Zaryae's expression was sad. "The ghosts watch and listen. Magic affects them. I can't dismiss the possibility that the Wraith Lord may also have influence. Whatever the reason, they chose sides."

"They drove Rostivan back," Ayers said. "And they killed quite a few of his men. Can they do it again?"

Zaryae looked as if she were listening to something the rest of them could not hear. Then she shook her head. "No, at least, not on the same scale. They expended nearly all of their power today. It will take them quite a while to build it back up again."

"It helped that one of the artifacts is a ghost portal," Rikard said.

"A what?" Niklas snapped.

Rikard nodded patiently. "They aren't common. I'd heard of them, but never seen one. It's a rather plain-looking piece, like a lady's hand mirror, only with the right magic it can open a door to the other side and make it easier for spirits to pass from that side into our side."

Niklas felt a chill down his spine. "It's secured?" He asked. "There may be less friendly 'things' waiting to get through."

"We thought of that," Leiv said. "And we have it sealed and guarded. That's one of the reasons Nemus isn't with us. He's on watch."

Niklas nodded. "Very well. Go on."

"The ghosts aren't pleased with Quintrel," Zaryae said. She held up a hand to forestall protests. "I'm not a necromancer, and I can't easily communicate with spirits. It's more like I listen in to conversations I can't help hearing."

"Why?" Ayers asked. "What's Quintrel done?"

Zaryae shrugged. "I'm not entirely certain, because the ghosts had no need to explain it to each other. But I gather that he has sacrificed men for magic, sent them to their deaths needlessly. Those spirits are restless and angry. The dead talk among themselves. We may find them to be valuable allies, if the opportunity arises."

"What of the *talishte*?" Niklas asked, looking at Geir.

Geir gave a quick recount of how the battle had fared for Blaine, the Solveigs, and Verner, and caught them up on the progress at Mirdalur. "So the chamber is ready, as soon as Blaine is able to bring his new Lords of the Blood," he finished.

"Are Dolan and the others sure it's safe?"

Geir gave a short, harsh laugh. "Safe? No working of this kind is safe. But everything the mages can find leads us to believe that if Blaine brings his twelve new Lords to the chamber, magic can be solidly anchored once more."

Niklas sighed. "Sad when that's the best we can get, but I imagine we'll need to settle for it."

"There's a bit more news to tell," Rikard said. "We've stumbled on some things you'll want to hear."

"Oh?" Niklas asked. The day had gone hard on him, and though the healers bound up his wounds and a good dinner along with a belt of whiskey took the edge off, he was exhausted.

"Leiv is a telepath," Rikard said, and Leiv nodded in agreement. "It's not a flamboyant magic, or one that's easy to use in the press of battle, but important nonetheless."

Niklas turned to Leiv, who seemed to shrink under scrutiny. "What did you learn?"

"I can't throw fire or rocks," Leiv began nervously, "but I can throw thoughts. That's what I do. I can rummage about in other people's heads, plant ideas, that sort of thing. So I spent most of today trying to find and attack Rostivan and his generals," the mage said.

Niklas smiled. "I like what I'm hearing. Go on," he encouraged.

"It's difficult to pick the right people in such a crowd," Leiv said apologetically. "But I made enough contact to do a bit of damage. I planted the idea with some of Rostivan's ranking men that you had dangerously powerful mages who could kill with their minds."

Leiv's cheeks colored. "A bit of an exaggeration, that. But I didn't figure it would hurt to inspire a little fear." He chuckled. "I touched their minds later, and everything that went wrong for them they figured we had hocused for them, whether we did or not."

Ayers gave a sharp laugh. "I like the sound of that."

Leiv nodded, gaining confidence. "Rostivan himself was difficult. He moved around a lot, and he's got unusually high shields, which makes him hard to read. But I picked up something that I think is important." He licked his lips. "Quintrel is controlling him with magic—dark magic."

Niklas leaned forward, fully attentive. "Oh?"

"Quintrel has somehow bound a *divi*," Geir answered. Everyone swiveled to look at him. "Dolan told us this when he returned from Valshoa." He paused. "It's an ancient spirit that never should have been summoned," he added. "Quintrel thinks he's controlling it, but odds are, the *divi* is riding Quintrel."

"What does that have to do with Rostivan?" Niklas asked, confused.

"Rostivan doesn't know he's being controlled," Leiv put in. "Quintrel's given him something that lets the *divi* 'manage' Rostivan's thoughts and actions." He met Niklas's gaze. "That means that Quintrel is the power to be reckoned with, not Rostivan," he said. "And from the glimmers I've picked up from Quintrel, you can count on him being insane."

Niklas exchanged a glance with Ayers. "Well now," he said. "That's interesting."

"We're working on how to break the *divi*'s hold on Rostivan,"

Rikard said. "It's possible that Quintrel has also used some of the *divi*'s power to put Lysander in thrall." He shrugged. "We've heard rumors, of late, that conversations were had." He shrugged. "It's logical."

"Can you do it?" Ayers asked, eyes bright with interest. "Can you disrupt whatever this *divi*-thing is doing?"

Rikard grimaced. "That's the hard part. We're working on it. *Divis* are old and powerful. They're known for being slippery. We don't have our manuscripts out here in the field, but we're doing what we can."

Niklas nodded. "Make it happen. If Rostivan finds out he's been in thrall to Quintrel, we just might see them turn on each other, and wouldn't that be a pretty picture?"

"There's one more thing you need to know," Zaryae said.

Something in her voice gave Niklas pause. He looked toward her, and met her gaze. "What?"

"I touched the minds of Rostivan's mages," Leiv said. "Just briefly." He met Niklas's gaze. "I picked up fear, distaste, and betrayal."

"Betrayal?" Niklas asked, raising an eyebrow.

Leiv nodded. "If I'm right—and I only touched their minds for a moment—Rostivan's mages are plotting against him. Perhaps even against Quintrel."

"Are you sure?" Niklas asked.

Again, Leiv nodded. "Yes. I saw a conspiracy. Rostivan is being undermined. We need to be ready to seize the moment when it happens."

"And hope that whoever's behind the plot doesn't have something worse in mind," Niklas added.

CHAPTER
TWENTY-NINE

WATCH YOURSELF! MORE *GRYPS* ARE COMING!"
Blaine shouted a warning to Piran and his men as
the leather-winged predators circled their soldiers. The *gryps*
shrieked, calling and answering to each other, skirling on the
air currents as they sized up their prey. With wings that were
easily as far across tip-to-tip as a tall man, sharp talons, and a
beak meant for rending meat, the *gryps* were nightmare creatures left over from the wild-magic storms.

Blaine vowed that once he and his men had eliminated the
gryps, he would happily slaughter the Tingur without a bit of
remorse, just for having driven the vicious creatures at him and
his troops.

He and Niklas had agreed before the battle that Niklas
would lead one-half of the army against Rostivan and Quintrel, trying to shield Blaine from the worst of the effects of
magic. Traher Voss's soldiers added much-needed reinforcements. Blaine led the other half of his army, backed up by the
armies of the Solveigs and Birgen Verner. So here they were,
arrayed on a wide-open plain halfway between Glenreith and

the Solveigs' holdings, facing down the largest army since King Merrill's soldiers went to Meroven.

"Watch out for the claws—they're poisoned!" Piran called out to the soldiers around them. Behind the front line, archers were readying their arrows. Thanks to Verran's spying, Blaine had known in advance that the Tingur had managed to collect and use the creatures in their attacks. And because of Blaine's previous run-ins with the beasts from the magic storms, he and his troops knew how to fight the things.

True to her word, Kestel rode with them. Since she was wearing the same dun-colored tunic and trews as the other soldiers, with her red hair bound up beneath a helm and her figure flattened by a hard leather cuirass, no one would be likely to give her a second look among the thousands of soldiers. That would be a mistake. Two bandoliers crossed her chest, each arrayed with dozens of dirks, throwing knives, and wicked circular blades. She wore two swords, and both a staff and a bow were lashed to her saddle along with a quiver filled with arrows and a covered bucket filled with pitch.

"We need those flaming arrows *now*!" Blaine shouted, fighting back the assault. Blaine could only guess how the Tingur managed to trap the *gryps* or tie heavy stone weights to their taloned feet, but he figured magic played a role. The weights were light enough that the *gryps* could still fly, and heavy enough to keep them near the ground where they could be 'herded' toward an enemy. From the bright glow coming from the Tingur line, Blaine bet the beasts had been prodded toward their objective with fire.

"Well then, we're about to start prodding back," he muttered. One of the *gryps* dove at Blaine, grabbing for his shoulder with its sharp talons. He barely evaded a nasty slice, and slashed with his sword, scoring a deep cut on the leathery talons. Foul-smelling ichor dripped from the wound. Steel glinted in the air, and one of Kestel's knives buried itself hilt-deep in the *gryp*'s side, forcing the creature to draw back and limiting the use of one wing.

Blaine and Piran each carried lances with torch-like tips soaked in resin and burning brightly. They spurred their frightened horses onward, charging at the *gryps* with their flaming pikes. Normally, the *gryps* would have arced high into the sky to evade them, but slowed and anchored by the heavy stone weights, the winged predators had limited mobility.

"I guess the Tingur found a disposable front line of their own," Piran muttered. Hobbled as the *gryps* were by the weights, killing them was easier than in the wild, though hardly without danger. But Piran was right: The only purpose for using the magicked beasts in battle was to wear down the enemy before the Tingur advanced, just as Lysander used the Tingur to protect his 'real' soldiers.

Blaine stabbed at the *gryp* with his lance, taking grim satisfaction at the way the beast screeched at the flames. The *gryp* flapped its wings madly. One of the foot soldiers dove for the heavy stone, anchoring the *gryp* further with his own weight.

"Get him, sir! I'll hold him!" the soldier shouted, ducking to avoid the thing's talons.

Lance in his left hand, anchored against his body, Blaine charged again, sword ready. Unable to fly, terrorized by the flames, the *gryp* tried and failed to snatch at the lance. Kestel sank two blades deep into the *gryp*'s body, one at the joint of its left wing and another in its belly.

Blaine stabbed the lance deep into the *gryp*'s gut, following through with a sword strike that tore its wing from top to bottom like a ruined sail. Pushed backward by the momentum of

Blaine's horse, the *gryp* flailed, and the soldier beneath it threw the rope-wrapped stone, managing to tangle the *gryp*'s talons in its own ballast. The creature fell heavily to the ground as the lance's fire burned it inside. The thing gave one last, ear-splitting shriek and collapsed. Blaine made sure of its death by bringing his horse's hooves down on its body, crunching bone.

"One down," he muttered, though at least a half dozen more still filled the sky.

A foot soldier to the left of Blaine screamed as a *gryp* raked him with its talons, opening bloody gashes from shoulder to thigh. Another of the soldiers battled back one *gryp* only to have a second snatch him up with its razor-sharp claws, tearing into him with its beak.

Down the line, *gryps* flew at the soldiers with talons out and beaks jabbing. The heavy stone weights added to the *gryps*' deadly arsenal, since the panicked beasts gyred and swooped awkwardly, trailing the swinging stones as they went. The weight-stones toppled two hapless soldiers who could not scramble out of the way quickly enough, sending them sprawling in a spray of blood as the heavy stones connected with skull and bone.

"We're losing men, and the real fighting hasn't even started yet," Blaine grumbled.

"I think that's the point," Piran responded.

Three flaming arrows soared into the air, over the injured soldier's head. Two of the arrows ripped through the skin of the *gryp*'s wings, but the beast managed to twist enough to evade the third arrow. Volley after volley of flaming arrows filled the sky as the *gryps* beat their wings furiously to get away.

Crowing a victory cry, Piran copied what Blaine had done, charging at the *gryp* with his lance while a soldier secured the anchor. The battle cry echoed down the line as horsemen leveled their flaming lances and rode for the *gryps* as foot soldiers in twos and threes ran to tackle the stone weights. The *gryps* shrieked and screamed, beating the air with their wings, but between the fiery pikes and the flaming arrows, the battle had turned. Blaine shook the ichor and soot from his vambraces and turned to survey the fighting. Kestel had slipped down from her horse, and was calmly retrieving as many of her blades from the fallen *gryps* as she could find, cleaning off the ichor on the dry grass.

"What in the name of Torven are those things?" a soldier near Blaine shouted in alarm. Beetle-like creatures the size of wild pigs skittered across the dry grass. Some of the beasts stopped long enough to rip flesh from the dying *gryps*, but the others, alerted to the presence of fresh prey by the soldiers' movements, swarmed toward the advancing line. There were too many to count, but Blaine guessed that there had to be at least fifty of the things, and untrammeled by stone weights, the creatures moved much faster than the *gryps* had done.

"They're *mestids*," Blaine shouted. "And they hate fire as much as the *gryps*."

"We've got more coming," Piran yelled, pointing to the strip of land between their forces and the Tingur. "And there's something else—are those *ranin*?"

"That's sure what they look like," Blaine said, refreshing the pitch and batting on his torch and lighting it afire. Kestel had swung up onto her horse once more, and was readying her bow with pitch-tipped arrows.

Pale, crab-like creatures scuttled among the *mestids*. If the *mestids* were the size of wild hogs, then the *ranin* were mastiff-sized, with oval bodies and bone-like carapaces. Six jointed legs clicked with every movement, tipped in sharp claws that looked as lethal as the *gryps*' talons. The *ranin* clattered their way toward the soldiers nearly as fast as a trotting horse, slashing at the slower *mestids* with their jointed legs.

"There are too many of them, coming too fast," one of the soldiers near Blaine shouted. Blaine looked down the line at the soldiers grimly braced for the onslaught, and a desperate idea formed.

"Light the grass!" Blaine shouted. "We want a line of fire! Do it!" Blaine used his flaming lance to catch the dry grass of the battlefield on fire, then he braced his lance like a pike behind the flames. Smoke rose in the cold air as the burning line spread down the front lines, and the archers shot one volley after another to rain fire down on the beasts. The clicking of the *ranin*'s carapaces and the clatter of the *mestids*' snapping claws and jointed legs filled the air.

The winter grasses caught quickly, and the fire spread rapidly. Confronted with a wall of flame, the *mestids* and *ranin* clattered to a halt, squawking and hissing. A gust of wind angled the flames toward them, and the creatures retreated, only to come into better range of the archers.

Piran sheathed his sword and grabbed the crossbow from his saddle. Down the line, Blaine spotted Borya and Desya doing the same, standing in their stirrups, taking aim.

The crossbow thudded, and a burning quarrel streaked through the air, catching one of the *mestids* at the jointed place where its front leg met its body. The arrow went deep, engulfing the *mestid* in fire. The insect-like creature screeched and scuttled backward, causing the other *mestids* and *ranin* to draw back from the flames. Already, its body was beginning to split with the heat, and an awful smell filled the air as the *mestid* exploded.

Another quarrel struck a *ranin*. The razor-sharp tip split the carapace and embedded itself deeply. Six legs flailed in vain as flames hissed, engulfing it in fire. Crossbows were able to pierce the heavy exoskeletons, and for every *mestid* or *ranin* that was felled by the quarrels, two or three abandoned their attack to gorge themselves on the smoking remains of the creatures as soon as the flames were extinguished.

Scrambling up the dead bodies of its comrades, one of the *ranin* launched itself at Blaine, managing to get its body briefly airborne to avoid the flames. Kestel lobbed one of her circular knives, a blade with sharp teeth like a saw blade, and it ripped easily through the *ranin*'s shell, spraying the ground with ichor as the beast fell, its legs clawing and spasming.

The bowmen quickly realized that regular arrows could not penetrate the beasts' natural armor, so they shot wave after wave of flaming arrows into the dry grass among the attackers, until the swath of land was engulfed in fire and the bitter, acrid smell of their burning flesh and shells filled the air with a choking haze of smoke.

Halted by the fire, panicked by the stench, the *mestids* and *ranin* ran. Flaming arrows pursued them until they were beyond archers' range, sending the creatures back in a deadly wave toward the Tingur who had loosed them.

Blaine took grim satisfaction in hearing the screams and shouts of the Tingur as the tide of enraged creatures swarmed toward them. To the left, Blaine could see that the Solveig army had begun to hem in the Tingur, while Verner's forces flanked them on the other side. As the fire burned out near Blaine's front line, his troops advanced, and his archers continued shooting their fire-tipped arrows just behind the *mestids* and *ranin*, forcing them to overrun the Tingur. With nowhere to run, the Tingur had no choice except to battle their own monsters, aware that once the beasts had taken their toll, soldiers awaited to finish the job. Unprepared, without ready access to fiery arrows or flaming pikes, the panic-stricken beasts caught up with the front line of Tingur as the rest fled for their lives.

"Lysander's biding his time," Blaine said as Piran rode up beside him. Piran's clothing was torn and soot-streaked, and Blaine guessed he looked much the same.

Piran nodded. "This was just the warm-up. Too bad we can't use the same tactic and have the Tingur turn on Lysander's troops."

"Something's happening. Look," Blaine said and pointed.

Pursued by the stampeding creatures, the Tingur fled toward Lysander's main army line. Yet even from here, Blaine could see that if the Tingur expected protection, their hopes were in vain. Lysander's soldiers blocked the Tingur's escape at sword's point, giving them the choice between fighting the creatures and being cut down by their own side.

"I guess Lysander doesn't want to dirty his hands dealing with the beasts," Blaine said, glad that the Tingur's folly gave his own side a chance to catch their breath. Blackened grass and the charred carapaces of dead monsters covered the open stretch between the opposing armies. A glance down his own line assured Blaine that although his vanguard had taken some damage in the fight, few of his soldiers had been seriously injured or killed.

"Hang on," Blaine said. "Here it comes."

Bellowing a war cry, Lysander's main forces charged toward the defenders' line. Horsemen led the way, with infantry not far behind. They rode through the battle between the Tingur and the beasts, trampling those who got in their way.

With an answering shout of their own, Blaine led their charge. The Solveigs and Verner followed a moment later.

Lysander's army bore no resemblance to the motley Tingur. Well armed and well armored, the attacking army moved with the skill of practiced fighters. And unlike the hapless Tingur, who had been carried into battle on raw emotion, it was obvious from the first sword's strike that Lysander's soldiers had a plan.

Warhorses thundered down the plain. Foot soldiers ran between the big horses, swords at the ready to engage. On horseback, Blaine had the advantage, and he used it to cut his way through the onslaught. Four men fell in quick succession, spattering Blaine's legs and his horse with blood.

Faces blurred as they rushed past him, but Blaine realized that many of Lysander's soldiers did not have the look of Donderan men. With a jolt, he realized that the warlord's army included recruits—or mercenaries—from the enemy kingdom whose mages had brought down the Great Fire and the Cataclysm on them all.

Piran came to the same conclusion, and rage colored his features. "Bloody Meroven mercs!" Piran shouted, following up with a string of obscenities. Piran was fighting a large man who was armed with a war ax, and it was taking all of Piran's skills to stay out of the way of the heavy ax long enough to get in a few strikes of his own.

Blaine faced down his own opponent, a seasoned warrior on a massive warhorse whose barrage of sword blows gave Blaine little time to worry about Piran. Blaine fended off the strikes, but he could feel the fatigue from the fight with the magicked beasts already taking its toll. He was mindful of the agate amulet at his throat, a talisman that deflected and minimized the drain of magic but did not remove it altogether. Remembering Carr's savaged features and tortured body ignited Blaine's anger, dispelling any tiredness, and he let that rage warm his body and drive him onward.

Strike. Parry. Strike. Block. Blaine and his opponent circled each other warily, each sizing up the other's strength, speed, and skill. Blaine saw cunning and dead-cold ruthlessness in the soldier's eyes, and he wondered what the other man made of him. Out of the corner of his eye, Blaine could see two other soldiers heading for him, but he dared not take his attention away from the man he battled.

His opponent landed a strike that got inside Blaine's guard, slashing down on his vambrace, but it was blocked by the heavy leather before it could damage skin and bone. Blaine swung, slicing into his attacker's arm, deep enough that the man drew back, but not far enough.

Blaine dug his heels into his horse's sides, and his mount jolted forward. Blaine angled his sword, and the horse's motion drove it into the gap above his attacker's cuirass, deep into the man's throat. Blood bubbled and gurgled as the soldier shuddered, alive enough to know he was dying quickly.

The soldier's horse panicked and bolted, nearly tearing Blaine's sword from his hand. His opponent clung to the saddle for a few strides, then toppled from his mount as the terrified horse galloped away.

Kestel had loosed her horse, and on foot she was deadly with her throwing knives, moving nimbly enough to evade the horses and ducking in and out of the action. Down the line, Blaine could spot Borya and Desya standing in their saddles, firing their bows with lethal aim. The twins galloped toward the enemy in a two-man offensive that took Lysander's soldiers completely by surprise for its boldness. Too late, as the astonished soldiers began to drop to the ground, arrows in their chests, did their companions realize that the twins posed a true threat.

Some of Piran's cursing was in Merovenian, the native tongue of the mercs, which seemed to rattle his opponent. To

Blaine's knowledge, Piran's fluency was limited to obscenities, but he could hold his own in at least half a dozen dialects. He switched between languages, keeping up a steady stream of curses.

"It's not enough for your mages to burn down the Continent!" Piran shouted as he landed a crazed series of sword strikes. "Now you've got to sell your swords to muck up what's left!" The speed of his blows, coupled with the unpredictability of his strikes as rage fueled his fighting, managed to get Piran inside his enemy's guard, and with a triumphant slash, he opened the soldier's belly.

"Take your guts and your stinking Meroven shit back across the border!" Piran screamed.

By now, the forefront of the battle had passed them by, and both Blaine and Piran slipped from their mounts, preferring the maneuverability of being on foot. They sent their horses running for the rear lines. Kestel joined them, and Blaine looked across the battlefield, taking advantage of a momentary lull.

Far to one side, he glimpsed the Solveigs' forces, which appeared to be holding their own. To the other side, where Verner's son, Birgen, led his father's troops, it was harder to tell which side was currently winning. One thing Blaine was sure of was that the wind had picked up.

"Temperature's dropping," Piran noted.

"Sky isn't looking good," Kestel added with a glance upward. Dark-gray clouds had massed, promising snow. "Zaryae said there would be storms."

One more thing that anchoring the magic might fix, Blaine thought.

"I could do without this," Piran grumbled. "It's not like I was homesick for Edgeland."

Blaine heartily agreed, eyeing the storm clouds warily. The battle was far from over, and an incoming storm would make it all the more miserable—and unpredictable.

"Trouble!" Kestel said, and Blaine turned to see three of Lysander's soldiers running toward them. The battle had shifted once more, coming back over the same few feet of ground it had just yielded, and Blaine knew they could take and lose the same thin stretch many more times before the day was over, at the cost of many lives.

In the distance, Blaine could hear his captains shouting orders and saw the units respond as he and Niklas had trained them. *We're holding our own,* he thought. *Let's see if it lasts.* His hand went to finger the magic-deflecting amulet at his throat. True to Rikard's word, the amulet had pushed aside the worst of the magic they had faced. All morning, Blaine had been alert for signs of magic, though he hoped that the mages had stayed with Rostivan and Quintrel. Lysander was known to be skeptical—even hostile—toward magic, and Blaine whole-heartedly hoped that rumor was true. So far, no major magic had been worked nearby, but surely that was unlikely to last the entire battle, and Blaine lacked assurance that the amulet could completely avert magic's effects, or protect him from its drain.

Blaine's attacker came at him with a morning star, swinging the spiked iron ball from its chain with one hand while he jabbed and thrust with a sword in the other. Blaine backed up a step and nearly fell over a corpse, but he glimpsed a metal shield in the dead man's hand and snatched it up in time to block the deadly morning star's strike. The ball hit the shield with a loud clang, leaving a dent Blaine was thankful was not in his helm or skull.

Piran took the offensive, charging his opponent before the fighter expected it. With his bald head, loud voice, and wild-eyed grimace, Piran looked like a maniac, and his penchant for risky moves made him unpredictable. Swearing in several different languages with curses that would have shamed the most hardened brigands, Piran came at his attacker with a berserker's frenzy. He landed three blows before the astonished soldier got his guard up, scoring a deep cut in his opponent's shoulder, a gash to the man's thigh, and a slice across his chest.

Kestel and the third man stalked each other warily. The attacker, eager for a fight, feinted to draw Kestel's strike, but she read the attempt for what it was and went in the other direction, moving inside the man's guard to score a deep puncture in his left shoulder. Enraged, the enemy soldier came after her with several pounding blows. Kestel.parried the first blow, then leapt backward over a fallen corpse to get beyond the man's reach as his swing went wild.

Even angrier now, the soldier stepped over the dead man and raised his sword for the kill. The movement left his chest open, and Kestel dodged out of reach of his sword. With a flick of her wrist, one dagger caught the soldier in his sword arm, while the second dagger buried itself deep in his chest. He fell across the corpse, and Kestel kicked his sword out of reach, then retrieved her blades, stopping to slit his throat before she cleaned the weapons on the dead man's cloak.

Blaine parried his attacker's sword, feeling the force of the blow reverberate up his arm. The morning star swung again, and once more Blaine deflected it with the shield, but the sharp points dug deep into the metal, and when the fighter yanked back his weapon, it jerked the shield from Blaine's hand, nearly breaking his fingers. His opponent chuckled, thrusting with his sword and almost getting inside Blaine's guard. The soldier's hand drew back, ready to let the morning star fly once more.

Blaine grabbed a broken pike from a dead soldier's hand and blocked the deadly blow, tangling the chain and jerking the weapon out of his attacker's hand. Blaine thrust forward, and his sword caught the soldier in the middle of the chest, dragging the blade down through his belly. The soldier gave one more savage swing with his sword, opening a deep cut on Blaine's shoulder before Blaine knocked it away with the broken pike and slammed the wooden pole against the attacker's head, dropping him to the ground.

Piran was making short work of his own opponent. The soldier tried to parry, but Piran's wild attack had rattled him badly. Cursing creatively, Piran scored a two-handed hit that cleaved the man from shoulder to chest.

"And your mother was a poxy whore!" Piran finished as he stepped back from the dead man, breathing hard.

"Bad form to keep insulting them after they're dead, Piran," Kestel said.

"That's the problem, Kestel. You've already heard all my good insults," Piran replied. "I've got to try them out on someone."

Snow was falling, a few flakes at first and then rapidly growing into a steady, heavy downfall. Coupled with the wind, it limited visibility, making it difficult to see where the next attack might come from.

"Something's happening," Blaine said, pointing. Lysander's troops were falling back, though the battle was far from decided. Not far enough for a retreat, but enough to put a few clear feet of space between themselves and Blaine's troops.

"Nice of them to give us a rest," Piran quipped suspiciously.

A sudden pounding in Blaine's head nearly made him cry

out. "Watch yourselves!" Blaine warned as one hand went to the pendant. Kestel stepped closer and grabbed his arm, and immediately the effect lessened, a benefit of the null talisman she wore.

"Now, would you look at that?" Piran said in a wondering voice. Blaine and Kestel turned, and Blaine lost contact with Kestel's grip. Piran was staring at the snow, and he reached a hand toward the snow as if to grasp something that only he could see.

Blaine frowned, then caught a glimpse of something in the curtain of shimmering snow. Shadows became faces, and Blaine gasped in recognition. His mother. Carensa. Servants, long dead, whom he had known since childhood. His hated father. Carr.

Carr's image triggered a jolt of rage, and Blaine blinked rapidly, struggling against the vision. He gripped the pendant tightly, and the vision blurred, sliding away from him as if the magic-dampening amulet had broken the spell. Kestel's touch on his arm cleared his head, and when he looked once more, the images were gone. Kestel grabbed Piran's arm, and he shook free of the illusion.

"They're regrouping, and they're going to attack while our men are woolgathering," Blaine said, glancing around wildly. "Noise! We've got to make noise."

Blaine grabbed his dented shield and the broken pike and began to hammer on the metal, shouting at the top of his lungs. "Wake up! They're coming!"

Piran snatched up three or four tin cups that had littered the battlefield, dropped or knocked from their owners' belts. Holding them overhead, he slammed them together over and over again as his rough voice carried over the wind.

Kestel ripped the dented helm from one of the dead men

and began to beat on it with the wooden handle of a fallen war hammer. "Danger!" she shouted. "Move!"

Blaine and Kestel ran along the line in one direction while Piran ran in the other, setting up as loud a clamor as they could muster. Blaine's head felt as if it would explode, both from the magic and from the cacophony. All around them, men roused from their vision, and the illusion faded.

Lysander's troops, cheated of their easy victory, readied for the charge, but this time, Blaine and his men beat them to it. Perhaps the illusion reminded the men too well of what they had lost or who was left behind. Or maybe, tired, cold, and injured, they were ready for a fair fight without tricks.

Whatever the reason, Blaine and Piran led the advance, rallying their spent troops behind them, swords in hand. Kestel snared the reins from a riderless horse and swung up to the saddle. Borya and Desya rallied the soldiers, much like they had long-ago herded errant livestock on the flatlands of their boyhood. Buoyed by rage, Blaine's troops closed the distance between themselves and Lysander's soldiers, fighting all-out and ready for vengeance.

Snow fell harder than before, and the wind sent icy gusts, reducing visibility a few inches. It was unlikely either side could prevail in these conditions. Blaine heard Lysander's commanders call retreat.

"Hold your ground!" Blaine ordered, and the command echoed down the line. "Hold steady!"

It was a fool's bargain to keep on fighting in this storm, and both Blaine and Lysander knew it. They would each lose as many men to exposure as to battle, and with no ability to see farther than the hand on one's arm, no strategy could suffice. Blaine had no doubt that Lysander and his men would return just as soon as the weather cleared.

"Are we certain mages can't affect the weather?" Kestel asked, riding up to join him.

Blaine shrugged. "So we've been told. If the storms really are a reaction to the old magic, then let's hope no one's foolish enough to add to the problem."

"I doubt this storm, at least, was sent by either side," Piran agreed. "After all, who benefited? Not Lysander—he was forced to retreat. Not us—we might have won the day if it hadn't started storming." He shook his head. "All the same, the sooner you get the magic straightened out, the happier we'll all be—and the longer we're likely to live."

CHAPTER THIRTY

"HOW WILL YOU KNOW WHEN IT'S DONE?" CONnor looked around the ritual chamber at Mirdalur and shook his head.

No one would mistake the large underground chamber for anything but a mage's lair. Torches in sconces along the walls lit the huge, windowless room. In the center of the open space, an elaborate labyrinth had been set into the rock, a twisting pathway that took up most of the area, leaving a narrow path along the outside.

The labyrinth had wider areas at intervals along its route: thirteen of them, Connor counted. The spaces would be just wide enough for a man to stand and a candle to burn. Along the walls of the chamber, sigils were marked into the stone, and Connor was certain that each marking had a match with one of the thirteen obsidian disks held by the Lords of the Blood.

"We can't be completely certain until McFadden walks the path and attempts to call down the magic onto his chosen Lords of the Blood," Dolan replied. "But the magic is no longer wild like what McFadden encountered on his first, unfortunate attempt."

Connor had heard the details of that attempt, and knew how close Blaine and the others had come to dying. Whoever created the Mirdalur ritual chamber did not want interlopers.

"What is it you want of us?" Connor's voice asked the question, but Dolan recognized the Wraith Lord's presence.

"You were one of the thirteen Lords," Dolan answered, meaning Kierken Vandholt, the man who became the Wraith Lord. "With Connor's help, you will participate again. You're the only one who has walked this labyrinth as a Lord of the Blood—other than McFadden—and the only survivor of the old ritual." He paused. "I would ask you to walk to your place in the path—just walk—and tell me what you feel."

The Wraith Lord chuckled. "Anxious to rid yourself of me, Dolan?"

Dolan looked aghast. "No, m'lord. And for safety's sake, you'll carry neither presence-crystal nor your disk. Our mages have walked the path and felt very little stirring of power. We fear we will only get one opportunity, and we have a minimum of information on which to draw."

Are you willing? The Wraith Lord asked in Connor's mind. *Since I require your body to comply with the request.*

So long as we don't get burned to a cinder or blown apart, I'm willing, Connor replied. *I didn't come this far to let Blaine fail.*

Connor had recovered from his battle wounds. As the Wraith Lord and Penhallow had promised him, his recovery was much faster than before Penhallow strengthened the *kruvgaldur*. *Then again, the injuries were that much worse, because I was able to withstand them,* Connor thought. Prudently, the Wraith Lord did not comment.

"What precautions have you taken?" Penhallow asked. He gave Connor a cautionary glance.

When Connor had staggered back after the battle, more

dead than alive, Penhallow had just been rising from his crypt. He had looked on worriedly as the healers labored, but Connor had declined more of Penhallow's blood since the wounds were serious but not mortal. Connor was still trying to decide whether, when the day eventually came that his injuries were beyond healing, he would accept Penhallow's offer of immortality. So far, he had thought no, but he was well aware the decision might look different when the moment was finally upon him.

"We've worked with extreme caution," Dolan assured him. "Mortal and *talishte* mages have warded the chamber inside and the structure outside. We have validated the translations of the manuscripts we seized from Quintrel, as well as those we took from the crypts beneath Quillarth Castle and the Citadel."

Penhallow nodded. "Very well. What of the presence-crystals? We believe Quintrel has been affected by a corrupted artifact. Are you sure, Dolan, that none of that taint affects the crystals?" He looked toward the crystals, which lay in a row on a narrow worktable in the rear of the chamber. Even from this distance, Connor could see a faint, pulsing glow.

Dolan hesitated. "We've tested to the best of our ability," he said. "But it's worrisome that Quintrel acquired a *divi* just at the time the crystals came to light."

"What's a *divi*?" Connor asked, pushing himself to the forefront of his consciousness for a moment.

Penhallow frowned. "*Talishte* are not the only immortals— nor are we the most dangerous, no matter what you may think. *Divis* are old spirits, perhaps old enough to have walked this world when it was formless and barren."

He seemed to carefully weigh his words before continuing. "They're not evil...not the way you would mean the word. They just don't care about anything that gets in their way. Power is what they crave. Valuing the lives of mortals—and even those of *talishte*—doesn't factor into their thinking." He met Connor's gaze.

"When you go for a walk, do you intend to step on small insects, crush the life out of plants? Does that give you joy?" he asked.

"Of course not!" Connor retorted.

Penhallow nodded. "Now imagine being the insect. Your intent—the fact that you didn't leave home looking forward to killing the insect and that you weren't going to enjoy it—wouldn't matter, would it?"

Connor took a moment to think about it, then shook his head. "No. I suppose not."

"To the *divis*, we are the insects, the beetle accidentally trodden underfoot on the way to achieving control. No harm meant does not mean no harm done," Penhallow replied.

"Is Quintrel strong enough to bind such a spirit?" Connor asked, eyes widening.

Penhallow gave a shrug, and even the Wraith Lord did not seem to know. "Doubtful," Penhallow said. "More likely, the *divi* has bound Quintrel without him knowing it. I would not be surprised that the old Valshoans had knowledge of many things lost to us now."

"They did," Dolan said, breaking his silence. "And they dabbled in things mortals—and perhaps immortals—ought not to touch. I thought that my Knights had destroyed or hidden those things." He grimaced. "Obviously, we did not succeed."

Penhallow shook his head. "Don't blame yourself. When a spirit such as a *divi* wishes to be found, it will arrange for it to happen. *Divis* are conscious and sentient, and the effects of their actions on 'weaker' creatures do not concern them."

Connor shuddered. The thought that the *divis* were powerful enough to group *talishte* and mortals together in their view of 'weak' was something he did not want to dwell on.

"Could a *divi* mislead a mage of Dolan's strength?" Connor asked.

Dolan gave a shrug. "It's possible. It would be quite presumptuous to declare myself too experienced to be fooled. It's certain that a *divi* misled Quintrel, because I doubt even he would give himself over to such a spirit if he knew the true cost."

Connor felt a chill go down his back. "Which is?" he asked.

Dolan met his gaze. "*Divis* feed on the energy of a soul. They're parasites. Quintrel is being consumed, little by little. No bargain is worth that."

Connor agreed, but he wondered if Quintrel himself would consider any cost too high. "What does Quintrel get out of the deal?" he asked.

Dolan grimaced. "When we left Valshoa, Quintrel planned to have his mages put a geas on Rostivan to assure that he would do Quintrel's bidding."

"Which would give Quintrel his own army," Penhallow replied. "And it appears to have worked."

The Wraith Lord directed Connor's attention to the presence-crystals. "Quintrel declared the crystals to be the solution to anchoring the magic," he said, "but how?"

"The crystals are the 'connection,' so to speak, between the power that flows through the nodes and meridians in the ground and the 'instructions' to bind the power that's contained in the disks," Dolan replied, gesturing toward the crystals. "We believe that each time the power has been bound, other objects have formed that connection. Perhaps the ritual destroys the connecting objects; we don't know what was used before."

"Carved stone wands," the Wraith Lord replied. "That's what

we carried four centuries ago when the working was done. I did not make the association with the crystals until now."

The Wraith Lord directed Connor to point toward the labyrinth. "We each had a thick agate 'wand' with runes carved into it," he recalled. "They cracked top to bottom when the magic was bound, and since they were no use after that, I assume they were discarded."

Dolan nodded. "Thank you. That confirms what I suspected."

Are you ready? the Wraith Lord asked Connor, who nodded. "Let's take that walk into the labyrinth now," he said to Dolan. "Since only McFadden and I are tied by bloodline to the prior workings, what say I return to the spot I filled the last time?"

For your safety, let me remain in control, the Wraith Lord warned Connor. *I don't trust Quintrel.*

Neither do I.

The Wraith Lord chuckled. *Then we are agreed.*

The Wraith Lord walked to the opening of the labyrinth and paused. He took a deep breath, letting it steady Connor's nerves. While the Wraith Lord might not have needed the breath, Connor certainly did. Carefully, the Wraith Lord entered the labyrinth, watching his steps so that he did not tread outside of the pathway.

I feel magic building, Connor thought.

Just a fraction of what will happen when the ritual is worked, the Wraith Lord replied. *But dangerous, nonetheless.*

He paused each time the path widened, and in those spots, Connor could see sigils etched into the rock. They matched the marking on the wall behind that spot, and he was certain there would be corresponding marks on each Lord's obsidian disk.

With every step that took them deeper into the labyrinth, Connor felt magic like a heavy blanket around him. No chanting or drumming sounded, no candles burned along the pathway, no ritual was enacted, and yet power was undeniable. Connor was relieved when they halted halfway into the labyrinth.

"This is the spot," the Wraith Lord said.

"Can you feel power rising?" Dolan asked. Nidhud and Dagur had joined Dolan.

"Yes. Don't let more mages enter; I fear it would feed the energy," the Wraith Lord cautioned. Dolan turned toward the door and shook his head. Connor guessed that other mages had gathered, hoping to see what transpired.

"Can you sense anything about the power?" Dolan questioned. "You're the only eyewitness we've got."

"It was a long time ago," the Wraith Lord replied.

Dolan nodded. "Yes. But please think: Does the power 'feel' right to you?"

The Wraith Lord held Connor completely still, every mortal sense on alert as well as the Wraith Lord's heightened *talishte* senses. Connor could hear his heart beating, and his breath seemed to echo in the stone chamber. Yet as he 'listened' to the power, as he focused his attention on it, he realized something was off.

"No," the Wraith Lord said. "It doesn't. I'm getting Connor out of here right now."

Even from a distance, Connor could see that one of the crystals pulsed more quickly than the others as it lay on the worktable. Twelve of the crystals glowed a muted golden. One throbbed a crimson color that began the shade of fresh blood and was growing deeper by the instant.

Can't we turn back? Connor asked, doing his best to remain calm.

That's not how the labyrinth works, the Wraith Lord replied. *Moving inward winds the power up. Moving outward releases the power. Even though this isn't the real working, power has been called and power must be dispelled. Otherwise...*

The Wraith Lord did not finish his sentence, but he didn't have to. Connor understood that the outcome would not be to his liking.

On the way into the labyrinth, the path had not seemed narrow. Now that the Wraith Lord was trying to navigate it quickly and without error, Connor felt as if it had become almost heel-to-toe, though the stone had not changed. Connor gave himself over to the *talishte* reflexes and dexterity of the Wraith Lord. Even so, he moved with caution; faster than a mortal, but hardly at full *talishte* speed.

Connor felt magic tingle on his skin, raising the hair on his arms and prickling on the back of his neck. Even with the Wraith Lord's presence, the farther into the labyrinth they went, the harder it was to walk, like trudging through hip-deep water. Connor labored to breathe, and his heart thudded in his throat. The temperature in the chamber plummeted, until Connor's nose and fingertips were numb.

Hurry! he urged the Wraith Lord.

I am endeavoring to do so.

The area outside the labyrinth had become blurred, as if Connor were looking through fogged glass. Still, he could tell that Dolan and the other mages huddled around the presence-crystals.

One of the crystals has been corrupted, the Wraith Lord said.

Can a divi's *power extend this far? We're nowhere close to Quintrel.*

The divi *only need be present once to do the damage,* the Wraith Lord replied.

Blaine will need the crystals to anchor the magic. If even one is corrupted—

It will not be our problem if we don't escape the maze. The Wraith Lord's voice was clipped, and Connor fell silent.

Voices hummed all around them. At first, Connor took it for the worried conversation of Dagur, Nidhud, and Dolan, bending over the tainted crystal. Then he realized there were too many voices to belong to the mages. The voices echoed from all over the chamber, growing in number until the whispers and chants clamored in his head.

Can you hear them?

Only through your gift, the Wraith Lord said. *Listen to them, Connor. They may be our salvation. What do they want?*

Connor strained to hear the murmurs clearly. Some spoke in accents strange to him, choosing words Connor had seen only in old manuscripts. *Ghosts,* he thought. *It's not enough to be possessed by one spirit. Now the dead are coming out of the rocks to have a go at it!*

Yet as Connor listened, the voices grew distinct, clearer. He did not fear them trying to seize his body. With the Wraith Lord in possession, that was not likely. The ghosts were calling to him, urging him on, leading him out of the labyrinth. As he reached the center and began the return leg of the maze, the voices grew stronger, and their forms began to take shape all along the outside of the labyrinth.

Power crackled in the air. Even with the Wraith Lord's control, he nearly stumbled, feeling as if the maze pulled life and breath from him. Live mages had joined their ghostly counterparts, and Connor realized that they were fighting to dispel the miasma projected by the tainted crystal.

Only a bit more, the Wraith Lord said, and Connor could hear the strain in Vandholt's voice.

If this had occurred to someone not possessed by a spirit of your strength— Connor began.

That person would be dead, the Wraith Lord finished.

Connor knew that the Wraith Lord's strength was sustaining him. Breath burned in his lungs from cold and exertion. His legs cramped from straining against the invisible force that did not want them to escape the maze. Blood welled beneath his fingertips as he dug his nails into his palms, willing himself to move.

Yet with every step that wound them out of the labyrinth, Connor could breathe a little easier. Halfway out, and the air had grown a bit warmer, though it was still frigid even for a subterranean chamber. The voices of the ghosts were clearer and louder now, and the chants of the living mages seemed to cut a path for him through the force that wanted to trap him within the maze.

Step by labored step, they struggled to reach the end of the labyrinth. Just an arm's length to go, and the vortex of power around the maze made one final surge to keep him captive. It took all of the Wraith Lord's strength to hurl Connor across the threshold. Behind them, the ghosts closed ranks, sealing off the labyrinth's exit.

For a moment, Connor lay panting on the cold stone. Then he realized that although he was out of the labyrinth, the power had not abated, nor had the freezing-cold air warmed. An answer impressed itself on him, spoken by ghostly whispers. Connor knew what he had to do.

Let the mages handle this, the Wraith Lord urged.

If they could, it would be handled by now, Connor snapped, unwilling to hesitate lest he lose his nerve.

You don't know this will work.

You can't say it won't, Connor challenged.

Dagur, Dolan, and Nidhud looked at Connor with alarm as he approached the table where the presence-crystals lay. One of them flared red, and the others' glow intensified, so that the twelve pulsed together in a different rhythm from that of the crimson crystal.

"The ghosts have a plan," Connor said, pushing past the mages.

"We've tried to counter it with all the different skills of magic we have among us," Dagur replied.

"Let an immortal handle this, Connor," Dolan said, trying to block Connor's path.

Connor moved around him. "I have the Wraith Lord with me. And the ghosts. They're all immortal."

Dolan grimaced. "You can still die."

"So can Blaine—and that's what will happen if we can't cleanse the thirteenth crystal," Connor said. "Now, move out of my way."

To his surprise, Dolan yielded, stepping back from the table. The mages drew away as the ghosts rushed forward. Dozens had become hundreds, though where they came from or how they knew to gather, Connor had no idea. Penhallow stepped up behind him.

"I will do what I can to help," Penhallow said. "Let's hope your ghosts are strong enough."

If the crystal is controlled by one spirit, let's see whether a hundred ghosts can crowd it out, Connor thought grimly.

Afraid that the *divi*'s power would try to push him back as it had hampered him in the labyrinth, Connor made a dive for the red crystal. As his hands closed around its cool surface, he opened his mind to the ghosts.

Fill me, he said. *Seize the stone.*

Spirits too numerous to count washed over him, entering his consciousness, streaming past the Wraith Lord, and through Connor's skin into the pulsing crystal. Never had he felt so much power flood his senses. Lifetimes blurred as the dead passed through his thoughts too quickly to grasp, leaving a shadow of themselves behind.

At the core of his being, Connor's essence clung to the spirit of the Wraith Lord like a man awash in a flood tide. The *divi* was not fully present in the crystal, yet the shred of itself tainting the stone was more than mere memory or the remnant of a spell. Souls poured through Connor's veins, seeped through his skin channeled by bone and sinew, through his hands into the glowing crystal. The *divi* howled in rage, and for a moment, Connor feared it would swell to its full power and retake the presence-crystal. Ghost after ghost crowded the stone, forcing out the *divi*'s power, and breath by breath, the crimson glare began to fade.

The rush of spirits pulled at Connor's soul, and had the Wraith Lord not managed to anchor him, Connor was afraid he might have been hollowed, his essence drawn out from him, leaving his body an empty husk. Kierken Vandholt held on to him, like a man caught in the storm surge, clinging to Connor even when the pain grew unbearable and Connor begged for death.

Teeth pierced Connor's arm, and as blood flowed, the *kruvgaldur* pushed to the forefront, binding Connor to his body and to his master. Joined by blood, Penhallow lent his strong, old spirit to the effort.

The *divi* shrieked in rage and pain one last time, and then was gone. Connor opened his eyes. Clutched in his hands so tightly he was not sure he could release his grip, the presence-crystal glowed with golden light. All around him, the ghosts poured from the crystal, relinquishing it now that their task was finished. Connor felt the *kruvgaldur* bond recede, though

Penhallow remained as vivid a presence in his mind as the Wraith Lord.

Strong arms encircled Connor from behind as gentle hands pried his fingers away from the cleansed crystal.

"Let go, Bevin. You did well. It's over. You won. Let go," Penhallow murmured over his shoulder. Dolan worked to loosen Connor's grip, and even his *talishte* strength was tested by the hold Connor had on the stone.

"I don't want to break any fingers," Dolan said. "It's safe now. The *divi*'s gone, and from the look of it, the ghosts intend to stand watch. Let me take the crystal. You need to rest."

Slowly, Connor willed himself to let go, although his fingers were cramped into claws and the muscles in his hands and arms ached when they released. He felt as if he had clung by his fingertips to a mountaintop in a raging storm. Dolan took the crystal from him and replaced it with the others. Only then did Connor feel the toll the night's work had taken. Even the Wraith Lord seemed spent, and Connor would have collapsed had Penhallow not caught him.

Dolan looked up as one of Voss's guards came to the chamber entrance. "Sorry to interrupt, but we've got trouble," the soldier said. "Hennoch's back—and he's bringing an army. It will arrive after daybreak."

CHAPTER
THIRTY-ONE

V EDRAN POLLARD HAD GROWN TO HATE
Mirdalur.

*A year ago, I could barely find the godsforsaken place on a
map. Now it haunts me at every turn.* His mood was sour as
he rode to the attack. The sky had grown dark, and another
nasty storm was certain. Lysander had accepted his offer of
an alliance, then promptly relegated Pollard and Hennoch to
the backwater, attacking Mirdalur and its handful of soldiers
while Lysander and Rostivan took on McFadden and the other
warlords.

The worst part of the slight was that Lysander's judgment
was sound. Pollard hated to admit it, but his troops were too
battered, too worn down by a string of defeats to go against a
strong, well-armed force. He knew it, and he hated it, just like
he hated Mirdalur.

Traher Voss's mercenaries tried to be inconspicuous. Pollard
snorted quietly, amused at the thought. Voss's pack of smash-
nosed bruisers could no more be 'inconspicuous' than a bull
could fly. Certainly the guards took pains to hide themselves,
trying to make the ruins appear deserted. Yet anyone who

glimpsed Voss's soldiers would have suspected that something was afoot, something that required the service of large, dangerous men with big, deadly swords.

And then there were the mages.

If it had been up to Pollard, magic would have died with the Great Fire, and Blaine McFadden along with it. That magic—and McFadden—survived were two more pieces of evidence that he had not found the favor of the gods.

Still, saddled with the reality that magic had returned, Pollard had done his best to acquire a cadre of mages, even if that meant having his *talishte* associates ambush some of those mages and turn them against their will.

Today the human mages made the first move. Pollard kept his troops out of range while the miasma of magic descended on the outbuildings around Mirdalur's ruined tower. It was two hours after dawn, when any *talishte* should be bound to their crypt. Pollard had no desire to test his mages or his fighters against the Knights of Esthrane. He did not doubt that the Knights fully deserved their reputation. Yet the *talishte* mages had to sleep, and when they did, they were vulnerable.

Pollard watched with grim satisfaction as the mages sent their illusion against the mercenaries. The fear-and-distraction spell should have sent Voss's mercs running in circles, shitting their pants and screaming like children.

"What in Raka is wrong with the spell?" Pollard demanded, watching from a nearby hillock. He hoped to see carnage, soldiers turning on one another in confusion and panic, an easy opening for him to lead the charge. Instead, Pollard saw Voss's mercenaries assembling with top speed from their hiding places, seemingly unaffected by the magic.

"It's either a powerful defensive warding or they're all wearing some kind of null-magic charm," the flummoxed mage reported. "I suspect the warding," he added. "Such charms are difficult to come by."

"Magic that suits my purposes is difficult to come by," Pollard roared. He had hoped to sweep in and seize the ruined manor with little opposition. Now, having lost the element of surprise, the assault would be that much more difficult.

Pollard's vexation found release in his sword. The soldiers who swarmed from cover to repulse Hennoch's attack looked too seasoned and too scarred to belong to McFadden. He guessed that they were Voss's troops, mercenaries Penhallow had somehow convinced to ally with his cause.

"Mercs bleed like everyone else," Pollard muttered under his breath as he brought his sword down in a crushing blow. The sound of snapping bone and the feel of a blade sinking deep into flesh assuaged Pollard's anger, barely. It would take more deaths, many more, to spend his fury. But as the soldier fell away, bleeding out onto the hard-packed ground, Pollard was one death closer, he thought grimly.

That he and Hennoch were personally present for this strike was galling. It should have been the kind of maneuver delegated to an underling, to a captain or even a lieutenant. Yet rumors persisted that 'something' was happening at the abandoned old manor, and that meant too much was at stake if Pollard and his allies wished to halt McFadden in his tracks.

"If I'd known McFadden would be this much trouble, I'd have killed him years ago," Pollard growled, though no one could hear him. Voicing his thoughts gave vent to some of the pain from his proxy wounds, which rubbed raw and sore beneath his armor. His injuries put him at a disadvantage, and he knew that willpower alone might not be enough to compensate for them.

Voss's soldiers, well trained and seemingly indifferent to

death, posed a challenge. He seemed to recruit only those who were the size of a bull, and nearly as strong. Yet Pollard was certain that a vicious mood could outfight experience and training every time, and he was doing well at proving his theory to be true.

This time, Hennoch brought close to one hundred men with him, surely enough, Pollard thought, to crush a garrison. His mages and the fighters had instructions to pin down the *talishte*. The living he could deal with.

What McFadden wanted with Mirdalur, Pollard could only guess, but his guesses were troublesome enough. It was enough that McFadden was interested in Mirdalur. For that alone, Pollard was determined to deny it to him.

A smash-faced soldier ran at Pollard with a guttural cry. Pollard met his charge head-on, blocking his swing and answering with a series of blows that took the fighter back a pace. All the while, a corner of Pollard's mind remained unperturbed, assessing the mercenary's fighting style. Only a few strikes had been traded when Pollard saw the weak point: a tendency to reach a little too far with the swing.

Pollard intentionally took a step back as the mercenary swung again; then he thrust forward, scoring a fatal strike. He jerked the blade upward, suspending the soldier there for an instant, satisfied at the astonishment on the dying man's face. Then Pollard lowered his blade, letting the body slide down the length of his sword, stepping over the corpse to engage the next mercenary who ran from cover.

The effort made Pollard stumble, and the new opponent saw weakness, scything his sword so close that it took a slice from Pollard's ear and grazed his hair. One of Hennoch's soldiers interposed himself, taking the brunt of the attack as Pollard teamed up for the fight. It galled Pollard to have to require anyone's assistance, yet the debilitating wounds acquired since Reese's capture meant that Pollard had neither the strength nor the stamina he possessed before.

In the distance, Pollard could see Hennoch setting about himself with a two-handed sword. He was a useful barbarian, Pollard thought, but a savage nonetheless. Hennoch would never be more than a wealthy man's attack dog. Lysander, on the other hand, was canny enough to be dangerous. He would bear watching when Reese returned. *If* Reese returned.

"Some fun," Nilo shouted, holding his own against a fighter who was a head taller and a stone heavier.

"Never better," Pollard muttered, taking the chance to bring his sword up sharply, biting into his opponent's sword arm and severing the bone midway between wrist and elbow. On the return blow, he cut clean through the soldier's neck, grimacing as blood spattered his cloak and drenched his arms.

"What anyone wants with this pile of shit is beyond me," Pollard grumbled. Mirdalur had been a ruin for generations. Long before the Great Fire leveled Donderath's grand manors and the Cataclysm laid waste to the kingdom, Mirdalur had crumbled in silence, overrun by weeds, retaken by the birds and foxes.

Once, it had been a place for kings. Pollard knew the legends. Four centuries ago, King Merrill's ancestor and his chosen noblemen bound the wild magic to their command in a secret chamber at Mirdalur. That story had drawn Blaine McFadden when he returned from exile, and Pollard nearly had him within his grasp, only to lose his prize to an unexpected interloper. That loss still stung, and Pollard was determined not to have it repeated.

Hennoch's troops fought well. Voss's mercenaries battled with a ferocity Pollard had only seen in mad dogs. Already, the courtyard was strewn with corpses, the ruined fountain in its center polluted with blood.

"Off with you!" roared a mercenary who seemed as wide as a wagon and as muscled as an ox. Despite the freezing cold, he wore only a leather cuirass over his tunic. Black hair formed a wild cloud around his blunt-nosed face, and his bare arms were covered with runes and drawings of the gods inked into the skin. The battle ax in his hands scythed dangerously from side to side, already bloodied to its hilt.

Pollard took two steps back. If he could not fight strong, he would fight dirty. A throwing knife from a hidden sheath slipped into his hand. As the lumbering giant raised his ax to attack, Pollard sent the blade flying. It sank to the hilt in the big man's groin, felling him with a howl of agony. He kicked the ax away and stood just out of reach of the fighter's grasping hands as the mercenary writhed in pain. Then with a sure, clean strike he sent the man's head rolling.

The mages concentrated their initial attack on a large cistern to one side of the courtyard. Pollard had given orders for them to begin their assault there, believing that the stone shaft hid access to Mirdalur's underground levels. Fire scoured the walls of the well, searing the dark tunnel with concentrated heat so that flames erupted from the mouth of the well, shooting up into the sky and illuminating the courtyard like a massive torch. Other mages sent tremors deep beneath the surface, in hopes of causing underground rooms and corridors to collapse.

The soldiers cried out in alarm and cursed in anger as the ground rumbled and trembled beneath their feet. A nasty grin spread across Pollard's face as he pictured the quakes burying the sleeping *talishte*. Focusing on his anger helped him deal with the pain from the raw sore in the center of his chest and the ceaseless itching from the rest of his skin, made worse by armor and violent movement.

One of Voss's men came at Pollard, and he waded into the fray, feeling his rage find its way into his sword, his anger spending with every swing and slash. Battle cleansed him, purging the dark thoughts—at least for a while—and reminding him with every spray of blood what it meant to be alive. Battle made him feel vital, yet the wounds he bore for his master took their toll. Nilo ran to join the fight, and Pollard knew that his second-in-command would not have done so had Pollard been at his former strength.

The mages had expanded their fiery attack, scouring every one of the stone buildings aboveground with flame. Voss's men, pushed from their hiding places by the mage-sent fires, took on Hennoch's troops with an edge that smacked of personal vendetta. This was the kind of fight Pollard relished, when combatants had a stake in the action, fighting not for gold or promotion but for the chance to thrash someone who had done them wrong.

"Go tell your biter masters that your little game is over," Pollard grated as he swung, parrying a blow hard enough to make his teeth rattle. He spun, blocking another strike, unsure just how long he could hold both men at bay, and committed himself to finding out.

"That's rich, coming from you, with a biter master of your own," one of the men growled. He made no pretense of technique, expecting sheer power to win the day, driving Pollard back several steps with a series of hard, fast strikes that tested Pollard's reactions.

Pollard struck high with the sword in his right hand, intending to thrust with the large knife in his left. The mercenary blocked the high strike, but before Pollard could score a fatal blow, the fighter swung his sword in an arc, striking the knife with such power that it numbed Pollard's hand and sent the blade flying.

Pollard and the mercenary circled each other warily, looking for weakness. The mercenary, with his broad shoulders and thickly muscled arms, likely outweighed Pollard by a good bit. Pollard was strong, muscular for a man his age, but not as massive as his opponent, who was likely half his age.

"Tired, old man?" the fighter taunted.

"Scared, young pup?" Pollard rejoined.

Pollard had regained feeling in his left hand, and he drew a shiv out of the folds of his clothing, letting it fall into his grip out of sight. He lunged toward the fighter, ignoring his pain and mounting an attack with his full strength and fury. Skill, training, and long practice fighting while wounded drove Pollard's movements, giving him a moment's grace to keep up the attack with his sword while awaiting the moment for the death strike.

The mercenary's attention was fully invested in tracking Pollard's sword. He never spotted the flick of the wrist that sent the shiv speeding toward him, or Nilo coming up from behind to stab him through the back. The fighter looked with astonishment at the hilt-deep knife protruding from his chest, staining his filthy shirt crimson. Cursing Pollard and consigning him to the depths of Raka, the mercenary stumbled, swinging wildly with his sword, before collapsing to his knees and falling facedown in the dirt.

Only then did Pollard realize that another, more dangerous enemy had arisen.

Heavy fog rolled in fast, blanketing the courtyard so thickly that Pollard could not see his boots. The day's weather had been cold, threatening snow, with no swing in temperature to cause the mist. The fog felt sticky, yet cold enough that Pollard wondered how it had not frozen. There was no wind, yet the fog moved swiftly, as if driven by a gale. The air took on an oppressive weight, and the cold went straight to the bone. Pollard fought off a shiver, aware that fear, more than frost, had set his teeth to chattering.

Figures were rising out of the center of the fog. Pollard could not be certain, as the mist billowed and roiled, whether it was one face, eyeing them maliciously, or many. At first, the fog was like a sheet of muslin, stretched tight over a corpse's face, rendering features hidden and distorted. Then the fog folded in on itself, and it seemed to Pollard that ranks of shadowed figures walked just hidden within the fog, blurred and insubstantial but no less real.

The fog was rising. It was up to the soldiers' chests, like a swelling tide, and Pollard heard muttering and curses among his men. Voss's fighters had withdrawn for the moment, making Pollard even more suspicious.

"Mages! We need light!" Pollard shouted, readying his sword should an enemy charge from the mist.

Obligingly, a glare of blindingly white light bathed the courtyard, and for a moment, Pollard and the others could see the shapes more clearly despite the fog, like figures backlit behind a scrim. Whatever walked toward them out of the mist was not human, or at least, was human no longer. Elongated arms with clawlike fingers hung at their sides, and their loose-limbed legs sauntered with the feral assurance of a big cat stalking its prey. Something about the heads was wrong, misshapen, with lantern jaws that could hold long, sharp teeth. Worse, in the glimpse they got of the fog figures, they looked distressingly solid, more so with every step they took, though it seemed to take them a while to emerge.

As if they're coming from a long way, Pollard thought. *As if they've walked here from the Unseen Realm itself.*

Something deep in Pollard's bones screamed for him to run. He started into the fog, terrified and curious, wondering whether the mage-warrior Knights of Esthrane had woken from their daytime slumber to somehow raise the dead. A disquieting thought occurred to him.

The Wraith Lord was cursed to walk the Unseen Realm. If he could cross that void, perhaps he could open the door for others to follow him . . .

"Retreat!" Hennoch's voice carried through the fog. "Fall back!"

Pollard felt a guilty rush of shame in the relief that flooded him, just for an instant, as he echoed the call. The things in the fog slowed their advance, as if giving the attackers one last chance at self-preservation.

Voss's soldiers had no such reserve.

Roaring like wild beasts, wide-eyed as berserkers, Voss's mercenaries came out screaming from the edges of the fog. Even they were careful not to slip among the shadow beings in the mist. Whether these were fresh soldiers or whether they had just taken new courage in the pause, Pollard did not know, but the mercenaries swept forward with savage purpose, battle axes and war hammers replacing their swords.

Pollard's soldiers fled, with Hennoch's men hard on their heels. Voss's soldiers ran fast enough to cut down stragglers from the rear lines, harrying them well past the boundaries of the Mirdalur walls. Those whose mounts awaited them nearly flew into their saddles before setting their heels to the horses' sides, while the foot soldiers ran for their lives.

Voss's men left off their pursuit at the edge of the forest, sending them on their way with catcalls and jeers, infuriating laughter and insults. The fog did not rest. Tendrils of heavy fog slunk around the horses' hooves, and wound in and out of the trees. Shadows moved in the fog, allowing disquieting glimpses from time to time, as if the ghosts of Mirdalur had taken it upon themselves to form an ethereal escort, to assure that none of the soldiers would double back to resume the fight.

There was little chance of that, Pollard thought bitterly. Their fleeing soldiers nearly outpaced the horses, which were unusually jittery and ill-tempered. The retreating army soon learned to keep to the center of the forest road after wisps of the fog spooked their horses. The horses bucked and sent their riders flying, landing in the hedgerow with broken bones and snapped necks.

Maybe the Wraith Lord means to hunt us down a few at a time, Pollard thought, aware that he gripped his reins white-knuckled. Inside, he was torn between shame at having run and resignation, aware that a seasoned soldier knows when to retreat to fight another day.

Fog made the forest miserably cold and damp, and it seemed to Pollard that the shadows were unnaturally dark for mid-day. It was as if the sunlight could not penetrate the branches, though Pollard had ridden this way many times in daylight and found nothing strange.

The road broadened when they emerged from the forest, and the fog hung back, its duty completed. Hennoch's men put on a burst of speed when the bright daylight came into view, riding at a gallop or running full-out to get out of the shadows and into the cold, clear light of day.

Pollard turned as he reached the crest of a small rise, and looked back at the forest. The fog lingered, stretching along the edge of the forest and filling the road as if to block it. No natural fog moved like that, confirming the certainty of every primal sense. Pollard did not know whether the fog could project emotions, whether it tinkered with their minds, but when he spurred his mount and rode down the other side of the rise, losing the forest to view, he felt a weight lift from his shoulders and the light, somehow, seemed brighter.

For a long time, the army rode in silence. None of the soldiers seemed disposed to the usual banter or bawdy comments, their way to celebrate a victory or take the sting from a defeat. The retreat hung heavily on all of them. Pollard brooded, steeping in self-recrimination and loathing as he rode. His wounds made it agonizing to ride or move, and he bit his lip to keep from crying out. Blood tinged the hem of the shirt he wore under his cuirass, not from battle damage but from the sore, and from where his skin was rubbed raw with the lesions. Cursing under his breath, he gritted his teeth and spurred his horse to catch up to Hennoch, who was near the front of the group.

"What now?" Hennoch asked, not making eye contact as Pollard joined him.

"We regroup," Pollard replied, having already replayed this conversation a dozen times in his mind before he rode forward.

"Against that?" Hennoch asked in disbelief. "I can lead an army against men. I can rally troops against *talishte*, though it's a suicide cause. But something powerful called those spirits, and it was too damn much for us to handle."

Pollard could hear the fear in Hennoch's voice, and recognized it as his own. Yet it would not do to allow his liegeman to see that. "There's always a way," Pollard said, voice rough with courage he did not feel. "*Talishte* aren't invincible and neither are mages."

"They don't have to be invincible," Hennoch replied. "They only have to be stronger than we are."

It was evening by the time they reached Solsiden, weary and defeated. Pollard did not look forward to recounting the day's misadventure to Lysander, and his temper flared at the expected humiliation of having been assigned an objective and failing to achieve it.

Pollard felt his spirits lift, just a bit, as they rode up to the front of the manor house. Despite everything else, he was home. His clothes were bloody from the fight and dirty from the road. Muscles and joints ached from the pounding of battle and the interminable ride, sorer than they should be from the fight alone. His proxy wounds were taking a steep toll, and it would likely be some time before he recovered enough to fight again. Worse, his battle wounds were serious enough to require the attention of a healer, and he loathed revealing his weakness. Most of all, Pollard wanted to pour himself some brandy and nurse his grievances in solitude.

Hennoch and his troops veered off before they neared the manor, returning to their camp. The mages went with them. Nilo accompanied Pollard to Solsiden, along with his personal guard.

"Was it the Wraith Lord, do you think, who summoned the fog spirits?" Nilo asked, now that they had some privacy for the first time since the battle.

Pollard shrugged ill-temperedly. "Perhaps. Who knows? I never heard that any of the Knights of Esthrane were necromancers, but then again, they've hardly trumpeted their abilities for all to know."

"What will you do about Lysander?" Nilo asked, undeterred by Pollard's foul mood. He had weathered many of Pollard's rages, and he met them all with an unflappable equanimity that got under Pollard's skin all the more for its affability.

Pollard let out a string of curses until his temper was spent, then sighed and shrugged. "Damned if I know, Nilo. Things went wrong today. Perhaps mages can't be conscripted, even if they're bound by the *kruvgaldur* to our *talishte*. Could they have done more to push back against those...things?" He shrugged once more. "Could they? Who knows. Perhaps."

"Then again, if it really was the Wraith Lord who pried the gates of the Unseen Realm ajar, could anyone have stood against it?" Nilo countered.

"Humph," Pollard said, unconvinced.

Nilo raised an eyebrow. "Look at it this way. There's no glory in leading an army into slaughter for ego's sake."

Pollard glowered at him. "Perhaps not," he admitted grudgingly.

Nilo let that go, perhaps realizing there was no good reply. But after a silence, Nilo slid a glance toward Pollard. "What of the wounds?" he asked.

Pollard took his meaning immediately. Nilo was not inquiring about the damage Pollard had taken in the battle: a few gashes and bruises that would heal. Pollard knew that Nilo meant the wounds he endured from Reese's captivity, which had grown steadily worse.

"Not good," he admitted. The wounds that mimicked his *talishte* master's torture wore at his body and soul. It was impossible to move, to think, to sleep without them at the fore-front of his mind. The skin lesions rubbed so against his tunic that without an undershirt of fine silk his skin was covered in a bloody sheen from even mild exertion. He was certain his shirt would be stuck to the blood when he retired for bed, after the action of the fight.

Worst of all was the sore on his chest. It ached to the bone with every breath. Pollard was certain that he would succumb to Reese's wounds long before the fifty-year imprisonment was over, even if his master did not.

"I just want sufficient brandy for the pain and a night's rest," Pollard said, certain Nilo could hear the weariness in his voice.

They rounded the bend, and found Solsiden bright with lights. Pollard felt his temper flare. "Who would dare—" he started, but before he could finish his sentence, he knew. *Talishte*, he thought. *For some reason, the* talishte *have come. I would know if Reese ceased to exist. So the alternative...*

"What do you want me to do?" Nilo asked quietly. He had intended to stay the night at the manor. Kerr would have been expecting both of them after the battle, and made ready with dinner and whatever healing supplies were necessary. These new, unwelcome *talishte* intruders called for a change of plans, and until he knew what they wanted, Pollard decided to keep Nilo clear of his new "guests."

"Go back to camp," Pollard said as they slowed their horses to a halt just beyond the manor wall. "I'll send for you in the morning, once I know what's going on."

Nilo nodded. "Very well," he said, turning his horse in the direction from which they had just come. "Good night."

Pollard gave a curt nod in reply, but he was certain his night would be anything but good.

Warily, Pollard rode the rest of the way in silence, accompanied by his guards. At the front of the manor, he saw no horses tethered, yet footprints marked the light dusting of snow that had fallen in the last candlemark. A groom ran out to grab the reins to his horse as Pollard swung down from his saddle. An effort of will was required not to wince at the strain the movement put on his wounds.

"M'lord," the groom said, rushing to his side. "Are you injured?"

"Not remarkably," Pollard replied, doing his best to mask the limp from a wound to his leg. He was quite aware that he looked like he had come from battle, and under other circumstances, that might have made for a triumphant entrance.

Tonight, he wanted to wash away the taint of failure and the smell of blood before having to face an audience.

Realizing how unlikely he was to get his wish, Pollard squared his shoulders and handed off the reins without a backward glance, striding toward the house on sheer strength of will.

Kerr awaited him at the door, looking worried. "M'lord," he said, taking in Pollard's appearance. "Do you require a healer?"

"Later," he replied. "Who's here?"

Kerr looked abashed. "*Talishte*, sir. Lord Reese's people, and they insisted that they be permitted to wait for your return." His expression showed his disapproval. "I tried to convince them to delay until you had the opportunity to have a proper return from battle, but they can be quite obstinate."

"We can be *very* obstinate, when we wish it."

Pollard recognized the voice. Vasily Aslanov stood in the doorway to the parlor, looking as if he owned the place. Tall and slender, with a mane of blond hair that fell to his shoulders and sharp, ratlike features with cold, dark eyes, Aslanov was trouble. Pollard had heard Reese speak of him on several occasions with grudging admiration, a powerful *talishte* not of Reese's get, and quite possibly one of the Elders. Pollard knew that while Aslanov and Reese had sometimes over the centuries been rivals, of late they had brokered a truce that occasionally found common rewards.

"Why are you here?" Pollard asked with as much cold disdain as he could muster. He knew that Aslanov could smell the blood from the battle and that his *talishte* senses easily read Pollard's injuries and weariness. Yet it galled Pollard that Aslanov stood between him and his brandy, and he was too tired and miserable to have any fear left.

Aslanov looked amused at Pollard's bravado. "We've come to discuss your long-overdue master," he said. "Join us."

Warily, Pollard followed Aslanov into the parlor. He bristled when Aslanov gestured for him to have a seat, and instead strode over to his brandy and poured himself a stiff drink. Only then did he sit down, and in his own favored chair, not the one Aslanov offered.

"I've just come from battle, and I'm not in a mood for company, so let's get down to business," Pollard snapped. After the cold day of battle and traveling, he took comfort in the fire that blazed in the fireplace, though its warmth meant nothing to the *talishte*.

Aslanov was one of five *talishte* who stood or sat in the parlor, likely the oldest of the group. *Even older than Reese*, Pollard recalled.

Another man, whom Pollard knew only as Kiril, leaned against the wall with his arms crossed over his chest. A woman he did not recognize sat in one of the chairs near the fire, watching them all with a bored expression. She had dark hair swept up in a knot and a thin, finely featured face, and Pollard wondered if she had been noble before she was turned. Perched on the corner of Pollard's desk was another stranger, a dark-haired man whose face was darkened with a hint of stubble, in his early thirties when he was turned, with the streetwise look of a pickpocket.

The fifth man Pollard recognized. Marat Garin was one of Reese's most loyal followers, and possibly one of the first Reese had turned. Garin's forehead was a bit too high, his eyes slightly too close together to look of Donderan blood. Garin often proved his loyalty to Reese by executing those who displeased Reese, whether mortal or *talishte*.

"We're going to get Lord Reese," Aslanov said as matter-of-factly as if he had proposed a trip to Castle Reach.

Pollard sipped his brandy, enjoying the feel of it burning down his throat. "Are you, now?" he said. "How's that?"

"We believe we've found a weakness in the manor where he's being held," Garin replied. "One we can exploit."

Pollard did not look up. He regarded the amber liquor and gave it a swirl, watching it catch the light. "Why come here? Why tell me?"

"Since Westbain has been seized by the enemy, and our resources are few, it makes sense to bring him here, now that Solsiden has been fortified," Aslanov replied.

"So bring him," Pollard said with a shrug.

Aslanov regarded Pollard for a moment, as if weighing how to reply. "Reese relied greatly on you," he said. "There is assistance—and protection—you can offer, being mortal, which we cannot. We wish you to prepare."

"In case you hadn't noticed, we're in the middle of a war," Pollard replied, taking another slug of brandy. "Against people Lord Reese regarded as his enemies. I can't guarantee his safety—or my own—if you bring him here."

"We will guard him," Aslanov said. "As for your war, I've already called more of his brood to join in the fight. It's nearing its conclusion. I believe that with our help, your master's enemies will be defeated."

"Why rescue him now, before the battle's won?" Pollard challenged. "Why not wait until the fighting's done so he can return with greater safety?"

Aslanov favored him with a thin-lipped smile. "Reese does not desire safety," he said reprovingly. "He intends to claim the spoils."

CHAPTER
THIRTY-TWO

I WANT TO MAKE A SWEEP OF IT," VIGUS QUINTREL said, eyeing his battle mages. "After this campaign, Rostivan will control a crescent from the Riven Mountains down to the sea," he said. His face was alight with excitement as he gestured at the maps he had tacked up on the wall.

Carensa could see the clearly marked sections that showed the bounds of each of the warlords' territories. To the northeast of Castle Reach, Rodestead House, Westbain, and Lundmyhre anchored the land protected by Lanyon Penhallow, Traher Voss, and Kierken Vandholt. Stretching north from there, anchored by Solsiden, were the lands of Pentreath Reese and Vedran Pollard, protected by Larska Hennoch's troops. Lysander's territory lay between the areas claimed by Rostivan, Verner, and the Solveigs, including the lands that had once belonged to the Arkalas, though the ambitious warlord clearly had plans to expand that.

Rostivan's lands were in the far north, up against the foothills of the Riven Mountains, but Quintrel's plans, if they succeeded, would give him a sickle-shaped swath that took the Solveigs' territory in the northwest down through Verner's holdings and Blaine McFadden's lands, seizing Glenreith, Quillarth Castle, and the seaport of Castle Reach.

The plan was audacious. It was also, in Carensa's opinion, suicidal.

"Yesterday decided nothing, yet a lot of men died," Guran pointed out. "There's little to be done until the storms lift."

Quintrel glowered, displeased with Guran's observation. "Nothing?" he challenged. "We probed the enemy's weaknesses. We learned what their mages were able—or willing—to do. Those dead men are that many fewer we have to kill to gain our objective. I would hardly call that 'nothing.'"

Guran inclined his head to show deference. "I misspoke," he said, hastily retreating. Carensa knew that Guran's opinion had not changed a whit, yet they gained nothing by antagonizing Quintrel, especially when he was already manic.

"Rostivan performed well yesterday," Quintrel said, beginning to pace. "Yet he lacks will. Several times, he would have drawn back had we not controlled him and pushed him to press on."

Rostivan is a seasoned commander, Carensa thought. *If he wanted to pull back, there was good reason. Vigus doesn't care how many men die so long as he gets what he wants. He's planning to make this battle his last stand.*

"What of Lysander?" Guran asked. "His troops engaged McFadden's and the Solveigs directly."

Quintrel's eyes were alight with the excitement of the fight. "Lysander has proven more malleable than I thought," he replied. "We're very happy with him." The *divi* orb pulsed beneath Quintrel's shirt. Carensa was grateful that her magic did not resonate with the *divi*. Something about its appearance reminded her of a large feline predator, content to wait for the right moment to kill.

"Lysander's Tingur proved useful," Quintrel said. "They and their beasts exacted quite a price from McFadden's forces. A shame they're used up now."

Used up, Carensa thought with disgust. *Not 'dead,' just 'used up,' like a tool. Expendable, like all of us.*

"What next?" Guran asked. Quintrel had summoned his senior mages to regroup over dinner. Esban had gone to make sure that the other mages were at work on their tasks. Half of the mages who had left Valshoa still lived. Several of those who had died were among the most senior practitioners, pushed to the limits of their ability by Quintrel. The rest of the mages were in their tents, preparing for the next day's battle. That left Carensa and Guran alone with Quintrel.

The *divi* was riding Quintrel hard, Carensa thought. Since the mages left Valshoa, Quintrel had grown thin and haggard. His skin now had a sallow cast, and his eyes shone with madness. Quintrel was fading, but the *divi*'s pulse grew stronger, yet Quintrel did not seem to notice.

"With McFadden tied up here, it's safe to say he's had no chance to use the crystals," Quintrel said. "And if he dies here, our problem has been solved."

"You sent Pollard to Mirdalur," Guran said. "Do you really think he can wrest the crystals back from the Knights of Esthrane and Voss's troops?"

Quintrel shrugged. "If not, and he dies, it's a rival eliminated. Without Reese, Pollard and Hennoch have only a fraction of their former power. If he succeeds, and we successfully eliminate McFadden, we are free to anchor the power as we will."

Carensa repressed a shiver. She had a growing sense that when Quintrel said 'we,' he did not mean the mages. She could not avoid a glance at the contentedly pulsing *divi* orb. She knew who 'we' really meant.

"If Pollard should by chance succeed, you'd gain both the crystals and Mirdalur's ritual chamber," Guran noted. "What then?"

Quintrel's expression was ecstatic. "Then we remake the Continent to our liking," he said, excitement clear in his voice. "If Dolan's gone to prepare the chamber, he won't last long. The taint in the presence-crystal will only activate in the presence of strong magic, so any attempt to work the anchoring ritual should trigger it. When the crystal activates, everyone nearby dies."

"You expected Dolan to steal the crystals?" Guran asked skeptically.

"Foresight warned me of betrayal," Quintrel replied. "I took precautions. The *divi* could lift the taint for those we choose to work the ritual without harm." He shrugged. "It would have also been easy to offer the crystals to McFadden and watch him take the bait."

"Without McFadden either as a willing partner or as a prisoner, how do you expect to make the anchoring work?" Guran probed. They had asked Quintrel the same questions directly and indirectly several times, and each time, Quintrel sidestepped the answer.

"We have everything we need," Quintrel replied, with a smile that gave Carensa no reassurance.

"Have you chosen your twelve?" Carensa asked. "Your new Lords of the Blood?" That was the missing piece. The thought had occurred to her in the middle of the previous night, when she lay awake listening to the sounds of the army camp, wondering how she had ever landed in the midst of such insanity. Quintrel's answer would make all the difference, because it augured the direction of Donderath's future.

"I've had a change in my thinking about that," Quintrel said.

"Anchor the magic to thirteen fragile mortals, and the cycle of destruction and chaos is set in motion all over again. Anchor magic to immortal spirits, and we never need endure anything like the Great Fire again."

"What do you mean, 'immortal spirits'?" Guran probed. "Ghosts? Souls?"

Quintrel shook his head impatiently. "My Guide," he said, reaching up to stroke the *divi* crystal, "has many brothers. Twelve more spirits await my call. Their magic, combined with ours, properly anchored, would make us invincible."

Carensa frowned. "But what of the blood?" she asked, fearing the answer even as she framed the question. "The ritual is bound to the bloodline of those who work the magic."

"As are the spirits," Quintrel replied, his face glowing with excitement. "The spirits join with their mortal hosts. Our blood is the catalyst, their magic binds the power."

"Thirteen mortals who are no longer exactly mortal," Guran repeated carefully as if he struggled to make certain he had heard correctly. "And the magic, controlled by the spirits, would pass from generation to generation?"

Quintrel nodded enthusiastically. "Yes. The spirit would pass from father to firstborn son when the father dies. Over time, the spirit would become one with its host."

Carensa struggled to hide her horror. The mental image of a *divi* abandoning the cooling corpse of its prior host and claiming an endless series of victims gave her chills. *That's what's happened with Vigus,* she thought, eyeing Quintrel and noting the changes in his appearance. *If that's how it would go for all the hosts, I don't imagine their lives will be long.*

Carensa had searched the manuscripts for any references to the *divi*. Most of the citations were oblique, vague references that seemed to expect the reader to already know something about the spirits, details that went unsaid but that she suspected were essential. Finally, she had found one old manuscript whose writer spoke plainly. He had written of the Genitors, the First Ones, monsters made not by the gods nor by magic, beings from the chaos that birthed the world.

Those Genitors, the *divi*, had eventually been rooted out at the cost of immense slaughter. The uprising against the spirits had cost the lives of thousands of mortals and hundreds of mages. And when the *divi* were bound, more lives were lost to work the type of forbidden spells necessary to send the *divi* to oblivion in the Unseen Realm.

Parasites, she thought. *That's what the* divi *were. And if the old manuscript is right, there won't just be thirteen of them. Once they control the magic, they'll bring their friends to feast on us.*

There had been another reason Carensa had lain awake the night before, and many other nights. Quintrel's lack of concern for life—the lives of his followers, the mages, and the soldiers—deepened her conviction that somehow he needed to be brought to heel. She and Guran, speaking briefly and always in code, had agreed on as much. Every night, Carensa tried to imagine a way even a small number of mages might be able to act against Quintrel, and every night she fell asleep without finding an answer.

She had realized months before that Quintrel was a danger, even prior to discovering that the *divi* controlled his thoughts. A mad mage was worrisome enough, but the danger grew when Quintrel bent Lysander and Rostivan to his will. Through Lysander, Quintrel had a hold over Pollard and Hennoch, and all of the mages not allied with McFadden, now that the Arkala twins were dead. Those forces were arrayed for this battle on the northern plains.

Verner's army had already been badly damaged. If the others

fell, there would be nothing in the way to keep Quintrel from carrying out his version of the ritual to bind the magic, and the *divi* spirits would return from their exile and find a world of potential hosts to be drained. Something had to be done. Somehow it had to be stopped. Carensa struggled to control her expression as inside she felt utterly at a loss.

"Lysander's mercenaries are a problem," Quintrel said, bringing Carensa's attention back to the conversation. "Damned border men. His messenger arrived a candlemark ago, and I can barely understand the man, with his backwoods talk."

"Carensa can be of help for that," Guran said, and as Carensa startled, she saw him meet her gaze. "She can make sure your orders are translated correctly, so there's no misunderstanding."

Carensa felt the missing piece slip into place at Guran's look, needing no telepathy or code to make his message clear. There was one way to damage Quintrel, one way to stop his vision. If he could be defeated in battle, despite the odds he had stacked in his favor, the *divis* would remain bound and Donderath would not face the caprice of an insane mage. But the price would be steep.

"How can I help?" she asked, managing a smile. She was grateful that Quintrel was not a telepath.

"I'll have a messenger bring you the orders I draw up for Lysander in a candlemark, once I finish. You'll translate them into that damned nonsense the border men speak so there's no misunderstanding," Quintrel said.

"What's the plan?" Guran asked.

Quintrel smiled. With his gaunt face and his hollow eyes, the expression was far more skull-like than Carensa remembered it being only a few months before. "Verner's troops continue to be the weak point in McFadden's front line. The beasts and Tingur hurt McFadden's troops, but the Solveigs are still quite strong.

"I'll keep Rostivan focused on Theilsson and Voss. I think our mages can break theirs with a little effort," he said, his grin becoming a smirk. "Lysander needs to smash the Solveig line. I believe that once the Solveigs fold, McFadden and Verner won't be able to withstand us on their own," he added. "And every day the magic remains unstable, it drains McFadden, perhaps to the breaking point."

"McFadden's a fighter, and Tormod Solveig's power is still an unknown," Guran said. "Are we certain there's no weakness of Lysander's that they might exploit?"

Quintrel seemed pleased by Guran's concern. Carensa read a darker meaning, that Guran was intentionally feeding her information. The battle was likely to be decided in the next day. What Carensa told the messenger could easily determine who won—and who lost.

"Lysander's spent his Tingur and their beasts, which will annoy him, because he doesn't like to use his soldiers until he's softened up the enemy," Quintrel remarked, and it struck Carensa that his talk of 'spending' lives made it seem like nothing more than coins. "He'll have to throw his best troops in up front, so I hope they haven't gotten soft, having the Tingur to lead the charge for them."

"What of his mages?" Guran asked. "Can they stand up to Tormod Solveig?"

Quintrel chuckled. "Oh, I think so. I've got a surprise planned for Solveig. Lysander's mages will loose a bit of the *divi* when Tormod Solveig uses his necromancy. *Divis* walk the Unseen Realm, like the restless dead," he said, warming to his subject.

"When Solveig opens himself to his magic, the *divi* will seize him, using the dead to drag his soul in to the Realm. Without Solveig, I don't think the others can last the rest of the day. They're counting on him to turn the tide." Quintrel looked quite pleased with himself.

He paused. "Now, if you'll excuse me, I need to finish writing the plan for Lysander, then meet with Rostivan. Watch for my messenger; he'll bring the plan to your tent," he said to Carensa.

Guran and Carensa walked together through the army camp in silence. *There were too many people nearby who would hear anything they might have said,* Carensa thought. And as she pondered her next move, she was not yet ready to talk, or perhaps afraid to say aloud the plans forming in her mind.

Guran stopped at the entrance to Carensa's tent. For a moment, she thought he might come in and set a warding to allow them to speak freely, but he did not. *No,* she thought, *it wouldn't do for us to make any move that might make Vigus suspicious, not now. Too much at stake.*

Instead, Guran managed a smile and met Carensa's gaze. "You've got important work to do," he said. "That message will determine the outcome of the battle, so you'll want to get it exactly right. You mustn't think about who will die. What matters is that the right outcome, the best outcome, is achieved." He nodded, but his smile did not quite reach his eyes. "I know that you'll do this brilliantly, and we'll all sit back and watch it happen together."

Carensa realized she was barely breathing. She felt cold in her marrow, something that had no connection to the temperature outside. Her heart was beating so hard she thought it might tear through her chest, and her mouth was dry. *He knows,* she thought. *And he is letting me know that the sacrifice is worth the outcome.*

Carensa reached out to squeeze Guran's hand. "Thanks," she said in a strangled voice. "I want to stand with you to watch it all play out."

"You will," Guran promised. "We're the guard of last resort. It's up to us to set it straight." He paused. "We'll be helping Vigus stay focused, so he's not distracted," he added with a meaningful glance. Carensa took his meaning immediately, that Guran and their other allies would try to divert Vigus's attention from whatever she did, for as long as possible.

Sweet Esthrane! Carensa thought. *It's come down to this. The outcome of the war, in our hands.*

There were a million things she wanted to say, but instead, she swallowed hard and nodded. "I'll wait for the messenger, then," she said. "And I'll stand with you in the morning." She ducked into her tent, and only then did she realize just how hard she was shaking.

Carensa paced her tent, thinking about her options. Every choice carried risks and consequences, and she knew there was only one chance.

We're plotting treason, or at the least, massive betrayal, she thought. *But when he accepted the* divi, *when he promised to give the magic over to those spirits, Vigus betrayed us. Vigus as the power behind the throne was bad enough. This...this would be intolerable.*

She had steeled herself to action when the messenger came to the door. To her relief, Vigus was not with him. "Come in," she said to the messenger. "This is going to take a little while."

"Master Quintrel says speed," the messenger said in broken Donderan.

"It must also be correct," Carensa said, summoning all her nerve to speak with authority. "Now, for me to put this into your language, I must hear you speak. Talk to me, and I will learn your words."

The messenger looked at her skeptically, but at her prompting, he told her of his journey from the front lines to Quintrel's position, of what he had seen and heard, and of his travels through the storm. Carensa listened intently, focusing her magic. She responded to his comments, at first a word or two, then short sentences, and finally, asking questions as naturally as if she had been speaking the messenger's border dialect all her life.

The man looked at her in wary amazement. "You talk like someone from my village," he said, a mixture of interest and fear clear in his eyes. "Yet before—"

"It's my magic," she said matter-of-factly, taking the folded parchment from him and sitting down at her portable writing desk. "Now I'll translate what Master Quintrel wrote so that your captains can understand."

If the messenger noticed her hand shaking as she took up the quill to write, Carensa hoped he would blame the cold. Carensa withdrew a clean piece of parchment and carefully smoothed it, stirred the ink, and set out the sand to blot. She forced herself to breathe, recognizing that if she succeeded, this paper would become her death warrant, and the order of execution for Guran and her allies as well as Quintrel and his *divi*.

With the messenger's dialect still clear in her mind, Carensa forced down thoughts of anything except the translation. She could not afford to dwell on the outcome, the loss, or her own willful betrayal. What mattered was the document, that it be clear and carry the force of legitimacy, and that it run completely counter to Quintrel's real orders.

Carensa looked up at the messenger, who stood a respectful distance from her writing table. "Did Master Quintrel review the plan with you?" she asked.

The messenger shook his head. "No, m'lady. It was sealed when I received it, and he said only that I must bring it directly to you for translation."

Carensa nodded and looked down, fearing her relief might show in her face. She broke the wax seal on Quintrel's document. "Very well," she said. It was unlikely that the messenger could read his own dialect let alone standard Donderan, but Carensa positioned the parchment so that Quintrel's plan was not visible to the man.

Quintrel's plan called for the mercenaries to make a lightning-fast charge against the center of the Solveigs' line while Lysander pounded away at Blaine's troops and Rostivan hammered Niklas and Voss. It was intended to force Tormod Solveig's hand, pushing him into expending his magic.

Carensa understood what Quintrel intended. Just as Lysander used the Tingur as expendable troops to wear down an enemy, Quintrel saw the mercenaries as equally disposable. Though Quintrel's plan did not say so, she knew that once Tormod Solveig had spent his most dangerous magic killing the mercenaries, Quintrel would use the mages to release the *divi* and kill the weakened necromancer.

I'm betraying Quintrel, Carensa thought, *but perhaps the mercenary should thank me. I'm likely saving his life and the lives of his companions.*

She wrote swiftly, afraid she might lose her nerve if she hesitated long enough to think. Magic supplied the translation and the words for Carensa to create false orders that would send the mercenaries in the opposite direction Quintrel intended. Once the troops were in action, there would be little Quintrel could do to stop them short of loosing his own magic against his ally's soldiers. If he did that, Carensa had no doubt that

Lysander's commanders, who were not under the control of the *divi*, would think it an enemy trick and fight to protect their warlord.

Quintrel ordered a rapid advance. Carensa's translation demanded a retreat. Quintrel intended to send the mercenaries like an arrow to the heart of the Solveig defenses. Carensa sent them against Rostivan's own rear flank. In the chaos, Rostivan's soldiers would defend themselves against what appeared to be Lysander's betrayal, diverting a goodly portion of Rostivan's army to fend off the attack.

The fighting was likely to push the front half of the troops into the forefront of the battle and deliver them into the sights of Tormod and Rinka Solveig and their army. Tormod Solveig, who had not yet loosed his full power in battle, Carensa suspected, would find a perfect target in Quintrel and her fellow mages. Once the mercenaries were deployed, Guran and their few allies would throw in their lot, doing whatever they could to undermine Rostivan and Quintrel until they were captured and killed. She could only hope Tormod would be able to withstand Quintrel's use of the *divi*.

We'll make our stand, Carensa thought as she blotted the ink with the sand and then carefully folded the parchment, melting wax to seal the document and pressing her ring into the wax to certify it. *And if we succeed, we'll die.*

CHAPTER
THIRTY-THREE

BLAINE MCFADDEN REELED, NEARLY LOSING HIS footing. His attacker's sword grazed Blaine's ear, landing a deep slice in his left shoulder. "You look tired," the Lysander soldier mocked. "Stand still, and I'll send you to your rest."

Blaine muttered a curse and brought his sword up sharply, knocking aside the soldier's blade and taking the man by surprise. He half lunged, half staggered forward to sink his second sword into the man's abdomen, nearly falling with the effort.

"The next fight will kill you," the soldier predicted as he fell, and Blaine feared he might be right.

Two days of battle against the combined forces of Lysander and Rostivan, and as yet there was no victor. Blaine's army defeated the Tingur advance force with their magic-born monsters, but Lysander's army was well trained and seemingly endless. Even with the Solveigs and Verner bringing their armies to bear, no one had yet punched a hole in the Lysander line.

Nightly runners brought updates from Niklas and the second front. Niklas's half of the army and Traher Voss's mercenaries battled Rostivan, backed by Vigus Quintrel's mages. What Rostivan might have lacked in sheer numbers he more than made up for in magic, and the last communiqué gave Blaine to understand Niklas was also at a stalemate.

"You need to tie up that gash," Kestel said, looking him over with a practiced eye. "Piran and I will cover you."

Blaine sank down to one knee, ripping a strip of fabric from his shirt to bind up the deep cut in his left arm. He felt light-headed, but he knew the injuries he had taken in battle caused only a portion of his problem. The magic was killing him.

Even though Niklas had volunteered to lead the assault against Rostivan—and therefore, Quintrel—to shield Blaine from the worst of the magic, nothing could protect him from it entirely, not even the magic-deflecting amulet Rikard had supplied. *If it weren't for the amulet, I'd probably be flat on my back—or worse—by now,* Blaine thought. The slash on his arm was just one of the many cuts and gouges he had sustained, plus more bruises and sore muscles than he wanted to think about. All of that he took in stride. But magic was not so easily dismissed.

Lysander's mages had kept up a near-constant barrage, requiring Blaine's mages to counterattack. Tormod Solveig had kept a low profile, but Blaine suspected that as the battle moved into the third day, Tormod would grow impatient with finesse. Rinka Solveig had already given up on restraint, leading her army in a headlong attack that almost broke the Lysander line. Almost, but not quite.

Across the valley, Birgen Verner's troops fought valiantly. Perhaps the son had more aptitude for warfare than the father, Blaine thought, because Birgen's tactics were daring, unexpected, and sometimes damn-fool crazy. *In other words, exactly what we need.*

Blaine realized early in the fight that Lysander really fielded three separate armies. The first, his Tingur allies, had been routed along with their beasts. The second group, made up of Meroven sellswords, swelled the ranks but fought without passion, as if they were counting the candlemarks until they received their pay, and were determined to live long enough to spend it. Blaine was sure that to Lysander, the mercenaries were as disposable as the Tingur, just better armed and somewhat better trained. The third group were Lysander's own soldiers, his elite crack troops, highly skilled but small enough in number that Lysander hoarded them like gold.

"Let me through!" A wild-eyed man careened through the fighting, face pale as death. He wore the tattered uniform of one of the Solveigs' men. "I've got a message for Lord McFadden."

Piran and Kestel stepped between Blaine and the newcomer, in case the messenger was not what he appeared to be. More of Blaine's soldiers circled them, added protection even in the midst of the battle.

"Get to the point, man. We've got a war going on," Piran said.

The messenger nodded, heaving for breath. "Tormod Solveig sent me. The ghosts of Quintrel's dead mages have betrayed their master. They were sent to him by our allies on the inside, with word that Quintrel intends to call a *divi* to use the necromancer's power against him."

"Can Tormod withstand that?" Kestel asked, eyes widening in surprise.

"He doesn't know whether he can or not, but he's asked for the help of all mages and those with magic, and he said to tell you that foreknowledge is the sharpest sword."

Blaine and the others exchanged glances, then Blaine nodded curtly in acknowledgment. "Very well. You've done your duty. Now, get behind the lines. It's suicide to try to return across the fighting."

Traitors inside Quintrel's organization? Blaine thought. *That has to be Carensa. And she got word to us the only way she could— by sending the dead to warn a necromancer. But how do we use what she's told us to block Quintrel's strike?*

The messenger had disappeared into the fray as the battle closed around them once more. Piran and Kestel battled two more of Lysander's mercenaries, and Blaine willed himself back into the fight, lunging in with a roar. The collective use of magic was burning him up, draining his energy and his life force faster than normal. And with every bone-jarring sword strike and every weary step, Blaine felt that drain in his marrow, despite the deflecting amulet.

"Not long now," Kestel said, with a glance at the orange gash of sunset. She saw an opening and went for it, finishing off her opponent with one strike that impaled his crotch while the dirk in her other hand slit his belly.

"I am so glad you're on our side," Piran said, dealing a powerful series of hammering blows that drove his enemy to his knees and then separated his head from his shoulders.

"Having fun," Kestel said with a grin that did not reach her eyes. They were all weary. Kestel was bleeding from half a dozen deep cuts, while Piran looked to have taken even worse damage. What they needed was something to turn the tide.

Lysander's mercenaries cursed in a language Blaine recognized as Meroven. He did not understand the words, but the intent was clear. Piran shouted obscenities back in the same language. Whatever Piran shouted brought three new mercenaries, faces red with rage, shouting and gesturing and swinging their swords to avenge their honor. Amid it all, Piran almost seemed to be enjoying himself.

"What are you saying to them?" Kestel asked, obliged to defend herself as Piran's barbs drew attackers.

"I may have commented about their mothers, their wives, their whores, and their manly inability," Piran replied, grinning.

Blaine was setting about himself in earnest, fighting off one particularly large man whose honor had been affronted. He apparently expected Blaine to understand the curses and imprecations he shouted, but the nuances were lost in translation.

"I've never actually heard anyone use that curse before," Piran called, clashing with his opponent. "It's forbidden by their priests. I must have really riled him."

"If anyone could make you lose your immortal soul from irritation, it would be you," Kestel replied, surprising her attacker with the skill and speed of her sword.

Blaine got inside his opponent's guard, striking his sword arm and opening a gash to the bone. His second stroke took off the mercenary's head. Within minutes, Kestel and Piran had also made short work of their attackers, and the three stood back-to-back, heaving for breath, awaiting the next attack.

"We need a sea change," Blaine muttered. "Something to shift the balance."

Hundreds of torches flared to life as darkness fell, and in the shadows, dark shapes came ghosting out of the twilight.

Blaine could just make out one of Lysander's generals astride a huge black warhorse. In the blink of an eye, the man was snatched from his saddle and carried up into the night sky. Simultaneously, more *talishte*, led by Geir, descended out of the darkening skies like the warriors of the gods, snatching predetermined targets—the commanders—from among the soldiers.

One after another, the black-clad executioners casually ripped the heads from the bodies, showering the soldiers beneath in their commanders' still-warm blood. They flung the bodies aside, dropping them into the midst of the panicking troops, then slung the heads with deadly aim and lethal force, shouting in triumph when they knocked another officer from his horse.

Again and again they dove, plucking the officers from their horses and making a show of discarding the bodies. Cast in torchlight, bathed in blood, Geir and his fellows embodied every nightmare vision Lysander's godsforsaken soldiers had ever dreamt. In the air, Geir's *talishte* forces battled the *talishte* Pollard had supplied, men from Reese's brood who were willing to fight in order to enjoy the bloody spoils.

Before Lysander's bowmen could collect their wits enough to shoot or the remaining officers could rally their troops, a frigid wind rushed toward the enemy line. Tormod Solveig rode at the head of an army of vengeful spirits. Some rode skeletal steeds, no more than bone and rusted armor, yet armed with blade and will. Other revenants charged on foot, wielding maces, axes, and morning stars that looked quite real. Their battle cry was the moan of the wind and the answering howl of wolves in the forest.

Rinka Solveig rode just behind the specters, clad in her blood-red leather armor, bloodied up to her elbows and spattered with gore. Rinka had none of her brother's magic, but she was fearless, and possibly crazy. She rode a massive white warhorse whose sides were streaked with blood, and the armor over the horse's head was designed to look like a skull. Rinka carried a sword in one hand and a chain flail in the other, making good use of both.

"Foreknowledge is the sharpest sword," Blaine repeated as a daring plan came to him. Daring, and quite likely suicidal. "Kestel, we've got to get to Tormod. My battle foresight might predict Quintrel's move, and if we use our amulets right, we might be able to limit the *divi*'s power while Tormod strikes it down."

Kestel gave him a wary look. "Or our amulets totally close down Tormod's magic and the *divi* eats all of us."

"You've got a better idea?"

Kestel shot him a feral smile. "Nope. Survival is overrated. Let's go for it!"

Piran swore. "Since you've both taken leave of your senses, I'll cover your asses while you do whatever you're going to do."

Together, the three of them fought their way across the battlefield toward where Tormod Solveig's spectral forces advanced.

"What in Raka are we going to do when a *divi* shows up?" Piran asked, slashing a path through the soldiers who had the bad luck to get in his way.

"We'll see how much juice the amulets really have," Blaine said, fighting back a foot soldier who lunged at him. "If Kestel and I work together, then even if the amulets can't hold back the *divi* completely, maybe we can weaken the spirit until Tormod obliterates it."

"So you're going to throw yourself in front of the monster, hoping your fancy necklaces keep it from killing you, until the necromancer can hurl magic at the monster over your head to destroy it, and hope you don't die."

"Basically. You've got something better?"

Piran shrugged. "I've got nothing. Let's hope you're smarter than your idea sounds."

As Tormod Solveig's ghostly army closed in on where Blaine and the others stood, the air in front of Solveig ripped in two, like fabric rent down the middle, exposing fathomless darkness beyond. Out of the darkness stepped a fearsome shape. This was no magicked beast, like the *gryps* and *mestids* and *ranin*. Blaine was certain that the monster in front of Solveig was a creature of the Unseen Realm. Even at a distance, power radiated from the being, dark magic as repugnant as putrefying flesh. Powerful limbs, talons like scimitars, and a maw filled with rows of razor-sharp, pointed teeth made it clear that the creature existed to devour.

The black rip in the daylight remained open behind the monster, and it rose up to its full height, standing in front of Solveig as tall as a man astride a warhorse. As Blaine watched the creature, it seemed both here and not here, as if its presence among the living wavered. Powerful, dark magic swept out from the monster toward Tormod Solveig, and Blaine knew, somehow, that the monster strove to turn the spirits of the dead against the necromancer, and to use them to draw Solveig into the limitless darkness beyond the rift.

Blaine gasped from the powerful magic, but his amulet deflected the worst of it. Piran stood guard, but their would-be attackers had run from the ghostly army and from Rinka's all-too-real assault.

"Go!" Blaine shouted. He and Kestel ran for the *divi*, one on each side, careful to keep a respectful distance. The *divi*'s power felt like a dark malaise, cold and stinking like an open grave. Blaine dodged closer, and the *divi*'s magic wavered, sliding aside, its strike against Tormod Solveig deflected by Blaine's amulet.

Blaine jumped back, and Kestel closed from the opposite side, careful not to get close to Tormod Solveig lest her amulet blunt his powers. For a moment, the *divi*'s power dropped out, as if a curtain of steel had fallen between it and them. It lunged at Kestel, and she danced out of its reach, releasing it from the grip of her null amulet.

The monster beckoned, and the ghosts wavered, torn between Solveig's call to them and the creature's infernal power. Again, Blaine ran forward, deflecting the power of the *divi*'s call. When the monster came at him, Blaine scrambled backward as Kestel ran forward, and the null amulet broke the *divi*'s hold on the ghosts, which had the good sense to disappear. Kestel and Blaine both fell back as the *divi* roared in rage.

Solveig muttered under his breath, and his hands wove a complex pattern in the air. The monster took a step backward, then dove forward, and it was Solveig who was forced back to avoid the creature's deadly claws. All around Solveig, the ghosts faded in and out, as if torn between the mortal master who called them from slumber and the beast that demanded their allegiance.

Blaine staggered from the flow of magic, but his amulet's protections deflected the worst of it. He felt the storm of magic surge toward them, power he was certain meant to kill. The magic was deflected when it came within range of his charm. Blaine steeled himself to feel the magic like a body blow, but his charm held, letting the wild power slide away from him and ricochet toward the monster. It was impossible to gauge surprise on the creature's inhuman features, but the thing fell back several steps, and its form wavered, as if crippled by its own magic.

"Now!" Blaine shouted to Solveig as he and Kestel threw themselves out of the way. Tormod Solveig's power swelled, and the ghost tide rushed toward the creature, sweeping it back toward the darkness. Blaine took back his position, so that the power echoed between him and the monster, magnifying the damage of Solveig's intent. The monster roared and shrieked as the ghosts pushed it into the darkness, and then the rift closed behind it, leaving only a patch of scorched ground in its wake.

Blaine wavered on his feet, and the tide of spectral warriors drew back. Kestel grabbed his arm, steadying him and extending the protection of her null amulet to shield him.

"Thank you," Tormod Solveig said. "I could not have fought the *divi* without help—at least, not without great cost."

"Don't let me stand in your way," Blaine said with a weary grin. "Go get those bastards." He stepped aside, and Solveig and his ghostly army swept by.

"*That's* a *divi*?" Kestel asked, eyes wide. "Quintrel controls that?"

Blaine nodded tiredly. "More likely, it controls Quintrel. I have the feeling that we haven't seen the last of it."

Piran ran up to them, anger and worry clear in his face. "You all right, mate?"

"Not exactly," Blaine replied, "but there's no helping it."

That was not entirely the truth. Blaine expected that being in the presence of magic would take its toll. He did not expect that he would be burning up with fever in a wind as cold as any on Edgeland. Nor did he think his head would swim and pound as if he had been dashed against the rocks, or that his blood would feel ready to boil while he labored for breath and struggled for the energy to move, let alone fight. It was growing rapidly clear that if he did not die in battle, magic itself would do the job.

Blaine's soldiers, having been warned of the *talishte* attack and the Solveigs' likely offensive, saw their chance and took it. Roaring like madmen, the soldiers swarmed forward, setting about mercilessly with swords and axes and descending on their panicked opponents like hornets.

Borya and Desya rode at the front, standing in their stirrups, howling like wolves. Borya's bow loosed arrow after arrow, firing into the fleeing Lysander ranks. Desya's bullwhip snapped from side to side, herding the enemy soldiers into retreat. The sharp metal tip set in Desya's whip dug deep into flesh when it struck, opening deep gashes and pulling strips of skin away with it when he cracked the leather free.

Blaine grasped the magic-deflecting amulet that hung

around his neck, wishing that it could do more, frightened to think about what a toll Tormod's sorcery and the *divi*'s attack would have taken without the charm. He felt a sudden quiet descend on him, as if someone had covered him with a large glass box that shut out sound and magic. He knew the respite could not last long, but while it did, his strength was replenished. Beneath it all, he felt his *kruvgaldur* bond to Penhallow like a thin, strong cord, shoring up his strength.

A few breaths later, the roar of battle returned, but by then, Blaine had regained his footing and enough stamina to rejoin the fight. All around him, soldiers cheered as they harried the enemy, excited that their fortunes had finally changed.

"What in Raka is going on?" Piran asked, pointing.

Amid the milling chaos of battle, half of Lysander's army appeared to be in full retreat. Archers fired sporadically at *talishte*, who for the most part easily dodged their arrows, only to swoop down again like raptors and snatch an officer from his horse. Soldiers shouted curses and shook their fists at the sky, or ran enraged at the enemy, while others made a hasty retreat toward the rear lines. Those officers who remained, mostly on foot, shouted in vain to regain control of their troops.

"They're running," Kestel said.

Blaine shook his head. "No, look. They're moving in an orderly retreat, watch them."

Kestel frowned. "Whatever their commander's doing, no one else seemed to expect it."

Blaine grinned. "Maybe not, but it opens a door for us. Let's go!" he shouted, rallying his soldiers to surge forward, giving chase to Lysander's retreating forces.

Blaine lost track of the candlemarks as they fought their way through the chaos. He was sticky with blood, covered in gore, but most of it was not his own. When the mercenaries retreated, they left a hole in the line between Lysander's army and Rostivan's troops. And before the mistake could be remedied, Blaine and Niklas sent their armies into the breach to make the most of it.

For the first time that day, Blaine let himself think about Carr. He had given clear orders that Quintrel was his to deal with, no matter what the mages had to do to shut down the man's magic. Carr would be avenged. After all they had endured, all that the battle had cost, Blaine intended to make Quintrel pay.

Verner's army stormed in along with Blaine's soldiers, their energy renewed by the unexpected stroke of luck. Blaine's troops rallied, despite being weary and wounded from days on the field. In the forefront, Rinka and Tormod Solveig cut a swath through the attackers as they ushered wave upon wave of the angry dead into the fight, enabling them to get their vengeance at last.

All the while, Blaine had searched the throng of soldiers for Lysander. This morning, Lysander might have expected an easy victory. Now, with his mercenaries in retreat and his army in disarray, hounded by the living, dead, and undead, Lysander would be lucky to secure a quick death.

It would be relatively easy for Geir or one of the *talishte* to snatch Lysander into the air and behead him, but that would make Lysander into a martyr, potentially a rallying point against those who would destroy the *talishte*. Blaine knew that his undead allies had endured enough at the hands of mortals without adding more to the legends to feed the fire.

Still, he was taken aback when Geir dropped down suddenly in front of him, Karstan Lysander firmly in his grip. Geir threw the black-clad warlord down so that Lysander landed on his hands and knees in front of Blaine. Kestel and Piran came to stand behind him, and Geir made no move to leave.

Lysander was weaponless and battered. Blood-spattered and bearing the gashes and bruises of battle, he nonetheless drew himself up to kneel with a straight back, head held high.

We all have parts to play, Blaine thought. *And play them we must.*

He withdrew his sword and moved to stand in front of Lysander. Unlike Quintrel, Blaine had no personal grievance against Lysander. His soldiers had fought admirably, and his strategies had been sound.

"Do you yield?" Blaine asked, his sword visible but not yet threatening.

Lysander regarded him with a baleful gaze. "What choice do I have?" He spat to the side. "I yield."

"Will you swear fealty, pledging your sword and loyalty to the House of Glenreith?" Blaine asked. He expected Lysander's answer, but his own sense of honor required him to ask.

"Go to Raka. I'm no man's liegeman." Lysander replied.

"Isn't it worth your life to swear fealty, man?" Piran asked.

Lysander glared at them both. "Torven take your souls. I'd rather die now than pledge my allegiance to any man."

"As you wish," Blaine replied. With one swift stroke, his sword parted Lysander's head from his body. When the body fell, a glass orb on a leather strap slipped from around his neck. The orb gave a faint, stuttering flicker, and Blaine ground it under the heel of his boot into dust.

Piran snatched up the fallen head and held it aloft by its hair. "Unless you want the fate of your dead lord, best you fall on your knees and confess allegiance," he shouted.

Only a remnant was left of Lysander's crack troops. Blaine

estimated that a few hundred enemy soldiers remained, perhaps fewer. Almost to a man, Lysander's troops knelt. Some fell to their knees and others bent grudgingly, but to Blaine's relief, only a small fraction preferred death to fealty.

Rikard and Leiv caught up to Blaine. Trying to minimize the impact of their magic on him, they had kept their distance during the battle. Both were red in the face from running, and despite the cold, Rikard mopped the sweat from his forehead with the sleeve of his robe.

"Can you bewitch the captives, make sure there are no surprises?" Blaine asked.

Rikard nodded. "That shouldn't be a problem." He glanced at the kneeling men. "I assume your soldiers will take precautions?"

Blaine motioned to a nearby captain. "March the captives behind the lines, build a stockade, and lock them up," he ordered. "Mage Rikard and Mage Leiv will keep them from causing trouble. We'll deal with them later."

The captain eyed the mages with suspicion, but nodded. "Aye, sir." He shouted for his men to surround the captives and begin tying their hands with their belts.

Rikard turned back to Blaine. "I'll magick them once we're clear of you... just in case."

Blaine nodded his assent and returned his attention to the battle.

The Solveigs had gone into a full assault on what remained of Rostivan's line as Verner's troops chased down strays from Lysander's army. Blaine's gaze sought the horizon, and Kestel moved up next to him.

"It's Quintrel you want," she said, watching his face.

Blaine nodded. "I can't bring Carr back, but I can avenge him."

Geir slipped up beside them. "I don't think you'll have long to wait," he said, a nod of his head indicating the direction of Rostivan's army. "They seem to be collapsing." He grinned, exposing the tips of his eyeteeth. "Nidhud spared me a few of his men. The Knights were mage-warriors, after all, and they hosted Quintrel's group in Valshoa long enough to get to know them. They'll help contain whatever Quintrel's mages throw at them, and tamp down the worst of it."

Blaine glanced at Geir. "Is everything ready at Mirdalur?" he asked.

Geir nodded. "Waiting for you." He shrugged. "Not that there haven't been a few bumps in the road, but we've gotten past them."

From the way Geir said it, Blaine was certain that the obstacles had been far greater than 'bumps,' but he let it go.

"Like?" Kestel asked.

Geir shrugged. "Some of Reese's brood decided to take this personally. Seems they've thrown their lot in with the other side—not a surprise, but hardly a welcome addition."

"You held them off?"

"Yes. But we could have done without the aggravation." Geir paused. "When you're finished here, I'm to bring you directly to Mirdalur. My orders, from Penhallow and Dolan."

Blaine managed a quiet chuckle. "Good enough. We wouldn't want to keep them waiting."

The battle shifted, and Blaine followed Geir's gaze. The Solveigs' army drove straight to the heart of Rostivan's forces. Niklas and Traher Voss followed with their troops, offering no quarter as they slashed a path through the broken line.

"Let's go. I want to be there when it falls apart," he said.

Blaine sent runners to Niklas with an update of what had happened, modifying the battle plan and providing new orders for the altered situation. He rallied his men, and they headed at a run for the action. Kestel, Piran, and Geir stuck close to Blaine, and he suspected that they could see the toll the battle had taken on him.

He felt worn and hard used. Tormod's magic, even at a distance, was a persistent drain. His fever had returned, and Blaine knew that nothing the healers could do would remedy it. Yet beneath the fatigue, Blaine could feel another presence, a silent strength, helping to shore up his defenses.

Penhallow. The kruvgaldur. *Very well. I'll take help wherever I can get it,* he thought, with a silent word of thanks for the bond that connected him to the *talishte*'s distant thoughts and immortal strength.

Stubbornness and rage drove him on over his body's protests. Carr's savaged face and battered body haunted his dreams, and now that Quintrel was nearly within his grasp, Blaine intended to have his revenge.

Neither Rostivan nor Quintrel was going to give in easily. Blaine's soldiers came pouring in behind Niklas's troops, joining their comrades with an earsplitting battle cry. With fresh soldiers swelling their ranks, Niklas's soldiers and Voss's mercenaries fought with new energy, leaving Rostivan's men no hope of reversing their fate and nowhere to run.

A soldier launched himself at Blaine, eyes narrowed with resolve. "We won't die easily," he muttered, coming at Blaine with a wild series of strikes and thrusts born of desperation. Blaine was certain that it was his battle magic that saved him, enabling him to anticipate the enemy's blows just an instant before the motion was made. He gave himself over to it, knowing the price, too weary to turn any boon away.

After a few rounds, the soldier's frantic press slowed, and Blaine held back, awaiting the next salvo, attuned to the heightened sense that saw the strike before it came. A heartbeat before the attacker lunged to the left, Blaine thrust forward, inside the man's guard, a blow that ripped his gut from side to side and spilled his entrails onto the ground. The soldier dropped his sword, pressing the edges of his opened belly together in vain, and as he sank to the ground, Blaine's sword swung again, severing the man's head from his neck.

Kestel and Piran had made short work of their attackers, while Geir had returned to the night sky, swooping down time and again to claw the throat from an unsuspecting soldier or snap a brittle neck. Shouts of panic echoed in the darkness, and Rostivan's terrified men ran, duty forgotten.

A victory cry rose from the direction of Rinka Solveig's troops. Blaine turned toward the commotion in time to see Rinka lift Torinth Rostivan's head on a pike, holding it over her head while fresh blood streamed down the wooden pole, and a spray of crimson showered her in gore.

Blaine and Kestel pressed forward toward a small redoubt in the rear made of hastily dug dirt mounds. "That's the mages," he said to the others. "I'm certain. If Quintrel's to be found, he'll be there."

"Then let's get the bastard," Kestel said, brandishing her swords.

They fought their way toward the mage's shelter, defending themselves against panicked soldiers already resigned to losing the battle. Blaine searched the fray for Niklas, finally spotting him surrounded by soldiers, who stepped aside when he and Kestel and Piran shouldered their way to the group.

Niklas managed a tired, lopsided grin. "Glad you could join us," he said. Three *talishte* stood with Niklas, clad in the uniform of the Knights of Esthrane. "You've got good timing. We're just about to storm the mages."

"I'm glad I didn't miss the party," Blaine said. Kestel gave him a worried look but did not comment. He could guess what she wanted to say, and shared her concern. There was a very real chance that putting himself in the thick of the magic could kill him, despite the amulet's protection. But he knew that he could not live with himself if he did not make the attempt.

"What's the plan?" he asked.

Niklas nodded toward the earthworks redoubt. "Jascha and Serg have been holding a damper on Quintrel's magic, while Gav strikes randomly, poking through with his magic to see where the weak points are." He shrugged. "From time to time, they switch roles."

"How's it working?" Piran asked, eyeing the redoubt with suspicion.

"We haven't been incinerated," Niklas replied blandly. "So I'd say offhand, pretty well." He grimaced. "On the other hand, we haven't broken them, either."

"Quintrel is sending most of the magic himself," Gav said, never taking his gaze from the redoubt. "I recognize the signature of his power."

"Is he alone? Surely he had other mages with him," Kestel asked, peering through the darkness for a glimpse.

Gav frowned. "There are others present but not active... what I can read is limited by the shielding, but I'd say they were injured."

Blaine narrowed his gaze, squinting to see. In the torchlight, it looked as if the dirt mounds had been scorched with fire and pockmarked with the impact of large, heavy objects. Yet the entire area seemed to be wreathed in a light mist, and Blaine could feel the magic of Quintrel's protections like a buzzing in his ears.

"One man can't be impossible to beat," he muttered.

"One man wouldn't be," Gav replied. "But Quintrel is no longer exactly human."

"The *divi*?" Blaine remembered the creature that had confronted Tormod Solveig on the battlefield, the monster that had stepped through a rift in the sky as if it were opening a door. *Thank the gods I didn't know what it was really like, or I might not have had the balls to throw myself in front of it.*

Gav nodded. "Quintrel's drawing on its magic, because no mortal should have been able to hold out against us this long."

"Won't it consume him, using that kind of power for so long?" Kestel asked.

Gav's expression was grave. "Oh yes, eventually. But Quintrel's already past the point of no return. Once a man commits himself to a *divi*, there's no turning back, even if he wanted to. The *divi* controls him, and for as long as he serves the *divi*'s needs, he'll continue to survive, as a useful tool."

Gav met Blaine's gaze. "It's the *divi* we're really fighting. Quintrel, as a mortal man, stopped existing quite a while ago, I would guess."

Blaine remembered the mages who had trusted Quintrel to protect them from the Great Fire, and Carensa, who had looked to Quintrel as a mentor and savior. *He's betrayed all of them,* Blaine thought, his anger flaring. *They depended on him, believed in him, and he sold them out to the* divi.

"What about the other mages?" Blaine asked. "Can you tell what injured—or killed—them?"

Anger glinted in Gav's eyes. "We haven't broken through his warding, so my guess is that whatever happened, Quintrel did it himself."

"Why?" Kestel demanded.

"Because someone betrayed him," Niklas replied. "I don't

think the Lysander mercs ran for the hills on their own accord. I don't think the ghosts brought their message about the *divi* to Tormod without being sent by someone. Someone Quintrel trusted didn't trust him back."

One possibility presented itself in Blaine's mind, and he shied away from it, unwilling to even consider the thought. *There's no way Carensa would have agreed to be a battle mage,* he thought. But he knew, even as he framed the thought, that she might have had no say in the matter. The likelihood made Gav's suspicion about the mages' fate all the more chilling.

"So how do we get in?" Piran asked, clearly tired of waiting.

"That's where I come in." Tormod Solveig looked like the Soul Reaper. His black leather armor was spattered with gore. His face was haggard, but his eyes blazed with purpose. Here and there on his armor, Blaine thought he saw the faint glow of runes and sigils, pulsing with inner fire and then going dark, only to appear elsewhere on the smooth black surface of the hardened leather.

"Rinka and Voss have the fighting well in hand," he reported. "I figured I'd be the most help here." He turned his attention toward the dirt mound and its warding. "Interesting," he murmured. "That's *divi* magic."

"Which is why Quintrel's still in there, and we're out here," Niklas replied ill-humoredly.

Tormod looked thoughtful. "Difficult, but not impossible." He looked to the others. "I think I know how to beat this," he said, a cold smile touching the corners of his lips, "but it's going to take all of us working together."

Half a candlemark later, everything was ready. Despite Tormod's warning and Niklas's urging, Blaine refused to leave, regardless of the effect the magic might have on him. Kestel had not tried to persuade him to retreat, but he could see the worry in her eyes.

Piran looked ready for a fight. "Never did like Quintrel, from the time we laid eyes on him," he muttered.

Tormod Solveig, Gav and the mages, and the three Knights of Esthrane took up positions at the four quarters around the redoubt. Niklas and twenty of his best soldiers formed a circle behind the mages, and Blaine, Piran, and Kestel stood back, watching and waiting. Blaine gripped his protective amulet, and Kestel laid a hand on his arm, supporting him with the null-magic charm she wore.

"Now!" Gav cried.

The air within the circle felt thick and heavy, like just before a storm. Blaine felt power coalescing around them, coursing through them, as if it descended from the sky and flowed upward from the depths. The magic-diverting amulet was protecting him, but even it had its limits, and fighting Quintrel might push it past its abilities. He gasped, but waved off any assistance from Piran. Kestel kept her distance from the mages, careful of her null charm.

The glowing thread that was Blaine's *kruvgaldur* link to Penhallow grew brighter, a supernatural lifeline linked to his blood. Blaine clung to the *kruvgaldur* bond, holding tight to ride out the magic that was brewing around him.

Power crackled from the upraised hands of the four mages, meeting with a sickly greenish glow as their magic and Quintrel's wardings collided. Tormod was chanting quietly, but although Blaine could not make out the words, the incantation sent a chill down his spine.

"The fog. It's back." Kestel's uneasiness was clear in her voice. Blaine glanced down and saw that the white mist was roiling around them, sweeping toward Tormod as if called to its master. The mist murmured like distant voices, and where it skimmed past Blaine's bare skin, it felt as if he was touched by grave-cold flesh.

The fog rushed toward Tormod until it enveloped him, swallowing him up in its cloud. Then it rolled left and right, encircling the redoubt, a wall of fog as high as a man's shoulders, gradually taking the ghostly shape of men.

Blaine felt a shift in the magic, and he had to struggle for a moment to catch his breath. Surrounded by the mist figures, Tormod's power and the power of the Knights of Esthrane had grown stronger. The blue-white energy that assaulted the redoubt's wardings and the green glow that countered it vied with growing tension, crackling and sparking like a lightning storm.

Tormod gave a sudden cry in a strange language, and the mages sent a pulse of blinding golden light at the green warding. Gav and the Knights added their power to his, and at the same time, the fog surged forward, straining against the green warding, unaffected by its snapping and spitting energy.

The green warding burst, shooting a spire of light upward, lighting the area bright as day. It struck Quintrel's redoubt, throwing dirt high into the air and collapsing one side of the earthen structure, which opened part of its roof to the sky. Tormod threw open his arms, and shouted a declaration, and the light vanished. Blaine felt the magic strain against his deflection amulet, and he clenched his teeth to keep from crying out or staggering.

A lone figure climbed to the top of the earthen wall. It was Vigus Quintrel, but his appearance was so altered that at first Blaine did not recognize him. Just in the months since Blaine and his friends had left Valshoa, Quintrel looked as if he had aged decades. His clothing was ripped and bloodstained and his eyes were bright with madness. Quintrel's features twisted in a snarl. Around his neck, gleaming brilliantly against the darkness, was a small glass orb on a strap that pulsed with the rhythm of a heartbeat, his link with the *divi*. Clutched in one hand was a larger, more brightly glowing orb with a mummified, withered hand—the *divi*'s anchor relic.

"I will not surrender!" Quintrel shouted, and he sent a barrage of lightning against all those gathered below. A circle of light flared from where Gav and the mages stood, strengthened by the spirits who had come to join them. The circle trapped the burst of power, and its energy sizzled and snapped as the two opposing magics warred against each other. Blaine's head throbbed, but the deflection amulet held.

Quintrel gave a howl of rage, descending closer, close enough that Blaine knew he could reach Quintrel in a few running steps.

Not yet, he told himself, itching for the opportunity. *Not until the magic settles, or I'll never make it to Quintrel. But soon...*

Quintrel snapped his right arm forward, palm out, blasting energy toward the Knights of Esthrane. The warding wavered, rippling in a translucent curtain of light that reminded Blaine of the Spirit Lights of Edgeland. Blaine feared the warding would break, but the protective curtain surged back to its former strength.

"Look at his orb," Kestel hissed. She and Piran had followed Blaine and stood just behind him.

Blaine stared at the rapidly pulsing light trapped in the large crystal globe. Just staring at the crimson light make the hair on the back of his neck stand on end. Even the magic-diverting amulet could not completely shield him from the power the *divi* exuded, energy that triggered every primal warning deep in his brain, screaming for him to flee.

"Vigus Quintrel, you have lost. Surrender," Niklas shouted.

Quintrel loosed a wave of fire in response, but the warding held, dissipating the wild energy as soon as it struck the shielding.

Quintrel staggered, stumbling a few more steps down the wall of the embankment, stopping just beyond the ghost mist. His entire form trembled, and his face twisted in excruciating pain and unrelenting rage. Quintrel raised his hands for one final salvo, and his entire body glowed, suffused with the *divi*'s energy. He sent a new fiery torrent, even stronger than the last, drawing on the *divi*'s magic along with his own.

The fire burned blue white, hot enough that it broke through the shielding of the mages at the forefront of Solveig's line, incinerating them where they stood. Both the larger orb and the small orb glowed with a blinding blood-red light. Blaine glimpsed a visage in the light, something that was not human and never had been.

Tormod, the Knights, and the remaining mages held their position. Strain was clear in their faces, and sweat ran down Tormod's brow. Quintrel alone would have been no match for the power arrayed against him, but the *divi* made it an unequal fight.

"If we could just break Quintrel's concentration, I think Tormod and the other mages could take him," Kestel said. Between her amulet and Blaine's, they held off enough of the power to keep Blaine conscious and functioning, although his head ached enough to blur his vision. They edged as close as they dared, nearing the front line off to one side, away from the full blast of the magical onslaught.

"Not if something doesn't change soon. Our mages are weakening, and Quintrel has the *divi* to draw from. All Quintrel has to do is outlast them, and he wins," Blaine replied.

Quintrel's magic punched through the mages' protective

warding again, cutting down the soldiers in the front lines and slamming into Tormod's shielding so hard it knocked him from his saddle and felled his horse. The Knights of Esthrane rushed forward to meet the onslaught, along with Gav and what remained of his mages. But Gav's contingent had taken losses, and even the Knights of Esthrane were showing the strain. Tormod was pale and haggard, as if the level of magic on which he drew was pulling from his own life energy.

Without warning, a streak of green fire flared behind Quintrel, looping and curling like a serpent around his body, snatching at the orb on the strap around his neck. An instant later, an arc of blue light struck Quintrel, too bright to look at for more than an instant.

"Look!" Kestel pointed. Two battered and bloodied figures had crawled from the ruins of the redoubt behind Quintrel. One held a bone as an athame, sending the blue flame against Quintrel, while the other loosed the green-flame serpent from a relic clutched in her hand.

Sweet Esthrane! Blaine thought. *One of those mages is Carensa.* "Give me your amulet," Blaine said, his gaze fixed on Quintrel. "If I hit Quintrel while he's weak, I might be able to take him."

"Or we'll roast like chestnuts," Kestel replied. "Let you charge him alone? Forget it! We go together."

Quintrel's power wavered, and Blaine saw his chance. "Now!" he said. He and Kestel took off running.

Quintrel howled in anger, and wheeled to strike at the mages who had betrayed him. He made a slashing movement, and the mage with the bone athame screamed as deep gashes opened up his body from shoulder to hip.

Just like he did to Carr, Blaine thought, intent on reaching the redoubt before Quintrel could react, praying to the gods for a miracle, that their two amulets might break Quintrel's power long enough for Tormod to finish the fight. *Even if it kills me and takes the magic with me to the Sea of Souls.*

Quintrel snapped his left hand toward Carensa, and the *divi* orb flared. Carensa did not lower her arm, and the serpentine power continued to strike at Quintrel, but smokelike wisps began to unravel from her form, pulled toward the power of the *divi* orb, and the orb pulsed brighter with every bit of smoke that entered it, while the green-fire snake dimmed with every breath. The *divi* orb absorbed the smoke wisps, drawing more and more of them from around Carensa and swallowing the smoke into the orb.

Carensa staggered, clearly damaged by the loss of whatever energy was being drained from her, but she never let the green fire waver, and her gaze was fixed on Quintrel with a look of pure hatred. Then her whole body trembled, ashen as a corpse, and as Quintrel's orb swallowed the last of the smoke wisps, the green serpent light flickered and died. Carensa fell to the ground and did not move again.

Blaine ran for Quintrel, sword in hand. At the last second, Quintrel turned and slashed with his hand, meaning to strike with the same invisible claws that he had used against Carensa. The deflection amulet held, and Blaine felt the power of the attack slide away without damage, though his head ached and pounded.

Quintrel held up the *divi* orb, and Blaine felt its power straining the amulet's protection, then sliding away before it could drain his soul as it had Carensa's. From the look on her face, he was certain Kestel felt the attack against her null amulet, but she kept moving forward as if buffeted by a headwind.

Blaine came at Quintrel with a sword in one hand and a knife in the other. Quintrel dodged at the last second, so the strike meant to cleave shoulder to hip only managed to sever

Quintrel's right arm. Kestel tackled the mage from behind, jamming the null amulet against Quintrel's back as she grabbed the leather thong of the *divi* orb and used it as a garrote.

Our amulets were never meant to take on a divi, Blaine thought. *But if they can buy us just a few seconds more, we might destroy him—or damage him enough that Tormod and the others can finish the job.*

Quintrel bucked against Kestel's grip on his throat as Blaine buried his knife in the mage's heart.

"Go to Raka," Blaine growled. "Torven take your soul." He twisted the blade, then yanked it free.

Blood bubbled at Quintrel's mouth, and his body convulsed. Quintrel struggled to mouth a curse, but all that came was a wheezing gasp. In one savage sweep, Blaine severed Quintrel's head from his body. "That's for Carr and Carensa," he muttered.

The small orb burst into fragments, but the larger orb began to flicker wildly.

"We've got trouble," Kestel said, grabbing Blaine and rolling with him over the lip of the redoubt as the large orb flared searingly bright, then exploded into a rain of glass, and the spirit of the *divi* burst forth.

Blaine clawed his way to the top of the embankment and stared at the fire-red spirit, but it was too bright to see clearly, save for the indelible impression of grasping tendrils and an open, hungry maw.

The Knights of Esthrane joined forces with Tormod's magic. So did Gav, the last of the regular mages still standing. Together, they sent a single, massive lance of power that struck the *divi* in its core. Silvery light suffused the *divi*'s form, driving out the crimson fire, and behind the trapped spirit, Blaine swore he saw a rift in the darkness that was blacker than the night.

Pain lanced through Blaine's head, threatening to black him out as the massive outpouring of magic overwhelmed the protections of his deflecting amulet. Even the support of the *kruvgaldur* and Kestel's null amulet seemed tenuous, strained by the maelstrom of power. Blaine clung to consciousness, watching through slitted eyes as blinding silver light pushed the *divi* back into the unnatural darkness.

Perhaps because he was so near to death himself, Blaine saw the ghost mist rise from Quintrel's corpse, struggling to uncoil itself from his body, twisting free only to be pulled into the *divi*'s grasp. Blaine heard a scream of utter terror, an earsplitting shriek from the *divi* that rent the night, and then both the *divi* and the rift were gone.

Blaine dragged himself over the edge of the embankment and crawled to where the two renegade mages lay. One was a man he did not recognize. Carensa's body lay next to the dead mage. Blaine turned her over gently, calling her name. Deep, bloody slashes savaged her chest and belly. Her skin was gray and she looked as drawn and gaunt as if she had been fasting, drained of her life by the *divi*. Carensa's head lolled and her eyes were wide and staring.

"Thank you," Blaine murmured to Carensa and the other mage as Kestel moved up beside him. The world reeled around Blaine. Blaine's heart pounded erratically and his head felt ready to explode. Even his *kruvgaldur* bond could not sustain him any longer. Exhausted, grief-stricken, and utterly spent, Blaine fell face forward onto the ground, giving himself up to the darkness.

CHAPTER
THIRTY-FOUR

———

SIX DAYS AFTER THE VICTORY AGAINST QUINTREL and the warlords, thanks to the healers and Penhallow, Blaine was ready to fight another kind of battle. The new Lords of the Blood gathered at Mirdalur for one more attempt to anchor the magic securely. Now, after all the preparation, it was finally time.

"Before you enter, the working demands blood." Blaine looked up to see Dagur holding a silver chalice and a boline knife. Rikard stood beside him, the sigil-carved wood held in his grip.

Blaine slid back the sleeve of his shirt, baring his left forearm. "Take it," he said.

Dagur drew the ritual knife across Blaine's skin, scoring deep enough to raise a thin stream of blood. He harvested it carefully into the chalice, and one by one the others offered an arm for the bloodletting.

When each of the thirteen had been bled, Dagur and Rikard moved to the opening of the labyrinth. Dagur murmured something, and runes appeared in the stone walkway, marking the first step of the maze.

Rikard held the sigil-carved wood over the marked stone. Dagur raised the chalice to each of the four quarters in turn, and then poured out the blood over the sigils. His chant grew louder as the blood spilled over the carved wood, and there was a rush of power, spreading from the first stepping-stone all along the pathway of the labyrinth as power called to power.

When the cup was dry, Rikard fit the carved wooden piece into a depression beside the opening to the labyrinth. He was bloody to the wrists, and the floor was stained crimson.

"Enter," Rikard said to the thirteen. "Carry the mingled blood on the soles of your feet. The chamber is ready for the ritual."

As Blaine and his companions wound their way into the labyrinth, Nidhud, Dagur, and the other mages began to chant. The chant was mellifluous, with a second and then a third group of chanters joining in the repetitive phrases like a round until the chamber seemed to swell with plainchant.

Blaine felt the magic rising with the chant, winding around them as they coiled their way into the heart of the labyrinth. The crystals, which had pulsed lazily before, now glowed brightly with amber light. Perhaps it was a trick of the torchlight, but to Blaine's eyes, the crystals seemed to be pulsing along with the chant.

The obsidian disk hung on a strap around Blaine's neck, over his heart. It had been cold to the touch when Blaine entered the labyrinth, but it grew warmer the farther along the path he went. Now the disk felt fevered, warmer than Blaine's skin, and the runes and markings etched into its glossy surface were pulsing with a golden glow from deep inside.

The last time Blaine had worked the ritual at Mirdalur, he had been alone inside the maze. Then, it felt as if the labyrinth was fighting him at every step, turning its magic against him. Perhaps it had been, trying to protect him from what was to come, from nearly being killed by magic too wild to be completely bound.

This time, among twelve compatriots, the magic of the labyrinth felt completely different. Instead of fighting him, the magic drew him forward, quickening his step so that if he had not been mindful of it, he might have ended up running. From the looks on the faces of his companions, Blaine was certain that at least a few of them could feel the pull of the magic themselves.

Of those he had chosen to become the new Lords of the Blood, most had some level of magic. Blaine's own magic, before the Great Fire, gave him an edge in battle, augmenting his natural agility and training, and since the ritual at Valshoa, he had felt the battle magic enhance his speed and strength. Since he had made the first anchoring, he had also gained a few seconds of precognition, knowing where the enemy would move and making it easier for Blaine to anticipate and block the strike. His *kruvgaldur* with Penhallow strengthened his endurance and made him harder to kill. And as Kestel had pointed out, awareness of where magic was being worked was a valuable early warning signal.

Blaine had no idea whether this night's working would allow him to keep those skills, strip him of his limited magic entirely, or change him in some new and unexpected way. The last time the magic was successfully bound, the Lords of the Blood gained new abilities, though it did not make mages of those who had not been mages before, nor had it turned the mages into gods. Blaine thought that he would be content to just live through the working and have it succeed.

Connor was a medium, and the Wraith Lord who possessed him qualified, to Blaine's thinking, as a magical creature in his wraith state, certainly supernatural. Borya's magic added to his acrobatic ability, while Dolan, a Knight of Esthrane, was a mage as well as a warrior and *talishte*.

Niklas had no magic. Neither did Piran, who made it clear that he thought that lack was a good thing. Verran's magic enabled him to pick locks and gain people's trust. Dawe's ability enhanced his talent for metalworking.

Penhallow was *talishte*, supernatural in his essence, and to Blaine's thinking, the *kruvgaldur* counted as magic, though Penhallow was vague on the matter. Blaine had no idea what magic, if any, Folville, Voss, and Verner possessed, though Tormod Solveig had clearly demonstrated just how powerful his necromancy was.

"Look at the walls," Niklas murmured.

The paintings of the constellations on the walls had begun to glow. Instead of the flat paintings that had been there a few moments before, the murals now seemed to be windows into the heavens, as if Blaine could reach his arm though the rock and into the cosmos.

The air itself was astir with magic. Perhaps it was a trick of the torchlight, but to Blaine's eyes, the air shimmered, as if someone had loosed gold dust on the wind.

"Overhead," Piran said in a low, warning voice. Blaine glanced up, and the dark ceiling of the underground chamber had been replaced by the coruscating colors and brilliance of the Spirit Lights of Edgeland.

One of the mages had begun a steady rhythm on a hand drum. The beat reverberated in the chamber. Censers set around the exterior of the labyrinth burned sage in smoky bundles, adding the candle smoke. Candles glimmered at intervals along the labyrinth, one at each circle reserved for a Lord of the Blood.

Blaine felt disoriented, as if, with the chanting and the

drumming, the glimmering light and the glittering air, power rose and fell with every breath. His head was swimming, his knees felt weak, and it was difficult for him to keep his focus, though he clung to the urgency of his mission.

Blaine inhaled the sweet sage smoke that hung in the air, breathing deeply, letting it fill his head and lungs, clearing his thoughts. His body felt light, as if he were not completely grounded in the world. He dared not turn to see if the others felt the same. Though the chamber was bounded by stone walls and the labyrinth was clearly marked in the rock floor, Blaine knew that if he took his eyes off the place where he must stand, he might lose his way. Time within the labyrinth seemed to move at a different pace.

After what seemed like forever, Blaine reached the spot where he had stood the last time, when the magic nearly killed him. In the paintings of the constellations, he could see the stars moving in their courses, like looking up into the night sky. A rain of falling stars glimmered across one of the portals. *Perhaps the boundaries between land and sky have been weakened by the magic,* Blaine thought. *Or maybe to magic, the boundaries are only in our imagination.*

Blaine glanced toward the others outside the labyrinth. Though the labyrinth was only a few strides across, from where he stood, it seemed as if Kestel, Zaryae, and the mages stood on the far side of a great chasm, farther away than the rock-bound room made possible.

Or else magic alters the space, once the power is invoked, and we are in a place that's not quite where we set out to go, he thought.

"Step into your circle," Dolan said.

Glancing at the others, assuring himself that they were all moving into place, Blaine drew a breath to steady himself, and stepped into the circle appointed for him.

At once, all of their presence-crystals flared with a deep-orange light. The golden runes on his onyx disk glowed brilliantly. From the ceiling of the chamber, the coruscating lights spread, dropping around them like a curtain to separate those within the labyrinth from those on the outside of the circle. Blaine caught a glimpse of Kestel's face, and saw the fear in her eyes, but there was no turning back.

Dolan had divined a word of power for each of the participants, an ancient word to speak aloud and activate the magic. Once spoken together, the words of power would bind the magic, tethering its wildness with stronger bonds than one man alone could forge. Through the ritual, the magic would be grounded and bound, to each of them and through each of them, altering them and placing a sacred bond and duty upon their eldest sons for all the future. For the *talishte*, the working bound them personally as guardians of the magic.

For a moment, the silence was unbearable. It was as if the cosmos, and not just those within and outside the circle, waited for the words to be spoken. The constellations bore witness, and the shimmering light, the runes, and the crystals all connected in the massing power that Blaine could feel crackling in the air, waiting.

"*Ahanthi!*" Blaine said in a loud, clear voice.

The others spoke their words just a breath after Blaine, each a different word, echoing through the chamber. Together, the syllables rolled like thunder, as if they were not meant to be spoken by mortals.

The many-colored lights curtaining off the circle flared so brightly that Blaine shielded his eyes with his arm. In addition to the sound of the mages' plainchant and drumming, Blaine swore he could hear the shimmer of bells and hundreds, perhaps thousands, of voices, an unseen choir of all those who had come before them.

The constellations whirled and spun, dancing in the cosmos, their colors brilliant and fantastic. The air smelled like the tang after a lightning storm. Beautiful, hypnotic, and utterly terrifying, the sounds, smells, and images were intoxicating. Blaine stood transfixed, waiting for what would happen next.

Blue-white bolts of energy rained from the top of the light-dome. Some of the bolts struck along the pathway, but thirteen of the bolts found their targets, striking each of the new Lords of the Blood in the crown of their heads and racing down and through their bodies into the rock beneath their feet.

Blaine's body was frozen in the arc of light. He expected to smell burning hair and searing flesh, to feel the energy burn him alive, and he readied himself to die.

In that instant, Blaine saw the others transfixed by the brilliant light, held immobile in its glare, eyes wide. Some looked frightened, others angry, some ready to flee if they could. Blaine wondered what they saw when they looked at him.

If the Wraith Lord expected this and didn't tell me, we're going to have a chat about this if we all survive, Blaine thought.

Blaine felt a wordless reassurance deep in his mind, something he had come to recognize as his *kruvgaldur* bond with Penhallow. He had a sense of Penhallow's presence, an infusion of resilience, and an unspoken certainty that he would be strong enough to endure.

Is that why Connor seems so at ease with all of this? Blaine wondered. *His bond must be many times stronger than mine, and he's channeling the Wraith Lord's spirit. It's nice to be able to draw on Penhallow's strength, but will it be enough? What if it isn't?*

The chamber faded from Blaine's sight, replaced by a vision of

Glenreith. This was the manor as he knew it before his exile, before the Great Fire, when the lands had been prosperous and the great house in good repair. Ian McFadden was beneath one of the trees in the orchard, and though his back was turned, from the way his fist rose and fell, it was clear even at a distance that something had drawn his wrath.

Blaine saw himself, a half-grown youth, come running down the manor stairs, shouting at his father. Ian did not pause or turn, and Blaine caught a glimpse of the victim of his father's wrath. Ian held Carr by one arm in an unbreakable grip, while the other large fist landed blow after blow. There was no sound in Blaine's vision, though the figures were speaking. Blaine did not need to hear them. He remembered.

In the vision, Blaine came running at Ian's back, roaring like a bull, and caught his father between the shoulder blades with his own shoulder, shoving him hard enough that Ian stumbled and let go of Carr's arm. Carr scrambled to his feet and ran off as Ian rounded on Blaine. Blaine had grabbed the nearest weapon he could find, a long, forked branch from a nearby tree, and he used it to keep Ian at a distance. Both exchanged shouts, red in the face with anger, as Ian attempted to dodge around Blaine's guard and Blaine kept his father far enough away to postpone the beating that was certain to follow.

Time in the vision slowed, freezing like the inlaid images in a mosaic. And in that moment, Blaine saw something in Ian's face he did not remember from the encounter long ago. Rage twisted Ian's facial expression, but in his eyes was naked fear.

He knew, Blaine thought. *Somehow, even then, he knew I would kill him. Before I knew, before it had even crossed my mind, he saw his fate.*

The vision shifted, as if someone had stirred the placid surface of still water. Blaine saw an unbroken expanse of white that stretched into the gray horizon, and more snow falling from slate-colored skies. He shivered as the snow fell on bare skin where his ragged prison uniform had been shredded by Prokief's beating.

A soldier on either side dragged him, one on each arm, with Blaine between them as deadweight, too injured to stand. It was Velant, one of many times Blaine had gotten on the wrong side of the prison colony's violent commander.

Blood dripped from Blaine's mouth into the snow, leaving a crimson path of droplets. Red stains trailed behind him from his injuries as the guards dragged him across the snow. The gritty ice burned against his raw wounds until his skin grew numb from cold. Blaine knew where the figures in the vision were going. To the 'Hole,' Prokief's oubliettes cut into the ice.

One guard removed the lid from the Hole, then the two guards heaved Blaine into the darkness. Blaine tumbled down, deep into the ice, as they replaced the lid and left him in blackness. He landed hard.

Prokief might have the soldiers haul Blaine out after a day or two, but he might leave him to die of cold. Blaine expected nothing. Then, as now, when he was dying, the visions had come to him, voices and bells and coruscating power, visions he did not remember until now, when he saw them anew.

I barely realized I had any magic at all, Blaine thought. *Not then. But the magic knew me. Meridians ran beneath Edgeland, perhaps beneath Velant. Perhaps that's why I survived. Could the power have recognized the bond in my blood, even then, and sustained me?*

As abruptly as the visions came, they vanished, and with them went the blinding light. Blaine fell to the ground, as if even breathing required more energy than remained. He was bleeding afresh from the cut on his arm and from his battle wounds, and every muscle and sinew ached. From what he could glimpse, the other twelve, even the *talishte*, had collapsed. Their bodies twitched, reassuring Blaine that they were alive.

The candles had guttered out. Gone also was the coruscating light curtain separating the labyrinth from the chamber. Blaine's presence-crystal lay where he had dropped it, but now it was nothing more than a carved piece of charred stone. The obsidian disk hung on its lanyard, flipped faceup against his shirt, dark.

As the shock of being alive receded, Blaine realized that the chant and drumming continued. Magic flowed around and through the chamber, through him and through the others, a silent, roaring river, and for the first time since the Cataclysm, that torrent felt clean and unimpeded.

We did it, Blaine thought wearily. *I don't know if it will work the same as it used to, but the magic is back. We did it.*

He made it to his knees before the chamber swam in his vision and he fell onto all fours, retching violently. Every muscle in his body tightened painfully, sending tremors that cramped his arms and legs and clenched his gut. His heartbeat stuttered and he labored for breath. Blaine fell forward onto the cold stone of the labyrinth, and fought to remain conscious.

Going into the labyrinth 'winds' the magic up, Blaine thought. *We have to walk the rest of the maze to release the power, or we'll die here.*

"Get up!" His voice was a harsh rasp. He managed to reach his knees, and then stood, swaying. "We've got to get out, or the magic will eat us alive."

One by one, the others stirred. Penhallow and Dolan were the first to regain their footing, followed by Connor. When Blaine was certain the thirteen men were conscious and able to move, they began the careful trek back to the outside of the labyrinth.

When they had gone in, the power had not fought them, but the return journey felt to Blaine as if they struggled against a headwind. He was utterly exhausted, and the half-healed battle wounds ached anew from the strain of the magic. Sheer willpower kept him moving, careful to stay inside the labyrinth path, one foot in front of the other. Yet with each step, the power captured in the maze dissipated, and Blaine felt the oppressive weight lift.

Outside the maze, the mages kept up the chant and drumbeat as Blaine staggered from the warded circle. Kestel was waiting for him, and he leaned hard on her as he stumbled. Mages and guards cleared out of their way as Blaine made his way to the rock wall, unwilling to collapse until he was certain the others made it out.

"When the power struck you, I thought you were going to die," Kestel admitted. Although Blaine leaned back against the wall, she stayed under his arm to keep him on his feet. The new Lords of the Blood looked as hard used as Blaine felt, even the *talishte*.

"So did I," Blaine replied. "But not this time. Not tonight." He smiled. "Tonight, we won."

CHAPTER
THIRTY-FIVE

————

I CAN'T BELIEVE WE'RE NOT ALL EITHER DEAD OR barking mad," Piran said.

"Who says we're not?" Connor replied.

A small group gathered in one of the underground rooms beneath Mirdalur after the ritual was over. The Knights had provided food and drink for the mortals and flagons of fresh deer blood for the *talishte*, as well as pallets where the participants in the night's working could rest.

Blaine agreed with Connor, though at the moment, he was too utterly spent to make a flippant remark.

"Here. Eat this. You'll feel better," Kestel said, bringing bread, smoked meat, and cheese to Blaine and Piran, along with hot cups of *fet*.

Blaine shook his head to clear it, and immediately regretted the action. "I really don't remember much after the lightning," he said. His voice was raspy, and his entire body ached. Still, he eyed the food hungrily, feeling as if he had fasted for days. Zaryae looked after Borya, Verran, and Dawe, and across the cramped room, the other mages brought food, drink, or blood to the rest of the weary participants.

"It was a lot like the last time," Kestel said, trying to keep her tone light. Blaine could hear the concern she tried to hide. "We were all on the outside of that curtain of power, totally helpless, and there was nothing even the mages could do except watch you twist and scream in pain." Her voice was steady, but Blaine saw the worry in her eyes.

"We had no idea whether when it was all done, you'd all survive, or whether there would be nothing left but ashes," she added, brushing a strand of red hair out of her eyes. "Dammit, Blaine! Don't you ever do that to me again!"

"And did I worry you awfully, Kestel?" Piran asked with exaggerated concern. Kestel rolled her eyes and punched him in the shoulder.

"You, not really," Kestel said with a forced chuckle. She sighed. "Honestly, it was awful. I didn't see how anyone could live through that."

"Neither did I," Blaine admitted, sipping his hot cup of *fet*.

"Good to see you awake, if not exactly up and around," Nidhud said, walking among the pallets to get to Blaine.

"Did it work?" Blaine asked, looking up.

"Mostly," Nidhud replied. "Dagur, Rikard, and the others are testing that now."

"What do you mean, 'mostly'?" Piran asked with a dangerous note in his voice.

Nidhud shrugged. "The magic appears to be stable. We'll have to test to see if that's really the case and whether it's temporary or permanent."

"Is the magic what it used to be?"

"Probably not," Nidhud said, and held up his hands to forestall argument. "Hear me out! You intend to rebuild much of what was destroyed in the Cataclysm, right?" he asked, and the others nodded. "But no one would claim that what is rebuilt would be exactly as it was before. For a lot of reasons, it can never be exactly as before, but it might be just as good, perhaps even better."

Blaine was silent for a few moments, thinking as he ate. To no one's surprise, Penhallow and Dolan were back on their feet the quickest. They were followed by Connor, the first of the mortals to recover. Blaine watched Connor with worried interest, wondering just how much his bond with Penhallow had changed him.

And how has it changed me, really? Blaine wondered. Even now, he could feel a hint of the *kruvgaldur* bond active in the back of his mind. He was too tired to argue about it, fearing that without Penhallow's assistance, he might collapse. Bits and pieces of memories came back to him from the ritual, of visions and nightmares, and of the underlying bond that held fast beneath them, like a lifeline.

Later, I'm really going to have to have a long talk with both Penhallow and Connor, he promised himself.

"What about the others?" Blaine asked, glancing around the crowded room. He had expected Piran and Niklas to recover rapidly since they did not have magic, and he guessed that the same might be true of Folville, Voss, and Birgen Verner. None of those men looked to have rebounded yet. Dolan and Penhallow walked over to join them, as did Connor.

"Do you remember the Wraith Lord telling you that the last time magic was anchored successfully at Mirdalur, the Lords of the Blood found themselves changed?" Dolan asked, having heard Blaine's question.

Blaine nodded uneasily. "Yes."

"Well, we think something similar happened today as well, but we're not sure just what," Dolan replied.

Piran looked at him as if daring him to make a response. "You're trying to tell me that because I got hit by lightning, now I can throw fire from my fingertips?"

Dolan chuckled. "Probably not. I think you're safe from that," he said. "But if the anchoring works as it did in the past, each of you now has some new magically enhanced ability, or a previous ability has been strengthened. It may take you each a while to figure out what that ability is, and how to use it." He shrugged. "Perhaps it's magic's way of assuring your survival, making you harder to kill."

Piran snorted. "After it did its best to kill us itself," he countered.

"The last time, how did the ritual change you?" Kestel asked Connor, addressing the Wraith Lord. He hesitated, and they could see a change come over his manner as the Wraith Lord took possession.

Vandholt looked thoughtful. "It was quite a long time ago," he said. "I have been trying to remember." He looked at Piran. "One thing I am certain of: It did not change the participants into mages."

"King Merrill could truth-sense, though he tried to keep that a secret," Kestel mused. "Were the abilities gained or enhanced on that level of magic?"

Vandholt nodded. "I agree with Dolan that the...alterations...were protective, but not of full mage strength." He frowned, thinking. "Foresight, touch magic to read the history of an object, the ability to talk with spirits—but not to summon them. Divination with fire and water. An ability to 'see' magic and supernatural power and thus evade traps. Being able to read another person's thoughts, heightened intuition, and in one case, as I recall, dreaming that enabled the person's spirit to travel the astral paths without his body. All abilities that were valuable for rulers. And all of the mortals gained an extended life span—not unlike the effect of the *kruvgaldur*."

"I don't feel any different," Blaine said. But upon reflection, he realized that was not entirely true. His senses seemed sharper, and his awareness keener than normal. Colors looked brighter, sounds carried farther, and his eyesight seemed to note details he might not have even been aware of before the ritual. *Perhaps that's also why I'm now so aware of the* kruvgaldur *with Penhallow,* he thought. *Usually, it's forgotten unless it's needed.*

"What about Solveig?" Blaine asked, noticing that of all of them, Tormod Solveig seemed to be taking the longest to rally.

"The Wraith Lord, Dolan, and Tormod were the only true mages among those within the circle," Penhallow replied, "and Dolan had his *talishte* strength to rely on. Solveig's magic is quite powerful, so I suspect that the ritual took a greater toll on him than on the rest of you."

"Will he retain his magic?" Kestel asked, frowning in concern.

"With luck," Nidhud replied. "The thing is, we don't know whether the changes from the ritual happen immediately, or manifest over time. It could be days—even months—before all of you truly realize how the ritual has changed you."

"If it's all the same to you, I'd rather not get into a battle to test the theory," Blaine said with a tired half smile. He fell silent, searching his thoughts. "And yet..."

"Oh?" Kestel said.

Blaine concentrated, listening for the magic he had learned to sense when he was its sole anchor. "I think the ritual changed my ability to know when magic is being worked nearby from a problem to a benefit. It doesn't drain me anymore, but I still know where magic's being used—a handy thing, especially in battle," he said finally, meeting Nidhud's gaze.

Nidhud nodded. "A change that might have some protective benefits, if it becomes permanent," he replied.

"What about the storms? If the magic's anchored, will the storms lessen?" Kestel asked.

The Wraith Lord, speaking through Connor, grimaced. "Not sure. That's one of the things it will take us some time to figure out. In fact, magic itself is going to require some refiguring, to see exactly what has changed with this new binding," he said.

"This upends everything, just as the Cataclysm did originally," the Wraith Lord continued. "We know we can't go back to what we had before, but what we have now remains to be seen." He gave an enigmatic smile that belonged to Kierken Vandholt, not to Bevin Connor. "These next few months are going to be very interesting."

Their speculation ended as Nidhud was called away by one of the mages, while a *talishte* guard beckoned to Penhallow and Connor.

"Should we be worried?" Kestel murmured, watching Penhallow and Connor in close conference with the guard.

"Probably," Blaine replied. "But right now, I want to go outside," he added, feeling suddenly claustrophobic. "I need some air."

Blaine and Kestel wound their way through the tunnels beneath Mirdalur until a set of stone stairs led upward into the night. Outside, the cold air was fresh and bracing, and for once, the sky was clear, filled with bright stars.

"How many days were we in there?" Blaine asked, leaning against one of the ruined stone walls.

"Three," Kestel replied. "You were all either unconscious or barely able to move for a long time," she said tiredly. She let out a long breath. "It seemed to take forever."

Soldiers patrolled the ruined grounds of the old manor.

Beyond the tumbledown stone walls, troops from each of the victorious warlords' armies stood guard to assure they would not be ambushed. Blaine's own men, along with those loyal to Traher Voss, the Solveigs, and Verner, presented a large, united force against anyone who might seek to interfere. Add to that *talishte* belonging to Penhallow and the Wraith Lord, and Blaine felt like he could rest easy, at least for a night.

Rinka Solveig spotted him as she gave orders to one of her commanders. When the soldiers were dismissed, she strode over with an expression of worry and anger.

"There you are!" she said, looking him up and down. "You survived? Good. What of my brother?"

Blaine told her what he knew, watched her dark eyes narrow as she considered his report. "But he still sleeps?" she questioned.

Blaine nodded. "Yes. Those with strong magic are taking longer to recover. And he may come away from the ritual with even more magic than he had before."

"Maybe a good thing," she replied, her face unreadable. "Maybe not."

"What happened up here during the ritual?" Kestel asked. "Any problems?"

Rinka gave a cold chuckle. "Nothing we couldn't handle."

Her red armor showed cuts and gashes from the battle on the northern plains, dark stains and splatter that did not beg close examination. Her skin was streaked with dirt and blood, and her hair was wet with sweat, despite the cold. It was obvious that she and the soldiers had fought a battle while the others were in the underground chamber. Rinka looked more haggard and gaunt than Blaine remembered, and he wondered if the twins shared a bond of their own, magical or not, that connected her to her brother's distress.

"What happened?" Blaine asked.

Rinka's smile was the expression of a predator. "Hennoch made an attempt to disrupt what we were doing. We did not permit that."

"Did he survive?" Kestel's interest matched Rinka's for deadly focus.

Rinka gave a contemptuous look. "That depends on how much blood he loses on his way home," she said. "We sent his troops running with their tails between their legs, like curs. I stopped the commanders from pursuing them because they weren't our priority, and I had no desire to be led into a trap."

"Lysander's survivors have scattered, and so have Rostivan's," Blaine replied. "They know they won't be welcome among our allies, which leaves Hennoch and Pollard—unless another warlord comes to the fore."

Rinka made a dismissive gesture. "There will always be men happy to snap up the scraps and cobble them back together." She shrugged. "No matter to us. If another power arises, it'll have to challenge us." She smiled, baring her teeth. "And we will kill them, like we've killed the others." They might have asked her more questions, but a captain called for her, and with a nod, she returned to her troops.

"Could it be that simple?" Kestel murmured as Blaine slipped an arm around her shoulders, partly in affection and partly because he was feeling the strain of standing.

Blaine sighed. "Probably not," he admitted, watching as the soldiers bustled around the courtyard and the perimeter. "Pollard's the power behind Hennoch, and Pollard won't give up until one of us is dead."

He let his gaze rise to the black night sky and the stars, which seemed even brighter and closer than usual. "Pentreath Reese was bound, but not destroyed. Until he's dust, I'm not counting him out. I don't think Penhallow and the Wraith Lord have forgotten about him, either."

Kestel leaned into him. "True. And if the survivors from Lysander and Rostivan join up with Hennoch, he might be ready to field an army a lot sooner than we'd like to think."

Blaine nodded wearily. "That's certainly possible. Probable, even. And we'll face the threat when it comes."

Donderath's harrowing was not over; not yet, but perhaps soon. And during it all, there were crops to plant and harvest, walls to rebuild, ale to brew, and a Continent to reclaim.

"It's time to be a lord for a while, instead of a warlord," Blaine said, pulling Kestel close, enjoying her nearness. "I'm ready to go home to Glenreith. There's work to be done."

EPILOGUE

———

Two weeks later

I F REESE IS STILL IMPRISONED, WHY DO WE NEED to see the Elders again?" Connor was seated across the table from Penhallow, and he was aware that the Wraith Lord's spirit hovered nearby. It was just a fortnight after the ritual at Mirdalur, and even though Connor knew that his strengthened bond with Penhallow would change him, he was amazed at how quickly his body had healed.

From having been a breath away from the Sea of Souls, Connor now felt healthy and strong. Even the memory of the horror of that night seemed to have dimmed. Connor fought to remember, unwilling to allow the event to recede in his mind.

"Because matters are not yet settled." The Wraith Lord's voice was a rough whisper, and Connor knew that Vandholt was doing him a kindness by refraining from possessing him until absolutely necessary. "Reese's maker has returned."

Connor could not repress a shiver. "Reese's maker still exists?"

Penhallow nodded soberly. "Thrane is as old as I am—perhaps

a bit older. He was a ruthless and violent man when he was alive, and centuries of undeath haven't improved him."

"Is Thrane an Elder? Or a lord?" Connor searched his memory, but he could not remember ever having heard that name at court.

"Perhaps you know him by his war name: Hemlock," the Wraith Lord replied.

Connor's eyes widened. "I thought Hemlock was a superstition, like Red Mariah—the witch who appears in mirrors if called thrice, and steals souls."

A look passed between Penhallow and the Wraith Lord, and Connor drew back. "Oh no, don't do it. You're going to tell me that Red Mariah isn't entirely a superstition either, aren't you? I don't want to hear it."

"Red Mariah was an insane—and bloodthirsty—conjurer who was cursed to wander the Unseen Realm for her crimes," Vandholt replied. "And as you'll recall, I, too, inhabit the Unseen Realm. I have seen her, unfortunately. She is no myth."

"Red Mariah is the least of our worries," Penhallow said. "But Thrane—Hemlock—is another matter. The fact that there are rumors that he's returned are worrisome, especially given how fragile the consensus of the Elders is right now."

"Returned from where?" Connor leaned forward.

"We don't know. That's the problem. Thrane disappeared nearly seventy years ago, without a trace," Penhallow replied. "He was not the type to avoid attention, so his absence—while not minded—was frequently remarked upon."

"And now he's back? Why?" Connor asked.

"That, m'lad, is the problem," the Wraith Lord said. "There have been rumors that Thrane has stepped in to take advantage of the opportunities now that Lysander, Quintrel, and Rostivan have been killed." He paused. "It's also likely that he'll try to enable Reese to escape. Reese has been a valuable servant."

"Can he do that? Reese, I mean. Can he get loose?"

Penhallow shrugged. "You were in the oubliette with Lorens. Despite the most stringent mortal precautions, Lorens managed to slip his bonds. Few of our kind supported Lorens. I suspect that Reese's support is somewhat broader, though many would hesitate to speak of it aloud."

"What does Thrane want from the Elders?" Connor asked.

"Knowing Thrane, he's got a long list of demands," Penhallow observed drily. "But I'm sure he will insist that Reese be released. He'll try to get sanctions against the Wraith Lord and me for having brought Reese to the Elders' attention."

"Would the Elders support him?"

"Doubtful," the Wraith Lord replied. "But if you recall, in the last vote among the Elders they were hardly united. Out of thirteen Elders, five voted to merely punish Reese and not require the final death, while three would have freed him without sanction and punished Penhallow and me for having brought the matter up." His spectral figure shook its head. "That's a thin margin."

"Are any of the Elders on our side?" Connor asked.

Penhallow chuckled. "On our side? Only Kierken here that we're sure of," he replied. "The others vote primarily for their own self-interest."

"But aren't the Elders supposed to rule for what's best for *talishte* as a group?" Connor asked. Yet he remembered the often-contentious debates within the King's Council, when nobles fought over petty issues when they, too, were supposed to be responsible for the welfare of the kingdom as a whole.

Penhallow looked resigned. "When the kings of Donderath

ruled, the Elders had a purpose. Under mortal rule, we needed a governing body of our own to enforce a code of conduct designed to avoid the kind of slaughter that happened when the Knights of Esthrane were banished, or when Lorens went on a rampage."

He shook his head. "Now there's no single mortal ruler. No recognized authority. The threat of organized extermination is not imminent. And some among our kind are thinking that it would be good if that situation remained permanent."

"It can't," the Wraith Lord replied. "Mortals outnumber us by too large a number. We will always be vulnerable. But there are fools who forget those constraints and dream of a world without rules."

Penhallow raised an eyebrow. "Any man who rails against the need for government bears watching very closely. Honest men appreciate the constables. Only those who wish to do something they should not be doing fear and hate the rule of law."

"So why are we going before the Elders again?" Connor asked.

"We're going before the Elders because someone has to stand against Thrane," Penhallow replied.

"We do have allies," the Wraith Lord said. "Silver, Onyx, and Gold all voted for death. They're the least likely to change their vote."

"It's the ones who voted for punishment we need to watch," Penhallow added. "Had Merrill still been on the throne and the kingdom been as it was, I am certain that several—maybe all—of those votes would have changed to 'death.'"

"And if Thrane gets his way, he'll try to change enough of those votes to get Reese released," Connor said. "Won't he?"

Penhallow and the Wraith Lord nodded. "And if he does, that means Reese will be out for revenge," Penhallow said.

*   *   *

Lundmyhre, the estate of the Wraith Lord, was a two-candlemark ride from Westbain. Connor rode alongside Penhallow, too preoccupied with his thoughts for conversation. Several *talishte* bodyguards followed them. The Wraith Lord had gone on ahead, unencumbered by the need for transportation.

I'm tired of nearly dying or being killed every other day, Connor grumbled to himself. *I just came back from battle, and then the ritual and Mirdalur, and here we go, riding into a confrontation with ancient* talishte, *who could squash me like a bug.*

The Wraith Lord's men were waiting for them when they reached Lundmyhre's boundaries. "My soldiers and I will wait for you here," Penhallow said. "And if we're needed, Kierken will be able to summon us."

The Wraith Lord materialized next to them. "The others will be here in a few moments," he said. "Connor—I fear this may go badly. That's why Lanyon has his soldiers present, and why I need your help."

Connor nodded. "If it keeps Reese locked up, count me in."

Connor gave his reins over to the *talishte* soldiers. He opened himself to the Wraith Lord's spirit, no longer surprised that the possession did not tax his energy as quickly as before his strengthened bond with Penhallow.

How will they know I'm you? Connor fretted as he walked on foot along the narrow path to the circle of standing stones where the Elders would convene their session.

Kierken Vandholt chuckled. *Ask your friends sometime whether they can tell the difference between us. I may share your body, but our mannerisms are quite different.*

The standing stones were large hand-hewn monoliths that

had been raised in their circle in a time long forgotten, even by *talishte*. Their builders were a matter of legend and argument. Mages, astronomers, and scholars debated their origin, but the common folk went out of their way to avoid the circles.

One by one the Elders assembled, each masked and robed figure standing in front of one of the thirteen standing stones. Connor watched as they took their places. Behind their jewel-toned masks, it was impossible to see the faces or expressions. Their masks made them even more intimidating, and far less human.

"Who summoned us?" Emerald was the first to speak.

"I did." A broad-shouldered man Connor had never seen before strode into the circle. He had dark hair and coarse features, with black eyes that missed no advantage. The man had a powerful chest and muscular arms, but he looked more like one of the ruffians hired to keep the peace in a disreputable tavern. "I am Thrane, but perhaps you know me better as Hemlock."

None of the masked figures spoke, but from their stance, Connor could see that the names were known to them. Some turned toward Thrane, eager to hear what he might say. Others leaned back, wary. Still more crossed their arms or turned away.

"Why have you asked for this convocation?" the Wraith Lord asked.

Thrane eyed Connor as if trying to figure out what to make of him. "What right does a mortal have to be here, let alone know my reasons?" Thrane retorted.

"He is my servant, my spirit-bearer, and it is my right to know," the Wraith Lord replied in a tone that made his anger at Thrane's lack of respect clear.

Thrane had the good sense to make a low bow in concession. "My apologies, Lord Vandholt. I did not recognize you."

"You have not answered my question," the Wraith Lord replied, sweeping aside the apology.

Thrane stood to his full height, and his chin rose. "You've imprisoned my blood son, Pentreath Reese," Thrane said, turning to take in the masked figures who encircled him. "I ask you to reconsider, and free him."

"Are you aware that it is a penalty worthy of death to convene the Elders without cause?" Onyx asked.

Thrane made a low bow. "Yes, m'lords. And I am quite fond of my neck. I do not risk it lightly. Yet here I am."

"We have already considered the evidence against Pentreath Reese and determined his fate." This time, it was Silver who spoke.

"We do not reconsider our judgments lightly," Gold added. "And we have rarely reversed our rulings. Why should we now?"

For someone whose fate hung on the forbearance of a group of immortal *talishte*, Thrane looked very much at ease. Connor watched Thrane, sizing him up as he paced back and forth in the center of the circle. The arrogance in Thrane's mannerisms reminded Connor of many nobles he had met when he was in Lord Garnoc's employ.

"Because times have changed, m'lords," Thrane said. "The Elders were gathered to protect *talishte* against powerful mortals." He turned in a circle, one hand out, palm up, as if to gesture toward the world itself. "Behold. There are no more powerful mortals. The kings of the Continent are dead, and there are no heirs. Much of the nobility is dead, and what remains is impoverished and disorganized. If the threat for which the Elders were gathered no longer exists, why are we bound by rules from a time that is no more and never will be again?"

As much as Connor disliked Thrane, he had to admit that

the man's natural charisma made it impossible to ignore him. He wondered if Thrane's charm might be a form of magic.

"Reese attacked me on my lands, and Penhallow in his crypt," the Wraith Lord countered. "Those actions alone are punishable by death."

"Yet we are so few now, aren't we?" Thrane asked, hands clasped in front of him like a barrister making a plea to the court. "So many of our number lost in the Great Fire, and before that, to mortals who hated and feared us. So many of our broods unable to sustain themselves after the Cataclysm. We're not as numerous as we once were—and we were never many. Can we afford to destroy our own kind?"

Thrane was eloquent, and his arguments came across as reasoned and sincere, yet Connor's intuition tolled a warning that grew more frantic with every word Thrane spoke.

"We have not ruled to destroy Reese, although many of our number believed he earned such a penalty," Silver replied. "If all is forgiven when centuries have passed, then what is a few decades' imprisonment? Merely a chance to reflect upon one's missteps and find resolve to do better, is it not?"

Connor could not see Silver's expression, but from the Elder's tone, he could have sworn Silver was enjoying baiting Thrane.

Is it possible that some of the Elders know Thrane? Connor asked the Wraith Lord silently.

Almost certain, the Wraith Lord replied.

Does Thrane know—or guess—that he has allies among the Elders? Aren't their identities supposed to be secret?

Connor heard the Wraith Lord's silent chuckle. *Immortality doesn't change human nature. All of the games, the intrigue, the petty competition that went on at court go on among* talishte— *only they play out over centuries, and at a much higher cost.*

"I did not vote for punishment, or death." Aubergine

spoke up. There was a tone in the Elder's voice that presumed vindication.

"Nor did I," Sapphire added. "Reese was impertinent, and he has been censured. As for his 'crimes'—this is a new era. New rules apply."

"I don't think we went far enough by half," Gray replied. "This isn't the first time Reese has overstepped his boundaries. He serves no one but himself, and his dealings will cause grief for all of us. I'd like nothing better than to see him turned to ashes."

"Kings are not the only ones who can wield power," Jade said, with apparent indifference. "The Knights of Esthrane have returned, and while their numbers are small, they are a powerful force to return the kingdom to stability."

"Lord Blaine McFadden, Lanyon Penhallow, and I have already made an alliance with General Dolan and his Knights," the Wraith Lord argued. "Together with McFadden's allied warlords, more than half of the kingdom is being returned to the rule of law, including Castle Reach. Reese has tried, and failed, to prevent that from happening. If you desire stability, there is no benefit to freeing Reese."

"The situation is still fluid," Thrane argued. "Why not allow Reese and his allies to fight for their vision of the future of Donderath and let the decisions about the future fall to the victor?"

"You mean, winner take all." The Wraith Lord's voice was cold. "Much like the 'decisions' that brought the kingdom to its knees in the Meroven War."

Thrane wheeled to face the Wraith Lord, and for an instant, Connor could see his geniality slip, revealing a canny predator beneath. "Yes, if that's the way you wish to put it. Let the strongest survive. Remove the most dangerous predator, and you have a war among the weak. That proves nothing. If the others wish to fashion the kingdom in their own mold, then let them emerge victorious."

"If the Elders had followed your logic, Reese would have been destroyed, not imprisoned," Silver replied disdainfully. "Reese's forces lost decisively at the Battle of Valshoa to McFadden and the Knights. By our own law—*talishte* law—Reese compromised himself when he sent his men to attack the Wraith Lord." Connor felt the Elder's anger and contempt for Thrane. "We have been merciful in our judgment. You are not wise to press for more."

"I agree with Thrane," Saffron said. Her voice was cold with anger and impatience. "The time of the Elders has ended. *Talishte* will find their place in this remade world, and we will not need to have a ruling body to keep our people from offending mortals. This time, we claim a seat at the table, instead of being the lackeys of the king."

"The last time magic failed, there was a century of bloodshed until the kingdom became stable once more," Brown replied. "I have no desire to return to constant warfare. I like being civilized, and civilization requires stability. The sooner Donderath's forces find balance, the better our existence becomes."

"If you'll recall, we existed on the edges of that civilization," snapped Amber. "Sometimes tolerated, often hunted, and our lands confiscated, our homes and resting places burned. I'm tired of looking to mortals for permission to exist. I welcome a change."

"As do I," Aubergine replied. "I see no further reason for the Council of Elders to exist."

"Then dissolve," Thrane challenged. "Your purpose was to protect *talishte* by making them invisible and harmless to mortals. We have no king left to fear. How can we emerge to own the future unless we seize our opportunity?"

Connor could feel the Wraith Lord's anger. Thrane's arguments were having an effect. Those among the Elders who had been unwilling to put Reese to death were clearly in support of Thrane's vision for the future. Even those who had voted to punish Reese seemed to be giving serious consideration to what Thrane said.

It was equally clear that others were growing increasingly angry with Thrane. "Enough," said Onyx. "You petitioned to speak to the Elders. You have made your argument, but we are not obliged to reconsider our decision. As for the role of the Council of Elders, that is not your concern."

"Maybe not," argued Emerald, "but he's only said aloud what we have each wondered privately. Without a king to persecute us, there is no central authority to fear. We need not dread the judgment of mortals; they are not strong enough to threaten us. That makes the Elders unnecessary. Let circumstances sort themselves out, and if there is need of us, then we can reconvene. I move to disband the Council."

Can they do that? Connor asked the Wraith Lord silently.

Technically, yes, the Wraith Lord replied. *Any member of the Council can bring up a matter for a vote.*

"I agree. Disband the Council." The second vote came from Aubergine.

"Our role in this new landscape may be different, but we are still a force for order, which is necessary even for *talishte* if we are not to become savages." Onyx crossed his arms across his chest.

"I rather like savages," Saffron replied. "They're tasty. I welcome the chance to operate openly, making no secret of who we are, using our abilities to carve out a piece for ourselves. I vote to disband."

"You are voting for your own downfall," Silver argued. "Even *talishte* need rules. No one is honest enough to remain civilized without some kind of sheriff waiting to punish wrongdoers."

"Who's to say what we do is wrong?" Red challenged. "Is the wildcat wrong because it kills a deer? We are the superior beings. We determine what is right and what is wrong. I vote to disband."

"We are not gods," Gray countered. "And whenever we have forgotten that, we have paid dearly. The Council keeps the actions of a few from jeopardizing the rest of us. I oppose disbanding."

"The Council exists because we will it to exist, and it ceases to exist if we declare it so," Sapphire said. "And I declare the Council disbanded." With that, Sapphire left the circle.

"Agreed," Red said, and walked off.

Saffron, Amber, and Emerald followed them without a word. Thrane glanced around at the empty places by the standing stones, and walked away, chuckling as he went.

Aubergine remained behind to savor the broken circle. "What becomes of your rule of law now?" he taunted. "You are no longer needed." With that, he headed into the darkness beyond the standing stones. Jade lingered a moment, and then followed.

Six of the original thirteen remained in their places. Connor did not need to see their faces to read the shock and confusion in their posture.

"What now?" Silver asked. Her voice was carefully neutral, but Connor could see the uncertainty in her stance.

"We could do exactly what Aubergine dared. We who remain are the Council. No one legitimized the Council's formation; we need no one to validate our continuance," Gray replied. It was clear to Connor that several of the remaining Elders were angry and ready for a fight.

"Even if we remain a body, our influence is diminished," Brown said. "We became Elders because we were the oldest of the *talishte*," Brown continued. "And because we had the largest broods, and controlled the most *talishte*. What we banned or what we permitted became the law to our own get. That accounted for the majority of *talishte* in the kingdom. And it still does."

"We can still exert influence, and that may be enough to change the tide," Onyx replied. Onyx was angry, as was the Wraith Lord.

"Without the full council, it would be a shadow of our former control," Gold replied. "Perhaps too little to matter amid such chaos."

"Maybe not," Silver challenged. "A boulder can change the course of a mighty river. Onyx still holds Reese prisoner, which alone could change the outcome."

"I agree with Brown," the Wraith Lord said. "We are not many, but our edicts control the allegiance and actions of hundreds of *talishte*. Just a handful of *talishte* can affect the course of a battle. We can still present an impact out of proportion to the size of our forces. It could well be enough to determine who becomes the next mortal king of Donderath."

"The remaking of the Continent will be like weighing beans on a scale," Onyx said. "At some point, one more bean throws the scales out of balance, but no one knows until it happens which bean will make the difference. Our small factions are like those beans, and sooner or later, one of us will tip the balance."

"Then we are agreed," the Wraith Lord said. "We may not be the Council of Elders, but we will remain a council of equals, and where we can lend our influence to restore a stable kingdom, we will seek alliance to do so."

"Agreed," replied Onyx. "And I shall do everything in my power to keep Reese imprisoned, according to his sentence."

"Yes," Silver said. "But more than that, we've let Penhallow's brood bear the brunt of the fighting thus far. If we expect to restrain Reese and Thrane, we'd best be willing to bring our own soldiers to the fray."

"We are agreed," replied Brown, after a murmured consultation with Gold. "Both against Thrane and with stepping into the fight with our own broods. We have remained on the sidelines too long."

"I don't know what game Thrane is playing, but I'm happy to be on the other side," Gray said. "Agreed to both propositions."

The Wraith Lord nodded. "Very well. Your broods become a thousand spies. If you have something of significance to report, summon the rest of us."

"Do you think Thrane will raise Reese's get to come against us?" Brown asked.

The Wraith Lord and Onyx both nodded. "I think it's entirely likely," Onyx replied.

Onyx gave the Wraith Lord an appraising look. "This McFadden you've allied with. He brought back the magic, and anchored it. But can he lead an army?"

"His forces did just fine at Valshoa, and again at the Battle of the North," the Wraith Lord replied. "If there's anyone who can unite a shattered kingdom, Blaine McFadden is our best chance."

"I never would have figured you for a kingmaker, Kierken," Onyx replied.

"I don't like the other options," the Wraith Lord replied with a shrug. "Penhallow and I have seen this kind of thing happen too often before, done nothing, and we found that we didn't care for the results. So this time, I'm not leaving it up to chance."

"That's a dangerous game," Gold warned.

"I don't think there are any other kinds left in Donderath," the Wraith Lord replied. "But I am quite certain that our fates hang on the outcome."

*   *   *

Later that evening, at Solsiden, Vedran Pollard looked up in annoyance as Kerr stood in the doorway to the study, a look of fear and chagrin on his face. "My lord," he said. "You have a guest."

"Who in Raka would be out on a night like this?" Pollard demanded. He rose to his feet, sword drawn.

A dark-haired man with shrewd black eyes strode into the room. He had the powerful build of a brawler and the pallor of a *talishte*. "Who in Raka, indeed," the stranger said. "I'm Lord Thrane, your new master. Most call me Hemlock, like the poison."

Thrane peeled off his still-dripping cloak and handed it without a backward glance to Kerr. The doors closed behind Kerr, leaving Pollard alone with Thrane, who had already taken a seat in the best wing chair and stretched out, looking deceptively vulnerable. Pollard did not rise to the bait.

"There are a couple of dead men you'll need to bury when the storm is over," Thrane added. "The others obligingly got out of my way."

"We had *talishte* at the doors," Pollard snapped. "They were supposed to stop unwanted guests."

" 'Unwanted'?" Thrane mused with a dangerous casualness. "You don't even know why I'm here."

"I'm not in need of a new master," Pollard replied. "I serve Lord Reese."

Thrane gave an eloquent shrug. "Ah well, there's been a problem with that. He's indisposed. But as the stake pierced his heart, I heard him scream through the *kruvgaldur*. And I came."

Pollard felt a cold dread that had nothing to do with the storm that howled outside. "That's impossible," he snapped.

An unpleasant, mocking smile touched the corners of Thrane's lips. "Oh, I assure you, it happened just that way." He eyed Pollard like a predator sizing up its prey. "I'm his maker, and I'm here to clean up his mistakes," Thrane added as the charm in his voice turned to steel.

"Can you prove it?"

Thrane gave an icy chuckle. "I could—but you would not appreciate it." He met Pollard's gaze. "You know what I'm saying to be true. You can feel it, through the bond."

"Reese told me about you," Pollard said, remaining where he stood. He sheathed his sword, knowing that it would be of little use against a *talishte* of Thrane's age and strength. "If you're who you claim to be."

Thrane gave him a leisurely glance that held an undertone of malice. "You know who I am. Reese was my get, and through him, you are mine."

Much as Pollard wished he could deny it, Thrane was right. The *kruvgaldur* conveyed a sense of *knowing*. The proof was indeed in the blood. "Reese told me he hadn't heard from you, hadn't seen you in nearly a century," Pollard challenged. "Why come back now?"

Thrane chuckled. "Because now is the perfect time. The Continent is ripe for the taking, even if Reese couldn't quite handle the task." He shrugged. "Never send a soldier to do a general's job."

ACKNOWLEDGMENTS

Thanks always to my readers, those who are just discovering my books and those who keep coming back for continued adventures. Because you read, I write.

Thanks also to my agent, Ethan Ellenberg, and his team. You've got my back, and I appreciate all that you do.

And thank you to my editor, Susan Barnes, and the whole Orbit crew, including Laura Fitzgerald, Ellen Wright, Anna Jackson, and Gemma Conley-Smith, and all the other folks who work hard to make my books happen and get them where they need to go.

Plenty of thanks as well to the wonderful folks at Arisia, Illogicon, Shevacon, Mysticon, Awesomecon, Capclave, Lunacon, Chattacon, Libertycon, Ravencon, Balticon, ConCarolinas, ConGregate, Dragon*Con, Atomacon, Philcon, Contraflow, Confluence, and the Arizona and Carolinas Renaissance Festivals, who have welcomed me as a guest author for so long—as well as the new conventions I have yet to experience. I truly appreciate the warm welcome fandom offers and the chance to participate in convention programming to meet wonderful people and give back to a community I love.

Thanks as well to my Thrifty Author Publishing Success Network Meetup group, for being an awesome group of writers. I have a blast working with you, and together we have all come so far.

Thank you to all of my author, artist, musician, performer, and reader convention friends and Renaissance Festival regulars who help me survive life on the road, to the fantastic bookstore owners and managers who carry on a valiant fight on the front lines of this crazy publishing industry, and to my social-media friends and followers, who are always up for some online mayhem.

And most of all, thanks to my husband, Larry Martin, who plays a huge part in bringing all the books and short stories to life. He's my best first editor, brainstorming accomplice, proofreader extraordinaire, and in 2015, he'll become official coauthor of our new Steampunk series. It wouldn't happen without him, and I'm grateful for his help. Thanks also to my children, who are usually patient with the demands of the writing life, and for my dogs, Kipp and Flynn, who are experts at dispelling writer's block. It takes a village to write a book, and I treasure every one of you.

extras

www.orbitbooks.net

about the author

Gail Z. Martin discovered her passion for SF, fantasy, and ghost stories in elementary school. The first story she wrote – at age five – was about a vampire. Her favorite TV show as a preschooler was *Dark Shadows*. At age fourteen she decided to become a writer. She enjoys attending SF/Fantasy conventions, Renaissance fairs, and living-history sites. She is married and has three children, a Himalayan cat, and a golden retriever.

Find out more about Gail Z. Martin and other Orbit authors by registering for the free monthly newsletter at www.orbitbooks.net.

if you enjoyed

WAR OF SHADOWS

look out for

THE FALCON THRONE

Tarnished Crown: Book One

by

Karen Miller

CHAPTER ONE

B rassy-sweet, a single wavering trumpet blast rent the cold air. The destriers reared, ears flattened, nostrils flaring, then charged each other with the ferocity of war.

"*Huzzah!*" the joust's excited onlookers shouted, throwing handfuls of barley and rye into the pale blue sky. The dry seeds fell to strike their heads and shoulders and the trampled, snow-burned grass beneath their feet. Blackbirds, bold as pirates, shrieked and squabbled over the feast as children released from the working day's drudgery shook rattles, clanged handbells, blew whistles and laughed.

Oblivious to all save sweat and fear and the thunder of hooves, the two battling nobles dropped their reins and lowered their blunted lances. A great double crash as both men found their marks. Armour buckled, bodies swayed, clods of turf flew. Their destriers charged on despite each brutal strike.

With a muffled cry, his undamaged lance falling, abandoned, Ennis of Larkwood lurched half out of his saddle, clawed for his dropped reins, lost his balance and fell. For three strides his horse dragged him, both arms and his untrapped leg flailing wildly, helmeted head bouncing on the tussocked dirt. Then the stirrup-leather broke and he was free. Squires burst from the sidelines like startled pheasants, two making for the snorting horse, three rushing to their fallen lord.

Heedless of the vanquished, the crowd cheered victorious Black Hughe, youngest son of old Lord Herewart. Hughe let slip his ruined lance, pushed up his helmet's visor and raised a clenched, triumphant fist as his roan stallion plunged and shied. The mid-afternoon sun shimmered on his black-painted breastplate, thickly chased with silver-inlaid etchings.

"Fuck," Balfre muttered, wishing he could reach beneath his own armour and scratch his ribs. "Did a more rampant coxcomb ever draw breath?"

Standing beside him, sadly plain in undecorated doublet and hose, his brother sighed. "I wish you wouldn't do this."

"Someone must," he said. "And since you refuse, Grefin, who else is there? Or are you saying our dear friend Hughe isn't ripe for a little plucking?"

Grefin frowned. "I'm saying the duke will be ripe to toss you into the dankest dungeon he can find once he hears what you've done. You know he's got no love for—"

"Aimery clap his heir in irons?" Balfre laughed. "Don't be an arse, Gref. His pride would never let him."

"And your pride will get you broken to pieces, or worse!"

Hughe had pranced his destrier to the far end of the makeshift tourney ground, so his gaggle of squires could prepare him for the next joust. Ennis was on his feet at last, battered helmet unbuckled and tugged off to reveal a wash of blood coating the left side of his face. Much of his close-cropped flaxen hair was dyed scarlet with it. He needed a squire's help to limp off the field. As the shouting for Hughe died down there came a scattering of applause for Ennis, no more than polite recognition. Harcia's rustics had little patience for defeat.

Balfre shook his head. "You know, if Hughe's a coxcomb then Ennis is a pickled dullard. Any donkey-riding peasant with a barley-stalk could push him off a horse."

"My lord!"

Turning, he looked down at the eager young squire who'd run the short distance from their rough and ready tourney-stall and halted at his elbow.

"What?"

The squire flinched. "Master Ambrose says it be time for your bout, and to come, my lord. If it please you."

"Tell Ambrose to polish my stirrups. *Fuck*. Does he think the joust will start without me?"

"No, my lord," said the squire, backing away. "I'll tell him to wait, my lord."

Balfre watched the youth scuttle to Master Armsman Ambrose. "Speaking of pickled dullards . . . " He grimaced. "I swear, Grefin, that turnip-head must've snuck into Harcia from Clemen. He's witless enough to be one of scabrous Harald's subjects. Don't you think?"

But his brother wasn't listening. Instead, Grefin was raking his troubled gaze across the nearby jostling villagers, and Ennis having his split scalp stitched by a tourney leech, and beyond him the small, untidy knot of lesser men who'd come to test their armoured mettle and now stood defeated, and the heavily hoof-scarred tilt-run with its battered wicker sheep-hurdle barrier, to at length settle on Hughe and his squires. The chuffer had climbed off his destrier and was exchanging his dented black-and-silver breastplate for one unmarked but just as gaudy. It would be a vaunted pleasure, surely, to dent that one for him too.

"Balfre—"

If this weren't such a public place, be cursed if he wouldn't hook his brother's legs out from under him and put his arse in the dirt where it belonged.

"Hold your tongue, Grefin. Or better yet, since you've no stomach for sport, trot back to the Croft and lift your lance there, instead. Plant another son in your precious wife. After all, you've only sired one so far. You must be good for at least one more."

"Balfre, don't."

"I mean it," he said, keeping harsh. Refusing to see the shadow of hurt in Grefin's eyes. "If all you can do is carp then you're no good to me. In truth, it havocs me why you came in the first place."

"To keep you from breaking your neck, I hope," said Grefin, still frowning. "What havocs me is why *you* came! Look around, Balfre. We stand in an open field, far from any great house, and those who cheer and groan your efforts are villagers, herdsmen, peddlers and potboys."

"So you'd deny the local churls an hour or two of entertainment? You're turning mean-spirited, little brother."

Grefin hissed air between his teeth. "It's a question of dignity. Aside from you, and Hughe, and Ennis, who of any note came today to break his lance? Not our cousin. Not even Waymon, and he's a man who'll wrestle two drunk wild boars in a mire."

"Come on, Gref," he said, grinning despite his temper. "Even you have to admit that was funny."

"Side-splitting, yes. And I'm sure the squires who broke themselves to save Waymon from being ripped wide from throat to cock laughed all the way to the bone-setter!"

"Grefin—"

"No, Balfre. You'll listen," his brother said, and took his elbow. "You're Harcia's heir. You owe its duke more than this joust against a gaggle of mudder knights fit only to ride the Marches."

Wrenching his arm free, Balfre looked to where Ambrose and his squires stood waiting. His stallion was there, his unbroken lances and his helmet. Catching his eye, Ambrose raised a hand and beckoned, agitated.

He looked again at his niggling brother. "Where and how I choose to romp is my concern. Not yours. Not Aimery's."

"Of course it's Aimery's concern. He has enough to fret him without you risking yourself here. Those bastard lords of the Green Isle—"

Familiar resentment pricked, sharper than any spur. "You can throw down that cudgel, Grefin. When it comes to the Green Isle, Aimery has his remedy."

"Balfre . . . " Grefin sighed. "He needs more time."

"He's had nearly two years!"

"It's been that long since Malcolm died. But Mother died in autumn, and here we are scant in spring."

"What's Mother to do with it? She wasn't his Steward!"

"No," Grefin said gently. "She was his beating heart. He still weeps for her, Balfre. And for Malcolm. Both griefs are still raw. And now you'd have him weeping for you, too?"

The chilly air stank of churned mud and horse shit. A troupe of acrobats was amusing the crowd as it waited for the last joust. Motley painted canvas balls and striped wooden clubs danced hand-to-hand and man-to-man through the air, the jonglers' skill so great they never dropped even one. From time to time they snatched a cap from a villager's head and juggled that too. The field echoed with delighted laughter.

Balfre glared at them, unamused. Aimery weep for him? That would be the fucking day. "I never knew you had such a poor opinion of my lance-skills."

"This has nothing to do with jousting," Grefin retorted. "Please, Balfre. Just . . . let it go. Who cares what a sophead like Hughe mutters under his breath?"

"I care!" Blood leaping, he shoved his brother with both hands, hard enough to mar Grefin's dark green doublet. "When what he mutters is heard by a dozen men? *I care.* And if you cared for me, *you'd* care."

"I do! But Balfre, you *can't*—"

"Oh, fuck off, Grefin! Before I forget myself and give those gaping churls reason enough to gossip for a week!"

Grefin folded his arms, mule-stubborn. "I don't want to."

"And I don't care what you want."

Holding his brother's resentful stare, unflinching, Balfre waited. Grefin would relent. He always did. There was a softness at the core of him that made sure of it. A good thing for Harcia he wasn't Aimery's heir. Such a softness would leave the duchy's throat bared to faithless men like Harald of Clemen.

At last Grefin huffed out a frustrated breath. "Fine. But never say I didn't warn you," he said, and retreated.

Still simmering, Balfre returned to Ambrose. The Master Armsman near cracked his skull in two, shoving his gold-chased helmet onto his head.

"For shame, my lord," Ambrose said in his rasping voice, come from a sword-hilt to the neck in the desperate, long-ago battle that had made Aimery duke. "Dallying like a maid. This might be a rumptiony shigshag we be at but still you should be setting of a timely example."

Balfre bore with the reprimand. The armsman had served two dukes of Harcia already, thereby earning for himself a small measure of insolence. With a nod, he held out his hands so the turnip-head squire could gauntlet him. The burnished steel slid on cleanly, cold and heavy.

Ambrose started his final armour inspection. "You been watching that rump Hughe?"

"I have," he said, twisting his torso to be certain of no sticking points in his breastplate, which was gold-chased like his helmet and worth more than Hughe's horse. "Nothing's changed since the last time we bouted. He still drops his lance a stride too soon, and sits harder on his right seatbone."

"True enough." Ambrose slapped his pupil's steel-clad shoulder. "And shame be on his tiltmaster. But for all that, he be a brutey jouster. You'll be kissing dirt, my lord, if you don't have a care."

"Then shame be on *my* tiltmaster," Balfre said, flashing Ambrose a swift smirk. "If I do kiss the dirt, I'll have to find myself a new one."

Because this was no formal tourney they lacked judges to keep time or award points and penalties. There was the lone hornblower, though, for the sake of the ragged crowd. As Hughe remounted his restive stallion, one of his squires ran to the man and gave an order. Obedient, the appointed villager blew his horn to alert the crowd to the next joust.

Balfre nodded at Ambrose, then crossed to the wooden mounting block where his destrier was held fast by two squires. As he approached, one of them was doltish enough to shift too far sideways. The stallion lashed out its foreleg and caught the man on his thigh with an iron-shod hoof. Squealing, the squire crumpled.

"Maggot-brain!" said Ambrose, hurrying to drag him clear. Then he gestured at turnip-head. "Don't stand there gawping, you peascod. Hold the cursed horse!"

The excited villagers set up another din of handbells and rattles and whistles. Stood at a distance in their second-rate armour, Ennis and the vanquished mudder knights cast envious looks at the stallion. Quivering with nerves, eager for the joust, the horse tossed its head and swished its thick black tail. As Balfre reached the mounting block it bared its teeth and snapped, strong enough to rip fingers from an unprotected hand.

"*Bah!*" he said, and punched the stallion's dish-round cheek. "Stand still!"

Walking to and fro, the hornblower sounded another rallying blast, coaxing more raucous cheers from the crowd. On the far side of the tourney ground Hughe kicked his roan destrier forward, scattering his squires like beetles. One tottered behind him, awkwardly carrying his lance.

Rolling his eyes, Balfre picked up his reins, shoved his left foot into his stirrup and swung his right leg up and over his jousting saddle's high cantle. The moment he settled on his destrier's back he felt the animal tense beneath him, its breath coming in angry grunts. Not even his heaviest gauntlets muffled its throttled energy, tingling from the curbed bit to his fingers. Through the steel protecting his thighs and lower legs he could feel his mount's barrel ribs expand and contract, and the pent-up furious power in the muscular body beneath him. This was his best horse, and they were well-matched in both temper and skill. Only for Black Hughe would he risk the beast here. But Hughe was owed a mighty drubbing, and to be sure of it he'd chance even this animal.

With a decided tug he closed his helmet's visor then held out his hand. "Lance!"

The weight of the carved, painted timber woke old bruises and strains. Stifling an oath, he couched the lance in its proper place, pricked spurs to his horse's flanks, then softened the bit's sharp bite.

The destrier leapt like a flycatcher, snorting. White foam flew from its mouth. Prisoned within his gold-chased helm, his vision narrowed to a slit and the crowd's roaring a hollow boom, Balfre laughed aloud. Aside from a writhing woman pinned on his cock, was there anything better in the world than a lance in his hand, a grand horse between his legs, and a man before him a handful of heartbeats from defeat?

No. There wasn't.

Snorting, ears pricked, the destrier settled into a stately, knee-snapping prance. He sat the dance with ease, guiding the stallion to the start of the tilt-run with nothing more than his shifting weight and the touch of his long-shanked, elaborate spurs. There he halted, and paid no heed to the crowd's wild cheering or the stallion's threatening half-rears.

"Black Hughe!" he called, loud enough to be heard through his helmet. "You stand ready?"

"I indeed stand ready, Balfre!" Hughe shouted back. "Do I have your pardon now, for the unseating of you later?"

"You'll have my pardon once you answer for your slur."

"My lord," said Hughe, defiant, then closed his own visor and demanded his lance.

As the hornblowing churl took his place midway along the rough tilt-run, horn ready at his lips, the watching villagers and mudder knights fell silent. Only the blackbirds kept up their squabbling, seeking the last grains of seed.

The horn sounded again, a single trembling note. Balfre threw his weight forward as he felt his stallion's quarters sink beneath him, felt its forehand lift, saw its noble head and great, crested neck rise towards his face. It bellowed, a roaring challenge, then stood on its strong hindlegs. Night-black forelegs raked the air. He loosened the reins, gripped the lance and spurred the stallion's flanks. The horse plunged groundwards, bellowing again . . . and charged.

Blurred, breathless speed. Pounding heart. Heaving lungs. Nothing before him but Black Hughe on his horse and the memory of his hateful taunt, dagger-sharp and unforgivable.

Seven thundering strides. Six. Five.

He tucked the lance tight to his side, closed his thighs, dropped the reins. Blinked his eyes free of sweat . . . and took aim . . . and struck.

A double shout of pain, as his lance-head impacted Hughe's armoured body and shattered, as Hughe's undamaged lance struck then glanced harmlessly aside. Pain thrummed through him like the ringing of a great bell, like the clashing of a hammer against the anvil of the world. His fingers opened, releasing the splintered remains of his lance. Then they closed again, on his dropped reins. He hauled on them, unkindly, and his destrier shuddered to a head-shaking halt. A tug and a spurring, and he was turned back to look for Hughe.

Herewart's youngest son was sprawled on the tilt-run's dirt like a starfish, his fancy breastplate dented, his helmet scratched, his brown eyes staring blindly at the sky.

"My lord! My lord!"

And that was Ambrose, the old, scarred man, running hoppy and hamstrung towards him. Turnip-head and another squire scurried at his heels. Hughe's squires were running too, the ones that weren't dashing after his ill-trained horse.

Ambrose, arriving, snatched at the destrier's reins. His pocked face, with its faded sword marks, stretched splitting-wide in a tottytooth smile.

"A doughty strike, my lord, *doughty*! The best from you I've surely seen! Lord Grefin will bite his thumb, for certain, when he's told what he missed."

Grefin. A curse on Grefin and his milksop mimbling. Balfre shoved up his visor, then kicked his feet free of the stirrups and twisted out of his saddle. The jar in his bones as he landed on the hoof-scarred ground made him wince. Ambrose saw it, but nobody else. He held out his hands for the squires to pull off his gauntlets, and when they were free unbuckled and tugged off his helmet for himself.

"Take the horse," he commanded. "I would speak to Black Hughe."

"My lord," said Ambrose, holding stallion and helmet now. "We'll make ready to depart."

The villagers and mudder knights were still cheering, the ragtag children shaking their rattles and handbells and blowing their whistles. He waved once, since it was expected, then turned from them to consider old Herewart's son. The lingering pains in his body were as nothing, drowned in the joy of seeing his enemy thrown down.

"Lord Balfre," Hughe greeted him, his voice thin as watered wine. His squires had freed him from his helmet and thrust a folded tunic beneath his head. "Your joust, I think."

With a look, Balfre scattered the squires who hovered to render their lord aid. Then he dropped to one knee, with care, and braced an aching forearm across his thigh.

"Hughe."

Black Hughe was sweating, his face pale beneath the blood seeping from a split across the bridge of his nose. More blood trickled from one nostril, and from the corner of his mouth. He looked like a knifed hog.

"I'm not dying, Balfre," Hughe said, slowly. "I bit my tongue. That's all."

"And to think, Hughe, if you'd bitten it the sooner you'd not be lying here now in a welter of your gore, unhorsed and roundly defeated," he said kindly, and smiled.

Hughe coughed, then gasped in pain. "My lord—"

"Hughe, Hughe . . ." Leaning forward, Balfre patted Black Hughe's bruised cheek. Mingled sweat and blood stained his fingers. He didn't mind. They were his prize. "I'm going now. Without your horse and armour. I didn't joust you for them."

"My lord," said Hughe, and swallowed painfully. "Thank you."

"Not at all. And Hughe, for your sake, heed me now. Remember this moment. Engrave it on your heart. So the next time you think to slight my prowess with my lance? You think again – and stay silent."

Hughe stared at him, struck dumb. Balfre smiled again, not kindly. Pushed to his feet, spurning assistance, gave Hughe his armoured back and walked away.

Temper sour as pickled lemon after his fractious dealings on the Green Isle, Aimery of Harcia disembarked his light galley in no mood for delay. Not waiting to see if his high steward and the others were ready, he made his way down the timber gang-plank, booted heels sharply rapping, and leapt the last few steps with the ease of a man half his age. The surety of steady ground beneath his feet at once lifted his spirits. Ah! Blessed Harcia! Never mind it was little more than a stone's throw from the mainland to the Green Isle. He'd stick a sword through his own gizzards before confessing to a soul how much he hated sailing.

"'Tis good to be home, Your Grace," said his high steward, joining him.

Staring at the busy harbour village of Piper's Wade crowded before them, Aimery breathed in the mingled scents of fresh salt air, old fish guts, people and beasts. Some might call the air tainted, a stench, but never him. It was the smell of Harcia, his duchy, sweeter than any fresh bloom.

"We're not home yet, Curteis. Not quite." He smiled. "But this'll do. Now, let's be off. I can hear the Croft calling."

His party's horses had been stabled against their return at nearby Piper's Inn. With their baggage to be off-loaded from the galley and transported by ox-cart, he led his people to the inn with purposeful haste, greeting the villagers who greeted him with a nod and a friendly word in passing, making sure they knew he was pleased to see them but alas, could not stop . . . only to be halted in the Piper's empty, sunlit forecourt by a wildly bearded man in embroidered rags.

"My lord! Duke Aimery!" Skinny arms waving, the man shuffled into his path. A soothsayer from the old religion, half his wits wandered off entirely. Lost, along with most of his teeth. Twig-tangled grey hair, lank past his shoulders, framed a seamed and sun-spoiled lean face. His pale grey eyes were yellowed with ill health, and sunken. "A word, my lord! Your pardon! A word!"

It was held bad luck to spurn a soothsayer. Aimery raised a warning hand to his four men-at-arms. "Keep yourselves. There's no harm here. See to the horses and you, Curteis, settle our account with the innkeeper."

They knew better than to argue. As he was obeyed, and his scribe and body squire hastily took themselves out of the way, Aimery turned to the ragged man.

"You know me then, soothsayer?"

The soothsayer cackled on a gust of foul breath. "Not I, my lord. The stars. The little frogs. The wind. The spirits in the deep woods know you, my lord. But they whisper to me."

"And what do they whisper?"

Those sunken, yellow-tinged eyes narrowed. "I could tell you. I should tell you. But will I be believed? Do you honour the spirits? Or . . . " The soothsayer spat. Blackish-green phlegm smeared his lips. "Are you seduced by the grey men, my lord?"

The grey men. The Exarch's monks, harbingers of a new religion. It had barely scratched the surface of Harcia, though its roots grew deep in other lands. The soothsayer stared at him, hungrily, as though his reply must be a feast.

"I'm seduced by no one," he said. "Every philosophy has its truth. Speak to me, or don't speak. The choice is yours. But I'll not stand here till sunset, waiting."

The soothsayer cocked his head, as though listening. Then another gusting cackle. "Yes, yes. I hear him. A needle-wit, this Aimery. Prick, prick, prick and see the blood flow." A gnarled finger pointed to the early morning sky, eggshell-blue wreathed in lazy cloud. "Three nights past, my lord. As the moon set. A long-tailed comet. The sign of chaos. Were you witness? It made the black sky bleed."

Three nights past at moonset he'd only just crawled into his borrowed bed on the Green Isle, head aching with arguments. "No. I didn't see it. I was asleep."

"Asleep then, asleep now." Eyes stretching wide, the soothsayer shuffled close. "Time to wake, my lord duke, and see the trouble festering under your roof."

A clutch at his heart. "What trouble?"

"There was a man who had three sons. Lost one. Kept one. Threw the third away. The fool."

"What do you mean? What—"

"Be warned, my lord duke," the old man wheezed. "Unless you open your eyes you will sleep the cold sleep of death." A rattle in the scrawny throat, a sound like the last breath of a dying wife. A dying son. "And no right to say you were not told. You have to know it, Aimery. A long-tailed comet cannot lie."

But a man could. A mad man, his wits scattered like chaff on the wind. Aimery stepped back. "Be on your way, soothsayer. You've spoken and I've listened."

"Yes, but have you heard?" The soothsayer shook his head, sorrowful. Or perhaps merely acting sorrow. Who could tell, with a mad man? "Ah well. In time we'll know."

It was nonsense, of course. He had little time for religion, old or new. But the soothsayer looked in a bad way, so he pulled a plain gold ring from his finger.

"Take this, old man. Buy yourself a warm bed and hot food. And when next the spirits whisper, whisper to them from me that a faithful servant should be better served."

The soothsayer's eyes glittered as he stared at the ring. Then he snatched it, and with much muttering and arm-waving hobbled out of the forecourt.

"Your Grace," Curteis murmured, arriving on soft feet that barely disturbed the raked gravel. "Is aught amiss?"

Aimery frowned after the soothsayer, an indistinct bundle of rags vanishing into the high street's bustle. Mad old men and their ramblings. Throw a stone into any crowd and you'd likely strike at least three.

"No. Can we go?"

Curteis nodded. "Yes, Your Grace. As it please you."

They rode knee-to-knee out of the inn's stable yard in a clattering of hooves, with his body squire and his scribe and his men-at-arms close at heel.

"Be warned, Curteis," he said, as they scattered pie-sellers and cobblers and fishwives before them along Piper's Wade high street, "and share the warning with them that ride behind. I wish to sleep in my own bed under my own roof sooner rather than later. Therefore we shall travel swiftly, with few halts, and should I hear a tongue clapping complaint I swear I'll kick the culprit's arse seven shades of black and blue."

"Yes, Your Grace," said Curteis, smiling. He was well used to his duke.

With the past two weeks fresh in mind, Aimery scowled. "I tell you plain, man, I've heard enough clapping tongues lately to last me till my funeral."

"The lords of the Green Isle were indeed fretsome, Your Grace."

"Fretsome?" He snorted. "Snaggle-brained, you should call them. Vexatious. Full of wind. Especially that cross-grained fuck Terriel."

"Your Grace," agreed Curteis. "Lord Terriel and his noble brothers farted many noisome words. But you set them well straight."

Yes, he did. And woe betide a one of them who again dared defy his judgement. That man, be he ever so lordly, even the great and grasping Terriel, would find himself so handily chastised there'd be scars on his great-grandson's arse.

Bleakly satisfied, still impatient, Aimery urged his iron-dappled palfrey into a canter, then swung left off the high street onto Hook Way, which would lead them eventually to his ducal forest of Burnt Wood. If the rain held off and no mischance befell them, with the horses well rested they'd be in and out of the forest by day's end. Spend the night in Sparrowholt on its far side, leave at dawn on the morrow, ride hard with little dallying and with fortune they'd reach the Croft before sunset.

And so it proved. But when he did at last trot beneath the arching stone gateway of his favourite castle's inner bailey, feeling every one of his fifty-four years, he found himself ridden into yet another storm. For standing in the Croft's torchlit keep, clad head to toe in unrelieved black velvet, was old Herewart of nearby Bann Crossing. He trembled in the dusk's chill, tears swiftly slicking his withered cheeks. Waiting with him, stood at a wary distance, Balfre and Grefin.

"What is this, Balfre?" Aimery demanded of his accidental heir, even as his gaze lingered on his youngest son. His favourite, now that Malcolm was dead. "Why am I greeted with such confusion?"

He'd sent a man ahead, to warn of his arrival and stir the castle's servants to duty. As they hurried to take the horses and relieve Curteis and the scribe of their note-filled satchels, and the men-at-arms waited with their hands ready on their swords, he saw Balfre and Grefin exchange disquieting looks. But before his heir could answer, Herewart let out a cry cracked-full of grief and approached without leave or invitation.

"Your Grace, you must hear me! As a father, and my duke, only you can grant me the justice I seek!"

"Hold," he said to the men-at-arms who were moving to protect him. Then he looked to his steward. "Curteis, escort Lord Herewart within the castle. See him comforted, and kept company in the Rose chamber until I come."

Very proper, though he was also weary, Curteis bowed. "Yes, Your Grace."

"Your Grace!" Herewart protested. "Do not abandon me to an underling. My years of loyalty should purchase more consideration than that. I demand—"

"*Demand?*" Summoning a lifetime's worth of discipline, Aimery swung off his horse to land lightly on his feet. "My lord, be mindful. Not even a lifetime of loyalty will purchase a demand."

Herewart's colour was high, his wet eyes red-rimmed and lit with a burning fervour. "A single *day* of loyalty should purchase the justice I am owed. And be warned, Aimery. Justice I'll have, as I see fit, and from your hand – or there will be a reckoning. This is not cursed Clemen, where *in*justice wears a crown!"

Silence, save for Herewart's ragged breathing and the scrape of shod hooves on the flagstones as the horses hinted at their stables. Aimery looked to his sons. Grefin stood pale, arms folded, lower lip caught between his teeth. There was grief for Herewart there, and fear for his brother. As for Balfre, he stood defiant. He knew no other way to stand.

Belly tight, Aimery looked again at Herewart. "What has happened, my lord?"

"My son is dead, Your Grace," said Herewart, his voice raw. "My youngest. Hughe."

The blunt words tore wide his own monstrous, unhealed wound. "I'm sorry to hear it, Herewart. To lose a son untimely is—"

"You must know he was murdered," Herewart said, bludgeoning. "By your son and heir, Balfre."

"*Liar!*" Balfre shouted, and would have leapt at the old man but for Grefin's restraining hand. "It was ill chance, not murder, and he'd still be alive had you taught him how he should speak of Harcia's heir! The fault is yours, Herewart, not mine, that your son's bed tonight is a coffin!"

Aimery closed his eyes, briefly. Oil and water, they were, he and this son. Oil and flame. *Balfre, you shit. When will you cease burning me?* "What ill chance?"

"None," said Herewart, glowering. "Hughe's death was purposed. Your son challenged mine to a duel and killed him."

"*Duel?*" Balfre laughed, incredulous. "It was a joust! I unhorsed him by the rules, and when I left him he was barely more than winded. How can you—"

"No, my lord, how can *you*!" said Herewart, a shaking fist raised at Balfre. "My son made a ribald jest, harmless, and *you*, being so tender-skinned and pig-fat full of self love, you couldn't laugh and let it go by. You had to answer him with your lance, you had to goad him into unwise confrontation in the company of churls and mudder knights and take your revenge by taking his life! He breathed his last this morning; his body broken, your name upon his blood-stained lips."

Pulling free of his brother's holding hand, Balfre took a step forward. "Your Grace, Hughe's death isn't my—"

Aimery silenced him with a look, then turned. "My lord Herewart, as a father I grieve with you. And as your duke I promise justice. But for now, go with Curteis. He'll see you to warmth and wine while I have words with my son."

Herewart hesitated, then nodded. As Curteis ushered him within the castle, and the inner bailey emptied of servants, squires, men-at-arms and horses, Grefin tried to counsel his brother but was roughly pushed aside.

"Balfre," Aimery said, when they were alone. "What was Hughe's jest?"

His face dark with temper, Balfre swung round. "It was an insult, not a jest. And public, made with intent. I couldn't let it go by."

"Grefin?"

Grefin glanced at his brother, then nodded. "It's true. Hughe was offensive. But—"

"But *nothing!*" Balfre insisted. "For Herewart's son to say my lance is riddled with wormwood, with no more strength to it than a pipe of soft cheese, and by lance mean my cock, never mind we talked of jousting, he questioned my ability to sire a son. He as good as said I wasn't fit to rule Harcia after Aimery. And that's treason, Grefin, whether you like it or not."

Grefin was shaking his head. "Hughe was wine-soaked when he spoke. So deep in his cup he couldn't see over its rim. He was a fool, not a traitor."

"And now he's a dead fool," said Balfre, brutally unregretful. "And a lesson worth learning. My lord—" He took another step forward, so sure of his welcome. "You can see I had no choice. I—"

"Balfre," Aimery said heavily, "what I see is a man possessed of no more wit and judgement at the age of three-and-twenty than were his when he was *five*."

Balfre stared. "My lord?"

"You killed a man for no better reason than he had less wit than you!"

"But Father – I was wronged. You can't take Herewart's part in this!"

Oh Malcolm, Malcolm. A curse on you for dying.

Aimery swallowed, rage and disappointment turning his blood to bile. "Since last you saw me I have done nothing but ride the Green Isle, hearing complaints and chastising faithless lords who count their own petty needs higher than what is best for this duchy. And now *you*, Balfre, you encourage men to defy my decree against personal combat. What—"

"It was a *joust!*" Balfre shouted. "You've not banned jousting. I was obedient to all your rules. I made sure of a tilt barrier, my lance was well-blunted, and I—"

"And you killed a man, regardless," he said, fists clenched. "Much good your obedience has done you, Balfre. Or me."

Balfre's hands were fisted too. "That's not fair. Father—"

"*Do not call me Father! On your knees, miscreant, and address me as Your Grace!*"

Sickly pale, Balfre dropped to the damp ground. "Your Grace, it's plain you're weary. You shouldn't be plagued with the Green Isle. Appoint me its Steward and I'll—"

"Appoint *you*?" Aimery ached to slap his son's face. "Balfre, if I let you loose on the Green Isle there'd be war within a week."

"Your Grace, you misjudge me."

"Do I?" He laughed, near to choking on bitterness. "And if I were to break my neck hunting tomorrow and the day after I was buried you learned that Harald of Clemen had yet again interfered with Harcian justice in the Marches? Tell me, would you tread with care or would you challenge *him* to a joust?"

"Harald is a cur-dog who sits upon a stolen throne," said Balfre, his lip curled. "Thieves and cur-dogs should be beaten, not cosseted. If Harald feared us he'd not dare flout your authority, or entice Harcia's men-at-arms to break your decrees, or demand unlawful taxes from our merchants and—"

"So you'd challenge him with a naked sword, and slaughter two hundred years of peace." Aimery shook his head, stung with despair. "Never once doubting the wisdom of your choice."

"Your Grace, there's no greater wisdom than overwhelming strength and the willingness to use it."

And so the decision he'd been avoiding for so long, like a coward, was made for him. He sighed. "I know you think so, Balfre. Grefin—"

Grefin looked up. "Your Grace?"

"The Green Isle has been left to its own devices for too long. Therefore I appoint you its Steward and—"

Forgetting himself, Balfre leapt to his feet. "*No!*"

"Your Grace—" Alarmed, Grefin was staring. "I'm honoured, truly, but—"

"Enough, Grefin. It's decided."

"No, it isn't!" said Balfre. "You can't do this. Like it or not I'm your heir. By right the Green Isle's stewardship is mine. You *can't*—"

Aimery seized his oldest son's shoulders and shook him. "I must, Balfre. For your sake, for Harcia's sake, I have no other choice."

"You're a duke," said Balfre, coldly. "You have nothing but choices."

"Ah, Balfre . . . " Run through with pain, he tightened his fingers. "The day you understand that isn't true is the day you will be ready for a crown."

Balfre wrenched free. "Fuck you, Your Grace," he said, and walked away.